MW00860701

WORD BEARERS
THE OMNIBUS

THE WORD BEARERS are a Legion of Traitor Space Marines fanatically devoted to the Ruinous Powers. Led by their Dark Apostles – charismatic and dangerous individuals who guide the warriors of the XVII Legion on vicious dark crusades against the Imperium of Man.

• DARK APOSTLE •

Driven by dark visions, Dark Apostle Jarulek and his Word Bearers lay waste to the Imperial planet of Tanakreg. Brutally enslaving the population, they set them to work building a monstrous tower. What is the traitors' vile purpose, and can they achieve it before the Imperial forces arrive to reclaim the planet?

• DARK DISCIPLE •

Marduk, aspiring Dark Apostle of the Word Bearers, strives to unlock the secrets of an ancient artefact. This quest throws him into a deadly warzone and a desperate battle between the armies of the Imperium, the alien tyranids and a third faction as sadistic as it is mysterious.

• DARK CREED •

Dark Apostle Marduk faces challenges from within his own Legion as he wages war with Space Marines of the White Consuls. Harnessing the power of the Nexus Arrangement, a powerful necron device, the Word Bearers can turn the tide. But as victory looms, an old enemy returns to throw the entire dark crusade into ruin.

By the same author

KNIGHTS OF BRETONNIA
(Contains the novels *Knight Errant* and *Knight of the Realm*
and the novellas *Questing Knight* and *Grail Knight*.)

MARK OF CHAOS
A Warhammer novel

EMPIRE IN CHAOS
A Warhammer novel

More Chaos Space Marines from Black Library

· NIGHT LORDS ·
Aaron Dembski-Bowden

Book 1: SOUL HUNTER
Book 2: BLOOD REAVER
Book 3: VOID STALKER (May 2012)

THRONE OF LIES
An audio drama

· IRON WARRIORS ·
Graham McNeill

IRON WARRIORS: THE OMNIBUS (March 2012)
(Contains the novel *Storm of Iron*, the novella *Iron Warrior*
and five short stories)

A WARHAMMER 40,000 OMNIBUS

WORD BEARERS
THE OMNIBUS

ANTHONY REYNOLDS

BLACK LIBRARY

For Graham, Anita, Evan, and the latest addition to the clan, Amber.
A family to walk the mountains with.

A BLACK LIBRARY PUBLICATION

Dark Apostle first published in 2007.
Dark Disciple first published in 2008.
Dark Creed first published in 2010.
This edition published in Great Britain in 2015 by
Black Library,
Games Workshop Ltd.,
Willow Road,
Nottingham, NG7 2WS, UK.

10 9 8 7 6 5 4

Cover illustration by Clint Langley.

Word Bearers Omnibus © Copyright Games Workshop Limited
2015. Word Bearers Omnibus, GW, Games Workshop, Black Library,
The Horus Heresy, The Horus Heresy Eye logo, Space Marine, 40K,
Warhammer, Warhammer 40,000, the 'Aquila' Double-headed
Eagle logo, and all associated logos, illustrations, images, names,
creatures, races, vehicles, locations, weapons, characters, and the
distinctive likenesses thereof, are either ® or TM, and/or © Games
Workshop Limited, variably registered around the world.
All Rights Reserved.

A CIP record for this book is available from the British Library.

UK ISBN 13: 978 1 84970 104 4
US ISBN 13: 978 1 78572 116 8

No part of this publication may be reproduced, stored in a retrieval
system, or transmitted in any form or by any means, electronic,
mechanical, photocopying, recording or otherwise, without the
prior permission of the publishers.

This is a work of fiction. All the characters and events portrayed
in this book are fictional, and any resemblance to real people or
incidents is purely coincidental.

See Black Library on the internet at

blacklibrary.com

Find out more about Games Workshop
and the world of Warhammer 40,000 at

games-workshop.com

Printed and bound by CPI Group (UK) Ltd, Croydon, CR0 4YY

IT IS THE 41st millennium. For more than a hundred centuries the Emperor has sat immobile on the Golden Throne of Earth. He is the master of mankind by the will of the gods, and master of a million worlds by the might of his inexhaustible armies. He is a rotting carcass writhing invisibly with power from the Dark Age of Technology. He is the Carrion Lord of the Imperium for whom a thousand souls are sacrificed every day, so that he may never truly die.

YET EVEN IN his deathless state, the Emperor continues his eternal vigilance. Mighty battlefleets cross the daemon-infested miasma of the warp, the only route between distant stars, their way lit by the Astronomican, the psychic manifestation of the Emperor's will. Vast armies give battle in His name on uncounted worlds. Greatest amongst his soldiers are the Adeptus Astartes, the Space Marines, bio-engineered super-warriors. Their comrades in arms are legion: the Imperial Guard and countless Planetary Defence Forces, the ever-vigilant Inquisition and the tech-priests of the Adeptus Mechanicus to name only a few. But for all their multitudes, they are barely enough to hold off the ever-present threat from aliens, heretics, mutants - and worse.

TO BE A man in such times is to be one amongst untold billions. It is to live in the cruellest and most bloody regime imaginable. These are the tales of those times. Forget the power of technology and science, for so much has been forgotten, never to be re-learned. Forget the promise of progress and understanding, for in the grim dark future there is only war. There is no peace amongst the stars, only an eternity of carnage and slaughter, and the laughter of thirsting gods.

CONTENTS

INTRODUCTION

Everyone loves a good villain.

Growing up, many of my favourite characters in novels, movies, TV shows and comics were (and still are) the bad guys: Dracula, the Joker, Captain Hook, Gollum, Roy Batty, Mr Hyde... the list goes on and on. All of these characters transfixed me – as despicable as they could be, I found them hard to turn away from, and given the choice I'd almost always choose to see more of Magneto than Professor X, more Darth Vader than Luke Skywalker, more Faith than Buffy, more Green Knight than Gawain, and more Iago than Othello; and I bet there are a lot of people out there who would agree with me.

I wouldn't go so far as to say that I'd always be cheering on the bad guys rather than the heroes, but the antagonists I particularly liked were scene-stealing characters that tended to overshadow the protagonist. They had their own motivations and goals, and I wanted to see more of them. I wanted to see *their* side of things; and yes, every now and then, I just really wanted them to come out on top and put those 'heroes' in their place. Keep 'em honest. So when I started thinking about a Warhammer 40,000 story that I'd like to tell, I naturally drifted towards the dark side of things.

Apart from a couple of notable exceptions (Graham McNeill's *Storm of Iron*, in particular) Chaos Space Marines in Black Library fiction had, at the time, been relegated pretty much into the role of antagonists to be overcome. The Warhammer 40,000 universe is a dark and twisted place, and its protagonists are rarely flawless shining heroes, but what I was interested in seeing was more from the perspective of the *really* bad guys.

So I approached the Powers That Be (otherwise known as Black Library's editors) with the notion of writing a Chaos Space Marine novel, and I got the thumbs up. From my three separate book ideas, the one that they liked best had the Word Bearers Legion as its focus: the initial pitch for *Dark Apostle* (the other two were about the Alpha Legion and the Death Guard).

It was at this point that I moved from the UK back to Australia, and with a plan for the novel agreed I promptly locked myself away in a dark room, turned the music up nice and loud (lots of Nine Inch Nails, Mozart's Requiem, and dark movie soundtracks like Dracula and Hellboy) and set to work. Three months later I emerged, wild-eyed and unshaven, the finished draft clutched in my trembling hands.

Dark Apostle was well received by the fans (that's you guys, and I owe you all a big thank you) and it sold well enough for Black Library to be keen on turning it into a trilogy. The story had been written so that it could work as a stand-alone book, but I'd always planned it to be the first part of longer story arc, so I was more than happy about this decision. A year later I started work on the second part of the trilogy – *Dark Disciple*.

I don't want to spoil it for those yet to read it, but I wanted to make things harder for the Word Bearers – the enemies were more dangerous and there was more at stake. Another year passed and I got to work on the final book of the trilogy, *Dark Creed*. Again, I wanted to up the stakes to a whole new level.

As I write this introduction, I realise that almost four and half years have passed since I wrote the opening sentence of *Dark Apostle*, and so I've been writing about Marduk and co. for almost half a decade. (As an aside, I lost count of how many times I re-wrote those first few paragraphs – the opening of a book is always the most difficult!) That time has gone by very quickly and, I must say, I've had a lot of fun writing about the Word Bearers along the way.

They are such an important Legion in the bigger picture of Warhammer 40,000, for the origins of the Horus Heresy lie with them. While my books do not dwell on the Heresy itself (see Aaron Dembski-Bowden's impressive novel *The First Heretic* for more on that), it's definitely been interesting to delve into the mindset of a Legion dealing with the fallout of those momentous events. They are consumed by hatred and bitterness about the way things turned out, but they still passionately believe that they are right; and as corrupted and tainted as the Word Bearers are ten thousand years after the Heresy (well, maybe less, since time flows strangely in the warp) they still fervently believe that they are the only ones who can lead mankind to salvation. Who knows, *maybe they are*.

As much as they are evil, reprehensible and loathsome bastards, I've grown to really like these characters. Maybe 'like' is the wrong word, but I certainly enjoyed writing about them – Burias and the Warmonger especially – and I hope that they conjure a little of the same kind of feeling in readers that I get when watching/reading about all the charismatic bad guys that I've always loved.

'Torment', the new short story included in this omnibus, brings this series to a close. I'd definitely like to write more about these characters that have really come to life for me in the last five years, and I certainly do have ideas about the direction that new story arc would take. But exactly when that will be, I cannot say – there are other stories that I'd like to explore first, but I am sure it will only be a matter of time before the lure of Chaos draws me back...

Once again, I'd like to thank all the readers who bought and enjoyed *Dark Apostle* and the sequels – if it wasn't for you, this omnibus edition would never have been printed. I'd also like to thank Clint Langley for the truly epic cover of this volume, and to Klaus Sherwinski for the awesome individual novel covers.

Until next time – *Death to the False Emperor!*

Anthony Reynolds
Sydney, March 2011

DARK APOSTLE

As Sanguine Orb waxes strong and Pillar of Clamour rises high,
The Peal of Nether shakes,
And Great Wyrms of The Below wreak the earth
With flame and gaseous exhalation.
Roar of Titans will smite the mountains and they shall tumble.
Depths of Onyx shall engulf the lands, and then exposed shall lay
The Undercroft,
Death and Mastery.

The door shall be opened to he of pure faith
Into Darkness two descend,
Apostate and he who would be,
Into madness and confusion descend,
Restless dead and creatures old,
The Undying One to face.

Master of the cog will come in chains and tattered robes,
To become Enslaved,
To unleash the Orb of Night and Breaking Dawn.

One shall fall, he of lesser faith, he unmarked by godly touch,
His fate to remain, trapped eternal,
And for one to flee with prize in hand,
Gatemaster,
He who bears Lorgar's touch.

PROLOGUE

MARDUK, FIRST ACOLYTE of the Word Bearers Legion, looked up. His noble, deathly pale patrician features, common amongst those imbued with the gene-seed of blessed Lorgar, were twisted in frustration and anger. Braziers burning within the darkness of the icy mausoleum lit his face, the flames mirrored in his eyes.

'I have read the portents. I felt the truth within the blood of the sacrifices on my tongue.'

He rounded on his silent listener, the ancient Warmonger.

'But this vision fills my head, and its meaning is unclear. I have recited the Curses of Amentenoc; I have supplicated the Great Changer with offerings and sacrifice. I have spent endless hours in meditation, opening myself up to the wisdom and majesty of the living Ether. But the meaning remains unclear.

'I am assailed by the dead, long dead, and they claw at my armour with skeletal claws. They scratch deep furrows into my blessed ceramite, but they cannot pierce my consecrated flesh. I begin to recite from the *Book of Lorgar*, the third book of the *Litanies of Vengeance and Hate*. "Smite down the non-believers and the deceived, and they shall know the truth of the words of oblivion."'

Marduk clenched his fist tightly, servo-muscles in his armour whining as his entire body tensed.

'I shatter their bones with my fists. They cannot stand against me. But they are many.'

'Calm your mind, First Acolyte,' boomed the ancient one. It was the sound of the sepulchre given voice, an impossibly deep baritone that reverberated through the still tomb, deep within the strike cruiser. Each word was spoken slowly and deliberately, amplified through powerful vox-units.

Once he had been a mighty hero who fought at the side of the greatest warriors ever to have lived. As a captain he had led great companies of the Legion against the foes of Lorgar and the Warmaster, and Marduk had studied all of his recorded sermons and exhortations. They were masterpieces of rhetoric and faith, filled with righteous hatred, and his skill at deciphering and predicting the twisting patterns of the future through his ritualised dream visions were astounding. He had fallen fighting against the arch-enemies, the deniers of the truth, those who followed the False Emperor in their ignorance and blindness.

'You fight your visions too hard. They are gifts from the gods, and as with all gifts bestowed from the great powers, you should receive them with thanks.'

The meagre physical remnants of the inspirational leader had been interred within the sarcophagus that lay before Marduk. Though his body was utterly ruined, he was destined to live on within the tomb of his new shell, and become the Warmonger. While the other Dreadnoughts of the Legion had slowly succumbed to madness and raving insanity, the Warmonger retained much of his lucidity. It was his faith, Erebus himself had stated, that kept him from slipping into darkness.

All the anger and frustration flowed out of Marduk, and he smiled. The face that had looked brooding and twisted with anger a moment before was darkly handsome once again, black eyes glinting.

'Pray for enlightenment, but do not be impatient and expect instant gratification,' continued the Warmonger. 'Knowledge and power will come to you, for you are on the path of the devout, and the favour of the gods is upon you. But you must let yourself succumb to the embrace of the great powers; they will buoy you, and only then will the veil be lifted from your eyes. Only then will you see what your vision means. You need not fear the darkness, for you *are* the darkness.'

The Warmonger flexed its huge, mechanical arms, hissing steam venting from the joints.

'My weapons ache for the bloodshed to begin anew,' the Dreadnought said, massive weapon feeds aligning themselves in anticipation. 'Do we fight alongside our Lord Lorgar this day?'

'Not today,' said Marduk quietly, recognising that the Warmonger's lucidity was slipping. It was often this way.

'And the Warmaster? Do his battles against the False Emperor fare well? Has he yet dethroned the hated betrayer, the craven abandoner of the Crusade?'

The mention of the Warmaster Horus pained Marduk. He longed for the simpler days of the past, when the victory of the Warmaster over the Emperor seemed like a certainty. The memories were fresh in his mind, and his anger, hatred and outrage burned within him stronger than ever. He wished he had been at the battle of the Emperor's palace on Terra alongside the Warmonger and most of the warriors that made up the Grand Host of the Dark Apostle Jarulek, but he had not. No, in those days he had been but a novice adept sent to serve under Lord Kor Phaeron. It was a great honour, but while he fought the hated Ultramarines of Guilliman on Calth with passion and belief, he longed to be fighting the battle at the palace that would determine the outcome of the long war. Or so he had thought. The war ground on, and would never end until the so-called Emperor of mankind was thrown down, and every cursed edifice that falsely proclaimed his divinity was smashed asunder.

'The Corpse Emperor sits on his throne on Terra still, Warmonger,' said Marduk bitterly, 'but his end draws ever nearer.'

BOOK ONE: SUBJUGATION

'From the fires of betrayal unto the blood of revenge we bring the name of Lorgar, the Bearer of the Word, the favoured son of Chaos, all praise be given unto him. From those that would not heed we offer praise to those who do, that they might turn their gaze our way and gift us with the boon of pain, to turn the galaxy red with blood, and feed the hunger of the gods.'

– Excerpt from the three hundred and forty-first
Book of the Epistles of Lorgar

CHAPTER ONE

KOL BADAR GLARED across the expanse of the cavaedium. The arena of worship, located deep within the heart of the strike cruiser *Infidus Diabolus*, was large enough to allow the recently swollen ranks of the entire Host to stand in attendance. Its curved ceiling stretched impossibly high, and immense skeletal ribbed supports met hundreds of metres above. The kathartes perched along the bone-like struts, daemonic, skinless harpies that flickered in and out of the warp. But Kol Badar's gaze did not rise to look upon the carrion feeders.

No, his scowling features were focused on the last of the warriors filing into the enormous room. From his vantage point, just one step from the top of the sacred raised dais that none bar the most holy of warriors would occupy, he could see the last of the Host's champions leading their warriors into the cavaedium, to take their places for the coming ceremony. The expanse was almost full. The entire Host had been gathered. Kol Badar let his gaze wander over the serried ranks, glorying in the strength and power that his warriors exuded. None could hope to stand against such a force of the devout, and his warriors would soon prove their worth once again.

His warriors. He grunted at his own hubris. They were not *his* warriors. If anything, they were the warriors of the Dark Apostle, though in his words they belonged only to Chaos in all its glory. The Dark Apostle claimed that he was merely the instrument through which the great powers directed these noble warriors of faith, and that Kol Badar was his primary tool to enact the great gods' will.

Kol Badar was the Coryphaus. It was a symbolic title, granted to the most trusted and capable warrior leader and strategos of the Host. His word was second only to that of the Dark Apostle. The Coryphaus was the Dark Apostle's senior war captain, but more than this, he was the voice of the congregation. The mood and opinion of the Host was delivered to the Dark Apostle through him, and it was his duty to lead the chanted responses and antiphons from the gathered Host in ceremonies and rituals. It was also his role to lead the responses within the true house of worship of the dark gods: the battlefield.

The processional corridor that ran down the middle of the nave remained clear as the cavaedium filled. Almost half a kilometre long and laid with black, immaculate carpet consecrated in the blood of thousands, none dared to step upon this hallowed ground, bar those deemed worthy, on pain of immortal torment. There were no seats within the nave; the warriors of the Legion received the word from the Dark Apostle standing, armed and armoured. Dozens of smaller sanctuaries and temple-shrines branched off from the ancient stone walls of the cavaedium, containing statues of daemonic deities, ancient texts and the interred remains of holy warriors who had fallen during the constant, long war.

An almost imperceptible, ghostly chanting whispered around the room. Lazily swooping cherubiox circled in the air, skeletal, winged creatures with sharp fangs set within childlike mouths, each carrying a flaming iron brazier. Odorous incense descended from the tusked maws of daemon-headed gargoyles towards the gathered Host. The clouds of smoke eddied and roiled in the wake of the gently weaving cherubiox.

Kol Badar stepped heavily down the altar steps, the joints of his massive, ornate Terminator armour hissing and steaming. He passed through the gates of the ikonoclast, the spiked metal barrier that separated the altar from the openness of the nave. Its wrought iron frame was decorated with dozens of ancient banners, twisted icons and trophies dedicated to the gods of Chaos, and upon its spiked and barbed tips were impaled the heads of particularly hated foes.

He prowled along the base of the altar, glaring at the warrior-brothers filing into the room, as if daring any of them to dishonour him in any way. The warriors of the Legion stood unmoving once they had taken up their positions. Almost two thousand warriors of the Word Bearers stood in absolute silence, and Kol Badar stalked back and forth along their ranks.

Two thousand was a particularly large number of warrior-brothers for a single Host. The ranks of the Host had swollen a century past, when the warriors of another Dark Apostle had been amalgamated into its ranks after their holy leader had been slain in battle. Ceremonies of mourning had lasted weeks as the Legion honoured the passing of one of its religious fathers. Jarulek had, of course, ordered the execution of all the captains of the leaderless Host for having allowed such a sacrilege to take place. It was deemed by the Dark Council on the revered daemon-world of Sicarus, the spiritual home of the Word Bearers Legion and the throne world of the blessed Daemon Primarch Lorgar, that Jarulek take in the leaderless Host, for he had an apprentice, a First Acolyte who would soon be ready to bear the mantle of Dark Apostle. When, and if, the First Acolyte became worthy of the title of Dark Apostle, then Jarulek would split the Host once more into two.

The thick features of Kol Badar's face darkened at the idea. The very thought of the bastard whoreson Marduk bearing the exalted title of Dark Apostle made Kol Badar's rage and bitterness burn fiercely within him.

The Anointed, the warrior-cult of the most favoured warriors within the Host, stood in neat ranks surrounding the raised pulpit of the Cory-phaus, and Kol Badar approached them. The Anointed looked like statues, utterly still and wearing their fully enclosed, ancient suits of Terminator armour. Each suit was a relic of holy significance, and to don the armour was a great religious honour. Once a warrior-brother entered the ranks of the Anointed, he was a member for life, and with lifespans extended indefinitely through a combination of their Astartes conditioning, bio-enhancement and the warping power of the gods of the Ether, the Anointed were only replaced on the rare occasion that one of their cult fell in battle. Many of them had fought alongside Kol Badar and their holy Daemon Primarch Lorgar at the great siege of the Emperor's palace, and he knew of no finer fighting force. Unsurpassed warriors with the hearts of true fanatics, the cult of the Anointed had won countless battles for the Legion. Their glories were sung in the flesh-halls within the temples of Sicarus, and their deeds recounted in the grimoire historicals housed in the finest scriptorums of Ghalmek. Kol Badar stalked through the ranks of the elite warriors and climbed the steps to his pulpit, there to await the arrival of the Dark Apostle.

The Dark Apostle; Jarulek the Glorified; Jarulek the Blessed, a divine warrior who heard the whispered words of the gods, and communed with them as their vessel. One of the favoured servants of the immortal daemon primarch Lorgar, Jarulek truly was a bearer of the word. His furious passion and belief had brought countless millions into the fold. Countless millions more, ignorant and resistant to the words of truth, had been slain in holy war upon his order.

As much as it furthered the cause of the Word Bearers for more sys-tems to be brought under the sway of Lorgar's word, Kol Badar much preferred the worlds that resisted. He enjoyed the killing.

Thin, spider-like limbs extended from the pulpit towards his exposed face. Fine, bladed hooks at their tips emerged and pushed into his flesh, latching beneath the skin. He closed his eyes. A large proboscis uncurled, and he opened his mouth to accept it. It entered his throat, and small barbed clamps latched onto his larynx. The proboscis expanded to fill his throat. His voice, enhanced by the apparatus, would not only carry through the vast expanse of the cavaedium, but also through the entire *Infidus Diabolus*, so that all within the cruiser might intone the correct responses.

He recalled the conversation he had had with the Dark Apostle mere hours earlier, and his face flushed with the thought of the rebuke he had received.

'Speak as the Coryphaus, Kol Badar, not as yourself,' Jarulek had scolded him gently.

Kol Badar had clenched his heavy jaw tight, looking down. 'What would you have me say, Dark Apostle?' he had asked, his voice sounding course and crude in his ears after Jarulek's velvet words.

'I would have you speak for the Host, as the Coryphaus. Does the Host accept him?'

'The Host follows your word without fault, my lord.'

'Of course. Meaning?'

'Meaning that they embrace and revere him, for it is your will for them to do so,' he had said, his voice thick.

'And speaking as yourself?' Jarulek had asked, softly.

'He is an upstart newborn risen beyond his position. He has not been with us from the start. He did not fight at our side as we assailed the cursed False Emperor's lapdogs on Terra,' Kol Badar had fumed. 'You should have let me kill him.'

Jarulek had chuckled at that. 'A newborn, I have not heard you call him that before. He has fought against the False Emperor mere centuries less than you and I, old friend.'

Kol Badar's face had darkened. 'He was not there at the start.'

'No, but a long time has passed since then: ten thousand years in the world of mortals.'

'We do not live in the realm of mortals,' Kol Badar had replied. Time held no sway over the warp; a warrior may spend a month within its unstable boundaries, emerging to find that the galaxy had changed, that countless decades had flown by. To Kol Badar, the siege of the Emperor's palace felt like mere centuries ago, not the staggering ten thousand years that had passed since that time, and his memories of it were strong.

'He has been chosen by the gods,' Jarulek had said. 'Do not struggle against their will, Kol Badar. They are unforgiving masters, and a soul like yours would be an exquisite plaything. You are my most loyal and honoured warrior – do not let your hatred of him be your ruin.'

A mournful, tolling bell echoed across the expanse of the cavaedium. Silence descended, and not a movement stirred through the massed ranks of the Word Bearers. This was the start of the exhortation, and the entire Host stood in silence, awaiting the arrival of the Dark Apostle.

Kol Badar was a warlord, a killer and a destroyer of worlds. But, along with the rest of the Host, he would wait, patient, unmoving and in silence, for the arrival of the holy Dark Apostle. If it took a minute or a week, he would stand immobile. And so he waited.

'Go,' SAID THE voice over the comm-channel. Reacting instantly, black-armoured figures of the Shinar enforcers stepped out of the gloom of the narrow alleyway. Lieutenant Varnus levelled and fired his combat issue shotgun at the heavy locking mechanism of the rusted door. The sound of the weapon echoed deafeningly, and a fist-sized hole was punched through the metal. Varnus slammed a heavy boot into the door, swinging it violently open, and surged through, the other enforcers close behind him.

The door opened to a refuse strewn corridor, dully lit by humming glow-globes. A man sitting with his feet up on the crude synthetic table looked up, eyes wide, lho-stick hanging limply from his mouth. A second blast from the shotgun threw him backwards, slamming him against the wall in a spray of blood.

'Entrance gained,' said Varnus, opening up the comm-channel.

'All teams have entered the complex. Proceed as planned,' said the captain in reply.

'Yes, sir,' said Varnus. He mouthed an obscenity under his breath once the comm-channel was closed.

Moving in a half crouch up the corridor, he stepped quickly over the scattered piles of twisted metal and broken masonry.

'Smells like a damn sewage pit,' muttered one of the enforcers. Varnus was forced to agree. He indicated sharply to a closed door as he passed it. A pair of enforcers behind him took up positions to either side of it. One kicked it open, and the two of them moved in, shotguns raised. The sharp, focused beams of light from their helmets swung around to locate any threats. The other two enforcers in the team moved up in support of Varnus. He paused at the end of the corridor, and glanced quickly around the corner: another empty, sparse corridor, this one with a single door leading from it. Glow-globes overhead flickered weakly.

Varnus stepped around the corner and moved forwards cautiously, the focused beam from his helmet piercing the dark corners that the weak illumination of the glow globes failed to light. Rodents scurried away from the brightness. The stench was overpowering.

'Who in the Emperor's name would want to hide out here?' remarked one of his team, swearing colourfully.

'Those who don't want to be disturbed,' said Varnus sharply. 'And cut the chatter, Landers. I'm sick of your whine.' The enforcer muttered something under his breath, and Varnus resisted the urge to turn on the big man. Focus, he told himself, and stepped towards the closer of the two doors. He heard the sound of muffled voices, a shout. He swore.

Varnus slammed his heavy boot into the door, and it collapsed inwards, its hinges long corroded. A pair of men were raising a heavy metal hatch in the floor of the room. One, his eyes filled with fear, dropped down into the darkness of the bolt-hole. The other raised an autopistol, face twisted in hatred, and raking fire spat from the end of the stub-nosed weapon. Varnus's shotgun barked, even as the bullets from the pistol ripped across his chest, and the man's head exploded in a splatter of gore.

Varnus fell back from the impact of the projectiles on his carapace armour. 'Get the other one,' he wheezed.

'I can't fit down there,' remarked Landers, shrugging his shoulders. He nodded towards the smallest of the four enforcers, a grin on his face.

'One of you damn well go! Now!' roared Varnus, pulling himself to his feet. The slight enforcer swore, seeing the eyes of the whole team on him. He placed his shotgun on the floor of the room, drew and cocked his autopistol and dropped into the darkness of the bolt-hole. The sound of the man scrambling through a metal duct echoed loudly beneath them.

Still wheezing, Varnus opened up his comm-channel.

'They are running. Undisclosed bolt-holes. Orders?'

Varnus pulled the bullets from his chest-plate as he waited for a response. He could feel the heat from the bullets through the leather of his gloves.

'Captain?' he said with some impatience. 'Did you hear me? What are our orders?'

There was a muffled grunt of pain from the bolt-hole, and then the sound of three gunshots. The enforcer reappeared a moment later. 'Bastard stuck me,' he said, his hand gripped around his left arm, blood seeping between his fingers.

'Hold position. Awaiting new intel,' came the captain's terse response, finally.

'Hold position? They will have cleared out by the time we wait for new intel!'

'Hold your position, lieutenant.' The comm-bead clicked closed in his helmet.

'Frek that,' said Varnus. Yanking the last of the autopistol bullets from his chest plate, he threw them to the ground. 'Right, let's move.'

'Lieutenant?' questioned one of the enforcers.

'The bastards are getting away. We close on the target position, now. If the Emperor wills it, we may yet salvage something from this mission. Move!'

'That's what the captain's orders are, are they?' asked Landers, disbelief clear on his face.

Varnus turned quickly, stepping in close to the bigger man, and slammed a clenched fist into his face. Landers fell back, a cry more of shock than pain escaping his lips.

'I am your lieutenant, damn you, you slimy arse licker, and you will do as I damn well say,' snarled Varnus. 'Now, all of you, let's move out.'

Leading the way, Varnus pushed on deeper into the stinking, crumbling complex. He heard the others falling in behind him, and heard Landers muttering to himself. He grinned. He had wanted to punch that man for months.

The enforcers moved on, covering each other as they ghosted through the corridors and down corroded metal stairways. Varnus heard running footsteps ahead, and raised a hand, crouching low. He turned off the light on his helmet, the other enforcers following suit, and they plunged into dim, semi-light. A figure ran lightly around a corner, and Varnus reared up, slamming the butt of his shotgun into the figure's head. There was a crunching sound, and the figure dropped. Clicking his light back on, he saw it was a woman, her hair clipped short. Her eyes were open and staring, and blood seeped from her head where Varnus had struck her. An autogun was clasped in her dead hands.

'We are close,' said Varnus.

Carefully descending another flight of metal stairs, the enforcer team could see a flickering of orange light coming from below. The stink of promethium filled their nostrils.

Reaching the landing below, the team was faced with a single, heavy door standing slightly ajar, its plasglass window smashed through. Flames could be seen on the other side.

'Quickly,' hissed Varnus, and the enforcer team entered the room. It was a large, square space, and one of the glow-globes in the ceiling exploded as flames touched it. Couches and chairs were ablaze, as was a low table covered in papers and documents. The walls were lined with bunks and desks, and a makeshift kitchen had been constructed in the eastern corner. The figure of a man, oblivious to the sudden appearance of the enforcers, was liberally upending the contents of a metal can across a table on the far side of the room.

Varnus hissed, motioning for his team to lower their weapons. 'Take him, no guns,' he mouthed to Landers. The enforcer nodded, the confrontation of minutes earlier forgotten, and moved swiftly towards the figure. Feeling the presence behind him too late, the man turned just as Landers's thick arms wrapped around his neck, locking him firmly. He was dragged back across the room, and slammed face first onto the floor, his arms held painfully behind his back. The man struggled in vain, and Landers dropped his knee into the man's back, pinning him in place.

Varnus ran across the room and picked up one of the sodden papers that covered the promethium doused table. It was a detailed schematic map. He swore as he saw what it detailed.

'Get these damn flames out now! This whole place could go up at any second!' Varnus hollered. He opened up his comm-channel. 'Captain, this is Lieutenant Varnus. You need to get in here. Now,' he said, moving back towards Landers and the captive.

He knelt down beside the pinned captive and turned his face roughly towards him. The man's features were twisted in hatred and pain.

'What in the Emperor's name were you planning here?' Varnus said quietly.

The captive spat, eyes blazing with fury.

'What do you make of these, lieutenant? Gang markings? I don't recognise them,' said one of the enforcers.

Varnus looked to where the man motioned with his head. A crude tattoo was visible where the captive's dark brown overalls had been torn at his left shoulder. Ripping the heavy cloth fully away from the man's body, he gazed upon the emblazoned design: a screaming, horned daemon head surrounded by flames.

'I don't recognise it either, but it looks like some kind of damn cult marking to me,' said Varnus. He swore silently to himself.

CHAPTER TWO

BURIAS WALKED WITH a warrior's grace as he stalked through the dark, musty smelling halls of the *Infidus Diabolus*, impatient for the slaughter that was soon to come. His armour was a deep, bruised red, edged in dull, brushed metal. It was an exhibit of exceptional craftsmanship, each heavy ceramite plate fitting perfectly over his powerful, enhanced body.

He could not recall a time when his sacred armour had not been a part of him. He had laboured over every coiling engraving covering the auto-reductive armour plates, had painstakingly whittled the words of blessed Lorgar along the burnished reinforcement bands that circled his forearms, and had carved the words of the gods themselves around the rim of his heavy shoulder plates. The sacred Latros Sacrum, the symbol that represented the Word Bearers Legion was embossed on his left shoulder. A bronze, stylised representation of a roaring, horned daemon surrounded by flames, it represented all that the Legion and Burias stood for, all that they believed in and all that they killed for.

He wore no helmet for the upcoming exhortation. His vicious, deathly pale face was unmarked by scars, a rarity for a warrior who had fought in as many campaigns as he had, and it was framed by long, oiled black hair.

With each step, the heavy butt of the icon that Burias held in his left hand slammed into the polished, black-veined, stone floor, the sharp sound echoing around him.

The icon was a thick staff of spiked, black iron. It was almost three metres tall, taller even than him, and loops of heavily ornate bronze encircled its shaft. These loops were inscribed with litanies and epistles, sacred words of the Daemon Primarch Lorgar. It was topped with a glistening, black, eight-pointed star, the points of the symbol of Chaos barbed and sharp. In the centre of the star was a graven image of the sacred Latros Sacrum.

Burias had received the honour of becoming Icon Bearer with great pride, and he had the privilege of walking before Marduk, the First Acolyte, and Jarulek, the Dark Apostle, leading them to their positions in the ceremonies of worship and sacrifice. He had performed this sacred duty for many years, and the esteem he had earned from his warrior-brothers as a result was great.

He paused before he began his ascent up a grand set of curving stairs. The staircase was wide enough for twenty Space Marines to walk side by side, and its curving balustrades were highly ornate and picked out in bronze, crafted by some unknown hand countless aeons past. Two intimidating statues glared at any wishing to climb the steps, monstrous, coiling daemons said to strike down those with unworthy hearts.

Raising his head high, Burias began the long climb, his footfalls on the cold stone echoing up into the gloom of the arching ceiling hundreds of metres above. Ghostly chanting flowed down upon him, the sound of dozens of servitor eunuchs, forever ensconced in hidden pulpit-casings, intoning the canticles of blessed Lorgar in never ending cycles.

Reaching the top of the grand staircase, Burias continued on towards a pair of gigantic, arched doors on the opposite side of a long gallery. Huge, stone tablets lined the walls of the gallery, each more than twenty metres in height and covered in intricate, precisely carved script, just a part of the Book of Lorgar, said to have been carved by the Dark Apostle Jarulek.

At the far end of the gallery, at either side of the great doors, stood a pair of warrior-brothers, the two chosen to act as the honour guard accompanying the First Acolyte to the exhortation. Each wore long robes of cream over their blood-red armour, and stood static in their positions, bolters held clasped across their chests. Tall curling horns extended from the helms of the warriors, and the pair made no reaction as Burias crossed the gallery to stand before the great doors.

A partially hidden side door clicked open, and a shuffling, robed figure emerged. Bent almost double, the figure's face was obscured beneath its hood, and it bore a brazier upon its back from which strong smelling incense smoke wafted in thick clouds. Sickly thin, grey-fleshed, shaking hands clasped a metal lidded bowl, and as the awkward figure hurried towards him, Burias raised his arms out to either side. The attendant lifted the lid on the bowl, revealing a stiff brush sitting in oil. Burias stood impassively as the shuffling figure daubed his armour with the sacred cleansing oils, stretching to reach his arms. Its duty done, the figure turned and retreated back within the sanctity of its den. Idly, Burias wondered for how many centuries the pathetic creature had performed this duty.

He pushed such thoughts from his mind as he strode forwards and placed a hand upon one of the great doors. Perfectly weighted, it swung open noiselessly at his light touch. Without pause, Burias entered the sanctum of the First Acolyte, the door sliding shut behind him.

The entrance room was sparsely decorated, with little ornamentation. Arched doorways led off to other parlours and rooms of worship, and on the other side of the large room hung a curtain of bone beads, leading to a smaller antechamber. Burias was always intrigued by the floor when he entered this room, and he stared down at it in awe. The entire floor space had been constructed in a clear, glass-like material, and beneath it was a gigantic stone carved, eight-pointed star. Around the star, a red liquid writhed and boiled with a life of its own, and as he watched, faces and hands appeared within the viscous substance, clawing at the smooth glass beneath him. He grinned at the pained and angry expressions of the beings within. He imagined that they looked at him jealously, walking freely without containment as he was. Once, he had asked Marduk what they were. Are they daemons trapped within, he had questioned? Marduk had replied that they were, in a sense. He called them the Imaginos, and he claimed that they were but reflections that mirrored the inner daemons of those that looked upon them. A face manifested itself right beneath Burias's feet, and ripped its smiling face open, revealing a snarling and spitting visage beneath. Burias laughed softly, and snarled back at the creature.

'Is it time already, Burias?' asked the powerful voice of Marduk, the First Acolyte, from behind the curtain.

'It is, First Acolyte,' Burias replied. He could just make out the shadowy form of his master behind the beaded curtain, a large, dark silhouette kneeling within the slightly raised small room beyond.

'A shame. I was experiencing some most lucid dream visions. Most enlightening,' said the voice. 'Come closer, Burias.'

Obeying his master's order, he strode across the room. Up close, he could make out the details of the bone beads, seeing that they were tiny skulls. Were they real, shrunken with sorceries? he wondered, as he had done a million times before.

'Surely the exhortation will be such that any regrets as to its timing will be soon forgotten,' suggested Burias.

'Sometimes I think you should lead the sermons, such a golden tongue you have,' said Marduk. The shadow of the holy warrior rose to its feet and rolled its shoulders, loosening muscles that had been immobile for long hours of prayer and meditation. He angled his neck from side to side, producing cracking sounds, and turned around. With an imperious sweep of a gauntleted hand, the First Acolyte brushed the beaded skull curtain aside and stepped down into the room. Burias instantly lowered his gaze respectfully. Coiling smoke followed in Marduk's wake, and Burias could taste the dry, acrid incense in the back of his throat.

Eyes downcast, he saw that the Imaginos had fled. He could feel the closeness of the First Acolyte: the charged air, the electric taste of the gods that hung upon him. Truly, he was chosen of the gods, and Burias relished the sensation.

'You can look up now, Burias, your reverential obeisance has been witnessed,' said Marduk, a sarcastic tone tingeing his words.

Burias raised his gaze to meet his master's flinty, cold eyes. 'Have I angered you, First Acolyte?'

Marduk laughed, a harsh, barking sound.

'Anger me? But you are always so careful with your displays of respect. How could you have possibly angered me, Burias?' Marduk held Burias's gaze, dark humour in his eyes. 'No, you have not angered me, my friend,' he said, turning away. 'My mind is… occupied. The dream visions are coming to me more frequently since leaving the Maelstrom, the closer we draw to the planet of the Great Enemy.'

'Your power grows, First Acolyte,' said Burias, looking at Marduk's strong profile, his skin so pale it was translucent.

'And yours with it, my champion,' Marduk growled.

Burias grinned ferally. 'That it does.'

Marduk's head was ritually shaved, except for a long, braided length of black hair that sprouted from his crown. A network of criss-crossing, blue veins pulsed beneath his flesh. Cables and pipes pushed through the skin at his temples, and his teeth had grown into sharp fangs over the centuries. He was truly a terrifying warrior to look upon, and his armour was bedecked with honorifics and artefacts of religious significance. Burnished metal talismans, tiny shrunken skulls and Chaos icons hung from chains on his ornate, deep red armour. A scrimshawed bone of the prophet Morglock was strapped to his thigh with padlocked chains, and extracts from the Book of Lorgar, scratched upon human flesh, hung from his shoulder pads.

'And how is Drak'shal today?' asked Marduk, looking deep into Burias's lupine eyes.

'Quiet. But I can feel he is… hungry.'

Marduk laughed. 'Drak'shal is always hungry. It is his nature. But I am glad he is not strong today; today is no time for him to come to the fore. Keep him in check. His time will come soon enough.'

'I look forward to it. He so likes to kill.'

'Yes, he does, and he does it very well. But come now, we must not keep the Dark Apostle waiting.'

The pair left the sanctum, Burias leading the First Acolyte in silence, the icon held out before him, reverentially clasped in both hands. The honour guard fell into position a step behind. They walked through twisting corridors and up further flights of stairs until they came to a great, golden door, details picked out in relief. Once there, all four of the Word Bearers warriors dropped to one knee and bowed their heads. They waited in silence for several minutes before the doors before them were thrown open.

'Arise,' said a dangerously softly spoken voice.

Raising his eyes, Burias looked upon Jarulek, the Dark Apostle of the Host. Bedecked in a black robe that covered much of his ancient, blood-red armour, he was neither particularly tall nor broad for one of the Legion. Outwardly, he projected none of the sense of brutal power that Kol Badar exuded, nor the potent vitality that Marduk possessed. Nor did warriors fear him for the lethal savagery that Burias knew lurked only barely beneath the surface of his own demeanour.

It was perhaps the confidence of one who knew that the gods themselves sanctioned his actions that made warriors tremble before him, or perhaps it was the absolute belief in what he did, the fire of faith that burned within his soul or whatever of it was left, for it had long been pledged to the ravenous gods of Chaos. Whatever it was, Jarulek inspired fear, awe and devotion in equal measures. His words were spoken softly and deliberately, but on the battlefield his voice would rise to a powerful howl that was terrifying and inspiring to hear.

Every centimetre of Jarulek's exposed pale skin was covered in the hallowed words of Lorgar. Tiny, intricate script was inscribed perfectly across his flesh. Litanies and catechisms ran symmetrically down each side of his pale, hairless head, and his cheeks, chin and neck were sprawled with passages and curses. There was not a place upon him where you could place a data-stylus and not be touching the hallowed words of the great daemon primarch. Devotions, supplications, orisons, they extended over Jarulek's lips, inside his cheeks and across his tongue. Not even his eyes had been spared, citations of vengeance, hate and worship scribed on the soft, glutinous jelly of those orbs. He was a walking Book of Lorgar, and Burias was in awe at his presence.

'Lead the Dark Apostle forth, Icon Bearer,' intoned Marduk. Six additional guards of honour stepped into place around Marduk and the Dark Apostle, and together with the pair accompanying Marduk they represented the eight points of the star of Chaos.

'First, we worship,' said Jarulek. 'Then we kill a world.'

'I RISK MY men in there, and I am told to forget all about it?' spat Lieutenant Varnus. 'There is some kind of cult organisation operating in Shinar, perhaps across the whole of Tanakreg. We are just getting close.'

Varnus glared across the plain metal desk at Captain Lodengrad. The captain looked of middling years, but it was hard to gauge. He could have been forty, or a hundred and forty, depending on how much augmetic surgery he had been subjected to. Certainly he didn't appear to have aged in all the time Varnus had known him.

There were no features within the blank walls of the interview room other than the desk, the two chairs and the door. One wall was mirrored, and Varnus stood glaring at his tired and angry reflection. He knew that a trio of conjoined servitor twins stood beyond the mirror, recording and monitoring every movement made and every word spoken in the room. His heartbeat, blood pressure and neural activity were being analysed and recorded on a spooling dataslate, the details noted down by fingers ending in needle-like stylus instruments.

'Sit down, lieutenant,' said the captain.

'You seriously want me to go back on patrol and just forget everything I saw in that damned basement?'

'No one said anything about you going back to work, lieutenant,' said the captain. 'You disobeyed a direct order, and you struck a fellow enforcer.'

'Oh, come on! If I had obeyed your direct order, *sir*, the whole place would have gone up in flames. And Landers is a loudmouth cur. He was questioning *my* order. And he reports directly to me, if I recall correctly.'

'Sit down, lieutenant,' said the captain. Varnus continued to stare at his own reflection. 'Sit *down*,' the captain repeated, more forcefully.

'So what, are you going to kick me out? Send me back to work the damnable salt plains? Like before you recruited me?' Varnus sat back down and folded his arms. 'You knew what I was when you gave me this job. If you didn't want that, then you should never have pulled me out of the worker-habs in the first place.'

'Forget about all that, lieutenant. I'm not getting rid of you just yet. I'm just telling you to forget everything you saw in that basement. It is no longer our concern.'

'Not our concern?' exclaimed Varnus. 'That was no group of isolated, small time, hab-gangers, captain. The information they had was highly classified material: maps, plans, schematics. They had plans of the damn governor's palace, for Throne's sake! You know what would happen if they managed to get explosives within the palace? They could knock out the entire city's power in one go, and what would happen then, captain? It would be bedlam: rioting, looting, murder. It would take a lot more enforcers than you have to put all that down. The PDF would have to be brought in. It would be absolute bedlam.'

'Are you quite finished, lieutenant?' asked the captain.

'Um, let me think. No. No, I'm not actually.'

'Well, hold onto those thoughts. There is someone here who may be able to answer them,' said the captain, rising to his feet. Varnus raised an eyebrow. 'I'm sick of listening to you, lieutenant. I'm going to get some caffeine. Wait here.'

The captain walked to the door and knocked twice. The door opened a moment later, and he left the room.

Varnus pushed his chair back and placed his feet on the table. He closed his eyes. He was so damn tired.

The door opened a few moments later. Varnus didn't bother to open his eyes. He sighed dramatically.

'It's Varnus, isn't it? Lieutenant Mal Varnus.' The voice was hard, and the lieutenant dropped his feet from the table, standing to look up into the face of the newcomer.

The man was big, bigger even than Landers, and he was dressed in the severe black uniform of an Arbites judge.

Throne above! An Arbites judge!

The blood rushed from Varnus's face, and he licked his lips.

The judge walked around Varnus and sat down in the seat recently vacated by the captain. His jaw was thick and square, his nose flat against his face and his brow heavy and solid. In all respects the judge looked hard and unrelenting. His intimidating physical presence was further enhanced by heavy ablative carapace armour and by the severe black uniform he wore over it.

'Sit down, lieutenant,' he ordered forcefully, his eyes cold and danger-ous, his voice deep.

Varnus sat down warily.

'What you discovered, it is not within the jurisdiction of local enforc-ers. It is within the jurisdiction of Imperial law, Arbites law.'

Varnus frowned darkly.

'However, I have been reading your record,' continued the judge. 'It was... interesting reading. The Arbites could use a man like you, lieuten-ant.'

Varnus raised an eyebrow and pushed himself back in his chair. 'Huh?'

The judge pushed something across the table towards him. It was a heavy round pin, embossed with the aquila. He stared at it, and then looked questioningly into the eyes of the Arbites judge.

'Tomorrow, come to the palace. I have matters to attend to there, but at their conclusion I wish to speak with you. Present this.'

With that, the judge rose to his feet, huge and imposing, and left the room.

Varnus sat still for long minutes. Then he picked up the pin. He stood, and turned to leave, halting when he caught a glimpse of his own reflec-tion. He snorted in amusement and left the room.

THE INFIDUS DIABOLUS left the roiling, familiar comfort of the warp, the realm of the gods, and burst into real space. Crackling shimmers of light, colour and sheet electricity ran along its hull as the last vestiges of the Empyrean were shaken off. The strike cruiser shuddered, its immense length creaking and straining as the natural laws of the uni-verse took hold of it once more.

Deep within the belly of the cruiser, Jarulek's grand Host of the Word

Bearers Legion joined together in worship of the gods of Chaos. It was a requiem mass, a celebration of the death that they would soon deliver, a promise of souls. It was a prayer in the darkness, a pledge of faith, an honouring of the very real, insatiable deities of the warp.

The huge mass of the *Infidus Diabolus* was tiny and insignificant in the vast, cold darkness of the galaxy. But to the doomed world that it ploughed silently towards it was death, and it closed towards the blissfully unaware planet unerringly.

CHAPTER THREE

THE PALACE OF the Governor of Tanakreg was a sprawling fortress bastion that perched on a long dormant volcanic outcrop overlooking the city of Shinar, the largest industrial city on the planet. Shinar rolled out to the west of the fortress. Any other approach to the palace was impossible, for sheer cliffs hundreds of metres high dropped down from the bastion walls into the blackened, acidic oceans that dominated the planet's surface.

Varnus held onto the railing tightly as he stared out of the vision slit of the fast moving tri-railed conveyance. The compartment was packed with adepts of the Administratum whose access level allowed them to move around the city freely rather than confining them to their workstations. Soft-skins, he thought derisively. They were uniformly scrawny, wide-eyed and pale-faced, weakling specimens of humanity. Their faces and hands were unlined and soft. Most of the citizenry had a wind-blown harshness to their craggy faces, and eyes that were practically hidden from squinting against the salt winds for years on end. Indeed, most living on Tanakreg succumbed to salt-blindness by the time they reached forty standard Imperial years of age. Their skin generally looked like dried, cracked parchment, the moisture slowly sucked from their bodies by years of exposure to the harsh, salt-laced air.

Varnus was full of scorn for the privileged soft-skins able to avoid the harshness of the land. Most of them had probably never felt the touch of the wind upon their skin. He glared at them occasionally, enjoying the uncomfortable shuffling it caused amongst the robed adepts. Though the compartment was densely crowded, the adepts left a good amount of space around Varnus, intimidated, he imagined, by the enforcer uniform. He was glad of the additional room. Shinar spread out beneath him as the tri-railed conveyance began its ascent to the palace.

He marvelled at the view. From this angle, the city almost looked attractive. Throne above, but it was an ugly bitch of a city from every other angle, he thought. From here, the angled sails were just rising. The winds were coming. Every building within Shinar was constructed with a metal sheet sail that would slide out to protect the building from the worst of the salt winds. Those winds were devastating. They could reduce a newly constructed building to dust within years if not adequately protected. Even as it was, most of Shinar was crumbling away. But then, it was cheaper to build anew on top of the ruins of the past than to properly maintain what was already built. He had never understood how that worked, but he accepted it nonetheless.

From his viewpoint, as the tri-rail climbed ever higher, the vision of a million sails rising in perfect unison was a deeply bizarre one. As the light of the blazing orange sun caught the sails, it looked for a moment as if the whole of Shinar was burning. Varnus shivered.

Shinar spread out like a growing cancer, each week encroaching further out into the salt plains, clawing its way ever closer to the mountains, hundreds of kilometres to the west. Varnus was thankful that he did not still work those damnable salt fields. He was certain that he would have been long-dead; a dried, desiccated husk had he not been picked out from amongst the other hab-workers.

The tri-rail came to a shuddering halt. A giant, tentacle-like satellite clamp reached out and fastened to the exterior of the conveyance, and the doors hissed open amongst blasts of steam and smoke. The adepts surged from the carriage, their reticence to be near Varnus apparently gone as they bustled and pushed past him, shuffling down the long corridor within the middle of the tube-like tentacle.

Filing along amongst the bustling crowd, Varnus was half carried to a great, domed reception hall. Around a hundred other tentacle tubes spilled out their cargo of humanity into the vast hall. It was seething with people, almost all garbed in robes of various shades, from grey to dark brown, and every variety of off-white and puce in between.

Looking up through the transparent dome-top, he could see the mighty walls of the bastion fortress, beyond which stood the palace proper. Those walls were immensely thick, some fifteen metres worth of reinforced plascrete. He could see half a dozen massive turrets, huge batteries of heavy calibre cannon pointing towards the heavens.

Thousands of workers, Administratum adepts, politicians and servants were joining long queues. Bored palace guards armoured in regal blue semi-plate oversaw the masses as they filtered past servitors processing their data passes. Only once through the checking station could they pass on into any of the hundreds of offices, temples, shrines or manufactorums that were located in the volcanic rock beneath the palace. It was a city within a city. Built far beneath all of this were the giant plasma reactors that powered all of Shinar.

With a sigh, Varnus joined the queue that he thought looked like it was moving quickest, though he knew it would doubtless turn out to be the slowest. He prepared himself for a long wait.

'YOU ARE CERTAIN that the traitor will succeed?' growled Kol Badar, his critical gaze watching the Legion's warriors in the vast bay below. Led by their champions, hundreds of Word Bearers marched in orderly squads up the embarkation ramps and entered the bellies of the transport craft. Most were Thunderhawks, their hulls the familiar clotted-blood red, some were older Stormbirds, but there were dozens of others that had been salvaged or claimed by the Legion on their many raids from the ether. More than one had been discovered adrift in the warp, their crews slaughtered by the denizens of the realm when their warp fields had failed. The *Infidus Diabolus* had no need of such warp fields, the Word Bearers embracing the creatures of that unstable realm.

'He will succeed,' stated Jarulek flatly.

'If the traitor fails then the enemy's air defences will be fully operative. The Deathclaws will be annihilated.'

Jarulek turned towards the towering form of his coryphaus, his eyes flashing.

'I have said that the traitor does not fail. I have seen it. Board your Stormbird. Go kill. It is what you do well.'

GOVERNOR THEOFORIC FLENSKE sighed and fingered the sugared sweet-meats on his tiny, porcelain plate. They were his favourites, and they normally gave him small moments of joy in his otherwise long, drawn out and exhausting days.

He had always known that being governor of Tanakreg was going to be a stressful and thankless task, and was quite comfortable with that. He knew that he was admirably suitable for the role, and that he had best served the Emperor by taking on the position. He was utterly devoted to the Imperium, and was very happy to serve it as best he could. But this accursed bickering! It was going to be the death of him! He popped a sugar-coated nut into his mouth and closed his eyes briefly. It was a moment of escape. He crunched down on the nut, the sound echoing loudly in his head. He opened his eyes quickly, flicking his gaze around the table to see if anyone had noticed.

Dozens of advisors, PDF officers, politicos, consultants and members of the Ecclesiarchy were sitting around the long table. This was a gathering of the most powerful individuals on Tanakreg, but for all their importance and rank they argued like children, and Governor Flenske felt a headache building behind his eyes.

'Some cool water, my lord?' asked a quiet voice at his ear. Flenske nodded his head, thankful as always for the attentiveness of Pierlo, his manservant and bodyguard. Each of the people sitting at the council table had a small team of aides standing to attention behind their high-backed, velvet seats, though these little coteries were each distinctly different from one another. Behind the colonel and his majors of the PDF were stern-faced adjutants, their uniforms crisp. Behind the jabbering politicos, bureaucrats, adepts and ministers were servitor lexographers that recorded their words, long mechanical fingers scratching their masters' diatribes onto tiny rolls of unfurling paper, and punching holes in data-coils. Lesser priests and confessors stood behind the high ranking members of the Ecclesiarch, their eyes downcast. Kneeling at the side of the cardinal, who was sweating in the full regalia of his office, were a pair of shaven-headed women, their mouths sewn shut. They wore the aquila upon their chests, and bore seals of purity stitched into their pale robes.

Sitting quietly at the table amongst the throng was the scarlet-robed Tech-Administrator Tharon. He wore a twelve toothed cog upon his breast, the symbol of the Adeptus Mechanicus, and his right eye had been replaced with a black lens piece that whirred softly as it focused.

The Arbites judge stood with his back to the proceedings, looking out through the tinted, floor to ceiling plex-windows over the city spread out below. His arms were folded and he made no move, nor any comment, as the items on the agenda were discussed. Barring his helmet, he wore his full suit of carapace armour beneath his heavy black coat. A large autopistol was holstered conspicuously on his hip; there was no one within the palace with the authority to claim his weapon. His immobile presence made Flenske sweat, and the governor dabbed at his forehead, glancing over at the judge's back every few moments. The presence of a member of the Adeptus Arbites spoke of serious matters indeed, but he had no idea what it was that the judge sought in his cabinet meeting.

'Friends, please,' he began, his trained and subtly augmented voice carrying out over the din. Despite his unease at the unexpected appearance of the judge, his voice was self-assured and practised. 'Adept Trask, please summarise your point concisely. Leave out the rhetoric,' he said, a generous smile upon his face. 'It seems to irritate the colonel.'

Polite laughter greeted his comment, and Adept Trask rose again to his feet, clearing his throat. He lifted a slate and began to read from it. The governor coughed markedly, interrupting the dull voice of the small man, who looked up from his slate expectantly.

'A *summary* of your point, minister,' said the governor, still smiling, 'as in one that you can say out loud in less than an hour of our precious time, perhaps?'

The adept did not know whether to be insulted or not, but seeing the governor smiling at him still, he gave a nervous smile of his own and flicked through the thick wad of papers on his slate. Moron, thought Flenske.

'In… in summary,' the adept began, 'there have been seventy-eight raids across Shinar in the last three weeks, and two hundred and twelve insurgents have been detained by the enforcers. The situation is under control.' The adept sat back down quickly.

'Under control? Are you of sound mind, adept?' asked a robed, skeletally thin bureaucrat. 'We are overrun with riots and demonstrations, all linked to insurgent activity, and getting worse every week! Situation under control? I beg to differ. The enforcers are unable to control Shinar any longer. I mean no slur against them, but they do not have the resources or men to contain the insurgents.'

The aging Minister for the Interior, Kurtz, raised his hand to speak. He was a stocky, powerful man despite his age, but he had lost the use of his legs decades earlier and was confined to his powered chair. Once he had been an officer in the PDF and a captain of the enforcers, before he had been deprived of the use of legs. He was a tough old fighter, renowned among Flenske's ministers for his stubbornness, and most considered him a crude man with none of the refinement that came from proper breeding. The governor sighed as he saw the thick pile of documents that Kurtz held in his hand.

'The honoured Bureaucrat of the Third speaks the truth. I have been reviewing the various reports that show the activities of these so-called insurgents. They are far more organised and widespread than any here give them credit for.'

There were snorts of derision from around the table, and the governor fixed his gaze on Kurtz.

'What is this evidence then, noble minister?' he asked, flicking a glance towards the judge.

'Extensive details of Shinar and the Shinar Peninsula. Focused map work showing the valleys and paths that lead through the mountains.'

There were more snorts of derision around the table.

'You mean the enforcers found some *maps*, minister?' asked the governor. 'They needn't have raided insurgents just to find *maps*, man. I'm sure that our cartographers could have loaned them some.'

'They have detailed layouts of your palace, governor, including,' Kurtz said firmly, looking down at a map layout in front of him, 'the location of passages that show up on no unclassified map of the palace. Passages leading into your bedchambers, for instance.'

The governor swallowed whole the nut he had been gumming, and several of the figures at the table stood, their voices raised. He felt his manservant Pierlo lean in close behind him.

'Shall I go and change the combinations on the access passage to your personal chambers, my lord?' he asked quietly.

The governor nodded, and the man slipped out of the room.

'From the evidence garnered by the enforcers,' continued Kurtz, raising his voice over the clamour in the room, 'it is my belief that these covert groups are coordinating acts of rebellion and sedition that threaten the stability of Shinar. These are not isolated groups of rebel salt workers that are trying to avoid paying taxes. This is a well supplied and armed group of organised insurgents that have integrated covertly into the institutions of Shinar and beyond.'

He held up a schematic map.

'This shows unsanctioned construction of a considerable size in the Shaltos Mountains, not three hundred kilometres from where we sit. I believe this is a staging post, a training facility perhaps.'

'Minister, these documents, I would like them to be studied by my own people. Please pass them on to my aide once this meeting is concluded.'

'Governor?' said Kurtz, his face incredulous. 'You… you do not wish to act upon the information I have gleaned immediately?'

'I will act, minister, when and if I deem it to be appropriate to do so,' the governor said forcefully.

'Now,' he said. 'Colonel? I hear that the PDF is having some problems at the present?'

'I regret that that is so, governor. The Commissariat has been forced to execute a number of officers for… various infractions. As for the *insurgents*, I recommend that we pull more of the PDF ranks into Shinar. I believe the popular unrest can be stemmed with a martial presence.'

'Popular unrest?' burst the minister of the interior. 'This is coordinated cult activity, governor, not *popular unrest*,' he spat. 'It is my belief that these insurgents are worshippers of the Ruinous Powers, and that…'

'That is *enough*, minister!' hollered the governor. He felt the pain behind his eyes increase, and he took another sip of water. 'I will not have such talk bandied without irrefutable proof!' He took a deep breath. 'Thank you, colonel,' he said. He turned towards the sweating cardinal. 'And the Ecclesiarch? Holy cardinal, what do you say?'

'More citizens are attending the sermons than ever, governor. I attribute it to the nearing conjunction of planets. Scaremongering propaganda has been spread through the lower hab-blocks claiming that it signals the end of the world. The superstitious salt farmers are afraid.' The cardinal shrugged his thick shoulders, 'Ergo, more citizens on pews in the daily hymnals.'

The governor grunted. 'It certainly seems to me that this rise in insurgency, the riots, the scaremongering, it all relates back to the conjunction. It's just a damn planet passing, for Shinar's sake! Why under Throne is it such a big deal?'

'The red planet of Korsis circles our system in an aberrant, elliptical orbit, and on occasion it passes extremely close to Tanakreg. On very rare occasions, Korsis passing us coincides with a conjunction of sorts, when all the planets in our system are aligned. The last time this happened was ten thousand, two hundred and ninety-nine years ago. Such a conjunction will occur in less than three months time,' said a bespectacled, robed man.

'Thank you, learned one,' said the governor sharply. The pain behind his eyes was becoming almost unbearable.

'If it pleases you, governor,' said the tech-administrator, 'I would like to return to the sub-station. I was in the process of blessing the machine-spirits of the turbines when your request for my presence came through.'

'Fine, fine, go,' said the governor, waving his hand.

The Arbites judge turned around, his face emotionless. The room went deathly quiet, and the severe figure let the silence grow. The governor felt his stomach knot.

'I have heard enough,' the judge said finally, the sound of his voice making Flenske flinch.

VARNUS WAS BORED. Once he had finally been filtered through the checking facilities on the sub-ground floor, then the third floor, the eighteenth and finally the ground floor of the palace proper, he had been subjected to a rigorous security check from the regal, blue-armoured palace guards. They had requested his weapons, and he had realised that he would be denied access if he refused to give up his side arm and his power maul. With some reluctance he handed them over. He had even been forced to relinquish his helmet – 'comm security', apparently.

He had been directed to a small alcove, there to await the Adeptus Arbites judge. It was a small corridor space linking two grand galleries, and there were dozens of other plaintiffs and officials already sitting there, their eyes glazed. He took a seat at the far end of the corridor alcove.

It had been hours, and he was deathly tired of the whole thing. There was an impressive staircase on the other side of one of the grand galleries that the alcove opened onto, and he watched it with boredom. A heavy guard presence prevented anyone from climbing the stairs. Those that even began to approach backed away after seeing the guards. At the top of the stairs was a massive pair of double-doors, with another set of guards holding tall, high powered las-locks, vertically to attention. They didn't move, and their faces were stoic. They must be as bored as he was, he thought.

With a click he saw one of the large doors open briefly, and a man exit. The guards barely looked at him as he lifted the hem of his red robe and quickly descended the stairs. Some tech, he thought, as he saw the Mechanicus symbol on his chest and the bionics of his left eye. The man looked flustered, and he hurried to the bottom of the stairs, looking left and right frantically. A man that Varnus had not noticed before stepped out to meet him, and the tech began to talk animatedly. The other man shushed him, and Varnus recognised him as the one who had exited the same room earlier. The enforcer instantly disliked him; he looked like yet another arrogant, officious noble. The pair hurried off, and Varnus sighed.

THE GOVERNOR LICKED his lips and a bead of sweat rolled down the side of his face as the imposing Arbites judge stared across the room at him, his face a cold, expressionless mask.

'The local enforcer units have been sapped of resources and manpower over the last decade as a direct result of the policies of the governorship, and as a result it is unfit to deal with the insurgent threat. This speaks of gross and inexcusable incompetence.'

The accusation hung in the air, and none around the table dared make a sound. Governor Flenske felt his world contract and heat rising up his neck. His eyes flicked around the table before him. No one met his gaze except Minister Kurtz.

'I'm… this… perhaps we… misread the severity of the… the situation. Nothing that cannot be rectified, I assure you,' said the governor, his voice sounding hollow and weak in his own ears.

'Shinar risks falling into anarchy and rebellion. The security of the city is compromised, and this is an unacceptable situation. The time for bureaucratic pandering is over. Governor Flenske, I find you in contempt of your duties. You are to be replaced by a stewardship until a more suitable governor can be instated. I am locking down Shinar in a state of martial law until the insurgency has been eliminated and the city secured.'

The governor's face paled, and he felt his chest tighten. He tried to speak, but he couldn't find the words, and his mouth flapped open and shut in rising panic.

The judge pulled his large, black autopistol from its holster and pointed it at the governor. Never before had a weapon been levelled at him, and Flenske felt rising warmth in his trousers. He realised that he had soiled himself, and he felt shame as he stared in horror and panic at the barrel of the pistol.

'With the power vested in me by the Adeptus Arbites I hereby remove Planetary Governor Flenske from his position.'

'No, no…' began the governor.

The autopistol barked loudly. Three rounds punched through Flenske's forehead and the back of his head exploded. His body was thrown backwards to the ground as his chair overturned beneath him. Three empty shell casings fell to the marble floor with a musical, tinkling sound, and smoke rose from the barrel of the gun before it was smoothly replaced in its holster.

The judge walked around the table, his boot steps echoing loudly across the room. Giving the governor's body a push with his heel, he righted his chair and sat down at the head of the table.

'I want all local PDF units retracted to Shinar,' he stated to the pale-faced group of individuals staring at him in shock and horror. 'I want a lock down of all traffic into and out of the city, and I want armed checkpoints set up along all main thoroughfares. I want an indefinite curfew instated; any individual found on the streets after curfew is to be shot. The palace is to be secured; I want no one coming in or going out without my say-so. Contact the twin cities and order their local PDF units to be recalled within the city boundaries. Tell them to be ready for potential hostile activity.'

He glanced around the table, his gaze hard.

'We have a lot of work to do, and I am not here to play your little political games. I am here to bring this city back to order in the name of the God-Emperor. I am here to avert disaster, if at all possible.'

Governor Flenske's blood pooled out beneath his body. There was shocked silence around the room. No one dared move. The acrid smell of the gun's discharge was mixing with the stink of blood.

'Tanakreg teeters on the brink of destruction,' said the judge. 'This group is its only possible salvation.'

Then the room exploded, turning into a roaring inferno. Everyone in the chamber was instantly slain as the force of the detonations ripped the room apart. The marble floor exploded into millions of tiny shards and the synth-hardened plex-windows shattered outwards. The force of the blast rocked the entire palace and oily, black smoke billowed from the rising ball of flame that burst from the shattered windows.

VARNUS WAS THROWN back through the alcove corridor from the force of the blast that smashed aside the huge doors, throwing them off their hinges and hurling the guards through the air like rag dolls. Varnus was thrown back over ten metres, flying clear of the corridor and smashing to the gallery floor, amid a tangle of burning rubble and flesh. Dimly, he heard blaring alarms, and then he heard nothing.

CHAPTER FOUR

KOL BADAR GLARED around at his warriors, all members of the cult of the Anointed. The most vicious, faithful and dangerous warriors within the Host, he had wanted them to accompany the Dark Apostle on his drop assault, but Jarulek would not hear of it. Their Terminator armour was too bulky for a lightning assault on the palace, he had said, and Kol Badar had reluctantly agreed with him. It just did not feel right, though. He had always fought at the side of the Dark Apostle with his elite brethren.

The horned helmets of the Anointed looked daemonic under the glowing, red lights within the cramped hold of the Land Raider, and Kol Badar knew that he too looked like some malevolent daemon of the warp in his ornate battle-helm. Barbed tusks protruded like monstrous mandibles from his ancient helmet, which was crafted in the likeness of a snarling, bestial visage. The massive tank roared across the plains of the planet Tanakreg, hauling its deadly cargo ever closer to the central battle lines of the pathetic Imperials.

He was disappointed with the enemy, but then, he could not expect any more from them. The Imperium had grown weak.

The Host was borne from the *Infidus Diabolus* in scores of smaller vessels, angry hornets swarming from their nest towards their foe. They had landed on the planet surface as the harsh, orange sun was setting and stormed the first defensive line, taking it within an hour. The Anointed, borne within the belly of revered Land Raiders, had assaulted up the steep embankments to take the most heavily defended sections, slaughtering all in their path.

The enemy artillery was next to useless against the powerful tanks, and the remainder of the Host rampaged through the breaches carved by the Anointed and set up their own heavy weapon teams atop the earthworks, raining death upon the Imperials mustered beyond. They marched relentlessly through the trenches, killing and mutilating, and taking bunkers and strong points at will. Kol Badar had been disgusted to see hundreds of the Imperials flee before the Legion, seeking the false safety of the second defensive line. That second line had fallen almost as quickly as the first, once its emplaced guns had been silenced. The third line broke almost as swiftly.

There remained only the last line, the one closest to the city. The glow of the Imperial city could be seen over the horizon. This last defensive line was the shortest of the four, and had more emplacements than the first. Kol Badar hoped that it would prove somewhat more of a challenge.

So far there had been little satisfaction in these battles; they had been nothing short of massacres. The estimate was somewhere in the realm of fifteen thousand enemy troops slain, and around five hundred tanks, aircraft and support vehicles destroyed. The losses amongst the Word Bearers had been minimal.

The lascannon sponsons of the Land Raider screamed as they fired. The tank did not slow, and hit a slight rise at speed. There was a moment of weightlessness as the front of the tank became airborne before slamming back down to the ground. Dull explosions and detonations could be heard, the sound muffled by the roar of the engines and the screaming of the lascannons. The vehicle rocked as explosive shells struck its thick, armoured hide, and Kol Badar growled.

The Land Raider began ploughing up a steep incline, and Kol Badar knew that they were at the earthworks. High calibre rounds pinged off the exterior but the powerful machine had carried the Word Bearers across much deadlier battlefields on a thousand worlds, transporting them safely against far worse than these weakling Imperials could muster.

A glowing, yellow blister light began to flash, and Kol Badar pulled off the hissing coupling that held him to his seat and flexed his power talons.

'In the name of the true gods, Lorgar and the Dark Apostle,' he roared. 'Anointed! We kill once more!'

The elite cult warriors roared back, and the assault ramp of the Land Raider slammed down as the immense tank drew to a sudden halt near the top of the incline, steam hissing out into the cold of night.

After the muffled dullness within the belly of the Land Raider, the noise of the battlefield was deafening, as cannons boomed, boltguns thumped rhythmically and the screams of dying Imperials echoed across the salt plains.

Kol Badar led the Anointed onto the field of war, roaring like a primeval god. His archaic combi-bolter, its muzzle sculpted to resemble the fanged maw of some fell creature, coughed fiery death as he strode heavily forwards. His first shots ripped a grey uniformed soldier in half, and dozens more were torn apart by the gunfire of the Anointed.

The night was lit up as thousands of weapons fired, and Kol Badar could see the immense enemy bulwark stretching from horizon to horizon. Tens of thousands of uniformed PDF troopers stood along the defensive line, and hundreds of tanks and armoured units added cannon fire to the barrage.

He had chosen this place to attack the enemy for it was their most heavily defended point along the bulwark. A decisive strike that shattered their defences here would demoralise them completely.

Streaming las-fire lit up the night as the Imperials tried desperately to drop even a single one of the Anointed. The hulking Terminator-armoured figures strode to the top of the bulwark, walking straight through the frantic gunfire. Their own weapons ripped through the cowering ranks of the lightly armoured PDF troopers, the protection of their dug-in positions rendered useless.

A score of Land Raiders disgorged more of the Terminators at the top of the earthworks, and the butchery began in earnest. Kol Badar dropped down heavily over the lip of the corpse-strewn defensive position and raised his bolter to mow down a team of men working to reload an artillery piece. They were ripped to pieces, blood spraying.

Reaper autocannons roared along the line of the bulwark, the rapid firing, high-powered weapons tearing through the lines of reinforcements rushing to stem the breach in their lines. The high velocity rounds from the potent weapons tore up the defensive line and reached a battery of artillery pieces. The guns were instantly engulfed in a huge explosion as the armour piercing autocannon rounds ignited stacks of high-explosive shells. The fireball rose high in the sky, and further explosions answered it as other Anointed warriors struck further gun batteries.

'Warmonger, lead the Host forward,' growled Kol Badar, opening a comm-channel to the Dreadnought. 'Come join the slaughter, my brother.'

'SIR! WE ARE being massacred! They won't die! Emperor save us, they just won't die!'

Captain Drokan of the 23rd Tanakreg PDF cursed and licked his dry lips as he ordered the comm-channel closed. What could he do? There must be a way to salvage something out of this disastrous engagement, but he was damned if he knew what it was. He turned to his adjutant, who looked absolutely terrified, his face pale and his eyes staring.

'Val! Anything from the colonel? From any of the damn officers?'

The pale-faced adjutant shook his head, and Drokan cursed once again.

There had been no warning of the attack. The Emperor alone knew what had happened to the listening posts that skirted the system; a sudden attack like this just should not have been possible!

But it was happening, and it was all too real. Somehow Drokan had found himself the most superior ranked officer, cut off from the upper echelons. Him, Anubias Drokan! Never a dedicated student of tactics or strategy, he had risen to the rank of captain more because of his family's status and his own skill with a sword than through any real competence. It was only the PDF, damn it! Father had wanted him to join the ranks to give him a bit of hardness about him, he had said. A few years of service; he had never expected to be on the front line of a full-scale planetary assault!

Think, man. Think! What should he do? He had four companies of the 23rd with him here (dying here, he thought), but what other regiments were close by? There was the 9th and the 11th, but his adjutant had been unable to contact them on the comms. He assumed they had already been engaged and destroyed by the enemy.

He had to get the other nearby regiments to pull away from the last line, pull back to Shinar. That's what his superiors would do, he thought. Shinar, the palace, the governor; they were what needed protecting. Feeling slightly buoyed, Drokan turned to his adjutant once more.

'Put out a blanket message to all Shinar PDF regiments. Tell them to pull back to the city. The 23rd will hold them here for as long as we can. We will buy them as much time as possible.'

The adjutant gaped. 'We are to hold here? That's suicide!'

'Pass the damn message! Shinar is more important than the 23rd!'

With shaking hands, the adjutant began to relay the message. The captain shouted to the driver of the Chimera to head towards the battle. The man gunned the engines and the vehicle roared across the salt plains.

The men of the 23rd had never seen active service. War had never come to Tanakreg, and the only time the PDF had been required to use live ammunition had been to quell a minor insurgency within Shinar some four decades earlier. Most of the PDF soldiers had never fired on a live target.

Still, Drokan felt clear-headed suddenly. Yes, he would hold the enemy here. He pulled his laspistol from its holster. Just like his men, he had honed his skills on the target field, though he had never fired a shot in anger or defence. But I am a renowned swordsman, he told himself, patting the ornate chainsword at his hip. He had fought in countless tourneys, and had won several medals.

'Ca… Captain Drokan?' said his adjutant. 'The other regiments… they are not responding. Not one of them. I… I think we may be the last regiment within a thousand kilometres of Shinar.'

The captain frowned. 'Ah,' he said, 'I see.' He felt strangely calm. 'Well, pick up my family standard. We go to fight alongside the men.'

The adjutant gaped at the captain.

'Come on, boy!' urged Drokan. The younger man unclipped his safety harness and scrambled across to the other side of the command Chimera. He opened a stowage compartment, and removed a long black case. He struggled with the ornate clasps, but finally popped them open, and pulled out the captain's family standard. It was furled tightly around a telescopic pole. With a nod, the captain leant back in his seat as his Chimera took them into the maelstrom of battle.

KOL BADAR STRODE along the fortified line, gunning down dozens of terrified PDF troopers, their puny bodies torn apart by the force of his combi-bolter. Reaching an enclosed bunker emplacement, he ripped the sealed blast door from its hinges and stooped to enter. It housed half a dozen men and three, rapid firing heavy bolters that were pumping fire into the advancing lines of the Host.

Kol Badar gunned them all down, the walls of the emplacement splashing with their blood as he raked them with fire. Ripping another blast door from its housing, Kol Badar exited the emplacement and began killing once more.

Looking down over the plains beyond the last defensive line, he saw scores of APCs moving forwards in a desperate last-ditch attempt to hold back the Word Bearers. Salt dust kicked up behind the approaching vehicles, and lascannon fire and krak missiles streamed towards the Imperial vehicles from the heavy weapon teams that had gained the bulwark. Several of the advancing vehicles exploded spectacularly, spinning end over end as fuel lines were penetrated.

The Chimera APCs roared to a halt, and over a thousand PDF reserve troopers emerged, las-fire stabbing towards the Word Bearers. Smiling, Kol Badar strode down to meet them.

He knew that subtlety and strategy were not needed, just killing and more killing. It was what his warriors excelled at.

He strode onwards through the hail of gunfire, spraying boltrounds left and right. The salt plains were turning a deep red colour as the porous granules soaked up the gore.

'TANAKREG 23RD!' SHOUTED PDF Captain Drokan. 'Drive them back!' The soldiers screamed as they ran, their lasguns firing and bayonets readied. The captain's adjutant found himself shouting along with them. Hefting the captain's unfurled banner in one hand he began firing his laspistol, even though he could not yet see the foe.

Suddenly he saw the enemy, and he wished that he had not. They were huge, making the PDF soldiers look like children.

They were all going to die, he realised.

* * *

KOL BADAR RAISED an eyebrow within his fully enclosed helm as he saw the soldiers running towards him, an officer at their forefront brandishing a roaring chain blade. The towering warlord didn't even bother to raise his combi-bolter, and he began stalking towards the fools running at him and his Anointed warriors. Las-rounds thudded uselessly into him as the distance closed. The officer lifted his chainsword high, his face defiant. Kol Badar almost laughed out loud.

The warlord swatted the blade away dismissively with the back of his power talon, breaking the man's arm in the process, and clubbed the officer down into the ground with a blow from his combi-bolter. He stamped down heavily on the mewling wretch, and the man's skull shattered like a pulverised egg.

The Anointed cleaved into the PDF troopers, ripping limbs from sockets, tearing heads from bodies. The Coryphaus saw Bokkar drive his chain fist into the body of the diminutive PDF standard bearer, lifting him up into the air before the whirring blades cut the boy in half. The Anointed warrior turned his heavy flamer on the fallen standard, the fabric consumed instantly under the intense heat.

Las-fire sprayed across his back, and he hissed in pain and anger as one of the beams caught him in the back of his knee-joint. He turned and gunned down one of the PDF troopers before they disappeared beneath an inferno of flames, screaming horribly. Kol Badar nodded his head towards the Anointed warrior Bokkar, who acknowledged the Coryphaus with a nod of his own, before his heavy flamer roared again, engulfing another group of soldiers.

Heavy footsteps made the ground tremble, and Kol Badar turned towards the huge form of the Warmonger, the Dreadnought dwarfing even him as it walked through the carnage, potent cannons pumping fire towards enemy vehicles in the distance.

'It is good to crush the enemy on the field of war once more, but this is no battle, Kol Badar,' the ancient war machine boomed. There were few within the Host that would dare call the warlord by his name, but the Warmonger was amongst them. They had fought at each other's sides for millennia. Indeed, Kol Badar had been the Warmonger's Coryphaus when the warrior had been Dark Apostle.

'The enemy is weak,' agreed Kol Badar. 'How I yearn to face a worthy foe,' he added, turning his gaze up into the void of the heavens.

'You think Astartes will come?' boomed the Warmonger hungrily.

'No, I think not,' sighed Kol Badar. 'As much as I wish to face them once more. The Dark Apostle has said that in none of his dream-visions did he see any Astartes come to this world to do battle with us.'

'But minions of the Corpse Emperor will come, will they not? They will come to do battle?'

'Oh, they will come, my friend. They will be marshalling their forces even now.'

'But not Astartes?'

'No, not Astartes.'

'Bah,' snorted the Warmonger. 'It will be just mortals then.'

'Yes, mortals,' said Kol Badar, still staring up into the night sky, as if he could pierce the heavens with his angry gaze. 'One can only hope that they will come in force. At least then there may be a worthy battle.'

The Warmonger stomped off, its cannons firing once more. He saw the daemon engines clawing over the bulwark, multi-legged and spitting great gouts of flame from their maws, while others busied themselves tearing apart enemy tanks with contemptuous ease.

Kol Badar began to follow the Warmonger, to rejoin the battle once again. No, he reminded himself, this was not battle. This was a slaughter.

VARNUS COUGHED, CAUSING a searing, sharp pain in his side. Smoke was all around him, and bodies. No, not just bodies: body *parts*. He pushed himself to his feet, gasping at the pain that seemed to erupt all over his body, and his head reeled. He put a hand to his forehead and felt wet blood there, but the worst pain was in his side. It was slick with blood, and he winced as he loosened the clips holding his chest-plate in place. He hissed as he pulled out a long shard of metal that had pushed up under the body armour and into his side. He dropped the bloody shard to the floor. Still, he was alive, which was more than could be said for the others splayed out on the chamber floor.

The blast had ripped through the palace, and smoke and dust rose from piles of rubble. The walls were blackened in part, and ancient wall hangings were ablaze. Many of the bloody bodies strewn around him were also on fire, and the stink of burning flesh and fat almost made him retch. Varnus coughed painfully and he felt the floor beneath his feet shake as another blast somewhere else in the palace detonated.

The sound of shouting reached him, and he staggered towards it, away from the inferno that was blazing behind him. A trio of palace guards ran past along an adjoining corridor, and he hurried along in their wake. He felt another explosion rock the floor beneath his feet and increased his pace, wincing against the pain. He had to get out of this part of the palace.

Staggering along through the smoke that seemed to be thickening around him, he followed the direction that he thought the guards had taken. He limped through a half open door, entering a service corridor usually closed to those frequenting the palace. He passed a palace guard lying dead on the ground, a gunshot wound in the man's head. He leant down and picked up the guard's long-barrelled las-lock. It was heavy and unwieldy in his hands, but it was a weapon none-the-less.

Rounding a corner, Varnus saw a pair of palace guards standing over a fallen man. He wore a plain, cream coloured robe, identical to any number of anonymous bureaucrats that worked within the palace. Seeing him, the guards shouldered their weapons. Varnus held up his hands.

'I'm an enforcer. What the hell is going on?' Varnus managed.

'Insurgents,' said one of the guards. 'Our commander has called us out onto the upper battlements. You had best come with us, enforcer.'

Varnus nodded his head and hurried along after the guards as best as he could. Through winding passages they passed, through hissing blast-doors that their pass-cards gave access to. They climbed a set of steel stairs, and finally passed through a heavy door to emerge upon the high battlements of the palace bastion. The door slammed shut with grim finality behind them.

It was night. No, it was almost dawn, Varnus realised. How long had he been unconscious?

He saw masses of PDF soldiers garrisoned along the battlements and smaller groups of blue-armoured guards. They were rushing all over the bastion, the whole area seething with soldiers. Many were firing over the battlements at unseen foes on one of the multiple lower terraces of the bastion, and streaking lasgun fire answered them. Men crouched behind other sections of the battlements as rocket propelled grenades struck the walls, and they were raked by heavy gunfire. Men were shouting, and with the cacophony of gunfire and explosions, it seemed to Varnus that he had escaped the burning section of the palace only to enter a hell of a different kind.

Pain lanced through his side and Varnus grimaced, holding his hand to the bleeding wound.

'I'm fine,' he wheezed as he saw the guards accompanying him hesi-tate, caught between aiding him and joining the gun battle.

'Go,' he said, making the decision for them.

Floodlights lit up the battlements as if it were daylight, and Varnus, leaning heavily on his salvaged las-lock, staggered across the open area to take cover below the thick crenellations. He risked a quick glance down towards the sprawling, ugly city.

There was a series of lower terraces below the battlements upon which he stood, but beyond them he could see dozens of fires burning all across Shinar, and he could hear a steady thump of explosions coming from all over the city. From over the horizon, he thought he could see dim flashes.

'Emperor preserve us,' said Varnus quietly as he crouched back down behind the crenellations.

He started as one of the enormous air defence turrets along the battle-ments suddenly came to life, hydraulic servos whirring as the massive cannons rotated, the barrels angled high. What next? thought Varnus, as more of the turrets rotated their giant cannons heavenward.

The floodlights that lit the whole area flickered suddenly, then died.

The lights of the entire palace turned off as the potent plasma reactors beneath it went dead. A fifty-block radius around the palace went black instantly, swiftly followed by the rest of the city. Las-fire and tracer rounds flashed through the darkness.

The air defence turrets went off-line.

Without the glare of the lights, crouching, as he was in pitch darkness, Varnus could see what the turrets had been turning towards before they had died.

They looked like stars at first, but they burnt bright orange, and they were getting larger. What the hell were they? Meteors?

Whatever they were, they were approaching the palace with sickening speed. Varnus could almost feel the heat of the objects as they plummeted from the heavens.

Death rained down upon Shinar.

CHAPTER FIVE

MARDUK SMILED, EXPOSING his sharp teeth as the Deathclaw drop-pod hurtled down through the atmosphere of Tanakreg. The First Acolyte felt savage joy as the g-forces pulled at him. Burias grinned back at him like some feral beast from across the other side of the plummeting attack transport. Marduk pulled on his helmet, hearing the hiss as it slid solidly into place around his gorget, and breathed in the recycled air of his power armour deeply.

He savoured these moments, the thrill just before battle commenced. He knew that Borhg'ash, the daemon bound within the archaic chainsword at his side, felt his anticipation for the bloodshed that was soon to erupt for the weapon was vibrating slightly. It too hungered for battle.

Warning lights flashed, and Marduk felt the powerful retro-thrusters scream as they kicked in. He howled, the vox amplifiers fitted to his ornate helmet further enhancing the potency of the daemonic sound. The other Word Bearers joined in with howls of their own as their systems were filled with a sudden rush of adrenaline administered by their power armoured suits. Marduk relished the sensation of the combat drugs flooding his system.

'Into the fray once more, my brothers!' bellowed Marduk. The other nine warriors strapped into the Deathclaw roared their approval. 'We are the true bearers of the righteous fury of the gods!' Another roar. 'And in their name, we kill! Kill! And kill again!'

With that the Deathclaw struck, smashing into the ground with bone jarring force, stabiliser claws embedding deeply. Infernal mechanics grinded as the drop-pod was lifted up on its four claws, and the bladed arcs of the circular floor slid back with a hiss.

Marduk was first out of the Deathclaw, his heavy boots slamming hard onto the cracked plascrete, the booming of his vox amplifiers sounding out over the barking of his bolt pistol.

'Hate the infidels!' he roared, his pistol kicking in his hands as he fired. 'Hate them as you kill them! Hate them with your bolter and hate them with your fist!'

The towering hulk of the Deathclaw had slammed into a crenellated, terraced balcony on the upper face of the palace. Other drop-pods screamed down from above, their hulls glowing with the heat of the rapid descent. Seeing the enemy around him and feeling the fear emanating from them, Marduk licked his lips.

He thumbed the activation rune blister on his chainsword and it screamed into life. He could feel it trembling in his hand with barely suppressed hunger, and he gritted his sharpened teeth as he felt the weapon bond with his flesh, tiny barbs piercing his armoured palm.

There were uniformed soldiers all around them, scattered across the cobbled open area atop the crenellated defensive structure. Not that it was any defence against enemies that landed in their midst, thought Marduk as he fired his bolt pistol into the soldiers. They were falling away in terror from the Deathclaws that were landing with titanic force all around them.

'Death to the False Emperor!' he roared, charging into the midst of the foe. He carved left and right, hacking and rending flesh with his screaming chainsword. Blood sprayed out as he tore through the PDF troopers.

Blood and brain matter sprayed across Burias's twisted visage as he swung the heavy, barbed icon two-handed into the face of a soldier, and Marduk knew that the change would be upon him shortly. Good, he thought. Let the mortals see the face of the daemon and know that hell beckoned them.

The Word Bearers ripped though the PDF troopers, and Marduk saw a group of blue-armoured warriors standing together, long lasrifles held to their shoulders.

'With me my brethren!' he roared as he raced across the blood drenched cobblestones towards them. The soldiers fired, and las-fire streaked past Marduk's head. With a roar of animal fury he was amongst them. His chainsword ripped flesh and armour apart with ease, and he felt that the beast bound within the chainsword was pleased at the bloodshed. It pulled at his arm, urging him to seek more death for its whirring teeth. It has been too long since you tasted the blood of the heathens, he thought.

Blood welled in the carefully designed catchments of the weapon and was sucked eagerly into its inner workings. Veins pumped and throbbed along the length of the chainsword as the beast within fed. Power surged through Marduk, flowing from the daemon weapon as it grew in strength. He cleaved Borhg'ash into the chest of another victim, its sharpened teeth ripping apart flesh and ribs in a shower of gore.

The change came over Burias suddenly. His face seemed to ripple and shimmer like a mirage on a horizon. His features flickered back and forth between his own and the horned, bestial face of the daemon Drak'shal. He opened his mouth wide as his lips curled back, exposing sharp fangs and a long, flicking, bruised purple tongue. His bolt pistol dropped from his hand and was instantly retracted to his hip, the length of chain linking the weapon to his belt withdrawing automatically. His index and forefingers fused into thick, bladed talons, and he gripped the icon two-handed once more. Burias dropped into a low, bestial crouch, even as he seemed to grow in stature as the daemon's power increased.

With a roar that was at once his own and the daemon's, Burias-Drak'shal leapt from his crouch, launching straight at a terrified PDF soldier who ineffectually fired off a frantic las-blast at the creature. Burias-Drak'shal smashed the icon down onto the man's head, killing him instantly. Nevertheless, the daemonically possessed warrior punched his fist through the man's chest and raised the dead body up into the air, letting out an ungodly roar that made the substance of the air ripple with warp spawned power.

'The gods themselves send us their aid to smite the infidels!' roared Marduk. 'Behold the majesty of their power!'

The battlements were almost clear. A blast from a lasrifle struck Marduk's helmet, and his head was jerked to the side. Snarling, he turned to face the attacker that had dared to shoot him.

VARNUS SWORE AS he waited for the las-lock to repower. Though they fired powerful single bursts of energy, the weapons were painfully slow between firing. Still, the shot had done little more than irritate the towering monster that was leading the power armoured killers, so one more blast would be unlikely to do anything but stall the inevitable. Varnus knew that death had come to Tanakreg and that he had but moments left to live. Emperor protect my soul, he prayed.

The palace guard were being slaughtered. He saw one man explode as a bolt-round detonated in his shoulder, spraying blood around him like a mist as he fell to the ground, the entire left side of his torso missing. He saw another die instantly as one of the enemy clubbed him in the head with a bolter, the force of the blow crushing his skull as if it were glass.

The hulking fiend he had shot rounded on him, stalking through the melee, and Varnus swore. The monster towered over him. Varnus was in no way a small man, but he barely came half way up the beast's chest. With a hum, the las-lock re-powered and he fired again at the huge Chaos Space Marine. The shot was taken in haste and was not on target. Nevertheless, it struck the beast in his wrist, and his accursed bolt pistol dropped from his hands.

* * *

SNARLING IN ANGER, Marduk cleaved the long lasrifle wielded by the infidel in two, and reached out and grabbed him around the throat with his empty hand. He felt blood seeping from his wrist where the wretch had blasted him, but it was already congealing. His hand almost encircled the man's entire neck, and he could feel the pathetic fragility beneath his fingers. Tendons and ligaments strained as he exerted pressure.

Lifting the man into the air, his feet kicking uselessly half a metre from the ground, Marduk drew him close to his helmeted visage.

'That hurt, little man,' he said, the vox amplifier booming his words into the face of the wretch, 'but this is going to hurt a lot more.'

With that, he hurled the man off the battlements.

'Your weapon, First Acolyte,' said one of the Word Bearers, and Marduk turned to accept his bolt pistol, held reverently in the warrior's hands. Without a word, he took the weapon.

Looking out over the battlements, Marduk saw scattered fighting on a lower tier of the bastion some fifteen metres below, where the broken body of the infidel he had hurled had landed. He could see fighting down there, but no Word Bearers. Curious, he thought.

'Warriors of the IV Coterie, with me,' he ordered. 'The rest of you, cleanse this level of the Imperial filth.'

'Burias-Drak'shal!' he roared, and the daemonically possessed warrior turned from his killing, gore dripping thickly from his icon, arms and mouth. 'With me.'

The twelve warriors of the IV Coterie extricated themselves from the killing, and jogged towards the First Acolyte. Burias-Drak'shal stalked along with them, breathing heavily.

Marduk launched himself over the edge of the battlements, dropping down towards the lower terrace. He landed in the midst of a firefight, and cobblestones cracked beneath his weight. He rose up to his full height as his brethren landed around him.

'Death to the False Emperor!' he roared. The shout was repeated by several dozen of the Imperial garbed warriors. Marduk saw that most of those that had shouted had ripped their clothing to expose a crude, tattooed representation of the Latros Sacrum on their shoulders, the sacred screaming daemon symbol of the Word Bearers legion.

He began laying around with Borhg'ash and his bolt pistol, carving flesh and planting bolt-rounds through bodies. He didn't pay too much attention to those he killed, and doubtless he and the warriors of the IV Coterie slew as many of their cult followers as the Imperials, but it mattered not – the souls of both would be welcomed by the gods of Chaos.

The gunfire suddenly ceased, and the remaining men dropped to their knees, gazing up at the towering Chaos Space Marines with awe and reverence. Several had tears in their eyes. The Word Bearers held their killing in check, waiting to see the First Acolyte's reaction.

All except for Burias-Drak'shal, who stepped forward and smashed the icon into the head of one of the cultists. The man's skull crumpled and he fell without a sound.

'Burias-Drak'shal,' said Marduk quietly, and the daemon warrior looked up, snarling. His entire body trembling, Burias-Drak'shal stepped back and dropped into a half-crouch, staring hungrily at the humans. Marduk too felt the urge to step forward and slaughter the weaklings, but he knew that they had their uses. Borgh'ash trembled in his hands, wishing to kill more.

'Which one here speaks for you?' asked Marduk. The cultists looked around at each other, and finally one man stood and stepped through the other cultists to approach.

'I do, lord,' said the man, his head held high.

Marduk raised his bolt pistol and shot the man in the face. Pieces of skull, brain matter and blood splattered over the remaining kneeling cultists.

'Lower your eyes when looking upon your betters, dogs, or I shall ask Burias-Drak'shal here to remove them,' Marduk snarled.

'Now, who here speaks for you?' he repeated.

A shaven-headed woman in beige robes stepped forwards, her gaze lowered. 'I do, my lord,' she said in a shaking voice.

'What is the fourth tenant of the Book of Lorgar, dog?' asked Marduk dangerously, fingering the trigger of his bolt pistol.

The woman stood in silence for a moment, and Marduk raised the pistol to her head.

'*Give up yourself to the Great Gods in body and of soul,*' she said quickly. '*Discard all that does not benefit their Greatness. The First thing to be discarded is the Name. Your Self is nothing to the Gods, and your Name shall be as nothing to You. Only once you have reached Enlightenment shall you Reclaim you Name, and your Self. Thus spoke Great Lorgar, and thus it was to Be.*'

Marduk kept the pistol raised to her head. 'What is your name?'

'I have no name, my lord,' the woman replied instantly.

'If you have no name, what then shall I call you?'

The woman faltered for a moment, biting her lip hard, acutely aware of the bolt pistol held a centimetre from her forehead.

'Dog,' she whispered finally.

'Louder,' said Marduk.

'Dog,' said the woman. 'My name to you, lord, is dog.'

'Very good,' said Marduk, lowering his pistol. 'You are all dogs, to me, and to all of my noble kind. But perhaps one day, with faith and prayer and action, you will rise in my esteem.

'Arise, dogs. Gather your arms, and prove yourselves. Walk before your betters. Joyfully take the bullets of our enemies, so that not a scratch need mar the holy armour of the warriors of Lorgar. Such is a noble sacrifice. Lead forth, dogs.'

* * *

JARULEK STEPPED CAREFULLY through the carnage, the script covered orbs of his eyes taking in all the details of the slaughter wrought by his warriors. Bloodied and broken corpses lay sprawled throughout the palace. The fortress was enormous, and every living soul within it had been slain or was in the lower atrium on the ground level in shackles. He had sent the cultists out into the city, to spread panic and misery amongst the populace, and to hunt down the last remnants of resistance. He didn't care if they succeeded or not; Kol Badar and the bulk of the Host were fast closing on the city, and they would smash any final resistance utterly.

The Dark Apostle was pleased with the attack. The palace had been taken with few casualties and the kill-count was exceptional: a good sacrifice to the gods.

Picking his way carefully up the nave of the heretical temple, he felt hatred as he raised his gaze to the towering, granite statue of the aquila that dominated the back wall. Both of the heads of the two-headed eagle had been smashed by his zealous warriors, and the tips of the wings reduced to dust.

Dozens of clergy members were nailed to the defiled aquila, thick metal spikes driven through their flesh and bone, and into the stone.

The First Acolyte, Marduk, stepped forwards to greet him. He joined the fingers of both hands together, making the stylised sign of Chaos Undivided, and bowed his head. When he raised his head, he was smiling broadly, exposing sharp teeth; the row of smaller, razor sharp incisors in the front and the larger, ripping teeth behind.

'We left them alive, mostly, Dark Apostle,' he said. 'I thought that might please you.'

Jarulek too smiled. The intense hatred that the Word Bearers had for the Imperium of man was as nothing compared to the exquisite hatred that they reserved for members of the Ecclesiarchy. He stepped closer to the debased aquila statue, looking up at the priests, who were groaning in agony. Rivulets of blood ran down the statue, funnelled by the carved eagle feathers, and Jarulek placed a finger in the crimson liquid. He raised the finger to his inscribed lips and licked it with the tip of his script covered tongue.

'It does please me, First Acolyte,' he breathed. He stepped back, hands on his hips, as if he were appraising and admiring a favourite piece of artwork. 'Yes, it pleases me very much indeed.'

'Then there is this pair,' said Marduk. Two men were dragged forward and forced to their knees with heavy hands upon their shoulders. They both kept their eyes low, not daring to look up at the Word Bearers around them. One wore a red robe, his bionic eye buzzing softly as the lens rotated. The other, the larger of the two, wore a robe of plain cream. Both had exposed their left shoulders, showing the leering daemon face of the Latros Sacrum tattooed upon their flesh.

'The one on the left disabled the air defence turrets,' said Jarulek, not taking his eyes off the priests impaled upon the statue. Marduk looked at the man. His left eye had been replaced with a mechanical augmentation.

'While the other,' said Jarulek, 'ensured that the Cultists of the Word gained access to the palace. I believe that he was the bodyguard of the governor of this backwater planet. Was that not so?' he enquired, turning his face towards the man.

He nodded his head, wisely not speaking out loud.

'I have seen your faces in my visions,' remarked Jarulek. 'And in my visions of what is yet to come, your face is there, treacherous adept of the Machine-God. But I regret to inform you, bodyguard,' he said calmly, 'that yours is not. It would seem that your part in this venture is complete.'

The man stiffened, but did not raise his head.

'But you are not yet to be made a sacrifice to our gods. No, you are not yet worthy of that honour,' said Jarulek in his velvet voice. 'Take him down to the atrium to join the slave gangs. He can spend the last weeks of his life in service to the gods, aiding the construction of the Gehemahnet.' The man was dragged away.

'You, administrator, you are to stay close to me. But first, you must remove that abomination that you wear upon your breast,' said Jarulek, pointing at the twelve toothed cog upon his chest. The man instantly removed the metal plate from around his neck and held it in his hands, not sure what he was meant to do with it now that it was removed.

'First Acolyte, take the accursed thing and see that you perform the Rituals of Defilement upon it,' said Jarulek. Marduk took the metal emblem, his face curled in disgust.

'It is no god, you know, that your erstwhile brethren pray to,' remarked Jarulek conversationally.

'My… my lord?' questioned the administrator. Marduk paused as he was turning to leave, a snarl on his face for the man daring to speak in the presence of the Dark Apostle. Jarulek raised a hand to halt the blow that Marduk was about to deal the cowering man.

'They are coming, you know, coming here, your erstwhile brethren,' said Jarulek, almost to himself, seeing the waking vision as it overlapped with his surroundings. 'Yes, they come soon. They fear that we will succeed where they failed.'

Jarulek came out of the vision, and saw that Marduk had paused, looking at him. That one's power is growing, he thought.

It was sometimes possible for one of powerful faith to experience, albeit considerably weakly, the visions that another experienced. How much had he seen? he wondered briefly, before discarding the thought.

It mattered not. What was to come was to come, and nothing could change the prophecy.

CHAPTER SIX

Days and nights blurred together into one long, nightmarish, pained existence. Varnus was plucked from death and his wounds had been tended by the horrific chirurgeons that served the Chaos Legion, even as he fought against their administrations.

They had borne him from where he had lain after the Chaos Lord had hurled him off the battlements, and placed him on an icy, steel slab. He was restrained with thick binding cords of sinew. Bladed arms had cut into him, and long, needle-tipped proboscises had plunged into his flesh. He screamed in agony as the skin and muscles of his shattered leg and arm were peeled back, and the splintered bones reset before being sprayed with a burning liquid. His veins burned with serums, and his eyes were held open with painful spider-legged apparatus, for what purpose he knew not, unless it was for him to witness the infernal chirurgeons at work.

The skin of his forehead was delicately peeled back from his skull, and a burning piece of dark metal in the barbed shape of an eight-pointed star was inserted there before the skin was returned to its position and stapled back into place.

A collar of metal the colour of blood was wrapped around his neck and soldered shut, and he was taken to join the tens of thousands of other slaves that the Chaos forces had rounded up once the occupation of Shinar had been completed. Heavy, spiked chains connected Varnus's collar to two other slaves. They too bore the mark of Chaos beneath the red-raw flesh of their foreheads.

He had found that within a few days he was able to walk, albeit with considerable difficulty and pain. He was made to work day and night, his efforts directed by horrifying, hunched overseers, garbed in skintight, black, oily fabric. The faces of the overseers were, thankfully, obscured by the same black material, though how the creatures were able to see was beyond him. Grilled vox-blasters were positioned where the creatures' mouths should be, and their fingertips ended in long needles. Varnus had felt the pain of those needles when he had stumbled one night, and the pain that they caused was far in excess of what he imagined a slaver's whip would deliver. The overseers stalked along the lines of slaves, their hunchbacked gait bobbing and awkward.

But far more terrifying than the overseers were the Chaos Space Marines. Whenever Varnus glimpsed one of them he was overwhelmed by the scale of the monsters and the pure aura of power and dread that they exuded.

The sense of oppression never lifted. For days, the sky was largely obscured by the immense shape of a titanic Chaos battle-barge hanging in low orbit, plunging most of the city into darkness. Enormous landing craft were in constant movement between the Chaos ship and the ground, ferrying Emperor-knew what down to the planet. Then one day it was gone. Not being able to see the battle barge of the Chaos forces in the atmosphere was a small blessing amid the horror that was Varnus's existence.

The great red planet of Korsis could be seen both day and night, getting increasingly larger as its orbit drew it ever closer to Tanakreg and the time of the system's conjunction of planets.

Varnus had watched as an area somewhere in the region of a hundred city blocks was levelled by heavy siege ordnance. In a short flurry of brutal devastation, hundreds of buildings had been demolished with ground shaking force. Dust had rushed across the landscape for hundreds of kilometres all around, Varnus guessed. He no longer knew if it was day or night, for the air was thick with dust and foul, heavy, black smoke that left a residue on every surface.

Giant, smoking, infernal machines had been brought in to push aside the debris of the demolition, and along with thousands of slaves, Varnus had been forced to follow in the wake of these mechanical beasts, clearing away the smaller rubble that the machines missed. His hands had bled, and chirurgeons moving through the lines of chained Imperials had sprayed them with a dark, synthetic coating, stemming the bleeding, but not the pain.

Monstrous, polluting factories, foundries and forges were constructed, vast, vile places filled with acrid black smoke, heat and the screams of those being 'encouraged' by the overseers and their needle hands. Titanic vats of superheated, molten rock were fed with the rubble of the demolished buildings, and what looked like bricks, though bricks on an insanely large scale, were being created in gigantic, black, metal moulds.

The corpses of those killed in the defence of Shinar were dumped in giant, stinking piles, and more bodies were pushed there by huge bull-dozers, black smoke belching from racks of exhausts. Varnus thanked the Emperor that he had not been assigned to one of the slave gangs forced to strip those corpses naked before they were deposited in vast silos. He had no wish to learn what abhorrence the enemy had planned for the bodies.

Other worker teams were busy in the centre of the vast open space that had been cleared, working with smoke-belching machinery, drilling down into the earth, creating a vast hole over a kilometre wide that sank lower into the planet's crust with every passing day.

The destruction of the city was not, it seemed, complete, and on what Varnus guessed was his second week of hell, more demolitions began. The rubble created from the demolitions was brought to the smelteries in cavernous vehicles and upon the backs of thousands of slaves. Varnus completely lost track of time as he dragged and hauled twisted metal, chunks of rockcrete and stone to the vast smelteries, there to be turned into ever more giant blocks.

A sudden weight pulled at the collar around Varnus's neck and he was hauled back a step, almost dropping the chunk of rock he was bearing. He tried to keep moving, but there was a dead weight on the chain attached to his collar, and he glanced around fearfully, trying to see if there was an overseer nearby. Seeing none, he turned around and saw that the man behind him had fallen. Swearing, Varnus dropped the stone he carried to the ground and hobbled to the fallen slave, trying to pull him to his feet.

'Get up, damn you,' he swore. The punishments exacted upon the entire worker gang if one of their number slowed their progress were harsh. The man didn't move. 'By the Emperor, man, get up!'

Sudden, wracking pain jolted through his nervous system, and he heard the rasping voice on an overseer. There was a slight delay as whatever fell language the overseer spoke was translated into Low Gothic by its vox-blaster.

'Speak not the name of the accursed one!' rasped the overseer, and slammed another handful of needles into Varnus's lower back. He had never felt such pain in his life, would not even have been able to conceive of such agony. He convulsed and jerked on the ground. Abruptly the pain ceased, leaving him feeling numb.

The overseer called out something in its own rasping dialect, and another of its kind stepped forwards with a las-cutter, as Varnus shielded his salt-sore eyes from the white-hot light. The chains connected to the collar of the man who still lay unmoving on the ground were cut, and Varnus felt his own chain go slack for a moment. Then he was pulled violently to his feet by the chain, as the severed links were fused together.

The slave was dead, or close to it, and was dragged away.

Two sharp notes were blown on a whistle, and Varnus quickly picked up his dropped rock and shuffled to the side of the ruined street with the other slaves of his worker gang. A detachment of blood-red armoured Chaos Space Marines marched past, and the other slaves kept their gaze lowered, as did the black clad, hunchbacked overseers.

The familiar burning feeling beneath the skin of his forehead itched, but Varnus resisted the urge to scratch at it. He had seen other slaves claw at the eight-pointed star symbols beneath their flesh, and terrible, painful welts had erupted.

A Discord, one of the floating monstrosities that accompanied every slave gang, blessedly silent for a moment as the Chaos Space Marines had walked by, began once again to blare its cacophony of unintelligible words and hellish sounds from its grilled speaker-unit. It hovered limply half a metre off the ground, dragging behind it an array of mechanical tentacles as it moved ponderously up and down the line of slaves. The sound was sickening, making Varnus's insides twist with nausea.

A long, drawn out whistle sounded, and Varnus once again dropped his stone and lowered himself painfully to the ground. An overseer walked along the line of seated slaves, holding a muddy brown bottle with a straw out to each of the men in turn. When it came to his turn, Varnus leant forward and sucked deeply from the tube. He almost gagged on the foul, thick liquid, but forced himself to swallow. He had no idea what it was that the bastards fed them, but it was the only form of sustenance that they were allowed.

'So, what were you before?' asked a low voice in a conspiratorial whisper, after the overseer had moved on.

Varnus glanced surreptitiously at the man next to him. They were now chained together, since the poor soul who had been chained in between them had just been dragged off. He thought that he recognised the man from somewhere, but he couldn't place the face.

'Enforcer,' said Varnus quietly.

'You got a name?' whispered the man.

'Varnus.' A whistle blew, and the slave gangers pushed themselves to their feet. 'Yours?' he risked, whispering.

'Pierlo,' said the man quietly.

MARDUK WAS FIRST off the Thunderhawk, striding purposefully down the assault ramp as it was lowered from the stubbed nose of the gunship. He removed his helmet and breathed in deeply. The air was thick with pollution, smoke and the taint of Chaos, and he smiled. Much had changed since he had left the city of Shinar.

For the past weeks he had been engaged against various PDF armies far from the city, ensuring that there was no military power upon the planet with the strength to launch a counter-attack against the Word

Bearers. While there were still dozens of areas of resistance scattered across the planet, there was no single force that would prove a threat.

The skies were scarred with dust and smog, and the first cautious rumbles of thunder rolled across the marred heavens. The fires of industry were burning fiercely in the city below.

The palace had changed. The spires and towers that had once formed the silhouette of the bastion had been ripped down, replaced with brutal spikes and barbed uprights, and corpses were strung up all over them. Marduk saw that the skinless forms of the kathartes, the daemonic, cadaverous furies that accompanied the Host, were perched amongst the corpses. The vicious harpies screeched and fought amongst themselves for the prime perches. The powerful air defence turrets had been returned to activation, and they scanned the heavens. That was good; it would not be long before the Imperial fleet arrived.

Purple-red veins pulsed beneath the surface of the once plain, pale grey, plascrete walls of the upper bastion, and Marduk was pleased to see the symbols of all the great gods of Chaos artfully painted in blood on the walls of the galleries he passed through.

He nodded to the honour guard flanking the vast glass doors, and walked past them out onto the large, opulent balcony. Jarulek, surveying the ruin of a city below, did not acknowledge his approach.

Marduk strode to the Dark Apostle's side and knelt down beside him, his head lowered. After a moment, Jarulek placed his hand upon the kneeling warrior's head.

'The blessings of the dark gods of the Immaterium upon you, my First Acolyte. Rise,' said the Dark Apostle. 'You return having accomplished that which I requested,' he said. There was no hint of a question in the remark, since there would be no need for Marduk to return had he not completed the task appointed him.

'There is no fighting force upon Tanakreg that can interrupt the preparations, my lord,' said Marduk. 'I bring with me near to five hundred thousand additional slaves to aid in the construction.'

'Good. The slaves of this planet are weak. More than a thousand of them perish every day.'

'The Imperials are all weak,' said Marduk emphatically. 'We will smash those soon to arrive, as we smashed the pitiful resistance on this planet.'

'I have faith that you are correct, we will smash these new arrivals. Individually they are weak, yes,' said Jarulek, 'but together, they are not so. It is only through division that we weaken them. This is why we must always propagate the cults. When the Imperium fears the enemies within its own cities, that is when it is the most vulnerable.'

'I understand, my lord,' said Marduk, 'though I do not believe that your Coryphaus sees it so?'

'Kol Badar does not need to. He is the warlord of the Host, and he fulfils that role perfectly. Rarely has the Legion seen such a warrior and strategos,' he said, turning his disconcerting gaze towards Marduk for the first time since they began speaking. 'He brought in well over a million slaves from his attacks against the cities in the north, you know,' said Jarulek softly, watching his First Acolyte carefully. 'He is and always will be a better warrior than you.'

Marduk tried to remain composed, but his jaw clenched slightly. He saw the dark amusement in Jarulek's eyes. The Dark Apostle kept watching him, seeming to Marduk to enjoy making him feel uncomfortable, as he always did.

'You still feel the shame, don't you?' asked Jarulek, cruelly.

'I could have beaten him,' said Marduk, 'if you had given me the chance.'

Jarulek laughed softly, a bitter, cruel sound. 'We both know that is a lie,' he said.

Marduk clenched his fists, but he did not refute the Dark Apostle.

Jarulek placed a forceful hand on one of Marduk's battle-worn shoulder pads and turned him towards the view over the ruined city.

'Beautiful, is it not? The first stones of the tower have been laid, the ground consecrated with the death of a thousand and one heathens, and the blood mortar is setting. The tower will breach the heavens, the gods will be pleased, and this world will be turned inside out.' He turned towards Marduk, a hungry smile on his scripture covered lips. 'The time draws near. *"As Sanguine Orb waxes strong and Pillar of Clamour rises high, the Peal of Nether shakes, And Great Wyrms of The Below wreak the earth with flame and gaseous exhalation. Roar of Titans will smite the mountains and they shall tumble. Depths of Onyx shall engulf the lands, and then exposed shall lay The Undercroft, Death and Mastery."'*

The First Acolyte's brow creased. There was not one of the great tomes of Lorgar that he had not memorised in its entirety, nor any of the scriptures of Kor Phaeron or Erebus that he did not know word for word. As First Acolyte, he was expected to know the words of the Legion as well as any Dark Apostle did. Any time that he was not killing in the name of Lorgar or aiding the Dark Apostle in the spiritual guidance of the Legion was spent in study of the ancient writings, as well as the required ritualistic penitence, self-flagellation and fasts. He prided himself on his knowledge of the Sermons of Hate, and the Exonerations of Resentment, as well as thousands upon thousands of other litanies, recitations, curses, denunciations and proclamations of the Dark Apostles through the history of the Legion. He had spent countless hours poring over pronouncements, predictions and prophecies witnessed in ten thousand trances, visions and dreams. Marduk had even studied the scrawled recollections and scribed ravings of those warrior-brothers possessed by daemons, words straight from the Ether, seeking the truth in them. Yet he had never before heard the prophecy that Jarulek quoted.

'It is not written in any of the tomes within the librariox aboard the

Infidus Diabolus,' said Jarulek, seeing the look on Marduk's face. 'Nor is it written anywhere within the great temple factories of Ghalmek or the hallowed flesh-halls of Sicarus. No,' said Jarulek smiling secretively, 'this prophecy is scribed on only one tome, and it resides in none of those places.'

Marduk felt his frustrations grow.

'A fleet of the great enemy draws close,' hissed Jarulek, his eyes narrowing.

'I have felt no tremor in the warp indicating their arrival,' said Marduk, knowing that he was particularly sensitive to such things.

'They have not yet left the Ether. But I feel their abhorrent vessels pushing through the tides of the warp. They will arrive soon. I have sent the *Infidus Diabolus* back to the warp.'

'You do not wish to engage the enemy fleet as it emerges?' asked Marduk.

'No.'

'You do not seek to engage them in the warp?' he asked, somewhat incredulously.

'No, I have no wish to risk the *Infidus Diabolus* in a futile battle of no consequence.'

'No battle against the great enemy is of no consequence,' growled Marduk. 'So Lorgar spoke, and so it is to be.'

'Speak to me in such a tone again and I will rip your still beating twinhearts from your chest and devour them before your eyes,' said Jarulek softly.

Jarulek held Marduk's gaze until the First Acolyte could look no longer and dropped to his knees, his head down.

'Forgive me, Dark Apostle.'

'Of course I forgive you, dear Marduk,' said Jarulek softly, placing his hand upon the First Acolyte's head.

Marduk felt a sudden lurch. By the way that the Dark Apostle withdrew his hand, he knew that he had felt it too. He had felt that same feeling countless times, though much stronger in intensity, as the *Infidus Diabolus* dropped out of warp space. Jarulek stepped away, and Marduk stood.

'The great enemy,' said the Dark Apostle, 'has arrived.'

CHAPTER SEVEN

Brigadier-General Ishmael Havorn of the 133rd Elysians crossed his arms over his chest as he surveyed the flickering pict-screen. The image was hazy at best– at worst, nothing could be made out at all. He shook his head.

'Your pict viewer is of inferior quality, Brigadier-General Ishmael Havorn,' said the techno-magos. His voice was monotone, and barely sounded human at all. 'The level 5.43 background radiation of the planet c6.7.32 and Type 3 winds disrupt its capabilities.'

'Thank you, that is most helpful, Magos Darioq,' Havorn replied.

'You are welcome, Brigadier-General Ishmael Havorn,' said the techno-magos, clearly not registering the sarcasm in the middle-aged general's tone. The large form of Colonel Boerl, the commander of the Elysian 72nd and Havorn's second in command smirked.

The techno-magos, one of the pre-eminent members of the Adeptus Mechanicus of far distant Mars, was a massive, augmented being. It was hard to know where the human ended and the machine began. No features could be discerned underneath the low hood, just an unblinking red light where an eye had once been.

From the back of his red robe, two huge, mechanical arms extended over his shoulders like a pair of vicious, stinging tails of some poisonous insect. Another pair of servo-arms extended around his sides. Formidable arrays of weaponry, heavy-duty machinery, power lifters and hissing claws were constructed into them. The staff of office of the techno-magos was incorporated into one of the servo-arms, a long-hafted, double-bladed power axe topped with a large, brass, twelve-toothed cog, the symbol of the Machine-God. Dozens of mechadendrites hovered around him: long, metallic tentacles fused to the nerve endings of his spine. They were tipped with dangerous looking, needle-like protrusions and surprisingly dextrous grasping claws.

The man's organic arms were wasted, useless things that he held crossed over his chest. It looked like they lacked the strength to grasp anything any longer, and they were held immobile. Clearly they had been made redundant by the hovering mechadendrites and servo-arms.

A diminutive, robed figure the size of a child stood before the magos, though nothing could be seen of its form within its deep hood. It appeared to be connected to the Mechanicus priest by cables and wiring. A floating servo-skull hung above the techno-magos, mechanics covering the right-hand side of its cranium. Its unblinking, red eye watched the goings on within the command centre unerringly.

With a slight shake of his head, Havorn squinted at the pict-screen again. Bleary images flickered across the viewer of massed bulk carriers sinking slowly through the atmosphere of Tanakreg, with escorts of gunships flying in figure-of-eight patterns around them. It was hard to make out, but Havorn had seen scores of similar landings, and he could see exactly what was occurring in his mind's eye.

Imperial Navy attack craft, a variety of interceptors, fighters and assault boats, would have swarmed from their launch bays aboard the twin Dictator Cruisers, the *Vigilance* and the *Fortitude*, like a cloud of angry insects. As the first of the mass transports detached from the cruisers and began sinking slowly through the atmosphere, it was these Imperial Navy craft that were its first line of defence.

As the atmosphere was broken, vast bay doors on the descending transports would retract, and flights of Valkyries would emerge like circling buzzards, descending towards the surface of the planet in advance of the wallowing mass transport ship. Thunderbolts and Lightning fighters would scream from the still-descending transport to ensure air superiority. The Valkyries would sweep low over the ground and the first Elysians to step foot on the world would rappel swiftly from the gunships to secure the landing zone.

A wide perimeter would be quickly secured, the rapidly deployed Elysians establishing strong points along their line with quickly dug-in heavy weapons. More troops would rappel to the surface and smaller, breakaway transports would detach from the massive bulk of the main ships on the descent, dropping in heavier support to bolster the perimeter defences: rapidly moving Sentinel walkers and Chimera infantry transports bearing cargos of specialist Elysians.

Havorn had no doubt that the landing was proceeding smoothly and as planned, and a glance at the data-slates being updated every few seconds with fresh information confirmed this. The perimeter had been established well within the usual expected time-frame, and Sentinels were already scouting beyond the landing zone, seeking out possible threats invisible from the air.

The pict-image flickered again, but it was clear that the last of the mass transports had landed. Dust rose around the ships as their immense weight was lowered onto the earth. Havorn could imagine the rumbling beneath the feet of the men already on the ground as the ships landed and their titanic cargo doors dropped open.

He raised a hand to his long, greying moustache. Landings were always stressful; the mass transport ships were such tempting targets. He was pleased, though somewhat surprised, not to have had any sightings of the enemy. That was a blessing. A shudder of revulsion ran through him as he thought of the foe that his soldiers would soon be facing.

Chaos Space Marines, the most dangerous and hated of foes: traitors and betrayers who had turned their backs on the light of the Emperor and sold their souls to devils and eternal damnation.

The Space Marines, were the most elite warriors of the Imperium, each genetically modified to become giants among men, perfect machines of death with bodies created to withstand wounds that would kill a lesser man ten times over. In every respect they were superior to regular warriors. They were stronger, tougher and faster. Add to that the awesome protective and strength enhancing properties of their power armour, their unparalleled training and the best weapons that the adepts of Mars could construct, and you had the most powerful fighting force in the galaxy, and the most dangerous.

The Space Marines were meant to be the warrior elite of humanity that brought stability to the galaxy with bolter and sword in the name of the God-Emperor of mankind. But more than half of their number had turned their backs on the Emperor, embracing the sentient darkness and malice of the Empyrean.

The Elysians were soon to face these accursed traitors on this dead-end planet. His men would be fighting the genetically modified monsters, the results of a deadly experiment gone horribly wrong when they turned upon the Emperor. Havorn had fought alongside loyalist Adeptus Astartes many times, and their involvement in those wars had ensured that tens of thousands of Imperial Guardsmen had lived, but he would never trust them as he would trust any of his men.

Why are we on this accursed planet? he fumed, his face impassive. He was not one to question orders from the Lord General Militant, but he resented being left in the dark as to the reasons. Still, it mattered little. The enemy was here, and wherever it raised his treasonous head, the snake must be cut down. It was just that Havorn knew that this world must be of some hidden importance for the 133rd and the 72nd, in their entireties, to have been drawn off from the Ghandas Crusade to retake it; important, but not important enough, it seemed, to have drawn one of the loyalist Space Marine Chapters to the world.

Tanakreg was a backwater planet dominated by black, acidic seas. There were only two main landmasses on the world, and only one of those was inhabited. An inhospitable and desolate land dominated by salt plains and high ranges of mountains, it seemed to Havorn to be a planet that the hated forces of Chaos could damn well keep if they wanted it so much.

The Planetary Defence Forces had been overwhelmed contemptuously quickly, a fighting force of two hundred thousand soldiers, defeated within days by a force that could not have been more than three thousand. But those three thousand were Astartes, he reminded himself, and he surmised that traitors on Tanakreg had aided them. It sickened him that people could turn on their own like that.

'Brigadier-general,' said Colonel Boerl, 'the perimeter is secured and primary bulk transports landed. The secondary perimeter is being established and will be operational at any moment.'

'Thank you, colonel,' said Havorn. He turned to the representative of the Mechanicus.

'Techno-Magos Darioq, you may order your own transports to descend, if you wish,' he said.

'Thank you, Brigadier-General Ishmael Havorn,' replied the magos in his mechanical monotone. 'I will leave you now to return to my ship, to oversee the landing.'

Gyro-stabilisers hummed as the magos turned to leave. His footsteps were slow and heavy, clanking loudly on the metal-grilled floor plates of the command station aboard the battleship. Clearly, his legs were either augmented or had been completely replaced with bionics in order to bear the colossal weight of the harness. Mechadendrites floated freely around him, and a small, wheeled contraption, joined to the Tech-Adept by ribbed cables and wiring, trailed behind him. The floating servo-skull hovered in the room briefly before following its master from the command station.

'A word, before you leave, Tech-Adept,' said Havorn. The red-robed, towering figure turned around slowly.

'Yes, Brigadier-General Ishmael Havorn?'

'I am intrigued; what is it about Tanakreg that interests the Mechanicus so? It is rare to see such a gathering of Martian power.'

'The Adeptus Mechanicus supports the armies of the Emperor in all endeavours, Brigadier-General Ishmael Havorn. The Adeptus Mechanicus wishes to support the battle against the enemy on this planet c6.7.32.'

'You bring with you a force the likes of which I have never seen on a battlefield before; why is it that this place, of all the planets in the galaxy, is of such particular interest to the Mechanicus?'

'The Adeptus Mechanicus supports the armies of the Emperor in all endeavours, Brigadier-General Ishmael Havorn. The Adeptus Mechanicus wishes to support the battle against the enemy on this planet c6.7.32.'

'That does not explain a thing and you damn well know it,' said Havorn, his voice rising. 'What I am asking is *why*?'

'The Adeptus Mechanicus supports–' began the techno-magos, but the brigadier-general cut him off.

'Enough! Leave my command station and my ship, and see to your damned landings.'

'Thank you, Brigadier-General Ishmael Havorn,' said the techno-magos.

The brigadier-general's face was hard as the Adeptus Mechanicus priest left. Then he swore loudly and colourfully.

THE CHAOS INFESTED, polluted atmosphere was killing him. The foul smoke from the infernal machines spewed into the skies, and Varnus's breath was heavy and wet with fluid. Several times he had thought he had felt *things* crawling within his lungs, and he had hawked and coughed until blood had run from his tortured throat. Then the cursed, black-clad overseers had inflicted pain on him, stabbing him with their needle claws, and he had writhed with agony.

His eyes were weeping constantly, and a painful, mottled rash had developed around his neck and wrists. The eight-pointed metal star beneath the skin of his forehead pained him, and he imagined that the hateful thing was fusing to his skull, becoming a part of him. The thought was sickening.

The broken bones of his arm and leg had healed well, however, and though they still pained him, he had almost regained his full range of movement.

He wiped the back of his mortar encrusted hand across his eyes as another layer of immense stone blocks slammed into place, the sound booming out over the ruined city of Shinar. The tower was being erected at a ferocious pace, one layer of the huge bricks at a time. Giant, insect-like cranes swung around and lowered their cables to the ground to grasp the next round of blocks in their barbed claws, belching smoke and dripping oil.

Varnus stared into the booth of the closest crane with his sleep deprived, exhausted eyes. The pilot of the machine may once have been human, but was far from that now. It hung suspended within its cabin prison by dozens of taut wires and cables hooked painfully through its skin with vicious barbs. Ribbed pipes extended from its eye sockets and from its throat. Its legs had atrophied to a point that they were little more than withered stubs protruding from its torso, and with long, skeletally thin fingers it plucked at the wires suspending it. He tore his eyes away from the foul sight.

A sharp note sounded across the worksite, and black-garbed overseers prodded thousands of slaves forwards, off the scaffolds and onto the top of the stone slabs. Varnus and Pierlo stepped onto the wall of the round tower, and waited for the mortar hose to swing in their direction.

Other slave teams within the shaft of the Chaos tower toiled far below. Though the tower was only around thirty metres from ground level, the inside of it had been drilled down into the core of the earth twice that distance, and Varnus felt a surge of vertigo pull at him. Every time he looked over that edge, he had an impulse to hurl himself over, but he resisted these urges. He would fight death for as long as he was able; he wanted to be alive to see the Chaos forces utterly destroyed. He believed fervently that help would come to deliver Tanakreg from this hated foe.

Other slaves had not been able to stop themselves leaping from the walls of the tower, but it gained them little. The chains that linked around the slave's necks were bolted to the scaffolds at intervals and those slaves that slipped, or hurled themselves off the edge, seeking an escape from their hellish existence, ended up dangling against the inside wall of the tower. Normally, they would drag a handful of other slaves with them. It was not usually enough to kill them. The only chance a slave had was to throw himself with as much force as he could muster and pray that his neck snapped. Still, if he survived, the punishments at the needle-clawed hands of the overseers were severe, and meted out not only to the instigator, but to all those who were dragged over the edge with him. Such was the fear of these punishments, that any slave that looked as if he might try to end it all was restrained by his fellow captives and forced to continue with his servitude.

The thick weight of the mortar hose swung into position above Varnus with much hissing and steaming of pistons, and Pierlo and he reached up, pulling the hose across so that it hovered above the middle of the stone block. Thick, gruel-like mortar began to emerge in congealed lumps from the end of the hose, slowly at first, then faster, piling in the centre of the stone block. A deep pile of the foul substance was deposited before the hose, clanking and steaming, swung away from them to a pair of neigh-bouring slaves. Varnus and Pierlo dropped to their knees to spread the mortar evenly across the surface of the stone with their hands.

The mortar that held the stones in place smelt foul and was a sickly shade of pink. Varnus tried not to look too closely at the disgusting sub-stance after he had found human teeth in it some time earlier.

That was where the dead of Shinar ended up, he had realised with hor-ror. They were ground up into a thick paste, bones and all, and turned into this foul blood-mortar.

He was smeared in the stuff, from head to toe, and he tasted the hate-ful, metallic tang of it on his tongue, and smelt its repugnant stink in his nostrils.

A Discord hovered nearby as the slaves worked, its tentacles hanging limply as it blared a hellish cacophony of sound from its grilled speaker. An evil collection of voices chanted something in a language that Varnus hoped never to understand amidst the garbled, daemonic sounds, bel-lows and sibilant whispers that blasted from the infernal thing. *Varnus*, he imagined a voice whispering sometimes amidst that din, his quietly spoken name almost hidden beneath the garbled, Chaotic roars and screams. Not a moment went by when the slave's eardrums were not assaulted by the insane sound. *Kill him,* he heard a reasoned voice say, in amongst the jumbled shrieks, horrified moaning, ceaseless chanting and the drone of static that was emerging from the Discord.

Varnus and Pierlo finished smearing the blood-mortar across the top of the stone slab just as another sharp note rang out, and they hurriedly stepped back onto the scaffold. Shrieks of agony rang out from those slaves that had been deemed too slow as they were disciplined by the overseers.

The slaves held onto the metal spars of the scaffold as it shook. The outside wall of the tower was not perfectly smooth, but rather was slightly stepped, each block overlapping the one below by half a hand-span. After every twenty layers of stones were laid, the mechanical scaffold would climb those narrow steps, pistons steaming as the spider-like legs of the framework pulled it further up the growing structure. It was an ingenious creation, Varnus had been forced to admit, though he hated it to the core of his being.

Varnus squatted atop the shuddering structure, holding on tight. Pierlo grinned at him, his eyes lit up feverishly. He guessed the man was losing his mind, for he almost seemed to be enjoying the hellish work. It took almost ten minutes for the framework of the scaffold to reposition itself, and it was the only real break that the slaves got until the shift rotation. The Discord blared its hateful sound.

'So what was it that you did before?' whispered Varnus. He knew his fellow slave's name, knew that he had lived his entire life in Shinar and that he had fathered no children. But he did not know what the man had done before the occupation. It was almost as if the man had been avoiding the subject, and Varnus had been waiting for this moment to ask him directly.

The blood-mortar smeared man looked away. 'What did you do?' whispered Varnus again, more forcefully. *Betrayer,* he thought he heard amidst the horrific sounds blaring from the speaker of the Discord.

'I was a manservant and bodyguard,' Pierlo said, his eyes flicking left and right madly, and it suddenly clicked where Varnus had seen him before.

'I have seen you before,' he said. Pierlo looked around sharply, his eyes blazing with unnatural heat. He shook his head vigorously.

'No, I have,' said Varnus, 'in the palace, right before the explosion.' *Kill him. Betrayer.*

Varnus shook his head and held his hands over his ears, moaning, trying to get the sound of the voices out of his head. This place and that damned Discord were driving him insane. Pierlo was not the only one losing his mind.

'You okay?' he heard Pierlo ask dimly, and he nodded his head.

'Someone will come,' Varnus said to himself. 'Someone will come to liberate Tanakreg.'

Pierlo giggled hysterically, shaking his head. 'No one will come. We will die here and our souls will join with Chaos.'

Anger filled Varnus suddenly, hot and quick. 'Don't say such things! The Emperor's light will protect us in the darkness.'

'Chaos calls us, brother. Can't you hear its voice?'

The Discord blared its monstrous sound.

Kill him.

Varnus closed his eyes tightly, and rocked back and forth slightly, trying to blot out the hideous din.

'Someone will come,' he said to himself. He felt the hated symbol embedded in his forehead writhe. He imagined that feelers from the vile thing were pushing through his skull, entering his brain.

He prayed to the Emperor, his mouth moving silently, but the harsh, discordant babble of the Discord seemed to get louder. The sound of the deep voices chanting within the noise pounded at his eardrums.

Someone will come, he thought. They had to.

A HISS OF pain emerged from Marduk's pallid lips as the chirurgeons removed the vambraces of his power armour from around his forearms with their spider-like, long, metal fingers. Patches of skin were ripped from his flesh as the curved armour plates were removed, and pinpricks of blood covered the areas of the skin that remained. Tiny, barbed thorns lined the inside of the vambrace; Marduk and his sacred armour were slowly becoming one. It was not uncommon amongst the Legion.

The hunched chirurgeons scraped and bowed before him, and shuffled off to place the bloody pieces of ceramite armour on a purple, velvet cloth alongside his gauntlet and under-glove. Marduk clenched his fists before him, looking at the translucent, bloodied and pockmarked musculature of his arms. They seemed almost unfamiliar to him.

Kol Badar led the morbid, monotonous chanting of the Host, and it carried across the open ground, accompanied by the pounding cadence of giant, piston driven hammers striking great metal drums. The roars and hellish screams of the heavily chained, restrained daemon engines mingled into the din of worship. Throughout the city, the sound of the ritual would be blaring from the daemon amps that accompanied the slave gangs.

Jarulek stood atop the altar, his blood-slick arms raised high as he rejoiced in the sound of worship washing over him. Burning braziers lit the altar and thick clouds of incense rose from the maws of bestial, brazen gargoyles. In the distance behind him was the Gehemahnet, the tower rising at a rapid pace. A hundred slaves knelt along the front of the altar, adding their own music to the cacophony of sound. They were restrained, their wrists bound to their ankles behind them, and they stared out at the gathered congregation of Word Bearers, their faces twisted in terror, anguish and despair.

Jarulek walked behind the line of kneeling slaves. He grasped the hair of one, pulled his head back and slashed his throat with a long, ceremonial knife. Already, hundreds of throats had been cut with that knife that day. The slave gasped, a wet, gurgling sound, and his lifeblood sprayed from the wound. He was pushed off the front of the altar by a pair of Word Bearers honoured to have been chosen for the duty, and the bound, dying man fell amongst the bloodless bodies piling within the metal trough at its foot. Hunched overseers dragged another slave forward to take his place, and Jarulek stepped to the next victim, swiftly cutting his throat, and he too was pushed from the altar.

The blood of the sacrifices ran down the inside of the trough and drained into a catchment where it pooled before being pumped through a twisted pipe that extended out to a large basin positioned before Marduk. It bubbled as it was filled with the warm lifeblood, and he dipped his bare arms into it.

Kol Badar was the first to step forward, still chanting, and Marduk reached up to the warlord's forehead with a bloody hand. He drew the four intersecting lines that formed the Chaos star in its most basic form across the Coryphaus's brow with his thumb. The huge warrior then closed his yellow, hate-filled eyes, and Marduk placed a bloody thumb mark on each eyelid.

'The great gods of Chaos guide you, warrior-brother,' Marduk intoned, and Kol Badar wheeled away. The next in line was Burias, the warrior's vicious, handsome face framed by his slick, black hair. He dropped to his knees before Marduk, an aspect of the ceremony that Kol Badar had been unable or unwilling to perform in his bulky Terminator armour. Marduk drew the star of Chaos upon his forehead and placed his thumbs to his eyelids.

'The great gods of Chaos guide you, warrior-brother,' Marduk intoned, and Burias filed away. The entire Host was to be marked, blessed by the gods before they entered sacred battle once more.

He felt the daemon stir within the chainsword at his side as blood dripped from his gore-slick forearms onto the hilt. Marduk smiled as he applied the blood to the face of a towering Anointed warrior. Soon, dear Borhg'ash, he thought.

Over the course of the next hour, Jarulek slashed the throats of hundreds of slaves, their sacrifice offered up to the glory of the gods of Chaos, and the stench of blood and death was strong. The droning chants of the Host continued unabated, and the last warrior-brother was blooded.

Jarulek descended imperiously from the altar, drenched in blood, and stepped lightly down the stairs, his long, ceremonial skin cloak flowing behind him. The entire Host dropped to one knee as the Dark Apostle reached the ground, and even the raging daemonic engines were cowed by the powerful figure. He walked towards Marduk, and the Dark Apostle raised the First Acolyte's head with gentle pressure under his chin.

Jarulek drew the lines of the Chaos star upon Marduk's forehead and placed his bloody thumbprints against the skin of his eyelids.

His skin burned where the blood was smeared, pulsing with energy and potency. Opening his eyes, he saw that colours appeared more vivid than before, and he could clearly see a shimmering aura, the power of Chaos, surrounding the Dark Apostle like a ghostly, gossamer shroud. That power could always be felt when in Jarulek's presence, but it was rarely seen.

'The great gods of Chaos guide you, warrior-brother,' intoned Jarulek, his voice silken. Marduk rose to his feet and followed Jarulek as he strode back in front of his gathered warriors towards the altar steps. Kol Badar fell into step alongside Marduk, and without missing a word, Burias took over leading the ponderous chant of the Host.

Solemn and in silence, the Coryphaus and the First Acolyte followed the Dark Apostle back up the altar stairs. The Dark Apostle turned to face the gathered Host, and the pair stood a respectful distance back from him.

A chirurgeon shuffled forwards, accompanied by hunched, robed figures dragging a stepped platform behind them. The platform was placed before the Dark Apostle, and the chirurgeon climbed awkwardly atop it. Hissing steam, the platform rose until the robed figure stood at chest height to the Dark Apostle.

The chirurgeon then set to work, the blades and needles of its fingers piercing the flesh of Jarulek's face. Biting claws gripped the skin, holding it taught as the black robed figure sliced through Jarulek's pale flesh, cutting a neat strip from first one cheek, then the other. Blood ran freely from the wounds, before its flow was staunched by the tainted cells within its make up. The chirurgeon bowed and handed the two strips of flesh to the Dark Apostle.

Jarulek stood, holding the two rectangular, bloody ribbons high in the air for all to see. The pounding of mechanical drums ceased and Burias led the chanting of the warriors to a close.

'I honour these two warriors with passages from the Book of Lorgar, carved from my own flesh,' Jarulek said, his voice carrying effortlessly across the gathered mass. Already the red-raw rectangles on his cheeks were healing. Within a day the skin would be smooth and unmarked: two small patches of pale skin amidst a sea of scripture.

Marduk stepped forwards in front of Kol Badar, smirking at the flash of anger in the Coryphaus's eyes, and the skin of his left cheek was cut away by the chirurgeon. Speaking a blessing, Jarulek placed the scripture carved from his own skin upon the wound. There was a tingling, painful sensation as the flesh of the Dark Apostle knitted to his own. Bowing his head, he stepped aside.

'Go forth, my warrior-brothers,' said Jarulek once the second scripture had been fused to Kol Badar's cheek. 'Go forth, and kill in the name of blessed Lorgar, and know that the gods of Chaos smile upon you!'

CHAPTER EIGHT

Icy winds whipped at Marduk as he stood silhouetted atop the mountain ridge watching the approach of the Imperial scout vehicles below. The two-legged walkers, each manned by a single crewman, were climbing along a rocky ravine, making far faster progress than could be achieved by a man on foot. Clearing over three metres with each step, the walkers were making good progress, stepping easily over cracks in the rocky ground that fell away beneath them for hundreds of metres.

He had no concern about being spotted. A mere human eye would be unable to pick him out at such a distance, and the rocky terrain and gale force winds would make the crude sensors of the sentinels almost completely ineffective.

'Shall we gun the fools down?' asked Burias. 'The havocs of the VI Coterie have lascannons trained on them.'

'No, let the dogs down there take them,' said Marduk, indicating with a nod towards the figures waiting in ambush.

The three sentinels continued along the ravine, completely unaware of the cultists waiting in the rocks. A screaming rocket streamed through the air, slamming into the exposed cabin of the rearmost walker, which was annihilated in the billowing explosion.

The cult warriors wore pale cloaks as camouflage against the densely packed rock salt that was as hard as any stone, and they billowed out behind the men as they peppered the sentinels with las-fire.

The Imperial walkers began to edge backwards and returned fire, strafing the rocks with autocannons. Several of the cultists fell back as bullets ripped through their cloaks, but they had chosen a good place from which to launch their ambush and the rocks took the brunt of the fire.

One cloaked figure sprinted across the lip of the ravine, bullets spraying at his heels, and threw himself from the high rocks. He landed sprawled atop the roof panel of a sentinel and rose to one knee, a long blade appearing in his hand.

The sentinel crewman leant from the cabin, an autopistol raised, and fired off a quick burst across the rooftop of his cabin. The cultist grabbed the man's arm, pulling him further out of the cabin, and plunged his knife down into the man's neck.

The autocannon on the last sentinel went quiet as a lucky shot slammed into its pilot's head.

'Not bad,' grunted Marduk, as he began the descent towards the victorious cultists.

KARALOS LOOKED UP sharply as he heard the shout. Brushing his long, unkempt hair back behind his ears with his blood-splattered hand, he sheathed his knife and stood atop the motionless Imperial sentinel. The mutilated, bloody corpse of the Imperial soldier was forgotten as he shielded his eyes to see what the commotion was.

His jaw dropped as he saw the two colossal, red-armoured warriors walking through the ravine towards his band of the faithful.

'Get everyone together,' he ordered. 'The Angels of the Word have come, as the Speaker foretold.'

THE CULTISTS' BASE of operations was high in the mountains, hidden from view from the sky by pale tarpaulins that draped over the low structures. Every member of the cult within Shinar had spent some time at the Camp of the Word, the old Speaker had told Marduk.

The Speaker was a withered man, the flesh all but wasted from his almost skeletal frame. He was blind, his vision long lost to the biting salt of Tanakreg. To Marduk he had looked pathetic.

'Bring me a hundred of your strongest warriors,' he had ordered the old man, 'and send the rest of your cultists out into the passes. The enemy will be soon be upon us.'

He had grown bored as the old man had babbled on, and had eventually put a bullet through his head. The one hundred men on their knees before him had not made a move as the shot had rung out, and Marduk had seen that Karalos had smiled as the old man was slain. Marduk liked the man; he had the soul of a true warrior of Chaos, even if he was just a wretched mortal.

'You men are blessed indeed,' Marduk said, 'for you have been chosen to receive a great gift, a boon of the great majesty of the warp. It is the Calling, and you are to be the hosts.'

Marduk began to chant, his voice effortlessly mouthing the difficult, unearthly language of the daemon. He felt the creature Borhg'ash within his chainsword stir at his words.

The kneeling men were surrounding by dozens of burning blood-candles, the light of their flames the only thing holding the darkness of the room at bay. They flickered as Marduk continued his incantation, the flames straining in towards the First Acolyte.

Whispers could be heard, flittering around the dark edges of the room, and Marduk welcomed them, for they spoke of the arrival of the Kathartes. The flickering of the candles increased, and a howling sound began to circle the gathered group as Marduk's voice rose.

The blood of the Speaker, pooling out on the floor of the room, began to bubble, and Marduk knelt and placed both hands in the rapidly heating liquid.

Marduk continued to speak the words of the Calling and stepped towards the kneeling figure of Karalos, placing a bloody hand on either side of the man's head. He held onto his head firmly, feeling the skull compress beneath his hands, and continued his complex incantation.

Karalos began to writhe and twitch, but Marduk did not release his grip, holding tightly to the man's head. The cultist's eyes began to bleed and blood seeped from his ears, but still Marduk continued to chant and clasp the man. He could feel the power of the warp opening up, its strength pulsing through his hands into the boiling brain of the man beneath him, but Karalos made not a sound, silently welcoming the beast that was emerging within his flesh.

With a final barked stream of daemonic words, Marduk pushed Karalos away from him. The man stood for a moment twitching, blood streaming from his eyes, before he fell to the ground, writhing and convulsing. A flickering blur seemed to overlap the thrashing figure, flashing between the body of a mortal man and the insubstantial form of something distinctly *other*. His tongue bulged from his mouth and he arched his back unnaturally, before breaking into severe muscle contractions that threw his body across the floor. Bones broke under his exertions and his spine twisted horribly, tendons and sinews tearing and ripping. The other men stood hurriedly and backed away from the wildly jerking man, horrified fascination and devotion on their faces.

The man's flickering flesh bulged unnaturally, as if things held within were trying to burst free, and he scratched frantically at the skin of his face, ripping bloody rents. The bones of his fingers lengthened and pushed through the skin of his fingertips, curving out into sharp talons, and he ripped at his skin and clothes, tearing them off in bloody strips.

He rolled over and over on the ground, ripping and tearing at his flesh frenziedly, every muscle of his body straining. Blood vessels bulged on his neck and at his temples, and he lacerated his skin with his long talons as he continued to spasm and convulse soundlessly. His teeth lengthened into fine points and he bit into his own shoulder, ripping off chunks of meat.

Marduk smiled and crossed his arms over his chest.

The thing that had been Karalos entered even more frantic convulsions, ripping and tearing at its flesh, until it finally went still. It lay for a moment, bloody and broken, before it picked itself up from the ground and crouched, its skinless face turned towards the First Acolyte, staring at him with eyeless, bloody sockets. Almost its entire bloodied musculature was displayed, and only patches of raw, red skin clung to its frame. The hazy flickering still overlapped the creature, blurring its image slightly and hurting the eye.

An extra, backwards bending joint had formed in the lower leg of the daemon creature, in the manner of a bird, and long talons emerged from its toes. With a sickening, wet cracking sound, a pair of long, skeletal wings unfolded from the monster's back, sheets of bloody skin hanging limply between the bloody bones.

Opening its sharp-toothed, lipless maw wide, the daemon creature hissed hollowly at Marduk, like some newly hatched chick crying to its mother for food. He smiled broadly, the flickering candlelight glinting in his eyes.

'Karalos is no more,' spoke Marduk. 'He gave up his mortal vessel selflessly that this katharte might come into existence.'

The gathered men stared at the daemon with wide eyes. The air tasted electric; like the taste of Chaos.

'Now, all of *you* will selflessly give yourselves up to Chaos as good Karalos did,' said Marduk, 'for that is what I wish, and through my words you hear the desire of the gods themselves.'

The gathered men glanced warily at each other

'Well,' said Marduk to the daemon clawing at the floor in front of him, licking itself with a long, barbed tongue, 'call the flock.'

The men in the room fell to the ground as one, blood running from their eyes and ears, and they began to convulse.

'IT'S NOT RIGHT,' said Sergeant Elias of the 72nd Elysian storm troopers, hotly. 'We are the damned *elite*. We are not meant to be the grunts of the Imperium, plodding through the mud and crap getting gunned down in droves. We ain't that kind of regiment. We are…'

'The glory boys?' suggested Captain Laron wryly. The captain was a big, blond haired soldier, born of pure Elysian stock. Brash, strong and proud, he was the perfect captain for the brash, strong and proud storm troopers of the 72nd. If any other soldier or officer had spoken to him in such a way he would have had the man disciplined, but Elias had been his comrade for decades. He had fought alongside the man long before he had been captain, or even sergeant.

'Damn right we are!' said Elias with considerable passion. 'It's the job of the other regiments to grind mindlessly up the centre. We are the elite, fast in and fast out.'

'I'm sure the camp women appreciate that, sergeant.'

Elias laughed at that. 'But you know what I mean, sir. We don't have the sheer number of men or tanks to fight a conventional frontal assault, not against this enemy.'

'Who said we would be fighting a conventional frontal assault? The brigadier-general is not a damn fool.'

'I know that he is not, sir, but… I still don't know why we didn't just drop on Shinar and have this whole thing over with as soon as possible.'

'We do that and the entire damn regiment would be slaughtered. The air defences of Shinar are strong. Don't be thickheaded, Elias. Use your brains for a change and stop thinking with your damn balls!'

Elias grinned suddenly. 'I do have a big old pair of balls though, captain.'

'The sentinels on recon reported yet?'

'Another hour before the next report, sir.'

'Well, keep Colonel Boerl informed. If they see any enemy movement, report in immediately. We must secure those highlands. The brigadier-general says the enemy may be up there already. If that's the case, then without artillery support to make the bastards keep their heads down, we will be weathering the storm trying to land. If they are up there, it is not going to be easy to take it off them.'

'If anyone can take it off them, it'll be the 72nd,' said Elias, turning towards his superior. The captain was looking out across the plains to where the Adeptus Mechanicus battle force was making ready to move out.

'What do you make of them, sir?' asked Elias, indicating the massing Adeptus Mechanicus tech-guard with an incline of his head. Ever more of the disturbing warriors and war machines of Mars were disembarking from the wide-bodied Mechanicus loaders.

Captain Laron curled his lip in distaste. 'Never seen a concentration of them like this.'

The earth boomed as another of the massive cargo-transports of the Mechanicus landed, throwing up a cloud of salt grit. Hulking, slow moving, tracked crawler vehicles emerged from transports that had already landed, each led by a procession of censor waving, red-robed adepts of the Machine-God. From others came more of the pale fleshed tech-guard soldiers, marching in perfect, rectangular phalanx blocks, ten deep and a hundred wide.

Those phalanxes that had already disembarked were arrayed in their rigid formations, standing stone still on the salt plains, awaiting further instruction. Laron was certain that if no instruction came, they would stand unmoving, arrayed as they were until the cursed salt winds buried them. Even then, he supposed that the mindless things would be still, awaiting instruction.

From a distance, they might have been mistaken for regular Imperial Guard infantry platoons, though an observant onlooker would see that they were far too still to be completely human. They stood in serried ranks with lasguns held motionless over their chests, and many of their faces were all but obscured by deep visored helmets.

On closer inspection, many of the tech-guard soldiers looked less like Imperial Guardsmen and more like semi-mechanical servitors.

Servitors existed in every facet of Imperial life, fulfilling all manner of menial, dangerous tasks, but to see so many of them gathered together in one place for the sole purpose of war was highly disturbing to the Elysians. Servitors were neither truly alive nor truly dead. They had been human once, but all vestiges of that humanity had been long lost. Their frontal lobes had been surgically removed and their weak flesh improved upon with the addition of mechanics. These varied depending on the task that they were required to perform. They might have had their arms removed and replaced with power lifters or diamond-tipped drills the size of a man's leg to work in one of the millions of manufactorums across the Imperium, or be hard-wired into the logic engines of battle cruisers to maintain the ships' support functions.

The tech-guard soldiers arrayed upon the plains were created specifically for the arena of war. Amputated arms had been replaced with heavy weaponry, and targeting sensors and arrays filled the sockets where fleshy eyeballs had been plucked. Power generators were built onto the shoulders of some, and they stood immobile beside gun-servitors, cables and wiring trailing between the pair. Others had single, large servo-arms replacing one or more of their removed limbs, giving them an ungainly, limping gait as servos struggled under the weight. These mechanical arms were as easily capable of ripping a man's head from his shoulders as lifting heavy equipment, and some bore oversized rotary blades or power drills that could cut or punch through the heaviest of armour.

Amongst the phalanxes were smaller contingents of heavier, tracked servitor units. The lower bodies of these servitors had been removed so that they had become one with their means of conveyance. These bore heavier payloads of ammunition that spooled into the large, multiple barrelled cannons that replaced the organic right arms of the servitors.

In between the ranks of Martian foot soldiers were tracked crawlers, one for every phalanx. They were Ordinatus Minoris crawlers, and each was the length of three Leman Russ battle tanks. They had two, wide track units, one at the front and one at the rear, and between these was supported the mass of the war machine. Heavy girders and steel struts supported huge weapons, and each crawler had dozens of red-robed adepts and servitors as crew. Steel ladders rose to the control cabins that were offset from the main guns. Laron did not recognise the weapons that these behemoths of steel and bronze bore, but the massive, steaming couplings and humming generators upon their backs spoke of immense contained power.

But these were as nothing to the sheer scale of the crawler that was emerging slowly from a lander of truly giant proportions.

'Emperor above,' said Elias. 'Would you look at the damn size of that thing!'

It bore a resemblance to the Ordinatus Minoris crawlers in the way that a fully grown adult bears a resemblance to its mewling newborn. It rolled forward on what must have been sixteen tracked crawler units, led by a stream of tech-priests. The size of the smaller tracked crawlers were rendered insignificant next to the immense vastness of the Ordinatus machine.

It was the size of a city block and was protected with thick layers of armoured plating. More than ten storeys of platforms rose up around the massive central weapon that the Ordinatus supported, a weapon the size of a small cruiser that ran down the entire length of the immense machine. Criss-crossing lattice works of steel supported gantries running around the circumference of the weapon, and a pair of quad-barrelled anti-aircraft guns rotated atop the control cabin above the highest deck level. Giant, claw-like, spiked arms were held aloft on either side of the Ordinatus, and Laron guessed that the huge piston engines behind them would drive them into the ground when the Ordinatus was readying to fire, to give the machine additional stability. That a thing that size needed stabilising legs was testament to the awesome power that it could unleash.

'Impressive,' said Laron somewhat reluctantly.

The sergeant put a hand to his ear as his micro-bead clicked.

'The Valkyries are ready and waiting, captain. They fly on your say-so.'

'Good. Colonel Boerl will be joining us on the drop.'

'I feel safer already.'

'Cut the crap, Elias,' snapped Laron. Even with Elias, he had his limits. The colonel of the 72nd was a hardened veteran, and he would hear nothing against the man.

'Let's go take those damn highlands.'

HE RAISED HIS crozius before him. Blood hissed along the length of the hallowed staff of office, boiling and spitting under the surging electricity coursing up the haft. Once it had represented faith in the Imperium, belief in the Emperor and the optimistic confidence that the Crusades pushing out from great Terra would bring enlightenment to the galaxy.

Spitting, he sneered at the pathetic sentiment. Now he stood on Terra once more, as the greatest battle in the history of mankind was unfolding.

His crozius was dedicated to beings of far greater power than the deceitful Emperor. It represented faith as it always had, inspiring devotion and fervour in the Legion as it smote the non-believers, but this was a far more pure faith than merely a shallow belief and optimism that looked to a bright future for mankind.

This was *true* faith. The Emperor had been wrong. There *were* omnipotent gods in existence, and they wielded power beyond imagining. No cold, distant deities that watched the plight of their followers from afar, these gods were active and could affect a very real physical presence in the galaxy.

His crozius had been consecrated in the blood of those sacrificed to these great powers, ignorant fools who would not accept or embrace the true powers within the universe.

Now he fought on Terra, alongside holy primarchs, mighty heroes and noble warriors who had embraced the true faith.

The eager young Captain Kol Badar looked at him, passion and fervour in his eyes. His First Acolyte, the clever Jarulek, looked to him for the word to engage. Raising his sanctified crozius of the true faith high into the air, he incanted from the Epistles of Lorgar. With a fiery roar, the Word Bearers of the XII Grand Company launched themselves once more into the bloody fray.

The Warmonger was stirred from his thoughts of battles long past as his receptive sensors picked up faint reverberations in the air from over the horizon to the east.

'The enemy approaches, First Acolyte Marduk,' he intoned via vox transmission. 'The brethren wait in readiness.'

BOOK TWO: CONTENTION

'Victory attained through violence is victory indeed. But when the enemy turns on itself – that is the essence of true, lasting victory.'

– Kor Phaeron – Master of the Faith

CHAPTER NINE

THE NIGHT WAS lit up with hundreds of lancing beams of lascannons and super-heated streams of plasma. Flames coughed from the barrels of autocannons, and fast burning missiles hissed across the sky, leaving spirals of smoke in their wake.

Storm clouds rumbled overhead, the sound all but drowned out by the din of battle. Rain began to fall over the mountains in driving sheets.

Massive, eight-legged daemon engines strained at the chained restraints locking them in place, each infernal machine overseen by a dozen attendants. They roared into the night sky, metallic tendons bulging, and blazing comets of deep red fire burst from the daemonic hell-cannons built into their carapaces, screaming up towards the Imperial aircraft as they strafed in once more.

Lascannons speared up through the darkness. Flames burst over one of the low-flying Imperial fighters as a wing was shorn off, and it spiralled down into a ravine where it exploded deafeningly. The cockpit of another was ripped apart as lascannons punched through it, and the fighter exploded in mid air, debris and flames raining down along the ridge top. The cover of night did nothing to hamper the warrior-brothers of the Legion, nor the daemons that infused their deadly war machines. The darkness was pierced equally well, whether it was due to genetic modification and acute auto-senses or daemonic witch sight.

A nearby ridge erupted in a series of rising explosions as a stream of bombs struck, and Marduk swore. The enemy had brought in far more air support than even Kol Badar had expected. The fool had not predicted this.

Arcing beams of spitting multi-lasers strafed along the ridge, accompanied by the resonant, barking thud of rapid-firing heavy bolters. Rock and dust were kicked up, and one of the daemon engines was obliterated in a screaming inferno. The fiery explosion rose high into the air, but was sucked back down sharply as the daemon essence of the machine was returned to the warp.

Marduk growled as bullets ripped up the earth less than a metre from where he stood, rocks ricocheting off his ancient, deep-red armour, but he continued to stare angrily down towards the broken ground below his vantage point. While the enemy occupied Marduk's forces, holding the high ground with strafing runs and bombing attacks, other aircraft had hovered briefly beyond the range of the Word Bearer's fire and disgorged their human cargoes. With his targeters at full zoom, Marduk had seen the Guardsmen rappel from these hovering aircraft, disembarking onto the rough ground. He had lost sight of them as they traversed the massive cracks and faults, but he knew that they were climbing slowly towards him in a vain attempt to take the commanding location. Doubtless, hundreds of similar aircraft had dropped their cargoes of Guardsmen all along the rough ground behind the ridges occupied by his warriors, and were even now climbing up. Fools, he thought. No matter how many of them there were, did they really think that mere mortals could dislodge Astartes? Their arrogance was astounding.

'We have engaged the enemy, First Acolyte Marduk,' came the vox transmission from the Warmonger.

'Acknowledged,' returned Marduk as yet another strafing run of aircraft screamed overhead, peppering the Legion with gunfire. 'Take them down, havoc teams,' he snarled into his local vicinity vox.

'Movement,' said Burias, his witch-sight keener than the eyesight of the other Chaos Space Marines.

'Where?' barked Marduk, squinting his eyes where the Icon Bearer pointed.

'There, lord. Looks like around… eight Imperial platoons, plus heavy weapon platoons.'

'Bah, the wretches won't get anywhere.'

Burias lowered his head deferentially, rainwater running down his pale face. 'With respect, lord, their mortars could prove… vexing. If they make the rocks there,' he said, indicating a crop of sharp boulders, 'they could lob their shells over the lip of the ridge, and it would be… irritating for us to remove them from the position. And they bear lascannons as well, First Acolyte.'

'You fear their guns, Burias?' asked Marduk.

'No, First Acolyte, I am merely making an observation.'

'It sounded weak to my ears,' growled Marduk, but he saw the sense in what his Icon Bearer had said. 'Choose a small team from one of the coteries. Get around behind those mortars and clear them out of the rocks, if they make it that far.'

Burias's face split into a feral grin. 'I will take members of my brethren, if it pleases you, First Acolyte.'

'Fine. Go.'

'Thank you, First Acolyte,' said Burias, handing his icon to Marduk. Its bulk would merely hamper his mission.

'Take out the guns, and then move to the rear of these weaklings. If there are any of them left,' remarked Marduk.

Burias dropped to one knee swiftly, before stalking off through the gunfire to gather his warriors.

'Good hunting, Burias-Drak'shal,' the First Acolyte said.

CORPORAL LEIRE PYRSHANK held the controls of the Marauder bomber tightly in his gloved hands as he guided the massive aircraft through the darkness. The dark clouds far beneath the aircraft crackled with lightning, and the massive red planet Korsis hung in the black sky overhead, so close that he imagined he could land the heavy bomber there if he wished.

He also wished that he couldn't hear a thing over the roaring drone of the four turbine engines, but unfortunately he could.

'You'd think they were the High Lords of Terra, the way they acted,' said Bryant's incessant voice in his ear. The navigatius operator seemed incapable of remaining silent for more than a few minutes at a time. 'Bit on the dim side, though. All brawn and light on the brain matter. Still, the way they held themselves, looking down on us Marauder crewmen, I was happy to clean them out. The stupid frakker couldn't have had nothin'! But he stayed in. I think it was only 'cos he was a damn glory boy storm trooper, didn't want to fold to the likes of me. He didn't say a word when I won, neither. One of his eyes just sorta twitched, and he stormed away from the table, taking his muscle-bound cronies with him. Five ration packs, a bottle of amasec and five lho-sticks I took off them. Oh, you missed a great game, Pyrshank, a great game indeed.'

'How far to the target?'

'A while yet. Man, it was good. Ended up drinking the whole bottle of amasec with Kashan, you know, that bomber-tech girl from the 64th? Did I show you the scratches she left on my back? That girl,' said Bryant, 'she's really something.'

'How about you cut the damned chatter and concentrate on your screens, huh?'

Bryant merely laughed. 'Thirteen five to target.'

The navigatius operator leant up against the side window of the cockpit and whistled in awe. 'Damn, I'm glad I'm not down there in that mess. I haven't seen a firefight like this since Khavoris IV, and the

Guard units there suffered something like eighty percent casualties. The whole mountain range is lit up. '

'It happens in times of war, Bryant,' said Pyrshank. 'I can't see a damned thing out here.'

'Just use the nav-screens. You don't *need* to see a damn thing. Ten five to target.'

There was a moment of blessed silence. If you could call the deafening noise of four "ear bleeders" silence. That was when he felt the cockpit rock, as if with a sudden impact.

'What the hell was that?' asked Bryant.

'I dunno,' said Pyrshank. 'Could have been some bird, I 'spose.'

'Pretty damn high for a bird,' replied Bryant. 'Have you seen any birds on this salt heap of a planet?'

'No,' said Pyrshank. The entire breadth of indigenous wildlife of the cursed planet seemed to consist of the brine-flies that thrived in vast clouds along the banks of the salt lakes, and the tiny grey lizards that ate the brine-flies.

The cockpit shuddered once more, and there was a tearing sound of shearing metal.

Bryant released the clips of the harness crossing his shoulders and removed his rebreather mask. He pressed himself against the cold side window, trying to look down the side of the bomber's fuselage.

'What in the Emperor's name was that?' he asked.

'Herdus, can you see anything out there?' said Pyrshank into his comm unit. There was no response from the front-gunner, who sat in the forward facing turret just below the cockpit.

'Herdus, can you see anything?'

Bryant swore, and Pyrshank looked over at him. His eyes widened as he saw the skinless creature grinning in at him from outside the cockpit window.

'Throne!' he uttered, recoiling from the hideous visage. Bryant fell back from the window, a cry of horror and shock escaping his lips.

The creature began scrabbling at the corners of the cockpit window, its long talons scratching at the edges of the clear panels. Finding no opening, it reared its skinless head back and slammed it into one of the panels of the window with sickening force.

Pyrshank swore as he realised he had turned the bomber into a dive, and he pulled sharply at the controls. He saw motion behind him and turned his head to see Bryant, a laspistol in his hand. Before he could shout, the navigatius operator fired, and a neat hole was seared through the window and into the creature. It screamed horribly, but the sound was lost amidst the roaring of the air rapidly evacuating the cockpit. The roaring died as quickly as it had begun and Pyrshank saw that the horrifying creature had inserted a long, bloody talon into the neat hole.

A second later, the entire window panel was ripped clear and the skin-less daemon crawled into the cockpit.

Without his harness, Bryant was ripped out of the bomber instantly, sucked out into the icy, airless night. Pyrshank struggled frantically with his own harness, escape from the hideous creature his only thought.

He felt his stomach heave and he vomited inside his rebreather unit. But it didn't matter. The daemon grabbed his neck, talons biting deeply.

With a powerful movement, Corporal Leire Pyrshank's throat was ripped out. As the Marauder bomber began its steep dive towards the gathering storm clouds and mountain peaks below, the katharte kicked away from the aircraft, leathery wings beating hard.

'SHALL WE ENGAGE them, First Acolyte? They are within bolter range,' said a warrior-brother by vox transmission.

'Not yet,' said Marduk. 'Wait until they are closer. Conserve your bolts.'

'As you wish, First Acolyte,' replied the man.

The aeronautical barrage had, if anything, intensified. They were trying to make them keep their heads down as the Guardsmen below advanced, Marduk reasoned. But then moments ago it had ceased entirely, just as the Guardsmen below were almost in position. It didn't make much sense, but then Marduk had long stopped trying to make sense of the Imperium. He would never understand those who chose to worship the shattered corpse of an Emperor whose time was long past rather than embrace the very real gods of Chaos.

From the reports coming in, it looked as if somewhere in the realm of a hundred aircraft had been confirmed destroyed. Around ten bombers had fallen from the darkness of high atmosphere, crashing to earth. Marduk had smiled as he felt the Kathartes kill.

He could see the Guardsmen clearly, their faces all but covered by their grey-blue helmets and dark visors. Sheets of rain drove against them.

Bolter fire barked suddenly, and Marduk turned with a snarl to see which champion had allowed his coterie to open fire.

"Ware the sky,' came a vox from the Warmonger, and Marduk cursed again. He looked up into the heavens to see hundreds of dark shapes dropping like stones. He raised his bolt pistol and began to fire.

COLONEL BOERL HELD his arms clasped tightly to his side as he plum-meted through the darkness out of the storm clouds towards the flashes of gunfire marking the target ridge below. Icy cold air and rain whipped at him as he fell, and his heart raced with the thrill.

Forty-two thousand, nine hundred and twenty-seven drops, and over three hundred combat drops, the most of any Guardsman within the 72nd. Still it gave him an adrenaline rush like nothing else he had ever experienced.

He and the other drop-troopers had launched themselves from their

Valkyries at extreme high atmosphere, around forty kilometres above the ground, higher even than Marauder bombers operated when unleashing their deadly payloads. It was necessary to jump from such a height in order to avoid detection. Breathing through respirators, their bodies enclosed in tight-fitting jumpsuits beneath their reinforced carapace armour, the storm troopers had been free-falling for well over five minutes, reaching terminal velocity within the first thirty seconds of the drop, and leaving the cracking sounds of sonic booms in their wake as they hurtled towards the ground at phenomenal speed.

The ground was rising up with astounding swiftness and Boerl made ready. The arms of the grav-chute were automatically timed to unfold and engage at the last possible moment, and he watched the click counter in his visor drop as he neared the ground.

Pulling his arms out and splaying his legs suddenly, he slowed his descent fractionally and spun himself expertly in the air. The grav-chute engaged, barely five metres above the ground, and his descent dropped in an instant to a safe speed.

His hellpistol was already in his hand, and Boerl rolled expertly as he hit the wet ground, rising to one knee and blasting the over-charged laspistol into the back of a towering, power armoured figure. With a flick of his hand, he nudged the release button on his bulky grav-chute, and it dropped to the ground behind him. His storm troopers landed around him, rolling smoothly to their feet, and began laying down a blanket of fire with their hellguns. Super-heated air hissed as Sergeant Langer unleashed the power of his meltagun, the white-hot blast scything through the ceramite armour of another enemy.

The other Guard units would be pushing up at the enemy from below, just entering range as the drop-troopers landed. They were well drilled, and he knew that the timing would be perfect. The micro-bead in his ear confirmed this expectation and he made his commands, short and clipped, as he ordered the platoons to converge. The enemy were strong, but they were vastly outnumbered. The Elysians would have the position within the hour.

He was leading one contingent of the 72nd storm troopers, the other two arms of the elite regiment landing at the other main targets.

Tearing the respirator mask from his face, it retracted automatically into the chest unit of his carapace armour. 'For the Emperor and the 72nd!' he bellowed, his powerful voice carrying over the frantic sound of battle.

He drew his power sword in one swift movement as a huge, dark-red armoured warrior lashed out at him with a screaming chainaxe, and he raised his blade to block the swing. The unholy strength behind the blow was immense and he was knocked backwards even as his humming weapon carved into the axe, sparks and shearing metal screaming as chain teeth were ripped apart. The massive brute raised its heavy foot surprisingly fast and kicked Boerl squarely in the chest.

He was knocked back once again, stumbling over the rocky ground. It felt as though a truck had hit him, all the breath knocked from his body. The Chaos Space Marine loomed over him, savouring the kill. He threw his sparking chainaxe to the ground and raised his bolt pistol to execute the colonel. A blast of las-fire struck his knee joint and Boerl heard a deep, rumbling growl of anger as the Chaos Space Marine's leg gave out beneath him. Swinging his bolt pistol around, the traitor fired and a storm trooper was killed instantly as the bolt-round exploded in his chest cavity.

His sacrifice was not completely in vain, however, for it allowed the colonel a moment to gather himself, and he surged forwards, slashing his shimmering blade across the warrior's chest, cutting through ceramite easily and scoring a deep wound.

The blow would have killed any lesser man, but the Chaos Space Marine was Legiones Astartes, and he grabbed Boerl around the throat, crushing the life out of him. Frantically, he thrust with his power sword, the blade entering the warrior's gut, sliding easily through his body and emerging from his back. Still the warrior continued to fight, and Boerl began to see stars before his eyes. He managed to raise his hellpistol, pushing it into the Chaos Space Marine's neck, slipping it between armour plates, and he fired once, twice. Hot blood spurted from the wound, spraying Boerl's face, his skin burning.

The grip around his neck slackened, and he kicked back from the massive warrior, who even on his knees was the same height as the colonel. Still the warrior was not dead, and he raised his bolt pistol. Gathering as much strength as he could muster, Boerl swung his power sword into the warrior's armoured head, the humming blade embedding deep in his skull. At last the warrior fell, the power sword slipping easily from the wound, blood spitting as it boiled on the super-heated blade.

Las-fire erupted as the other Guardsmen arrived, lending the storm troopers additional weight of fire. There was a roar of daemonic fury, and Boerl saw a Guardsman lifted five metres into the air by a pair of immense, mechanical claws before being ripped in half and hurled into the darkness. His eyes widened as he took in the mass of the hellish thing.

It was a massive, eight-legged machine. No, not truly a machine, he realised with horror as he saw the fleshy torso that erupted from the body of the beast. Four times the size of a man, its black skin covered in glowing, blasphemous runes, the beast seemed to blend into the armoured machine that dwarfed it. The metal plates on the infernal thing rippled like muscle, and blood hissed from wounds scored on its armoured hide.

It stepped forwards, its eight metal limbs ripping free from chains that bound it to rune-encrusted stone blocks. Black-clad figures recoiled from the thing, and several of them were instantly killed as it impaled their bodies on spiked claws that unfolded from its legs. Flames belched from its weapon units, engulfing a group of Guardsmen who screamed in agony as the flesh dissolved from their bones.

'Langer!' roared Boerl. 'Take that thing out!'

The Guardsman at his side blasted another searing beam of death with his meltagun and nodded to his colonel.

'Storm troopers, with me!' shouted Boerl, and with Langer at his side, he charged towards the towering daemonic war engine, blasting at Chaos Space Marines that moved to intercept them. Several of the storm troopers were hacked to the ground by sweeping blows from the massive warriors, and others were torn to shreds by bolter fire. Langer ducked beneath a swipe from a Chaos Space Marine's barbed, short blade, and Boerl carved his power sword through the warrior's leg as he barrelled past, neatly severing the limb at the thigh. Still the warrior did not drop its weapons, despite the horrendous wound, and it fired as it fell, bolt-rounds thudding into the storm trooper beside Boerl, exploding his chest.

A shot smacked into Langer's leg and he screamed in pain as he fell, his leg shattered. A power armoured foot slammed down onto his neck, silencing him instantly, and another running storm trooper was felled by the Chaos Space Marine's swinging forearm, his neck cracking audibly. Boerl stumbled, a fortunate accident that saved his life as self-propelled bolts screamed just over his head. He fell to his knees before the monster, and a burst of lasgun fire smashed it backwards. Boerl rose from the ground, impaling the Chaos Space Marine through the neck with his humming blade. The stink of the monster was staggering, and he gagged as he ripped the power sword free.

Dropping his hellpistol and sheathing his blade, Boerl swept up the meltagun from Langer's lifeless hands and scrambled to his feet, continuing his advance towards the towering war machine that was killing his men in droves.

Its back was to him. He raised the powerful weapon, aiming towards the beast's horned head. Wires sprouted from the back of its blasphemous cranium. He squeezed the trigger. The searing, white-hot beam of super-heated energy screamed towards the target, but as if alerted by some daemonic prescience, the creature merely swung its head to one side and the blast passed harmlessly by.

An explosion detonated behind Colonel Boerl and he was thrown through the air, arms and legs flailing. He crashed to the wet ground, still clutching the meltagun, and grazed one of the war engine's spider-like legs. Pain ripped through him as his shoulder was sliced open by the sharp blades positioned on the daemonic machine's leg. Oblivious to him, it took another step, and Boerl found himself directly beneath the massive thing, lying flat on his back as hissing blood-oil dripped down upon him.

Without hesitation he swung the meltagun and shouted wordlessly as he fired it straight into the underbelly of the mechanical beast. The searing beam tore up through the creature, and a splash of hot liquid washed over the colonel, burning his skin and hissing on his armour.

The daemon engine roared horribly and its legs began to buckle. Scrambling frantically, Boerl pushed himself from beneath the monster before it fell. With the roaring, sucking sound of air filling a vacuum, the daemon essence of the machine vacated its host, and Boerl felt himself reel, his head spinning. A blast of energy knocked him from his feet, and all the Guardsmen within a radius of twenty metres of the departing daemon spirit were thrown to the ground. The Chaos Space Marines were buffeted, but retained their feet, and they fired into the prone Elysians, executing them mercilessly with head shots.

Colonel Boerl was spared this fate as a platoon of Elysians swept into the area, las-fire pounding into the Chaos Space Marines. It took dozens of shots before any of the traitors fell, and they exacted a heavy toll on the Guardsmen, killing more than ten for each one of their own that succumbed to the weight of fire.

'Facing heavy resistance,' came Captain Laron's voice through Boerl's micro-bead. The captain had led one of the other assaults, targeting an area some five kilometres away.

'No shit,' he muttered as he picked himself up from the ground, retrieving a lasgun from a fallen Elysian and firing it into the Chaos Space Marines.

BURIAS ROSE FROM his position and moved swiftly across the rocky ground, running low and fast. He covered the open ground quickly and dropped behind a group of boulders.

Pausing for a moment, he looked out through the darkness that was as clear as day to his eyes. Rain and wind whipped at him, but he didn't care. The other members of his team were all but invisible, even to his eyes, as they moved through the night. They were spread wide and were closing on their prey swiftly. They had fanned out in a wide arc, heading away from the enemy, racing through ravines and massive cracks in the mountainous terrain before swinging back around to encircle the foe.

This was the kind of warfare that Burias lived for, and he excelled at it. He had built a fierce reputation amongst the Host for his hunting and stealth missions, and the Coryphaus would often utilise his particular talents to sow terror and throw the enemy into disarray while the warlord led the main attacking force into the heart of the enemy's battle force.

Burias scrambled on all fours over the rain-slick boulders and ran into a tight ravine that rose up on either side. Water was flowing down through the ravine. He moved swiftly and quietly despite the bulk of his power armour, leaping lightly from rock to rock and stepping easily over cracks that dropped hundreds of metres beneath him.

Anthony Reynolds

The walls of the ravine dropped away in front of him suddenly, exposing a massive drop, and without hesitation Burias leapt, clearing the five metre expanse with ease, landing smoothly and continuing his kilometre-eating pace. His mental map of the area told him that they were close. He heard the heavy thump of mortars and picked up his pace, snarling.

He scrambled up a steep, near vertical, rain-slick incline without pause and leapt from the top to a nearby boulder, and from there to another. Up and down the broken, steep ground he traversed, leaping and rolling, always in motion. The mortars thumped again, closer this time, and he leapt onto a steep wall of rock, pulling himself swiftly up. The cliff-face angled beyond vertical, a dangerous overhang with a drop of hundreds of metres. With a snarl, he kicked off the rock face, lunging for a handhold near the lip of the rock. He grabbed it one-handed and hung there for a moment before he secured another handhold and hauled himself over the edge.

Burias paused, crouching for a moment, scenting the air. The rain dulled his senses somewhat, but the taste of meat in the air was strong. Then he was moving again, running along a thin ridge of rock barely two hand spans wide. The drop on one side must have been almost a thousands metres, but he traversed it at a full run before dropping behind some boulders. Glancing down, he grinned and looked back the way he had come, seeing the dark shapes of several of his brethren racing swiftly across the rocks. The thud of mortars was right beneath him.

He leapt from his position out over the drop, landing on a ledge on the other side. He waited for a few breaths, and then launched himself over the edge. He landed behind some large rocks and waited for the heavy weapons to fire once more. As they did, he rose from his position and ghosted up behind the Guardsmen, who were still oblivious to their imminent demise and were quickly reloading the six powerful mortars set on the rocky ground.

Grabbing the first Guardsman from behind by his helmeted head, Burias pulled him violently backwards, ramming his massive knifeblade into the base of his neck. The blade, easily the length of a man's forearm, severed the spinal cord and continued up into the brain. Burias hurled him away.

The other Guardsmen gaped in horror at the red-clad devil in their midst, even as Burias leapt amongst them. He ripped his blade across the throat of one and plunged it into the neck of another with the return, backhand motion.

Another Word Bearer loomed up behind the group, and a further Guardsman died as a bony, bladed arm was rammed into his back. The daemon within that warrior-brother had already surged to the fore, Burias saw, as the possessed Word Bearer ripped the fallen Guardsman's throat out with a tusk-filled, gaping wide maw.

Feeling Drak'shal begin to surface as the daemon responded to the presence of its kin, a jolt of daemonic power and adrenaline shot through Burias's body. He snarled and leapt at the remaining Guardsmen, who had recovered themselves enough to have drawn laspistols, at least those that were not already scrabbling over rocks in a vain attempt to escape.

Las-fire streaked past Burias's head, singeing the skin, and he grabbed the offender's hand, crushing bones as he turned the pistol away from him. Pulling sharply forwards, he ripped the man's shoulder from its socket and drove his blade up into the man's stomach, twisting it mercilessly.

A blast of las-fire struck him from behind and Burias turned, hurling the body of the man he had just gutted into the shooter. The power of the daemon within rose screaming to the surface and Burias-Drak'shal leapt on the man as he tried to rise. He lifted the trooper into the air, holding him by the head and the groin, and he brought his hands together sharply. The man was neatly folded, his back cracking sickeningly under the force.

Other possessed Chaos Space Marines leapt from the rocks above, crashing down through the rain to land amongst the enemy, hacking and slaughtering, ripping and rending. Blood sprayed the rocks as the Guardsmen died.

Letting the power of the daemon overcome him, Burias-Drak'shal and his possessed comrades slew until there were no more foes to kill. He stood, chest heaving for a moment before leaping off through the darkness on all fours, scenting other enemies nearby. He howled into the night and felt the rest of his pack spread out to either side of him, to encircle the next gathering of meat.

HEAVY BOLTER FIRE tore through the Guardsmen, taking down five men in a screaming burst. Their bodies were ripped apart, bolts tearing through armour as if it were made of paper, and punching through the soft flesh beneath. Blood sprayed out, and Boerl swung his head to see a massive armoured shape turning its rapid-firing guns in his direction. It was at least five metres tall and nearly as wide.

'Emperor above,' swore Boerl as fresh shells fed into the twin-linked heavy bolters of the Dreadnought, and it unleashed its barrage of deadly fire. He leapt to the side, rolling as the heavy bolts tore through more of his men, and came to his feet running.

He blasted a Chaos Space Marine in the head with his lasgun as he moved, the shot striking the warrior's helmet, rocking him backwards but failing to pierce the powerful armour. Ignoring the reeling Chaos Space Marine, Boerl charged towards the towering Dreadnought. He reached to his belt and pulled loose a melta bomb as he neared the hellish machine annihilating his men.

The thing was huge and the ground reverberated with its step, servos whining. Skulls and helmets, rammed upon black iron spikes, adorned the machine's shoulders. There were helmets of loyal Space Marines there as well as dozens of skulls, some human, but many from various xenos creatures.

The Dreadnought swung a heavy, taloned fist at Boerl, flames gushing out from the underslung flamer on the massive, armoured arm. Ducking the blow, the colonel hissed as the flames washed over his back, and he almost fell to the ground as overwhelming pain assailed him. Gritting his teeth, he flicked the activation switch of the deadly melta bomb and hurled it onto the armoured bulk of the machine. It struck a pitted and inscribed armoured shoulder plate above the heavy bolters that continued to roar, flames spitting from the barrels. It clanked loudly as it stuck fast, the powerful electro-magnets adhering to the metal.

Boerl ducked another swinging arm that would have ripped his head from his shoulders and leapt away before the melta bomb did its destructive work. Rolling to see the results of his handiwork, his heart sank as the Dreadnought picked the grenade off its armoured bulk and flicked it away with its surprisingly dextrous power claw.

Boerl scrambled to his feet just as the Dreadnought swung its heavy bolters around to bear, and dozens of shots ripped through his armour. The Dreadnought continued to pump shot after shot into the colonel long after he was dead, keeping his body dancing in the air for a moment. Colonel Boerl's body was finally torn completely in half, and it fell to the ground, bloody and unrecognizable.

'DEATH TO THE False Emperor!' roared the Warmonger as it stepped forwards. It smashed a mechanical foot down onto the shattered body of the pathetic wretch, grinding it into the wet ground.

Where was this battle taking place? The thought swam through what remained of the Warmonger's ancient mind. Where was Lorgar? He scanned the battlefield quickly, but could see no sign of the revered primarch. No matter. Here were enemies of his lord, and he would allow them no quarter.

The Warmonger opened up once again with his heavy bolters, seeing the weakling men before him ripped apart as he unleashed his deadly salvo. He began to advance once more, death roaring from his guns. One lightly armoured soldier stumbled too close, and the Dreadnought swept him up in its massive power claw, lifting the wretch high, so that all his brethren could see his demise. The Warmonger squeezed, servos in his claw whining, and the man broke. He was hurled to the ground, a bloody and very dead corpse.

'For the Warmaster!' roared the Dreadnought, and continued to kill.

MARDUK CHANTED FROM the *Epistles of Lorgar* as he killed, filling the Word Bearers with fiery hatred for the weakling foe as they slew. He saw the Guardsmen fall away from him in horror, and he imagined that in death they heard the truth in his words: that the Emperor was a false deity, a fraud and a traitor, and that the bearers of the truth were murdering them. They cried out to their fraudulent god for mercy, but his impotence was clear when no salvation came to save them. In death they could see that only the gods of Chaos were worthy of worship.

The sheer audacity and arrogance of the foe astounded Marduk. Against any other foe, a combined assault of air-lifted infantry, supported by heavy weapons and timed to strike in unison with an elite force dropping from the sky, may have worked. To hammer the foe first with barrages from the air, these *were* good tactics against any *other* foe. Indeed, they were tactics that Kol Badar made use of frequently.

But to have the misconstrued belief that these tactics would work against the Word Bearers, Chaos Space Marines, and that these pitiful men could drive them from their positions was beyond the First Acolyte's comprehension.

It was true that the enemy were great in number. Hundreds more troops were dropping through the storm clouds every minute, though they were not as heavily armed or armoured (he scoffed at this even as he thought it) as were the first to land. These men were regular Imperial Guardsmen. But numbers meant nothing against Chaos Space Marines, and Marduk was certain that the battle would soon be over.

The daemon within his chainsword was feeding well. He carved the screaming blade down into the collarbone of another Guardsman, its teeth biting deep, ripping and tearing through armour, bone and soft flesh. His strength was behind the blow, and the eagerness of the daemon drove the whirring teeth deeper. The man fell to the ground, a bloody rent ripped to his sternum.

Marduk swayed to the side and a missile screamed past him. He continued quoting from the Epistles without pause.

'The favoured son of Chaos, Our lord and our mentor, The bearer of truth. He is with us today, And upon all the battlefields where we strive, Bringing faith to the faithless, And death to the heedless. Always he watches, and lends us his strength.' he quoted.

'Hear me, my brothers! Lorgar watches us! Make him proud!' roared Marduk, blasting the head from an enemy with his bolt pistol and hacking down another with his chainsword.

The Word Bearers fought with a fury and hatred that had been nurtured for thousands of years, and despite being heavily outnumbered, they were butchering the Imperials that continued to drop in.

The dark shape of a possessed warrior-brother appeared atop a rocky outcrop, and it leapt through the air, smashing into a Guardsman plummeting towards the ground, his grav-chute yet to activate. Other shapes leapt from the rocks to snatch more drop-troopers out of midair, and Jarulek smiled.

Burias-Drak'shal's hunt had gone well.

CHAPTER TEN

'So, THE ENEMY still holds the high ground. Emperor-knows how many men we lost. A formation of Marauders is missing, presumed shot down, though Throne only knows how. There are at least forty Valkyries either destroyed or needing serious repairs,' snarled Brigadier-General Havorn, his tall, gaunt form trembling with rage. 'And to top it all off, Colonel Emmet Boerl of the 72nd was killed in action.'

Captain Laron stood before the glowering brigadier-general, his gaze fixed forward. Alongside him were the other captains of the 72nd. Laron was the only one of them to have been engaged in the failed attempt to take the mountain highlands. Indeed, he was the only captain to have returned of those who had attacked the mountains, and he felt that most of the brigadier-general's ire was directed at him.

'I ought to have the lot of you executed on the spot, care of Commissar Kheler here,' he said gesturing to a black-clad officer behind him. Laron flicked a glance towards the commissar. The man returned his stare coldly.

'But I will not, as I find the 72nd has a sudden lack of officers,' said Havorn.

He towered over Laron by half a head, though what the captain lacked in height he made up for in brawn. The brigadier-general was a lanky man, and he truly was one of the ugliest individuals that Laron had ever seen.

Where Captain Laron represented physically everything that the Elysians were famed for, the muscular build, the blond hair and the grey-blue eyes set in a handsome, chiselled face, Brigadier-General

Havorn was the polar opposite. Tall, thin and dark haired, his eyes were as black as sin and his face was narrow, long and just plain ugly. His hair was clipped to the scalp, and scars riddled his face and head, curling his lip into a permanent sneer. His one extravagance was the long, grey moustache hanging to either side of his scowling mouth.

'Captain Laron, I am instating you as acting colonel of the 72nd,' said the brigadier-general. Laron felt a flutter of pride rise within him, but he tried hard to make sure it didn't reach his face.

'With an emphasis on the word *acting*,' continued the brigadier-general. 'You are only in that position because there is no one better, for the time being. Once we are done with this cursed planet and return to the main crusade fleet, I will request a more suitable replacement for Colonel Boerl.'

The taller man leant down and forward so that he was looking directly into Laron's eyes, his hooked nose only centimetres from the captain's face.

'I don't know you well, Laron, but Colonel Boerl rated you highly. Do not dishonour his memory,' said the brigadier-general quietly, before turning away.

'I am assigning Commissar Kheler to keep watch over you. He has been a trusted advisor of mine for over a decade. His grasp of tactics and morale is strong. If there is ever a moment when it looks as if your arrogance or your pride are going to make you do something stupid that will get good men killed, the good commissar here will take steps to rectify the situation, with a bullet through your head.

'Do I make myself clear, *acting* Colonel Laron of the 72nd Elysians?'

The muscles in Laron's jaw clenched and he felt his cheeks redden.

'Yes, brigadier-general, I understand your meaning perfectly, sir.'

'Good,' said the tall man, turning and walking around his desk before sinking into his leather chair.

'You are dismissed, officers of the 72nd. Not you, acting colonel.'

His face burning, Laron stood motionless as the other men filed out of the room.

'Now,' said the brigadier-general, 'we need to establish how to get a victory after your devastatingly average attack against the highlands.'

THEY HAD AWOKEN him and the other surviving members of his worker team from their allocated two-hour rest break by throwing a bucket of warm water over them. Or, at least Varnus had thought it was water at first, until he tasted it on his tongue; it was blood, fresh and human. The overseers coughed vilely, what passed for laughter amongst them, and jerked at slaves' neck chains to get them to their feet.

The dreams were getting worse. The blaring of the Discord never ceased, and he heard it as he slept, the hideous sound seeping into his brain like a vile parasite, twisting and corrupting within him. It was no release from torment when he closed his eyes and fell into fitful sleep. No, if anything, his dreams were worse than his waking life. He saw a world utterly consumed by Chaos, its sky a roiling miasma of fire and lava. The land was not truly rock or soil, but a pile of skinless, moaning bodies that stretched as far as the eye could see in all directions. For all he knew, the planet was made entirely from these mewling, bloody wretches. Every one of them had a metal star of Chaos bolted to its forehead, the same mark that he also bore. Endless, monotonous chanting filled his head, intoning words of worship and praise. He saw this place every time he closed his eyes, not just when he slept, but every time he even blinked his eyes against the sulphurous, polluted air.

Praise ye the glory of Chaos screamed the Discord in his mind, blurred with hateful screams, words and bellows. *Kill him!* they said. *Traitor!*

Varnus stumbled along with the other slaves. He looked around in confusion as they turned off the well-worn path leading towards the tower that rose nearly a hundred metres into the air and headed off in a different direction. He saw his confusion mirrored in Pierlo's wild eyes, his only true companion here in this living hell.

Someone is here already, he said to himself. He could feel it in the air. Liberation was at hand. He prayed to the Emperor, *curse his name*, that his hated captors would soon be blasted from the face of the planet by the force of the Imperium.

He grinned stupidly at the thought.

Dully, he came to his senses to find that the line of slaves had stopped.

'On your knees, dogs,' said an overseer in his grating voice, the translator box over its mouth vibrating.

Without thought, he dropped to his knees. The overseers produced long, rusted metal spikes, and walked behind the line of slaves. They pulled the chains backwards violently, dropping the slaves onto their backs. Standing on the chains to either side of each slave, they hammered the heavy chains to the ground with the thick spikes.

Within moments, Varnus heard screaming from other slaves, but from his position he could not see what was happening. All he could see were the slaves directly to either side of him. On one side, a man cried, his eyes tightly closed as he mouthed the silent words of a prayer. The star upon his forehead was clearly visible, and steam seemed to rise from the skin around it, forming blisters. The stink of burning flesh reached Varnus's nostrils. Needle-tipped fingers plunged into the man's neck abruptly and he convulsed frantically, his prayer forgotten. His head stopped steaming and Varnus realised that it must have been the prayer that had caused the reaction.

Turning to the other side, he saw Pierlo looking at him closely with his crazed eyes.

'What now?' hissed the man. He didn't seem overly distressed to Varnus, but perhaps that was his way of dealing with this horror. He envied the man, briefly. *Kill him*, came the voice within the blare of the Discord.

'What new torture is this?'

The dark figures of chirurgeons loomed over Varnus. They were loathsome creatures, their hunched forms covered in shiny, black material. There was an unholy stink about them that made him gag, and their arms ended in arrays of needles, clamps and syringes.

Something was writhing in the hands of the hateful surgeons and he felt sickness pull within his gut at the sight of the vile, wriggling thing. It was a small, mechanical, flat box that looked somewhat like the translator machines that the overseers spoke through. However, the thin sides of the box were coated in a smooth, black-oily skin that pulsed with movement from within. Four short, stubby tentacles waved from the corners of the box, fighting at the chirurgeon's grasp. His gaze was forcefully removed from the vile blend of mechanics and daemon spawn as a further pair of black-clad chirurgeons pulled his head around.

'Open your mouth,' came the voice of an overseer at his ear, but Varnus resisted. Pain jolted through him as the overseer ran one of its needle fingers along his neck, and he opened his mouth wide in a cry of pain. The chirurgeons darted eagerly forwards with their mechanical hands, whirring power clamps gripping his front teeth. Without ceremony, the teeth were ripped from his jaw. Blood poured from the holes in his gums and he groaned in pain.

Yet the chirurgeons had not finished their brutal surgery. Gripping his head tightly, one of them leant forwards with another mechanical device, and Varnus tried to pull away from it desperately, blood running down his throat and spurting over his chin. He could not escape the attentions of the twisted, hunched chirurgeon, however, and as its partner hit Varnus's lower jaw to close his mouth, the first sadistic creature slammed its mechanical device into the side of his face.

A metal, barbed staple, half a hand-length wide, punched through the bone of Varnus's jaw and cheek, pinning his mouth closed. The metal bit deep into the bone, and Varnus gargled in agony. A second staple punched into the bone on the other side of his face.

That was when the black, tentacled thing was brought towards him. The chirurgeon thrust the fighting thing at his face and Varnus screamed, his jaw stapled shut, in pain and terror. He tried to turn away, but his head was held tight and the box was placed over his mouth.

He screamed and screamed as the four questing tentacles probed his skin, the touch stinging and burning his flesh. The tentacles felt their way across his face, and with horror he realised there was a fifth, thicker tentacle pushing through the gap in his front teeth and into his mouth. No, it wasn't a tentacle, he realised as his tongue touched the vile thing. It was a hollow, fleshy tube, and as it entered his mouth it began to expand and push itself down into his throat, flattening his tongue against the base of his mouth.

Two tentacles latched under Varnus's jaw, burrowing into his flesh to secure a tight hold, and the remaining two leech-like appendages wriggled across his cheeks, probing at the corners of his eyes before burrowing agonisingly into the skin at his temples. He roared in excruciating pain, the sound alien and strangely mechanical to his ears, altered by the thing clamped firmly over his mouth and nose. He breathed in deeply, which was heavy and difficult, and he felt a foul, sickly sweet taste in his mouth and nose.

White-hot pain shot through his head as the tentacles burrowed further into his flesh. They ceased wriggling within him, but the pain remained. His breathing was laboured and the figures above him went hazy, spots of light appearing before him, and he fell into the nightmare of his unconsciousness.

THE WARRIORS OF the Adeptus Mechanicus stepped inexorably forwards, like a seething, relentless carpet, spread out across the hard-packed salt plain. Some amongst them were almost human, though even these were hard-wired into the weapon systems they bore, their brain stems augmented with mechanics and sensors. The Coryphaus had seen their like before. He had fought against loyalist members of the Cult Mechanicus on their Forge Worlds during the advance on Terra ten thousand years earlier. More recently, he had fought alongside those members of the Machine Cult that had long sworn their allegiance to the true gods, the powers of Chaos.

Sheer cliffs rose up on either side of the valley, their tops hidden by dark, brooding, heavy cloud. The rumble of thunder boomed from the heavens and flashes punctuated the dark, threatening sky. The insides of the massed, bulbous clouds lit up as lightning crackled within, arcing, skeletal fingers of electricity that clawed across their surface.

The rain had been falling for almost an hour, hard and driving, lashing down upon the servitors as they plodded forwards at the impulse of their masters. The ground beneath their feet was pooled with salt sludge. The grinding tracks of weapon platforms and hissing crawlers ripped up the ground, creating mires in their wake as they slowly advanced amongst the serried cohorts of mindless and augmented servitors.

Visibility was poor across the open ground, as waves of driving rain were driven into the valley by the fierce winds that were picking up.

Screaming shells descended out of the gloom, accompanied by the constant rumble of artillery that was almost indiscernible from the sound of the building storm. They fell from the high ridges to either side of the valley, obscured by cloud and rain, and detonated amongst the ranks of servitor warriors, sending flesh and mechanics flying in all direction. Red blood and pale, unnatural fluids mixed with the pooling waters underfoot. They made no cries of fear or pain as they were destroyed, though even if they had they would not have carried through the pounding torrents of falling rain.

While visibility was poor for the Word Bearers, who were barely able to see the advancing enemy just rounding the dog-leg of the valley, the wretched slaves that Kol Badar had brought with him were virtually blind. They stood close together, weeping and terrified, shivering in the icy wind and rain that battered at them. They were chained together still, in long lines, clustered in front of the massive Word Bearers, who stood oblivious and uncaring of the hardships they endured at being exposed to the elements.

Kol Badar ordered the advance. Confused and deafened by the sheer fury of the downpour, they looked around blankly. Word Bearers pushed them roughly forward with the barrels of their bolters. A few shots into their midst soon had them moving, and almost five thousand slaves were goaded on through the torrential downpour. Scores of them fell, bustled by their terrified comrades. They were crushed underfoot, many drowning in the pooling, ankle deep water as their desperate companions scrambled over them, their only thought being to keep in front of their tormentors. Their limp, lifeless bodies were forced along with the push of humanity and dragged by the chains secured to their necks.

The Word Bearers advanced behind the seething mass of terrified slaves. They intoned from the Book of Lorgar as they marched through the strengthening rain, while the melancholic phrases recited by those warriors within their Rhino and Land Raider transports blared out from amplifiers on the outsides of the vehicles. Ancient, holy Predator tanks, their mighty turrets and weapon sponsons decorated with scriptures, bronze daemonic maws and icons scrawled in blood, rolled forwards at the wings of the Word Bearers, alongside Defilers and other daemon engines. The howls of the machines rose through the rain that hissed and turned to steam as it neared the infernal hulls of the hellish creations. Dreadnoughts were guided forwards by black-clad handlers, screaming insanely or reliving ancient battles long passed. Kol Badar and his Anointed warriors walked in the centre of the line.

The bombardment from the ridges above continued unabated, but Kol Badar was furious. There should have been more fire coming from above, and he was still angered by his earlier conversation.

'Unacceptable losses against a weakling foe,' he had growled through the vox-unit.

'My warriors hold the ridges still, Coryphaus,' was the snarled response from Marduk, the First Acolyte.

'The barrage will not be as effective as anticipated. Your failure will cost the lives of more of our brethren,' retorted Kol Badar.

'You did not predict an attack of such strength,' snapped Marduk. 'If there has been a failure, it has been yours.'

Kol Badar lashed out in anger towards an attendant daubing fresh sigils on his armour, but pulled the blow just before it connected, and merely clenched the talons of his power fist tightly, instead. The robed figure flinched backwards, then tentatively continued with its work. If the warlord had continued through with the strike, it would have instantly killed the attendant.

'You go too far. One day soon there will be a reckoning between us, whelp,' Kol Badar had promised, before severing the vox transmission.

The slaves stampeded ahead of the Word Bearers, running blindly through the rain. They began to die before they even glimpsed their killers.

A thick beam of white energy surged out of the gloom, cutting through the ranks of slaves. Their bodies burst into blue and white flames that rose fiercely, melting the chains binding the wretches to dripping liquid. A millisecond later, the flames all but died away, leaving piles of white ash in the shapes of the victims. A second later the morbid statues crumbled as they were trampled by the press of bodies that filled the sudden gap in the ranks.

As if the shot was the clarion call announcing the commencement of battle, the gloom was suddenly ripped apart as the guns of the Adeptus Mechanicus spoke. Blasts of plasma screamed through the air, massive rotating assault cannons upon the back of tracked units roared as they began to spin, and salvoes of hellfire missiles were launched.

The slaves surged through the inferno of death, hundreds of them slaughtered within the first second of the barrage. Those at the rear turned to flee from this new threat, but the bolters of the Word Bearers barked, dropping them in droves. The slaves surged forwards once more, running towards those that they would call allies, who were cutting them down mercilessly, killing them in droves.

A barking roar was unleashed as the Skitarii fired. Heavy bolters tore through the flesh of the slaves, and flashes from thousands of lasguns streaked through the rain.

The chained slaves surged towards those who appeared, through the gloom, to be Imperial Guardsmen, clearly not registering that their saviours were to be their executioners.

Kol Badar laughed as the Cult Mechanicus wasted its ammunition. All the while, the Word Bearers marched relentlessly forwards, shielded by the flesh of the Imperial slaves.

The Chaos Space Marines began to fire their own weapons. Lascannons from the lower reaches of the ridge seared down through the gloom, spearing into the heavy weapon platforms grinding along slowly. Predators of ancient, extinct design and Land Raiders daubed with Chaos sigils added their own weight to the fire, and the demented Dreadnoughts and daemon engines roared in excitement, bitterness and anger as they sighted the foe. Battle cannons boomed, autocannons shrieked, missiles screamed through the rain and heavy bolters barked.

The Anointed opened up, cutting down the last of the slaves as they neared the true foe. Striding forwards, Kol Badar saw the approaching ranks of Skitarii through the press of frantic slaves and impatiently shot down those in his way.

The front rank of the foe consisted of heavily augmented servitor warriors with massive shields built into their mechanical arms. These shields shimmered with power as they deflected bolter shots, protecting them and those in the ranks behind. They advanced slowly step by lumbering step, a walking barricade, firing their lasguns through the slaves and into the advancing Word Bearers. The top right corner of each shield was cut down to allow the larger guns of those behind to fire. The two opposing forces were close, and the fusillade was furious. Kol Badar grinned as he powered unscathed through the carnage, the revered plasteel plating of his Terminator armour absorbing the incoming fire.

He had ensured that his most vicious, blood-hungry warriors, those who strayed closest to the dedicated worship of blessed Khorne, were the first wave of Word Bearers to engage the enemy, and they cleaved into the foe with brutal force. The heavy shields of the front line of the enemy were hacked down with powerful blows from chainaxes and spiked power mauls, and bolter fire tore into the flesh of those behind. The shield-servitors were slow and lumbering, though they took a lot of punishment before they stopped moving. Kol Badar saw several of them fighting on, even with limbs hacked off and bolt having removed parts of their skulls.

Lasgun shots peppered off Kol Badar's armour like flies, and he punched his talons through a heavy shield, sparks flying and power conduits screaming as the blow impaled the Skitarii through its neck. With a flick of his arm, he hurled the servitor warrior over his shoulder, and unleashed his combi-bolter on full auto into the packed Skitarii ranks behind. These were softer targets. They had been augmented in lesser ways, not taking them fully down the path to becoming mindless servitors. Targeting sensors had replaced their left eyes, and the left halves of their heads were a mass of wiring and mechanics, but their bodies were easily torn apart by the bolter fire of the advancing Word Bearers.

At a distance, they would be dangerous foes, for many of them carried heavier armaments than a humble Guardsman would be able to bear, but up close they were slaughtered by the brute force and speed of the Word Bearers. The Anointed bludgeoned their way into the heart of the Skitarii formation. It mattered not to these elite killers that the enemy fought on after having sustained wounds that would drop a regular human. The Word Bearers, and the Anointed in particular, were far from regular humans themselves – they were demi-gods of war, and they tore apart the Skitarii with fury and passion.

Within ten minutes, as if a switch was flicked inside the mechanical heads of the thousands of remaining Skitarii, they began to re-form, walking steadily backwards as one, while continuing to lay down their withering fire into the Chaos Space Marines.

With a surge of his servo-enhanced muscles, Kol Badar pushed forwards into the retreating foe, punching the whirling chainblade that served as a bayonet upon his combi-bolter through the pudgy white face of another foe, and ripping the head and spinal column from another, electrodes and sparking fuses still attached to the vertebrae.

Heavily armoured servitors moved to the fore, stalking forwards between the ordered ranks of the lesser warriors, and Kol Badar was pleased to see that these foes were more to his liking. Around the height of a regular Chaos Space Marine, these were heavily armoured in thick, dark, metal armour. The mechanics of their left arms ended in spinning cannons that roared as they pumped fire from their multiple barrels. Ammo-feeds smoked as fresh bullets were fed to the guns from heavy integrated backpacks.

Concentrated bursts from the weapons were carving through power armour, and Kol Badar hissed in anger as he was rocked backwards by their force, though his Terminator armour was not breached. He fired his combi-bolter, blasting the gun-arm from a warrior in a shower of sparks, but it kept coming at him swinging its other arm towards him in a murderous thrust as the drill-arm began to spin. Metallic tentacles attached to the Skitarii's spinal column reached forwards to ensnare him, but Kol Badar had no intentions of backing away from the machine warrior.

With a backhand swipe of his power talons, he smashed the whirling, industrial drill away and fired his combi-bolter into the chest of the foe. Mechadendrite tentacles latched onto his chest and shoulder plates, and small drill pieces whined as they began to bore neat holes through the ancient suit. Firing his bolter again into the chest of the warrior, he ripped at the tentacles. Their grip on him was stronger than their binding to the warrior's spine, and he ripped them free of the Skitarii's back. Firing again, its armour cracking and shattering, the Skitarii fell onto its back. Kol Badar ended its struggles by slamming his heavy foot down into its head, pulverising the human skull and brain within its blank, metal faceplate.

Ripping off the tentacles still attached to his armour, he saw with pride that not one of his Anointed had fallen to these warriors, though several power armoured warrior-brothers had succumbed to their weaponry. He saw one of the Skitarii warriors torn apart by the fire from the reaper autocannon of one cult member, its chest a ruin of armour, machinery and seeping blood.

The enemy continued to retreat, but the thought of calling off the battle never entered Kol Badar's head. He would push on, deep into the foe, and inflict as much damage as possible, only calling off the attack when the terrain began to favour the Imperials once more. Even then, calling off the slaughter would be difficult, nigh on impossible, for the frenzied Dreadnoughts that were ploughing into the enemy.

One of the insane war machines broke into a lumbering run, smashing aside a warrior-brother in its eagerness to reach the foe. It was roaring incoherently, and gunfire leapt from its twin autocannon barrels and from the underslung bolters beneath its scything array of war blades. Other, swifter warrior-brothers backed out of the way of the charging machine, and it ripped into the Skitarii, its war blades cutting down four of them with one scissoring blow.

The Coryphaus recognised the Dreadnought as housing the corpse of Brother Shaldern, who had fallen against the hated coward Legion of Rouboute Gullimen, the Ultramarines, during the battle on Calth. His sanity had long since abandoned him. Such was the way with those entombed within the sarcophagi of the dangerous war machines, and Kol Badar wondered briefly if he would rather die upon the field of battle than suffer endless torment within one of those cursed engines. Few retained any semblance of rationality. That the Warmonger maintained as much lucidity as he did was a testament to the intense faith and belief that the Dark Apostle had wielded in life, and had taken with him into his hateful half-life.

The machine ploughed through the enemy and a great roar went up from the Word Bearers.

'Forward, warrior-brothers!' Kol Badar bellowed. 'For the glory of the Legion!'

CHAPTER ELEVEN

MECHADENDRITES ATTACHED TO the spinal column of Techno-Magos Darioq stretched out before him. Needle-like electro-jacks emerged from the tips of these mechanical, clawed tentacles and plunged into circular plugs around the base of the cylindrical device rising smoothly from the floor of the control room. Each of the electro-jacks was around fifteen centimetres in length, and they rotated as the magos connected with the machine-spirit of his command vehicle.

The room was dark and claustrophobic, with exposed pipes and wires lining the walls and twisting across the low ceiling. Eerie light spilled from the screens around the room as lines of data flicked across their surfaces. Hissing steam vented from latticed grills in the floor plates, and thick, ribbed tubing snaked from the grills to climb the walls and disappear amongst the dense, confusing network of conduits.

Pilots and technicians hard-wired into the control room were built into the walls, their forms almost hidden amongst the mass of coiling pipes that engulfed them. Insulated wiring entered the fused hemispheres of their brains through eye sockets, nostrils and ears. They manipulated controls through cables that plugged into the remnants of flesh that remained of their mortal bodies, and from each fingertip spread a spider web of intricate cables, attaching them directly into the holy machine that they were a part of.

Darioq muttered the incantation of supplication to the machine-spirit and recited the *logis dictates* that would ignite the spark of connection as his electro-jacks continued to manipulate the inner core workings of the command column. Speaking blessings to the Omnissiah, he tripped the internal switches within his own mechanised form, and his spirit joined with that of his flagship in a surge of images, information and release.

Hovering fifty metres in the air, the bloated airship that served as Darioq's command centre was as stable as the ground, despite the torrential downpour of rain and the sharp burst of wind that the magos felt buffeting its banded sides. Connected to the huge machine's spirit, he felt the rain and wind on its thick sides as if it were an extension of himself. Massive rotating spotlights that cut through the darkness were his eyes, and endless feeds of information flooded through the multiple logic engines within his construction, filing through the domed hemispheres of his 'true' brain, which then filtered relevant data out into the charged liquid housing domes that enclosed his secondary brain units.

He felt the smooth running engines that powered the mass turbines keeping the hulk airborne, and sensed the holy oils lubricating the cogs and gears slipping through the mechanics, as the dictates required. He could feel the scurrying feet of servitors, Skitarii and priests through the labyrinthine tunnels within the airship's underhull, and the spark of sensation as these servants of the Omnissiah plugged themselves into the vast machine, linking them to him and him to them. He could see through the augmetic eyes of these lesser minions and feel the twitch of their vat-born muscles.

His spirit reached out through the thick, insulated cabling that fed from his control station, travelling through the circuitry and carefully constructed piping that linked the airship to the Ordinatus *Magentus* far below. He linked himself to the intractable spirit of that great creation and whispered a prayer to the shrine-machine as he flowed through its holy workings.

Probing at the plasma-reactor at the core of the *Magentus*, he felt the contained power within, a blessing from the Machine-God. Back in his command station, he felt the vibratory impulse that pre-empted a vox transmissions arrival. An electro-pulse fired within Darioq's true brain and the magos recognised the sensation as irritation. He retracted his spirit from that of the *Magentus* in an instant and returned to his flagship. Though he remained in connection with the airship, he allowed his physical faculties to come to the fore and received visual stimulus through the glowing crystals of his augmetic right eye, and through the blearing, inferior gaze of his left, organic eye.

With a twist of one of his mechadendrites, Darioq turned a function dial on the command pillar and a hololith atop the pillar sparked into life. A three-dimensional image of an Imperial Guard officer sprang into existence, his every feature picked out in the intricate network of crisscrossing green lines. It showed the man's head and shoulders, and extended down to his chest.

'Blessings of the Omnissiah to you, Brigadier-General Ishmael Havorn,' said Darioq.

'Blessings of the God-Emperor to you, magos,' said the green rendering of Havorn, the sound issuing from the speaker box built into the command pillar slightly out of time with the movement of the lips.

'Your tech-guard suffer many losses, my reports tell me.'

'The losses of the servitors and Skitarii units is acceptable, Brigadier-General Ishmael Havorn. The Hypaspists and the Sagitarii units are replaceable. The Praetorians' destruction was necessary to conduct the falling back of the cohorts. The loss of several of the Ordinatus Minoris machines of the Ballisterarii is regrettable, but predicted by my cogitator engine. The Omnissiah has reclaimed their spirits unto the bosom of Mars.'

'And are your preparations for the second push proceeding as planned, magos?'

'The *Exemplis* advances, Brigadier-General Ishmael Havorn, and a larger concentration of cohort units advances beneath its hallowed shadow. My Cataphractarii lead the holy procession.'

'Six companies of the 133rd will accompany your tech-guard. They are advancing as we speak. Alongside them are heavy armour squadrons,' said the image of the Elysian commander. 'Members of the 72nd will re-engage the foe within the highlands to coincide with our combined assault.'

'I will accede to your wishes, Brigadier-General Ishmael Havorn. Your flesh units and heavy armour will accompany the second push.'

The image of Havorn's face frowned darkly, but Techno-Magos Darioq had long passed the point of being able to read facial expressions. He could read more from a blank data-slate or the turning of an engine than he could from the facial contortions of the fleshed.

'Never have I heard of such willingness by the Mechanicus to throw its tech-guard at an enemy, bar one threatening one of the Forge Worlds. You can understand my… confusion, magos.'

'The Adeptus Mechanicus supports the armies of the Emperor in all endeavours, Brigadier-General Ishmael Havorn. The Adeptus Mechanicus wishes to support the battle against the enemy on this planet c6.7.32.'

'Yes, as you have said, magos. I just wish to the Emperor that I knew why.'

'To many within the Cult Mechanicus, the Emperor of Terra and the Omnissiah are one. They would say that the Imperial Guard and the regiments of Mars enact his will equally.'

The image of Havorn raised its eyebrow at a figure off-screen.

'It is usual for brothers in arms to share pertinent information regarding their purpose.'

'The Adeptus Mechanicus wishes to support the battle against the enemy on this planet c6.7.32. That is the purpose of this expedition force.'

'Expedition force? This is a war zone!'

'You are correct, Brigadier-General Ishmael Havorn. Your voice has risen by 1.045 octaves, and my logarithmic codifier indicates that your volume has increased by 37.854 Imperial standard decibels. Are you unwell, Brigadier-General Ishmael Havorn?'

'What?' asked the Imperial commander.

'Your voice has risen by–' began Darioq before he was interrupted.

'Emperor above!' exclaimed Havorn.

'The mnemo-strands within my logic engines suggest that some savage cultures within the Imperium believe that the Emperor *does* exist beyond the atmosphere of their home world. Do you believe this, Brigadier-General Ishmael Havorn? Is that why you speak the words "Emperor above"?'

'Are you attempting a joke, magos? I thought such a thing was beyond one such as you.'

'I do not understand the concept of humour, Brigadier-General Ishmael Havorn. My memory functions contain the information pertaining to the notion, but I have erased my memories of such a notion as inconsequential to the Omnissiah.'

The image of Havorn stared fixedly at the inscrutable visage of Darioq. The magos waited patiently for the Elysian commander to speak once more.

'Move the *Exemplis* to the front line. We attack before dawn,' he said, and cut the connection.

Darioq removed his mechadendrites from the command pillar and the image of Havorn, frozen in a scowl when the Elysian severed the connection, disappeared. A ghostly after-image remained for a second before it too faded.

He stood motionless for a moment, his brains alight with sparks of thought. For a few moments the eyelid of his weak, organic flesh-eye flickered as he accessed information stored deep within one subsidiary cortex, and he plunged the blade of the electro-jack on the tip of one of his mechadendrites back into the column.

Another green-lined image sprang up, hovering above the surface of the command column. It showed the rotating sphere of a planet, a stark, rocky and lifeless world. Polar ice-flows spread out across much of the land. Temperature indicators marked the planet as being far below a temperature that was able to sustain life. A light flashed beneath the hovering image of the planet. It was a date, in standard Imperial time, and it indicated that this was the representation of a planet almost two thousand years in the past.

With a twist of his mechadendrite, Darioq caused a second planet to be projected alongside the first. This was a world dominated by water, seas covering the length and breadth of the sphere, bar two continents. With a further twist, Darioq brought the two glowing planets together, so that they overlapped each other perfectly. The mountains of the two images locked together like pieces of a puzzle. They were a perfect, identical match.

He rotated the overlapping spheres and magnified the image tenfold, zooming in on the north-western tip of the larger continent. The mountain plateau above the sea level rose to a point and then dropped off beneath the oceans. The cliff faces were almost sheer and fell into a series of deep undersea valleys, thousands of metres beneath the ocean. He zoomed closer, focusing on one particularly deep, abyssal chasm.

He abruptly retracted his mechadendrite and the green, three-dimensional depiction disappeared. Only the after image of the overlapping planets remained for a fraction of a second, along with a small line of digits beneath the spheres: c6.7.32. A moment later, they too faded.

IT WAS ALMOST midday, though it may as well have been midnight for all the light that penetrated the thick, roiling, black storm clouds. Torrential, blinding rain still lashed the high peaks of the mountains, and ravines and cracks were flooded with streaming water. In the valley below, vast moving rivers of water cut across the landscape, seeking the lower ground of the surrounding flat lands. Even the highly attuned sensors of the Word Bearers were becoming blocked by the high amount of water and electricity that coursed through the air.

The battle raged on, frenzied and devastating, and the bodies of Guardsmen floated through the mire. The wrecked shells of burned out vehicles and tanks were dragged through the rising waters. The Word Bearers strode through the shallower, knee-deep waters, firing into the massed ranks of the enemy.

Experimental weaponry of the Adeptus Mechanicus crackled and roared, ripping apart traitor vehicles and Dreadnoughts, and shells fell among both battle lines, causing torrents of water to explode into the air along with shattered bodies and armour. Coalescing arcs of energy streamed from the weapons borne upon the backs of tracked crawlers that inched forward through the mire of bodies and rain water.

Kol Badar had seen some of those weapons before. Many were weapons developed to be borne by the colossal war machines of the Titan Legions. Without the technology to continue to construct these behemoths of war, many of which were over a hundred metres in height, the Adeptus Mechanicus had clearly deemed it fit to mount these artillery pieces upon tracked crawler units, but the effectiveness of the weapons remained awesome.

Missiles streamed through the rain, exploding in white-hot blasts of super-heated energy. The ground was ripped apart in deep furrows that were instantly engulfed with water as other esoteric batteries fired, throwing warriors and vehicles aside as if they weighed nothing at all. Giant gouts of liquid flame roared through the darkness, engulfing scores of soldiers on both sides and heating the streaming waters of the valley to boiling point.

Casualties were rising, though the Imperials were losing scores of warriors for every Word Bearer that fell. The fervour, or impatience, of the Imperial commanders was strong. Despite their air raids being almost neutralised by the worsening weather conditions, they drove their forces ever onwards in a grinding battle of attrition, desperate it seemed to push the Legion back.

The Coryphaus had ordered the reserve of the Host forward, to reinforce the line of Word Bearers holding the valley. He had also demanded that Marduk leave the command of the ridges to the Warmonger, and for him to bolster the valley. While the lighter Imperial aircraft had been forced to pull out by the buffeting, gale force winds and lightning that had ripped many of their fighters from the air, the heavier Thunderhawks and Stormwings of the Word Bearers were able to remain airborne, albeit for only short flights before they retreated from the heart of the storm.

Marduk had fumed at the condescending tone of the order, but could recognise the danger. Holding the Imperials back was imperative, or the losses that they had already suffered were for nought, and the determined drive of the Imperials threatened to push through the Word Bearers' defence.

Roaring barrages continued to rain down from the ridge-tops, and lascannons and missiles lanced out of the darkness from the cliffs, targeting the tracked vehicles of the Mechanicus and the battle tanks that were rolling into the fray. Soaring missiles and rockets returned fire against the warriors under the Warmonger's command high above, but there was little that could truly reach them, high in the rocks. Nevertheless, it seemed not even to slow the ponderous advance of the Imperials, as ever more troops and vehicles filtered into the valley.

Chimera APCs spat sharp bursts of las-fire from their turret mounted multi-lasers, and strong waves were created as they ploughed through the deeper rivers that flowed across the battlefield. Easily as capable in the deep water as on land, the vehicles churned through the corpse-strewn mire to unload their cargoes of Guardsmen. Smoke-launchers fired, cloaking the battlefield behind white smoke that blocked even the auto-sensors and targeting arrays of the Word Bearers, but Marduk laughed as the smoke almost instantly dissipated in the gale. Several of the Chimeras were halted in their tracks as missiles and autocannon fire raked their hulls. The men scrambling to vacate the sinking metal coffins were gunned down by bolter fire. Another of the Chimeras was lifted into the air as it reached more solid ground when a Dreadnought struck its side with a massive siege ram before unleashing a flurry of missiles into another vehicle.

A formation of tracked units advanced through the gunfire, bolter fire pinging off their armoured forms. Humanoid upper bodies were integrated into the mechanised units and cannons protruded from the stumps of their arms. Marduk hacked through the metallic torso of a servitor warrior, spraying oil and blood, and broke into a loping run towards the strange, centaur-like creatures.

He felt the presence of Burias-Drak'shal at his side, the daemon soul of the warrior burning hotly. Two coteries of Word Bearers launched themselves forward in support of the First Acolyte and the Icon Bearer, bolters barking as they tore through the Skitarii warriors towards this new enemy,

Their movements jerky, the tracked centaur units fired controlled bursts from their rotating cannons as they rolled forwards. Their bodies were a mass of augmetic, metal body plating, and their heads were almost completely hidden in dark metal encasings, the only exception being the dead, staring left eyes that peered out from white flesh.

The lead unit turned its head jerkily in Marduk's direction and he felt the warning buzz from his auto-sensors as the mass of targeters arrayed over the servitor's right eye fixed on him.

With a snarl, Marduk threw himself into a roll as the mechanical warrior jerked the rotating barrels of its weapon in his direction and bullets began to spray towards him. They clipped his shoulder pad, taking chips out of the thick ceramite plating, and he fired his bolt pistol as he rose. Two bolts slammed into the face of the mechanised warrior, blowing a crater out the back of its head.

The other machines fired into the Word Bearers with short, sharp bursts. Marduk saw the chest of one warrior-brother ripped to shreds and the head of another pulverised.

With a roar, Burias-Drak'shal leapt onto one of the tracked machines as it rolled slowly forwards. He drove the daemon talons of one hand into the side of the Skitarii's head with such force that it punched through metal and bone, and pulverised the fused brain-hemispheres within. A burst of fire slammed into his lower back and the daemonically possessed warrior staggered. With a bellow that came from the pits of the Immaterium, Burias-Drak'shal spun and hurled the icon of the Host through the air like a spear. It slammed into the chest of the tracked creature that had shot him, impaling it on the large spikes that made up the eight-pointed star. Fluids ran from the wound and sparks engulfed the torso of the tracked machine, and it began to twitch convulsively. At a barked command from Burias-Drak'shal the icon ripped free of the malfunctioning machine and flew back to its master's hand.

Marduk launched into the *Catechism of Hate* and raising his daemonic chainsword high into the air, led the Word Bearers forward into the enemy. He pumped shot after shot into the mechanised torso of one of his foes, scoring deep craters across its armour. His chainsword bit through the thick tracks of the machine, and it floundered. Its expressionless face looked down upon him as it brought its weapon to bear, but Marduk moved swiftly around the immobilised machine, holstering his pistol. He pulled a krak grenade from his belt, pressing its igniting rune, and thrust it into the spinning cog-wheels of the damaged track unit.

He drew his pistol again as he charged towards the next machine, and the grenade detonated behind him. Flames washed over another machine, liquefying its flesh, but it fought on, its spinning cannon ripping the legs from a charging warrior at Marduk's side.

The press of the enemy was heavy, as other cohorts moved inexorably to support their kin, and Guardsmen pushed desperately forwards, vainly trying to drive the Word Bearers back. Las-bolts struck Marduk's armour and flames washed over him. Rapid firing rounds from the tracked machines raked him and he hissed in pain as one cracked a chink in the armour of his chestplate.

His fiery words drove the Word Bearers on and they fought deep into the enemy formations. Blood flowed freely as he carved his screaming chainsword through the head of a Guardsman. A man stumbled towards him, his arm missing from the elbow down, and Marduk smashed him to the ground with the butt of his pistol before putting a round through the back of his head.

He felt savage joy as he slaughtered any who drew near him. He stumbled suddenly as a las-bolt pierced the armour of his thigh, searing the muscle beneath. He shot another man in the chest, his ribs exploding outwards as the explosive bolt detonated within.

An explosion tore the life from a pair of Word Bearers, and Marduk was rocked by the sudden blast, staggering to keep his footing as shrapnel scored across his armour. He saw a battle tank advance, the barrel of its turret smoking.

A heavy blow from his side smashed him to the ground and he felt the blessed ceramite of his shoulder pad compress as it absorbed the force of the blow. A servo-arm clamped around his torso as he tried to rise and he hissed in pain under the pressure. Power assisted pistons hissed as the clamps of the servo-arm tightened, and Marduk felt his ancient ceramite begin to buckle beneath the force.

He swung his chainsword into the neck of the servitor, and flesh and mechanics were ripped apart by the whirling teeth of the weapon. The fused bones of his ribcage strained as the pressure increased and he tried to bring his bolt pistol around for a shot, but the hold the combat servitor had on him made it impossible. Marduk pushed with all the force of his arm, driving his chainsword deeper into his foe's neck, but the crushing force did not relent.

A combi-bolter was placed into one the armature joints of the servo-arm, and bolts tore into the weak point, severing the limb. The combat servitor reeled backwards, the stump of its servo-arm spraying oil and milky liquid as it waved ineffectually, before another blast from the combi-bolter tore the servitor's head from its shoulders.

'One day the pleasure of killing you will be mine, and mine alone,' came a snarling voice. 'None will steal that prize from me.'

Marduk looked up at Kol Badar, standing over him. He could just imagine the smirk on the whoreson's face beneath his quad-tusked helmet, and he rose to his feet quickly, his face burning with shame and fury. His hand tightened around the grip of his chainsword, and he felt the daemon Borhg'ash willing him to lash out at the Coryphaus.

Kol Badar laughed as he turned away from the First Acolyte, his combi-bolter tearing another enemy to shreds. With a swat of his power claw he sent one of the tracked units toppling onto its side, where an Anointed cult member turned its head to molten metal and liquid, burning flesh with a searing blast from the meltagun slung beneath his bolter.

Simmering with anger, Marduk watched as Kol Badar grabbed the track unit of the battle tank in his massive power talons, ripping it clear in a shower of sparks and smoke. As the tank jerked to a halt, the warlord of the Word Bearers clenched his talons into a fist crackling with energy and, with a roar, smashed it into the armoured plating of the vehicle. The reinforced armour buckled under the power of the blow. The second blow punched straight through the armoured hull and Kol Badar wrenched his fist free, tangled metal screeching horribly. Placing the muzzle of his combi-bolter through the hole, he unloaded his clip inside the tank. The bolt-rounds ricocheted around the enclosed space deafeningly and there were screams from within.

As if feeling Marduk's gaze, Kol Badar turned towards him, and pointed at the First Acolyte with one of his crackling power talons. The message was clear: *your time will come.*

I welcome that time with open arms, thought Marduk, flushed with anger and bitterness.

THE IMPERIAL FORCES were being butchered. Despite their efforts to drive against the traitor Legion, they were making no ground. Worse, they were *losing* ground, being slowly pushed back by the fury of the Chaos Space Marines' resistance.

But that was soon to change.

The earth shuddered with each step of the *Exemplis.* It rose out of the gloom like a colossus of the ancients, a towering behemoth of awesome power. The mountains shook to their foundations as thousands of tonnes of metal slammed into the hard, salt packed earth of the flooding valley with each titanic step.

Those legs alone were mighty bastion fortresses, complete with battle cannon batteries and crenellated walls from which soldiers could pour fire into the foe. Within each leg was a demi-cohort consisting of Hypaspists and the elite biologically and mechanically enhanced Praetorians. But the leg bastions were the least of the weapons of the *Exemplis.*

Heaving some of the most powerful weapons ever conceived by the

Adeptus Mechanicus, entire traitorous planets had surrendered at the mere appearance of the *Exemplis*. With weaponry the size of towering building blocks, each capable of demolishing cities and laying ruin to armies, the *Exemplis* had been in operational use by the Fire Wasps of Legio Ignatum since the time of the Great Crusade.

The plasma reactor, burning with the contained energy of a sun, roared with terrifying power as a fraction of its energy was siphoned into the giant weaponry of the god-machine.

The *Exemplis* was one of the last remaining Imperator Titans of Legio Ignatium of Mars and was worshipped by the adepts of the Cult Mechanicus as an avatar of the Omnissiah. With thundering steps, it strode to war once more against the traitors that had turned their back on the Imperium of Man.

CHAPTER TWELVE

THERE WAS SOMETHING distinctly *wrong* about the tower, something far more perverted and unearthly than Varnus could truly conceive. It was almost as if it was a sentient being, that it had thoughts and ambitions of its own, and that these thoughts and ambitions were seeping into the slaves that laboured over its living form.

It was large on an unfeasible, maddening scale, and continued to rise hundreds of metres into the sky with every passing change of shift. It was so high that were it not for the vile, living re-breather masks that had been attached to the slaves' faces, they would start to struggle for oxygen in the increasingly thin air, not to mention the noxious fumes that blanketed the shattered city. The smog fumes seemed inexorably drawn towards the tower, and they circled it lazily.

At times, the tentacles of the creature burrowed deeper into his skull, wriggling and twitching agonisingly. It could not be removed. He wondered if it could ever be removed, even under surgery, and he had seen more than one slave die while trying to tear the thing from their face. They ended up choking to death, blood seeping from their ears and eyes as the powerful, leech-like tentacles burrowed through their brains, seeking solid purchase, and the tubular, living pipes that ran down their oesophagi clenched shut.

The appearance of the slaves was drastically altered by the foul masks; they looked more like devotees of the dark gods than Imperial citizens, and Varnus realised that he too must resemble one of the hated ones.

The work on the tower was never-ending and the slaves were worked at a brutal pace, the overseers viciously punishing those that failed to meet their exacting demands. It was as if the whole operation had gone into overdrive, that there was a looming deadline fast approaching and the tower had to be completed. There must have been around two hundred thousand slaves working atop the walls alone, he estimated, and many more hundreds of thousands working down in the sink-hole that disappeared inside the shaft of the tower, burrowing ever deeper into Tanakreg's crust, down into the depths of the planet. All told, he estimated that there must have been a million slave workers toiling over the construction at any one time. More crane engines had been constructed, and along with thousands of slaves, they were strengthening the base of the tower, making it thicker with additional layers of bricks even as the tower soared up towards the heavens. In addition, they began work on a massive spiralling walkway, wide enough for a battle tank, that coiled its way around the exterior of the tower. It was a mammoth undertaking, but one that progressed at an astonishing pace.

There must have been dire sorceries involved, for the tower had already surpassed the height of the greatest construction that he had ever heard of, and logic dictated that it simply could not rise higher without toppling, or collapsing beneath its own weight. But rise higher it did, defying the laws of the material universe.

Although he loathed the monstrous tower as he hated his overseers and captors, he could not help but have strange paternal feelings over the mass of rock and blood mortar. It was a repulsive moment of self-awareness, but the actions of the other slaves, particularly the ex-bodyguard and manservant, Pierlo, who he was chained alongside, had alerted him to it.

There had been an incident two work shifts earlier. Was that two days past? Two hours past?

The man Pierlo, Varnus had ascertained, was barely holding a grip on his sanity. He had overheard the man whispering to himself, having one side of a conversation that only he could hear. The living, black module that was attached to his face strangely distorted his voice, making it guttural, thick and oddly muted. In fact, it sounded uncannily like the voices of the cruel overseers. Varnus knew that his voice had undergone a similar change.

As he talked quietly to himself, Varnus had noticed that the man was tenderly stroking the stone beneath him, as if he were petting a beloved family salt hound. It was unnerving, but since he heard voices constantly through the blaring cacophony of the Discords, he thought little of it. At least he had so far resisted the desire to talk back to those voices.

As Pierlo stroked the harsh stone, Varnus had heard a wailing cry and had swung around to see the commotion. A block of stone, one of the millions that made up the growing tower, was being lowered into position, but through some mishap, it had not been positioned correctly. It had crushed the legs of three slave workers and was teetering on the brink of tipping off the high wall. One of the spider-limbed cranes strained as it tried to reposition the stone, but it was clear that it would fall. Pierlo and several other slaves had risen to their feet, crying out in horror, and Varnus felt a pang of anguish and terror.

The stone slipped in the claws of the crane and dropped over the outside edge of the wall, spinning and smashing against the stones below. A hundred tonnes of rock, it tumbled end over end, down and down, before disappearing in the low hanging smog clouds. The men whose legs had been shattered wailed, but not in pain. They clawed their way to the edge of the wall, their legs twisted horrifically beneath them, as they watched the descent of the block, eyes already brimming with tears of loss.

Pierlo had fallen to his knees, crying out to the heavens. Varnus's stomach churned, and he felt such a hollow loss within his chest that he thought he would weep. He shook his head as he realised what he was thinking, but the pain remained. All around the tower, slaves cried out in anguish.

He also knew that this was no doubt some further degradation of his sanity, for how else could he imagine that a construction like this had self-awareness? But of that he was convinced. The tower had been distraught when the stone had fallen and the slaves that had tended it had picked up that emotion. It was the kind of feeling a parent has when its child is in pain but cannot be helped.

He hated the tower, but when the time for the shift change came, he found it difficult to leave. The ride down the rickety, grilled elevator that climbed down the narrow steps of the tower on mechanical spider legs was hard, and the pain of separation was strong, even though it repulsed him. Other slaves cried out and wept openly, pushing their hands out through the grill to touch the stone of the tower, often losing a finger in the process.

Sleep was still no respite for Varnus, as every time he closed his eyes he revisited the hellish landscape of skinned corpses. Only now, there were towering buildings made out of the corpses, huge edifices that reached to the roiling heavens. From these buildings came the tolling of bells and the sound of monotonous chanting. He awoke covered in sweat, and instantly the pain of separation struck him; he longed to be back atop the tower, working.

Discords blared and told him that the tower had a name. They told him that it was a Gehemahnet. He did not know the word, but it felt right.

It seemed to him that the Gehemahnet breathed, and that he could feel the pulse of its massive heart reverberating through the stone beneath his touch.

He prayed to the Emperor when he thought such things, but it was increasingly hard to remember the words of worship that had been drummed into him by the priests of the Ecclesiarchy.

He looked at Pierlo as the man worked, smearing the blood mortar across the stone face. The man's robes had fallen open and there was something underneath, a shape on the man's shoulder that even the lumps of congealed mortar could not hide.

'What's on your shoulder?' he hissed, his voice alien to him.

Pierlo looked up in irritation, as if rudely interrupted mid-conversation. He pulled at his tattered robe, covering up the mark, and continued with his work, head down.

Varnus risked a glance around and saw that there was no overseer anywhere nearby. His mind feverish and the din of the Discord blaring, *kill him*, Varnus scrambled over to the slave and grabbed at his robe. Pierlo clawed at his hands, trying to fend him off, but Varnus ripped the robe from the man's shoulder.

There was a symbol there on the meat of his shoulder, a symbol that he recognised, for he had seen it hundreds of times every day. It was embossed on the sides of the spider cranes and it was stamped into the foreheads of some of the head overseers. He had seen it on the shoulder plate of every cursed traitor Space Marine on the planet. It was a screaming daemon's face and he knew exactly what it proclaimed.

'You are one of them!' he hissed. Instantly the pieces fell together in his mind. He had seen the man leave the meeting room in the palace just moments before it had exploded. He was one of the traitor insurgents that had aided the forces of Chaos.

Pierlo's face twisted hatefully as the two scuffled. Dully, Varnus heard the yells of other slaves, but he paid them no heed. All he could hear was the pounding of blood in his head. This bastard was one of those who had opened the door to the invaders. Hatred swelled within him. His hand snapped out towards Pierlo's face, fingers spread like claws.

The man was no stranger to unarmed combat and he grabbed Varnus's hand as it came close, twisting his wrist painfully. Pierlo's other hand slammed into his solar plexus, fingers extended, and all the breath was driven from him. He sank to the stone. Where Pierlo was of high birth, and had clearly been trained in the arts of combat, Varnus had learnt how to brawl on the streets of Shinar, and he knew that fighting as an art form and fighting tooth and nail for daily survival were two very different things. Varnus had suffered countless beatings in his youth as a hab-ganger and had dished out far more. Even when he had tried to go straight and had secured a job on the salt plains, he had fought in bare-knuckle brawls at night to supplement his meagre income. All that had changed when he had been recruited into the Shinar enforcers, but his skills had come in just as useful there.

Varnus surged up suddenly, landing a fierce blow to Pierlo's chin, quickly followed by a vicious swinging elbow that connected sharply with the man's head. He reeled backwards, about to fall off the wall and probably drag Varnus and half a dozen other slaves with him. Varnus grabbed the thick, spiked chain, yanking the man back onto the stone and straight into a knee that he slammed into Pierlo's groin.

As Pierlo bent forwards in pain, the ex-enforcer drove the point of his elbow down onto the back of his head, dropping him to the stone.

Pierlo was motionless, but Varnus had not finished there. His hatred suffusing him, he made a loop with the spiked chain and hooked it around Pierlo's neck, placing a foot on the back of the man's neck. He crossed the chains in his hands and strained, pulling on the chain with all his strength. Though Pierlo wore the same blood-red metal collar as all the slaves, the chain bit deeply around his throat, cutting off his breathing as the spiked barbs sank into flesh. Blood ran from the man's throat, mixing with the mortar atop the stone.

Pain jolted him as the needles of the overseers plunged into his flesh, but he didn't care. His muscles bulged as he hauled on the chains one final time before the searing pain the overseers delivered made him collapse, twitching and convulsing, to the stone alongside Pierlo.

In his mind's eye he saw the sky running red with blood. He knew that Gehemahnet was pleased.

He smiled as he looked into the dead eyes of the traitor.

THE EARTH SHOOK, and as Marduk ripped his chainsword from the guts of a Guardsman he raised his head to pierce the gloom. Rain still lashed the bloody battlefield, but he sensed, as much as he felt, something approaching, something *huge*.

Lightning flashed, silhouetting a shape that Marduk had initially mistaken for a mountain. This was no mountain though, for it moved inexorably forwards, and the earth shook as it took another laborious step. With a curse on his lips, Marduk's gaze rose as the immense shape of the Titan was revealed.

IT WAS LIKE some ancient, primeval god from an antediluvian age that continued to stalk the lands long after its kin had passed into myth and legend.

Its metal hide was pitted and scored by wounds that it had suffered during the battles it had waged over its ten thousand year lifetime. It's leering, dull metal face was fire scorched and scarred, though its eyes still burned with red light. Within that metallic cranium sat the Princeps and his Moderati, psychically linked to the Titan. They felt its pain as their own and experienced savage joy as the behemoth laid waste to everything before it.

Advancing through the press of soldiers and tanks, it dwarfed everything in its path. A multi-towered bastion the size of a walled stronghold sat atop its massive, armoured carapace shell. Siege ordnance and battle cannons, of such size that a small tank could drive through the barrels, were housed within this massive structure, and the pennants and banners that adorned it whipped around in the gale. Scores of symbols were emblazoned on the ancient kill banners that hung from the pair of monstrous main guns that the Imperator Titan wielded in place of arms, marking the enemy Titans and super-heavy vehicles that it had destroyed throughout its long history. The air around the giant war machine shimmered with the power of its void shields.

The siege cannons upon the hulking shoulders of the Imperator thumped as they launched their first salvo, and the air was filled with screaming shells that erupted amongst the Word Bearers. Warrior-brothers were thrown through the air and tanks smashed asunder beneath the barrage, but that was as nothing compared to the awesome destruction that was to come. Super-heated plasma fed into the annihilator cannon on the beast's right arm, filling the air with potent hissing that hurt the unprotected ears of the Guardsmen, and the massive barrels of the deadly hellstorm cannon began to rotate, the wind beating fiercely as it picked up speed.

The hellstorm cannon let loose with a torrent of fire from the spinning barrels that tore along the line of Word Bearers, cutting from one side of the valley to the other, ripping through warriors and vehicles alike. The plasma annihilator cannon flared with the power of a contained sun and a gout of white-hot energy roared from its barrel, engulfing a handful of tanks that were instantly returned to their molten base elements.

The destruction that the Imperator wrought was awe inspiring, and a roar rose from the ranks of Imperial Guardsmen as their god-machine unleashed the power of its weapon systems upon the hated foe.

MARDUK BARED HIS sharp teeth, hissing up at the monstrous, unstoppable beast. Stabbing beams of energy flashed from the mountainside as the lascannons of the havoc squads positioned there targeted the Imperator. The powerful blasts looked like little more than pin-pricks of light as they strobed towards the Titan. Scores of predator tanks, Land Raiders, Dreadnoughts and daemon engines added their fire to that of the havoc squads as they directed their heavy weapons fire towards the towering behemoth. Missiles, lascannon beams, heavy ordnance shells and streaming plasma speared towards the Titan. Its void shields flashed as they absorbed the incoming firepower, leaving the deadly machine unscathed, and it returned fire with dozens of battle cannons situated in the leg bastions.

The ranks of the Imperial Guard renewed their attack, bolstered by the arrival of the Titan that unleashed the power of its plasma annihilator once more, firing up into the darkness and blasting away a ridge top, causing salt rock, debris and daemon engines to crash down the sheer cliff in a mass avalanche. Its hellstorm cannons smoked as they spun, tearing along the ridge. Rain turned to steam as it lashed against the super-heated barrels of the mega-weapon. Barrages of ordnance continued to pound at the void shields atop the carapace of the Titan, and they flashed with a myriad of colours as they deflected the incoming fire.

Marduk swore again and fired into the press of bodies around him, feeling the shifting tide of the battle turn against his Legion. There was just not enough firepower to take down the Imperator's shields, let alone damage the Titan, not while they were already engaged with the Guard and Skitarii forces.

But to fail in their duty to hold the valley was to face a fate far worse than death. If it was necessary, every Word Bearers Space Marine would willingly give his life in this battle at his word. Though it was Kol Badar's place as Coryphaus and strategos to organise the complex, interwoven battle lines, the carefully planned advance, fire support and overlapping fields of fire, it was Marduk's place, in the absence of the Dark Apostle, to be responsible for the Host's spiritual leadership. If he gave the order to stay and fight to the death, for that was what the gods of Chaos wished, then his word would be obeyed without question. The warrior-brothers would sell their lives dearly but willingly, taking as many of the enemy with them as they could, before their own life essences were freed from their earthly forms.

But Marduk could not see how a noble sacrifice could be made against this ancient war god. No, there could be no proud last stand. There would be only death and destruction, swift and ignoble. They would not be able to buy the time that the Dark Apostle needed to complete the construction of the Gehemahnet, and that was paramount. If the building work was interrupted then the whole attack against the planet was rendered pointless, and the Council of Dark Apostles upon Sicarus would be most displeased. That was truly something to be feared, for even in death, the Council would reach into the abyss of the Immaterium and seek out the souls of those who had failed them. The endless torment that they would orchestrate was too horrific to even contemplate.

He felt anger build within him and hacked around in a fury, shattering bones and slicing through flesh as he fought in the rising water. Many of the enemy were wading almost to their stomachs through the fast moving flow, and the corpses of the slain floated face down, their blood leaking out like an oil slick. Another blast from the Imperator obliterated a section of the battlefield with the power of its weaponry, and the whooshing sound of water instantly turning to steam was mixed with the roars of the dying and the detonations of the fuel lines and ammo-banks of vehicles.

'We must pull back, First Acolyte,' Kol Badar growled over the vox.

'The great war leader Kol Badar, ordering a retreat from Imperial Guard,' remarked Marduk. 'I can hear them laughing at us already.'

'Let them laugh. They won't have the chance to savour their victory for long.'

'For them to be able to savour any sort of victory against the Legion of Lorgar shames us all,' snarled Marduk.

'You wish to die here, whelp? I will joyfully oblige you if that is what you truly desire. And nobody will save you this time.'

Burias-Drak'shal cleaved his icon into the chest of a Guardsman, splattering blood across Marduk's helmet.

'The battle is good,' he growled, the thick daemon teeth within his shifting jaw making his speech awkward. He was not privy to the private vox transmissions passing between Kol Badar and Marduk. 'Is this the day to give our lives to Chaos?'

Marduk shook his head at the possessed Icon Bearer and snapped a barbed response to Kol Badar.

'The gods of Chaos would curse you if you dared try, warlord. Your failure mars us all.'

'And I will stand with my head held high before my lord and accept any punishment that he metes out. I would not try to wheedle out of it like you, whelp.'

'You admit your failures then, mighty Kol Badar.'

'I listen not to your spineless taunts, snake. As the gods are my witness, I will see that damned Imperator fall. I am still warlord of the Host, and you will do as I command.'

'I look forward to seeing you grovel and lick the ground at the Dark Apostle's feet as you beg for mercy,' snarled Marduk.

'Never going to happen, snake,' said Kol Badar. The vox-channel clicked as it was opened to the champions of the coteries.

'Fighting fall-back,' ordered the Coryphaus. 'Front coteries detach, third and fourth lines lay cover. Second and fifth lines, intersect with the first, overlap and close out. Third and fourth, then detach. And pull back those damned Dreadnoughts and daemon engines.'

Burias-Drak'shal snarled in frustration, ripping a man in two as he enacted his dissatisfaction.

'We flee from these?' he said as he broke the back of another soldier.

'No,' said Marduk. 'We flee from that.'

'Bah! We have taken down Titans before. The Coryphaus is weak.'

'Eyeing his position already, Burias-Drak'shal?'

The possessed warrior grinned ferally before he allowed the daemon within him to reassert itself, and he was transformed beyond being able to communicate. With a roar of animal power, he launched himself back into the fray.

Marduk felt shame and resentment build within him. It was not the way of the Legion to back off from a battle against the soldiers of the Corpse Emperor, though he knew that Kol Badar's orders were the best path of action for the Host.

Still, it would be a pleasure to see the arrogant bastard taken down a peg when the Dark Apostle received word of the setback.

THE WORD BEARERS' retreat was perfectly executed as the lines of coteries fell back in textbook order, laying down fields of overlapping fire to cover those that backed away. Those coteries in turn then planted their feet and covered their brethren. Fallen warriors were dragged back, for to leave them upon the field of battle would have been a gross sacrilege, and in addition, the wargear and gene-seed of the Legion were far too precious to abandon. Vehicles rolled slowly backwards, firing their weapon systems towards the Titan.

Most of the daemon engines and Dreadnoughts were dragged out of the fighting by massive chains hooked to heavy, tracked machinery, though they fought and struggled to rejoin the fray. Several of them turned against their minders, killing dozens of the black-robed humans that strained to rein them in, and tipping over several of the heavy vehicles hauling them backwards. Others ripped free of their restraints and launched at the foe, ripping, tearing and roaring, flames and missiles streaming from their weapons before they were inevitably silenced by the guns of the Imperator.

Kol Badar felt the shame tear at him, but he could not allow the Host to be destroyed. The losses had been high, however, and this day would long be lamented.

He had of course made preparations for a fall-back if it was needed, it was just part of the canon of engagement to be ready for any eventuality, but to order a retreat was not something that he had been forced to do for millennia.

With withering, concentrated fire, the Word Bearers drove the enemy back. The Legion slowly retreated, their bolters creating a swathe of death.

Ground-hugging, eight-legged machines skittered forward from the Chaos Space Marine lines. They were smaller than the towering defilers, and operated by beings that had once been lowly humans. Now they were forever linked to the machines through mechanical hard-wiring and black sorcery, the corrupted flesh of their bodies contained within domed, liquid-filled, blister-like eyes at the front of the constructions.

The bloated abdomens of the machines pulsed as circular mines were excreted from their rears, jabbed downwards through the water and into the earth. They scuttled forward, their oversized bellies shrinking as they laid their deadly cargos just beneath the crust of the hard packed salt rock, placing thousands of the mines across the entire breadth of the valley.

Other, longer legged constructions strode through the deepening water, like perverted, multi-limbed water fowl. They liberally spewed a thick, glutinous, oily liquid across the top of the water flows, spurting it out past the Word Bearers that backed away, out into the no man's land between the two forces.

The Imperials' fire destroyed dozens of the twisted creatures, and entire sections of the valley were still exploding beneath the horrendous force of the Imperator's weaponry, but they were disposable and Kol Badar did not care that they were destroyed. They were performing their allotted tasks and their destruction was of no consequence.

The Titan took another massive step forwards, the huge, multi-tiered metal foot slamming down with thundering force, firing its weapon systems at the retreating Word Bearers. Battle cannons atop the Titan's carapace turned, tracking the Thunderhawks and Stormbirds as they screamed through the storm, veering out towards the ridge-tops.

The words of the First Acolyte rang in his head and his anger grew. Such a victory for the Imperials should never have come to pass and he felt frustration weigh heavily upon his massive shoulders. He had wanted more time to scout out the enemy, to assess its strength and composition, but the Dark Apostle's wishes had been clear, and time had been a critical factor. To properly evaluate the enemy would have meant facing the foe deeper in the mountains, and he had felt that such a strategy would not have been to the Dark Apostle's liking.

'You are too cautious, my Coryphaus,' Jarulek would have said. He had insinuated it before.

His caution would have spared the lives of many warrior-brothers this day, however, for the arrival of the Titan had been an unexpected shock. Now he was forced to fight a retreat.

Still, he would damn well ensure that the enemy took as many casualties as possible during the Host's withdrawal.

As flames and shrapnel fell upon the thick, oily soup spewed forth by the twisted, long-legged walkers, the valley erupted into tall flames. Burning fiercely, they roared across the entire width of the valley, engulfing dozens of the walkers. They squealed horribly as they perished, legs kicking in agony as flames licked at them. The burning liquid gruel had covered hundreds of mindless Skitarii as they had continued their relentless advance after the retreating Chaos Space Marines, and the flames dissolved their flesh as they marched. Pieces of machinery, having lost the flesh that bound them together, slipped beneath the streaming waters, though they continued to burn, even beneath the surface.

The first tanks reached the mines secreted beneath the salt rock and were thrown into the air as the powerful weapons detonated. Having seen their power, the Imperials would be loathe to continue their advance until minesweepers had been brought forward to clear a path, and the princeps of the Imperator Titan would have no wish to risk his colossal war machine.

He had bought the Legion time, but it was time that he would have to use carefully, to plan and plot the demise of the Imperator Titan. Strategies and ploys were already swimming through his mind. He knew the place where he would face it, having already noted, on his flyover, the narrowing of the valley some five kilometres back.

He raised his bitter gaze to the heavens that were being ripped apart by lightning and falling shells, and repeated the oath he had sworn to the First Acolyte.

'I will see that god-machine fall by my hand,' he swore, 'or may my soul be damned to torment for all eternity.'

Thunder boomed overhead, as if in response to his oath.

He would break the machine-spirit of the beast, and once victory had been achieved, he would stand before Jarulek, the Dark Apostle, and accept whatever punishment he deemed suitable for his failures this day.

THE BATTLE WAS long over, and the intense storm overhead had abated. The waters had receded, flowing further down the mountains, leaving a mire of destruction across the valley. Bodies were strewn all across the battlefield, and burned out vehicles and wrecks scattered the field. Few enemy casualties remained, most having been hauled from the fire-fight, though Elysians wielding flamers torched those that were left behind. All avoided the blackened hulls of the enemy vehicles and cursed engines, for to destroy them utterly would be too labour intensive. Teams of Elysians bearing heavy arrays of detection sensors inched forward, removing thousands of landmines from the ground. They were far slower than the bizarre minesweeper vehicles of the Adeptus Mechanicus that fanned the ground with great sweeps of mechanical analysis arms. But the orders of the Elysian command were clear: the army would advance as quickly as possible, and every man equipped to detect the mines, whether Elysian or mindless servitor, would be employed.

Under the shadow of the stationary Imperator class Titan *Exemplis*, the adepts of the Mechanicus swarmed over wrecked Imperial vehicles, salvaging precious machineries and supplicating the dead or dying spirits of the vehicles. To Brigadier-General Havorn, they looked like nothing more than clusters of carnivorous ants tearing apart the carcasses of dying prey. The adepts swiftly stripped weapon systems from tanks and Ordinatus Minoris crawlers with focused energy, and loaded them alongside working engines, track-works and control systems onto the backs of hulking hauler vehicles for reuse.

Industrious servitors worked tirelessly, hefting heavy pieces of equipment with servo-arms and harnesses under the watchful eyes of the adepts, and the fallen Skitarii were likewise gathered up and taken to rolling factories that followed in the wake of the main army. There they were dropped onto mass conveyer belts and taken inside for recycling. Havorn was unsure what that entailed. He imagined that the weapons of the tech-guard warriors were torn from the dead flesh of their hosts, but he did not know the fate of the dead flesh. Only when the Techno-Magos Darioq had made a cold entreaty to him had he learnt what happened to those desecrated bodies.

'A request, Brigadier-General Ishmael Havorn,' said the techno-magos in his monotone voice. 'It is my understanding that the flesh bodies of your inactive soldiers are being gathered. Are they to be taken to the reprocessing factorum units of your regiment? I was not aware of the presence of such facilities within your expedition force.'

'Tokens of Elysia will be placed upon the eyes of my fallen soldiers and their flesh will be consumed with cleansing flame. The priests will guide their souls on their way to the Emperor's side,' replied Havorn, unsure of what the techno-magos spoke. 'It is the way of the Elysians. Each man carries with him his twin tokens of Elysia,' he explained, reaching beneath his robe and jangling a pair of round metal coins that hung around his neck, a fine chain running through the holes in their centres. 'This has long been the custom of my people. We specialise in drop attacks, and it is seldom possible to extract our dead, but it matters not where the body lies, merely that the spirit is guided on its way.'

'The dead flesh husks are burned? That is illogical. It is a waste of resources, both of promethium and of the flesh husks. And what of your flesh units that have been rendered inoperative but not yet fully non-functional?'

'My wounded, you mean?' asked Havorn, his voice icy.

'If you wish.'

'My wounded soldiers are removed from their platoons and taken to the medicae facilities. Those with fatal wounds are comforted as much as possible before their spirits are guided on their way.'

'I would make a request of you, Brigadier-General Ishmael Havorn.'

'Ask away,' said the Imperial commander, though he felt wary, not knowing where the magos was leading.

'It is illogical and irrational to dispose of your non-functional flesh units as you do. I would ask that upon the conclusion of your priestly rituals, that the flesh husks are collected for reprocessing by my adepts.'

'Reprocessing into what?'

'Into a semi-liquid, protein based nutrient paste.'

Havorn blinked as if he could not possibly have heard correctly.

'You… you wish to turn the bodies of honoured Elysian soldiers who have fallen in battle against the enemy into *paste*.'

'It is a logical use of limited resources. My Skitarii cohorts are well fuelled, but a replenishment of feed levels would be advantageous.'

'There really is not an ounce of humanity left in you is there, you wretched, base machine?' said Havorn, his voice trembling with emotion.

'Correction. There are exactly thirty-eight Imperial weight units of living flesh and tissue upon my frame, Brigadier-General Ishamel Havorn. I am neither wretched nor base, although their usage in such a context is a new piece of data memory to be stored. And I thank you for calling me "machine", though I am not yet so fully esteemed within the priesthood of Mars as to become truly one with the Omnissiah.'

'Your answer, *magos*,' said Havorn, 'is that you can go and burn in hell before I hand over any of my soldiers to you, dead or alive.'

Seeing no immediate response forthcoming from the magos, he added, 'That means no, you cold-hearted bastard.'

CHAPTER THIRTEEN

'WE HAVE IDENTIFIED the location from which the enemy has chosen to face us, brigadier-general,' said Colonel Laron.

'Show me,' said Havorn. The large table between the pair lit up at Havorn's word, thousands of twisting green lines of light springing up to show a detailed schematic map of the surrounding area. At Havorn's instruction, the crouching servitor built into the table's base manipulated the rendered image, scrolling it across the surface of the table and zooming in on valleys and ravines. At another word, the densely packed lines began to rise above the table, giving a three dimensional view of the mountains.

Taking a moment to study the detailed map, Laron pointed.

'We advance along this main valley bed here. Our scouts move along the ravines here, here and here,' he said, indicating two thin valleys a few kilometres away from where the main force advanced. 'And our drop-troopers have landed at these points,' he said, picking out a dozen key, strategic high points.

'As you have read in my reports, our attacks to take the high lands up to here,' he said, indicating, 'have been fierce, but a success.'

'The enemy has defended them half-heartedly,' said Havorn. 'Your men took them too easily, and I mean no slur upon them. When they choose their place to stand and fight, then they will face far stiffer competition.'

'My sentiment exactly, brigadier-general, and I believe we have found that place. Early forays to take these points here,' he said, indicating the ridges some ten kilometres into a particularly thin stretch of the valley, 'show high concentrations of the enemy. Our attacks have been rebuffed.'

'And with high casualties, I see,' growled Havorn.

'Indeed, the enemy will not budge. That is where they will make their stand.'

'It is a good place for it. The twisting valley is at its narrowest there. There is not a straight line of fire longer than a kilometre, rendering our ordnance of limited use, but their warriors will excel. It means that the *Exemplis* will have to get close to them to engage, rather than blasting them from five clicks out. It is a cunning place to make their stand. But it could be a ruse. Have you scouted for ambush points ahead of this position?'

'I have, brigadier-general. The valley thins some ten kilometres further up, here. It shrinks to a width of less than a hundred metres at several points; that's a tight fit for the Imperator. That would be the place to launch an ambush, but there are more than forty places where the valley contracts in such a way.'

The brigadier-general grunted.

'Any sign of enemy movement? If we walked into that valley and the enemy had control of those ridges, we would suffer heavy casualties.'

'None, sir. I have sentinels scouring the region, but they have engaged nothing more than cultist outrider vermin that were skulking parallel to the valley. They were all slain.'

'The enemy commander is no fool. If I were him, I would plan something here,' said Havorn, pointing towards one of the narrower areas of the valley. 'The minesweepers have found nothing as yet?'

'No dedicated minefield, only mines scattered every hundred metres or so.'

The Imperial forces had been slowed to a crawl behind the sweeper units. Though no further minefields had been discovered, the traitors had placed sporadic patches of mines down, just enough to force the Imperials into scanning their entire advance.

'A series of cracks riddles the cliff faces all along this stretch. I have ordered flame units to advance along the cliff walls and cleanse any cave systems. Scanner teams are accompanying the flame units, sweeping the area for life-signs and power outputs.'

'Order demolition teams to cave in the larger crevices,' said Havorn.

'Yes, sir.'

'They will wish to wipe the history books clear of the shame they were dealt at the hands of the *Exemplis*,' said Havorn. 'They may well have chosen this place to make their stand against us. If that is so, they will fight to the last.'

KEEN AUTO-SENSORS ALERTED Kol Badar to the questing machine-spirit of an enemy auspex, and the last systems of his Terminator armour were automatically shut down. He was barely breathing, and his twin hearts beat but once per minute. He had long ago shut off his air-recycling units, and the massive weight of his armour hung upon him as the last of the servos were deactivated.

Dully he heard the muffled thump of detonations, and dust and rock crumbled down upon him as the ground beneath his feet rumbled. Heavier chunks of salt stone broke upon him, but still he stood immobile in his state of semi-suspended animation. It was not the deep slumber that the Legion was capable of, for that would require the attentions of the chirurgeons to reawaken him, and would not allow him to remain at least partially alert for the signal that his prey was near. It was however a deep enough state that any auspex sweep of the enemy should not detect his life signals, particularly while he was shielded behind the thick, insulating plates of his sacred armour.

An indeterminable amount of time passed, and flames washed over him. His heartbeat increased as he registered the brightness of the promethium-based conflagration lapping over him and the sharp rise in temperature. The heat was almost unbearable, the inbuilt heat regulators of the suit having been shut down along with all its other functions, so as not to give off any tell-tale signs of radiation.

The flames lit up the narrow cavern brightly. He could see other members of the cult of the Anointed, immobile as he was, flames licking at them. He saw the external ribbed piping of one warrior-brother's early mark Terminator suit flare brightly as it melted, and the warrior pitched backwards to the cavern floor, his lungs undoubtedly on fire. Kol Badar was pleased to see that he did not cry out as he perished.

As his breathing became more regular in conjunction with the quickening beat of his heart, he began to use too much oxygen, and there was not a lot of that remaining in his suit. He settled his breathing and his heart slowed until once again it almost stopped.

'WHAT WAS THAT? You picking something up?' asked the weary Elysian trooper, looking back at his companion. The half-sphere of the heavy auspex disc was a weight in his arms. Trust him to get stuck doing the lifting rather than the easy job of keeping an eye on the data-screen on the attached feedback unit.

'I thought there was something for a second, but its gone now. Must have been a glitch.'

'Time for us to swap, eh?' he said hopefully. His team member laughed out loud.

'Not a chance. You lost, fair and square. Come on, let's move on. There's nothing here.'

KOL BADAR'S CONSCIOUSNESS was roused as the cavern shook and crumbling salt dust dropped down upon him. There was a pause of almost thirty seconds before there was another booming sound like thunder, closer than the first, and more dust rained down. His yellow eyes flickered and he powered up his suit's basic functions. He reasoned that after the enemy had swept the area and declared it clear there would be little in the way of further scans, so powering up his Terminator armour was but a slight risk. Air began to circulate once more, stale and dry, and he breathed in deeply, flooding his oxygen starved body. His senses came instantly to their full capacity.

His prey was near.

He took in his surroundings, turning his head from side to side as he familiarised himself once more with his situation as his suit's diagnostics ran. The cavern was cramped and demolitions had caused cave-ins in several places, where chunks of rock lay strewn across the uneven floor. Massive blocks leant against several of the Anointed and parts of their blessed ceramite were chipped and dented. Many of his brethren were half-buried beneath the collapse, but it mattered not.

The cavern branched off a deep chasm that split the cliff face of the main valley. He had seen the narrowing of the valley and noted its suitability as a place to face the enemy, but he would never have discovered this cave system in the limited time that he had to prepare the ambush. One of the cultists had brought it to the attention of the Chaos Space Marines, one of the wretched dogs that doted on the First Acolyte.

Branching off the sheer-faced chasm, the entrance to the cave system was hidden from view, and unless someone knew of its location it would be nigh on impossible to discover. Still, the flames of the enemy's weaponry had found the entrance, even if their bearers had not, and his armoured suit was blackened from the blasts of blazing promethium.

The demolitions that had followed had completely caved in the chasm as the seismic charges shook down rock from above. No exit from the cavern could be accessed by a warrior in Terminator armour. But if the enemy became complacent because they believed their flanks were secure, then all the better.

There was another booming sound and the ground shook. Though the area was most likely not being scanned, it would be too much of a risk to chance vox communication. The First Acolyte whelp should be moving the cultists forwards. If he mistimed the advance, the Anointed would be left terribly exposed to the guns of the cursed enemy. He ground his teeth. Were the whelp to fail in his duty, he and his brethren would almost certainly be annihilated. Not even the upstart Marduk would knowingly leave the Anointed to perish, though he was certain the thought had crossed the bastard's mind.

Still, this was the only chance the Legion had of destroying the Imperator-class Titan without the loss of hundreds of warrior-brothers. It was a risky venture, but Kol Badar found a glimmer of excitement at the prospect. He had thought that such battle hunger was long lost to him, faded over the great expanse of time he had been fighting for the glory of Lorgar. He welcomed the feeling like a long-lost comrade.

Dozens of sharp, red lights began to flash against the cavern wall as the ground once again rumbled beneath him. The shifting of rock caused another avalanche of stone and dust to fall, and Kol Badar smirked as he realised that there was every chance that the whole cavern might cave in at any moment, trapping him and his warriors beneath thousands of tonnes of mountain. That would be an inglorious death indeed, and he could just imagine the derision that would be heaped upon him by the bastard Marduk if such a fate was his destiny.

There was yet another crashing impact nearby. He estimated its distance. It was difficult to determine, but he judged that after two more impacts, it would be time to detonate the impact charges.

The red lights of the charges blinked rhythmically in the darkness. They were designed to explode outwards in one direction only, and he had organised their placement carefully. An expert in siege demolitions, he had spent several hours studying the fault lines and angled layers of the rock face so that the powerful explosives would have the desired effect. Just one misplaced charge would bring the mountainside down upon them, and he would allow his fate to be determined by none but himself.

With his savage anticipation building, Kol Badar listened for the heavy impacts that would signal the launch of the ambush.

THE COMMAND CHIMERA rumbled forward slowly in the shadow of the *Exemplis*. No matter how many Titans Brigadier-General Havorn had seen, he was still awed by the sheer scale of them, and this, an Imperator-class no less, was amongst the largest Titans ever constructed. From his position in the cupola of his Chimera, he had a good view of the massive war machine as it strode forward. He could understand why the twisted adepts of the Mechanicus worshipped it as an avatar of their god, for it was a powerful, primal thing of epic proportions.

From behind, he could see many of the oiled workings of the god-machine, as its rear was not as well armoured as its front. Pistons the size of buildings rose and fell as the behemoth lifted its huge, bastion legs, and eddies of super-heated smoke and steam blasted from the exhausts in its back. Higher still, pennants were whipped by the bustling breeze atop the arched architecture of the fortress that the Titan bore upon its massive shoulders. Battle cannons and siege ordnance was housed there, along with temple shrines to the Machine-God and mausoleums that held the remains of past princeps.

The narrowness of the ravine made him tense and uneasy. It was more like a chasm than a valley, the sides sheer and close. They seemed to loom in threateningly, and if the enemy moved onto those ridges, they would be able to rain fire down upon the convoy with impunity. Still,

Laron's 72nd held those regions and were pushing forwards along the ridge tops ranging out ahead. The point of the Mechanicus forces was moving forward slowly through the ravine and it seemed that the enemy were content to wait for them up ahead. Still, he half expected something to happen, some ploy to be launched, and he had learnt long ago to trust his instincts.

'Rachius,' he called down into the Chimera, 'run another sweep.'

'In progress, sir,' said his communications officer.

The Chimera was outfitted with an array of sensors and powerful vox-units to allow the brigadier-general's commands to be conveyed to his captains, and tall aerials and dishes rose from the rear of the APC.

'I'm picking up faint radiation from the cliff face, sir, The exact position is unclear.'

'Damn it!' he said. He felt his tension rise. This was the critical moment. The diminishing width of the pass had forced the Imperial regiments to spread out in a long, unwieldy convoy. If an attack was launched it would be difficult to bring up support and the rest of the regiments behind would grind to a standstill.

'From the cliff face you say? The demolition teams didn't leave any chasms clear, did they Rachius?'

'No, sir. My reports say that all were collapsed. Could just be geothermals.'

'Try to pinpoint the location. And order the Chimeras to close formation. Tell the commanders to be ready for action.'

The hyper-efficient officer swiftly carried out his orders. Donal Rachius was a fastidious man, utterly fixated on his appearance. A crease in his uniform upset him, and he was exact and precise in everything he did. Havorn tolerated his eccentricities because the man was exceptional and his perfectionism, though irritating on a personal level, made him ideal for his role.

The Chimeras behind his command tank revved their engines and advanced, drawing level with his own. There was not room in the ravine for even twenty of the vehicles to advance alongside one another. Still, they kept a wary distance from the Titan. One descending foot of that monster would easily crush a tank flat.

When the attack came, it was almost a relief. But it came at the front of the armoured column, the strongest point in the Imperial line.

He heard scattered bombardments up ahead and saw the column slow.

Instantly, Havorn dropped his lanky frame down through the cupola, swinging his legs around beneath him as the powered semi-lift lowered into the Chimera proper. It was cramped with communications equipment, a small team of officers and a very large ogryn hunched in a specially constructed bucket seat, his head stooped but still pressed against the roof.

'Report,' he ordered.

'The techno-magos informs us that his Skitarii units have engaged the foe.'

'What, the enemy has advanced to meet us?'

'It would seem so, sir. They have rounded the bend here,' said Rachius, pointing to a data-slate with a simplified overhead map that glimmered with points of light that indicated troop formations.

'But that makes no sense. They will be butchered without the support of their bigger guns, which are all positioned back here, are they not?' replied Havorn, pointing along the ridge tops some kilometres around the bend in the ravine.

'They are. We have received no intelligence to indicate otherwise.'

'They want us to engage, halting the column.'

'The Mechanicus have already halted, sir. The *Exemplis* is readying its weaponry.'

'Tell the magos to advance. Tell him his god-machine is in danger,' said Havorn as he climbed once again into the cupola to survey the situation.

He raised the hatch of the Chimera to see the Titan's legs planted firmly, and support pinions locking into place as it readied its weapons. The air was charged with power as its plasma reactors burned hot, making ready to unleash a fusillade of destruction. He lifted a pair of long range magnoculars to his eyes, scanning along the cliff walls ahead. There was nothing there, no entrance from which a hidden force could emerge.

'We have enemy movement, sir! They are pushing forward along the ridges! And more of the enemy are moving along the ravine at pace! They are moving for a full attack!'

What the hell are they doing? thought Havorn. They will be slaughtered in their droves by the massive guns of the *Exemplis*. Still, this new development gave him no comfort and his unease rose.

'FORWARD!' ROARED MARDUK. 'The eyes of the gods are upon you and their judgement awaits. Prove your worth before them, and take your hatred to the infidel corpse worshippers!'

The cultists advanced before his fiery oratory, but Marduk despised them, every one of them. The gods were watching, it was true, and they would laugh as these wretches were led to the slaughter to accomplish the goal of the true favoured ones, the Word Bearers.

'Onward, warriors of the true gods! Glory and ascension awaits you! Fear not the guns of the enemy. Embrace destruction, for with your deaths the aims of the gods are accomplished. Give up your mortal bodies unto Chaos, and your souls will soar in the realms of the deities this night!'

Five thousand cult warriors advanced into the tight ravine, towards the waiting guns of the looming Titan in the distance. They screamed their devotion as they marched forward.

Leaving a considerable gap behind the Cultists of the Word, Marduk ordered the remainder of the Host forward, giving up on any further pretence that they were going to wait for the enemy to come to them.

He saw the Imperator Titan plant its feet as the cultists drew within range of its weaponry, just as Kol Badar had predicted. Now was the time for the Coryphaus to act. His gambit needed to work, else the entire Host would be at the mercy of the Titan's guns.

'I still think we should have held back,' snarled Burias. 'Let that bastard Kol Badar face the enemy alone and blast him back to hell.'

'Burias,' laughed Marduk, 'your choler is in the ascendant. You speak these words because you believe they are what I wish to hear?'

'A statement of my feelings, First Acolyte, nothing more. The bastard ordered a retreat against the foe. He deserves death.'

'Maybe, my Icon Bearer, but you would have us abandon the Anointed?'

'The Anointed are Kol Badar's pets. They worship him with nearly as much fervour as they worship the Dark Apostle.'

'And you are bitter at having not been indoctrinated into the cult,' said Marduk. The Icon Bearer made no reaction, save a slight tension in the muscles of his neck, which Marduk observed. He laughed.

'You are an ambitious, black-hearted one, aren't you, dear Burias. And you hold some resentment towards me, is it not true?'

'First Acolyte?' asked Burias in a slightly hurt tone. 'I am your devoted warrior, always.'

'But you blame me for your not having been embraced into the cult of the Anointed. You think it is a subtle insult directed at me from Kol Badar, an insult that you must pay the price for because of our comradeship.'

'The thought… had crossed my mind, First Acolyte.'

'It pleases me that you can at times be honest, Burias,' said Marduk lightly. Before the Icon Bearer could respond, he continued, 'Is it the lure of Slaanesh, your endless desire to raise yourself, to better yourself?'

'It is not perfection I seek, First Acolyte, as you know. I don't need perfection to attain that which I desire.'

'No, you just need to be on the good side of one who would become a Dark Apostle. Do not become complacent, dear Burias. When the time comes for me to take on the mantle of that position, I will choose only the most suitable warrior to become my Coryphaus.'

'My suitability is in doubt?' questioned Burias, trying to keep his pristine, handsome, pale face devoid of emotion, but Marduk saw a flash of Drak'shal's fury in his eyes.

'No, Burias, but nothing beneath the gaze of the gods is certain. Do not allow your hubris to one day shame you.'

'Nothing will bring shame upon me, just as I will never bring shame upon the blessed Legion of Lorgar,' said Burias severely.

Marduk smiled and placed his hand upon the Icon Bearer's shoulder.

'I believe you may be right, Burias, old friend. You said the same words on Calth while we battled the cursed warriors of Guilliman.'

'And you said that one day you would lead one of the grand companies, with me at your side,' said Burias.

'That is true.'

'If this… trick of Kol Badar's goes badly, then there will be too few warriors within the Host to justify splitting it, as the council on Sicarus ordered, especially after the casualties we suffered against the Titan. There will be little need for a second Dark Apostle.'

'That thought had crossed my mind,' snarled Marduk, his mood darkening. 'Regardless, one way or another, I *will* become a Dark Apostle.'

'Always I have fought at your side, First Acolyte, long before I called you such. And I will fight there, always, whatever may come.'

Marduk placed a hand upon Burias's shoulder.

'I would expect nothing less of you, my friend. Now, order the last of the Host to advance. We fight them here, and pray to the gods that Kol Badar succeeds, else we will all be slaughtered and seeing them sooner than expected.'

'What if it is the will of the gods for us to die here, First Acolyte?'

'Then it is their will, but that is not what I have foreseen. The twisting paths of the future are never set, but of the thousands of coiling threads that I have followed in my dream visions, we were slaughtered here in less than half of them.'

'That is of… great comfort, First Acolyte,' said Burias dryly.

Marduk laughed again, his black mood evaporating in the blink of an eye.

In the distance, the Titan's guns flared brightly as they were unleashed, followed half a second later by the cacophony of the barrage as it echoed up the narrow ravine. Hundreds of cultists were instantly slain in the devastation. The timing for the Word Bearers' advance was critical. If Kol Badar timed it wrong, it would result in the destruction of hundreds of the Legion's warriors. If he timed it just right, then the slaughter of the enemy would be great.

Gods of the Ether guide me, he prayed, and he closed his eyes. A waking vision assailed him the instant he closed his eyes, the image sharp and painful, leaving a dull ache in his temples. He wiped a droplet of blood from his nose and watched as it instantly congealed to a dried crust upon his finger. He would need to discuss this vision with the Warmonger at battle's end, for its meaning was obscure and disturbing.

'Come,' he said, 'let us release our anger upon the foe.'

* * *

'I'VE GOT A lock, sir!' shouted Rachius. 'Emperor damn them, there are more than fifty of the bastards in there! Vector 7.342.'

Havorn swore and swung his magnoculars around towards the location that Rachius had indicated. 'Get the Chimeras moving,' he shouted, but the words were lost as a series of detonations ripped apart the mountainside, rocks exploding outwards spectacularly. One sizeable chunk of rock smashed onto the front of his Chimera, denting the thick armoured plate, and others smashed harmlessly against one of the massive feet of the *Exemplis*, no more than thirty metres from the explosion. At such a range its void shields were useless. They were only effective from a certain distance, and anything within them would be able to attack the god-machine directly.

With this thought running through his mind, he swore again and slammed his fist down onto the top of the Chimera as he saw the dark shapes emerging from the cloud of dust surrounding the point of the explosion.

Clattering gunfire erupted from weaponry as the figures stamped heavily through the rubble. They were huge individuals, their armour plate thick and nigh on impervious to harm: Terminators, the enemy's elite.

Havorn banged on the top of the Chimera.

'Go!' he shouted. 'Intercept them! And get some heavy support over here now!'

The engine of the APC roared as the tank surged forward over the hard packed earth. The other Chimeras were already heading towards the foe, and Havorn saw one of them explode, oily, black smoke rising sharply above the orange conflagration.

'Sir, you should come down here,' said Rachius from below, concern in his voice, but Havorn ignored him, instead grabbing the pistol-grip of the pintle-mounted storm bolter. He swung the powerful weapon in the direction of the Terminators and squeezed the trigger.

KOL BADAR ROARED as his combi-bolter barked fire at the enemy. He was in the middle of the foe's colonnade, surrounded, and he saw vehicles and soldiers rushing towards him from left and right. But the true target of his wrath stood before him: the massive Imperator Titan.

Grand steps descended from arched gateways upon the foot of the immense war machine, and he strode towards them. Covering fire from reaper autocannons swept across the approaching vehicles and Skitarii units, and raking fire tore down the enemy infantry that ran across the salt packed rock to intercept their progress.

Nothing would keep Kol Badar from his target, however, and he strode relentlessly forward through the increasing weight of incoming fire, driven on by steely determination and anger. The defensive batteries built into the Titan's leg bastion unleashed their wrath, engulfing the advancing Anointed, ripping through even mighty Terminator armour

with the force of their detonations. Air bursting shells exploded overhead, scattering red-hot, scything shards of shrapnel down onto the
warrior-brothers and Kol Badar hissed as a shard the length of a man's
hand slammed into his helmet, cutting through his armour and piercing
one of his eyes. Blood welled and congealed in the wound and he broke
off the end of the piece of red-hot shrapnel with a swat of his power
talon, leaving the tip embedded in his eye.

Such a wound would not keep him from his prize and he roared
wordlessly as he continued his relentless advance.

Arched doors ten metres up the Titan's foot were thrown open and
Skitarii warriors stepped out onto the steps, firing their inbuilt heavy
weapons down into the terminators. Kol Badar aimed his combi-bolter
into the throng of the enemy and strode on.

Enemy Chimeras screeched to a halt and blue-grey armoured Guardsmen emerged, firing their lasguns into the mass of Terminators. Bolter
fire ripped through the soft targets and heavy flamers roared as they
engulfed swathes of them in deadly infernos. Combi-meltas hissed as
they targeted incoming vehicles, and tanks were rendered into burning
shells as they detonated, their crews screaming in pain as they died.

A Chimera with arrays of aerials caught the Coryphaus's eye and he
recognised it as belonging to an officer of high rank.

'Take it down,' he ordered. Reaper autocannons swung around, spraying bullets from their twin barrels.

Bolter shells struck Kol Badar, knocking him back a step, and he
snarled and squeezed a burst of fire from his combi-bolter at the figure
manning the pintle-mounted weapon, forcing him to duck back into
the Chimera. He swung his heavy head back towards the target. Only
twenty metres now. The Skitarii spilled steadily down off the steps of
the Titan's foot as more emerged and others advanced around from the
limb's three further assault ramps.

'Keep on the target!' he roared, knowing that if the Anointed were
held for too long, the Titan would simply walk away, leaving them horribly exposed.

The Skitarii marched straight into the advancing clump of Terminator-
armoured warriors, attempting to keep them away from their charge
through sheer weight of numbers and the power of their guns. The steps
were packed with the enemy and they unleashed a storm of fire upon the
Anointed, each tech-warrior firing over the heads of their companions as
they stepped slowly forwards.

Rotating cannons tore through more of the Word Bearers, ripping
through ancient plasteel plating and flensing flesh from bone.

High above, steam and smoke was expelled sharply from pistons and
locking mechanisms ground as they were released. Kol Badar recognised
the signs of the Titan preparing to move.

With a roar he smashed into the ranks of Skitarii, battering them out of his path with sweeps of his power claw and ripping through them with his combi-bolter on full-auto.

'Forward, Anointed! For the glory of Lorgar!'

THE CHIMERA SLEWED to the side as it took heavy incoming fire and one of its tracks was ripped to tatters. Armour piercing rounds tore through the shell of the APC and two officers within slumped in their seats, their blood splashing the interior. Havorn slammed his fist onto the glowing rune-plate and the release valves of the assault hatch hissed as the ramp swung down. He was exiting the Chimera even as the ramp was still falling and he flicked his plasma pistol into life.

'Sir, let us at least take the lead, since you seem set on this course,' said Rachius in his concerned voice.

Havorn's ogryn bodyguard emerged from the confines of the Chimera and breathed deeply, its eyes narrowing. It stepped protectively in front of the brigadier-general, shielding him from fire with its muscled bulk.

'We must stop the enemies from reaching the Titan! Why in the Emperor's name hasn't it moved yet?' Havorn shouted.

'Our units are converging on them, sir. You do not need to enter the battle!'

'They are coming too slowly,' shouted Havorn. 'We move, now!'

With that, the Elysian commander pointed the way and the ogryn began loping towards the enemy who were climbing the stairs on the Titan's leg battlement.

They were too late, Havorn thought. The Terminators were already past them and his body was old and slow. He cursed the debilities of age and pushed himself on. Fallen Elysians and Skitarii lay strewn across the ground, as well as the occasional bulky form of a fallen enemy. Few of them were truly dead and they lashed out, grabbing and killing any foe within their reach. Even at the point of death they were more than a match for a Guardsman.

The ogryn raised its heavy ripper gun, a thick finger pulling the trigger. Empty shells scattered in its wake. It did not roar or bellow as it charged. Such base, animalistic behaviours had been erased from its simple brain-pan, but no amount of augmetics could improve the aim of the ogryn and the bullets from its ripper gun sprayed the area, hitting nothing.

Havorn snapped off a shot with his pistol, the streaming blue-white bolt of plasma dropping one of the Terminators.

Bolter fire raked towards him, striking the hulking abhuman, who grimaced in pain. Chunks of flesh were torn from its arms and chest, but the three metre creature that dwarfed even the Terminators did not slow. It lowered a shoulder and smashed into one of the enemy, knocking it from its feet. Raising the butt of its heavy ripper gun, the ogryn began caving in the helmet of the fallen warrior, smashing it down onto the prone traitor again and again.

Skitarii and Guardsmen were all around Havorn, filling the air with las-fire and high velocity bolts. The traitors were on the steps and held a tight defensive formation. More than half of the bastards had been taken down, most from the devastation wrought by the Titan's cannons and the powerful weaponry of the elite tech-guard warriors. It would be but moments before they breached the blast-doors that led into the Titan.

'Take them down, men of Elysia!' he hollered, his steely, field parade voice carrying over the din of battle.

Suddenly, victory was snatched away as the Titan raised its massive foot high up into the air, carrying with it the traitor Terminators and hundreds of tech-guard warriors still fighting upon the steps. Many of them were knocked off as the *Exemplis* raised its leg, falling ten metres to the valley floor as the foot was raised higher and higher.

'Damn it!' swore Havorn.

'WE ARE THROUGH, Lord Coryphaus,' reported one his Anointed brethren. The chainfists had made short work of the blast-doors that had sealed the entrance to the leg bastion, carving through the thick metal with a minimum of fuss.

'Into the breach!' roared Kol Badar as he crushed the augmented, semi-mechanical skull of a Skitarii warrior and hurled it over the edge as the Titan's leg continued to rise. At his command, the Anointed entered the Imperator class Titan.

CHAPTER FOURTEEN

FLAMES ROARED UP the spiralling metal staircase, clearing the way. Two abreast, the Terminators had been climbing for what seemed like an age, assailed from above and below by an apparently never ending stream of Skitarii warriors. Inbuilt defence turrets were stationed at every second level, their hard-wired servitor controllers built into the heavy wall panels of the interior staircase, and they swung their weaponry upon the intruders, filling the cloying, hot air with shells and gunsmoke.

It was hard going, the Word Bearers forced to fight for every step of the mammoth climb up the interior of the Titan's lower leg. Kol Badar's destroyed eye, still with the shrapnel shard jutting from the socket, was throbbing in his head, but he pushed the sensation away as he stamped up the heavy, grilled stairway, blazing away with his combi-bolter.

He was at the front of the line of Terminators, the heavy-flamer wielding Anointed warrior Bokkar at his side. Between the flames of his comrade and the bolts of his combi-weapon, few of the Skitarii could stand against them. Those few that survived were ripped apart by the warlord's power claws and hurled over the railing to fall down the open expanse in the centre of the spiralling stairwell to join a growing pile of sparking, shattered corpses.

The resistance from above slackened. Clearly the last of the Skitarii had been neutralised, leaving just the inbuilt, servitor-guided sentry guns to hamper their progress. The going was unsteady as the heavy Titan foot smashed down into the ground with devastating force and rose once more into the air.

Kol Badar allowed a pair of cult members wielding reaper autocannons to advance past him, for their powerful guns were able to rip through the armoured plating protecting the sentry guns far more efficiently than flame or bolt. It was a torturous task, for they had to advance up through a barrage of gunfire before they could get a clear shot at the servitor housed just beneath the turret, but time was of the essence.

Up and up the Terminators wound, under constant, desperate attack from the Skitarii climbing behind them and the sentry turrets. Ammunition was running low, and with a blast of fiery promethium directed down over the open stairwell to melt the exposed flesh of a dozen enemy machine-warriors, the last of the heavy flamer reloads was expended. Even if they had not a bolt shell remaining, Kol Badar would fight on and succeed. He would die, with all his Anointed at his side, before he would allow the bitch of a Titan to best him once again. He would rip it apart piece by piece with his bare hands if need be.

The noise of turning machinery became increasingly loud as the Terminators neared the Imperator's knee joint. Abruptly, the last sentry gun was silenced, the milky life-blood of the servitor dripping down through the latticed grill to fall upon its brethren advancing from below. At Kol Badar's direction, blinking demolition melta-charges were attached to bulkheads where he indicated, as scattered gunfire roared up from below, shearing through the metal stairs. Scores of charges were placed, four times the amount that were used to blast away the mountainside. Kol Badar was taking no chances.

He nodded as he studied the placement of the blinking charges.

'Commence the descent,' he ordered and the Anointed warriors began to fight their way back down the staircase that they had just fought so hard to ascend.

'WE ARE ENTERING the range of the Imperator, First Acolyte,' hissed Burias. The massive Titan had already blasted every cult warrior apart.

'If he's failed, this war is going to be over very quickly,' replied Marduk.

He climbed atop a rocky outcrop, allowing the ranks of the Host to advance past him. Vehicles rumbled forward slowly, and Dreadnoughts and Defilers stalked across the broken ground. Burias climbed up behind him, planting the icon in the ground at the First Acolyte's side.

The Imperator raised its leg for another step. A series of internal explosions suddenly burst out around its knee-joint. Flames and smoke erupted from the mechanical joint, a mass of detonation within ripping through the thick, reinforced metal. The bastion foot touched down on the floor of the ravine and a secondary flash of timed demolition charges erupted. For a moment it looked as though they had had no effect, until the knee joint gave way beneath the immense weight of the Titan and it lurched to one side as if in slow motion, thousands of tonnes of metal teetering over the battlefield.

Its weapon arms flailed out as if trying to steady the toppling god-machine, but the Titan was falling, gaining speed as its weight bore it down on the ground. There was silence as it crashed to the ground, until the bastion of one shoulder slammed into the sheer cliff face, causing the mountain range to shudder beneath the impact, and an avalanche of rock was sheared from the cliff. Off balance, the impact caused the Imperator to swing towards the ravine wall and the leering head of the great machine smashed straight into the rock face with a resounding crash. The other leg of the Titan, bearing the entire weight of the colossal machine, buckled suddenly with a screeching sound of wrenching metal. The Imperator slammed to the ground with a deafening boom that echoed through the ravine. The impact caused avalanches of rock and rubble, and hundreds of Guardsmen and Skitarii were slain. A rising cloud of dust obscured the fallen, broken Titan.

As one, the Word Bearers roared victoriously at the sight of the mighty war god dying and Burias raised the Host's icon high into the air for all to see.

'Advance and kill!' roared Marduk and the Host descended upon the shattered vanguard.

AFTER KILLING THE traitor Pierlo, Varnus had expected to be slain by his captives, but if anything, his action seemed to have garnered a kind of hateful respect from the hunched, black-clad overseers. Oh, they had hurt him as they prised him off the corpse of the traitor, filling his body with agonising torment as the vile serums that filled their needle fingers assaulted his nerve endings, but he had been expecting far worse.

But no, he had been dragged from the tower and placed on the chirurgeons' familiar, cold, steel slab. There was no Discord there and he felt naked without it speaking to him. There the spindly creatures had prodded and probed him. They seemed particularly interested in the symbol beneath the skin of his forehead, chittering excitedly amongst themselves. They drew blood from him and fed burning black liquid into his veins. Small, black leech creatures with orange patterns on their backs were attached to him and he howled as they burrowed their heads into his skin. They were pulled back out, bloated and fat, some time later.

The joy of killing the man had filled him with warmth. The traitor had turned against the blessed, *hated*, *False* Emperor and had deserved death. Taking his life had been a great release and it made him feel strong and rejuvenated.

The enemy had taken him back to the tower, transporting him back to the top, now hundreds and hundreds of metres above the ground. He was to work alone. Perhaps the overseers feared that he would kill again if he was teamed up with another slave, and perhaps he would have.

The tower was above the level of the black pollution hanging over the city, and it swirled beneath him. The mighty winds that were building didn't seem to touch the tower; it was as if he stood in the middle of the eye of one of the dust devils that raced across the plains, spinning the salt up in twisting cones of wind. The noxious fumes whipped around the tower and it looked to him like a great, black, whirlpool that stretched out as far as the eye could see.

He felt strange without the cover of the smog overhead. Now he could see the blaring white sun during the day and the stars by night. Always there was the red giant planet Korsis, drawing ever closer. It was so large that it almost filled the skyline and Varnus could see valleys, craters and channels criss-crossing its surface.

The brightness pained his eyes and the lack of oxygen made them heavy and sore. Twice a day he was held down as red-black, stinging drops were inserted into the centres of his eyeballs. He screamed as the sharp needles pierced the aqueous humour of his orbs and injected the substance that squirmed and burned within him.

Tirelessly he worked, doing the job of two men, but the toil no longer drained him as it once had. Indeed, time seemed to pass quickly and he was barely aware of the fall of darkness as the white sun disappeared over the horizon and rose again as he worked, smearing the blood mortar over the stones.

A Discord seemed to favour him, if such a thing was possible, and it hung at his side for hours on end, pounding his eardrums with its blare. He could hear the voices talking to him, teaching him and bolstering him when he felt weak.

Sometimes he shook his head as if waking from slumber and the horror of his predicament washed over him. He would cry out at such times, longing for the Emperor's soldiers to rescue him and his world. He would kick out at the Discord and it would retreat from him. But these moments passed quickly and Varnus would recover himself and be somewhat confused. He couldn't remember why he had been angry and he set back to work with vigour, the feel of the blood mortar familiar and comforting beneath his hands. The daemon speaker would hover slowly forward until it floated less than a metre from him once again. Sometimes its usually limp tentacles would reach forwards and touch him on the neck or the back as he worked. He would recoil in shock and the thing would retreat once again. Over time, he came to ignore the touch of the thing and in a way he found it almost comforting. He felt a strange, warm, buzzing sensation at its touch, but it was not unpleasant.

The Discord told him many interesting things: what the other slaves were thinking, that the overseers were afraid of him and that his power was growing. It talked of the early years of an ancient hero who had been turned into an immortal godling and lived on in a great palace far away, and the warriors that he had trained to spread his word. He wondered if it was the Emperor, but his head had begun to hurt when that thought had crossed his mind and he quickly dismissed it.

Yet even as he had come to bear his hellish existence, he prayed for release. Not death, no, he had lived through too much to simply perish. He was filled with a new vitality and fervour that made him determined to cling to life for as long as he was able, to see this through one way or another.

He prayed for deliverance and tears ran down his face as he felt himself becoming lost. Had the Emperor forsaken him? Did His light no longer shine upon Tanakreg? Had he been abandoned to his fate? For the first time since the occupation, Varnus felt true despair pull at him. He prayed vainly to the Emperor, but felt no comfort in his soul. No, he felt nothing but emptiness.

The next moment he had forgotten why he had been crying and wiped away his tears in bafflement. Shrugging, he continued his work. The Gehemahnet needed tending.

THE SLAUGHTER HAD been immense and the valley was filled with the dead and dying. A cloying stink rose as the temperature soared, the hot-white sun overhead baking the earth. The wreck of the Titan was like the discarded shell of some giant colossus and scattered debris littered the ravine floor. The battle had been intense. The Word Bearers advanced into the confused Imperial lines after the Imperator's fall, killing thousands of their foes as they tried to realign their battle line and draw support up past the massive frame of the *Exemplis*.

The enemy had inflicted a terrible blow and had retreated once the Imperial reinforcements were brought forward. They had suffered relatively few casualties.

A day had passed and the giant Ordinatus *Magentus* rumbled towards the valley. It was so massive that it was barely able to fit through the ravine and there was no possible way that it would be able pass the fallen Titan. It came to a halt some kilometres back, where the valley was wider.

A dozen, giant, spiked stabiliser legs unfolded to either side of the titanic vehicle, steam hissing out into the hot air as their mechanics were engaged. They reached out to either side of the massive structure and drove down into the ground.

The air tingled with power as giant energy cores were readied and the massive ribbed cone of the Ordinatus's main gun was raised. A sound like a thousand jet engines began to whine, soon reaching a screaming intensity that reverberated through the earth. Elysians within a kilometre of the giant machine clutched hands to their ears as the giant creature made ready to unleash its power.

The air around the ribbed cone-tip of the giant weapon began to shimmer and waver and then the Ordinatus fired.

A deafening, sharp crack like the sound of a planet ripped in two resounded through the valley. Pre-warned, all the Elysians in the vicinity had engaged the sound mufflers within their helmets, but even so the blast of sound was deafening, making Havorn's eardrums vibrate painfully. An ungodly silence followed as if all noise had been sucked out of the valley by the focused blast of sonic energy, and the air between the gun and the valley wall wavered and reverberated.

The effect was astounding. Where the centre of the focused beam of sound struck the wall the rock was turned to dust, exploding outwards in a massive blast as it was shattered down to the molecular level. A wave seemed to spread from the epicentre and the rock rippled as if it were liquid, huge cracks appearing in its wake. Vibrating and shattered, the entire rock face broke apart and fell to the valley floor with a crash that rumbled along the entire mountain range. A huge cloud of salt dust rose up into the air.

CHAPTER FIFTEEN

THE BATTLE FOR Tanakreg had ground down into a brutal war of attrition. Within five days, the ravine had been levelled by the sheer power of the Ordinatus machine. Its sonic disruptor had reverberated through the mountains, shattering stone to powder and causing vast avalanches that could be felt halfway across the continent. Laron had only ever read about such a weapon and to see it in action was awe-inspiring.

The steep cliff walls had been reduced to dust and the valleys were filled with crumbled salt rock, creating a vast expanse that the Imperial Guard and Mechanicus forces rolled across. The going was difficult, but with the steep ravine walls reduced to nothing, they were able to attack on a wide front. The enemy was unable to contain the sheer number of the Imperial troopers and they were relentlessly pushed back.

The enemy had launched several vicious assaults to destroy the potent weapon, but Havorn had charged Laron with the protection of the Ordinatus and he had coordinated effective battles to stall the attacks. He had used his Valkyries effectively, rapidly redeploying units of his 72nd to launch counter-attacks into the flanks of the foe as they advanced, while the tech-guard of the Mechanicus had taken the brunt of the frontal attack. As he dropped more troopers into the flanks of the enemy, Havorn had directed heavier support forwards. Assailed on all sides, the enemy advance had been quashed time and again. He relished these battles. Now that the terrain had been levelled out, he had found the enemy much easier to deal with.

He snorted, easier to deal with indeed. He had fought the Traitor

Astartes only once before and they were the toughest and deadliest foes that he had ever encountered in all his days of soldiering. Still, without having to advance up narrow defiles, the small number of the enemy meant that the vast Imperial war engine could grind on. Though their attacks on the traitors became more directed and hate fuelled, they were unable to close on the Ordinatus *Magentus*.

Tens of thousands of Imperial troopers had been slaughtered and, wherever the enemy dug in for a concerted battle, they inflicted horrendous casualties. But it was not enough to halt the never ending tide of Guardsmen, Skitarii warriors and vehicles. The foe was spread too thin and their flanks were surrounded and overrun. It was simply too wide a front for them to cover and there were too few of them to fight the type of war that suited the massed ranks of the Imperial Guard so well.

Laron had capitalised on this and had ordered hundreds of Valkyries ahead of the main Imperial entourage. Already his storm troopers had assaulted and destroyed several of the enemy anti-aircraft guns emplaced on the foothills of the mountains and he knew that the time would soon come when the Imperials would be able to push forwards and take the fight onto the plains.

Vast lines of siege tanks ground inexorably forward behind the infantry, pounding the enemy with ordnance outranging anything they had.

Slowly the enemy had been driven back, pushed out of the mountains and onto the salt plains that spread out like a rippling blanket towards Shinar. If they could push the foe back to the peninsula on which Shinar sat then they would eventually grind them down and destroy them utterly. Though he saw that the old brigadier-general grieved for every soldier that they lost, he could also see that the Imperial commander was confident of their eventual victory.

It was not the type of war that Laron liked, for it was more suited to the style, or lack of it, of other Imperial Guard regiments. His soldiers of the 72nd were drop-troopers, and in this war of attrition, the unique skills and talents of his units were not being utilised to their full capacity. As soon as the battle reached the plains though, it would be a different matter.

The sheer number of casualties amongst the tech-guard had been staggering, but ever more of the mindless tech-soldiers marched from the vast factorum crawlers that ground over the earth in the wake of the army.

Laron had seen the mechanised enhancements and weapons of fallen tech-guard servitors being recovered as the Imperials pushed ever forward and he knew that they were used to create more lobotomised, unfeeling soldiers. Brigadier-General Havorn had spoken of what became of the flesh of the fallen tech-guard and Laron had been horrified.

It was like some archaic necromancy, he thought, to reuse the flesh and armaments of the dead to create new soldiers to throw thoughtlessly at the enemy. It was morbid and repugnant, and he tried as best he could to keep his men away from them. What was it that the magos called them? Skitarii? They were unnatural and they made his men uneasy. Hell, they made *him* uneasy. Soldiers that had no notion of fear or self-preservation, he was certain they would all march straight off a cliff to their doom at a word from the magos.

Soldiering was meant to be glorious; heroes were made on the battle-field and the victories of those heroes would be recorded for ever more back on Elysia, recounted in song at the great banquet feasts and balls of his home world. War was a noble act where one could gain honour and standing. There was no such honour or heroism amongst the Ski-tarii. They were little more than automata, playing pieces of their callous masters. What honour was there to be gained fighting alongside such as them?

He had been fascinated and horrified in equal measures when he had first seen inside one of the mobile factorum crawlers. The motionless shapes of pale-fleshed humans were held in vast aisles of bubbling vat-tanks, kept in a dormant state. That single factorum must have held ten thousand inert bodies, or 'flesh units' as the magos called them. Darioq had coldly explained that while the Mechanicus was capable of creat-ing its own vat-grown host bodies, it was time consuming and resource heavy, so most of these soldiers were from the other Imperial Guard units within the Crusade. They had suffered grave injuries, leaving them alive, but brain-dead. Others were criminals and deserters, and the pun-ishment for their crimes was to be turned over to the Mechanicus.

They were destined to become battle servitors, all semblances of their former selves erased with mind-wipes and the removal of their fron-tal lobes. Indeed, Darioq had stated, the entire right hemisphere of the brain was removed from all but a few, those used as shock-troops and specialists, where a certain degree of adaptability and autonomous deci-sion making, albeit severely limited in nature, was required.

Such concepts as creativity were clearly frowned upon within the Mechanicus and Laron had found this galling, for it was anathema to the way that the Elysians operated. Adaptability, being able to react to changing directives, objectives and situations, and the ability to operate effectively deep behind enemy lines with little or no direction from the upper echelons of command, were all favoured skills in the ranks of the Elysians. Those same traits were deplored as dangerous and heretical amongst the adepts of the Machine-God.

'Deep in thought, acting colonel?' asked a voice behind him and Laron turned to see the approach of the leather-clad figure of Kheler walking towards him.

'Commissar,' said Laron in acknowledgement. The commissar had been his shadow ever since Havorn had assigned him to watch over Laron and he had certainly not been lax in his duty. Wherever he turned, the man was there, watching and listening, waiting for him to slip up.

'Survived another day without getting shot then, acting colonel?'

'The day isn't over yet, Kheler.'

The commissar chuckled. It was insulting and belittling to have the man watching over him and the threat of his presence was obvious. His uniform demanded respect, yet he was a canny warrior and a highly capable officer.

The swiftness and the severity of his judgement was shocking. The commissar had been smiling and talking with one of Laron's men, but had executed that same man without a thought not an hour later when the trooper had turned to flee because his lasgun's powercell had run dry. A laspistol blast in the man's head had shown all the troopers that cowardice of any kind would not be tolerated.

'You do not flee the enemy under any circumstances!' he had roared. 'The Emperor watches over you! If your power cell runs dry, you pick up the weapon of a fallen comrade. If that runs out of ammunition, you draw your pistol. If you have no pistol, you fight with your knife. If your knife breaks, you fight with your bare hands. And if your hands are cut off, still you do not flee, you attack the enemy with any weapon that you have. You bite their damned kneecaps off if that's all you can do!'

That had got a scattered laugh and Laron had marvelled at the commissar's skill. The man had just killed one of their comrades and he had got them to laugh.

'But you do not flee!' Kheler had shouted severely, his eyes wide and threatening. 'Or I promise you, as the Emperor is my witness, I will gun you down like traitorous dogs.'

'Motivation,' the commissar had explained to Laron. 'That is what I provide to the regiment. The threat of a bullet in the back of the head is good motivation not to turn tail and run.'

The man switched from jocular comrade to ruthless executioner in a second. Even knowing this, Laron found it hard to dislike the man.

'Aren't you hot in all that get up?' asked Laron, motioning towards the commissar's long, black, leather coat and hat. The temperature over the last days had soared and any sign of the storms of the week before were long passed.

'Hot, acting colonel? Yes, I am damn hot, but do you think I would look such a commanding figure if I were stripped down to my undergarments? And besides, I look damn good in black. Dashing is a word that springs to mind.'

Laron snorted and shook his head.

'We are only flying to the front to see if the enemy truly are retreating into the plains, or if it is some ploy.'

'Must keep up appearances, acting colonel,' replied Kheler.

'Hold on to your hat, commissar,' said Laron as the dark shape of a

Valkyrie approached overhead and the Elysian clicked his visor down over his eyes.

The screaming reverse thruster jets of the Valkyrie blew salt dust up into the air as they rotated towards the ground. Laron smirked as the commissar shielded his eyes with one hand while the other was clamped down on his leather hat to keep it from blowing away in the hot blasts of air coming from the engines.

The aircraft touched down onto the ground and its door slid open. With a nod to the men inside, Laron climbed aboard and turned to help the commissar. The man fell into his seat, blinking salt dust and grit from his eyes. Laron stood in the open doorway grabbing the overhead rail tightly as the Valkyrie left the ground and began a vertical ascent into the air, turning slightly.

The Imperial battle force was spread out beneath him. Lines of tanks rolled towards the front and tens of thousands of men marched in snaking columns over the rough ground below. Free of the constriction of the ravine, the army moved forward quickly and in good order. It was surprisingly tiring to organise the dispositions and lines of advance, but no doubt that was why Havorn had ordered him to do it, to test how he progressed.

It was certainly very different from being a captain. He had not thought it would be quite as difficult and exhausting as this. A lot of thankless organisational and logistical work required his attention, and he found that he was weary beyond words. He was far more tired than he had ever been when engaged on the front line, or even more than when he had been when engaged in deep missions in enemy territory. At those times he would snatch sleep when he could get it, an hour here, a few minutes there, but at least that sleep had been deep and restful, even if it was in the middle of a siege barrage. Now he felt as if he hadn't slept for weeks and when he did sleep he was still filled with concerns and worries.

There were a thousand and one jobs that needed his agreement, his sign-off and his input, and he had found it overwhelming. He was floundering and he couldn't see how he could get on top of it all. It was difficult at first to know what truly needed his attention and what could be delegated to his captains. His respect for Havorn had grown immeasurably as he realised the responsibilities of command that must weigh upon him. But he never showed it. He was always the tough old campaigner and none doubted his judgement.

His captains; it still sounded strange to him. He was no longer one of them. Now he was their colonel and the easy camaraderie he had once shared with them was long gone. He grinned at that. In truth, there had never been any easy camaraderie with most of the other captains. They had always seen him as an arrogant bastard, the 'glory boy' captain of the storm troopers; and they were mostly right.

It felt good to be in the air again and away from the pressures of his position, and he hated slogging along on foot. That was grunt's work. He was a glory boy, damn it, and if they were going to say it anyway, he might as well live like one.

'You think the enemy is truly retreating, colonel?' asked the commissar, though Laron knew that he already knew the answer. This was for the benefit of the men around them. He noted that in the presence of other members of the 72nd the commissar left out the *acting* part of his title. No doubt that was something else to do with motivation. He was a clever bastard.

'It's been hard and we have lost a lot of good men, but the enemy are falling back. I just want to see the traitors fleeing with my own eyes. The Emperor is with us! We will make them pay for the deaths of the men of the 72nd.'

He saw a slight smile in the eyes of the commissar as he played along.

'Motivation is vitally important,' the commissar had said earlier, 'whether it comes from the threat of a bullet, the impassioned speech of an officer, or propaganda from the mouth of a commissar, it doesn't matter. All that matters is that your soldiers fight and that they have fire in their bellies. For some that comes from faith, for others it is from outrage. It doesn't matter. But you must never miss an opportunity to inspire your men. It's not much, but a word here and there goes a long way with the common soldiers.'

These conversations with the commissar had been playing on his mind and he had begun to wonder if that was another reason why Havorn had attached the commissar to his staff, to teach him the power of motivation in all its forms.

'By the Emperor's name, they will pay,' said Laron once more.

THE VIEW ON the grainy, black and white pict screen had been astonishing as Marduk's Thunderhawk made its approach into Shinar. It was almost unrecognisable from the original Imperial city. From this high in the air, nothing of it could at first be seen, bar the immense Gehemah-net tower that rose into the atmosphere. It was as if some astral deity had hurled a mighty spear into the planet, skewering it. It could be seen for thousands of kilometres all around when the air was clear.

Beneath the tower, lower in the atmosphere and hanging directly over Shinar, was a thick, oily, black smog. It was roiling and contorting as if alive and it was swirling around the tower that rose in its midst. The tower was the very centre of the gaseous maelstrom and the fumes were thickest there, the winds strongest.

Nothing could penetrate the thick, noxious smog cloud, not even the Thunderhawk's sensitive, daemon infused sensor arrays. Marduk knew that the Gehemahnet was creating a wide cone of warp interference that spewed out through the atmosphere and beyond. This interference would effectively make the entire side of the planet all but invisible to the enemy. Just as he thought of this, the Thunderhawk's pict screen flickered and degenerated to static. The power of the Gehemahnet was indiscriminate in whose equipment it affected. The gunship was still around two hundred kilometres from Shinar, but had clearly entered the wide cone of disruption. The Thunderhawk had no need for concern – it did not rely upon technical arrays and its witch-sight saw all the more clearly within the warp field.

Marduk felt the field close over him and his twin hearts palpitated erratically for a moment, his breath catching in his chest. It was joyous to feel the power of the Immaterium wash over him. He heard the whispers of daemons in the air. He felt his sacred bond to the warp strengthen and his power with it. The Dark Apostle was wielding some powerful faith to have created a warp field of such potency.

Movement flickered at the corner of his eyes and he felt presences brush past him. The barriers between the realms of Chaos and the material plane were thin. He could almost make out the daemonic entities straining from beyond to cross the thin walls and enter the physical world. Soon, he whispered to them. Soon the barriers would be stripped away like flesh from bone and then they would be able to take corporeal form and bring hell to this world.

He felt a certain amount of apprehension as he approached Shinar and the Dark Apostle. To wield such power! Never had he been witness to such a feat of strength from the holy leader as this. He had not imagined that Jarulek would have been able to create such a powerful Gehemahnet. He had believed that the Dark Apostle had long reached the apex of his rise and that his own rise would eclipse Jarulek's power over the next millennia. Could he have underestimated him?

An uncomfortable and uncharacteristic flicker of doubt squirmed within him. Could he wield such power? He knew that he could not, not yet, but he was certain that his powers would treble once he passed the full indoctrinations required to become a true Dark Apostle. He would take up that mantle and soon, no matter what the cost or sacrifice required. Long had he waited for his moment to arise and he would be damned before he saw his opportunity splutter and die out like a bloodwick before it had even begun to blaze.

He was rocked as strong winds buffeted the Thunderhawk. The engines screamed as they fought against being sucked into the swirling morass rotating around the Gehemahnet. The speed of the wind whipping around the tower must have been immense. Pushing these thoughts from his mind, he closed his eyes and let his spirit break free of his earthly body.

Invisible and formless, he soared from the Thunderhawk, passing through its thick, armoured hull and out into the atmosphere beyond. The powerful winds touched him not at all, and with a thought he hurtled across the sky towards the rising Gehemahnet, faster than any crude mechanical aircraft ever could. This was the way of the spirit and with his insubstantial warp-touched eyes he saw the world in a different light.

The material world around him was shadowy and dim, a pale and dull land. With his sight he saw not the light of the sun, nor the colours of the mundane world, all was but shades of grey, lifeless and monotone. There was movement all around, the movement of daemons separated from the mundane world by only a micro-thin layer of reality. He flew somewhere in between the two worlds, neither truly in the real nor the Ether, but he could perceive both.

He heard nothing but the scraping, garbled cacophony of noise that was the sound of Chaos. A million scrambled, screaming voices mixed with the roars and whispers of daemons. It was to Marduk a comforting, neutral sound in the back of his mind. It was too easy for the unwary or uninitiated to be forever lost in the sound. If you listened too closely, it would draw you into it and never let you have peace.

Marduk willed himself on, drawn towards the massive Gehemahnet tower that rose in both the material world and the warp. It existed in both planes and it was not a monotone shadow like the rest of the world he passed over. Far from it, for the Gehemahnet tower was ablaze with light and colour. Deep red and purple shades blurred across its surface amid flashes of metallic sheen, like those created by oil on water.

Tiny pinpricks of light, countless thousands of them, marked the soul fires of the mortal worker slaves who toiled over the physical construct of the Gehemahnet. They were like tiny burning suns. Some burnt bright and fierce, their spirits strong, while others grew pale and faltering. Carrion daemons of the warp clustered around each burning soul fire, along with an endless myriad of daemons of other bizarre and horrific forms. They clumped around the souls of the living like cold children around a campfire in winter, struggling against each other to be the closest to the blaze. The mortals were completely unaware of the attention that they received, save perhaps for an occasional feeling of coldness, or a flicker of movement in the corner of the eye.

The kathartes were there, clustered around the bright soul lights, and they raised their beautiful, pristine and predatory feminine faces at his approach. They kicked away from their vigils and soared towards him upon glowing feathered wings. In the Ether they were angelic and alluring – it was only when they breached the material plane that they became twisted hag furies.

As he drew nearer the pulsating Gehemahnet, he saw the soul fire of one of the slaves flicker and dim as the man gave up his hold on his mortal body. Instantly, the pale light of the spirit was set upon by the daemons huddled around it and its light was hidden amongst the dense ball of daemons that were wild in their ravenous feeding frenzy as they consumed the unfortunate soul.

The soul fire of one slave drew his attention, for it was different from the others. It was bright and fierce, with a grand cluster of over a thousand ethereal denizens of the warp around it, and Marduk could feel their expectation. This one was favoured indeed, he thought.

A sudden tug upon his spirit pulled at Marduk and he allowed himself to be drawn towards the calling. In an instant he had passed through the walls of the shattered palace of Shinar and hovered before the Dark Apostle. He was infused with light, a strong presence in the warp as in reality. He turned his earthly eyes to look at Marduk and smiled.

'Welcome, my First Acolyte. I thought I felt your questing spirit lurking nearby.'

I wished to see the glory of your Gehemahnet with more than the limited faculties of my mortal being, my lord.

'Of course. Its power waxes strong.'

It does, my lord. It is nearing completion?

'It is close, but I need your strength, First Acolyte, to complete the rituals of binding. This is why I recalled you from battle.'

The battle fares poorly. It is shaming.

'I would sacrifice the entire Host in order to fulfil the will of the Dark Council, if such was needed.'

And the warrior-brothers of the Legion will lay their lives down if that is what is required of them.

'Yet you struggle, First Acolyte. Why is that?'

The Coryphaus must be punished for his failures.

'Must? You would make demands of me, First Acolyte?'

No, my lord.

'I have faith in my Coryphaus, First Acolyte. To doubt his abilities is a reflection of your doubt of me, for he is my chosen representative in all matters of war. You would insult me in such a way, dear Marduk?'

No, my lord.

'Do not defy me, young one. You are no Dark Apostle yet, and I hold the key to your future within my hand. I can destroy you at my will.'

It will be as you will it, Dark Apostle, said Marduk, and took his leave. His spirit soared high into the upper atmosphere. Hundreds of daemons were drawn to him, feeding upon the hot emotions of hate and anger flowing from his spirit.

THE TENT FLAP was thrown open and Havorn stooped to enter the shelter. The air was heavy and cloying with the stale smell of sweat. It took a moment for his eyes to adjust to the gloom before he could make out the three medicae officers standing over the cot in the corner. One of them approached him, saluting, and he recognised the man as Michelac, the chief surgeon of the 133rd. His black rimmed eyes were tired.

'It's not good, sir,' he said.

'What the hell happened?' asked Havorn.

'Astropath Klistorman collapsed late yesterday afternoon, as you know. He was ranting and was suffering severe convulsions, and he was bleeding from the nose. I suspected an internal haemorrhage within his brain; such a thing could have been building there for months. But he seemed to regain his strength this morning and he seemed to have suffered no ill effects. This afternoon, however, he has had a series of episodes. He is sleeping now, but they are getting worse.'

'There are other astropaths with the fleet. This is war, medic, and people die. Why did you call me down here?'

The medicae officer licked his dry, cracked lips.

'His ranting has disturbed me. He has spoken of things that chill my soul.'

'You fear possession?' asked Havorn sharply, his hand falling to his holstered weapon.

'No sir, not that, thankfully,' said the man hurriedly. 'But... I know that astropaths are powerful psykers, sir. I am no expert in such things, but I am of the understanding that they are able to see things that humble men like I cannot. In my opinion, that is not a blessing but a curse.'

'So what has he been speaking of?'

'When his words are decipherable, he has been speaking of some construction of the enemy. It will erupt with power when the "Red orb waxes strongest" I believe were his words. Given that there is a damned big red planet hanging in the sky, I thought that you might wish to know what he said.'

Havorn walked to the side of the cot and looked down upon his astropath. The man was skeletally thin, his skin ashen. He wore a metallic, domed helmet over his head and his eyes were concealed beneath it, though there were no eye slits or visor. Pipes and wiring protruded from the back of the helmet, disappearing beneath his high-necked, sweat soaked robes. He was bound with leather straps, holding him firmly upon the cot.

'I didn't want to remove any of his accoutrements. I feared that I might harm him, or me,' muttered the medic. 'I ordered him restrained so that he did not harm himself if he had another seizure.'

Havorn nodded.

'Did he say what would happen when this power he talked about was unleashed?' he asked.

'He was not particularly lucid, sir. Most of his words were gibberish. He did, however, talk of hell being unleashed and of this world being turned inside out.'

The astropath coughed suddenly, blood and phlegm on his lips, and then he began to go into severe convulsions. The muscles in his neck strained as his entire body went rigid and shook, and the medic pushed a piece of leather between his teeth to stop him from biting though his own tongue. He twitched spasmodically for thirty seconds before going limp, his breathing heavy and ragged. He spat the leather from his mouth and turned his sightless gaze towards Brigadier-General Havorn.

'It draws near!' he said in a coarse whisper, flecks of foam spitting from his mouth. 'As the red orb waxes strong, it will erupt! Damnation! It will awaken Damnation! Destroy it before the time comes. It is...' The man's words dissolved into unintelligible gargles as another fit took hold of him.

'See to him as best you can,' said Havorn and he took his leave. Walking out of the tent, he raised his gaze to the giant red planet Korsis looming overhead. He had been told that it would be at its closest to Tanakreg in five days time.

Five days to wipe the enemy clear of the planet before whatever it was that the astropath had seen would occur. He wished that he could discount the man's fevered words as those of a diseased mind, but he felt that there was something in them.

Damn it, was he getting superstitious in his old age?

His gaze turned towards the insane construction that rose like a needle into the atmosphere. It was hard to believe it was over a thousand kilometres away.

It had to be destroyed. Five days, he thought.

'I AM WITHDRAWING the Host back to the defensive earthworks and bunkers outside the ruins of the city, my lord,' growled Kol Badar. He squeezed the trigger of his combi-bolter and ragged fire ripped apart the chest of yet another enemy trooper. There were thousands of them advancing all along the battle front and the Coryphaus's armour was slick with gore and the foul, milky, nutrient-rich blood of the Skitarii.

'I cannot hold them at the mountains with the valleys destroyed and our numbers are too few to halt them on the salt plains,' he said as he gunned down more soldiers advancing relentlessly into the Word Bearers' fire. The ground was liberally littered with the dead, yet the enemy continued to advance, stepping over the bodies of their fallen comrades. Others were crushed beneath the rolling tracks of battle tanks and mechanised crawlers. Earth and bodies exploded around him as shells from battle cannons pounded the line. Searing lascannons silenced a Leman Russ tank, blowing its turret clear of its chassis and Kol Badar heard the roars of the Warmonger nearby as the revered ancient one relived some long past battle as it killed.

The voice of his master, the Dark Apostle, throbbed in his head.

The time of the Gehemahnet's awakening draws near. Allow it to be interrupted and your pain shall know no bounds, my Coryphaus.

'I would gladly give my life in sacrifice for my failures, my lord,' said Kol Badar as he stepped slowly backwards, snapping off sharp bursts of fire left and right.

'Seventh and eighteenth coterie, close ranks and give covering fire,' he ordered, switching his comm-channel briefly. 'Twenty-first and eleventh, disengage and back off.'

You have a duty to perform, Kol Badar, and you will have no such release while it remains unfulfilled.

'Burias, ensure they do not encircle us with their light vehicles. Engage and destroy them,' he ordered before closing the comm once again.

'My lord is merciful.'

No, I am not. Your failure will not go unpunished, nor will it be forgotten. Allow none to assail the Gehemahnet. Sacrifice every last warrior-brother before you allow a single enemy to launch an attack against it. Do this and the Dark Council will be pleased. Fail again and eternal torment will be yours.

'I will fight them every step of the way, my lord,' swore Kol Badar. 'I have ordered Bokkar and the reserve to strengthen the defences, preparing for the arrival of the Host. We will hold.'

Succeed in this, my Coryphaus, and I will give you what you most desire. I will give you the First Acolyte, and you can finish what you once started.

Kol Badar blinked his eyes in surprise. He clenched his power claw tightly, the talons of the mighty weapon crackling with energy as he slew another pair of enemy soldiers, his fire cutting through their midsections. He chuckled in anticipation and felt a savage joy fire within him.

'I will not fail, my lord. I swear it before all the great gods of Chaos. I will not fail.'

BOOK THREE: ASCENSION

'With victories over others, we conquer. But with victories over ourselves, we are exalted. There must always be contests, and you must always win.'

– Kor Phaeron – Master of the Faith

CHAPTER SIXTEEN

The Imperial Dictator-class cruiser *Vigilance* moved soundlessly through the void of space as it rounded the war-torn planet, dropping into close orbit. The calculations had to be absolutely precise and the logic engines housed within the bridge had been working constantly to provide the complex algorithms calculating the exact moment for the barrage to be unleashed.

The area of jammed communications was broad; to risk the *Vigilance* entering the field was testament to the severity of the threat. All sensory equipment was rendered useless as soon as they entered the zone. Even the astropaths were unable to pierce the gloom projected up from the planet's surface. Once within the field, the *Vigilance* was utterly cut off from the outside world. The only guiding light was that of the Astronomican, which Navigators could still thankfully perceive.

Nevertheless, to launch an orbital bombardment essentially blind was highly unorthodox and the risks were high. However, the Admiral had been insistent and the cogitators had been consulted to predict the exact mathematics required to plan such an endeavour.

The approach of the cruiser was painstakingly enacted. If it were but a fraction of a degree off its angle of approach, if its speed was slightly out and the tip of the massive cruiser off by the smallest fraction then the bombardment would miss the planet altogether, or would fall far from the target. Worse, it could fall upon the Imperial Guard on the planet's surface far below.

With its holo-screens blank and its sensor arrays rendered inoperative, the Dictator cruiser advanced into position. Muttering prayers to the Emperor that the algorithms he had been provided with were accurate and that his team of logisticians had coordinated them exactly, the ship's flag-captain breathed out slowly as the gunnery master initiated the launch sequence. The port battery, housing hundreds of massive weapons that could cripple a battle cruiser, were activated. Thousands of indentured workers slaved to match the exact range and trajectory initiated by the gunnery crew as they readied to fire. The gunnery captain prayed that his barrage would fall against the target.

His worry was in vain, for the *Vigilance* never had a chance to unleash its orbital bombardment.

A surge of warp energy from the infant Gehemahnet surged from the tower, creating an opening to the Ether for the smallest fraction of a second. In that brief flicker, the darkness of space was replaced with the roiling, red netherworld, a place of horror where the natural laws of the universe held no sway, and the nightmares of those of the material plane were given form. It was filled with screams and roars and the deafening, maddening blare of Chaos. It lasted but the blink of an eye, but when it passed, the *Vigilance* had gone with it, dragged into the realm of the Chaos gods.

Without the protection of its Geller field, which it had no time to erect, the cruiser was overrun with hundreds of thousands of daemonic entities, its structure turned inside out. The physical forms of those unfortunates within the Dictator cruiser were driven instantly insane at the exposure to the pure energy of the warp, their bodies mutating wildly as Chaos took hold. Their souls were devoured and their screams joined with those of countless billions who had been consumed to feed the insatiable gods of the realm. Within the blink of an eye the *Vigilance* was no more.

MARDUK WAS ROCKED as the fledgling strength of the Gehemahnet surged. Such staggering power!

Only once before had he witnessed the birthing of a Gehemahnet, for to construct one of the potent totems was a draining experience. Only the most powerful Dark Apostles would even attempt to create one, and the process would often leave them shattered wrecks, weak shadows of their former selves.

Jarulek's presence was evidence of the truth of this. Marduk had been shocked by the appearance of his master when he had arrived back at the ruined shell of the once prosperous Imperial city.

Jarulek seemed to have aged several millennia. His skin was sunken and wasted, and bones and spider-web lines of veins were clearly visible beneath translucent, script inscribed flesh. His lips were thin and drawn back from his teeth like those of a long-dead corpse. Deep, dark, sepulchral sockets surrounded his eyes, though they flashed with defiant strength.

He is weak, thought Marduk, licking his lips.

'You feel the awakening, First Acolyte,' said Jarulek.

'Yes, Dark Apostle. It is… astounding,' Marduk replied truthfully. 'It must have taken much of your strength to imbue the tower with such potency.'

Jarulek waved a hand dismissively.

'The great gods gift me with the power to enact their will,' said the Dark Apostle lightly, but Marduk could see that he was almost utterly drained.

Jarulek saw Marduk's narrowed eyes and raised an eyebrow on his skeletal face.

'You have something to say, First Acolyte?'

'No, my Dark Apostle,' he said. It would not be wise for Marduk to antagonise his master, not yet. 'I am merely in awe of the power of your faith. I aspire one day to reach such glorified heights.'

'Perhaps, but the path to enlightenment is a long and painful road. Many fall along the way to eternal damnation and torment, seeking that which they desire too quickly, or by taking up challenges that are far beyond their reach,' said the Dark Apostle evenly, his velvet voice enunciating the words carefully.

'With your guidance, lord, I hope to avoid falling prey to such temptations,' said Marduk.

'As I would expect, my First Acolyte. The Imperials draw near?'

'They do, my lord. The Coryphaus pulls the Host back from its advance.'

'I do not require the Host to hold them indefinitely. It is but days until the conjunction. That is when Korsis will be largest in the sky and the seven planets of this system will be aligned. We need but hold them until then. The Coryphaus understands my needs.'

'To be pushed back at all is an insult to the Legion. It shames us all.'

'To expect the unattainable is foolish, my First Acolyte. I never asked Kol Badar to destroy the foe, it is unnecessary. He must merely hold them until the alignment and buy time for the Gehemahnet to be completed.'

'And it is nearing completion, my lord?'

'It is. That is why I have called you back from the front line, to aid me in the final stages of its summoning. This Gehemehnet is to be different from any other totem that has been constructed before, for I have called it forth not to turn this planet into a daemon world, but to shatter it utterly,' said the Dark Apostle with a smile on his face.

'My lord?'

'It must be complete for the alignment. When the red planet is high, the Daemonschage will toll, signalling the death of this planet, and a great treasure will be revealed, a treasure that will be unlocked by the Enslaved.'

'The Enslaved?'

'One who will come to us. With the secrets unlocked, we will launch a new era of terror upon the followers of the Corpse Emperor. We will take the fight to those we hate the most.'

'The arrogant, cursed offspring of Guilliman,' said Marduk.

'Indeed.'

'First Acolyte, a question.'

'Yes, my lord?' asked Marduk, frowning.

'Have any holy scriptures appeared on your flesh yet?'

'No, my lord. I bear none but the passage that you honoured me with,' he said, indicating his left cheek where the skin of the Dark Apostle had knitted with his own.

'Tell me immediately if words begin to form upon your skin, First Acolyte. They… they mark your readiness to proceed with your induction into the fold.'

'Thank you, my lord,' said Marduk, bemused. 'I will consult you immediately should such a thing occur.'

'THEY ARE PLANNING to pound us into the ground with their artillery,' commented Burias, standing atop the first defensive line and watching as the Imperials advanced slowly. 'Are we just going to cower back here and allow them?'

The salt plains were spread with Imperials as far as the eye could see. They advanced in a massive, sweeping arc towards the curved first line of the Word Bearers' defence. The first bulwark was wider than the other three that guarded the crumbled remains of the Imperial city and, but for the reserve led by Bokkar, every warrior of the Host stood upon it awaiting the enemy. Havoc squads hunkered down within those bunkers that were intact, placed at one hundred metre intervals.

Burias and Kol Badar stood side by side as they watched the advance of the foe. A mass of salt dust rose up behind the advancing army.

Kol Badar swung around, his one good eye staring coldly down at the Icon Bearer. His other eye, shattered by shrapnel, had been replaced with an arcane augmetic sensor by the chirurgeons.

'You question the orders of your Coryphaus, whelp?' he snarled.

'No, Coryphaus, but I feel Drak'shal raging to be unleashed.'

'Keep a rein on your daemon parasite, Burias. Its time will come soon.'

'I shall, Coryphaus.'

'They have more ordnance than we.'

'There is no sign of that Ordinatus machine, though.'

'No. Its range is not as great as their artillery's. If it advanced ahead of the main battle line, it would sustain damage. The methodology of the Adeptus Mechanicus is rigid. They deviate not at all from their ritual tenets and the modes of behaviour programmed into their mechanical heads. They will not risk damage to the machine.'

'You know a lot about the followers of the Machine-God, my lord?'

'I have learnt much from the Forgemasters of Ghalmek. And I fought alongside Tech-Priests of the Mechanicum during the Great Crusade, marching to battle alongside blessed Lorgar and the Warmaster,' he said, bitterness in his voice. 'And afterwards, I fought against them.'

'I am sorry to have dredged up painful memories, Coryphaus.'

Kol Badar waved away the words of the younger Word Bearers warrior-brother.

'Bitterness, anger and hatred is what fuels the fires within. If we forget the past then we will lose the passion to dethrone the False Emperor. To lose the fire is to fail in our sacred duty; the Long War,' growled Kol Badar. A thought struck him, was the Dark Apostle fuelling his own hatred of the First Acolyte to keep the fires within him stoked? He dismissed the thought instantly as irrelevant to the situation at hand.

The Coryphaus placed the talons of his power claw upon Burias's shoulder plate and exerted just enough pressure for the ceramite to groan.

'No, we do not attack just yet. But when we do, Burias, *you* will lead it,' he said generously.

'You do me much honour, Coryphaus,' said Burias, surprise on his face.

'You may be the lackey of a wretched whoreson, but you should not be held in the shadows because of it,' said Kol Badar.

Burias tensed and the warlord could see the daemon within flash in his eyes.

'The First Acolyte is on the cusp of greatness,' said Kol Badar, 'though it is a dangerous position and his fate is not yet determined. He may yet be deemed unworthy. Your precious master may fail at the last. Be wary, young Burias. Make sure you know where your loyalty lies, with the Legion, or with an individual.'

Burias stared at the Coryphaus for a moment before he gave a sharp nod of his head and Kol Badar released his crushing grip on the Icon Bearer's shoulder.

'Do well, and I will see you initiated into the cult of the Anointed,' said Kol Badar and he was pleased to see fires of ambition and greed come to life within the younger Icon Bearer's eyes. He had him.

'Go now. Gather the most vicious berserkers of the Host. I want eight fully mechanised coteries ready to roll out on my word. I feel that the enemy will bring the fight to us, and when they do, I want you ready to meet them head on.'

MARDUK WALKED WITH the Dark Apostle towards a small, twin-engine transport, the pair of holy warriors accompanied by an honour guard. Daemon heads spewed smoke as its engines were revved and the doors hissed shut behind the Word Bearers. Marduk saw the Dark Apostle's eyes close in prayer or exhaustion.

On the short journey to the base of the Gehemahnet, Marduk marvelled at how the Imperial city had been transformed. From a bustling city of millions, it had been rendered into a wasteland of industry. Every building had been levelled and the fires of the Chaos factorums blazed in the dim light, spewing fumes and smog into the roiling sky. The ground was black with oil and pollution, and lines of slaves, each a thousand strong or more, wound through the black detritus and slag piles like multi-legged insects. Huge pistons drove up and down, conveyor belts piled with rock and bodies fed into hissing, steaming vaults and furnaces, and chains with links larger than battle tanks wound around immense wheels, turning the machineries of Chaos. It was almost like an infant version of Ghalmek, the daemonic forge-monastery world, one of the great stronghold worlds of faith and industry of the Word Bearers, deep in the Maelstrom.

Black dust was kicked up as the shuttle landed and the honour guard stepped to the ground, scouring the area for any threat before they stood to attention. Marduk allowed the Dark Apostle to alight first and his dark eyes followed the movement of the older warrior priest as he stepped out of the shuttle. Even his movements were stiff, he thought. Truly it seemed the Dark Apostle was drained almost to the point of exhaustion. He smiled to himself.

They marched across the blackened earth towards the vast doors of a roaring furnace factorum, ignoring thousands of slaves and overseers that dropped to the ground to grovel before their master. Gears and chains groaned as the sliding doors were dragged aside and a blast of intense hot air radiated out from within, making his vision shimmer.

Workers prostrated themselves on the ground as the Word Bearers entered the massive factory. Huge vats of liquid metal were being poured into a vast mould, along with other liquids that flowed from dozens of spiralling tubes and distillery pipes. The super-heated liquid metal was doused with blood and clouds of heady steam rose.

'Now this, this is what sets my Gehemehnet apart from any other,' said Jarulek, his eyes alight.

A dozen huge chains lifted the mould into the air and it swung across the factorum to hang overhead. With a nod from Jarulek, it was released and it fell with bone shaking force ten metres to the floor of the factory. The entire area shuddered as it landed. The floor of the factorum cracked beneath the impact and small, spider web cracks spread across the surface of the mould. Searing light spilled from the branching cracks. Without the benefit of its inbuilt reactive auto-sensors in his helmet, Marduk squinted his eyes against the glare. More of the miniscule faults appeared across its surface, spilling light in all directions, and the mould began to crumble into tiny granules, falling to the ground, smoking and hissing.

The black mould exploded outwards suddenly, spreading scalding hot granules across the factorum, and blinding light filled the area. Overseers and slaves screamed and recoiled as burning particles seared into their skin and their retinas were burned away.

Even to Marduk the glare was painful and he hissed as super-heated granules burned the skin of his face. Still, he did not flinch, for he was determined not to show any weakness before the Dark Apostle.

A towering, glowing shape stood in the middle of the factorum.

'You have made a bell,' he said dryly.

Jarulek laughed, though the laughter tailed off into a hacking wheeze.

'A bell, yes. With this Daemonschage the power of the Gehemehnet will be harnessed. When that power is unleashed, it will shatter the planet's core. Come,' he said, motioning Marduk forward.

The pair approached the glowing bell towering over them. The intensity of the light it projected was dimming, so that it was bearable to look upon, and Marduk saw that it was smooth and the colour of blooded steel. Tiny script-work wound around its circumference, covering most of the bell. Waves of hot emotion, hatred, jealousy, anger and pain emanated from the Daemonschage.

'Place your hands upon it,' ordered Jarulek.

Marduk moved a hand tentatively forwards and touched his fingers gingerly upon the metallic surface.

'It's cold,' he said and placed both his hands firmly upon its surface. There were presences there. A myriad of voices screamed painfully in his mind and he pulled his hands back sharply.

'I have already bound the Daemonschage with the spirits of over a thousand daemons.'

'Such hatred I felt,' said Marduk. 'This is a powerful binding.'

'The daemons are angered that they are within the physical realm, yet they cannot manifest,' chuckled Jarulek. 'But it needs more daemons bound within this prison before it is complete. My strength wanes. It falls to you, First Acolyte, to complete the ceremonies of binding.'

'You honour me, my lord.'

'The construction of the Gehemehnet is all but complete and that is where my strength is needed. The Daemonschage is to be transported to the top of the tower. You will complete the summoning there, Marduk, and then the Daemonschage will sound and this world will be ripped asunder.'

THE THUNDER OF ordnance was constant. The lines of artillery and siege tanks boomed one after another, billowing smoke covering their positions. The shells had been hurled relentlessly towards the traitor lines for almost three hours and the salt plains and earthworks were pockmarked with craters. It was impossible to gauge enemy casualties, though Laron guessed they were few. The armour of the enemy, together with the defensive bulwarks and bunkers, would most likely ensure protection against most of the incoming fire.

He was pleased however that the brigadier-general was pushing for the war to come to a head. A long, drawn out siege was not a war for an Elysian. Surgical strikes, lightning raids and daring attacks deep into enemy territory: that was how the warriors of Elysia were meant to fight and it seemed that at last they would have the chance.

Still, it would not be easy and the loss of the Imperial cruiser had been a shock, its destruction testament to the unholy power of the enemy.

'Looks like the brigadier-general has had a change of heart,' said Captain Elias. Laron had promoted the man from sergeant when the brigadier-general had given him the mammoth task of becoming acting colonel. He nodded his head.

'Shinar's air defences are famed throughout the sector,' said Elias. 'You were the one that reminded me of that, sir. Won't we be blown out of the air on the approach?'

'It *is* going to be bloody, no two ways around it, Elias, but the brigadier-general feels that such a risk is necessary. The threat the enemy poses is far greater than was first understood. It is not going to be pretty, but this is war and it is what the Emperor demands of us.'

That suits me fine, thought Laron. The frustrations and stresses of the previous week had built up, and he longed for the simplicity of leading his men into battle once again.

Elias was right though, they would be at the mercy of the enemy guns until those emplacements were silenced. He prayed that their objective was achievable, else the 72nd and the 133rd would be slaughtered.

CHAPTER SEVENTEEN

THE GEHEMEHNET ROSE almost fifty kilometres into the atmosphere. Black, oily clouds circling the tower far below hid the land from Varnus's eyes, making him feel dizzy and disoriented. The giant, red planet Korsis dominated the sky above. It hung so close that it was an intimidating, looming presence.

Hot vapours rose from the hollow shaft of the Gehemehnet in long, steaming exhalations. The breath of the gods themselves, the Discord had told him, and its touch was intoxicating. It came from deep within the planet, for Varnus knew that the shaft plunged far beneath the earth, into the fiery heart of Tanakreg.

He noticed that there were fewer than a hundred slaves atop the tower: those that had proven to have the strength and will to survive its completion. Each man was crouching on his haunches, accompanied by an overseer who stood just behind him. Looking around at them, Varnus felt sickened. They all looked like worshippers of the Chaos gods, far from the industrious servants of the Emperor that they had once been. Varnus knew that he too must look like one of the cursed, *blessed*, followers of the ruinous powers and he seethed.

He knew that he had changed. Outwardly, the change was obvious, but the most damaging changes had occurred within him. His blood ran thick with serums concocted by chirurgeons and his mind was filled with hateful visions of darkness and death. Voices spoke within him constantly, chattering maddeningly, and heretical thoughts plagued him. He wanted to embrace the gods of the Ether, to allow himself to succumb utterly to their will, and he knew that the last barriers of resistance were being eaten away.

The tower spoke to him, its voice soothing him.

A massive, black-girded construction was brought over the lip of the tower, held aloft by a trio of spider-legged cranes, and Varnus stared at it in wonder. Its shape was bewitching to the eye and it was swung over his head to hang over the top of the open shaft. It had eight black, iron legs, the first of them touching down on the stone only metres to Varnus's left.

It was an eight-legged armature that rose to a point, like the frame of a giant, triangular tent. That point was embossed with beaten metal the colour of blood,and thick, spiked chains swung from the legs, hanging down into the vast emptiness of the shaft within the tower. Seeing the chains made Varnus put a hand to his neck, feeling around the circumference of his collar. He realised that he no longer wore a chain around his neck, though he had no recollection of the overseers having removed it.

He felt the Gehemenhet beneath him tremble and the feet of the black frame sank into the stone as if it were made of quicksand. Varnus blinked his eyes, as if they were deceiving him. *He saw fields of the skinless dead beneath a burning daemon sky.* But the stone was once again solid, holding the frame tightly in place.

There was a trembling in the air and a feeling of anticipation built within him. He felt a rumbling bass note shudder through the tower and the ceaseless blare of the Discord began to blend into a monotonous chant that rose up loudly around him. His internal organs shuddered as the intensity of the volume rose and the black arms of the armature began to resonate with power, chains shaking and clinking.

Darkness spilled from the centre of the Gehemehnet, fingers of shadow clawing out over the top of the stones and questing out in all directions. The gloom engulfed Varnus and he began to shiver. He saw flickers of movement in the darkness, shapes clustered all around him, and he felt their hot breath on his neck. They whispered to him and their talons brushed against him, painfully cold and ethereal. He could see the blood-red glow of their eyes in the netherworld staring hungrily out at him and he felt nausea and disorientation.

A trio of Discords rose from within the Gehemehnet, rising up out of its hollow shaft, their tentacles playing out around them like gently waving undersea fronds, angelic voices blurring with daemonic roars and melancholic chanting that boomed from their speakers. Beneath the cacophony of voices was the rhythmic grinding of machinery, the pounding of metal drums and the deep reverberations of pipes. Varnus felt the hairs of his body rise with the potent sounds.

Behind the Discords came a red, armoured figure, arms outstretched to either side, appearing out of the darkness like some devil arisen from its hellish realm beneath the earth.

Varnus was in no doubt that this was a priest of the ruinous powers and he felt awed and horrified in equal measure. Faith and power, these were the two things that the warrior-priest radiated. He saw the shadowy, insubstantial shapes of daemons circling the warrior. He could feel their excitement and relentless hate being strengthened by the priest's radiance.

The warrior was huge and his ornate, red armour was scarred from battle. He wore no helmet, but appeared to suffer no ill-effects from the scarce amount of oxygen. His eyes were closed as he chanted, his voice powerful and deep. Varnus did not understand the meaning of the words the priest spoke, but he knew them well, having heard them for weeks on end within the roar of the Discords.

The chains hanging from the black frame began to rise and their barbed tips began to wave around in the air like the searching heads of serpents. They reached out towards the slaves, who were all face down bar Varnus. The tip of one of the chains approached him and it hovered in the air. The barbed tip was the size and length of his forearm and he saw that the dark metal was covered in tiny script. It swung back and forth before him, mesmerising and moving gently in time with the rhythms of the Discords, as if held in thrall by some fell snake charmer.

With the speed of a striking serpent, the chains struck down into the backs of the slaves, driving through their bodies and ripping out through their chests. The slaves were lifted up into the air, transfixed upon the living chains running through them. The bladed tips of the chains coiled around and lunged again, stabbing again and again the bodies of the slaves impaled on other chains, until no body was pierced fewer than a dozen of times.

The blade hovering before Varnus hung in the air before him, waving back and forth before it too plunged forward, but not into him, instead it descended into the back of the overseer at his side. The black-clad slaver squealed horribly as the bladed chain tore back and forth through its body, and it was lifted high in the air, along with all the others, black blood showering Varnus.

The chains began to knit together, forming an intricate pattern within the eight-legged frame above the hovering priest, who continued on with his intonation, uncaring of the mayhem that had been unleashed around him. The chains bound together tightly until they resembled a giant spider web, complete with grisly trophies. The bodies of the slaves and the overseers hung impaled and wrapped within the chains, and Varnus was horrified to see that most of them were not yet dead. They twitched and moaned, and their life blood dripped down onto the Chaos Space Marine priest beneath them.

He stood atop the Gehemehnet walls, his limbs shaking as he realised that he stood alone. Every other slave and overseer was within the sickening chain-length spider web, dying. Only he had been spared.

The priest's eyes opened and fell upon him. He felt as though the warrior's gaze pierced his soul and he cowered before him. Though the Chaos Space Marine continued to chant his monotonous incantation, Varnus felt a voice throb within his mind.

The Gehemehnet has chosen you to witness its birth. You are privileged, little man.

SCREAMING SHELLS RAINED down upon the Word Bearers, throwing up great explosions of earth as they struck at the embankments. The bombardment had increased in tempo and they detonated across the entire length of the Shinar peninsula.

The Warmonger stood atop the battlements in the centre of the first line of defence, uncaring of the mayhem exploding around him. The enemy's pitiful shells could not harm him and he stood motionless in the midst of the bombardment, surveying the battlefield coldly.

The other war machines and daemon engines of the Legion had been pulled back to the second line. Their unarmoured attendants would have been slaughtered beneath the fury of the attack and the daemon engines would have stormed forwards across the plain, eager to get to grips with the enemy. They would have been uniformly destroyed. None bar the Dark Apostle would be able to restrain them.

The Dreadnought's augmetic senses pierced the fire and smoke that surrounded the first line, and he saw a series of detonations erupt further out along the salt plains, several kilometres away. This was no bombardment of the Word Bearers, and the Warmonger was momentarily confused. Not even the pitiful gunners of the Imperial Guard could be so inaccurate with their fire. A second line of explosions ran out along the salt plains, this time two hundred metres closer to the Word Bearers' lines. His senses could not pierce the vast clouds of smoke that rose from the detonations.

'Kol Badar, the enemies of the Warmaster are on the approach. They mask their advance with ordnance and blind grenades.'

'Received, Warmonger,' came the vox reply. 'Incoming aircraft have been picked up. Be ready.'

'The blessings of the true gods upon you.'

'Kill well, old friend.'

'THE ENEMY HAS made its move, Icon Bearer. Your time has come,' said Kol Badar.

Burias bowed his head to the massive, Terminator-armoured war leader.

'You do me a great honour, my Coryphaus,' he said.

'Remember it, Burias,' growled Kol Badar. 'Do the Legion proud. Do not make me regret giving you my favour.'

'You will not, Coryphaus,' said Burias, his handsome, pale face serious with devotion. 'My first kill will be dedicated to you, my lord.'

He could not gauge the reaction of his words upon the Coryphaus's face, hidden as it was beneath his quad-tusked helmet, but he thought the warlord's posture showed that he was pleased. Good, thought Burias.

He turned away from the Coryphaus with another bow of the head, to face the gathered warriors below him, on the off-face of the embankment. Explosions detonated around them, but the warriors were unflinching, their helmets turned up towards him, awaiting his order.

Burias slammed his icon into the ground and the warrior-brothers stood motionless in rapt attention.

'My brothers, the time has come for us to ride out and face the enemy head on,' he roared, the daemon Drak'shal giving his voice unholy resonance and power.

A huge roar of approval rose from the gathered, since many of their voices were also enhanced by the daemons lurking within their souls.

'The Coryphaus honours us with this sacred duty,' Burias continued, which was met with another roar from the gathered warriors.

'Do the Coryphaus proud, my brothers, and kill in the name of Lorgar!'

The gathered warriors roared the name of their daemon primarch, their voices mingling with Burias's bloodcurdling bellow, screaming to the heavens so that their lord might hear their devotion.

The gathered Coteries intoned prayers to the dark gods as they climbed into their transport vehicles. A pair of Land Raiders would lead the Rhino attack column and the assault ramps of the monstrous tanks hissed as they slammed open to receive the warriors honoured to be carried within. Engines revved in anticipation and the lascannon turrets of the Land Raiders swivelled as the daemon spirits controlling them expressed their impatience.

'The smoke the Imperials use blocks our sight, but it blocks theirs as well, Burias. Go forth. Tackle them head on. They will not see you coming.'

Burias snarled a wordless reply. Drak'shal was rising within him. With a final nod, he turned and jogged towards the awaiting Land Raider. Before the assault ramp had even hissed completely closed, the column of tanks roared forwards, climbing the steep embankment quickly amid the explosions of incoming barrage fire. Engines screamed as the massive Land Raiders reached the apex of the climb and rose over the lip of the embankment before the tanks thumped down on the other side. They rolled towards the enemy, hidden behind a wall of smoke and ash that was drawing closer with every falling barrage.

Drak'shal's daemon essence pumped strength through his veins and his muscles strained within his power armour.

To become one of the Anointed had been his dream since his inception into the Legion. He knew that his relationship with Marduk had kept him from being embraced into the cult, for his prowess was fault-less. Long had it been a source of dishonour for Burias and he had at times hated the First Acolyte for it. He had no idea what had occurred on the moon of Calite, but the hatred between Marduk and Kol Badar had been palpable ever since.

Curse him and his feud with the Coryphaus! Burias thought. If the warlord would allow him to be embraced into the cult of the Anointed then he would relish the opportunity and grasp it with both hands.

The Coryphaus was right, the future of the First Acolyte was far from certain, and to throw his support behind Marduk without consideration of this would be foolish. No, he would wait for the right moment to make his decision about where his loyalties lay.

Such thoughts left him instantly as he heard the mechanised, insane whisperings of the Land Raider cease for a moment. The vehicle's machine-spirit had been merged with the essence of a daemon upon the factory world of Ghalmek, bound within the casing of the tank by the fabricators and sorcerers of the Legion with the aid of the chirumeks.

'Entering the blind cloud, Icon Bearer,' said the drawling twin voices of the Land Raider's operators, warriors who had long ago become one with the machine.

The daemonic, mechanised whisperings of the tank began again, the voices agitated and excited.

'COMMAND? COME IN! Damn it!' swore the Valkyrie pilot. He could make no sense of the garbled nonsense being broadcast through the vox sys-tem. His sensor arrays had turned to darkness minutes earlier and he was flying completely without their assistance. Now the vox-caster was playing up and he was completely cut off from the rest of the squadron, not to mention base command. Damn it, he couldn't even commu-nicate with the drop-troopers behind him, for even the closed circuit comm-transmissions of the unit were spewing nonsense.

He knew that the other Elysians were trying to make contact, but their voices morphed into hellish, bestial screams and roars. He wondered if that was how his voice sounded to their ears.

The closer they got to the damned insane tower of the enemy, the more garbled and chaotic the sounds became. He switched the system off, reasoning that he would rather hear nothing than that hellish blare. Yet even with the systems disabled, his earpieces blared with the evil sound and he slammed his fist into his helmet in desperation to get the insane noise out of his head.

You are all going to die, the voice said to him.

The Valkyrie was ripped apart as it was struck by anti-aircraft fire and the pilot was certain that he heard laughter in his ears, even as the cockpit exploded into a billowing fireball.

TANK COMMANDER WALYON grinned as he stood in the cupola of his Leman Russ battle tank, the wind and smoke blowing in his face. The lowered visor of his helmet protected his eyes, not that there was anything to see as the tank thundered through the smoke.

He glanced out to either side. He could dimly make out only the closest tanks, but he knew that there were scores of vehicles spread out on each wing. He was at the point of the arrowhead, roaring towards the enemy, and his heart was racing.

He had been waiting for this day for decades. He knew that being a tank commander within the Elysian ranks was regarded as a dubious honour; all good Elysians dreamt of attacking via drop-ship, for that was the rhetoric drilled into the soldiers from day one. But tanks had always been Walyon's true love and he had accepted the post with relish. The tank company within the 133rd was regarded as little more than a joke; few Elysian regiments even had a tank company. The other officers regarded the position as a dead-end and he knew they sniggered behind his back – promotion out of harm's way, they said. Walyon did not care, for within the ranks of the tank company he had found his home.

However, what had followed was years of boredom and resentment. Time after time the 133rd were launched into battle, but the armoured divisions were held back.

Finally, his time had come and he would be damned if he wasn't going to enjoy it. He smiled like a child given his first exhilarating trip on the harbour shuttle of his home city-hive of Valorsia, and he screamed with exhilaration into the whipping wind.

Somewhere far overhead the Valkyries were disgorging their living cargos. Drop-troopers would be falling through the atmosphere towards their target, the second line of the enemy's defences. Somewhere behind, the Gorgons of the Mechanicus were grinding forwards in the wake of his battle tanks.

An echelon of low-flying Thunderbolt heavy fighters screamed overhead, dull shapes in the haze, utilising the same cover of smoke as the battle tanks, and Walyon punched his fist in the air as they passed, willing them on.

He grinned wildly, feeling as though he were screaming through a vacuum of white smoke. The feeling was not unlike falling blindly through clouds on a combat drop, but this felt much more secure, for he had a giant battle tank steed beneath him. Excitement building, he pulled out his shimmering sabre and levelled it out in front. He felt like one of the daring cavalry marshals of history and he screamed wordlessly, glorying in the sensation of speed.

That was when he saw the massive, red shape looming out of the smoke ahead of him, and the next second of his life seemed to occur in horrifying slow motion. He dimly registered twin flashes of searing white lascannons and the battle tank to his right exploded in a rising ball of black smoke.

Walyon ducked back within the cupola as heavy bolter rounds ripped across the hull of his tank. The command tank's driver must have seen the Land Raider at exactly the same moment and the Leman Russ slewed to the side in an attempt to avoid the massive shape. The move was one of desperation and instinct and the Land Raider turned into it, smashing into the side of the Leman Russ at full speed.

The force of the impact slammed the battle tank onto its side with the sickening sound of crunching metal. The front of the Land Raider rose up into the air like a looming monster of the depths as the impact and its momentum lifted it. The Leman Russ rolled onto its top and the massive traitor tank smashed down upon it, engines roaring as its tracks spun wildly, gaining no traction.

Metal screamed as it buckled beneath the weight of the giant and Walyon was buffeted from side to side, smashing his head on the inside of the cupola, the hot taste of exhaust fumes in his mouth. The next moments of his life were a blur as the Leman Russ rolled wildly across the salt plain, flipping and finally coming to rest upright.

Dazed and shell-shocked, blood running from nose, Walyon called out weakly to the crew within the tank. Pulling himself upright, wincing and feeling as if every bone in his body had been smashed by the severity of the impact, he looked across the smoky void of the salt plains. He couldn't see far, but now that the Leman Russ engine was dead, he could hear the roar of engines, the chatter of gunfire, the heavy boom of battle cannons and the hissing scream of lascannons. Explosions rocked the earth and rising plumes of oily, black smoke and bright orange fireballs pierced the haze. He coughed painfully, spitting blood, and he closed his eyes against the burning pain in his ribs.

An enemy Rhino screamed out of the smoke and Walyon dimly saw Chaos Space Marines standing in the open top of the vehicle, weapons raised. His vision was blurring before his eyes and he barely saw the plume of white-hot plasma screaming towards him, nor the meltagun that blurred the air as it fired upon his beloved tank.

Walyon died, his flesh burning and liquefying, and a moment later the Leman Russ exploded violently, throwing the blackened hull into the air.

A BATTLE CANNON shell detonated on the flank of the Land Raider's hull, spinning the behemoth to the side, its momentum lost.

'Out!' roared Burias. 'Lower the attack ramp!'

Leading the coteries from the Land Raider, desperate to get to grips with the enemy, Burias swung his head from side to side as battle tanks roared past them. Snarling, he snapped off an ineffectual shot with his bolt pistol.

One of the tanks spun amid a rising cloud of salt dust as its track was blown clear by a meltagun shot and the coterie broke into a run towards the slowing vehicle, roaring to the heavens.

One of the tank's side sponsons screeched as it rotated and unleashed its salvo into the Word Bearers, ripping apart bodies. Burias leapt over the fallen warrior-brothers.

Drak'shal surged to the surface of the Icon Bearer's being and his shape blurred as muscles bulged within his power armour. Bunching his legs beneath him, he leapt through the air, landing atop the Demolisher tank. He gripped the hatch atop the cannon turret and ripped it clear of its housing in one brutal movement, wires and cables sparking as the metal was wrenched out of shape, and he hurled it aside. Thumbing a pair of grenades into his hand, he hurled them into the exposed interior before leaping from the tank.

The grenades detonated behind him, but his focus had fixed on something new, and he stared into the impenetrable smoke cloud, his nostrils flaring. A giant shape appeared, roaring towards the Word Bearers.

Larger than even a Land Raider, a super-heavy Gorgon transport vehicle loomed out of the smoke. A giant, angled assault ram of thick metal protected its front, and the gunfire of the coterie pinged off its surface. The metal turned molten beneath the touch of melta weaponry, but even that was not enough to penetrate the thick armour.

Chattering gunfire ripped up the ground around the coterie and a spray of autocannon shells smashed Burias back a step. He felt his anger grow. Lascannons from the Land Raider pierced the metal side of the massive super-heavy vehicle, but it did not slow, and Burias once again tensed his leg muscles, making ready to spring.

With a roar, he leapt as the massive tank bore down on him and he landed on the upper side of the assault ramp, the force of the impact causing him to hiss in pain. A second later, the Gorgon slammed into the wreckage of the Demolisher, smashing the battle tank aside with contemptible ease, nearly crushing Burias. He pulled himself up over the lip of the giant dozer blade. The vehicle was open-topped and he snarled in pleasure as he saw the score of heavy battle servitors packed within. Several were borne upon large tracked units, while others were bipedal, easily as large as a Space Marine, held in place by large clamps around their waists. Autocannon fire slammed into one of Burias's arms, shattering the ceramite, and he lost his grip momentarily, sliding precariously. With a roar he pulled himself up and, kicking off with one foot, he descended into the midst of the heavy Praetorian battle servitors. They raised their massive inbuilt weapon systems towards him, though they were hampered by the tight confines of the Gorgon.

Spinning cannons screamed, the heavy calibre gunfire tearing armour and flesh from Burias-Drak'shal's body, but he was amongst them in an instant. The holding clamps hissed open, releasing the Praetorians.

Their immense weight and solid construction ensured they did not lose their footing, despite the speed the Gorgon was travelling at. He ripped the augmented head from the shoulders of one of the warriors as he landed, and protein rich, sickly, white synth-blood, sucrosol, sprayed out, mixing with spurting oil and Burias-Drak'shal's sizzling, scarlet vital fluids.

Another three possessed Chaos Space Marines launched themselves over the side of the Gorgon, landing amidst the Praetorians, roaring their dedications to the Chaos gods. Chainaxes and power swords rose and fell in bloody arcs and their bolt pistols barked as they fired into the tight press.

The enemy was all around him and Burias-Drak'shal lashed out blindly, ripping mechanical arms from torsos and punching his talons through chests. The Praetorians were the most highly advanced servitors created by the Adeptus Mechanicus, fitted with neuro-linked targeting processors and enhanced combat brain-stem implants, as well as heavy weaponry and powerfully armoured shells. They were easily a match for a Legiones Astartes warrior-brother.

One of the berserkers was clubbed to the ground by a heavy blow from a chaingun, mechanics and augmetics whirring as they lent immense power to the blow. Placing a heavy foot upon the downed warrior's chest, buckling his power armour, the Praetorian levelled its cannon towards the Word Bearer's helmet, which was torn to shreds beneath the power of the burst of fire it unleashed. The headless corpse twitched as it died.

Burias-Drak'shal caught a swinging, metal arm in one hand and with a powerful twist ripped it from its mechanical socket. Lashing out with his other hand, he slashed his claws across the head of another, tearing its red blinking eye free and ripping away a chunk of skull and brain with it. A spinning cannon was levelled at his back, but he spun around, the daemon within him sensing the danger. He knocked the weapon to the side using the Skitarii's dismembered arm as a club. Gunfire burst from the barrels, tearing apart a pair of Praetorians.

A heavy blow smashed into his head and Burias-Drak'shal staggered to the side, straight into another swinging metal arm that smashed into his high gorget. He was slammed backwards, falling to the floor of the roaring Gorgon, and a multi-barrelled cannon swung around towards him. The barrels of the gun were shorn off with the sweep of a power sword and a burst of bolt fire knocked the Skitarii backwards, allowing Burias-Drak'shal the time to regain his feet.

He came up fast, the talons of one hand swinging up in a slashing uppercut, ripping the head from a Praetorian, even as the warrior-brother that had saved him was slain, a hole appearing in his chest as a burst of cannon fire ripped through him. Holy Astartes blood splashed over Burias-Drak'shal's face, congealing even as it landed on his pale skin, and he grabbed the rotating cannon in his hands as it swung in his direction. The barrels halted instantly under his daemonic, crushing grip. He wrenched the metal out of shape and smoke rose from the mechanics of the weapon.

With a barked roar, he slammed his fist into the Praetorian's head, pulverising its skull. Burias-Drak'shal hurled it into one of its comrades, slamming it against the thick metal interior of the Gorgon.

The next minute passed in a flurry of bloodshed and gunfire. Burias-Drak'shal alone stood on his feet. Every Skitarii had been ripped and hacked apart, and lay twitching and sparking on the floor of the super-heavy vehicle. His fallen brethren lay unmoving, their souls having passed on to the Ether.

Burias-Drak'shal reached out and gripped a heavy, metal hatch, the metal bending out of shape beneath his grip as he wrenched it from its hinges. A withered servitor was revealed, hard-wired into the cabin of the vehicle, its sightless eyes staring forward and its arms connected directly to the gearshift and steering column of the tank. He grabbed the wretch around its throat and ripped it out of the cabin amid a shower of sparks and pale, sickly blood. It was ripped in half, its lower torso still attached to the machine, and its mouth moved soundlessly as milky fluid rose in its throat. The super-heavy vehicle came to a halt.

Burias intoned the words of binding and Drak'shal was pushed back within, fighting against the strength of its master. The overgrown tusks that protruded from his mouth retracted painfully and his long talons receded back into his hands. His posture straightened and he was once again the elegant, controlled warrior, though his body was ravaged and exhausted, the after-effects of possession.

'Coryphaus,' he spoke.

'Speak, Icon Bearer,' said the vox reply.

'Met the foe, head on,' said Burias, breathing heavily. 'My warriors fought well. More have advanced around us. Beware the Gorgons.'

'Acknowledged.'

'You wish me to return to the bulwark, Coryphaus?'

'No. The enemy has committed to the attack. They may have left their command unprotected. Continue your advance. Drive through them and kill their commanders. Succeed and the Cult of the Anointed will embrace you, young one.'

Wiping blood from his face, his breathing having almost returned to normal, Burias nodded his head.

'It will be done, my Coryphaus.'

CHAPTER EIGHTEEN

THE ANTI-AIRCRAFT BATTERIES tore the heavens apart overhead, but the Warmonger was focused only on the Leman Russ battle tank climbing the embankment towards him. The Dreadnought stood motionless as a battle cannon shell streaked past its shoulder and its armoured plates were peppered with explosive heavy bolter rounds.

The Warmonger stepped heavily to the side, into the path of the tank. As it breached the top of the battlement, its front lifting up into the air, the Dreadnought reached up with its massive power claw and brought the vehicle to a screaming halt. Servos groaned as it held the tank and its huge mechanical feet slid backwards beneath the vehicle's weight and momentum. Its underbelly was less armoured than its front and the Warmonger fired its weaponry, the rapid firing rounds punching through the undercarriage, shredding the weakling mortals within and tearing through the Leman Russ's vital systems.

The Chaos Dreadnought's servos whined as it exerted its strength and pushed the tank back the way it had come, sending it toppling end over end down the embankment to smash into the front of another battle tank.

'Kill for the Warmaster!' the Dreadnought roared as it refought the battle for the Emperor's palace in its damaged mind. 'Destroy the Emperor, the betrayer of the Great Crusade!'

BODIES FELL ALL around Kol Badar. Many of them were already dead, though their timed grav-chutes were in operation and slowed their descent mere metres above the ground. Still, thousands of living drop-troopers were landing all along the second tier and the open space behind the first, and he fired off controlled bursts left and right as he killed.

The attack had been well coordinated, timed to perfection. The first drop-troopers had landed just as the line of tanks had emerged from the cloud wall and just after a scything attack run by air that had cost him many warriors and war machines of the dark gods.

It was a well-organised attack, but one that was ultimately flawed. Given an inordinate amount of time, the enemy would prevail, for their numbers were great, but time was not on the Imperials' side. Even he, Kol Badar, who felt the touch of the dark gods only faintly, could feel the birth tremors of the Gehemehnet. He knew that the enemy would feel it too. They would be fearful and rightly so.

In the meantime, the enemy would die upon his warriors' blades.

THE HAEMONCULUS ATTACHED to Techno-Magos Darioq via aqueduct cables flooded his system with suppressants and holy vital fluids, filtering his veins and cables for viruses. Red robes hid the tumorous, cancer-ridden flesh of the stunted creature that had been bred in the nutrient tanks of Mars. It diverted the diseases and weaknesses of the flesh into itself so that they did not afflict him; such was its purpose in life.

He quoted the fifteenth Universal Lore to himself, 'Flesh is fallible, but ritual honours the machine-spirit', and he intoned a prayer to the Omnissiah as his system was cleansed.

Nevertheless, he recognised something amiss within the frail remnants of his flesh body and he opened up the cortex channels to the right-hand side of his brain in order to determine its purpose. Synapses sparked and he realised that what he felt were crude and fleshy emotions: tension, trepidation and anger.

Such base, human things, emotions, yet he found them intriguing as well as deplorable.

It had been a long time since last he had stepped foot upon planet c6.7.32, what the Elysians called Tanakreg. He accessed the hard memories of his secondary brain units and one of the myriad arrays of screens within the control centre of his airship flashed with data.

It showed his report to the Fabricator Tianamek Primus, dated over two thousand years earlier, though his current brain units had no record of him having scribed them.

Access to primary expeditionary focus/purpose denied. Magos Metallurgicus Annonus unable to determine material make-up of structure. Impervious. Logis cogitator augurs recommended path – terraform c6.7.32 and dissemble discovery. Magos Technicus Darioq to fabricate auditory station, and post watch over c6.7.32.

That was the source of the alien emotions of tension and trepidation that he had felt in the past two millennia. None had sought out that which he had been unable to breach, yet here was a powerful enemy of the Omnissiah on c6.7.32. It was imperative that they did not uncover the structure that he had gone to such pains to eradicate from all Imperial and accessible Mechanicus records.

But anger had nothing to do with the exploratory expedition he had led. That strange, hot temper had been brought upon him by the nature of the foe. He could feel the affront to the Machine-God in their essence, in the unholy constructions that they had defiled beyond all heresies.

Their machines, infused with the essence of daemonic warp entities, were the greatest corruption that the adepts of Mars could contemplate, a blasphemy that made all other blasphemies pale. All thinking machineries of the Mechanicus had souls within their flesh, for a soulless sentient machine is the epitome of true evil; and upon the battlefield, raging beyond the concealing clouds of blind-smoke, were machineries that had been polluted by their merging with the soulless entities of the warp. A soulless sentience is the enemy of all.

Such heresies were utterly wrong and Darioq was both revolted and horrified by how low the Legion of the Word Bearers had stooped. He shut off the receptors and synapses that synched his right brain hemisphere and the uncomfortable feelings instantly vanished. All that remained was the irrefutable fact that the enemy made use of sacrilegious, dangerous machineries that were an affront to his god and that they needed to be neutralised, their heresies eradicated and their hold over c6.7.32 removed.

His mechadendrites plugged into the central control column and, connected as he was to the delicate sensors on the outside of the hull, he registered the field of disruption that spread out in a cone from the enemy's tower. At his impulse, the command ship was lowered towards the ground. It was imperative for him to maintain contact and hence control over his thousands of Skitarii warriors. If he were cut off from them and his adepts then his entire army would grind to a halt.

Vast turbine engines rotated in their housings as the airship began to descend, the linking cable that connected it to the holy Ordinatus *Magentus* drawing it in towards the docking station on its upper deck.

One of the servo-arms of Darioq's quad-manifold rotated, whining softly, and its clamp-like jaws eased open.

'Enginseer Kladdon, open the hiemalis chamber and bring forth my blessed cogitation units.'

One of the red-robed junior priests behind him lowered the head of his power halberd in respect for his master's order and stepped towards one of the walls of the command centre. He spoke the words of awakening as he pressed the buttons of the hiemalis unit ritualistically, timing his speech to coincide with the correct sequence of buttons. With a blessing to the machine-spirit he gripped the sunken circular handle and, as he incanted the correct words beseeching the unit for its acquiescence, he pulled the drawer open.

Fog billowed from the unit as the ice-cold air within reacted to the heat outside. Held within a long shelf were over a dozen carefully stored bell jars. Within each jar was a blessed brain hemisphere held in static charged null-liquid. One of Darioq's servo-arms reached forward, hovering over several of the jars before the magos selected the required unit, and his servo-arm gently lifted it free.

Another servo-arm folded down and grasped the top of one of the bell jars protruding from the massive power generator he bore, and as he muttered the required intonations of supplication, mechadendrites whirred as he loosened the cog-shaped bolts fixing the bell jar to him. Needle-like incision spikes clicked out of the centres of other mechadendrite tentacles and were carefully inserted into the cog-shaped holes revealed with the removed bolts. They turned and with a hissing sound the bell jar was lifted clear. He felt the loss of information and processing power of the brain unit like a vague emptiness within him.

Swiftly and precisely he placed this brain unit within the gap in the hiemalis unit and attached the new bell jar to his core systems. Fresh information that he had not accessed for many centuries flooded through him, including memories and algorithms that had departed from him completely when he had disconnected the brain unit.

Much of the content of this brain unit would have been classed as heretical by some of the priesthood of Mars, but Darioq had felt driven to re-synch with the hemispheres within the bell jar. This was the unit that he had utilised when he had been part of the explorator team that had first investigated planet c6.7.32, and it had none of the synapse burns that altered and neutered many of the right brain functions.

This was a *creative* brain unit. Only a few secretive and covert members of the priesthood would dare to access such a component. *The knowledge of the ancients stands beyond question*, the tenets said, and for him to utilise a creative thinking brain unit to make adaptations and improvisations to mechanics, as he had done in the past when wired into this particular bell jar, was at best the height of hubris and, at worst, heresy of the worst kind.

His devotion to the Machine-God, Deus Mechanicus, and its conduit manifestation, the Omnissiah, was unwavering. To deny the effectiveness of such a creative drive when prescribed methodology would fail was abject foolishness, but even as these thoughts ran through his mind, he recognised the danger inherent within them. He must not utilise this brain unit for long periods, or he risked his whole being. Such dogmatism is folly, he thought. I must retain my dogmatism. The conflicting impulses gave him pause, but the new addition was the more dominant presence.

'Tech-priests, go forth and ready the plasma reactors of the Ordinatus.

And bring the void shields up to full power,' Magos Technicus Darioq said. The robed figures bowed their cog-bladed power halberds in compliance and left the command shrine.

His cogitator units had judged the potency of the weapons of the enemy and calculated the likelihood of damage to the blessed Ordinatus. Any moderate risk of damage was to be avoided, thus spoke the tenets, and he had previously determined not to advance the giant war machine until the enemy forces had been pushed back by 7.435 Mechanicus standard units, back to the third defensive tier.

Now he thought differently. He remodelled the algorithms of trajectory and manifest firepower, and a flurry of numbers scrolled down the screens lining the walls of the command shrine.

If the energy of the rear void shields was redirected to the frontal arc then the probability of success rose exponentially the more power that he diverted there. Such a thing may be deemed heresy, for the STC explicitly stated the correct shield levels and to alter them was to ignore the teachings of the elders. But if his mission on planet c6.7.32 was compromised then it would be of no matter. He deemed the minor heresy a lesser evil than what would occur if the enemy breached the walls of the xenos structure, and he began the complex calculations necessary to adapt the systems of the Ordinatus to his will.

SCORES OF VALKYRIES were being ripped apart by the relentless anti-aircraft fire that speared up through the roiling black clouds. Thousands of the Elysians drop-troopers were slaughtered as they plummeted down through the atmosphere at terminal velocity, but still others survived and Laron prayed that the other storm trooper platoons were amongst them.

It was a baffling experience, to be falling alongside something so massive. They had launched from their Valkyrie above the tower and he had been falling past it for the last few minutes. That such a thing could be so high was inconceivable, the engineering impossible, but there it was in front of his eyes. It made him feel physically ill and he could hear strange voices in his head. The thing seemed to exert a gravitational pull of its own and he angled away from it, so as not to be drawn too close.

'Keep your distance from the tower,' he said into his micro-bead, but the thing merely fed back a blare of roaring, horrifying sounds in his ears and he doubted that any heard his order.

He angled further away from the tower, hoping that his storm troopers would follow his lead, but even as he did so he felt something tugging at him, pulling him in closer, towards the hateful construction.

He muttered a prayer to the Emperor and felt the pull slacken enough for him to angle as far from the tower as was feasible while staying on target. The surface of the tower seemed to pulse and waver, and he felt hot blasts of air spilling from it, disrupting his descent, bustling him from side to side.

He was rapidly closing on the roiling, black smog clouds circling the tower and he was pleased to have his rebreather mask. As soon as he hit the smoke he felt terror rise within him. There were *things* within the oily cloud and they slashed at him with their claws, their red, glowing eyes burning fiercely in the gloom as he screamed past them.

Wind whipped at him, drawing him off course, and he cried out as something raked a series of deep cuts across his arms and chest. It was more from shock than pain, for his heavy carapace armour ensured the wounds did little real damage, but such an attack startled him. He had the impression of insubstantial creatures flying alongside him.

Pushing these thoughts from his mind, he turned into a steep dive, legs held together and arms clasped tightly to his sides, and prayed that he would escape the hellish clouds alive.

MARDUK CHANTED AS he held his hands out towards the Daemonschage. As he bound each additional daemon essence within its structure, another tiny line from the Book of Lorgar flashed into existence upon its surface.

The true names of the daemonic entities contained within appeared between each line of the holy script and the beings of the warp screamed in hatred as they were sucked from the Ether and sealed within. The bell was vibrating slightly, creating a low hum that would have been impossible to hear with mere human ears.

His hands shook with the power of the summoning, and a bead of sweat rolled down his forehead from the exertion. He was vaguely aware of explosions in the skies above and of dark shapes falling around him, but his entire concentration was focused upon the Daemonschage, and its complex binding incantations.

The pressure in his head increased and he felt the strength of the warp building within him. Still, his faith was unwavering and he bound the daemons of the warp to his will with the power of his word. The corners of his mouth rose in a smile as he incanted, relishing the feeling of sheer joy that came with control over the entities of Chaos.

VARNUS CROUCHED, UNMOVING atop the towering Gehemehnet wall, enthralled and horrified. The air at the top of the tower was electric and he could see dim, shadowy shapes of daemons being pulled screaming and clawing into the massive bell that hung over the endless drop of the tower's chimney. The corpses hanging in the chains twitched and convulsed, and he reeled backwards in shock as a body fell from the sky to land upon that spider web of chain, crashing amongst the corpses with bone breaking force.

The body jerked as the chains broke its fall and the man's back, and the body hung for a moment before it continued downwards, spiralling madly, down into the depths of the planet. A moment later, a roar of hot air was expelled up the hollow shaft, and Varnus saw more bodies falling around him. He decided that he must truly have lost his sanity, if he was seeing men falling from the heavens.

Still they fell, some tumbling down into the gaping maw of the Gehemehnet, as if it were drawing them to it, and others flashing past him, smashing into the outside of the tower. He jumped to his feet as a figure fell directly towards him, scrambling out of the way as it smashed into stone with a sickening sound. The man lay broken and very dead, his legs and arms bent beneath him, blood splattering out over the stones and across Varnus's legs. He stood, looking down at the helmeted corpse dumbly. It was Imperial!

Another figure landed beside him, though this one's descent was slowed by a tech-device upon its back. He landed awkwardly, one of his legs buckling beneath him with a sickening, cracking sound.

The figure cried out in pain and fell to one knee. He held a lasgun in his hand and Varnus could see his pale blue eyes behind his visor. He saw the twin-headed eagle symbol of the aquila pinned to the man's chest and he felt a surge of recognition. This was an Imperial Guardsman! The Imperium had come to liberate Tanakreg!

He shouted out in joy and dropped to his knees to help the man, but the man scrambled back away from him.

'I am a friend!' Varnus called out, holding his empty hands up, showing the man he was unarmed. 'I am a citizen enforcer of this planet! Thank the Emperor you have come at last!'

GUARDSMAN THORTIS CRIED out in pain and pulled the rebreather mask from his face. His leg was a shattered wreck beneath him, but he pushed back with all his force away from the vile figure. His heart was thundering in his head and his stomach churned with the absolute *wrongness* of everything around him.

Insane daemon speakers blared a deafening, evil cacophony of hatred and corpses were strewn up in chains. A devil Legiones Astartes chanted vile words that made his skin crawl and *things* unnatural and maddening flickered at the corners of his vision.

The wretched follower of the ruinous powers clawed at him, his eyes as red as a daemon's and a burning eight-pointed star upon his forehead. His mouth was nothing but a grilled speaker-box amidst a tight fitting, black mask, and he spoke in the foul language of Chaos.

Amid the hateful, guttural speech of the traitor, he heard the word *Emperor*.

'Speak not His name, enemy of mankind,' Thortis spat and levelled his lasgun at the hated foe.

THE SPOKEN WORDS of the Guardsman meant nothing to Varnus, the sound coming out of the man's mouth little more than a garbled mess of childish sounds to his ears. In confusion he saw the hatred burning on the man's face and he saw the lasgun lower towards him.

A flash of anger burned hot within him, and he felt his blood pounding in his head. He had offered his hand in aid to this soldier, and he was turning his weapon on him! The shock of betrayal quickly changed to anger and his hand flashed out, knocking the barrel of the gun to one side. The lasgun blast seared across his shoulder and he hissed in pain. Without thinking, his survival instinct taking over, he drove the fingers of his other hand up into the man's throat, crushing his windpipe. He stepped in close and slammed his elbow into his head.

The Guardsman fell heavily, choking, his pale blue eyes bulging, but Varnus hauled him back to his feet.

'I was trying to help you and this is how you repay me?' he roared, weeks of repressed rage and shame rising to the surface. Holding onto the man's jacket front with one hand, he thundered a punch into the man's face, splattering his nose.

'I curse you!' Varnus shouted and landed another punch into the soldier's face, ignoring the man's feeble attempts to deflect the blow. He pulled the helmet off the man's head with a sharp rip and threw it over the edge of the Gehemehnet tower. He saw that the man's hair was sandy blond, and for some reason even this made him angry. He saw nothing but red, felt nothing but rising hatred, loathing and rage, and gripping the man with both hands, he smashed his forehead into his face, and let him fall to the stone.

'I curse you,' he screamed once more, kicking the soldier hard in his side. He knelt down on top of the man and gripped his head in both hands.

'And I curse the False Emperor!' he screamed as he slammed the soldier's head into the stone.

LARON LANDED SMOOTHLY, rolling to his feet and flicking the release of the heavy grav-chute with one hand, while he blasted his hellpistol into the face of an enemy Chaos Space Marine. His ornate plasma pistol appeared in his other hand and he fired it into the chest of a second enemy warrior, the screaming plasma searing through ceramite, flesh and bone. Superheated air vented from the potent weapon, hissing like an angry serpent.

Storm troopers were landing all around him, laying down a withering hail of fire from their overcharged, gyro-stabilised hellguns. All vox communication was jammed and Laron wondered how many of his soldiers had survived the drop even if their Valkyrie had not been gunned down on the approach.

Thousands of drop-troopers were descending through the hellish clouds above and falling along the ridge of the second enemy embankment, just behind the long first line. Some squads of Laron's storm troopers had been briefed to attack along the second tier, targeting the enemy's static war machines with melta weaponry, but the majority of his elite cadre were targetting the bunkers along the first battlement.

While Laron's squad laid down a protective curtain of fire, one of his men knelt and stuck a melta charge to the thick door of the bunker.

'Clear,' yelled the man, stepping back, and the charge detonated inwards, melting the thick metal to liquid.

A second storm trooper stepped forward, kicked the heavy, metal door open and filled the interior with a spray of roaring promethium from his flamer, before pulling back, allowing Laron to lead the hellgun-armed soldiers in.

The walls were scorched black from the flames and the advanced auto-sensor systems in Laron's helmet adjusted to the gloom instantly. He fired both his pistols into the massive shape of the first Chaos Space Marine and his soldiers' hellguns shot down the next, even as the enemy swung their weapons to bear.

A blast from a lascannon, blindingly bright in the confines of the bunker, ripped a head-sized hole through one of his men and tore the arm off another, before striking the bunker wall behind them. A pair of enemy warriors had thrown down their missile launchers and hurled themselves at the storm troopers, their armour blackened and still burning in places.

Laron ducked beneath the huge slashing knife of the first and fired his plasma pistol into the giant Chaos Space Marine's groin, followed by a sharp double-tap from his hellgun into the traitor's head as he fell back.

Four hellgun shots slammed into the second enemy warrior, but it did not slow him, and he barrelled into the storm troopers with a daemonic roar. The traitor rammed two men back against the thick wall of the bunker with the sickening sound of breaking bones and swung his fist into the face of another as he rose, shattering the bones of the man's jaw.

The lascannon-wielding enemy swung the heavy weapon like a club, sending Laron flying into a wall. He slid to the ground gasping for breath. Raising both his pistols from his prone position, he fired into the chest of the Chaos Space Marine, who twitched and fell.

Laron pushed himself to his feet to see the last traitor fall to his knees. Even as the Chaos Space Marine died, he broke the neck of a storm trooper, before a trio of hellgun shots took him in the head.

Four of Laron's men were dead, but the bunker had been neutralised.

'Out,' he shouted. 'To the next one.'

CONCENTRATED HEAVY WEAPON fire ripped through the Imperial armoured advance and the embankment was littered with scores of motionless and burned out vehicles. Battle cannons roared and the heavy siege shells fired at close range, obliterated dozens of bunkers.

The south end of the embankment was overrun, armoured vehicles rolling up and over the defensive position. Hellhound tanks spewed sheets of flaming promethium, engulfing dozens of Word Bearers before heavy weapons pierced their fuel tanks and they exploded in rising balls of fire, sending the searing, flammable liquid spraying out in all directions.

Hulking, super-heavy Gorgon assault tanks roared up the steep embankment, their side-sponsons spewing flaming death and autocannon turrets raking along the ridge top.

Streaking lascannon beams and smoking krak missiles zeroed in on the Mechanicus vehicles, but nothing was able to halt their advance. As they reached the top of the tier, their huge assault ramps were dropped and the heavy battle servitors within surged out, chainguns spinning and multi-meltas hissing.

'The reserve is committed, my lord. Have engaged the enemy behind the second tier,' said the growling voice of Bokkar, Kol Badar's Anointed sergeant, across a closed vox-channel.

'Understood,' replied Kol Badar. The reserve had occupied the third tier, guarding against the enemy dropping in behind the main battle force of the Host.

The Kataphractoi followed in the wake of the Gorgons, Skitarii warriors hard-wired into tracked units. They roared forward, heavy bolters barking and missile pods sending streams of self-propelled explosives towards the Word Bearers.

Echelons of Thunderbolts screamed through the air, flying low, tearing up the ground with their strafing gunfire. Several of the fighters were blown out of the sky, lascannon fire and anti-aircraft cannons tearing through wings and cockpits, and they smashed down into the ground, carving burning furrows through the earth and killing all in their path.

Still more drop-troopers fell from the sky, though for every soldier who landed ready to fight, another four smashed lifeless into the earth. Marauder bombers and Valkyries descended in flames through the wildly circling black clouds overhead to crash amid the chaotic battle.

Kol Badar grinned at the spectacle of carnage around him as he gunned down dozens of enemy Guardsmen as they landed. There would be no break in the fighting until victory was achieved and all his enemies were dead or dying upon this field of battle.

Flames washed over him, but he stepped through the conflagration and smashed the weapon out of a Guardsman's hands, placing the barrel of his combi-bolter against the chest of the soldier, relishing the look of terror on the man's face. He pulled the trigger and the man was smashed to the ground, his chest blown open.

'Captains of the Legion, pull your warriors back to the second tier.'

The evacuation of the first line of defence was methodical and organised. The Coryphaus had dictated his orders to his underlings and each enacted his designs with practised efficiency.

Under the covering fire of the restrained Dreadnoughts and war machines of the Host, the warrior-brothers pulled back. They walked with unhurried, measured steps as they laid down overlapping enfilades of fire against the combat servitors emerging from their transports, specialist weaponry destroying vehicles and tanks.

Kol Badar and his Anointed stood at the base of the second tier, clearing the area of incoming drop-troopers, their roaring weapons ripping easily through the lightly armoured foe. They were practically immune to the Guardsmen's fire and carved through them with ease, though the number of the foe was starting to clog the open space with bodies.

He saw the Warmonger stepping resolutely backwards, his roaring cannons ripping apart the foe, and the heavy flamer slung beneath his power claw engulfing dozens in flames.

LARON DROPPED OFF the stepped rampart of the embankment, snapping off shots with his pistols at the retreating enemy, before taking cover behind the wrecked chassis of a Gorgon. They were masterful in their order and precision. Each squad that backed off was supported by angled lines of troops firing their bolters in controlled bursts. It was like attacking a damned fortification. The lines of the enemy were angled like those of the greatest fortresses, with the strongest points, the 'towers', being squads bearing heavy weapons. The Guardsmen were naturally drawn towards the apparently weaker points, veering away from the heavy weapons, but this brought them into the deadly killing ground where the enemy's guns were able to assail them from both sides.

'Where is that damned infantry?' he snarled. He desperately needed the massed ranks of the Skitarii foot cohorts to arrive, for he had not the men to tackle the retreating foe, and the incoming Elysians were being cut down in swathes.

As if on cue, the first ranks of the tech-guard cohort appeared over the edge of the battlements, tracked weaponry rolling forward at their side. They began to fire as they marched resolutely forwards.

The tracked units of the tech-guard unleashed the power of their arcane construction at the Chaos Space Marines as they backed away. The air crackled with energy as coruscating lightning leapt from humming bronze spheres to strike the foe. The ground was ripped up as bizarre weapons fired, causing great rents to rip along the ground, tossing the enemy into the air. Heavy, quad-barrelled cannons pumped fire into the foe, but the traitors, recognising the new threat, began to target the tracked units of the Mechanicus with missiles and other heavy weapons fire.

Laron's eyes flashed to the timer counting down in the corner of the head-up display in his helmet and he swore. The second wave of drop-troopers was about to be launched and the anti-aircraft fire from the palace had not yet been silenced. The first wave had been devastated and it looked as though the second would face a similar barrage.

Time was running out.

CHAPTER NINETEEN

Brigadier-General Havorn cursed as the pict-screen before him flickered, the detailed map-schematic shorting out. The Chimera bumped its occupants about as it rolled across the salt plain in the wake of the tech-guard cohorts. Sweat was dripping down Havorn's face.

Bestial roars and screaming mixed with hissing static blared out of the vox-unit suddenly, replacing the relayed chatter of the senior captains.

'What the hell's all that?' Havorn snarled.

'I don't know, sir, but its been flooding the less powerful voxes for the past hundred metres or so,' replied his adjutant. 'I thought my set-up would be too powerful for it. Damn enemy's jamming our comms somehow.'

'Perfect. Looks like the rest of this war is going to be fought deaf, dumb and blind.'

'Your officers are good men, sir,' replied the man. 'They know their orders.'

'Move us up closer to the front, Kashar. I want to at least be able to see what the hell is going on.'

'Is that wise, brigadier-general? You would be exposing yourself to unnecessary danger.'

'What do you think is going to happen if we lose this battle, Kashar? We lose this battle and we are all dead men. Move us up closer. I want to be able to see the outcome with my own eyes.'

Burias-Drak'shal hacked left and right, smashing the Skitarii out of his way with sweeps of his spiked icon. At the Coryphaus's order he had remounted his Land Raider and led his warriors straight into the massed ranks of the enemy cohorts, meeting them within another of the slowly dispersing cloud walls. The vehicles had ploughed through the enemy ranks, crushing hundreds beneath their heavy tracks.

The Rhinos disabled by the foe were left behind, the warrior-brothers within abandoned to their fate. They would kill many before they fell. It was an honour to die for the Legion.

They had ridden deep into the heart of the enemy formation, until his Land Raider was finally brought to a halt, its hull pierced by countless melta-blasts, its tracks torn and ragged, and its engine reduced to molten metal.

Even then, Burias-Drak'shal refused to be slowed, leading his coterie of warrior-brothers out of the ruined vehicle, roaring and screaming their battle-cries. He pulverised the enemy in his path, shrugging off countless wounds and gunshots that would have killed any other warrior-brother within the Host. The Word Bearers carved a bloody swathe through the Skitarii cohorts, urged ever onwards by the Icon Bearer, following the frenzied warrior deeper into the enemy formation. These were the regular troopers of the Adeptus Mechanicus, indentured warriors who had only minor augmetic enhancements: eye-piece targeters, altered neural pathways, enhanced lungs and such, and they died easily beneath the fury of the possessed warrior and his battle-brothers.

Hissing ichor dripped from his wounds and his armour was cracked and blistering, yet Burias-Drak'shal continued on, ploughing through the enemy, bashing them out of his path. His warriors' chainaxes rose and fell, and bolt pistols blasted as they followed behind him.

Burias-Drak'shal blocked a swinging double-handed axe with the shaft of his icon and grabbed a hovering metallic tentacle attached to the red-robed Tech-Priest's spine, pulling the adept towards him. He leant forwards, snarling as the priest stumbled, and ripped out his throat with a bite, tasting putrid oils and blood-replacement fluids in his mouth. Knocking the priest to the ground he continued to run, impaling a gun-servitor upon the point of the icon and hurling it into the air as its heavy bolter armament ripped chunks out of his shoulder pad.

He saw armoured personnel carriers through the press of bodies up ahead and roared as he sensed that the prey was close, sprinting on with renewed vigour. With a flick of his talons he decapitated another foe, and smashed another out of his way with the return blow, a brutal backhand swing that almost ripped the head of another Skitarii from its shoulders.

THE FIGHTING BETWEEN the first and second tier was brutal and bloody. The daemon engines of the Word Bearers unleashed countless barrages of warp infused shells into the no-man's-land, killing thousands. The Skitarii warriors marched in perfect unison into the guns of the Word Bearers protected behind the fortified bulwark of the second embankment and hundreds of them were torn apart by the concentrated fire.

'Ancients of battle,' roared the Warmonger, 'be released from your shackles and kill once more in the name of Lorgar!'

Thirty Dreadnoughts roared and screamed wordlessly, straining against the inscribed chains that bound them. The chains were suddenly released and the bloodthirsty machines, all semblance of their sanity having long abandoned them, were unleashed on the enemy as they pushed up the second tier.

They surged over the parapet, their ancient weapons roaring and booming, and they slammed into the enemy, hurling them into the air with great sweeps of their power claws and piston-driven siege hammers. Multi-bladed power gauntlets scythed through the front ranks of the foe, cleaving men and Skitarii in half, and screaming chainfists the length of two men carved down through the bodies of others, throwing blood and chunks of flesh in every direction.

Dreadnoughts stood atop the bulwark, missiles firing from their inbuilt weapon systems, detonating amongst the foe in fiery blasts. One Dreadnought, screaming insanely, turned its rapid firing autocannons upon power armoured warrior-brothers, his ability to distinguish between friend and foe lost in the madness of battle.

The Warmonger strode towards the machine and struck it to the ground with one mighty sweep of its arm. It kicked and screamed madly as it tried to right itself, and the Warmonger unleashed the power of its guns into the sarcophagus casing of the Dreadnought, seeking to put an end to its struggles. Its kicking ceased and its screams became a gurgled hiss. A cadaverous, jawless head could be seen within the cracked sarcophagus, the skull malformed and covered with bony, spiny growths coated in sickly pus.

'You are released from your bondage, warrior-brother,' intoned the Warmonger before it turned its guns once more towards the numberless enemy swarming over the barricade.

'CORYPHAUS, THE SMOKE-WALL is abating. The Ordinatus is come,' said Bokkar.

'What?' growled Kol Badar. 'The Mechanicus would never risk the war machine until its safety was assured.'

'Nevertheless, it is advancing across the salt plain, my lord. It will be in range of the daemon engines within the minute and will be ready to fire upon the palace within ten.'

'A curse upon them! Pull out from combat, Bokkar. Take a Thunderhawk and slow the damned thing down! Get the daemon engines to target it.'

'As you wish, Coryphaus.'

* * *

MY LORD JARULEK, *it is done. The Daemonschage is ready.*

Good, my acolyte, Jarulek replied. *Everything is set in motion. I will join you shortly.*

Jarulek opened his eyes from the deep trance. He sat in the restoration chamber, blinking against the thick, viscous liquid that he was immersed in. His arms were bare, the script-covered, pale and heavily muscled limbs pierced by dozens of pipes and needles, pumping him with biologics and serums. He had no wish for his underlings to realise just how taxing the creation of the Gehemehnet had been on his system, but the last twelve hours in the tank, deep in a trance and communion with the higher powers, had rejuvenated him.

The thick liquid evacuated from the chamber, sucked into gurgling pipes, and he sank to his feet. Chirumeks clustered around him, pulling free the tubes and pipes inserted into his veins and muscles, and he flexed his fingers. The time to rejoin the Host had come. It was mere hours until the alignment of planets took place, until the Gehemehnet awoke.

TECHNO-MAGOS DARIOQ STOOD impassively upon the secondary gantry deck of the Ordinatus as heavy calibre anti-aircraft batteries directed fire towards the Thunderhawk. The enemy's barrages had been as nothing to the Ordinatus, the incoming ordnance soaked up by flashing void shields, and its return fire darkened the air, overloading the gunship's shielding with ease.

The critically damaged Thunderhawk turned towards the Ordinatus, its pilot clearly fighting with its controls to guide it towards the target. It passed through the giant vehicle's void shields as its left wing tore loose, sending the gunship spinning, and the concentrated, servitor aimed quad-cannons ripped the hull apart, tearing the bulky aircraft in two. The rear half was engulfed in flames and exploded as the fire reached its fuel lines. The front half of the gunship fell from the sky, plummeting towards the Ordinatus, propelled by its velocity and the force of the explosion.

Techno-Magos Darioq calculated the trajectory and velocity of the incoming debris from his position and stood stone still as it slammed into the upper deck above. The metal grid was smashed asunder by the massive incoming weight and it skimmed along the metal, raising a shower of sparks as it ploughed through barricades and crane-structures. It screeched through one of the cannon batteries, instantly crushing a pair of ogryn servitor loaders, before careening off the edge and falling to the secondary gantry where Darioq stood.

The front section of the Thunderhawk screeched across the metal latticework towards him, but he did not move, and it ground to a halt just metres from him, as he had calculated.

Servitors rolled forwards on tracked units, dousing the flames with foam.

'Life signs remain,' said Darioq as he scanned the Thunderhawk, and the servitors retreated from the wreckage instantly. Heavy combat servitors rolled forwards, weapons raised, scanning for the enemy.

Red-armoured Chaos Space Marines emerged from the flames and the servitors fired upon the survivors. Several of the servitors were ripped apart by bolt fire, but others rolled forwards even as their fallen comrades were dragged aside by tentacled scavenger servitors for re-manufacture.

Darioq's four servo arms unfolded like the legs of a gigantic spider, the weapons systems built into their design humming into activation. Four of the enemy warriors were ripped apart by the fire from his potent weaponry.

With a roar, a bulky shape emerged from the wreckage, smashing through twisted, burning metal. Flaming promethium from this warrior's heavy weapon system engulfed the servitors, turning their flesh to liquid and detonating their ammunition drums.

BOKKAR ROARED AS he smashed his way towards the magos. Plasma pierced the reinforced plasteel plating of his Terminator armour and heavy bolt-rounds tore through his chest plate.

He unleashed the fury of his heavy flamer and roaring promethium engulfed the magos, hiding him from view. As the inferno dissipated, Bokkar could see that the flames had washed harmlessly over a bubble of protective energy surrounding the cursed Mechanicus priest, and he powered forwards, intent on smashing the magos apart with the force of his chain fist.

Bokkar stepped within the boundaries of the tech-priest's protective field and swung his chain fist around in a murderous arc. The blow never landed, as one of the servo-arms, hanging over the magos's shoulder like the barbed tail of a scorpion, snapped out and grabbed his arm, halting it mid-swing.

The servo-arm over the other shoulder grabbed his other arm, and he felt his blessed Terminator armour crack beneath the immense pressure that the whining arms exerted. The servo arms pulled out to each side sharply and both of Bokkar's arms were ripped from his body, spraying blood out in both directions.

He stared down dumbly at his armless torso and was cut in half by the magos's swinging power halberd, the cogged blade hacking through his midsection. He fell to the metal lattice floor.

He had failed his Coryphaus, failed his Legion and only damnation awaited him.

THE AIR TURNED electric as the massive plasma reactors roared to full power in readiness to fire. Fashioned from the same STC templates from which the grand Ordinatus Mars was constructed, the giant weapon's humming increased to painful decibels as it drew the reactors' energy into its power drums.

The pitch of the weapon rose beyond that of human hearing and the entire colossal structure of the Ordinatus began to shudder.

'Dispose of this in the inferno chambers,' said Darioq as he dropped the severed arms of the traitor Terminator beside the severed torso. The armour had been constructed by Mechanicus Forge Worlds over ten thousand years ago and he was loathe to destroy such a revered piece of artifice, but the enemy had long tainted it with its corruption.

He registered the rising pitch of the sonic destructor cannon, and reran the trajectory algorithms. Satisfied, he waited until the warning beacon began to flash within his inner systems, indicating that the Ordinatus was ready.

'Targeting locked, magos,' said the mechanised voice of one of his Tech-Priest subordinates.

'Initiate firing sequence,' Darioq intoned.

THE PALACE THAT had stood upon Tanakreg since it was populated two thousand years previously shuddered as the focused sonic beams ripped through it, shattering its structure at a molecular level. Fully three kilometres long from one end of the structure to the other, and rising hundreds of metres above the low-lying salt plains, the structure began to vibrate as its rocky substructure was rent with hundreds of cracking faults and weaknesses.

One section of the palace collapsed with a thundering roar that echoed across the battlefield as the cliff walls beneath it gave way. The fortified battlements atop the sprawling defensive structure were shattered and the anti-aircraft turrets and batteries ripped from their plascrete housings as more of the palace collapsed.

The whole mountainous outcrop from which the palace was carved disappeared beneath a rising cloud, and the thunder of its collapse made the earth beneath the feet of the battling armies shudder. The potent guns of the palace were silenced as the entire structure smashed to the ground.

A subterranean explosion rocked the earth and Darioq's delicate sensors picked up the faint hint of radiation as the plasma reactor buried deep beneath the ground was breached. A secondary subterranean explosion roared as the palace settled, and rock and debris was hurled hundreds of metres into the air.

A shockwave rippled out from the detonating plasma reactor, hurling tanks and men into the air as it whipped across the land before its power was spent.

The enemy's giant tower shook, dried mortar cracking and slipping from between its massive stone bricks, and a shudder ran up its length. Yet, denying the laws of the physical universe, it remained standing.

'WHAT IN THE Emperor's holy name was that?' asked Havorn as the Chimera ground to a halt. He scrambled out of the command tank, his blinking advisors and adjutant at his side, and the ever-present bulk of his ogryn bodyguard behind him.

Putting his magnoculars to his eyes, he saw the rising dust cloud where a moment before the towering presence of the palace had been located.

'Emperor be praised,' he exclaimed.

He laughed out loud in surprise and astonishment.

'When's our second wave of drop-troopers inbound?'

'Now sir, they should be falling as we speak,' answered his comms officer, who had been staring blankly at his useless machines since his vox communication had been silenced.

'And now they are safe from the wretched fire from those air turrets,' exclaimed Havorn's young adjutant. 'This is a good day for the Imperium indeed! Victory is assured!'

'Victory is never assured,' said Havorn as his eyes fell on the red-armoured Chaos Space Marines fighting their way free of the tech-guard cohorts. His augmented, ogryn bodyguard growled menacingly and took a step in front of the brigadier-general.

'Quick, sir!' said his adjutant, urgently.

'We have not the time,' said Havorn flatly, seeing the enemy carve a bloody exit from the mass of bodies and begin hurtling across the salt plain towards them. He pulled his gold-rimmed plasma pistol from his holster.

His entourage raised their weapons and sprayed the approaching warriors with gunfire. The ogryn roared as it planted its heavy feet and empty shells streamed from its ripper gun as it fired the weapon wildly. The Chimera behind them rotated its turret and multi-laser fire peppered the traitors, cutting several of them down. Only six Chaos Space Marines reached the brigadier-general's command group, but it was enough.

The first Chaos Space Marine ducked under the ogryn's heavy swinging arm and leapt forwards, smashing its tall, spiked icon into the head of Havorn's adjutant, pulverising his skull.

A burst of fire tore apart another of Havorn's men and the brigadier-general fired his plasma pistol in response, knocking back a chainsword wielding foe as the shot took him in the shoulder. He fired again quickly and despatched the traitor, streaming plasma engulfing his helmet.

This was the end, he thought. An ignominious end to his thirty-seven years within the Imperial Guard, hacked apart by brutal warriors behind his battle lines.

'Damn you, you traitorous whoresons!' he muttered and fired his pistol twice in quick succession, felling another of the two and half metre behemoths.

Two more of his entourage were hacked down and he backed further away.

He saw the loyal ogryn fall to the ground with a bestial roar. He wasn't a sentimental man by any stretch, but he felt pain as his faithful bodyguard fell to the ground, coughing blood from his lungs.

Havorn fired his pistol again and again, and felt the rising pain beneath his hand as the pistol overheated, venting super-heated air. With a snarl, he hurled it to the ground and drew his long bladed combat knife. It had been more than twenty years since it had tasted blood, back in the days when he was a captain of the storm troopers.

Only two of the enemy remained standing and they stalked towards him, wordlessly stepping away from each other to take him from both sides.

Havorn kept his eyes on the foe so as not to attract their attention to the massive form of the ogryn picking itself up behind them, blood running from the wounds on its arms and chest, and spilling from its mouth.

With a roar, the ogryn picked up one of the traitors, one massive hand upon the enemy's backpack and the other between his legs. It lifted the Chaos Space Marine high into the air and slammed it head first into the ground, cracking its neck.

The second traitor turned with a snarl and swung its icon two handed into the ogryn's legs, driving it to its knees. Releasing his grip on the haft of the hateful symbol of Chaos, the Chaos Space Marine leapt at the ogryn, its long talons extended for the killing blow.

Havorn cried out and surged forwards, but he was too slow and he saw the bodyguard fall, its throat ripped completely out, blood spurting from the fatal wound.

He drove his combat knife through a crack in the traitor's ceramite back plate, the blade sinking deep. Blood spurted from the wound, burning through Havorn's leather glove, and the enemy spun, his fist smashing into the brigadier-general's cheek, shattering the bone.

Pain exploded in his head and he fell back from the force of the blow. He saw the ogryn's large, mournful eyes as it tried desperately to aid its master before the Chaos Space Marine reached down and broke its neck with a brutal twist.

'Traitorous hellspawn,' spat Havorn.

'Hellspawn yes. Traitor, no,' replied the hateful, possessed traitor, his fang-filled maw forming the Low Gothic words with difficulty. The fangs retracted and the warrior shook his head, his daemonic visage melting away to leave a cold, pale handsome face.

'The Word Bearers Legion, blessed of Lorgar, are no traitors, wretched fool,' growled the warrior as he stalked towards Havorn.

'You and your wretched kin turned your back on the glorious Emperor and all of humanity to embrace damnation,' said Havorn, crawling back towards his fallen adjutant and the dead man's laspistol.

'The Emperor turned his back on us!' raged the traitor. 'Only through the unified worship of *true* divinities can mankind be saved. Your False Emperor is nothing more than a rotting corpse perched atop a golden high-chair, a puppet for bureaucrats and taxmen. And you pathetic humans pray to him? You are the lowest of scum, ignorant and embracing that ignorance.'

Havorn's hand slid behind him and closed on the grip of the laspistol.

'Your soul will be damned when you leave this world, while I will go to the blessed Emperor's side in glory and light,' said Havorn, trying to keep the bastard distracted.

'I say my soul is already damned in *this* world, and that there will be nothing but hell waiting for *you*,' said the traitor.

'I'll see you there,' said Havorn and he swung the laspistol up, firing it straight into the face of the Chaos Space Marine. The traitor fell backwards with a cry of anger and pain, and lay still.

Havorn pushed himself to his feet, pain throbbing from his shattered cheek-bone, and he began to stagger away.

A clawed hand wrapped around his neck from behind, and he was lifted into the air and turned to face the traitor. The wound on the traitor's forehead was closing as he watched, the bone knitting together and flesh re-forming over the bullet hole, leaving not a scratch upon the traitor's darkly handsome face.

'YES, I WILL see you in hell, human,' said Burias-Drak'shal as he plunged his clawed hand through the brigadier-general's chest. With one decisive wrench, he pulled the Elysian commander's still-beating heart from the old man's broken ribcage and watched as the life left his eyes. He held the beating heart to his mouth, tasting the sweet, warm blood, and threw the lifeless corpse dismissively to the ground.

The Chimera slammed into Burias-Drak'shal with shocking force, sending him flying out in front of the armoured personnel carrier. As he tried to rise to his feet it slammed into him again, and he disappeared beneath its whirling tracks, sixty tonnes of Imperial tank rolling over him.

A RIPPLE OF movement spread out from the base of the Gehemenhet, the blackened earth around the tower shimmering and wavering. Electricity coalesced down the tower and surged across the surface of the ground before dissipating. Glowing light began to spill from the mortar between the massive stone blocks, which began to bulge and warp like molten rubber. A daemonic, fanged face appeared within the stone, pushing outwards, straining to break into the mortal realm.

'Not just yet, precious,' said Jarulek, caressing the daemonic manifestation. Claws appeared in the stone, reaching out towards the Dark Apostle and he chuckled. He spoke a word in the language of the daemon and the creature recoiled, its face a mask of childish, shamefaced repentance.

'Not just yet,' he repeated and the daemon retreated back within the Gehemehnet.

CHAPTER TWENTY

FOR A DAY and night the Chaos Space Marines held the Imperials at bay, though they were driven slowly back, unable to contain the sheer numbers of the foe advancing against them. There were moments of brief respite in the action, as the Elysians gathered themselves for another push forwards, but always there were skirmishes and minor actions. The Skitarii tech-guard cohorts advanced tirelessly. Without the threat of the potent air defences that had been housed within the palace, the heavens were filled with Elysian and Imperial Navy aircraft, and Elysian drop-troopers descended through the darkness above to fall behind the enemy lines. Laron felt a touch of admiration and awe for the enemy, for they fought without rest as never-ending waves of the Imperials attacked, and they resisted every push and new attack with great fervour. He dismissed the thought as soon as it formed. To even think such a thing bordered on heresy.

Arcs of lightning reached out from the tower to ensnare Valkyries, Thunderbolts and drop-troopers that strayed close, and they were dragged through the air into its sheer stone sides. Pilots fought with their controls as the circuitry of their aircrafts was fried and they were drawn in towards the tower. There were no explosions, however; they merely disappeared as they should have struck stone, sucked into the Ether, to be fed upon by the army of daemons waiting just beyond the thin membrane separating the physical world from the warp.

Missiles screamed from beneath the wings of fighters, detonating explosively into the side of the daemon tower, and keening, high-pitched, maddening screams echoed across the skies. The attacks caused great rents to appear in the side of the tower and dark blood seeped from the wounds, thick and glutinous. Bombardment from the advancing Imperial line joined with the attack and battle cannons and siege ordnance were directed towards the giant tower as they too came into range, and bleeding pockmarks appeared across the sheer walls of the tower.

The tower's pain resonated within the soul of every warrior on the battlefield. The traitorous enemy seemed to become enraged by the power of the cries and they attacked with renewed fury. Laron staggered beneath the twisting power of Chaos that burst in waves from the tower, his head spinning and nausea making bile rise in his throat, and he knew that every Elysian on the field of battle suffered. Even the tech-guard warriors of the Adeptus Mechanicus seemed affected, pausing mid-battle in confusion at the unwholesome stimuli washing over them.

The Ordinatus continued its relentless, unstoppable advance and it levelled great sections of the Chaos defences with every titanic blast from its sonic weapon. Laron swore as enemy warriors and Elysians alike were caught in the blasts, their internal organs exploding and their bones shattering as the resonating blast ripped through them. The foes' ancient ceramite power armour shattered into millions of tiny shards beneath the potent Mechanicus weapon.

Clearly recognising the threat that the Ordinatus posed, the Chaos Space Marines hammered thousands of rounds of fire into its void shields, overriding them completely several times. Little damage was sustained by the behemoth before dutiful Tech-Priests and the army of servitors that swarmed over the machine restored the shields and it continued its relentless advance. Soon it would be within range of the cursed daemon tower. Laron prayed to the Emperor that the war machine would fell it.

The enemy was pushed back to the third tier and then back to the fourth. Here it seemed that they had determined to make their stand. They would hold the fourth tier or they would be slaughtered to a man. That suited Laron just fine. It was brutal, gritty fighting, but he took heart in the fact that they *were* grinding the enemy down, though it was a slow process. The enemy were being beaten, individual by individual, even though Imperial losses were horrific.

Communications remained completely inoperative and Brigadier-General Havorn's corpse had been found behind the tech-guard cohorts. Colonel Laron had donned a black armband in mourning for the old general, but he had taken over as the overall commander of the Elysian 72nd and 133rd with some reluctance. He set up crude communications using runners, flags, loudhailers and searchlights to organise attacks and retreats across the peninsula. Commissar Kheler proved an admirable and forthright advisor. Kheler tempered Laron's more foolhardy attitudes and the acting colonel developed an appreciation of Kheler's uncompromising expectations of the captains of the regiments. He allowed no talk of retreat and shot any man who showed the slightest sign of doubt or reluctance to perform his duties.

It will all be over soon, thought Laron. The enemy could not hold out for longer than hours at most. They would be victorious and they would return to the Crusade bearing Havorn's body with full honours.

This was the final push. They just needed to break the enemy from the fourth tier of defence and that would allow the Ordinatus to begin its barrage upon the cursed tower. It was unholy, the massive thing that rose up and pierced the skies over head. It must have been over a kilometre in diameter, and the aura of *wrongness* that it exuded made him feel physically sick. It must be destroyed.

If there was a portal to hell, it was surely this damned tower. With a nod to his subordinates, he indicated the commencement of the final push against the enemy. Flags were raised and powerful spotlights flashed the signal along the Imperial line.

The final chapter of the war would be played out in the next hours of engagement, for better or for worse.

VARNUS PACED BACK and forth behind the picketed slaves, a lasgun in his hands and his mind seething.

Blood filled his thoughts, anger and bitterness infusing him.

A hundred thousand workers, the last remaining Imperial subjects enslaved by the Word Bearers, had been herded together and picketed along the top of the third tier. Their chains were bolted into the plascrete battlements atop the earthen bulwark. There they stood, forming a living shield of bodies.

The red-armoured priest had dragged him there. Varnus's thoughts were confused and tormented. He had not realised at first what was going on. All he could hear were the voices of Chaos in his head and the pounding of blood, and he had stared at his bloody hands in dumb incomprehension.

A small shuttle had risen to the top of the Gehemahnet tower and a glorious, terrifying figure had emerged. Without any conscious will, he had dropped to the ground before this warrior-priest, screwing his eyes tightly shut and trying desperately to maintain control of his bodily functions. The figure radiated power and the essence of Chaos and Varnus found his insides twisting within him, his skin crawling and his head aching. He felt as if he was being turned inside out and pain wracked his body before he passed out.

He had awoken to find the first warrior-priest dragging him across the earth and he was deposited at the top of the fourth defensive line with the other slaves. The warrior had left him without a word, going to join in the raging battle.

The overseers had tried to chain him with the others, but they soon backed away from him after he had killed two of them and turned their needle-fingers upon them. Some of the slaves had cheered at that, but their cries died in their throats as Varnus looked at them. Perhaps they saw the same thing that made the overseers back away.

So he had waited with the slaves, unchained but bound there nonetheless. To go forward was to die, but to go back would only be to lengthen his torment. No, this was the battlefield where his eternal fate was to be determined and he waited whatever was to come with little care of the outcome. He stalked back and forth, letting his anger and bitterness build.

He raged as he felt the pain of the Gehemehnet and cried out in anguish as each shell screamed over his head to strike against it. The child was strong and it would take more than humble shells to destroy it, but still he roared with anger at the pain it endured.

Even here on the battlefield, the Discords blared at the slaves and Varnus knew now that they spoke the truth.

The Emperor was no god; he was a shattered corpse that clung to a last vestige of life by feeding off the deaths of those dedicated to him, and he cared not at all for Varnus or any of the other wretched, deceived slaves that invoked his name in prayer.

But there were true gods in the universe, ones that took an active interest in the lives of mortals: gods that granted strength to their followers and brought ruin upon their foes.

He had been blind, but now his eyes had been opened wide. He didn't hate the Imperial Guardsmen for their ignorance, for he too had been duped into believing the lies of the Ecclesiarchy. He hated them for betraying him and all these poor chained-up individuals. They had waited for liberation, enduring hell at the hands of their captors, and now they were being killed by those they had waited so long to save them.

He had picked up a lasgun from a corpse and he stood waiting for them to come to him. He would damn well kill as many of the bastards as he could before he was overcome. It would not be long before the fighting was upon them once more. The Chaos Space Marines were even now pulling back towards the fourth line and it was time for the slaves to do their part.

The overseers had attached the slaves' chains to dozens of massive living machines of horrific power and brutal will. These daemonic, infernal creations roared as they fired their ordnance into the advancing Imperial ranks and the closest to them were deafened by the sound. Scores more slaves were killed by the daemon engines, dragged beneath their claws and within reach of snapping mouth-tentacles of flesh and metal.

Varnus could feel the ceaseless anger of the daemon essences bound within the vehicles and he felt somehow akin to them. At some unheard command, the daemon engines were released from their bindings of words and shackles, and they surged over the barricade of the fourth and last defensive line, dragging the slaves forward between them.

Varnus screamed his hatred and pain, and followed, clutching his lasgun.

MARDUK STOOD ATOP the fourth and final embankment, watching as the enemy began its final push. The bombardment of artillery began afresh and the lines of the Host were hidden beneath plumes of smoke and flame. An endless wave of enemy troops and tanks spilled down into the open ground between the third and fourth lines of embankments, the intensity of gunfire lifting dramatically as they came into bolter range.

'The end is nigh,' commented Burias.

'It will be a close run thing. This will be the final battle' said Marduk. He glanced over at the Icon Bearer. 'Watch out for your nemesis, Burias. Fear the dreaded Chimera.'

Burias laughed out loud and rubbed his unmarked head with one hand.

'Damn thing hurt,' he said. He had returned to the lines of the Word Bearers, driving a battered enemy tank through the ranks of battle servitors, crushing them under its tracks, but they did not target it. It was an Imperial tank and it was not in their programming to raise a weapon against it. As it drew near the Host's lines a missile had sent it spinning into the air. Burias had crawled from the flaming wreckage and told a laughing Marduk of his tale.

He had gripped onto the tank as it thundered over him and had crawled across its hull before ripping away a hatch and slaughtering the occupants. Then he had ripped the driver's seat from its housing so that he could fit his bulk into the compartment before driving back towards the lines of the Host.

'I saw you speaking with the Coryphaus,' said Marduk.

Burias looked over at him and Marduk raised his eyebrows.

'Yes, First Acolyte.'

'Of what were you speaking?'

'Things of little consequence,' said Burias. 'The deployment of our Havoc squads, the use of the slaves.'

Marduk narrowed his eyes. The Icon Bearer was concealing something. He was a conniving snake, and Marduk had no doubt that he would turn on him if that would benefit him.

'The Dark Apostle comes!' Marduk heard one of the warrior-brothers exclaim, and he turned, his thoughts pulled away from Burias, inclining his head to witness his lord's arrival.

He floated out of the roiling, black, lightning filled clouds, surrounded by a glistening nimbus of light, descending gently towards the battle like a glorified angel. He was borne aloft upon a disc-like daemon pulpit, one hand upon the spiked railing at its front. Daemons swirled around him, filling the air with their keening screams as they scythed around the Dark Apostle in intricate weaving patterns.

They were daemons blessed by Tzeentch, the Great Changer of the Ways, and their bodies were long and smooth, rimmed with thousands of jagged barbs. Hunters of the Ether, they resembled the ray-fish that existed in the oceans of countless worlds, sleek and deadly. Their bodies were ovular in shape and long barbed tails swished behind them as they cut through the air, fleshy wing tips rising and falling deceptively slowly. Colours played over their dark hides, glistening patterns of iridescent shades. Each was the length of three men and they cut through the air in a deadly dance, spiralling down in steep dives before turning into climbing corkscrews, interweaving with the paths of others of their kind.

Smaller versions of the screaming daemon-rays, no larger than a hand span across, whipped around the Dark Apostle, spiralling around him like a dense shoal of frenzied fish.

Jarulek held his crozius of the dark gods high before him and a roar rose up to greet him from the assembled Host.

He certainly knew how to make an entrance, Marduk thought wryly.

'The way you appear to the Host is paramount, First Acolyte,' he remembered Jarulek lecturing him. 'Always you must project an aura of authority and religious awe. We are beyond the warrior-brothers of the Legion, we are the chosen of the gods, exalted in Lorgar's eyes and raised beyond the morass of the lower warrior. Our warriors must worship us. And why? We must appear glorified and exalted so that always we can inspire utter devotion in the Host. A warrior fuelled with faith fights with twice the hatred and twice the strength of one that does not, and he will fight on past the point when he would otherwise give in to death. A Dark Apostle must always inspire such devotion in his flock,' said Jarulek, his eyes filled with passion and belief.

'That is the reason that we need a Coryphaus, Marduk. The Dark Apostle must be separate and aloof from the Host to maintain the utter devotion of the warrior-brothers. He must not be one of them, he must be beyond them. The Coryphaus is the war leader of the Host, but he is also the conduit through which the Dark Apostle can gauge the feeling of the Host. For once you take on the mantle of Dark Apostle, you must be one apart from the Legion. Always you must project a holy aura that will inspire utter, fanatical loyalty and devotion.'

The full power of the Dark Apostle's words were driven home to Marduk as he felt the spirit of the Host rise as Jarulek made his descent upon the back of the hellish daemon construct.

The daemon pulpit was a work of mad genius, formed from the lucid dreams of the Dark Apostle's mind and birthed in the Immaterium before it had been dragged into the material realm to serve his will. Its skeleton was of blackest iron and the ribs of the metallic frame formed an eight-pointed star beneath his feet. Between these was living, red-raw flesh and muscle, and it was upon this that the Dark Apostle stood.

The whole daemon construct was disc shaped and razor sharp barbs of black iron lined its edges. Black, iron rib work rose up at the front of the pulpit, curved to either side of the Dark Apostle like a chariot of old, and living, bloody flesh filled the gaps between the struts. An ancient book bound in human leather was open before him and a pair of burning braziers trailed oily, black smoke in his wake.

He held his arms out wide to receive the praise of the Host, a rapturous smile upon his upturned face. He glided down until he was hovering just above the heads of the warrior-brothers and his velvet voice swept out before him as he spoke.

'Let the infidel worshippers of the Corpse Emperor witness the power of true gods!' he said, his words carrying easily over the throng of battle, though he seemed barely to raise his voice. 'Show them the power of the warriors of true faith! Let them not defile the sacred monument of the Gehemahnet! Slaughter them with the words of blessed Lorgar upon your lips! Feel the power of the gods surge within you! Kill them, my warriors! The gods hunger for sacrifice!'

The Dark Apostle lowered his defiled crozius arcanum in the direction of the enemy and his daemon pulpit began gliding forwards over the heads of his warriors. The scything daemon rays of Tzeentch screamed ahead of him, weaving deadly patterns and glowing with iridescent light.

The explosions of incoming shells erupted around the Dark Apostle, but he emerged unscathed, protected by a nimbus of light that surrounded him.

As one, the Host of the Word Bearers gave a roar of devotion and hatred, and surged forwards. The Gehemahnet rumbled behind them and Marduk could feel the presence of thousands of daemons struggling to enter the physical realm. Its time was almost upon them.

There was no glory to be had in waiting behind walls for death to come. No, the final battle would be a full attack against the enemy. Havoc squads would hold position upon the fourth tier, but the remainder of the Host was to attack in one powerful wave and engage the enemy in the open.

Marduk lifted his daemon weapon, feeling its power building as the Gehemehnet neared its awakening, and he leapt the barricade.

'Purge them of their heresies!' he roared. 'Death to the followers of the Corpse Emperor!'

The Host surged towards the enemy behind the advance of the slaves, bolters barking. Marduk was pleased to see that many of the slaves picked up weapons from fallen enemy soldiers and put them to use, shooting at their erstwhile allies. Some turned these weapons back to shoot at the Word Bearers, but they were few, and they were clubbed to the ground and murdered by their fellow slaves.

Marduk always found it pleasing to see former heathen worshippers of the False Emperor turn to Chaos, embracing the truth and becoming true converts, proselytes of the true Gods. The corruption of the innocent some would say, but he knew that it was something far more worthwhile. He was seeing enlightenment come to those who had been exposed to lies and falsehood for their entire lives. It was liberation and it was salvation.

The daemonic war engines that the slaves were chained to bellowed and roared as they clawed up the earth beneath them and filled the air with sprays of shells, flame and missiles. They smashed into the enemy foot soldiers and began ripping them apart and crushing them beneath their weight. Hundreds of slaves were injured as they were dragged into the fray and their chains snapped tight between the machines, entangling them with the foe.

The Host followed closely, firing into the mayhem, not caring who they killed. Thousands dropped beneath the roar of bolters, and as chains were driven into the ground and snapped, the Host broke into a run. They fell amongst the slaves and enemy, hacking and cutting with chainaxes and swords, bludgeoning with bolters and burning with roaring flamers.

Marduk saw Jarulek enter battle ahead of him, shooting down from his floating pulpit with a monstrous, daemon-bolter that caused hideous mutations in those it struck. The screaming daemons of Tzeentch scythed through the enemy, their razor-edged forms cutting limbs from bodies and cleaving through heads. The smaller daemons whirled around the Dark Apostle, eviscerating anything that came close.

Marduk saw a warrior raise a hand to hurl a grenade at the Dark Apostle, but his forearm was cleanly severed as he pulled it back for the throw. It fell to the ground as his feet. Marduk laughed as he saw the look of frantic panic on the man's face before he was hurled through the air by the force of the explosion. A pair of screaming ray-daemons cut through the air and sliced into the flailing body as if playing with a new toy and he fell to the ground in pieces.

Give them a taste of the power of Chaos that will soon come, said the voice of Jarulek.

Marduk fired his bolt pistol into the face of an enemy as he formed the complex words of a passage from the *Enumeration of Convocation*, an inspired work that blessed Erebus had crafted in the language of the daemon. He spoke the difficult words easily, his chainsword hacking into flesh and his bolt pistol blasting through bone.

A searing beam of white-blue energy from a Skitarii weapon caused the flesh and blood of several Word Bearers to boil within their power armour, and Marduk rolled to the side as the beam swept towards him, almost stumbling over the words of the complex enumeration. The results of such a slip could be catastrophic, but he picked up the incantation smoothly once again as he rolled to his feet, cleaving his weapon across the throat of another foe.

He barked out the guttural words of the enumeration, feeling the power of Chaos building, tapping into the excessive amounts of energy waiting to be released. Burias-Drak'shal's horned head lifted as the possessed warrior crouched over a kill, nostrils flaring as it scented the build-up of warp energy.

With a wave of his chainsword, Marduk ordered the warriors around him to form a circle, with him as its centre. The power armoured Chaos Space Marines of the Legion planted their feet, facing outwards, mowing down any that drew near their First Acolyte.

Burias-Drak'shal stalked through the maelstrom of battle. His whole posture was altered once the change had taken him. From a tall, proud and graceful warrior, he became a hulking, stooped, feral creature that oozed power and barely suppressed rage. He roughly shoved a Word Bearers warrior-brother out of his way to take his place beside the First Acolyte, who was drawing near the end of the enumeration, and planted his icon firmly into the ground.

Reaching out with one hand, Marduk gripped the icon, directing the building power of Chaos through its black metal. He gripped the icon tightly and closed his eyes, still speaking in the contorting language of the warp. When he opened his eyes they were as black as pitch.

He barked the last words of the enumeration and, in the moment of silence that followed, he and Burias-Drak'shal raised the icon high before slamming its butt down into the ground, steam rising from where it touched the earth.

The air around the icon shimmered as if with the heat of a star-engine and the long, spiked haft began to vibrate. A swirling vortex of darkness suddenly opened, and the surrounding air was sucked towards it. The kathartes screamed into reality from within the portal. Scores of them hurtled up into the sky from the rift in real space.

Their exposed muscles were slick with blood and they beat their powerful, flayed wings as they coiled overhead before descending upon the battlefield. They plummeted into the Elysians, talons curled forwards like those of an attacking bird of prey, hooking and ripping into flesh. Some men were grasped by the shoulders and lifted into the air before other kathartes screamed into them, ripping at them and squabbling over the pickings. Guardsmen were torn apart as the kathartes fought, and Marduk could feel the rising terror and fear of the soldiers, their resolve wavering.

'Fear not the devils! Faith in the Emperor will protect your souls!' came a shout from a leather-clad individual with wide, mad eyes and Marduk laughed at his folly. The man screamed an oath to the Emperor and shot down one of the katharte daemons. The shot broke one of its wings and it fell into the crush of men.

Marduk roared and leapt towards the figure, smashing aside those in his path, but the black-clad commissar was lost amongst the melee. Marduk swore in anger and continued to slaughter those around him.

* * *

LARON SMILED AS he saw the enemy surge forward. This was the moment he had been waiting for. He commanded his signal communicators to order the attack. They had stormed forward from their final defensive line. Now the sheer weight of the Imperials must surely prevail.

Laron raced back down the embankment towards the waiting Valkyries. He leapt aboard the closest aircraft and hooked himself onto the rappel line attached just inside the open bay door, nodding to Captain Elias. The aircraft's engines roared as it took off and the flight of thirty Valkyries rose just high enough to clear the embankment of the third defensive line before screeching over the heads of the frantically battling combatants in the no-man's-land below. The crewmen manning a pair of secured heavy bolters opened fire as the Valkyries swooped low over the field of battle. Laron's storm troopers, kneeling in the open doors and secured with rappel lines, fired their hellguns down into the melee, picking out targets amongst the chaotic battle surging below.

A hellish shape burst through the open bay door, ripping with daemonic claws, and blood splashed across the close interior of the Valkyrie. The stench of the creature was foul and it slashed around frenziedly, ripping at the storm troopers and hacking through rappel lines as if they were twine. Two storm troopers fell from the aircraft as it roared across the battlefield, jinking from side to side to avoid incoming fire. They fell into the mayhem below, and another's face was ripped off as the creature's tri-hinged jaw snapped.

Laron clubbed the hateful thing in the face with the butt of his pistol. Its head swung towards him, eyes burning with flames and steam emanating from the twin gashes that marked where a nose should have been. Its foetid breath made him gag and he saw that its tongue was made up of a thousand wriggling worm-tentacles as it reached for him. He jammed his melta pistol into the daemon's mouth and pulled the trigger. The thing was lit up from the inside before it broke up into a million tiny pieces of ash and was blown out of the aircraft.

Laron grimaced as he spat the foul ash from his mouth, before grinning at the surviving storm troopers.

The Valkyries carried large cases packed with explosives. The Ordinatus might well destroy the tower, but he wasn't taking any chances and he didn't like the idea of their victory relying upon the disconcerting Adeptus Mechanicus magos. This might have been an old-fashioned way of blowing something up, but sometimes that was the best way.

'HAVOC SQUADS, SHOOT them down,' ordered Kol Badar as the Valkyries appeared over the ridge, flying fast and low over the top of the raging battle, fire pumping from their forward-mounted guns and from their open doors.

Shells smashed down along the defensive tier as carefully timed and targeted artillery fire was unleashed, and an echelon of thunderbolts screamed along the line, peppering the heavy weapons teams with their intense strafing runs. The Havoc squads took down over a dozen of the Valkyries, but the relentless attacks forced them to take cover, and the remaining Valkyries screamed overhead, past the fourth defensive line, heading towards the base of the Gehemehnet.

'Rearguard, incoming,' Kol Badar said as he ripped through a pair of enemies with his combi-bolter.

'Acknowledged, Coryphaus,' came the response.

VARNUS COULD SEE nothing but red as his rage lent him strength and he swung his lasgun into the face of the Elysian, smashing his visor. He leapt upon the Guardsman as he fell and smashed the butt of his lasgun into his face again before rising from the kill and gunning down another.

Something struck him from behind and he was thrown forwards, falling at the feet of a man dressed in black. A commissar, he recognised dimly, seeing the man level a pistol at his head. He stared back at the commissar hatefully, awaiting the shot that would end his life.

But it never came. The commissar's hand was hacked off by a chainsword and Varnus surged to his feet.

'This one is mine!' he roared and the Chaos Space Marine towering over him turned its helmeted head in his direction. With a dignified nod of its head, it left the wounded commissar to Varnus and leapt back into the fray, its twin chainswords whirring.

Varnus stood on the one good hand of the commissar as he scrabbled for a weapon and the man turned his face towards him, twisted in hatred and pain.

'Where is the Emperor now?' asked Varnus in a language the commissar could not understand. 'He has abandoned you, just as he abandoned me.'

Varnus placed the barrel of his lasgun against the commissar's forehead. The man's eyes were defiant till the last and Varnus pulled the trigger. He watched as the life faded from his eyes and a pang wrenched inside him. He dropped to his knees over the dead figure, confused and lost. The anger drained from him and was replaced with self-loathing, guilt and anguish.

He caught the sight of his own reflection in the highly buffed, silver pin on the commissar's hat and he lifted it up, staring at his own hate-filled visage.

What had he become? This was the face of the enemy. *The False Emperor is the enemy!*

He looked upon the two-headed eagle symbol upon the black leather hat he held in his hands and he felt duel emotions: hate and sadness. *They betrayed you! The worship of the False Emperor is a lie!*

Maybe it was a lie, but was this a better alternative? This embracing of evil and slaughter?

Slaughter is the holy sacrifice that the gods demand.

The madness was descending upon him again and he had not the strength to fight it any longer. He would continue to fall into damnation. No, he would not fall, he would embrace it. He felt the rage building within him and it terrified him that it was not unpleasant. He would be lost and he would not care that he was lost.

With the last vestiges of himself, he lifted the pistol from the commissar's hand and raised it to his head. Emperor, save me, he thought. Before the unrelenting rage descended upon him once again and he was completely lost, he pulled the trigger.

At last he had found release from the sound of Chaos in his mind.

'GET THOSE DAMNED explosives set! We ain't got much time!' shouted Laron as he hunkered down behind the Valkyrie. His storm troopers were firing on the incoming enemies, but they would be on them in a moment. Bolter rounds impacted against the aircraft, and the crewman operating the heavy bolter flew backwards as a bolt shell detonated in his skull, splattering Laron with blood. He swore and took the man's position, swinging the heavy weapon towards the enemy. A missile slammed into one of the other Valkyries, which detonated explosively, throwing flaming debris in all directions.

Laron pressed the twin thumb triggers of the pivot mounted heavy bolter and fired a spray of heavy calibre rounds towards the incoming foe, dropping several of them. Rhinos could be seen cutting towards the storm troopers from further off, and Laron swore.

'Set the damned timers! Move it!' he roared in between bursts of fire.

'Sir, we have incoming hostiles from the east,' said a wounded storm trooper as he pulled a piece of metal from his shoulder.

'Just great,' muttered Laron as he gunned down another enemy.

'All set,' Captain Elias shouted.

A sudden scream from the base of the tower made Laron glance around and he did a double take as he saw the scene unfolding. A long, spined arm had reached out of the stone of the tower, grabbed one his men around the throat and was dragging him towards the wall. Another storm trooper was hacking at the arm with his knife, and hissing ichor dripped from the wound. Fleshy, hooked claws burst from the wall and latched onto another man. He was pulled off balance and tumbled into the wall. He half disappeared into the surface of the stone, and tentacles and claws gripped his armour and hauled him fully inside as he screamed.

The storm troopers backed away from the wall and began firing at the things materialising out of the stone surface. Hissing, fanged faces pushed out, bulbous, mutated eyes opened up all over the stone. A flickering figure of a huge, horned daemon with a twisting blade of fire in its hand strained to escape the stone, and hellguns blasted as the soldiers targeted the emerging monster.

'Back! Get back to the Valkyries!' shouted Laron, ducking down behind the heavy bolter as rounds of incoming fire peppered the aircraft.

One of the storm troopers shot their comrade who was still being pulled into the tower. It was a mercy killing, to end whatever cruel fate had awaited him.

A heavily muscled humanoid figure pulled free of the wall and ran at the storm troopers, hefting a heavy, archaic broadsword in its muscular red arms. With one sweep of the blade it carved a man in half from shoulder to waist, and it roared, flames spilling from its eyes and throat.

Laron swung his heavy bolter around and unleashed a long burst of fire into the daemon's chest. It was driven back several steps by the impacts, though it appeared unharmed. It turned its snarling head towards Colonel Laron and began to advance through the barrage.

'Go!' he shouted to the pilot as the surviving storm troopers scrambled aboard, and the Valkyrie lifted straight up into the air, its powerful vertical thrusters roaring. Boltgun fire ripped through the undercarriage of the aircraft as it lifted and several men were killed, their blood spraying the roof.

'The charges blow in ten, sir!' shouted one of his men, and Laron nodded as he fired upon the Chaos Space Marines below. More things were emerging from the walls of the tower.

The Valkyrie turned steeply, and a missile destined to smash into its side flew through the open doorway, screaming over Laron's head and miraculously passing straight out of the other open doorway, filling the interior with the smoke of its propulsion.

Open-mouthed, Laron turned.

'The Emperor protects!' shouted Elias, laughing at the sheer improbability of the occurrence.

'It certainly seems that way,' agreed Laron, shaking his head in utter disbelief.

He didn't see the hulking, winged daemon pushing out of the wall behind the turning Valkyrie. Nor did he see it leap towards the aircraft, nor hear the power of its roar over the screaming engines. But he felt the impact as it struck.

The tail of the Valkyrie tipped earthwards with the sudden additional weight, and the pilot struggled to keep it airborne. The head of a giant axe slammed through the raised rear assault ramp, smashing it asunder. The ramp was ripped from the aircraft as the axe was pulled free, and it tumbled end over end to the ground below.

The daemon roared as it pulled at the tail of the Valkyrie, its wings beating furiously and its infernal muscles straining to bring the aircraft down to the ground. It was thrown off as the Valkyrie's jet turbines kicked in, but with a beat of its powerfully muscled wings it turned in the air and its whip flicked out, wrapping around the tail of the aircraft, pulling it sharply downwards.

With its engines roaring, the Valkyrie screamed up into the air as its tail tipped beneath it, and the pilot lost control. The aircraft slammed into another Valkyrie before flipping upside down and plummeting to the ground. Laron leapt from the aircraft as it slammed into the earth, rolling into the dust.

The daemon landed atop the flaming wreck, its massive hooves twisting the metal beneath it. It seemed impervious to the flames, and Laron scrambled backwards as the malevolent thing stepped out of the inferno, its burning eyes fixed upon him.

It was over twelve feet tall and it seemed to flicker as if it were not fully there. Its skin was as black as pitch and a burning symbol was emblazoned on its chest, the mark of one of the ruinous powers.

'Emperor, protect my soul,' whispered Laron.

The charges exploded. Both man and daemon were ripped apart by the force of the detonations.

But the tower still stood.

THE ORDINATUS FIRED upon the Gehemehnet, enormous amounts of energy focused into a deadly frequency that held the power to shatter mountains and crush bones to powder. The air shimmered as the ultra-high and ultra-low frequencies screamed over the top of the chaotic battle and roared towards the fifty kilometre high structure. It struck the side of the tower some forty metres up, and stones were ruptured from within as they were shaken apart. They exploded into sand and were blown out of the other side. A hole the size of a building was driven through the tower.

Impossibly, the tower still stood, despite the lack of integrity holding it together, for it was no longer bound by the rules of geometry or gravity. The tower was a gateway to the warp beyond, and through the hole blasted in its side the roiling darkness and liquid flame of the Ether could be seen.

With a roar that came from the throats of a million infernal entities the Gehemehnet awoke and the barrier between the realm of the daemon and the material plane was stripped away. Energy roared outwards from the Gehemehnet, throwing dust up into the air and hurling men to the ground. It made the black seas beyond the Shinar peninsula rise in a giant tidal wave that roared out from the tower, and lightning tore apart the heavens. Rumblings shook the ground, and daemons screamed into being.

They emerged from within the tower, thousands of straining hellish entities clawing out of living stone, and they roared their pleasure as they manifested. Thousands of others flew from the rent in the tower's side, held aloft by pinioning wings or twisting, contorting winds of fire. Screams and roars thundered across the Shinar peninsula and tens of thousands of daemons poured from the gateway, descending on the mortals.

The Ordinatus machine fired again, but this time the force of its attack seemed to rebound from the tower and it hurtled back towards the behemoth, smashing into its void shields and ripping them apart, the fury of its own power turned against it. The void shields crumbled one by one beneath the onslaught, robbing the energy of its force, but still enough power hurtled into the Ordinatus to rip it apart.

The Ordinatus was rocked by the force of its own weapon, though even this was not enough to destroy it completely. Plumes of smoke wreathed its iron sides, and metal scaffolds and gantries were shattered. The great weapon housed upon its back, greater than even those of a mighty Titan, was torn from its housing and collapsed beneath its own weight. Blue fire spurted from breaches in the plasma core powering the machine and tech-priests wailed as the machine-spirit groaned in agony.

Daemons streamed across the battlefield, hacking, slashing and ripping. Thousands of mortals were slaughtered in the first moments of the insane combat, their limbs hacked apart by brutal hellblades, their bodies turned to liquid by blasts of yellow and pink unearthly fire and their souls ripped from their still warm bodies by lascivious, hateful daemons.

The clouds overhead were sucked suddenly inwards, towards the Gehemehnet, and fierce winds pulled at everyone battling upon the plains. Tanks slid across the ground under the force of the sudden gale and men were sent flying through the air.

As suddenly as they came into being, the daemons of the warp were sucked back towards the Gehemehnet, screaming in rage as the fabric of their beings was stripped away like melting wax, and the energies that composed them was drawn back into the tower.

The heavens were cleared of darkness and the great orb of the red planet Korsis could be seen large overhead.

'The conjunction comes,' muttered Jarulek in awe, down on one knee as he strained to resist being pulled back by the roaring gale, his daemonic pulpit having been sucked back to the Gehemehnet by the force of the Daemonschage. He put a hand out to break his fall as the wind stopped abruptly and silence descended across the peninsula, except for one sound.

At the top of the Gehemehnet, the Daemonschage bell tolled as the twelve planets of the Dalar system drew into line and the energies of the ten thousand daemons contained within the tower were propelled down the shaft into the core of the planet.

The dense rock that formed the mantle surrounding the absolute centre of Tanakreg was ripped apart by the unholy power and the land above was shattered.

Massive fault lines ripped up the continents as tectonic plates shifted and smashed into each other. New mountains were instantly formed as shifting rock plates collided and were thrown up into the sky, and existing mountain ranges disappeared as they sank into the vast chasm opening up beneath them.

Earthquakes rolled across the planet, throwing up giant tidal waves that roared across the earth, destroying everything in their path and creating new oceans as plains were overrun with the deluge. New continents were formed as the oceans roiled and great up-thrusts of rock climbed into the sky.

Volcanoes spewed lava and ash into the atmosphere, and acidic seas boiled away as they were exposed to rising streams of liquid iron from the planet's core. Deep, subterranean avalanches at the core mantle boundary, far below the planet's surface, disrupted the planet's magnetic field, and the integrity of the planet as a whole wavered.

The gravitational pull of Korsis strained at the weakness of the planet and Tanakreg was tipped off its axis, sending a new shockwave through it, and triggering a second wave of earthquakes.

Great cracks appeared across the Shinar peninsula and the mountains to the east were lost to oblivion as the continental plate sank. The peninsula was lifted up into the air, throwing the Gehemehnet off at an oblique angle, though it still stood. Water rushed across the plains as it vacated the seas below the peninsula, boiling and rising into scalding steam as it touched the rising lava spilling up through the cracks in the earth.

Ash, dust and gases filled the skies, covering the hot, white sun and obscuring Korsis once more.

The Ordinatus slipped into a giant chasm that opened up beneath it, falling into the molten magma rising from below, even as the airship docked upon its back lifted off and rose into the air, smoking and labouring to stay airborne. It drifted sluggishly through the air, hanging heavily to one side where its gyro-stabilisers had been destroyed, passing over the shattered battlefield. Missiles impacted with the undercarriage of the airship and it dived down over the edge of the cliff, flame and smoke spewing from it.

The Word Bearers backed towards the base of the Gehemehnet, though scores of their vehicles and daemon engines were lost as they fell into chasms that opened beneath them, or were swept away by the black acid sea.

At last the continents settled.

Below the peninsula where the Gehemehnet had been built, deep in an abyssal channel that just moments before had been hidden beneath kilometres of inky black, acidic waters, was a structure.

It was a black-sided pyramid, its sides perfectly smooth and gleaming. The burning, shattered airship descended into the chasm before smashing upon its floor.

'And that,' breathed Jarulek as he stared down at the structure hungrily, 'is what I have come to find.'

CHAPTER TWENTY-ONE

THE CULT OF the Anointed stood to attention upon the deep, abyssal chasm floor. The glossy black sides of the pyramid rose up some two hundred metres behind them. Nothing upon its sides gave any indication as to its origin and it was unmarked by scratch or blemish.

The Dark Apostle strode imperiously down the assault ramp of the Stormbird, flanked by his First Acolyte and the Icon Bearer. He wore his ceremonial cloak of skin, the inside lined with golden thread, and his head was held high, for this was the moment of his success.

Twenty of the Anointed formed a corridor that the trio strode along, each slamming a heavy foot down onto the earth as they passed. They advanced towards the bulky form of Kol Badar, standing at the head of the two hundred Terminators arrayed in serried ranks, who awaited the arrival of their lord in silence. All two hundred warriors stamped their feet into the ground as the Dark Apostle halted before them.

The Coryphaus spread his arms wide, palms up, the power claw on his left arm dwarfing the right, as he intoned the ritual greeting.

'The Cult of the Anointed greets the revered Dark Apostle with open arms and beseeches the Dark Gods to bless him for time eternal.'

'And the blessing of the Ether upon you, my loyal Anointed warriors,' said Jarulek, concluding the ritual.

'My lord, we have secured the area and I have inspected the outside of the structure. There appears to be no entrances to its interior.'

'The door shall be opened to him of pure faith,' said Jarulek, a knowing smile on his face.

'Yes, my lord,' said the Coryphaus, bowing his head to Jarulek's proclamation. 'Our auspexes and sensors are unable to scan within. It gives off nothing, my lord.'

'And what of that?' asked Jarulek, pointing towards the black smoke rising in the distance that marked where the airship of the Mechanicus had gone down. 'Did you ensure it was destroyed?'

'I did, my lord. There was a survivor from the crash. I brought it back alive, for I thought it would interest you.'

'Master of the cog will come in chains and tattered robes, to become Enslaved,' quoted Jarulek, a smile upon his script covered, pale face.

'And so, the prophecy comes to fruition.'

JARULEK STRODE FORWARDS, raising his cursed crozius arcanum high into the air as he neared the base of the black, flawless structure. Not a mark could be seen upon the pyramid's slick surface, not a crack or a join – it was as if the whole structure had been carved from one gigantic piece of some midnight, glossy mineral.

As he neared it, a green light began to glow, dimly at first and then more fiercely. The light coalesced into strange symbols running vertically down the surface in front of the Dark Apostle, hieroglyphs the likes of which Marduk had never seen before. It appeared to be a form of early picture writing, consisting of circles and lines, but it was utterly alien in design.

The green light grew in intensity until the glare spilling from the strange glyphs was almost blinding. More light began to appear upon the surface of the pyramid and Marduk clenched his hand around the grip of his daemon-blade, feeling the reassuring connection as the barbs of the grip pierced his armour and flesh.

A circular symbol appeared, and lines that could have been representations of sunbeams spread from its circumference. Without a sound, the circle sank into the black surface of the stone and the panels created by the 'sunbeams' slid to the side, revealing a dark entranceway within the structure, almost five metres in height. Air was sucked into the open gateway, as if the inside of the structure was a vacuum, and icy coldness exuded from within.

The Anointed moved up protectively around the Dark Apostle, combi-bolters and heavy weapons swinging towards the open gateway. Jarulek turned towards Marduk, a smile upon his lips.

'Come, my First Acolyte. Our destinies await us.'

Allowing a dozen members of the Anointed to take the lead, Marduk and Jarulek entered the ancient, alien pyramid.

A searing pain flared on Marduk's head beneath his helmet as he crossed the boundary into the pyramid, and he dropped to one knee, eyes tightly shut. It felt like someone had pressed a red-hot brand against the flesh of his forehead.

'What is wrong with you?' snapped Jarulek.

Marduk concentrated hard, mouthing the scriptures of Lorgar to shut off the burning pain, and pushed himself back to his feet.

It felt as though his skin was being melted away from the bone and he gritted his sharp teeth as he mouthed the sacred words.

He knew what the feeling was – it had been described to him – and he had read of it in countless accounts of Dark Apostles.

Jarulek's words came back to him.

Have you had any holy scriptures appear on your flesh yet?

He pushed the pain deep within him, feeling a surge of pride. He could still feel the searing pain, but it would not dominate him. He rose to his feet.

'Nothing, Dark Apostle,' he said, and the Word Bearers pressed on into the alien pyramid.

'THERE IS NOTHING here,' said Kol Badar. They had been walking through the darkness for what seemed like hours, passing through endless, smooth corridors flanked by columns of obsidian, descending deeper into the stygian blackness. They must have been far beneath the ground, thought Marduk. How large a structure was this unearthly, black pyramid?

'That which I seek is here,' said the Dark Apostle. 'I have seen this place in my dream visions.'

Marduk could sense something, but what it was he didn't know. His skin prickled with vague unease. He ran his hand along the smooth, black stone, feeling the icy chill within.

The corridor was wide enough for four Terminators to walk side by side, and the Dark Apostle was flanked by warriors who formed a shield of ablative armour around him. They had passed dozens of other corridors and passages that bisected their own, but Jarulek had never once paused to consider the way forward. He strode onwards, his head held high, as if he had been here before.

'This place is ancient,' said Marduk. 'What manner of xenos created this structure?'

'Creatures long dead,' said Kol Badar, his deep voice ringing out from the speakers concealed beneath the quad-tusks of his helmet.

'Maybe,' said Marduk, but he was not so certain. This place certainly felt dead, but unease nagged at him.

'DRAK'SHAL IS WRITHING within me,' snarled Burias. His eyes shone with daemonic witch-sight, like silver orbs in the gloom.

'Keep control of yourself, Icon Bearer,' replied Kol Badar sharply.

'The daemon is… repelled by this place,' said Burias.

A whisper of air brushed past Marduk and he swung his helmeted head to one side, scanning for movement or heat signals that would indicate an enemy presence. There was nothing. Another wisp of air shadowed by him and he raised his bolt pistol, scanning to the left.

'Something is in here with us,' he hissed.

'Anointed, be vigilant, possible hostile presence,' said Kol Badar, his words carrying to each of the Terminators through their internal comm-system. The Terminators turned left and right, weapons panning.

There was a sudden shout and the darkness was lit up as combi-bolters roared. There was a crunching sound followed by a wet splash and more bolter-fire barked.

Marduk felt a shadow rise behind him and he spun to see a towering shape looming out of the gloom, something that did not register on any of his heat or life sensors. Even with his advanced vision and the keen autosenses of his helmet, the shape was still little more than a shadow, a tapering coil of darkness that rose up to a hunched pair of shoulders. Skeletally thin arms whipped out, plunging down into the body of an Anointed warrior-brother, skewering him, and blood splashed out across the slick, black walls.

With a shout, Marduk fired his bolt pistol into the shape and he saw a shadowy face turn towards him, pinpricks of green light marking eyes amidst the darkness. With inhuman speed the creature was gone, leaping straight into the smooth, black wall, its tapering shadow tail whipping behind it as it disappeared.

The Anointed warrior fell to the ground, dead.

'They are coming out of the walls,' roared Marduk, spinning as he felt another shadow flash past him. He thumbed the activation rune of his daemon-blade to life and the chainblades roared.

Shouts and gunfire erupted as more shadowy forms appeared all along the corridor, plunging their long arms into the bodies of the Anointed, killing and rending, before disappearing like ghosts.

A pair of green, glowing eyes appeared as a shape rose out of the floor before Marduk, and he swung his chainsword towards it. He saw a dark, metallic, skeletal face as the thing opened its mouth in a soundless hiss. It reared back out of range of his attack, its shadowy torso held aloft upon a long, flexible spinal cord that tapered into darkness.

He fired his pistol towards the thing's head, but the bolts passed through it as it turned to black smoke. In an instant, it had regained its metallic, physical form and lunged at him, preternaturally fast arms plunging down to impale him. He lashed out with his chainsword and threw himself into a desperate roll beneath the descending ghost creature, feeling the teeth of his weapon bite against something solid. As he came to his feet, the creature was gone.

The Terminator to his left staggered to his knees as shadowy blades punched through his head, and Marduk lashed out with his chainsword once more, the blade passing harmlessly through the shadowy, serpentine spinal cord of the creature before it disappeared back within the sanctity of the black walls.

'We have to get out of this corridor, we need more space!' yelled Burias, flailing to defend himself against a shadow that emerged to his right.

'Warriors of Lorgar! Advance, double time!' roared Kol Badar.

Marduk saw a creature descend from the darkness above, coiling down to impale another warrior upon its skeletal arms, and the man was lifted up into the air, legs kicking.

'Gods of the Ether give me strength,' Marduk heard the Dark Apostle spit, and he saw him smash his cursed crozius into the enemy. A burst of hot electric energy crackled over the dark shape as the weapon made contact, and it was smashed to the ground, its metallic limbs and long, serpentine spine thrashing feebly. The skull of the creature caved in with the Dark Apostle's next blow and the green glow of its eyes faded to darkness.

'Move out! Protect the Dark Apostle,' roared Kol Badar as he turned to give covering fire to those warriors behind him. More of the Anointed were slain as wraiths appeared out of nowhere and drove their bladed, shadow-arms through armour and flesh.

One warrior, walking resolutely backwards, his reaper autocannon roaring, caught one of the shadowy creatures in a blast of heavy fire and it was ripped apart by the awesome force of the weapon.

'Enkil, turn!' roared Kol Badar as a wraith dropped down from the darkness behind the warrior. The Coryphaus stepped forwards, pumping fire towards the dark shape looming over the warrior, but the shots passed straight through the creature. Enkil turned, swinging his heavy weapon around to bear, but the shadow was too quick and it drove twin-bladed arms through his body. He fell to his knees, blood pumping from the wounds. Kol Badar roared as he stepped forwards, his combi-bolter barking as the injured warrior tried to push himself to his feet. Three wraiths appeared around him like looming spectres of death, their arms raised, poised for the kill.

The Coryphaus took another step towards the fallen warrior, but a hand on his arm halted him.

'Coryphaus, we must leave this place,' said Burias, his eyes glittering like molten silver.

With a snarl, Kol Badar shook off the Icon Bearer's hand, but nodded his head.

'The gods be with you, Enkil,' he said, firing a final burst towards the gathered wraiths as they killed the warrior. He turned and moved as swiftly as his armour allowed him, passing the rearguard walking steadily backwards, fire barking from their weapons.

MARDUK RAN AHEAD of the Anointed warriors, unencumbered by the bulky Terminator armour they wore, and the corridor gave way to a vast open area. Steps rose to a large circular dais that dominated the room, surrounded by dozens of columns glowing with green hieroglyphs. A black-sided pyramid stood in the centre of the dais, a miniature replica of the structure they were within, some ten metres in height.

He scanned left and right as he ran, seeking out any sign of the enemy, and he leapt up the steps and onto the circular dais. He circled and realised that dozens of corridors similar to the one he had just exited, branched off this large, circular room, spaced evenly around the perimeter. Darkness, impenetrable even to his eyes, was beyond these corridors, but he had the impression that they all led back up towards the surface. Everything was perfectly symmetrical and it made sense that none of these corridors led further down. The circular room rose up high into darkness – no ceiling could be seen – and the cylindrical open space projected straight up what Marduk guessed was the centre of the structure.

He approached the central pyramid warily, weapons ready. It began to silently rise, green light spilling from beneath it. Whatever mechanism or sorcery lifted the massive weight was powerful indeed and the smooth black pyramid rose high into the air, steadily and silently. He realised that it was not a pyramid at all, but rather an immense diamond shape, and he squinted against the green glare that spilled from beneath its bulk, his bolt pistol scanning for movement.

'The gateway to the ancients,' breathed Jarulek as he came up beside Marduk. There was nothing holding or supporting the giant, black diamond shape as it rose, neither above nor below. It lifted higher and higher into the vast empty space above them, hanging suspended in the air.

The Coryphaus entered the room, Burias at his side, and Marduk's eyes narrowed.

'We hold here. We are right where we are meant to be,' ordered Jarulek.

With a nod, Kol Badar quickly ordered the Cult of the Anointed into positions around the edge of the circular dais, guarding the corridor entrances, forming a protective circle around the Dark Apostle, facing out.

'The shadow wraiths seem unable or unwilling to enter this room,' said Marduk.

The Dark Apostle made no response, his eyes fixed on the expanse vacated by the diamond that had come to a halt, hanging ten metres above them. The green light had dimmed and from the smooth, black sides of the angled hole that the diamond fitted perfectly into, wide steps appeared out of the seamless, black stone. A section of the black stone sank away and a gateway was revealed at the foot of the steps, green light spilling from the same sun and lightbeam icon that had appeared on the outside of the pyramid.

There was a shout for silence from the Coryphaus, and Marduk ripped his eyes away from the newly exposed gateway. A dim, rhythmic and repetitive sound could be heard in the silence that followed, something akin to metal striking stone. He realised that it was getting louder and he turned around, trying to get a lock on where the sound was emanating from. It seemed to be coming from all around.

'What in the name of the true gods is that?' he said.

'Something comes,' hissed Burias.

He could see nothing at first, but then he saw green lights, eyes of the enemy, appearing within the darkness of one of the corridors, no, from *all* of the corridors. They were completely surrounded. His first thought was that the shadow wraiths had returned, but these creatures were not ethereal shadows; their bodies were very real.

They were the walking dead and Marduk jolted as the force of his recurring vision entered his head. *Assailed by the dead, long dead, and they claw at my armour with skeletal claws.* This was his vision come to life.

But it was different. These creatures were not formed of bones held together by desiccated, dried skin. Their skulls glinted with a metallic sheen and their eyes glowed with baleful green light. That light matched the coiling, green energy that was contained within the enemies' weapons, held low in their skeletal hands as they trudged forward. The creatures were formed of dark metal and the green glow spilling from their weapons was reflected upon their ribs and bony arms.

The first were smashed apart by the guns of the Anointed, falling silently to the floor where they were stepped over by others of their mechanical kind. There were scores of the creatures spilling from each corridor, marching in perfect unison, shoulder-to-shoulder, silent except for the sound of their metal feet clanking rhythmically on the stone floor.

On and on they came, walking slowly into the torrent of gunfire laid down by the Anointed, and still they did not raise their weapons. Marduk saw one of the fallen creatures, its head shattered by autocannon rounds, begin to rise to its feet once more, its eyes, which were black moments before, glowing once again. The damage done to its cranium repaired before his eyes, the metal knitting back into shape. Its skull was smooth and immaculate, and it stepped back into line with its companions.

Liquid promethium from heavy flamers roared as it was unleashed, as the walking corpse-machines drew ever nearer to the Terminators, but the flames did nothing to halt their progress.

As one, the front rank of the corpse-machines raised their weapons and blinding, green light roared from their barrels. Marduk saw the thick Terminator armour of one warrior-brother flayed instantly to nothing beneath the searing light. Skin was torn away, exposing first muscle tissue then inner organs then nothing but bone, before even that was seared away.

Several of the Anointed fell beneath the blasts, though return fire smashed the first line of the foe away. The second line stepped forwards, lowering their weapons, and a second barrage of green light spewed from the barrels of their potent weapons.

'First Acolyte, we are entering that gateway. Hold them here, Kol Badar,' Jarulek said into his comm unit.

Kol Badar broke away from the circle of Terminators and approached the Dark Apostle, the armour of his left shoulder pad sheared away from a glancing shot, exposing servos and insulation beneath.

'My lord, the Cult warriors can hold here. I shall accompany you,' said the Coryphaus.

'No, you will not,' said Jarulek, stepping close to the big warrior.

Marduk turned away from the pair, scanning the area. There seemed to be no end to the undead warrior-machines entering the room. The Anointed were the finest fighting force within the Host, but he could see that even they would eventually be slaughtered by this relentless foe.

This will be our tomb, he thought.

'MY LORD?' SAID Kol Badar. Always he had fought at the side of the Dark Apostle. He was his champion, his protector. To allow the holy leader to face some unknown enemy without him was unthinkable. The life of a Coryphaus who allowed his master to fall in battle was forfeit. The Council would see him dead were Jarulek to fall.

'What I go to face is not for you to be a part of,' hissed Jarulek, his voice low, his eyes resolute. 'This is one battle that you cannot win, Kol Badar, and it is one foe that you cannot face.'

Doubt plagued the Coryphaus.

'My place is at your side, my lord,' he said. 'You would take the wretched whelp with you, but not me?'

'I am telling you that, for now, your place is not at my side. Hold the line here. The Anointed need you. This battle will not be easily won. Await my return.'

'As you wish, my lord,' said Kol Badar, fuming. The Dark Apostle stepped in close to him, looking up at him with eyes ablaze with faith.

'If we both return, then you may kill Marduk, my Coryphaus. Your honour will be fulfilled.'

A surge of pleasure ran through Kol Badar at the Dark Apostle's words and he smiled beneath his quad-tusked helmet. At last his hand that had once been stayed was free of constraint. At last, he would kill the whoreson whelp, Marduk.

'We shall hold, my lord. I await your return with great expectation.'

'The blessings of the dark gods upon you, my Coryphaus.'

'And with you, my lord. May the gods be at your side as you walk into darkness.'

Kol Badar watched as the Dark Apostle and the First Acolyte descended the stairs. The panels of the gateway slid aside soundlessly and the pair of Word Bearers stepped inside, disappearing into the inky blackness as if consumed. The panels flicked back into place. There was no way of following them now, he thought. He just had to wait and hold off these forsaken corpse-machines long enough for him to be able to kill Marduk.

He rejoined his warriors, racking the underslung mechanism that activated the meltagun attached to his bolter.

'They are gone, Coryphaus?' asked Burias as he fired his bolt pistol into the head of an enemy, knocking it back a step.

'They are, Icon Bearer. The fate of the Host hangs in the balance.'

CHAPTER TWENTY-TWO

THE PANELS SLID shut behind them, cutting off all noise of the raging battle, and they stood in absolute darkness. Not a sound pierced the pitch-black night that descended on them. The silence was heavy, claustrophobic and dense. Marduk was utterly blind. Never before had he experienced such all-encompassing darkness.

He felt lost, adrift, his connection to the warp severed, and he panicked for a moment as his head reeled as if with vertigo, though it was impossible for him to experience such a sensation.

Marduk wobbled, though his senses came back to him in an instant, and his faculties returned. He saw a dim light, though perhaps it had only just begun to shine. It reached out towards them from below, a slowly pulsing beam.

He looked at Jarulek beside him, whose face showed tension and wariness.

'It felt as though we just travelled an infinite distance in the blink of an eye,' said Marduk quietly, unwilling to break the oppressive silence. The gateway they had come through was sealed shut, though the sun icon emblazoned upon it glowed dimly with light. He pushed against it, but it would not budge. As the pulsing light increased, he saw that the black stone wall in which the gateway was positioned rose impossibly high above them. They stood on a bridge of black stone that seemed to hang in the air. There were sheer drops to either side, and it was joined by dozens of black staircases. These in turn were linked to other bridges, gantries and platforms, all formed of black stone and all hanging in the air without any clear support.

'This place is insane,' he hissed. 'It is madness.'

Marduk had encountered many landscapes and worlds that most would consider maddening within the warp, where the rules of the physical world held no sway, but here he felt no touch of Chaos. Far from it, this place felt like it actively kept Chaos out. It was sterile and lifeless, devoid of any touch of the warp.

'Is it some trick of the Changer?' asked Marduk, speaking of Tzeentch, the lord of the twisting fates and one of the greater gods of the Ether. He knew as he spoke that it was not, for even the great Changer of the Ways would surely be unable to create such a place, so cut off from the essence of magic.

'Far from it, First Acolyte,' said Jarulek. 'This is the antithesis of the Great Changer and indeed of all of Chaos.'

'And what you seek is here, in this place? It would seem that anything here would be better destroyed than utilised.'

'Much can be tainted and changed by Chaos, Marduk. Turning an enemy's weapons against them is the greatest strength that we have.'

'And you have foreseen this place in your dream visions?'

'This place, no. It has always been hidden from my sight. I foresaw our entrance through the gateway, but never what transposed beyond it, only what occurs afterwards.'

'You have seen our return from this place?'

'Sometimes. The future is fickle and unclear. In some twists of what may come to pass we return with our prize. In others, we do not and the Anointed are destroyed. The guardians assailing them return to their eternal rest. In others I have seen just myself return. In others, just you.'

'I would not abandon you here, Dark Apostle,' said Marduk. Jarulek chuckled.

'We need to move,' he said.

'Which way?'

'Down.'

It seemed that they had been walking for days on end, or perhaps it had been but minutes. Marduk was not sure anymore. This place was maddening in its power to disorient, and he had long since lost a sense of his bearings. They had walked down stairways only to find themselves walking up, had crossed straight walkways only to find themselves somehow turned around and walking back the way they had come, and more than once they had descended staircases only to find themselves higher up than they had been before the descent.

'This place affects our connection with the blessed Ether,' said Jarulek.

'It does,' replied Marduk. 'It is as though this place muffles it. I can still feel it, but it is distant, and faint.'

'It is an unholy place,' said Jarulek. 'What do you feel from your daemon-blade?'

'I feel... nothing,' said Marduk, placing his hand around the thorn-covered hilt of his chainsword. There was none of the tingling sensation that usually announced the essence of the daemon Borhg'ash merging with his own. There was no indication of its presence at all.

'It is as though the daemon has escaped its binding, but that is not possible.'

They continued their descent towards the slowly pulsing light below. After what seemed an age, they could discern a circular platform beneath them, though it was certainly not the bottom of the expanse. Marduk wondered if there truly was a base to this maddening place, or if it extended forever. Or perhaps if they continued down they would find themselves back where they had started.

Shaking his head, he concentrated upon the circular platform. It seemed that it was covered in silver waters that rippled with movement. As they descended, he realised that it was not liquid.

THOUSANDS OF TINY, crawling insect creatures swarmed away from the Word Bearers as they stepped down from the last of the maddening steps onto the slick, black, circular platform. The creatures scuttled away on metallic, barbed legs, making a sound like gentle ocean waves crashing, as their metallic carapaces scraped and millions of tiny metal legs scrambled for purchase. Their glistening carapaces were dark and the smallest of them was no larger than a grain of sand.

Marduk bent and grasped one of the larger, scuttling beetle creatures, lifting it up between his thumb and forefinger for closer inspection. Dozens of glowing green eyes were arrayed upon its segmented head and its wickedly barbed mandibles clicked as it tried vainly to bite him. Its eight-spiked legs kicked and pushed at him, surprising him with their strength as it tried to get free. Its carapace was of dark metal and a golden emblem, the now familiar sun circle with light beams streaming from it, was emblazoned across it.

He turned it over in his hand to get a look at the creature's underside, but its sharp mandibles bit into him, gripping onto the ceramite protecting his finger. It could not pierce his armour, but it would not let go. He flicked his wrist as he lost interest and patience with the creature, sending the mechanical bug flying. It unfurled wafer-thin membranes of metal from beneath its thick carapace and flittered through the air to join its fleeing companions. It landed amongst the scuttling mass of creatures moving like a living, metal carpet away from the intruders who had entered their realm. They streamed towards a sunken, circular pit that lay before the pair, crawling over its lip and down into its protective darkness.

There must have been tens of thousands of the creatures, and they swarmed towards the pit from all directions. Marduk stepped forwards and the living mass of mechanical insects surged away, parting before him.

Stepping to the edge of the hole, he looked down into the darkness. It was impossible to guess its depth.

He felt a presence behind him and quickly turned, moving away from the edge of the abyss, seeing Jarulek smirk at his discomfort. Marduk glared hatefully at his master from within his helmet. Not long, he thought.

The pair of unholy warriors stalked warily around the edge of the pit. Curved walls rose up around the platform, rising high into the air above. The floor gave way a metre before the wall and it fell down into darkness. They walked carefully around the ring of stone towards the pulsating light throbbing from an adjacent chamber.

A short, enclosed passageway linked the two rooms, and the Word Bearers stepped along it warily. Marduk was uneasy, but it was good to feel solid walls on each side rather than an empty expanse. The second chamber was small and its glossy, black walls reflected the glaring, green light of the glowing object suspended in mid-air in the centre of the room. Pulsing light spilled from it as it spun slowly, floating above the tip of a metre-high black pyramid set in the floor. Light rose in a shaft from the tip of the pyramid, encasing the spinning orb in its beam.

It was a captivating piece of mechanical artistry of utterly alien design, and it revolved slowly. Its centre was a glowing ball of harnessed energy, around which revolved a series of metal rings that spun in all directions around the sphere in a complex weave. The rings overlapped and swung around the glowing centre of the sphere, forming intricate and mesmerising patterns. Marduk could not be certain exactly how many rotating rings there were and he saw that glowing, alien hieroglyphs shone across their flat surfaces. He thought he could see something solid within the ball of energy, but the light was too intense for him to be sure.

He was pulled away from the fascinating object by a hand on his shoulder and he snapped his gaze away, a dull pain in his head.

'Do not look too closely,' warned Jarulek. 'It will ensnare you.'

Marduk nodded, his temples throbbing.

'This is the object you have come to find,' he said finally.

'It is. This is the artefact spoken of in the third book of the *Oraculata Noctis*.'

Marduk's eyes widened.

'And with the Nexus Arrangement one shall wield great force, and he shall open and close the portals to the netherward and become Gatemaster,' quoted Marduk. 'You believe that *this* is the… the Nexus Arrangement?'

'It is,' said Jarulek, his eyes alight with faith and passion. 'And long have I waited for its discovery.

'The Nexus Arrangement is the tool, it is said, that will usher in a new age of destruction. But it is unclear about the destruction of *what*, or of *whom*.

'It is the same as any weapon. It has no will of its own, but is directed by he who would use it. A boltgun is indiscriminate in who it kills, the one who pulls the trigger is the killer. It is a holy weapon to those who use it as such and it is a tool of the great enemy.

'But *this*... this is something far more potent. With this, we will be able to strike at our enemies without fear of reprisal.'

'Open and close the portals to the netherward?'

'That's right, my First Acolyte,' laughed Jarulek. 'Entire systems could have the warp closed off to them, allowing nothing to pass in or out of the region. Imagine it: systems unable to receive reinforcements, communications, supplies, munitions. Imagine, if you will, if this were activated near ancient Terra,' said Jarulek, an evil grin upon his face. 'Terra itself, closed to the warp, the cursed light of the False Emperor effectively kept in shadow, his ships, blind and lost in the turmoil of the Immaterium...'

'This could bring about the end of the Imperium,' Marduk breathed, awe and lust in his soul.

'And it is foretold that it may only be removed when in the presence of a master and an apprentice, holy warriors of Lorgar both. Our being here was prophesied and now that prophecy is complete.'

The Dark Apostle whispered an entreaty to the dark powers and reached his hands slowly forwards, into the light projecting up from the top of the pyramid, reaching towards the revolving sphere. Instantly the light from the pyramid dimmed, plunging the room into darkness, but for the green light emanating from the glowing sphere.

Holding his breath, Marduk watched as the Dark Apostle's hands neared the spinning rings, reaching underneath the orb to cup it. The spinning rings began to slow. Each pulse of light was timed with the revolutions of the rings. There were seven rings, he now saw as they slowed to a standstill, and they seemed to melt together, their edges merging, so that within seconds all that remained was what appeared to be a solid sphere of dark metal. The green hieroglyphs faded away and darkness descended. The blackness was not complete, for now that the glare of the room had faded, a dim light could be seen emanating from the pit in the adjacent chamber, where the scarabs had retreated.

Jarulek lifted the metal orb out from where it hovered above the black pyramid, awe upon his face.

It was the size of grown man's heart and he cradled it in his hands like a newborn child.

Marduk felt greed and desire rise within him. He licked his lips and toyed with the activation rune of his chainsword as he stared at his master. As the Dark Apostle had said, the prophecy had been fulfilled.

A flicker of movement in the corner of his eyes drew his attention and he spun towards it.

A dark shape was rising from the circular pit in the adjacent chamber and Marduk thumbed the activation rune of his chainsword, snarling.

His gazed shifted between Jarulek, who was focused on the sphere in his hands, and the rising shadow that blocked their retreat.

The shape was roughly humanoid, though it was covered in thousands of the metallic scarabs, or more correctly it was *formed* from them. They skittered over the humanoid torso, rising slowly and silently from the pit, their body mass creating the shape of a man.

'Jarulek,' he hissed. The eyes of the Dark Apostle flashed with outrage that he dare use his name, but then he too saw the rising shape.

As they watched, the skittering bugs came to rest as they aligned in their appropriate positions, and their bodies merged, like droplets of water that were sucked together to form a greater mass. Thousands of metallic insects blurred together, their individual shapes and limbs moulding like liquid metal to form the immaculate and perfect form of a skeletal torso, gleaming silver.

Black, carapaced scarabs gave up their physical uniqueness, forming a black chest plate over the silver ribs of the cadaverous, ancient lord rising up out of the light below. A golden sun gleamed on the centre of the black, lustrous armour plate, golden lines representing the sun's rays spilling from it. The corpse-machine's head was down, its chin lowered, and its eye sockets were dark and hollow.

A long-hafted weapon was formed in the creature's metallic hands, as hundreds of scarabs gripped each other with claw and mandible to form a solid shape. They blurred as they melted together, creating an arcane and impressively sized weapon, a pair of curving blades at each end of a long shaft.

Marduk and Jarulek raised their weapons as one, the Dark Apostle supporting the heavy weight of his archaic bolter on his forearm, the orb still held in his hand. They unleashed a salvo of barking shots towards the forming corpse-machine. Bolts smashed into its gleaming, silver skull, blasting chunks of metal away, and others caused chips of black stone to crack from its chest plate.

These pieces of metal and stone landed on the black, glossy surface of the floor and immediately returned to their metallic scarab forms. They skittered about for a second before launching themselves into the air, wafer-thin metallic wings clicking out. They hovered over the deathly machine before settling on the damage done by the guns of the holy Word Bearer warriors. The metallic insects disappeared as they melted into the metal body of their master, leaving no appearance of the damage that had been caused.

'The Undying One,' said Jarulek.

A scarab with a gleaming, golden carapace skittered over the skull of the forming creature, and it melted to become a shining circlet upon its forehead, glittering with intricate, alien line work. It was an alien yet clearly regal device, and Marduk was left in no doubt that this was some lord of the undead, living machines.

Swarms of smaller insects, some barely large enough for the eye to discern, glided over the silver bones of the creature and blurred together, forming a semi-opaque, wafer-thin, billowing shroud that whipped around the skeletal form. This cloak had a dark, metallic sheen as if it had been woven of infinitely fine mesh, and it shimmered like liquid metal. It fluttered as if caught in a breeze, though there was no movement of air. From beneath the deep hood, the darkness of the creature's eye sockets began to glow a baleful green and it raised its chin to look upon the interlopers trespassing on its ancient realm. A feeling of dread washed over Marduk. He gritted his sharp teeth in anger at the unwelcome and uncommon feeling.

The creature rose higher out of the pit, accompanied by a rhythmic humming noise, and the light beneath it grew stronger, throwing its skull into deeper shadow beneath its billowing shroud. Rather than ending in hips and legs, the metallic spinal column of the creature merged into a bulky shape that was not dissimilar to the armoured carapace of one of the diminutive scarabs, though on a colossal scale. Thousands of teeming insects scrambled over each other and moulded together to form this lower body, and eight barbed legs hanging beneath the bulk of its armour took shape. The light filling the room came from beneath this carapace, shining out below it and throwing its upper body into gloom.

The creature rose into the air, hovering above the open pit as it awoke, its silver, insect legs curling and clicking beneath it, the humanoid torso flexing as the ancient, unliving being rolled its shoulders. It did not move in the same manner as the skeletal machines guarding the upper chambers of the pyramid. Where they were mechanical and jerky in movement, this creature was fluid and supple, its limbs moving smoothly and in perfect balance.

It spun the staff before it, the twin blades humming through the air. It seemed ignorant or uncaring of the Word Bearers as it went through a series of lithe movements with the double-headed blade, spinning the haft of the weapon around in its metallic hands with consummate ease.

Intent on the monstrous creature, Marduk failed to see Jarulek raising his ornate bolter towards his head.

'And this, my First Acolyte, is where your education comes to an end,' breathed the Dark Apostle, and pulled the trigger.

CHAPTER TWENTY-THREE

MARDUK THREW HIMSELF to the side, servo-muscles straining, but he could not avoid the burst of fire at such close range. The mass-reactive tips of the bolt-rounds impacted with the side of his helmet as he dodged and their explosions tore the right side of his helmet and face apart in a gory mess of blood and sparks.

He fell, smashed to the ground by the impact. The inside of his helmet was awash with blood and he ripped it from his head, hurling it away from him as he staggered backwards on the floor.

He could feel that the left side of his skull was shattered and he could not see from his left eye. He felt fragments of bone and tooth in his mouth, and he spat them to the floor amid blood and saliva. He tongued the inside of his mouth and felt that the teeth on his left side had been shattered, and where he should have felt the inside of his cheek, he felt nothing. The flesh had been completely blown away. He heard a chuckle.

'*One shall fall, he of lesser faith, he unmarked by godly touch,*' Jarulek said. 'Did you think that I did not notice your treacherous intent, whelp? Your usefulness passed as soon as you fulfilled your role in the prophecy.'

Marduk blinked blood from his working eye. He scrabbled on the ground around him, but realised that he had lost his grip on his bolt pistol and it lay out of his reach. He felt dizzy and disoriented.

Jarulek stood with his bolter pointed at Marduk. The metal sphere was still in one hand and the bolter was supported upon his forearm. He stared down the stylised daemonic maw that was the barrel of the archaic weapon and Marduk knew that he was too far from the Dark Apostle to be able to rush him without taking a full clip of bolts.

'What damned prophecy?' he spat, his jaw not working properly, spraying blood.

'Why, the Prophecy of Jarulek, dear Marduk: the prophecy that appears on only one page: my flesh, the prophecy that I have lived with since the fall of the Warmaster. The prophecy says that only one of us will leave this place and I intend that to be me.'

Marduk tensed himself to leap. He wiped the blood from his face quickly with his free hand and he saw Jarulek's eyes widen in shock.

A searing beam of green light slammed into the back of the Dark Apostle and ripped through him, boring a fist-sized hole from abdomen to lower back.

The bolter in Jarulek's hand barked as Marduk leapt from the floor, bolts ricocheting around the chamber. With a roar of pure hatred, Marduk swung the blade of his chainsword towards the staggering Dark Apostle, but Jarulek managed to bring his arm up before him and swipe the blade away, though it tore a chunk of armour and flesh from his arm. Marduk felt the faint presence of the daemon Borhg'ash rouse within the weapon as it tasted the sacrosanct blood, and it lent him strength.

'The mark! This cannot be!' screamed Jarulek, his eyes locked to Marduk's forehead, where pain still seared him.

Another blast of green light speared towards the pair and Marduk rolled to the side to avoid it, coming to his feet quickly, positioning himself so he could see both enemies with his limited vision.

The skeletal, ancient xenos lord was hovering towards them, its dark shroud whipping around it furiously. The tips of its double-bladed staff were glowing with power and it thrust one end forwards, a searing beam lancing from the weapon. Marduk swayed to the side, the blast just grazing against his chest plate, searing a groove along it as the super-hard ceramite was stripped away.

Bolts impacted with his chest a millisecond later, slamming him back against the wall. He snarled, his attention swinging towards Jarulek.

'I'm going to rip you apart, you whoreson,' he spat.

'Not the way one should speak to his holy leader. Mark or no mark, you are dying here,' said Jarulek. Seeing movement, he turned and fired a burst towards the advancing alien machine-creature, the bolts making its head reel back, but not slowing its advance.

Marduk rolled as another green lance of light streaked towards him, and came up in front of the Dark Apostle. His chainsword roared and he ripped it up in a murderous arc as he rose, carving it between Jarulek's legs. Pre-empting the attack, but with nothing to defend against it, the Dark Apostle released his grip on his bolter and grabbed the whirring chainblades with his hand, halting its progress before it struck.

Blood and ceramite sprayed as his hand was ripped apart, but the move had taken Marduk by surprise, and the Dark Apostle slammed a kick into the outside of his knee. The leg collapsed beneath him. Jarulek followed the attack with a thundering elbow that struck Marduk in the head, cracking the bone, and he fell heavily.

Switching the precious sphere into the crook of his other, now hand-less, arm, Jarulek swept up his discarded bolter with his left hand and fired towards the closing skeletal alien, hefting the kicking weapon with difficulty in one hand. Bolts hammered into the creature's arm, sending its next shot wide. The Dark Apostle hurled the bolter aside, its ammo spent, and pulled his crozius arcanum from where it hung on his hip, the spiked head of the holy weapon crackling with energy as it came to life. He sprang directly towards the hovering, monstrous creature, a curse on his lips.

Marduk scrambled to his feet, swept up the Dark Apostle's discarded bolter and slammed a new clip into its base. He looked up to see the hovering, skeletal machine fire a blast of green energy towards Jarulek, who swayed to the side with nigh on preternatural speed, and leapt forwards with a shout, swinging the crozius towards the foe.

The enemy lowered itself towards the ground, so that it hovered less than a metre above the floor, its claws clicking and flexing beneath it. Its shimmering shroud whipped around it and it flashed out with its double-bladed staff, blocking Jarulek's attack with a screech of sparks and crackling energy. The other end of the staff swept around, its long curved blade slicing towards his throat. The Dark Apostle swayed beneath the lightning quick repost and swung his crozius again. The heavy blow was deflected easily and he stepped to the side, moving further around the flank of the creature and closer to escape.

Marduk broke into a run, invoking the gods of Chaos, and fired the bolter one-handed. If the Dark Apostle escaped then his life was forfeit. The bolts slammed into Jarulek's lower back, pitching him forwards. He roared in despair as he lost his grip on the metal sphere, and it flew through the air away from him.

The hovering corpse-machine swung its weapon in a wide arc as the Dark Apostle fell, the blow carving through the chest armour just below the fused ribcage. Blood sprayed from the wound and from the blade as it passed through the Dark Apostle's body and out the other side, severing his torso. Jarulek flailed frantically for the spilled sphere as he fell to the ground in two pieces, his lifeblood flooding the floor beneath him.

Marduk leapt, landing with his right foot on the carapace of the enemy and hacked his chainsword into its head. Chunks of metal were torn loose by the whirring chainblade, turning almost instantly into tiny, metallic flying scarabs, and the death's-head visage of the foe was snapped back by the force of the blow. Pushing off with his other foot, Marduk leapt through the air, his good eye focused on the falling sphere, and his hand reaching out vainly to catch it.

The metal ball slipped beyond his reach and hit the ground with a heavy, reverberating thud. It did not bounce, but began to roll straight towards the pit from which the cursed alien creature had emerged. Marduk hit the ground and slid after the ancient artefact. His hand closed on it just as it rolled clear of the edge and the unnatural weight of it almost took him with it.

He saw Jarulek's eyes glaring at him, filled with bitterness and hatred. The Dark Apostle clawed his way towards him, pulling his legless torso across the blood-slick floor.

'*He unmarked by godly touch,*' spat the Dark Apostle. 'You deceived me, Marduk. Somehow, you kept that mark concealed.'

Jarulek was silenced as his head was skewered upon the blade of the massive skeletal creature. It lifted his severed torso high into the air and the dark crozius slipped from dead fingers to the floor. The Dark Apostle was hurled through the air, thudding wetly against the curving wall of the chamber. He slid down its slick surface and disappeared into the abyssal darkness.

Marduk attached his daemon-blade to his waist and staggered forward to retrieve the fallen crozius. He raised it before him and it crackled to life, arcing blue electricity shimmering over its spiked head.

He felt the baleful gaze of the enemy fall towards him and he turned and ran.

MARDUK STAGGERED FROM the gateway, falling to his knees, the ice-cold sphere cradled under his arm.

Had the Undying One allowed him to leave its realm? No, he told himself, my faith brought me back from that ungodly place.

Gunfire blared around him and he stumbled up the black steps to the top of the dais. The Anointed, their ranks more than halved in number, had fallen back, forming an ever-tightening circle of warriors.

Kol Badar spun as he saw the First Acolyte rise from the steps, and took a few paces forward, lightning crackling across the talons of his power claw, but he slowed his advance as he drew nearer.

'Where is the Dark Apostle?' he thundered.

'Dead,' spat Marduk. 'He sacrificed himself that I may escape to lead the Host.'

'That is a lie!' roared Kol Badar, stepping forward to smash Marduk with his powerful fist. He halted his movement as Marduk lifted the crozius up between them.

'The Dark Apostle gifted me this, his sacred crozius arcanum,' said Marduk, his voice raised loudly to carry to all the Anointed. 'He told me to lead the Host to Sicarus, to see me sworn in as Dark Apostle. He sacrificed himself that I could escape with that which we have fought so hard, my brothers, to attain. Come,' he said, as more of the Word Bearers were cut down by the scything green flashes of the xenos weaponry, 'we must vacate this world.'

Kol Badar clenched his fist but did not move. Did he know that Jarulek had always intended to see him dead, pondered Marduk? Most probably, he surmised.

'The Host must honour the Dark Apostle's last wishes, else his sacrifice has been made in vain,' said Marduk loudly, a smile curling the right side of his mouth. The left side of his face was a mess of torn and missing flesh. 'Come, Coryphaus, we must leave here.'

Kol Badar's face twisted in anger and hatred, and he lashed out violently with his power claw, the talons curling around Marduk's neck, crushing the ceramite of his gorget and lifting the smaller Word Bearer up into the air before him like a child. The muscles of his neck straining against the immense grip, Marduk still managed a crooked smile.

'Just like our encounter upon the cursed moon so many years past, Coryphaus, and all because I killed your worthless, heathen blood-brother.' Marduk's face turned red as Kol Badar tightened his grip. 'He was a worthless dog, not fit to be named Word Bearer,' gasped Marduk. 'He brought nothing but shame to the noble Host. Lorgar himself would have done as I did that day.'

'Your words are poison. They mean nothing to me,' snarled Kol Badar, exerting even more force, hearing the enhanced muscles and vertebrae of the First Acolyte groan in resistance to his pressure.

'You would try to kill me here, Kol Badar?' snarled Marduk, his voice strained.

'You wouldn't be able to stop me,' growled the big warrior.

'No,' said Marduk, with difficulty, 'but *he* would.'

Kol Badar glanced to his side to see Burias-Drak'shal's hulking form beside him, staring at him. Great horns rose from the possessed warrior's forehead and his corded muscles were tense. His massive clawed hands clenched and unclenched as he stared at the Coryphaus with glittering, daemonic eyes filled with bestial rage.

The possessed warrior rose to his full, towering height, his chest rising and falling heavily as he drew breath, steam billowing from his flared nostrils. He was quivering with anticipation for the kill, veins bulging within his hyper-tense muscles.

'You would stand against me, Icon Bearer?' growled Kol Badar.

'I would not stand against the holy leader of the Host,' replied Burias-Drak'shal, forming the words with some difficulty, his jaw having altered in form to contain his thick, tusk-like teeth.

'And this is not he!' thundered the Coryphaus.

'The Dark Apostle entrusted me with his holy writ,' said Marduk. 'Go against me and forfeit your life. Choose your words carefully.'

The Coryphaus was silent. The sound of bolters firing echoed from the glossy black walls, accompanied by the death groans of falling Anointed warriors.

'We cannot leave this place without the Dark Apostle,' Kol Badar said, at last.

'He is dead!' snarled Marduk.

'Then we must bear his holy body back to Sicarus,' roared Kol Badar, his grip around Marduk's neck tightening. Burias-Drak'shal hissed and grasped Kol Badar's arm, his claws digging deep, cutting into the thick armour. Their strength was evenly matched.

'You would dare put hands upon me,' Kol Badar growled. Burias-Drak'shal snarled, digging his talons in deeper, blood pooling around them and flowing over the Coryphaus's sacred Terminator armour.

'And you would dare defy my command?' asked Marduk. 'Your life is on tenterhooks, Kol Badar. We leave this place, *now*. Choose your path. Follow me, or die here in this tomb. Your name will be cursed by the Legion for time immaterial, a traitor to the Legion and a traitor to Lorgar.'

Kol Badar stared at Marduk, who returned the glare, staring back at himself in the eyes of the Terminator's helmet.

'Choose swiftly, Kol Badar. The warriors of the Legion are dying.'

'This is not over,' growled Kol Badar, releasing his grip around Marduk's neck with a shove. 'Remove your hands, Icon Bearer.' Burias-Drak'shal looked to Marduk, who nodded, and the possessed warrior released his grip, blood upon his talons.

Kol Badar swung away, shouting orders.

'We leave, now!' he roared. 'Form up!'

'Your forehead,' growled Burias-Drak'shal. 'You bear the mark of Lorgar.'

The burning pain on his forehead was as nothing to the pain covering the rest of his head, but it was worth the feeling of satisfaction that he felt as he looked upon the crozius in his hands.

'Let us leave this forsaken world,' said Marduk. 'It has served its purpose.'

AT MARDUK'S PSYCHIC call, the *Infidus Diabolus* returned to the shattered wreck of Tanakreg, tearing a rift in reality as it emerged from the warp to meet the Thunderhawks, Stormbirds and other landing craft streaming up from the planet's surface.

The Imperial ships that had remained in orbit around the planet moved to engage, though they were sluggish to respond to its appearance. Their astropaths' senses were dulled by the warp field projected by the Gehemehnet and they had no warning as to the strike cruiser's sudden appearance. The Imperial ships kept a respectful distance from the field of unbridled Chaos energy that the tower continued to project into the outer atmosphere. Flights of fighters swarmed from the bowels of the *Infidus Diabolus* to slow the enemy's approach, though the Chaos ships were outnumbered and outclassed by those of the Imperial Navy.

Several transportation craft were destroyed as they sought to dock with the *Infidus Diabolus* and the powerful strike cruiser took damage from incoming torpedoes fired from an Imperial Dictator class warship.

The Host had suffered heavy casualties and many of the holy suits of armour worn by the Anointed had been lost in the xenos pyramid. The revered religious leader of the Host had fallen, and long would be the requiem services dedicated to his honour. The First Acolyte, mourning the loss of his master and spiritual guide, would lead these ceremonies of lamentation and grievance.

The *Infidus Diabolus* returned to the roiling seas of the Ether, forging a path towards the Eye of Terror and Sicarus, the world claimed by the Daemon-Primarch Lorgar, and the religious seat of the Council of Apostles. There Marduk would face trial, to prove his worth to be embraced into the fold and become a true Dark Apostle of the Word.

EPILOGUE

THE TWITCHING MAGOS was held against the back wall of the cell, deep within the *Infidus Diabolus*. His legs had been sheared off above the knees, and he hung suspended by dozens of chains. His wasted arms, covered with cancers and black malignancies, were outstretched and clamped with spiked manacles attached to further chains. Those arms had not been moved or utilised for centuries, and they were little more than canker ridden, skin-covered bones. They had broken as they had been pulled away from their position across the magos's chest, where they had been held unmoving for countless centuries.

Marduk moved beneath the sole, flickering glow-globe that buzzed overhead. The entire left side of his face was covered in augmetics and the skin around these bionics was puckered and a deathly shade of blue. His left eye was an angry, lidless, red orb, the pupil slender and slitted like a cat's. He had rejected the bionic eye replacements that the Chirumeks had offered, instead demanding this daemonic flesh hybrid, and he was pleased with the chirurgeons' efforts.

The sparking stubs of four mechanical servo-arms flailed spasmodically from the priest's shoulders and the remnants of mechadendrites quivered. Most had been ripped from the magos's spine and those that remained were little more than shorn off, useless protuberances. The haemoncolyte that had been attached by umbilical tubes to the machine priest had been severed from him and its repulsive, diminutive form opened up by the chirurgeons for study. It had squirmed as their knives had cut into its cankerous flesh. Large bell jars filled with viscous liquid

244

protruded from the hunched back of the magos, though several of them had been smashed open, leaking pungent green-blue liquid, and sparking electricity flashed from within them occasionally. The contents of the jars had been placed under close scrutiny to try to tease the secrets from the preserved, ancient brains.

The red robes of the magos had been stripped from his mechanical body, and without its all concealing hood, the priest's head was exposed. Little human flesh remained of its face, and what existed was corpse pale and twitched uncontrollably. Tubes and pipes fed via thick needles had been shoved into his exposed flesh, pumping him with serums and foul secretions.

'It would seem that it has some kind of protective field generator around it,' Kol Badar had explained when the magos had first been discovered amongst the wreckage of the crashed airship.

'I would presume that this is what enabled it to survive the crash,' he had said. 'Allow me to demonstrate.'

The Coryphaus had fired a burst of fire from his combi-bolter towards the magos and an energy bubble surrounding the priest of the Machine-God shimmered as it absorbed the momentum from the incoming bolt-rounds, slowing them enough for them to fall harmlessly at the magos's feet.

But this device did not protect him any longer. No, the device had been prised from his flesh and the Chirumeks of the Host were even now examining its workings. Marduk could do whatever he wanted to the magos, who now had no defence.

'Greetings Magos Darioq.'

'I will not aid you Marduk, First Acolyte of the Word Bearers Legion of Astartes, genetic descendant of the traitor Primarch Lorgar. My systems are failing. This flesh unit is dying and I shall soon become one with *Deus Machina*.'

'You *will* aid me, and you will *not* be granted release. Yes, your flesh is dying since we removed your filthy dwarf clone, but soon you will be… changed. A daemon essence is being nurtured especially for you; you should feel privileged. Soon it will merge with you. Daemon, human and machine will become one within you. You will become that which your order loathes.'

Marduk smiled, the buzzing glow-globe lighting his face daemonically.

Soon you will be a puppet, dancing to my words, thought Marduk, and then you will beg to do my bidding. You will unlock the secrets of the Nexus Arrangement and a new era of destruction will be unleashed upon the Imperium of Man.

DARK DISCIPLE

PROLOGUE

It FELT LIKE his body was on fire. Every nerve ending was awash with agony. He had never dreamed that such excruciating torment could be possible.

A shadow leant over him, the image of death itself: skeletal, hateful, merciless. Eyes as black as pits bored into him, savouring his torment.

'Your suffering is only just beginning,' it promised, its voice matter-of-fact and even.

Needles plunged into his veins.

Then the prisoner heard a cry, the bestial roar of an animal in pain, and it took him a moment to realise that it originated from his own raw throat.

Blades slid from the tips of Death's long fingers and sliced through his skin, each deft incision drawing forth a wave of pain. Blood welled beneath each cut and was hungrily sucked up into tiny tubes attached to the grooved scalpel blades. The tubes ran along the back of Death's fingers and joined the protruding veins on the backs of his hands, feeding the filtered vitae into its bloodstream.

'Give in to the pain,' it said calmly. 'Beg for mercy.'

He gritted his teeth, and felt the metallic taste of blood on his lips. The vision of death leant closer.

'Fear me,' it whispered, and fresh agony jabbed through his body.

A needle appeared in front of his left eye, its barbed tip dripping with fluid. His muscles strained to turn away, but his head was held fast, and he could do nothing as the needle was pushed agonisingly slowly into the soft tissue of his eyeball. He hissed as it slid through his pupil and deep into his cornea.

The prisoner whispered something, and his tormentor turned, straining to hear.

'You will never break me,' the prisoner said again, this time with more force. 'Pain holds no fear for me.'

'Pain? You know nothing of it yet,' said his tormentor calmly.

Flaps of skin were teased back, exposing the vulnerable flesh beneath. Nerve endings were seared and his body jerked spasmodically as agonised muscles tensed involuntarily. His primary heart palpitated erratically and the needle in his eye twisted, grinding against the inside of the socket.

'You *will* come to fear me, in time,' mused the softly spoken image of death, plucking at his captive's exposed tendons, making the fingers of his left arm twitch. 'We are in no rush.'

Memories struggled to surface on the edge of the prisoner's mind. He tried to grasp them, but they were as elusive as shadow, taunting him, just out of reach.

Fresh agonies assailed the captive as dozens of barbed needles stabbed into his spinal column, sliding between his vertebrae and plunging into the tender flesh within.

Darkness rose to claim him, but he fought it with all his being, straining to possess the elusive memories that hovered just beyond his reach.

Abruptly, a name rose to his lips from the very depths of his being.

His name.

'Marduk,' he whispered. Fresh strength flowed through him as the dam holding his memories at bay broke. He smiled, his sharp teeth stained with blood.

'My faith is strong,' Marduk whispered hoarsely. 'You will not break me.'

'Every living thing can be broken,' said his tormentor, black eyes gleaming. 'Everything begs for death come the end. You and I, we will find that point together. You will beg come the end. They all do.'

'Not in this lifetime,' snarled Marduk. Then his eyes rolled back in his head and he succumbed to darkness, a bloody grin on his face.

BOOK ONE: PERDUS SKYLLA

'In true faith there is enough light for those who want to believe, and enough shadow to blind those fools that don't.'

– Apostate Evangelistae Paskaell

CHAPTER ONE

MACHION-DEX, PROCURATOR OF the Adeptus Mechanicus archive facility of Kharion IV, strode across the grilled deck, his footsteps echoing loudly through the enclosed space. Ten expressionless skitarii warriors marched in a protective cordon around him, hellguns hard-wired into their brainstems held at the ready in black-gloved, augmetic hands.

The procurator came to a halt mid-deck, alongside an array of cogitator banks that rose from the floor. A blank data-screen reflected his image back at him. A servitor, nothing left of its original body other than a head and torso of morbidly pale flesh, was plugged directly with the logic-engines. Ribbed tubes connected its eye-sockets to the data-slate, and clusters of wires and cables ran from its severed torso into the machine's innards.

The skitarii warrior-units broke into two groups and stepped out to either side of Machion-Dex to form a corridor, their movements in perfect, robotic synchronicity. They moved to within a metre of a strip of yellow and black hazard stripes upon a plate bisecting the room. Their heavy boots stamped as they came to attention, awaiting their next command.

Machion-Dex folded his arms across his chest. He wore a vermillion tabard over a black bodysuit, its hems stitched with bronze wire, and his head was shaved to the scalp. Cables and clusters of wires sank into the flesh around the base of his skull, and a tattoo of a cogwheel, half black and half white, was emblazoned on his forehead.

'Initiate lock-down,' he said to the servitor, which twitched in response.

A series of red glow-globes began to strobe, and to the sound of wailing klaxons, heavy-duty plasteel blast-doors, half a metre thick and containing a sandwiched core of interlaced adamantine, slammed down from the ceiling in front of the procurator and his entourage. Secondary layers of reinforced ceramite dropped down on either side of the main blast-doors with a crash, and tertiary armoured plates of thirty-centimetre thermaplas slid from wall recesses, slamming together with titanic force.

Pistons wheezed as arcane locking mechanisms rotated and clinched shut, sealing off the sole entrance into the installation of Kharion IV. Not even half a kiloton of military grade explosive would be able to penetrate those doors without destroying half of the asteroid that the installation was embedded within.

The blaring klaxons stopped abruptly, along with the flashing red warning lights.

'Connect screen feed,' said Machion-Dex, and the servitor twitched again.

The blank data-screen before the procurator burst into life, covered in a snowstorm of static. Machion-Dex murmured a blessing to the Omnissiah and pressed a ritualistic sequence of buttons upon the data-slate's side panel. A green, pixellated image of the room beyond the blast-doors appeared on the screen's surface.

The procurator folded his arms, and the fingers of his right hand began to tap a nervous rhythm on his bicep as he waited for his guest's arrival.

The walls of the room beyond the blast-doors were scorched black, and half a dozen automated heavy flamers rotated in their mounts, aiming towards the circular bulkhead on the far wall. The pilot-flames of the weapons burnt hot white on the green data-slate screen.

There was a shuddering clang beyond the bulkhead as the access artery connecting to the docking facility clamped into position. There followed a burst of super-heated steam that partially obscured Machion-Dex's view of the audience room, and a pair of lights located above the bulkhead began to rotate, sending shadows dancing across the fire-blackened walls.

The circular locking mechanism located in the centre of the bulkhead clicked outwards and rotated a full turn clockwise, before turning half a turn anticlockwise and sinking back into its recess. Then, with a shuddering groan, the bulkhead doors slid aside.

There was a hiss as atmospheric pressure equalised, and Machion-Dex leant forwards, squinting at the image on his data-screen. At first, nothing could be seen beyond the gaping aperture revealed by the parting bulkhead doors, and the darkness there was heavily pixellated and vague. Then a bulky robed and hooded shape appeared.

A single, unblinking light shone from beneath its hood, positioned where a left eye would have been. It limped down the fire-blackened steps to the metal grilled mechanical floor. Four massive individuals accompanied it; they too were heavily robed, their faces obscured by deep hoods. They turned their heads to regard the heavy flamers that rotated to fix upon them.

The lead figure limped across the room, unconcerned, and came to a halt before the blast-doors.

'Blessings of the Omnissiah upon you,' it intoned , looking up at the armoured relay camera box positioned above it. Up close, Machion-Dex could see the cogged wheel symbol of the Adeptus Mechanicus upon its chest.

'And upon you, servant of the Machine God Incarnate,' replied the procurator, speaking into a grilled vox-unit.

'Knowledge is the supreme manifestation of divinity,' said Machion-Dex, invoking the sixth of the Mysteries, one of the sixteen Universal Laws memorised by all adepts of the Cult Mechanicus.

'Comprehension is the key to all things,' came the reply.

'The Omnissiah knows all,' said Machion-Dex.

'The Omnissiah comprehends all.'

Satisfied, Machion-Dex keyed a sequence of commands into the data-slate, and a control pillar rose from the floor beside the image of the hooded figure beyond the blast-doors. The procurator saw a mechanical tentacle emerge from within the figure's robes. It lifted up before the camera, its mechanical claws snapping open and shut. A thirty-centimetre data-spike slid from the centre of the snapping claw, and it was thrust into the control pillar.

A flood of data flowed over the data-screen in front of Machion-Dex, the apparently never-ending stream of scrolling information overlaying the motionless image of the hooded figure. The procurator's eyes flicked left and right, and his mouth moved soundlessly as the internal processors built into the left hemisphere of his brain-unit registered and recorded the flow of data.

The information was quickly processed and Machion-Dex blew out a slow intake of breath, impressed. With a click of a button he dismissed the stream of information from the screen.

'Deactivate weapon hardware,' he said, and the heavy flamer units went offline, their pilot lights cutting out. They turned away from their targets and retracted back into their housings.

Machion-Dex cleared his throat and leant forward to speak once more into the vox-unit.

'Access granted, Tech-Magos Darioq. Welcome to Kharion IV.'

MAGOS DARIOQ STOOD stock still, his features hidden in the darkness beneath his hood as the blast-doors were opened. Steam from the disengaging lock mechanisms vented around him.

'Revered magos,' said the procurator, bowing his head and touching his fingers to the symbol of the Adeptus Mechanicus, 'your visit is most unexpected.'

Darioq remained motionless as his four companions jerked into motion, marching suddenly forwards. Each of them stood almost two and a half metres in height, and their massive shoulders were twice as wide as the procurator's.

Machion-Dex's eyes flicked between the intimidating figures in alarm. He had thought them combat servitors, but he saw now that their movements were arrogant and self-assured, far from the ungainly, stilted gait of a servitor.

Robes were thrown aside and archaic bolters raised, and before the skitarii warriors' targeting arrays registered a threat, the first of the weapons began to roar.

Fire burst from the barrels of the ancient weapons. The sound was deafening, filling the enclosed space and echoing painfully off the walls. Fully half the skitarii were destroyed in an instant as high explosive shells tore through their bodies, ripping them apart in bloody explosions of armour and flesh.

Machion-Dex stumbled backwards, falling to the ground, his face a mask of horror as he gazed upon the massive, augmented beings. Their armour, inscribed with heretical symbols and litanies, was the deep red of congealed blood, and they fired with controlled discipline, eliminating each target with practiced efficiency.

The remaining skitarii brought their hellguns to bear, energy capacitors humming as the weapons surged into life. Electric-blue las-beams stabbed from the barrels of their guns, knocking one of the towering warriors back a step, searing holes through his robe and leaving smoking black impacts on his armour.

Two more of the skitarii were cut down, one of them spinning as a bolt slammed into his shoulder and exploded, severing its arm and leaving a gory head-sized hole in its torso. A bolt round detonated in the brainpan of the other and its head exploded, spraying blood, brain matter and splinters of skull in all directions.

A las-blast struck one of the warriors in the helmet, jolting his head backwards. With a snarl of anger, he ripped the skitarii apart with his return fire.

The firefight was over in seconds. The acrid smell of gunfire rose from smoking, silent barrels, and two of the giant warriors moved in to inspect the kills. One of the skitarii, who had been cut in half by a burst of gunfire, was still twitching. His movements were halted as a heavy armoured boot slammed down on its head, crushing its skull like a nut beneath a hammer.

Machion-Dex lay on his back, his breath coming in short gasps as he stared up at the terrifying figures. Each was massive, their every movement filled with power, and their inscrutable, Heresy-era Astartes helmets extensively modified to make them all the more fearsome in appearance. One had been fashioned in the likeness of a snarling daemon, and others had fierce sets of curving horns and tusks that gave them a brutal, barbaric look.

One wore no helmet at all, but its true face was far more terrifying than any of the helmets. The left side was a mess of scar tissue and augmetics, and its skin was so pale as to be translucent; blue veins could be seen within its flesh. A lidless, baleful red orb had replaced its left eye, and an infernal glyph of the ruinous powers was emblazoned prominently in the centre of its forehead. The figure snarled down at him, lips pulling back to expose sharpened teeth.

'Area secure,' growled one of the warriors, and the one standing over Machion-Dex nodded, not taking his eyes from the procurator.

'The location of the target will be found here, Enslaved?' he said over his shoulder, his voice filled with power and authority.

'That is correct, Marduk, First Acolyte of the Word Bearers Legion of Astartes, genetic descendant of the traitor Primarch Lorgar,' replied Magos Darioq in his monotone voice.

'Then let's get this done,' replied Marduk. He stepped towards the cowering form of Procurator Machion-Dex, and looked down at the terrified man.

'Do you need this one?' he asked over his shoulder.

'His continued existence is not required in order to retrieve the information held within the logic-centres of this installation,' replied the magos.

Procurator Machion-Dex gasped and began to scramble backwards, desperate to get away from the image of death looming over him.

Marduk's bolt pistol was levelled at the procurator's head and he froze.

'No,' begged the man. 'Omnissiah, protect your servant.'

Marduk smirked.

'Your profane god does not heed your cry, heathen,' said Marduk. 'You have devoted your entire, pathetic, worthless life to the worship of a false deity, a silent, profane image of the unbelievers. I will show you the path to the true gods. In death, you will bear witness to the glory of the true gods. They will feed upon your soul, and you will cry out in your torment. Embrace it, little man. Embrace your damnation.'

He shot the procurator in the head, and blood and gore splashed across the grilled floor.

'Glory be to the true gods,' declared Marduk.

MARDUK STOOD WITH his arms folded, deep in the bowels of Kharion IV. He stood upon a grilled gantry within the hollowed core of the asteroid, a massive pillar of machinery rising from the roughly hewn floor before him, glittering with lights and dials.

The magos stood before the humming pillar, fluid leaking from the severed input-jacks in his spine. He was connected to the pillar by the one mechadendrite tentacle that had been re-grafted to his body, and his pallid, dead lips twitched as he extracted information from the heart of the installation's data-library.

At last, the flexible tendril was retracted, and Magos Darioq jerked spasmodically as the connection was severed.

'Well?' growled Marduk.

'I have disabled the automated defence system that protects the installation,' said Magos Darioq, 'and initiated the self-destruct mechanism, so that our presence will not be transmitted to the god-cogitators of Mars.'

'Good,' said Marduk. He grabbed the waving mechadendrite tentacle with a violent motion and gave it a solid wrench. It was ripped from the magos's spinal column, writhing in his hand like a serpent. Darioq twitched, and milky liquid seeped from his mouth.

'You have the information we need?' asked Marduk, ignoring the mixture of blood, oil and protein-fluid that dripped from the thrashing mechadendrite onto his boots.

'That is correct, Marduk, First Acolyte of the Word Bearers Legion of Astartes, genetic descendant of the traitor Primarch Lorgar,' replied the magos. 'I have identified the location of the one in whom the forbidden knowledge of xenos tech devices is installed. With this knowledge obtained, Darioq will be able to unlock the xenos tech device.'

It was an odd quirk of the daemonic essence growing within the magos that he had begun to refer to himself in the third person. Marduk found this amusing, but at this moment he was concentrating fully on the words of the corrupted magos.

That the magos had not been able to unlock the device himself was infuriating, but it seemed that he could do little other than find the one of whom it spoke.

'Where?' snapped Marduk in impatience.

BENEATH THE SURFACE of Perdus Skylla, tens of thousands of people surged down access tunnel 25XI, a never-ending stream of humanity, desperate and fearful. They were crushed together like animals being led to the slaughter, and the air, stale and hot, was filled with shouts and curses.

Mothers clutched wailing children to their chests, and men barked at each other, pushing and shoving. Some stumbled and were trampled underfoot, while others were pressed against the rockcrete walls, crushed by the relentlessly driving push of humanity. Others fainted, overcome by the heat and the lack of oxygen. The crowd was so tightly packed that, unable to fall, their limp bodies were carried along in the suffocating press.

The stink of sweat and oil was heavy, the turbines of the labouring air recycling units unable to cope with the demands required of them. The rockcrete ceiling, above which was half a kilometre of solid ice, pressed down oppressively.

The access tunnel was some forty metres wide and bisected by barriers and rockcrete pillars. Beyond these barriers, traversing down the centre of the corridor, was a sunken area of open space in which wide-gauged tracks were embedded. People pushed, shoved and cried out as they were carried along the platforms on either side of the rail tracks.

With a blast of solid displaced air, a high-speed automated carriage sped by, gushing superheated steam and making the access corridor reverberate as it screamed along the slick, steel tracks. Knocked back a step by the force of the conveyance, people covered their eyes and gazed ruefully at the mirrored sides of the carriage as it passed. Only the wealthy guild masters and their staff had the funds and access privileges to use the high-speed conveyances.

It was a two hundred kilometre journey to Phorcys, the sole starport off Perdus Skylla within five thousand kilometres. Access tunnel 25XI was the only link between Antithon Guild and Phorcys, unless one wished to traverse across the frozen surface of the moon. Few ventured up to the inhospitable surface of Perdus Skylla other than outcasts; those unlucky enough not to be born into any of the great guild-houses, or who had been exiled from them for serious infractions.

Twelve other mining guilds were connected to Phorcys, each of the proud guilds situated around the starport like the points of a compass and connected by artery tunnels like the spokes of a great wheel.

Most of the people of Antithon Guild had never left the hab-blisters deep in the ice other than to commute to the mining facilities some five thousand kilometres below. Fewer still had been to Phorcys, and few amongst the tide of humanity had any real understanding of the distance involved. To them, Antithon Guild and its environs was their world and universe, harsh and uncompromising, but familiar and safe, and they had no need to know of anything beyond its boundaries.

Or at least it had been safe until the first of the sirens had begun to wail and the pict broadcasts had declared that Perdus Skylla was being evacuated.

No reason for the evacuation had been issued from the guild master general's office, and the twenty-three million strong population of the moon had been in shock. Shock had quickly descended into panic as rumours spread of an imminent xenos invasion, rumours that were not in any way refuted by the Administratum.

Groups of the Skyllan Interdiction Force pushed through the crowds, attempting to maintain order. They wore their customary white body armour over sky-blue uniforms, and held high-powered laslocks across their chests. Snarling, shaggy-coated mastiffs with gleaming mechanical eye-augments strained at their leashes, sensing the tension in their masters.

An armoured Catalan-class squad vehicle moved slowly along one of the platforms, its white, high-compound plasteel chassis gleaming beneath the humming strip lights overhead. Its flashing lights and blaring siren urged people out of its path, but its progress was slow, for there was no room to allow the vehicle through.

The winged emblem of the mercenary force was resplendent across the broad grill on the front of the heavy vehicle, and a pair of armoured soldiers stood in its dual turret at the rear, swinging the massive twin-linked heavy bolters left and right. Their faces were all but obscured by their white helmets, and black visors hid their eyes from view.

For twenty-five generations, Perdus Skylla had employed the Skyllan Interdiction, an outside mercenary agency funded by the wealthy mining guild conglomerates. They served as the military force protecting the guilds' assets in lieu of a Planetary Defence Force, while simultaneously acting as local law enforcement. Better trained and equipped than most Imperial Guard regiments, the hiring of the Skyllan Interdiction Forces had allowed the mining guilds to concentrate on their endeavours without having to draw away any of its skilled workforce to form a PDF.

Still, even with the mercenaries present within the tunnel to help restore order, the flow of humanity was little short of a rout.

One of the long-furred mastiffs let out a long growl, eyes locked on the ceiling. Seeing nothing, its master jerked its chain hard, silencing the beast.

A creature of shadow clung to the ceiling of the corridor, virtually undetectable to the naked eye or the sophisticated targeting matrices built into the helmets of the Skyllan Interdiction Force. It moved like a spider, making its way across the ceiling with slow, purposeful movements. Its lean, black armoured body disappeared for a second, its menacing form turning as insubstantial as smoke, only to reappear within the shadow of a grilled turbine further along the roof.

The creature's skin was inky black, and elegant runes of alien design were cut into its flesh. The runes glowed with a cold, inner light.

Turning its gaze downwards, it peered malevolently over the sea of humans with eyes that were milky white. It paid particular attention to the armed forces of the Skyllan Interdiction, and its limbs quivered with barely contained bloodlust. The blades running up its forearms hummed in anticipation.

The mastiffs below went into a frenzy of barking as the creature's scent carried to them, and their handlers struggled to control the powerful beasts. The creature disappeared into shadow once more as eyes scanned the ceilings, straining to pick out what had disturbed the dogs.

The air recycling turbines cut out, abruptly. The few who registered the sudden change in air pressure gazed up at the slowing fans in concern. Without the recycling units, the air in the tunnel would turn to poison within hours, as all the oxygen was used up and replaced with the toxic carbon dioxide exhaled by the masses.

Skyllan Interdiction Forces tapped their helmets as their communications went down, as if jammed by interference.

Then the first of the lights went out.

First, one of the lights faded to darkness, then another. The strip lights began to fail, one after another, in both directions, like a wave. People screamed as darkness engulfed them. The lights were going dark faster than a man could run, and within less than a minute every light in sight was dead.

The darkness was complete, all consuming and as black as the abyssal depths of the oceans below. People clutched at one another in panic, unable even to see a hand waving in front their face, and the crowd surged. Spotlights on the Skyllan armoured vehicle clicked on, and they wove back and forth, piercing the darkness like beacons.

People pushed towards the light sources, like moths being drawn to an open flame, and their panicked faces shone like ghosts in the cold light. They pressed against the armoured vehicle as if it was a talisman, those at the front crushed against its armoured sides by those pushing from behind.

Overhead, the nigh-on invisible figure had reappeared, and the runes carved into its flesh glowed with power. Still hugging the ceiling in defiance of gravity, it slid a curved, double-bladed punch dagger from its sheath. Other blades slid from the back of its hands, jutting forward over its fists like the talons of a great cat, and a low hiss of anticipation passed its lips as it waited for its dark kin to arrive in response to its summons.

It did not have to wait long.

A ball of lightning appeared, hanging in mid-air for a fraction of a second before it exploded outwards, blinding those nearby with the sudden burst of energy and throwing them to the ground. The crackling energy was gone in an instant, and an impenetrable void was left in its wake. It was like an inky black pool of water, though it was vertical and hung in mid-air, a plane of absolute darkness no thicker than a single molecule.

Ripples appeared across its surface, as if a pebble had been tossed into its centre, and whining shapes sped from the rent in real space, hurtling up the access corridor at tremendous speed. They screamed overhead, slicing like knives through the darkness. Blades cut through flesh, and hot blood splattered into the faces of hundreds of people, who screamed in terror. Many threw themselves to the ground in fear and were trampled to death by their brothers, sisters and wives in their panic to escape. However, with no lights, and with the tunnel packed from wall to wall with terrified people, there was nowhere to run.

The spotlights atop the armoured Skyllan Interdiction vehicle turned frantically, trying to lock onto the enemies that screamed past them, but they could only hold the speeding shapes in the light for a fraction of a second. A shape dropped from the ceiling, landing lightly atop the vehicle, and the troopers saw a shadowy blur in the rough outline of a humanoid figure perched on the roof of the armoured car before the spotlights were shattered.

The panicked troopers manning the turret-mounted heavy bolters opened fire into the darkness, and muzzle flare lit the area.

A sleek black shape hurtled past, and the mercenaries chased it with high-explosive rounds. They hit nothing but the walls and pillars of the tunnel, ripping away head-sized chunks of rockcrete.

The troopers' mastiffs had erupted into frantic barking and were fighting at their chains. Their masters turned around on the spot, laslocks held to shoulders as they struggled to sight the enemy. Dark shapes were zooming through the tunnel, but the troopers' targeting systems were unable to lock onto the targets.

There was a blur of movement and one of the troopers was sliced open from groin to throat. He squeezed the trigger of his weapon as he fell, blasting into the crowd of surging people, cutting several of them down.

People screamed and ran as the sounds of gunfire echoed deafeningly, fighting each other in their desperation to get to safety. The other troopers turned left and right, trying desperately to hold their targets in sight. A shape screamed overhead, and a trooper's head was severed from its body. The shape was a hundred metres further up the tunnel before the head hit the ground.

Streams of tiny bladed splinters spat out of the darkness towards the mercenaries manning the turret of the armoured vehicle. The razor-sharp shards sliced through their armour and flesh, and blood sprayed out across their pristine white armour.

Their gun silenced, the darkness was once more complete. Screams of terror and pain accompanied the speeding shapes, invisible in the darkness, as they cut through the air. There was a sudden gust of displaced air as another high-speed carriage screamed along the tracks in the middle of the tunnel, the lights from within the automated, servitor-controlled conveyance shining brightly, sending shadows dancing.

Tall-helmeted figures were visible in the flash of light, dragging people kicking and screaming back into the darkness.

A beam of pure darkness stabbed into the high-speed transport, rocking it. The beam tore through the fore-carriage, cutting through the engine block, seats and half a dozen occupants before passing through the roof, leaving a scorched black ring on the ceiling of the tunnel.

Two more searing beams struck it, and the front carriage was knocked off the rails. With the squealing of protesting metal, it slammed into the side-barriers, tearing through them in a shower of sparks. Striking the raised platform at speed, the conveyance tilted up on its nose, and the second and third carriages buckled behind it and rolled onto their sides.

The whole machine flipped onto its side and smashed over the platform's edge, tearing the barrier fully away and smashing through the surging masses. Hundreds were crushed as the carriages flipped across the platform to the sickening sound of metal being wrenched out of shape and scraping across the hard platform surface. It slammed into the tunnel wall, crushing more people between its bulk and the rockcrete walls, and finally came to rest. Electricity discharged across ruined metal wheels and sparked from the rails that had been half-ripped from the floor.

In the wake of the mayhem and silhouetted against the sparks, more black figures advanced through the press of bodies, smashing people to the ground with sharp blows before dragging their semi-conscious bodies back into the darkness.

Mastiffs yelped as they were torn to shreds by concentrated bursts of deadly fire. A blurred shape, little more than a vague, hazy outline, moved like quicksilver through the press of humanity, slicing and cutting, and the last of the Skyllan Indictment Forces were slaughtered without holding any of the enemy in their sights long enough to fire upon them.

A trio of shapes, in tight formation and moving impossibly fast, veered around the wreckage of the ruined rail conveyance, banking over the heads of the terrified masses as they screamed towards the rear of the Catalan-class armoured vehicle. It was peppered with spitting gunfire and detonated as its fuel tanks ruptured, exploding in a blinding fireball that hurled the vehicle across the seething platform.

The three sleek shapes sped through the inferno unscathed and gunned their engines, hurtling once more up the tunnel into the darkness, travelling hundreds of metres in seconds.

THE BLADES OF the turbine fans began to spin once more, and the strip lights flickered falteringly before humming back into life. The carnage unleashed in the last twenty minutes was revealed under the cold light of the glow-strips.

Hundreds of bodies were strewn across the floor, blood pooling beneath them where they had fallen. The blackened shell of the Catalan-class vehicle was upside down against a wall, pinning half a dozen charred corpses beneath it. Sparks burst intermittently from the rails, which had buckled and been torn from their housings.

The ruin of the conveyance's carriages was testament to its speed when it had crashed, for they were wrenched out of shape, and their plasglass windows were shattered ruins. Its curved roof had been half ripped off, and the shattered barrier it had crashed through was twisted beneath it. Bodies, their heads smashed and limbs severed, were spread around the wreck, either crushed when the conveyance rolled off the tracks, or thrown from their seats inside. Blackened holes the size of fists showed where the vehicle had been struck by dark-matter weapons.

There was no sign of any living thing within the tunnel, and not one of the corpses twitched or groaned. Where earlier the tunnel had seethed with life, now it was utterly bereft, and the only sounds were the humming of the strip lights, the reverberations of the recycle units and the odd spark from the ruined tracks.

Of the thousands of people not slain, there was no sign. Nor was there any sign of their attackers. Only the carnage left in their wake was evidence of their having existed at all.

CHAPTER TWO

STARING THROUGH THE twenty-metre wide observation portal of the bridge, Admiral Rutger Augustine looked out over the vast length of his flagship vessel, the mighty Retribution-class battleship *Hammer of Righteousness*.

She looked like an immense, armoured Imperial cathedral, majestic and of such a scale as to be almost incomprehensible. Six kilometres from stern to prow, hundreds of spires ran along her length, joined together by flying buttresses and archways, and she bristled with the finest weapon systems that the Imperial Navy could boast.

Hundreds of close-range turrets were set across her armoured hull, each the size of four super-heavy battle tanks, and a dozen torpedo tubes, each gaping almost forty metres wide, were inset into her sweeping, massively armoured prow. It was in her broadside batteries, however, that the *Hammer of Righteousness's* true power lay.

Running almost the complete length of the battleship, the starboard and port batteries were capable of unleashing an incredible amount of firepower, easily enough to cripple even the largest warship with a single barrage, or lay waste to entire continents if she entered the upper atmosphere of a rebellious planet. Indeed, the resistance of entire planets had crumpled merely at her appearance in their sub-system, fearful of the wrath that she could unleash.

Tens of thousands of indentured workers and servitors slaved within the confined gun decks to load and ready the batteries for firing, and Admiral Augustine was proud to know that his gunnery crew, under the stern guidance of his master gunner and master of ordnance, were amongst the most efficient in all of Battlefleet Tempestus.

He never grew weary of looking out across the *Hammer of Righteousness*, and he knew in his heart that he never would. Even after all these years of service, the power and scale of the battleship filled him with awe. Set against the sheer scale of space with its untold millions of solar systems, she was tiny and insignificant, but it was her duty to protect Imperial space from all threats, xenos or otherwise.

Constructed in the Adeptus Mechanicus shipyard moons of Gryphonne IV over a period of a thousand years, *Hammer of Righteousness* had been in commission, defending Imperial space for nigh-on eight thousand years. Admiral Augustine had served on her for almost one hundred and fifteen years, first as a junior officer before moving steadily up through the ranks. He had served on two other ships after fulfilling his commissioned appointments on the *Hammer of Righteousness*, first as a flag lieutenant on the Lunar-class cruiser *Dauntless*. After a tenure of fifteen years he had been promoted to flag captain of the recommissioned *Emperor's Wrath*, which had recently been reassigned to Segmentum Tempestus. Augustine served aboard this Overlord-class battle cruiser – a famed veteran of the Gothic wars – for ten years, before he was reassigned back to the *Hammer of Righteousness*, the ship where he had began his naval career.

He had held the rank of admiral for forty-two years, and at the age of one hundred and sixty-two, he was one of the most experienced officers in the fleet. No one knew the nuances and quirks of the ancient battleship like he did, save perhaps for the ship's long-serving flag lieutenant, Gideon Cortez. Only two other ships assigned to Battlefleet Tempestus were of comparable size, and they were facing off against the xenos menace in distant sectors of the segmentum. The eastern expanses were his responsibility, and it was here that he had formed his blockade.

He could not see the enemy with the naked eye, for they were still millions of kilometres away, but he knew that they were out there and closing on them inexorably. He could see flashes in the distance. From here, they looked almost incongruous, but he knew that more of the enemy bio-ships were being subjected to concentrated barrages of ordnance.

His fleet was making a good account of itself in this engagement, the most recent of dozens over the last months, having destroyed two dozen hive-ships for no losses. Still, the xenos fleet continued to plough relentlessly on into Imperial space. The losses they had suffered made no discernible impact on the vast tyranid hive-fleet.

Vile bio-organisms that consumed everything in their path, like the locusts of Augustine's home world but on a galactic scale, the tyranid menace was a very real threat to the Imperium as a whole.

Four years previously a new hive-fleet had been identified, dubbed

Hive Fleet Leviathan. It was a fitting name. Already billions had lost their lives to its insatiable hunger.

Admiral Augustine stared balefully out into the darkness. For all his years of service he had proudly defended the reliant worlds of the Imperium from its enemies. Now he was tasked with destroying those same worlds that he had dedicated his life to protect.

By Lord Inquisitor Kryptman's order a galactic cordon stretching before the encroaching xenos fleet was formed. The band of worlds directly in front of the cordon were evacuated, and many of them utterly destroyed, in order to deny the hive fleet raw organic matter. Any world already under tyranid invasion was to suffer Exterminatus – the theory being that the xenos would expend much energy in claiming a world, only to have all living things on the world exterminated. The inquisitor believed that by stalling the hive fleet's advance, it would eventually turn aside, towards more lucrative killing grounds, and thus save the Imperium from devastation. However, it was a cruel and callous strategy, and not one that sat well with Admiral Augustine, even if it was humanity's only hope of stalling the hive fleet. Billions of Imperial citizens had already been evacuated, their home worlds destroyed, and hundreds of millions had perished, killed by orbital barrages and virus bombs launched by those sworn to protect them.

He turned away from the observation portal, his movements, like his appearance, crisp and precise. He strode back along the command deck, his expression unreadable. His staff upon the bridge went about their work with practiced efficiency and calm, talking in low voices. Several of them looked up as their admiral passed them by and were greeted with curt nods. Banks of logisticians, hardwired into the battleship's logic engines and monitoring a constant flow of technical data, murmured as stylus-fingers traced the mnemo-papers feeding from skull-faced machines. A pair of enginseers were reporting to the flag lieutenant, Gideon Cortez, and humming cogitator arrays flickered with updates from the fleet, the eyelids of servitors flickering as information was relayed.

Augustine moved to the holo-table positioned within a sunken recess in the floor, stepping down to look upon the position of his fleet. The table was criss-crossed with a grid of glowing green lines, indicating spatial parameters, and scale models of the entire fleet were positioned across its smooth expanse.

He took a moment to study the formations. Most of the fleet, seventy-two vessels of escort class and higher, had formed a bulwark spreading across the system with the *Hammer of Righteousness* at its centre. The cruiser *Valkyrie*, accompanied by three squadrons of smaller frigates and destroyers, was out in front, slowing the vanguard of the tyranid fleet to enable the pleasure world of Circe to fully evacuate, formless black spheres being placed on the table to represent the known enemy forces.

More of them were being put on the table all the time, placed there by lobotomised servitors hanging like twisted marionettes amid the gently hissing mechanics above the table.

The bio-mechanical amalgamations had no lower torso or legs. Their upper bodies, replete with wires and cables protruding from their pallid flesh, were attached to multi-jointed mechanical armatures that whirred and hissed as they extended and retracted, accurately moving and placing the fleets, accordingly, as fresh data was transmitted into them. Augustine was so used to their movements that he barely registered their presence; they were merely part of the ship; one more tool to help him with his strategy.

Two other cruisers with squadrons of smaller escorts clustered in front of other populated worlds, the agri-world Perse, and the mining moons of Perdus Skylla and Perdus Kharybdis, rotating slowly around the uninhabitable gas giant, Calyptus.

Small, featureless scale models, representing a host of transports and carriers engaged in the evacuation efforts, were positioned touching the inhabited worlds. Several other models representing similar transports were positioned en route to the blockade. Almost two hundred million people were being evacuated from this system alone. Already, there had been problems with some of the mass transports associated with the fleet, as riots had broken out within the civilian populations already evacuated. He pushed these thoughts out of his mind; it was his job to enact the strategy laid down to him and see the worlds evacuated safely, not to police those populations once they were safely onboard the mass transport ships.

As he watched, an Imperial light cruiser was placed on the table on the lee-side of Perdus Skylla, and then removed. The arm of the servitor jerked spasmodically, and it placed the light cruiser back down upon the table.

'What's that?' asked Admiral Augustine, pointing towards the ship, which was once again removed from the table.

One of his aides, a junior lieutenant, shrugged.

'It's been doing that for the past hour, admiral,' he said, 'interference from the hive fleet, or a radiation field, perhaps. The flag lieutenant thinks it may be nothing more than a technical glitch in the servitor unit. He is speaking to the enginseers about it.'

Admiral Augustine raised an eyebrow and regarded the peculiar behaviour of the servitor with a frown. Once again it put the ship back on the table, and then removed it.

'Useless bastards,' said Cortez, shaking his head as he extricated himself from the enginseers and walked to Augustine's side. 'They say the unit was serviced last week.'

The servitor-unit seemed to be operating as normal, again, and the phantom ship was nowhere to be seen on the table.

'Give me an update on the evacuations, Cortez,' said Augustine.

'Circe is almost completed, admiral,' said Cortez. 'The *Valkyrie* will be disengaging and pulling back within the hour.'

The flag lieutenant was a stocky man of indeterminable age. A livid scar tracked across his chin, and a gleaming, bronze-rimmed lens stared from the hollow socket of his left eye. He was a natural officer and Augustine's closest confidant, the one and only man that he would class as his friend.

'And the evacuations of Galatea? And the Perdus moons?' asked the admiral.

'Galatea goes well; the moons of Calyptus less so. There are not enough transports. It's going to take those transports that are available three trips to complete the evacuation of Perdus Skylla and Perdus Kharybdis.'

'Three trips,' mused Admiral Augustine. He hissed through his teeth, gauging the position of the moons and the advancing enemy hive fleet. 'It's going to be tight.'

'If the evacuation is not completed before a ground invasion commences, anybody still on the moons must be forgotten,' said Cortez, moving to the opposite side of the table to the admiral.

'We shall buy the moons as much time as we can,' Admiral Augustine said, 'but you are correct, I cannot risk the fleet for the benefit of two moons. Our orders are clear.'

His orders *were* clear, as much as they rankled with him. They were the same orders that all of the fleets engaging Hive Fleet Leviathan had been issued, and he knew that they were being enforced all across the warfront.

The tyranids were a deadly menace, there was no disputing that, but it sat badly with the admiral that they were giving way before the xenos forces rather than making them fight for every bit of Imperial space. Of course, he would not allow his personal feelings to colour his judgement, and he would never go so far as to voice his feelings in front of his officers. Their orders were clear. He had sent an astrotelepathic message to the lord admiral on receiving the dictate, but once confirmation of the order had been returned, his path was set.

The new tyranid advance was potentially more catastrophic than any ever seen before, and the strategy that had been decreed to be used against it was similarly extreme.

It was genocide. Those worlds that were already suffering under the first waves of ground assault were effectively condemned to death, along with their Planetary Defence Force and any force of the Imperial Guard that could not be extricated.

Admiral Augustine knew that the political ramifications and backlash from this modus operandi would be devastating, but he also knew that no fleet captain would fail in his duty. They would carry out their orders, and leave the politicking to the bickering bureaucrats of the Administratum.

Cortez cursed, and Augustine shook his head slightly as the malfunctioning servitor unit once again placed the phantom Imperial light cruiser back on the table.

'Have a destroyer do a sweep around the moon, just to be sure,' said Augustine, and Cortez nodded his assent, even as he was shouting for the engineers to be returned to the bridge.

Augustine's gaze focused on the spherical representations of the twin moons of Perdus Skylla and Perdus Kharybdis.

The evacuation of the moons would continue, and he would hold the fleet in position for as long as possible. However, looking again at their position, and the advance of the tyranid fleet, he knew instinctively that it would not be long enough.

Before the week was out, he would be ordering their Exterminatus.

THE CHAMBER WAS a shrine to death. Part of Marduk's personal quarters within the labyrinthine *Infidus Diabolus*, its high, domed ceiling was formed from the ribs of sacrifices, and eight pillars, each constructed from thousands of bones, rose into the gloom. Oily candles had been set into the hollow craniums of the skulls set into the pillars, and an infernal glow exuded from fire blackened, hollow sockets.

Braziers of black iron burnt low, and black, acrid smoke rose from the smouldering coals. Hunched figures, their abhorrent faces hidden from view beneath deep cowls, stalked the darkness outside the circle of pillars, swinging heavy censors from which thick, heady incense spilled.

Inside the pillars, the floor was rough granite, carved into the image of a holy eight-pointed star, the symbol of Chaos in all its guises. A massive figure stood at its centre, his augmented arms raised out to either side as he was prepared for the forthcoming ceremony.

Marduk was silently fuming, still angry at Magos Darioq's inability to unlock the secrets of the Nexus Arrangement. Silently incanting the Nine Levels of Enlightenment, he forced himself to calm. From the archive facility of Kharion IV, the magos had identified the location – a backwater Imperial moon called Perdus Skylla – of the one whose knowledge would release the artefact's power, and Marduk forced himself to breathe evenly. Be patient, he reminded himself.

More than a dozen hooded figures, stunted creatures that stood not even to the mighty warrior's chest, clustered around their master, making him ready for the ceremony. Their eyes had been ritually sutured closed with thick staples, for it was regarded as a sin for them to look upon such a revered warrior. They brushed his blessed armour with sacred unguents, and fixed icons and holy charms to his armour.

Marduk, First Acolyte of the Word Bearers Legion, acting Dark Apostle of the Host, stood over two metres tall, his limbs encased in thick reinforced plate the colour of congealed blood. His holy power armour had been worked upon by the artisans of the Host in recent months, the plates rimmed with dark meteoric iron, and battle damage repaired.

Marduk had meticulously scrimshawed hundreds of thousands of words across them in tiny script, scriptures and sacred litanies of Lorgar that he knew by heart. The entire third book of the Tenets of Hate was inscribed around the armoured vambrace encasing his left forearm, and the titles of the Six Hundred and Sixty-Six Enumerations of Erebus were carved across the curved mass of his left shoulder pad.

The left shoulder pad had been dutifully painted black, as had those of the entire Host, in mourning for the loss of their revered leader, the Dark Apostle Jarulek. That Marduk had been integral to Jarulek's death made the symbolic act particularly ironic, and he smirked.

Over his painstakingly worked armour, Marduk wore a bone-coloured robe, tied at his waist with chains hung with icons of dedication to the dark gods of the ether. A book of hymnals and battle-prayers from the Epistles of Lorgar hung at his side, its dusty pages bound in human leather.

His head was bare. A bolt round fired by his former master, the Dark Apostle Jarulek, at point blank range had rent the helmet beyond repair, and Marduk's features bore testament to the damage that the shot had wrought. The entire left half of his face had been blasted away, and it had taken all the skill of the Host's chirurgeons and chirumeks to rebuild his facial structure.

Adamantium had been fused to his skull, and he had grinned as the procedure had taken place. Pain, it was taught, was a blessed gift that fortified the spirit and brought one closer to the gods. As such, it was a sensation to be welcomed. No proud warrior of the Legion would ever consider allowing a chirurgeon to distance him from the blessed pain of his battle wounds with narcotic opiates or psychotropic injections, for such a thing was regarded as blasphemy.

His shattered left cheek was rebuilt, and the muscles and tendons of his face re-grown or replaced with bionic implants. Marduk's skin had yet to grow across this new facial structure, and the ceramic gleam of his sharpened teeth could be seen through the strands of muscle tissue that linked his upper and lower jaws.

His left eye socket had been blasted to splinters, and the eye turned to molten jelly by the concussive force of the bolt round. Once the socket had been reconstructed, a replacement eye grown in a culture of amniotic-fluid infused with warp energy was surgically attached to his brain stem. The daemonic flesh hybrid replacement stared out from his adamantium eye socket, an angry, red, lidless orb. The pupil was little more than a sliver, like that of a serpent's eye, reflecting all that it saw.

For all his reconstructive surgery, Marduk's face bore the patrician features that spoke of his genetic ancestry. Every warrior in the Legion bore the genetic makeup of his lord, the blessed daemon primarch Lorgar, and the similarity between them was marked, characterised by their pale skin, their noble profile, their proud bearing and their hair, which was as black as pitch.

Marduk's long black hair had been combed and oiled by his robed attendants, before being tied into a long braid and secured behind his head, atop the cluster of cables that entered his flesh at the base of his skull. A cloak of matted fur, skinned from a blood-beast that Marduk had slain on the death world of Anghkar Dor, was draped over his shoulders and fixed to leering, daemonic bronze faces on his breast-plate. The inside of the fur was lined with velvet, and symbols of Chaos resplendent had been scorched into the fabric.

Holy scriptures of Kor Phaeron, cut into the flayed flesh of innocents, were driven onto the spikes rimming his shoulder pads, and fresh blood, drawn from the bodies of mewling sacrifices artificially bred in vats on the lower decks of the *Infidus Diabolus* for that sole purpose, was daubed reverentially onto his gauntlets.

One of the attendants lined his right eye with coal, and smoke rose from the holy mark of Lorgar on Marduk's brow as the servant's withered hand brushed it. The stink of scorched flesh rose from the attendant's hand, and it pulled it back sharply as smoke rose from the mark. Marduk growled in annoyance, and the attendant was dragged away into the darkness by two of its kin. Its flesh would be consigned to the cleansing fires, its body fed to its kin and its soul, if it had one, subject to eternal torment for displeasing its master.

Marduk's eyes lit up as his weapons were brought forth, led by a procession of censer-bearing attendants. They were the tools with which the Dark Faith was delivered to the heathen masses of the galaxy and as such, they were borne with reverential care. They lay upon black cushions, and were carried upon the backs of creatures whose flesh was completely swathed in black cloth to hide their obscene forms.

Marduk picked up his customised bolt pistol, its squat barrel protruding from the carved maw of a daemon. It felt natural and light in his hand, though a mere mortal would struggle to bear its weight, and he rammed a sickle-shaped clip into place before holstering it at his hip.

Even in times of relative peace the brothers of the Host bore live weapons, for though they were disciples and custodians of the Dark Creed, they were holy warriors first and foremost, and it was part of their tenets to be always reminded of the Long War against the cursed Imperium, to be ever in readiness for holy battle. Bitterness fuelled their beliefs and passion, and the holy bolter and chainsword were the tools with which the proper order of the galaxy would be instated. No warrior could forget the betrayals of the Corpse Emperor, or the fallacy of his church, while they held their sacred weapons.

Next, he lifted his archaic chainsword from its cushion. His grip closed around the hilt of the weapon, and he felt the familiar rush as it bonded with him, barbs piercing the flesh of his palm. The power and rage of

Borhg'ash, the daemon eternally bound within the chainsword, surged through him, and he restrained the urge to lash out, to feed the beast's hunger. The blood of thousands had been shed beneath its biting teeth, and it was with some reluctance that he sheathed it, allowing the locking clamps to secure it at his waist.

'Soon you shall feed, dear one,' said Marduk to appease the daemon, and he felt a twinge of unease as his bond with the daemon weapon was severed, as if a part of his body had been cut from him.

Marduk dismissed his servants with a wave of his gauntleted hand. They retreated into the dark recess-hollows in the chamber walls, disappearing from mortal sight.

Whispering a prayer, he turned and walked across the chamber. The great doors reared up before him, intricately carved into a representation of the maelstrom, replete with daemonic forms and the souls of mortals writhing in agony. The amorphous carving shifted maddeningly, souls screaming out in silent torment as flames consumed them and devils cavorted.

Pressing his palms against the doors, Marduk pushed them open, and they swung aside soundlessly.

An entourage of twelve chosen warriors knelt upon the flagstones beyond the doors, their heads bowed low. At their fore was the Icon Bearer, Burias, his head lowered to the ground before his master.

'Arise, my brothers,' said Marduk.

THE DEVOTIONAL CEREMONY lasted for twelve hours, and the mournful voices of the Host rose and fell as they intoned their hymnal responses. The morbid peal of bells echoed out across the cavernous expanse of the cavaedium, signalling the end of the communal worship of the gods. Marduk's throat was raw from his elocutions and recitals from the books of Lorgar, but he felt refreshed and invigorated by the communion with the great powers of the ether. It was always this way for him.

For three months it had been this way, with prayers, sermons and services dominating the lives of the Word Bearers as their ship, the *Infidus Diabolus*, ploughed its way through the roiling sea that was the warp. The Host was eager for battle, for the fields of war were the truest halls of worship to the gods, but these hymnal services served their needs, while not engaged against the enemy, and they fuelled the hatred and stoked the fires of vengeance that burnt within the breast of every warrior-brother.

Warp travel allowed the *Infidus Diabolus* to travel vast distances in months or years rather than decades or more, but Marduk would allow none of his battle-brothers to enter stasis while on these journeys, for these times were important lulls during which affirmations could be renewed and dedications and oaths of servitude to the great gods blooded anew.

As the Host filed away, returning to their cells for individual, silent communion, reading of scripture, the blessings and refitting of holy bolters and other daily rituals, Marduk found himself gazing upon the blessed crozius arcanum, lying dormant upon a plinth at the front of the alter overlooking the nave where the Host had gathered.

The crozius arcanum was the hallowed staff of office of the Dark Apostles, the bearers of the true faith. Once it had symbolised belief in the Great Crusade, in the Imperium of Man and the optimism of the Crusade bringing enlightenment to the galaxy, but the Emperor's lies had long been revealed.

The Emperor had claimed that gods did not exist, that they were merely the creations of weak minds. Hypocritically, it was this same Emperor, though his body was now a mere rotting corpse, that the Imperium prayed to as their patron deity. The fallacy of the lie and its hypocrisy filled Marduk with bitterness and rage. In truth, that anger had not waned with time, but rather had grown stronger and deeper.

In ignorance, blindness or perhaps fear, the Emperor had proclaimed that there were no great godly powers in the universe, but he had been wrong. He had *lied*. There *were* deities in the depths of the warp, tangible and very real, and they were more powerful than anyone could have imagined. It was to these ancient gods that the Word Bearers had pledged their allegiance, and it was the faith in them that they sought to bring to the universe.

Once the Great Truth had been revealed, the Legion had thrown off the repressive, enslaving beliefs of the Imperium and dedicated themselves fully to their holy cause.

The crozius arcanum had been sanctified to the true gods, and it was a potent symbol of the Dark Creed and faith. It had been purified in the blood of millions, and countless unbelievers had been smitten beneath it.

Its haft was as black as ebony and studded with spikes. Marduk longingly traced the blood-red veins that ran up its length with a finger, marvelling at the workmanship. The hilt of the crozius was bound in the tanned skin of a cursed unbeliever, the Chaplain Atreus of the cursed Ultramarines Legion, who had been flayed alive on Calth by Lord Kor Phaeron. The head of the holy weapon was like a flanged mace or power maul, eight raised, spiked wedges forming its shape. When activated, the spiked head was wreathed in energy, and it would sunder the foes of Lorgar with the selfsame potency of a power talon.

Marduk longed to lift the weapon up in both hands. Only two Dark Apostles had wielded this mighty weapon: the ancient Warmonger, long since interred in the sarcophagus of his mighty Dreadnought, whose sanity was only barely kept in check; and Jarulek: Jarulek the Blessed, Jarulek the Glorified, beloved of the gods.

Not anymore, thought Marduk with savage relish. This was *his* time. His star was in the ascendant, and once he had faced the Council of Sicarus, he would be allowed to wield this potent artefact himself. As it was, he had held it in his hands once, when he had rescued it from oblivion within the xenos pyramid, but even he was loathe to break the taboos and traditions of his order by bearing the holy weapon into battle before he had been fully embraced into the fold by the council.

He felt the approach of his underlings behind him, and his eyes narrowed. Running his hands lingeringly over the crozius, he left them waiting for a moment, to reinforce their place, and his.

At last, he turned towards them. They stood at the foot of the raised platform, and with a gesture, he beckoned them closer.

They ascended the steps side-by-side, and though they both bore the hallmarks of Lord Lorgar's gene-seed, they were as different in appearance as night and day.

Kol Badar was ancient, having been a captain of one of the great battle companies of the XVII Legion long before the great Warmaster Horus had aligned himself with the true powers of the universe. His face was broad and bullish, though his flesh was wasted almost to the point of emaciation, and creases so deep they looked as if they had been carved with knives lined his face. His head was bald, and pipes and cables sank into his cranium, connecting him to his immense battle suit. He wore archaic, age-old Terminator armour and towered over Marduk by half a metre. He walked with heavy steps, his every movement filled with power and weight.

Kol Badar was the Host's Coryphaus: strategos, war leader, and the voice of the battle-brothers. It was his role to lead the chorus of hymnal responses in prayer, and to act as the link between the Host's Dark Apostle and his warriors. At his side, dwarfed by his sheer bulk, swaggered the Host's icon bearer, Burias.

Where Kol Badar was all brute power and smouldering anger, Burias walked with a warrior's subtle grace, his movements relaxed and fluid. He was wolf-lean and darkly handsome, his full head of pitch black, waist-length hair oiled and scented. His pale face encapsulated all the noble bearing of his heritage, and it was said that he resembled Lorgar, before he had ascended to daemonhood.

Burias was the epitome of the warrior ideal: a consummate, balanced warrior. His body was as proud and strong as his faith, and though he was young in comparison to Kol Badar, he had been blooded in battle across a thousand worlds. He was quick to smile, though there was a lingering, dangerous intensity in his wide eyes, just a hint of the power lurking within, straining to be released. Burias was one of the possessed, and though he kept the daemon Drak'shal at bay with sheer force of will, he willingly gave way to the beast once the fires of battle were met, and the results were invariably bloody.

Burias bowed low, dipping his tall, eight-pointed icon before him, and Marduk acknowledged him with an incline of his chin. Kol Badar bowed his head, carefully measuring the movement to be at once mildly insulting, yet not overtly disrespectful.

'The Enslaved one is requesting that he be allowed to reconstruct his armature arrays, that he may continue his work upon the Nexus Arrangement, lord,' said Burias, his voice neutral.

'It is foolishness to allow it such privileges,' said Kol Badar.

'Walk with me,' ordered Marduk, turning on his heel and striding away. He did not speak as they exited the cavaedium by a side portal within the sacristy, walking up corridors lined with skulls.

One of the kathartes, skinless daemonic furies that inhabited the *Infidus Diabolus*, perched upon the shoulders of a winged angel of death statue above them, baring its teeth at their passing. Marduk flicked his gaze up towards the daemon, and it lowered its head, whimpering like a dog beneath the switch. Blood glistened across its exposed musculature, and it shimmered like a distorted pict image before disappearing once more into the sea of souls that was the warp. Immersed in the tides of the ether buffeting the *Infidus Diabolus*, the katharte would take on its truer form, that of an angelic maiden, as dangerous as it was alluring, propelling itself through the formless other world upon feathered wings, its siren call signalling the death of those of weak mind that heard it.

They passed dozens of dark arches, each leading off into different areas of the labyrinthine ship. Warrior-brothers stood aside, their heads lowered, as they passed. Black-cloaked slave-creatures scurried out of their path, while others prostrated themselves pathetically, faces pressed to the floor. Moans and tortured cries came from darkness beneath the walkways, and wasted, skeletal fingers extended through the metal grids in appeal. Thousands of wretched slaves were kept aboard the *Infidus Diabolus*, existing in the darkness and squalid conditions below deck in order to perform all the horrific and mundane jobs required to keep the ship running. They were condemned to a lifetime of servitude, and they cried out for death.

'The priest-magos of the Machine-God is necessary,' said Marduk finally, as the trio walked the musty halls of the strike cruiser. 'The Nexus Arrangement will never be unlocked without him; he is the Key-master,' he said, referring to a prophecy that told of one, the Enslaved, who would unlock the potent device that the Host had uncovered from a xenos pyramid upon the shattered Imperial world of Tanakreg. It would be a powerful weapon in the arsenal of the Word Bearers, and much favour would be granted to he who controlled it.

'The Key-master?' scoffed Kol Badar. 'The wretch has proven useless in unlocking the device thus far. He cannot be trusted.'

'The magos is mine,' said Marduk. 'He is my puppet, and will do exactly what I want.'

MAGOS DARIOQ WAS changing. At first, the effects on his body had been subtle, barely noticeable, but, as the daemon took further control of his purged system, the change was coming on with alarming, exponential swiftness.

Stripped of his robes and chained to the wall of his cell, he shuddered in torment as the carefully cultured daemon essence writhed within him. He opened his mouth soundlessly, exposing a secondary set of teeth, thick and sharp, pushing up through his bleeding gums behind his own.

His flesh was wasted and pallid, though most of his body had long been replaced with mechanical augmentations. His entire lower body had been replaced with heavy-duty bionic replacements, immensely powerful leg-units with inbuilt gyro-stabilisers that enabled the magos to bear almost two metric tonnes of weight upon his frame. This was necessary, for with a fully activated servo-harness, the magos weighed as much as a small tank. Black tendrils crawled and pulsed beneath his skin, and his flesh rippled from within as the daemon made its claim on him.

Augmetic telescopic braces were fused to his spine for stability and strength, but the distinction between mechanical augmentation and flesh was blurring. Blood dripped from rents in the metal.

The heavy bulk of Darioq's servo-harness was clamped between his hips and his shoulders, and again, the hybrid amalgamation of fusing metal and flesh could be seen. Fleshy muscles had grown over several of the pistons, enhancing their mechanical strength with that of the daemon and giving the corrupted magos an even more hunched appearance. The four servo-arms of his harness had been sheared away, along with half a dozen mechadendrites that plugged into the nerve endings of his spinal column, and they wept blood and ichor as their stubby remnants twitched and jerked spasmodically. Two of the severed mechadendrites had already re-sprouted, fleshy tentacles of glistening muscle growing from his spine. Plugs and sockets covered his wasted skin, and from some of these leaked a milky ichor that hissed as it hit the floor.

With his hood and robes stripped away, Darioq's head was laid bare. Only a fraction of his original face remained, the rest encased in mechanics. A grilled voice box was implanted in his throat, and his left eye was an impressive display of sensors and optical arrays.

The distinction between the mechanical and the human was blurring all over the corrupted magos's body. Even as the trio of Word Bearers watched, the metal cranium of the magos swelled and rippled like water, and a curving horn pushed up from the righthand side of Darioq's skull. Its tip was hard and bony, but clearly organic.

His right eye, which had been milky and blind when the Word Bearers had first captured him, was now solid black. His brain units, held in protective bell-jar casings that protruded from behind his hunched shoulders, were filled with dark, writhing clots, and black, oily tentacles burrowed through them, like a mess of bloodworms.

'Magos Darioq is no more. This,' said Marduk with a wave of his arm, 'is Darioq-Grendh'al.'

CHAPTER THREE

GUILDMASTER POLLO SCANNED the latest despatches, blinking his augmented silver eyes intermittently to record their contents. After several minutes of reading and recording, he dropped them onto his desk and leant forward to pour himself another drink from the half empty crystal decanter in front of him.

He raised his glass up to his eyes, gazing at the play of light upon the ruby liquid as he sloshed it around the ice. Then he knocked the drink back, savouring its bite. He placed the glass down on its coaster, and rubbed at his temples with both hands, his eyes closed.

'Bad news, guildmaster?' ventured a voice.

Pollo turned to face his young adjutant, Leto. He was little more than a boy, barely having the need to shave yet, and his eyes flicked around nervously as he waited for his answer. He was young, but he was a good officer and had a mind like a sponge. He knew that in time he would have made a suitable guildmaster, but such a thing was not to be.

'You should have gone with the others, Leto,' he said, his voice tired.

'I will leave when you leave,' replied his adjutant.

When the first astrotelepathic despatches had come, warning of the xenos hive fleet's approach, Pollo's distaff had been aghast. That had quickly descended into panic when the extreme dictate to combat this threat had been transmitted, and that panic had not been aided by the sudden departure of the Administratum's advocate of Perdus Skylla.

'This world has been condemned to death,' the administrator had whined as he frantically gathered up his possessions. 'You are a fool to stay behind,'

'I will not leave until the guilds are fully evacuated,' Pollo had replied, his voice unwavering. '*I* will not abandon my post and leave those who depend upon me to their fate.'

'Do not judge me, guildmaster,' the administrator had snapped. 'I am a servant of the Administratum, and with the mining facilities abandoned I see no purpose in my remaining here. If you have any sense at all, you will leave Perdus Skylla immediately. Coordinate the evacuation from space if your conscience demands such a thing.'

Guildmaster Pollo had wanted to strike the man, but he had held his anger in check. He had turned his back on the administrator, and had watched as his shuttle left the moon for the safety of the Imperial blockade. He had ordered his distaff to vacate Perdus Skylla, and he had seen the relief in their faces at his order. He did not think badly of them as they saluted him and boarded the first chartered evacuation ships.

'Why will you not go?' Leto had asked him.

'I swore an oath of service to the guilds of Perdus Skylla. My leadership will be needed in the evacuation effort. It sends a message to the guilds, and the populace, if I remain.'

'Then I shall remain with you, sir,' said the boy.

Pollo had promoted him to be his adjutant, and had been pleasantly surprised to find that the young man adapted to his role admirably.

Pollo sighed, picked up the reports and flicked them to Leto. The young man caught them awkwardly, and scanned their contents. The guildmaster poured himself another drink as his adjutant looked at the first of the reports. Leto looked up in shock, his face pale.

'Keep reading,' said Guildmaster Pollo.

The reports contained disturbing information: evidence of slaughter in three of the main mid-ice access highways that linked the Phorcys starport to the guilds. The attacks had occurred just hours earlier, and there had been no survivors nor any eyewitnesses. It was impossible to gauge the number of casualties, but there was something in the realm of twelve thousand citizens reported missing. Thousands more had been killed in the stampede to get out of the tunnels, and the Skyllan Interdiction Forces had shut the access tunnels down, pending an armoured investigation.

Three guilds, two of them major houses, had no direct access to the evacuation freighters. That translated as almost four million people, trapped on Perdus Skylla until the tunnels were opened, for it would be almost impossible for them to make the journey on foot.

Three days had been the estimate before the xenos fleet made planetfall. It had been a logistical impossibility to evacuate all of Perdus Skylla in that time, but now with access tunnels locked down?

Guildmaster Pollo was a realist. He did not delude himself into thinking that he ever had even half a chance of getting more than perhaps twenty per cent of the population of Perdus Skylla off-world; there were just not enough ships to facilitate the evacuation. He cursed the bureaucracy of the Administratum that had given his world such callously short notice of its doom.

He had finished his glass of amasec by the time his adjutant had read through all the despatches.

'What does it mean, master?' asked Leto, his face pale.

'It means,' said Pollo, cradling his empty glass, 'that there are enemy forces already on Perdus Skylla.'

'The… the tyranids?'

'I don't think so, no,' said Leto. 'Something else entirely.'

WITH A SOUND akin to the birth-scream of a fledgling god, the *Infidus Diabolus* ripped through the skin of the warp and entered real space. Flickering arcs of energy danced across its hull, coalescing over the towering spires and cathedrals devoted to the dark gods of the ether. The full awesome majesty of the strike cruiser slipped from the protective womb of the immaterium, and the rift was sealed behind it.

Within the bridge of the colossal vessel, Marduk and Kol Badar leaned over the flickering data-screens before them, studying the stream of information being relayed. They saw an image of the sub-system, spinning slowly, and flashes of light began to appear, marking the positions of planets, ships and radiation fields.

Remnants of the warp remained within the ship, and scenes of depravity and bloodshed flashed up over the screens, momentarily disrupting the feed of information. For a fraction of a second, the screens showed a skinless face, its eyes on fire and its cheeks pierced by blades, before they returned to normal. A moment later, the screens flashed again, and an image of a writhing, blood-soaked figure appeared on the pict screens for less than a tenth of a second, accompanied by the blare of static, overlaid with unholy roars and screams.

The pair of Word Bearers ignored the distractions, peering through the ghost-images of daemons ripping apart flesh and bubbling blood that appeared on the screens, focusing on the wealth of sub-system information being picked up by the daemonic sensor arrays protruding from the prow of the *Infidus Diabolus*. They saw the conglomeration of Imperial vessels forming an unbroken line across the system and the flickering waves of warp energy that marked jump-points, and located the position of the target; the moon the Imperials called Perdus Skylla.

The sounds of Chaos croaked from grilled vox-speakers and discords throughout the ship, a blaring cacophony of madness and rage. Bellows and screams were overlaid with inhuman screeches and hateful whispers, and the painful squeal of scraping metal blurred with the relentless pounding of hammers and gears, the sound of flesh being rent by steel, the roar of the fires of hell and the plaintive weeping of children. It was a beautiful din, one that calmed Marduk's mind, though to listen too deeply was to give yourself over to insanity.

A face appeared on the central pict screen, its eyes black as pitch and its cheeks carved with bloody sigils, and it opened its mouth wide, exposing a mass of writhing serpents, spiders and worms.

'Enough,' barked Marduk, banishing the daemon with a wave of his hand. Instantly, the snarling image disappeared.

More flashing lights and runic symbols appeared on the representation of the surrounding galactic plane, and both Marduk and Kol Badar leant forward to peer upon them. Kol Badar snorted and leant back. A bitter laugh burst from Marduk's lips, the sound making the image on the pict viewers shimmer with static.

'It would seem, Coryphaus, that the Imperium is engaged in a war in this little solar system,' said Marduk, 'and they are losing.'

'ADMIRAL,' SOMEONE SHOUTED.

Rutger Augustine pulled his gaze away from the scale model representations of the fleet and turned to see one of his petty officers moving towards him.

'Go ahead,' he said.

The petty officer was flushed and he carried a transmission card, its waxy surface punched with a series of holes. He thrust it towards the admiral.

'Sir, Battle Group *Orion* has picked up a warp-echo emanating from jump-point XIV. It has been verified by our own Navigatorii.'

Augustine frowned at the transmission card, and then turned and fed it into the chest-slot of the servitor unit wired into his command console. The servitor jerked, and its needle finger began to punch away at a set of keys in front of it. Ignoring the drooling servitor, Augustine looked at the transmission data as it was relayed onto the screen.

'What is it?' he asked. 'A rogue hive ship? Don't say the bastards have got behind us.'

'No sir. Initial sweeps indicate a vessel of cruiser mass, but it is not an organic entity.'

'No? Probably another trade vessel come to aid the evacuations. Why are you bothering me with this?' asked Admiral Augustine. 'The fleet is engaging the xenos threat, petty officer!'

'I'm sorry, sir, and it may be nothing, but the long-range scan that Battle Group *Orion* performed seemed to indicate that the vessel may be an Astartes strike cruiser or battle-barge.'

Augustine frowned.

'I was notified of no Space Marine presence inbound, though we could do with their aid.' He rubbed a hand across his freshly shaved chin. 'Have *Orion* send a frigate squadron on an intercept course with the vessel, and keep me informed of any updates.'

With that, the admiral turned away from the petty officer.

'Yes, admiral.'

THE INFIDUS DIABOLUS ploughed through the vacuum of space, its plasma-core engines burning blue-white as it closed towards the vast red giant sun around which the solar system rotated. Solar flares a million kilometres in height burst from the daemonic red corona, leaping up from around dark sunspots that blemished its unstable surface.

The sun was dying. Five billion years earlier it was less than one hundredth of its current size, though it had burnt over ten times as hot. Having exhausted its gaseous core, it had expanded exponentially, engulfing its nearest planets. Even as it grew in size, it was diminished in mass, and the outer planets circling it began to pull further away, its gravitational hold over them weakening. Now it burnt the colour of hell itself, but in another billion years it would be no more.

The *Infidus Diabolus* dropped closer to the hellish, glowing corona, buffeted by solar winds. There, with intense spikes of radiation spilling around her hull, she drew anchor.

'I WOULD HEAR your council, revered Warmonger,' said Marduk. He ran the fingers of his hand thoughtfully along the surface of a stone column. A cold wind gusted through the darkness, tugging at Marduk's cloak, and a mechanical scream of insane rage echoed from deeper within the crypt.

Marduk and Kol Badar stood beneath the shadow of a wide archway, facing into a cavernous alcove set into the side of the expansive passageway. They were deep within the depths of the *Infidus Diabolus*, in the undercroft that housed those warriors of the Host that had long ago fallen in holy battle, but had not been allowed to pass on into blessed oblivion.

The damned warriors lived on in the deepest labyrinthine catacombs of the strike cruiser, condemned to a tortured limbo, neither living nor dead, the shattered remnants of their earthly forms interred in great sarcophagi that they might serve the Host even after their time had long passed.

A delicate mural decorated the back wall of the alcove, detailing the great moments of the Warmonger's life before he had been condemned to an eternity of servitude within the towering mechanical form of a Dreadnought.

Once he had been amongst Lorgar's most favoured and devout chaplains, the first Dark Apostle of the 34th Company Host that Marduk now led. He had fought alongside the god primarchs, and counted such exalted heroes as Erebus, Kor Phaeron and Abaddon as his battle-brothers. Marduk had listened in awe to the scratchy vox-recordings of his passionate sermons, and had pored over a thousand volumes of his thoughtful scripture, and his fiery rhetoric and hate-filled sermons never failed to inspire.

Though the other warriors interred within the Dreadnoughts of the Host had long ago lost any semblance of sanity, cursed as they were and unable to attain oblivion yet denied the physical sensations of holy war, the warmonger retained a coherent self-awareness, and was a source of great wisdom and council.

It was his unshakeable faith that kept him lucid, Holy Erebus had once said, the power and conviction of his rapturous belief that kept him from toppling off the precipice into madness.

A thousand blood-candles ringed the mighty warmonger, tended day and night by a pair of slave-proselytes to ensure that the flames never died, and their light cast a divine glow over the Dreadnought's sarcophagus.

It towered over Marduk, even Kol Badar, standing over five metres tall with the armoured sarcophagus that held the Dark Apostle's shattered remains at its heart. The Dreadnought stood on squat, powerful legs, and immense arms bearing ancient heavy weapons systems were held immobile at its side.

For hundreds of years at a time the Warmonger stood motionless within its own death shrine, lost in contemplation, waiting for holy battle to be joined once more.

'It is pleasing to my soul to see you once more, First Acolyte Marduk,' boomed the Warmonger, its voice a deep reverberating baritone, the words spoken slowly and deliberately, 'and you, Kol Badar, finest of my captains.'

The two warriors bowed their heads in deference.

'The loss of Jarulek pains me,' continued the warmonger. 'Though in you I see a worthy successor, young disciple Marduk.'

'Jarulek's death cuts me deeply as well, revered warmonger,' said Marduk. A slight smile curled his lips as he felt Kol Badar's anger at his words. 'I am honoured to fill the role of religious leader of the Host, though I feel... unworthy of such a hallowed duty.'

'It is only right that you step into the breach and guide the flock,' said the warmonger. 'Your star is in the ascendant. Feel not unworthy of the duty; be humbled by it, but never doubt your right to serve. The gods have ordained it.'

Marduk turned his head to Kol Badar and smiled.

'I fear that some amongst the Host feel I am not ready for such an exalted position, my lord,' he said.

'Tolerate no insubordination, First Acolyte,' boomed the Warmonger. 'Crucify any who seed dissent, for theirs are the voices of poison and doubt.'

'I shall heed your council in this matter, revered one,' said Marduk.

'You are walking the black path, Marduk,' said the Warmonger. 'You are the dark disciple, moving towards the light of truth, and you shall, in time, be granted enlightenment. You did not, however, come here for my acceptance, for you already know that you have it. What is it you would ask of me?'

'I had wished to descend on the Imperial world of Perdus Skylla with the full force of the Host, laying waste to the world and claiming that which is needed. While it pleases me to see the Imperium weakened in their battles with the xenos, for it will make our eventual victory in the Long War come all the sooner, the size of the battlefleet here in this sector forces me to change my intentions. Mighty as she is, the *Infidus Diabolus* would not survive long enough to get us to the Imperial moon.'

'I say we abandon this fool's errand here and now,' growled Kol Badar. 'Let us return to Sicarus and leave the Imperials to wage their war against the xenos hive-creatures. We will recoup our strength in the Eye while the Imperium suffers.'

'Kol Badar speaks, as always, with wisdom,' said the Warmonger, and for a moment Marduk thought he had horribly misjudged the way this conversation would go. He felt a flicker of unease at having instigated it in the presence of the Coryphaus as Kol Badar flashed him a look of triumph.

'And yet,' continued the Warmonger, 'Jarulek saw in the xenos device something of great import. He was always a gifted zealot and the power of his gods-gifted dream visions were stronger than my own. If he saw that the item was worth waging war for, then it is an artefact of great importance, and is destined to further the spread of the holy Word of Truth.'

'We already have the device in our possession,' said Kol Badar. 'We need not tarry here and risk it further.'

'We have the device, that is true,' admitted Marduk, 'but as it is, it is worthless to us; its secrets are locked within it. It is nothing more than a xenos curio, an inert and useless sphere of metal.'

'The chirumeks of the Legion will unlock its secrets, whatever they may be,' said Kol Badar.

I will not return to Sicarus in anything but glory, thought Marduk fiercely, glaring at the Coryphaus. Were he to return empty-handed, he feared that the council would not endorse his rise to Dark Apostle. With the secrets of the Nexus Arrangement unlocked and his to command, they would be forced to heap honour upon him.

'You know that the knowledge that will unlock the device will be attained upon this Imperial world?' asked the Warmonger.

'I do,' said Marduk. 'It is held within the mind of a servant of the false Machine-God.'

'You base that belief only on the word of another servant of the

Machine-God,' snarled Kol Badar. 'The Enslaved's loyalty does not lie with the Legion. For all you know, he may be leading us into a trap, to deliver the device unto his Mechanicus brethren.'

'The Enslaved is mine,' growled Marduk. 'It has no will of its own any more. It is not capable of such duplicity.'

'Speak with respect to your First Acolyte, Kol Badar,' chided the Warmonger. 'Marduk, if you trust the knowledge you have, then the path is clear.'

'The *Infidus Diabolus* cannot approach Perdus Skylla,' said Kol Badar, changing tack. 'If anything, we should return to the Eye and gather the Hosts to our cause. Then we can return, and take the moon by force.'

'The xenos threat will have obliterated it by then,' snapped Marduk. 'We have both seen worlds ravaged by their kind; nothing is left behind. The secrets will be lost forever.'

'You do not need my council, then, disciple Marduk. Kol Badar, if brute force will not suffice, explore more subtle ways of gaining victory for your First Acolyte.'

Marduk smiled as he saw Kol Badar's jaw twitch in anger.

'As always, Warmonger, you are the voice of wisdom,' said Marduk, bowing. 'My purpose is clear; you have allayed my fears and stripped away the shadow of doubt. I am confident that my *loyal* Coryphaus will find a way forward.'

'One last thing, Marduk. I am disturbed that there are those within the Legion who doubt your holy right to lead them. I would have it known that I fully endorse your appointment.'

The Warmonger shifted its immense weight, servos and gyro-compensators hissing. It turned on the spot, each step making the floor shudder, and reached out with its immense power claw, scooping something up in its grasp. Then it turned back towards Marduk, and the First Acolyte strained to see what the Warmonger held.

The sickle-bladed talons of the Dreadnought's power claw opened, and Marduk saw a gleaming helmet, its porcelain features moulded into the form of a grimacing skull. An eight-pointed star of Chaos was carved into its forehead, and its sharpened fangs were fixed in a grinning rictus. A crack, not battle damage, but rather a carved affectation, ran across the left brow and continued below the glimmering eye-piece onto the cheek.

It was a revered, ancient artefact of the Legion, and had been crafted by the finest artisans of Mars in the years before the commencement of the Great War for the Warmonger himself.

Marduk stared at the sacred helmet with covetous eyes.

'I ordered my helmet removed from its stasis field within the bone ossuary,' said the Warmonger, 'though at the time I did not understand what it was that urged me to do so. I see clearly now that it was the will of the gods for you to have it, young Marduk.'

The First Acolyte stepped forwards and lifted the helmet from the War-monger's outstretched claw, marvelling at the mastery with which it had been rendered. The morbid visage, a dark reflection of the helmets worn by the chaplains of those blinded Legions that had not joined with the Warmaster, was a potent symbol of death, the face of damnation for all those who refused to cow to Lorgar's word.

Marduk placed the helmet over his head, and he heard a mechanical whine as it adjusted to fit his cranium. It fitted firmly in place, and there was a hiss as coupling links connected. Then all sound was blanketed out, before the integrated auto-senses powered up and his hearing returned. He breathed deeply, sucking in a lungful of recycled air, and registered the flickering array of sensory information and integrity checks being relayed onto the front of his irises. Servos whined as he stretched his neck from side to side, and an enticing targeting matrix appeared before him, locking onto Kol Badar as he turned to look upon the Coryphaus. The towering war leader was scowling, and Marduk grinned. He dismissed the targeting matrices, somewhat reluctantly, with a blink, and dropped to one knee before the warmonger.

'I have not the words to express the honour you do me, Warmonger,' he said, his voice growling from the vox-grills cunningly concealed behind the fangs of the death mask.

'Leave me now, my captains,' said the Warmonger. 'The preparations for the final push against Terra must be made. Join your brothers, and rejoice in prayer and exaltation for within the month, we shall assail the walls of the Emperor's Palace.'

'Rest well, Warmonger,' said Marduk, and he and Kol Badar backed away from the towering Dreadnought, recognising that the ancient one's lucidity was slipping. Often it was this way, as the Dreadnought relived battles of days past.

The pair left the crypt, leaving the Warmonger to relive his memories. Marduk strode out in front, a triumphant strut to his walk. Kol Badar stalked behind, a deep scowl on his face as he glared at the First Acolyte's back.

COWLED SLAVES PUSHED the skull-inlaid doors wide, and Marduk stalked out into one of the expansive docking bays of the *Infidus Diabolus*. The entire Host was gathered there, and, as one, the warrior-brothers dropped to their knees as the First Acolyte strode through their serried ranks, heading towards the stub-nosed transport ship, the *Idolator*.

Indentured workers, their bodies augmented with ensorcelled mechanics and their eyes and mouths ritualistically sutured shut, hurried to ready the ship, pumping fuel into its gullet through bulging intestine-hoses and daubing its armoured hull with sacred oils and unguents. Four Land Raiders, massively armoured tanks that had borne the warriors of the Host into battle on a thousand worlds, were moved into position beneath the stubby wings of the *Idolator*, and reinforced clamps locked around them from above, securing them for transport.

Marduk was wearing the deaths-head helmet gifted to him by the warmonger for the first time in front of the Host, and he felt awe and reverence ripple out across the gathered warriors. Passages freshly scribed upon the flayed flesh of slaves hung from devotional seals fixed to his armour, and he felt savage pride as he looked upon the warriors of the Legion.

He stalked to the front of the assembly, where a group of thirty warrior-brothers knelt facing the rest of the Host. These warriors uniformly bowed their heads as Marduk came to a halt in front of them, his gaze, hidden behind the inscrutable red lenses of his helmet, sweeping over them.

With a nod to Burias, the icon bearer stood to attention and slammed the butt of his heavy icon into the floor. The sound echoed loudly, and with an imperious gesture, Marduk motioned for the thirty warriors to stand. Kol Badar stepped out of their ranks and began to prowl along the lines, inspecting them with a grim expression on his broad face.

The thirty warriors were gathered into four coteries and Marduk's gaze travelled over the waiting warrior-brothers, reading their eagerness for the forthcoming descent towards the Imperial planet in their faces and their stances.

Each holy Astartes warrior stood armed for war, his helmet held under his left arm, and weapons readied. They stood motionless and attentive as they awaited Marduk's word, their heads held high. Each was fiercely proud to have been selected to accompany the First Acolyte.

Including Marduk, Burias and the enslaved daemon symbiote Dar-ioq, they would number thirty-two. It was an auspicious number that equalled the number of the sacred books penned by Lorgar. It augured well. Marduk had read the sacred number in the entrails of the squealing slave-neophyte he had butchered in the blooding chamber not an hour earlier, and he knew that the gods had blessed his endeavour.

'Brothers of Lorgar,' said Marduk, addressing the thirty, though his voice was raised, so that it carried to every member of the Host, 'you are blessed, for amongst all the glorious Host you have been chosen to be my honour guard, to accompany me in doing what must be done to ensure that victory is ours, for the glory of blessed Lorgar.'

Marduk strode along the line of warriors, seeing the fire of religious fervour and devotion on their faces. They stared at him passionately, fanaticism in their eyes.

Each member of the four coteries was a veteran of a thousand wars fought across a thousand battlefields, and each had been tested and found worthy time and again in the forge of battle. These were the most vicious, fanatical and devoted of all the vicious, fanatical and devoted warriors of the Host. Each was a holy warrior, who would follow his word without question, for his was the voice of the gods, and through him their infernal will would be enacted without question and without remorse. Devout, holy warriors, they would not flinch in their duty, and their fervour lent them great strength.

Each of the four coteries was led by a favoured warrior champion of the Host.

Kol Badar stood before four of his anointed brethren, each of them enormous in their heavy Terminator armour. The other coteries consisted of eight warriors each. Towering Khalaxis, his cheeks covered in ritual scars, stood before his 17th coterie, brutal warriors all. Namarsin, shorter than his brothers, though he made up for this deficiency with sheer bulk, stood before his warriors of the 217th coterie, Havoc heavy weapon specialists. Last of the champions was Sabtec, who led the highly decorated 13th coterie. Neither as tall as Khalaxis, nor as broad as Namar-sin, Sabtec was a lean warrior whose tactical nuances had won countless glorious victories for the Host. A row of horns protruded from the skin across his brow, a clear mark of the god's favour upon him, and his hand rested upon the hilt of his power sword, gifted to him by Erebus.

'Kneel,' commanded Marduk, and the gathered warriors dropped to their knees instantly. He placed his fingertips upon the forehead of each champion in turn, murmuring a benediction. He felt heat radiate beneath his fingers, and the smell of burning flesh rose. The imprint of his fingertips remained on each champion's brow, five searing points where the skin had blistered away to the bone.

Having completed the ritual, Marduk turned towards the remainder of the Host, gathered in silence as they witnessed the blessing. He saw yearning and jealousy in the eyes of the warrior-brothers who had not been chosen to accompany him. Their champions would castigate the coteries not chosen, and when next they entered the field of war, they would fight with redoubled ferocity.

'Look upon your chosen brothers and feel pride, my brethren,' roared Marduk, spreading his arms out to each side. 'Glory in their successes as if they were your own, for they fight as representatives of you all. Pray for them, that your strength may buoy them in the days to come, for they will return victorious or not at all. In the true gods we place our trust.'

Burias slammed the butt of his icon onto the floor once more, and the Host as one hammered their fists against their chests in response, the sound echoing through the docking bay.

Turning back towards the chosen thirty, Marduk dropped to one knee and drew forth his serrated *khantanka* knife. Thirty other blades were drawn instantly. Each warrior of the Host carried a sacred blade, and it was with his own khantanka knife that each warrior-brother had been blooded when first inducted into the Legion. Each khantanka blade was individual, fashioned by the warrior it belonged to, and it was said that the true essence of the warrior could be read in its design.

Marduk's blade was curved and serrated, while Kol Badar's was broad and heavy, bereft of ornamentation. Burias's blade was masterfully fashioned and elegantly curved, and its hilt was fashioned in the shape of a snarling serpent.

'Gods of the ether, we offer up our blood as sacrifice to your glory,' growled Marduk, cutting a deep vertical slash down his right cheek. The gathered warriors echoed his words, mirroring the First Acolyte's action. Blood ran from the wounds, running down the faces of the warriors before the powerful anti-coagulants in their bloodstreams sealed the wounds.

A pair of murderous khatartes flickered into being high above, the skinless daemons circling down over the congregation, borne upon bleeding, leathery wings, and settled upon the *Idolator* to witness the ritual.

With his sacred blood dripping from his jaw and onto his armour, Marduk carved a horizontal line across his cheek, bisecting the other cut to form a cross.

'Garner us with strength, and let your dark light flow through our earthly bodies,' intoned Marduk as he made the incision. Again, his words and actions were replicated by the chosen thirty, and more of the khatartes flickered into being, breaching the skin between the real and the warp.

'We give of ourselves unto you, oh great gods of damnation, and open ourselves as vessels to your immortal will,' said Marduk, making a third cut that bisected the other two diagonally.

'With the letting of this blood, we renew our pledge of faith to the Legion, to Lorgar, and to the glory of Chaos everlasting,' said Marduk, completing the ritual and making the final cut upon his face, forming the eight-pointed star of Chaos upon his cheek.

A flock of thirty-two khatartes had gathered atop the *Idolator*, silent witnesses to the conclusion of the ritual. They kicked off from their roost, and circled low over the heads of the Host, blood dripping from their skinless muscles, and their hideous faces contorted as they screamed. Then they scattered, filling the air with their raucous cries, and one by one they flickered and disappeared, rejoining the blessed immaterium.

Again Marduk raised his arms up high, and his vox-assisted voice boomed out across the docking bay.

'The portents bode well, my brothers, and the true gods have blessed this venture; let us go forth, and kill in the name of Lorgar.'

'For Lorgar,' echoed the Host, their voices raised, and Marduk smiled.

'Let's get this done,' snapped Kol Badar, and the thirty warriors boarded the *Idolator*. Darioq was brought forth from a side-door, having been rightly excluded from bearing witness to the khantanka blooding ritual, and was marched towards the waiting transport ship. Marduk had allowed him to reconstruct his servo-harness armatures, though he had ensured that the weapons systems of the unit had been stripped, and had personally branded an eight-pointed star upon his hooded forehead.

The First Acolyte was the last to enter the transport ship, and the engines roared as the boarding ramp slammed shut behind him.

'Gods of the ether, guide us,' he whispered to himself.

THE THREE FIRESTORM-CLASS frigates of Battle Group *Orion* sent their sweeps out in front of them, searching in vain for the suspected Astartes vessel. Every scan came back negative, and attempts to locate the ship through astrotelepathic means proved equally fruitless. It was as if the ship had never existed.

'It could be a ghost-image from a jump a thousand years ago,' remarked the captain of the *Dauntless*, the lead ship of the patrol. 'There is nothing out here.'

With reports of the escalating engagement with the tyranid hive-ships coming in and eager not to miss out on the hunting, the captain ordered the frigates to come around and rejoin the rest of the battle group.

Unseen and invisible in the radiation field of the red giant, an Imperial-class transport vessel blasted from the hangar decks of the *Infidus Diabolus* and began to make its way across the gulf of space, heading towards the Imperial blockade and the moon of Perdus Skylla beyond.

CHAPTER FOUR

MARDUK FELT HIS anger rising as he stared out at the Imperial armada. He could see dozens of ships, ranging in size from immense battleships bristling with weapons to small civilian transports. The warships were long, inelegant vessels with thick armoured prows, like the ironclad ships that he had once seen ploughing the oceans of the Imperial world of Katemendor, before that world had been put to the sword. Cathedral spires rose behind the giants' command stations, immense structures that housed thousands. Marduk clenched his fists in hatred as he looked upon the giant twin-headed eagle effigies at the tops of the spires, and snarled a benediction to the gods of Chaos.

They glided by the vast and silent Imperial ships, and Marduk stared at the immense cannon batteries, torpedo tubes and lance arrays. If the enemy suspected them, they would blast them to pieces in an instant, and nothing could be done to stop them. The shields of the transport vessel were enough to protect it from showers of small meteors and other space-born debris, but a single broadside from even the smaller battle cruisers would easily overpower them, and the ship would be ripped apart.

'This is insanity,' said Kol Badar.

'Have faith, Coryphaus,' said Marduk mildly, masking his own unease.

At the dawning of the Great Crusade, before the Warmaster Horus had led his divine crusade against the Emperor of Mankind, the Legion had been outfitted with hundreds of Stormbird gunships, impressively armed and armoured transport ships that doubled as attack craft. Borne

291

within the Stormbirds, the Word Bearers had sallied forth from the docking bays of their strike cruisers, bringing the word of the Emperor to the outlying planets on the fringe of the empire. As the crusade ground on, many of the Stormbirds were replaced with the newer Thunderhawk gunships, which were less heavily armed and had a smaller transport capacity, but had the benefit of being quicker and cheaper for the forge-worlds to manufacture.

With the advent of the crusade against the Emperor, the Adeptus Mechanicus forge-worlds that had thrown their weight behind the war-master produced more of the Thunderhawks for his Legions, and the Stormbirds were all but fazed out within the XVII Legion. However, with the shocking defeat of Horus, and the subsequent retreat to the Eye of Terror, the majority of the forge-worlds that supplied the Legions of Horus were virus bombed, and thus the Word Bearers Legion had no way of replacing its lost attack craft.

Few original Stormbirds remained in service within the 34th Company Host. Those that remained had had their hulls patched and repaired a hundred times. Many of the original Thunderhawks were still serviceable, though they had been altered and modified over the millennia to fit the needs of the Host and as a response to limited manufactory facilities.

The flotilla had also been increased with vessels stolen from enemies. One Thunderhawk gunship, a new model fresh from the forge-worlds of Mars, had been claimed from the loyalist White Consuls Chapter, out on the fringe of the Cadian Gate, and an ancient, near fatally damaged Stormbird that had been claimed from the cursed Alpha Legion in a raid upon one of their cult worlds was currently being refitted for use.

As well as these original Astartes-pattern attack craft, there were dozens of recommissioned civilian transports, assault boats, refitted cargo ships and auxiliary vessels that had been captured by the Host, rearmed and armoured for use as makeshift assault craft. These had all been modified and refitted by the chirumeks of the Host, and some of them barely resembled their original model.

Marduk and his hand-picked entourage of Word Bearers were aboard one of these salvaged and refitted vessels as they made their way towards the Imperial moon of Perdus Skylla.

It was an ugly brute of a ship, a squat, stub-nosed vessel that the Host had crippled and boarded centuries earlier. Dubbed *Idolator* by its new owners, it had been part of a small convoy used by smugglers running the blockades of Imperial space, rogue traders that had been circumventing Administratum taxes on the outskirts of the Maelstrom. The *Infidus Diabolus* had scattered the convoy, emerging from the darkness behind a shattered planet and ripping two of the ships apart with full broadsides. The *Idolator* had been crippled with lance strikes, and a single Dread-claw been launched from the *Infidus Diabolus*. The boarding pod latched onto the hull of the *Idolator* like a limpet, cutting through its armour with ease, and a boarding party of Word Bearers, led by Kol Badar, had stormed aboard. The crew were slaughtered, and the reeling vessel claimed by the Host.

Marduk stood with Kol Badar looking out through the curved blister portal of the bridge of the *Idolator*. Behind them, serfs of the Host were guiding the ship to its destination, directing it in towards the Imperial moon. They had once been men, but their humanity had all but abandoned them. Their flesh was stretched and covered in vile, cancerous blemishes and the hands of the pilots had become fused to their controls. Tears of blood ran down their cheeks.

The bridge was dim, the only light coming from the crimson-tinged sensor screens, bathing the room in a hellish red aura.

The Coryphaus glared balefully out at the Imperial vessels, and he clenched and unclenched the bladed fingers of his power talon unconsciously.

'If they realise what we are, all the faith in the warp will not save us,' he snarled.

'They will not,' said Marduk calmly. 'We are but another transport vessel, aiding the evacuation efforts.'

'Such deception is beneath us,' said Kol Badar. 'It belittles the Legion. We are the sons of Lorgar; we should not need to conceal ourselves from the enemy.'

'Were we to have an armada of our own, I would joyfully engage them,' said Marduk, 'but we do not. Have patience, Coryphaus; we will take the fight to the cursed Imperium soon enough.'

One of the Imperial cruisers, not one of the larger vessels by any stretch, though it dwarfed the *Idolator*, rotated on its axis and moved above them, throwing them into deep shadow as it blotted out the system's dying sun. Its port weapons batteries came level with them, and Kol Badar hissed.

The cruiser continued to turn, and its weapon arrays slid away from the *Idolator*. They passed beneath its mass, and though hundreds of kilometres of empty space separated the two ships, it seemed that every intricate detail of the cruiser could be made out. It felt close enough that Marduk had but to reach out his hand to touch it, and he wondered if people aboard it looked even now upon the *Idolator*. Did any of them realise that their mortal enemy was passing beneath them so close?

The shadow of the cruiser passed, and Marduk nodded his head to the Coryphaus. Kol Badar barked an order, and the *Idolator* turned onto a new bearing. The engines were fed more power, and the ship pushed through the blockade of the Imperial cordon and began to power towards Perdus Skylla.

It looked so insignificant from here; a tiny white moon circling in the orbit of a green gas giant.

'Five hours until planetfall,' said Kol Badar, consulting a glowing data-slate built into the command array of the bridge.

'See that the warrior-brothers are ready. I want to move out as soon as the landing is made,' said Marduk, not looking at the Coryphaus.

Kol Badar's lips curled back, and his ancient eyes burrowed into Marduk's face.

'What?' asked Marduk, turning to face the larger warrior-brother. 'I am your master now, Kol Badar. Be a good dog and do as you are told.'

Kol Badar struck with a speed that belied the bulk of his Terminator armour, wrapping his power talons around Marduk's throat, his eyes blazing in fury.

Marduk laughed in his face.

'Do it,' he barked. 'Do it, and be cursed by Lorgar.'

Kol Badar released Marduk with a shove.

'Know your place, Kol Badar. Jarulek is dead. This Host is mine now, mine alone,' said Marduk. 'Just as *you* are mine.'

'The Council of Sicarus will repudiate your claim over the Host,' growled Kol Badar. 'They will strip you of your brotherhood, flay the flesh from your bones and have your eyes burnt from your sockets. Bloody and blind, you will be cast out into the corpse-plains, where the souls of the condemned will torment you, and the kathartes will strip the muscles from your limbs. You will wander in agony for ten thousand years, unable to die, your mortal body a wretched shell, your soul stripped and gnawed upon by the denizens of the darkness. All this awaits you, Marduk. Such is the punishment for one who plots against his Dark Apostle.'

'Jarulek groomed me as a sacrifice,' said Marduk, 'and I know that you were party to his schemes, but I do not hold a grudge against you for that; you were following your Dark Apostle's orders. The gods of Chaos chose for Jarulek to fall, however, and for me to flourish. They abandoned him in favour of me.'

'You fear to return there, and that is why we have not gone back,' said Kol Badar.

Marduk laughed, genuinely surprised.

'I fear to return there? I think not, my Coryphaus. I *yearn* to return, but I will not return without the secrets of the Nexus unlocked. I thought that you merely wanted me to return a failure, with a lifeless hunk of xenos metal, with no knowledge of what it did or how it is activated. I had no idea that you thought that the council would punish me. Punish me?' Marduk laughed. 'The council will *honour* me.'

'You are a dreamer and a fool, then,' said Kol Badar, turning away.

Marduk moved in front of the Coryphaus, standing in his way. He stared up at the older warrior, the light of fanaticism in his eyes.

'Look into my eyes, Kol Badar, and tell me that the gods do not favour me. Ever since we left Tanakreg, I have felt their favour upon me. My skin is crawling with their power. I can feel it writhing within me.'

Something moved beneath the skin of Marduk's face.

'I am the favoured of Lorgar, and the council *will* embrace me. Tell me that you do not see the gods' favour upon me. Even you, who can barely feel the touch of the warp or the gods, must surely sense my growing favour. Tell me that you cannot.'

Kol Badar clenched his jaw, his eyes blazing with fury, but he did not speak. Marduk laughed softly.

'You *do* sense it then,' he said, as the Coryphaus stalked past him. Kol Badar barged his shoulder into Marduk as he passed, knocking the smaller man aside, but Marduk merely laughed again.

The Coryphaus turned at the doorway.

'Maybe you could trick the council,' he said, 'but you have to make it there alive first.'

THE ARMOURED NOSE of the *Idolator* glowed red hot as the ship screamed down towards the surface of Perdus Skylla.

'Unto those who in ignorance and stubbornness refuse the Word, bring the fires of hell. Sunder their flesh, and burn them of their impurity. Take vengeance upon them for their failings, and teach them the weakness of their false idols,' roared Marduk, the vox-amplifiers built into his skull-faced helmet booming his words through the enclosed space of the transport. 'Thus spoke Lorgar, and so it shall be done. Open their veins that the truth might enter them. Cut upon them and let their blood flow. With holy bolter and chainsword we shall slaughter the unbelievers, and usher the word of truth into the world!'

Strapped into their harness restraints, the warriors of the Host roared their approval as the G-forces assailed them, the words of their holy leader fuelling their hatred and religious fervour.

'No mercy, no remorse,' barked Marduk. 'Such things are for weaklings. We are the faithful, Lorgar's chosen! None shall stand against us. Give praise to the gods of Chaos as you kill. Death will be our herald, and all who look upon us will know fear.'

The *Idolator* broke through the upper atmosphere of Perdus Skylla, streaking down through the darkness like a fiery comet from the heavens.

'Let us pray, brothers of the Host, and let the gods bear witness to our eulogies and bless us with their holy strength,' bellowed Marduk. 'Great powers of the warp, guide the arms of your servants that they might let the blood of your enemies in your honour. Gird us with the strength and fortitude to do your bidding, and let our faith protect us from the blows of the faithless. Let your dark light shine upon us, filling us with purpose and belief. With thanks, we give ourselves unto you, pledging body and soul to your glory, for now and for time immaterial. Glory be.'

'Glory be,' came the response from the warriors of the Host, led by Kol Badar.

'And unto those who would do harm to your faithful servants,' said Marduk, locking eyes with Kol Badar, 'bring an eternity of torment and pain.'

The *Idolator* continued its descent until, after several minutes, the relentless g-forces began to ease and the transport started to level out. Flying low, it screamed across the frozen wasteland, kicking up a great turbulence of snow and ice in its wake. Powerful winds rocked the transport, jolting its occupants from side to side, as it roared into the face of a fierce ice storm. Sudden drops in pressure and blasts of wind made the *Idolator* rise and fall by ten metres at a time, threatening to slam the ship into the ice crust at any moment.

Marduk grinned fiercely, exposing sharpened teeth. Adrenaline pumped through his system.

Kol Badar had plotted the approach course that the *Idolator* was now following with keen tactical acumen. They had entered the atmosphere along the equatorial belt of the moon, four thousand kilometres from the closest Imperial listening post, and they were now approaching the northern polar cap on the lee side of the moon, under the cover of darkness. The Imperials were based solely at the extreme northern and southern tips of the moon, where they had mining colonies, starports and fortress bastions. Immense defence lasers protected these settlements, each of which Kol Badar had estimated consisted of between eight and twelve million people, living beneath the ice.

Virtually nothing lived on the surface, its conditions too severe to maintain life or even any permanent structures other than the bastions. Even the starports were carved into the ice. Reinforced titanium roof structures covered the circular starports, protecting them and the vessels within from the harshest of weather conditions, and those roofs would open like the petals of a flower to allow transport vessels and freighters to dock.

From the information garnered from the Adeptus Mechanicus archive on Kharion IV, the most recent location of the explorator who held the secrets of the device had been ascertained, and it was towards this bastion station that the *Idolator* was bound.

They would get as close as they were able to the Imperial bastion, flying low across the windswept landscape and using the sweep-jamming ice storms to conceal their approach. Kol Badar had factored in the swirling eddies of low pressure, continent sized cyclones that wracked the empty wasteland, in order to further conceal their approach, though he had loudly voiced his displeasure at such subterfuge.

Regardless of the Coryphaus's misgivings, Marduk could not fault Kol Badar's execution. They would be upon the bastion long before their presence was known, and it would be a simple matter of breaching its defences and locating the custodian. The portents had boded well, and Marduk felt assured that it would be a simple undertaking.

He freed the restraints that locked him to his seat, and stood up, easily compensating for the roll of the transport as it was buffeted by howling winds. Stretching out his shoulders, his gaze wandered up the rows of seated Word Bearers, assessing them each in turn.

Khalaxis's teeth were bared, his aggressive nature mirrored in the expressions of his members of the 17th coterie. He jerked his head to the side, flicking his braided hair out of his eyes, concentrating on his knife as it carved into his flesh. He and his warriors had removed their left vambraces and were cutting ritualistic slashes across their forearms. Always the first into any breach, and the last to be extracted, his warriors were lethal combatants all.

Namar-sin, in stark comparison to Khalaxis, was composed and silent, though his one eye gleamed with a fervour no less passionate than Khalaxis's. His Havocs were dutifully tending their weapons, apparently oblivious to the shuddering transport and the roar of the engines. They went about their duties with utter focus, silently incanting benedictions of the dark gods upon their revered heavy weapons.

Brother Sabtec's face was serious, his stoic demeanour familiar and unwavering, and he led the hallowed 13th coterie in a low chant as they checked over their life-systems, and ensured that grenades, spare ammunition clips and devotional chapbooks were secured at their sides.

The final coterie, Kol Badar's veteran Anointed, glared ahead blankly, their expressions grim. Their faces were covered in ritual tattoos and each in turn lowered his head in deference as Marduk looked upon them.

Burias was looking at his hand as the fingers fused and elongated into talons, before he forced the daemon Drak'shal back and his hand took on its natural form once more. Marduk realised that his control over the daemon was growing. Often the possessed would become little more than screaming wretches, their will enslaved to one of the myriad entities that inhabited the warp, but Burias's mastery over Drak'shal was almost complete. Again, Burias let Drak'shal begin to rear within him, and his hand blurred into daemonic talons, before he reasserted his dominance and pushed the daemon back within him. Feeling Marduk's gaze upon him, Burias's eyes flicked up, and he winked at the First Acolyte.

Darioq stood apart from the brothers of the Legion. The corrupted magos could not sit even had he wished too; his mechanical body was not constructed to accommodate such luxury, and the bulk of his servo-harness would have made it impossible. The activated electromagnets within his heavy, augmented boots kept him locked to the floor, and his four mechanical servo-arms were braced between two bulkheads. Weighing well over a metric tonne, nothing was going to move the techno-magos.

'You have a wish to converse, Marduk, First Acolyte of the Word

Bearers Legion of Astartes, genetic descendent of the traitor Primarch Lorgar?' said the magos. The timbre of his voice was different, a growling, daemonic presence underlying his usual robotic monotone.

'Speak the word "traitor" once more when referring to the blessed daemon-lord of our Legion, Darioq-Grendh'al,' said Marduk, 'and I shall allow Kol Badar to rip your limbs off one by one, and no, I have no wish to converse with you.'

The *Idolator* made its way through the darkness across the featureless surface of the moon for two hours, and as they drew near the target, Marduk intoned a final benediction, and the warriors of the Host made ready to disembark. With his skull-faced helmet in place, Marduk ritualistically ran through his final diagnostics, checking his life-systems and those of his revered power armour.

At last, throbbing blister-lights warned of the final approach, and Marduk rammed a fresh sickle-clip into his bolt pistol. Retro-blasters fired, slowing the *Idolator*, and the nose of the transport craft lifted as its momentum dropped.

Kol Badar relayed his debarkation orders with curt commands, ensuring that each of the four coteries knew their position.

Restraint harnesses were thrown off as the rear landing legs touched down, and the vacuum seals of the rear embarkation ramp were released with a hiss. Before the *Idolator* had even settled, the ramp was thrown outwards, and snow and ice blasted into the interior, swirling around in blinding eddies.

'Get him moving,' shouted Kol Badar over the screaming of engines and the howling of wind, pointing towards Darioq, and two members of Namar-sin's coterie urged the corrupted magos towards the lowering ramp.

The first warriors were already pounding down the ramp, moving towards their allotted positions, filing off left and right. Marduk stomped down the assault ramp and stepped onto the frozen surface of Perdus Skylla. The enhanced auto-sensors in his helmet allowed his sight to pierce the raging blizzard, though mere mortal eyes would have seen nothing but a blinding sheet of white.

Marduk filed off to the right just as the Land Raiders, two tucked beneath each stubbed wing, were lowered onto the ice. They growled like angry war-beasts as they were released from their locking clamps. Their engines revved, and smoke billowed from their daemon-headed exhaust stacks. Marduk ducked his head as he entered the armoured hull of the closest Land Raider and locked himself into a seat. Burias slammed into the seat opposite, a feral grin upon his features. As usual, he did not deign to wear his helmet; his witch-sight easily the match of any automated sensors. Long strands of oiled black hair that had escaped their binding whipped around his head like a gorgon's serpents.

Brother Sabtec and his esteemed 13th joined them, piling into the

Land Raider and taking their seats, and the assault ramp was slammed shut. The frenzied wind died away instantly, and the shower of snow and ice settled on shoulder pads and greaves.

The Land Raider's massive tracks spun on the ice for a second before catching, and the heavy assault tank lurched into motion. Less than thirty seconds after the *Idolator* had landed, the four Land Raiders, each filled with blessed warriors of Lorgar, were speeding across the surface of Perdus Skylla.

Marduk was shaken as the assault tank hit a bank of snow, and there was a moment of weightlessness as the front of the vehicle lifted up before crashing down again with titanic force.

'Twenty minutes to target,' growled Kol Badar over the vox.

Burias's features shimmered like a faulty pict viewer, and the face of the daemon Drak'shal was momentarily superimposed over his features. Tall, uneven horns rose from his brow, and deeply slanted, hate-filled eyes blinked. Then Burias shook his head, pushing the daemon back within, and the image was gone.

'Not long, Drak'shal,' said Marduk in the guttural tongue of the daemons. Burias grinned at him once more.

CHAPTER FIVE

HUNDRED-KILOMETRE WINDS WHIPPED across the ice flow, and the roar of the storm was such that no human ear would have heard any shout or the staccato reverberations of gunfire. The darkness would have concealed anything from the naked eye, and the blinding swirl of ice, snow and fog was such that all but the most sophisticated sensor arrays were rendered useless. Still, Marduk was taking no chances as he elbowed his way cautiously forwards, edging nearer to the Imperial bastion.

He could see the dark shadow of the structure rising before him, though even his advanced auto-sensors and magnifier auspexes had difficulty piercing the blinding gale. It was built into a massive pinnacle of rock that pierced the thick ice, the first geological landmark that the Word Bearers had thus far seen on Perdus Skylla. Marduk snarled up at the hateful silhouette of the fortress. It had been constructed in the form of an immense aquila, the two-headed eagle that was the symbol of the Imperium and the Emperor's rule.

It rose some three hundred and fifty metres above the ice plains, the highest point on all of Perdus Skylla. If the weather had been clearer, it could have been seen for kilometres all around, an immense structure that dominated the landscape. Doubtless it had been built to remind the populace of Perdus Skylla of the Emperor's authority, to cow the people it loomed over and never let them forget who it was that ruled their lives.

To the ignorant people of Perdus Skylla it might have been a symbol of reverence, but to Marduk it represented all that he hated about the

Imperium, all that he desired to see toppled.

What sort of empire would allow a lifeless corpse to be venerated as a god, and let pompous fools and bureaucrats dictate how a galaxy was to be run? For the millionth time, he cursed the holy warmaster for being laid low by the trickery of the enemy. Had Horus overthrown the Emperor, the galaxy would never have fallen into stagnation and torpor. The Great Crusade would still be underway, wiping all xenos and non-believers from the universe. Humanity would be united in faith.

Marduk froze, pushing himself flat to the ground as his keen auto-senses flashed a warning before his eyes. The massive gates of the bastion began to open, folding in upon themselves and sliding into a hidden recess within the rock. Four armoured vehicles emerged, the sound of their engines lost in the howling wind.

They were non-standard template vehicles protected by thick plates of white-painted armour. Marduk's targeting arrays locked onto the fore-most vehicle, and a flood of data streamed in front of his eyes. A heavy weapons sponson unfolded from behind the main engine block, sliding forward and locking into place, and the weapon panned left and right. They were light vehicles, roughly the size of Rhino APCs, and they were clearly built for traversing the ice flows, with heavy, thick tracks at the rear and a single upwards flaring ski as broad as the tank at the front.

If it came to it, they would easily be neutralised by his Land Raiders, but he had no wish for the enemy to know, prematurely, that they were under attack.

The vehicles moved up the steep ramp of ice and snow that led from within the bastion, heavy weapons turrets rotating with precise, mechanical movements.

They turned to the north-west, and soon disappeared into the storm.

'Do not engage,' said Marduk.

'Acknowledged,' came Kol Badar's response, his voice blurred by static.

Resuming his advance, Marduk elbowed his way closer to the enemy fortification.

The aquila fortress reared up above him, its twin heads glaring out into the darkness. Despite his anger, disdain and disgust as he thought of what could have been, *should* have been, it gave him perverse pleasure to see how far the Imperium had fallen. This world was evidence of its failings. It was being abandoned, as was the entire sub-system, in the face of a xenos threat. He shook his head in mockery at such weakness.

The long, insulated barrels of defence lasers rose up behind the aquila structure, angled towards the heavens. He knew that the vast power source for the formidable weapons would be located deep within the rock below. They were weapons of awesome potency, though useless against an enemy that had already landed.

Marduk advanced a further two hundred metres, assailed by the relent-less wind and biting ice. The brutal environmental conditions did not concern him. His archaic power armour, a bastard hybrid of marks IV, V and VI, was capable of withstanding far more demanding situations.

Within fifty metres of the enemy structure, Marduk hunkered down to assess the defences of the bastion. Snow began to settle on his power armour, so that he was almost completely concealed. Indeed, a human could have stood five metres away and not have seen him, blinded by the gale and the fog.

His gleaming, black, reflective eyepieces panned upwards, targeters locking onto autocannon turrets and demolisher cannons built into the sides of the rock face. Had the weather been less severe, the static defences would have taken a heavy toll on the Host as it approached. Such a thing was unacceptable, for Marduk had brought less than thirty warrior-brothers with him on the mission to Perdus Skylla.

In ideal circumstances, he would have descended upon the moon with the entire Host, and the taking of the bastion would have been a simple thing. However, with the size of the Imperial blockade in the sub-system such an endeavour would have been folly, for the *Infidus Diabolus* would have been annihilated long before it reached the moon's atmosphere. As such, he had chosen to lead just a small strike force onto the surface of the moon, and slipped unseen through the Imperial cordon.

It was not the way that he would have liked to have achieved victory; for Marduk, like Kol Badar, would have been more pleased to have laid waste the Imperial world, to unleash the full force of the Host and leave nothing but corpses and edifices to the great gods behind. Victory here was important, however, and the manner in which it was achieved, less so.

Pushing his extraneous thoughts aside, Marduk turned his attention to the task at hand.

Two twin-linked autocannon turrets guarded the approach to the bastion gates, and they panned back and forth across the open ground before them. Each was restricted to a ninety-degree firing arc, though the arcs of the two turrets, and the others nearby were overlapping, ensuring that no enemy could approach the bastion from any angle without coming under fire. Heavier siege cannons protruded from the rock face above the gates, but they were of less interest to Marduk, for he was below their arc of trajectory. They were designed to fire upon enemy two hundred metres and further out, not at a foe already at the base of the bastion. Still, he opened up a visual feed with Kol Badar, allowing the Coryphaus to see what he did, so that the war leader was aware of what he would be riding into once the gates were breached.

'Brother Namar-sin,' said Kol Badar in a growled response to the visual feed. 'Move your coterie into position and target the turrets. Fire on the First Acolyte's command.'

'So it shall be, Coryphaus,' came the response. Somewhere behind Marduk, invisible even to his augmented sight, the Havoc Space Marines of Namar-sin's coterie would be targeting the autocannons with their ancient heavy weapons.

Marduk again looked up, peering through the blinding ice storm.

'Come on, Burias,' he hissed in impatience.

Two HUNDRED AND fifty metres up, Burias scaled the vertical rock face, hauling himself up hand over hand. Kol Badar had identified one last possible escape route from the bastion, and it was the icon bearer's duty to close it off.

He had allowed the change to come over him, bringing the daemon Drak'shal to the fore, and great horns rose from his head. Hellfire burnt within his eyes, and his teeth were bared, exposing a double row of serrated shark-like teeth. Impossibly, his darkly handsome, immaculate features could still be seen beneath the image of the daemon, as if both beings were coexisting in the same space.

Bunching his leg muscles, Burias pushed off from the rock face, leaping upwards. He grabbed a rocky overhang with one hand, and for a second he hung there over the vertical drop. The ground could not be seen below, lost in the swirling storm, though the glow of lascannons could be dimly discerned. Hauling himself over the edge, the heat of his breath clouded the air around him, and feral eyes locked onto the hateful shape of the giant aquila that reared above him. He dug his taloned hands into stone carved in the form of feathers and continued his ascent.

Up above, roughly a hundred metres away, the twin eagle heads of the colossal stone aquila glared out across the landscape, one facing east, and the other west. A bright light shone like a lighthouse from the eye of the right eagle head, while the eye of the left head was dark and blind.

Burias ascended towards the shining eye, his talons easily finding handholds between the massive carved feathers. He ascended the sheer exterior of the immense statue, swiftly, barely pausing as he climbed, like a dark stain upon the noble eagle's body. The wind howled around him, buffeting him and threatening to rip him loose, and ice and snow drove into him at gale force.

Climbing swiftly and surely, he scurried up the curving neck like a spider until he was directly below the head. With a snarl he sprang out, twisting in mid-air, and one hand locked around a feathered grip three metres higher. Without pause, he continued up beneath the immense head, crawling upside down along the underside of the monolith. He paused as he reached the beak, for the stone was as smooth as glass and there were no handholds. He changed the angle of his climb, and scrambled up the vertical eagle head, being careful to stay out of sight of the shining eye, and pulled himself atop the massive structure.

Oblivious to the danger the winds presented as they assailed him, Burias threw his head back and roared into the gale.

Dropping to a crouch, Burias made his way on all fours towards the eagle's shining eye. Cautiously, he peered inside.

He saw a man sitting at a desk, an almost completely empty decanter of dark liquid in front of him. By his manner of dress, he was clearly a high-ranking official; and another man, young and awkward, stood at his side. The two appeared to be engrossed in conversation, and they did not notice the daemonic vision of the possessed warrior glaring in at them. There were two exits from the room: an elevator lift that would descend into the body of the aquila, and a heavy blast door.

Climbing backwards, Burias-Drak'shal reached the top once more, looking down. On the back of the eagle head, fifteen metres lower, was a protected platform where a small shuttle was docked, and where the blast door led.

Burias-Drak'shal perched some ten metres above the blast door, and settled down to wait. If any eye had been able to pierce the darkness and the howling gale he would have looked like a malicious gargoyle, crouching motionless as he awaited his prey.

'In position,' he growled, his fang-filled mouth forming the words awkwardly.

'Received, Burias-Drak'shal,' replied Marduk. The snow settled over him, so that only his baleful skull-faced visage peered from beneath the white blanket, his black eyes staring hatefully at the enemy structure.

'217th Havoc coterie, split,' Kol Badar ordered. 'Heavy weapons, hold position. Namar-sin, move the rest of your squad forward to support the First Acolyte, and ready melta bombs. Move on the First Acolyte's word.'

'Forwards on me,' motioned Marduk as Namar-sin and three of his coterie emerged from the blanketing gale behind him, crawling stealthily forwards, their horned helmets covered in a thick layer of snow.

Marduk resumed his advance, inching his way forwards. Imperial sweeps arced across the ice three times, and the Word Bearers froze each time, instantly cutting relay feeds and vox-transmissions to make themselves all but invisible.

The distance to the closest turret was no more than twenty metres, and the bastion gate was less than forty. Metre by metre, Marduk and his chosen brethren crept forwards. The wind suddenly dropped, and warning sensors flashed in Marduk's helmet. Without the interference of the billowing ice-crystals in the air, the turrets swung towards the Word Bearers and opened fire.

A fraction of a second before the autocannons unleashed their fury, Marduk rolled to the side and high-calibre rounds ripped up the ground where he had lain. One of the Havoc Space Marines was hit by the opening salvo, his helmet smashing apart beneath the heavy weapons fire, staining the snow with his blood.

'Now,' barked Marduk into his vox-relay, and a beam of light stabbed out of the storm as one of the heavy weapon-armed Havocs of the 217th coterie fired his lascannon, and one of the turrets fell silent. A stream of white-hot plasma engulfed another turret, and plasteel and rockcrete ran like liquid as it was destroyed.

Marduk was up and running, roaring a catechism of devotion as he unslung his chainsword. Autocannon rounds screamed past him, and one of them clipped his shoulder, jerking him to the side, but not halting his progress. Another lascannon beam stabbed from the gale, and a third turret was destroyed, detonating from within as its ammunition cache was hit. The resulting explosion threw chunks of rock in all directions. Marduk swayed his head to the side as a piece of red-hot rockcrete the size of a man hurtled past him.

Marduk was five metres from the last remaining turret, and he threw himself forwards into a roll as its barrels swung towards him, spitting a torrent of high-velocity rounds. He came up to his feet beneath it, and grabbed one of the barrels. Servo-muscles straining, he pushed upwards with all his might, overextending the automated turret housing, exposing cabling and ammo feeds. Sparks spattered off Marduk's skull-faced helmet, and he slashed his chainsword across the turret's internals. The whirring chain links tore through the cables, and oil gushed like blood. Releasing his grip on the barrel of the weapon, the turret flopped lifelessly to the side.

More turrets, higher up on the bastion's face, were opening fire, raining down a hail of gunfire, which was answered by the heavy weapons fire of those warrior-brothers further back. One of Namar-sin's coterie was caught in a fusillade from two directions, and fell to one knee as his body was pierced a dozen times. Still, he refused to fall, and pushing himself back to his feet, he ran on towards the bastion gates.

Bullets glanced off Marduk's shoulder plates, and a round caught him in the chest, knocking him back a step, though it did not penetrate his thick ceramite armour. With a hiss of anger, he lurched forwards, running down the incline towards the bastion gates. Beneath the overhanging lip, he was protected from the worst of the fire, and Marduk pulled a melta bomb loose from a chain around his waist. He whispered a prayer to the Great Changer as he primed the potent grenade and slammed it onto the thick door, placing it over one of the locking mechanisms. Electromagnets held it firmly in place, and a red light on the melta bomb began to flash.

'On approach,' said Kol Badar, his voice overlaid with static and interference.

As another melta bomb was slammed into place by a warrior of the 217th coterie, the champion Namar-sin staggered into the protection beneath the gateway, smoking bullet craters across his armour. His left arm was gone, blown clear by autocannon fire, and his armour was awash with blood.

'You took your time,' growled Marduk.

'I apologise, my lord,' he said. The powerful anti-coagulants in the warrior's blood had already stemmed the flow, and formed a thick crust around the shocking wound.

'I can still do my job,' said Namar-sin defensively, feeling Marduk's gaze on his injuries. Gritting his teeth, the champion primed his melta bomb somewhat awkwardly with one hand, before slamming the bulky grenade into position.

More lascannon beams stabbed from the ice storm towards the bastion's defences as the Land Raiders approached. In response, the first of the battle cannons spoke, firing blindly into the gale, the ensuing reverberations shaking the ground.

The melta bombs detonated, and the metre-thick gates buckled inwards. The force of the super-heated explosions was directed inwards, searing through the reinforced metal barrier. It was not fully breached, but as he lowered the arm that shielded his face, Marduk recognised instantly that its integrity was compromised.

'Twenty seconds,' said Kol Badar's voice in Marduk's helmet.

Lascannons fired from the blinding gale, and then the dark shadow of the first Land Raider could be seen, driving at speed for the gatehouse. An explosion slammed into the ice beside the behemoth, knocking it to the side, and for a second its left-hand tracks lifted, spinning wildly before it slammed back on the ground and corrected its angle of approach.

Marduk moved to the side, his back to a rockcrete support buttress, as the immense Land Raider gunned its engines. Its ancient hide was inscribed with passages from the books of Chaos, and symbols of devotion and allegiance marred its clotted-blood coloured armour plates. Autocannon rounds ricocheted off the Land Raider, unable to penetrate, and heavy bolter rounds were deflected off its angled plates. Its side sponsons lit up the darkness as they stabbed into the gates, further weakening them, and Marduk pressed himself backwards so as not to be struck by the monstrous battle tank as it dropped down the incline towards the entrance to the bastion.

It slammed into the weakened gates with the force of a battering ram, and they collapsed inwards. Another Land Raider bedecked with chains from which severed heads and limbs hung followed the first, its daemon-headed exhausts spewing black smoke as it roared down the incline and into the belly of the bastion, followed by the third. The last of the Land Raiders would hold position, scanning for any sign of the enemy out on the plain. With the enemy bastion breached, the heavy weapons toting Havocs of the 217th coterie pulled back towards the Land Raider, as per Kol Badar's orders, though their champion Namarsin was to enter the bastion alongside the First Acolyte.

As the third Land Raider roared past, Marduk broke into a run behind it, using it as moving cover. He drew his chainsword as he ran, and felt the impatience of the daemon Borhg'ash within the daemon weapon.

Already he could hear the sounds of gunfire, the hiss of lasguns and the whine as they repowered, and the deep percussive boom of heavy bolter fire.

The ramp descended into the interior of the bastion, which had been carved into the solid rock. The interior was not unlike the hangar deck of the *Infidus Diabolus*, with high ceilings and various levels and gantries running around its walls. Around thirty APCs, light scout vehicles and a couple of heavier tanks, all armoured in the same uniform white plates, were lined up in serried ranks, and white-armoured soldiers were running forwards. Officers were shouting, and men were running in from portals in the north and south. Others were taking up positions upon the gantries lining the walls, firing down at the Word Bearers.

The two Land Raiders had ground to a halt, heavy bolters built into their hulls pumping explosive rounds into the enemy, ripping men apart in bloody detonations. The frontal assault ramps slammed down onto the rockcrete floor, and the bulky forms of the warriors of the Host appeared from the red-lit interiors, smoke billowing around them.

Kol Badar strode from the lead Land Raider, his face hidden beneath his quad-tusked helmet and fire spitting from the barrels of his archaic combi-bolter. The Coryphaus roared, the daemonic sound resounding from vox-grills as he cut a white-armoured man in half with bolter fire. Behind him, the four warriors of the Anointed, the warrior elite of the Host, stalked forwards heavily. The servos of their ancient Terminator armour hissed and vented steam as the Anointed advanced from the interior of the battle tank, their weapons roaring.

Sabtec and Khalaxis emerged from the other Land Raiders, leading their respective coteries. The 13th instantly took cover, bolters spitting death as they coolly split into two teams and manoeuvred into good firing positions. As Sabtec's warriors laid down their hail of suppressing fire, Khalaxis and his 17th coterie disdained any attempt to seek cover, and raced headlong towards the enemy, revving the motors of their chainblades and snapping off shots with their pistols.

A portal lifted beside Marduk, and he swung his bolt pistol around and fired. A troop of white-armoured soldiers ran at him, and his first rounds took one of them in the chest. He fell with a strangled cry as his ribcage was shattered. A second enemy dropped as his head exploded, and Marduk pumped another pair of shots into the body of a third warrior.

The soldiers halted, those in front dropping to one knee as they raised their lasguns. Others sought cover against the pipes protruding into the corridor, and they fired as their sergeant shouted an order.

Las-rounds impacted with Marduk's chest and shoulder pads, knocking him back half a step. They left blackened scorch marks on his armoured plates, and Marduk snarled in fury as he leapt forwards, his chainsword roaring.

More las-rounds pinged off his armour as he closed the distance, and he began to recite the Litanies of Hate and Vengeance, barking the words like a mantra. Several of the enemy soldiers baulked and stumbled back from his charge as his vox-enhanced voice made their eardrums bleed. Marduk blew the arm off one of them with his bolt pistol fired at close range, and then he was amongst them.

His chainsword hacked into the neck of the first, teeth biting through armour, flesh and bone, and hot blood splashed across Marduk's tabard. Blood ran down the feeder grooves carved into the sides of the chainsword and was sucked into the internals of the weapon, and Marduk felt fresh power and strength flow through him as the daemon Borhg'ash fed. Veins pulsed along the length of the ancient weapon, and the daemon urged Marduk on to feed it further.

He dropped to one knee, and a las-bolt seared above him where his head had been a fraction of a second earlier. He hacked out again, cutting through another soldier's leg, the bone ripped apart by Borhg'ash's eager teeth. He fired his bolt pistol, and another enemy was slammed backwards into its comrades as the back of its head exploded outwards.

Brother Namar-sin was at Marduk's side, and he buried his axe in the chest of another of the soldiers, the pain of his severed arm lending him additional strength and fervour. He planted his boot on the chest of the man and ripped his axe free, kicking the soldier to the ground. He hacked his axe into another man, severing his arm and cutting half way through his torso.

Another warrior of Namar-sin's 217th fired his bolter at point blank range, blasting the soldiers back, chunks of flesh and blood spraying in all directions. One man, his lifeblood running from his wounds, was on his knees before the warrior-brother, and his skull was pulverised by the butt of a bolter.

Marduk continued reciting from the Litanies of Hate and Vengeance and rammed his chainsword into the gut of another enemy. The whirring, barbed links of the weapon ripped the soldier in two, cutting off his pitiful cries of agony.

Borhg'ash was gorged with blood, and it leaked from the internals of the chainsword like a syrup, but the daemon still hungered for more. Marduk felt the sentience within the chainsword urging him to kill again, and he gladly indulged its will.

Having emptied his bolt pistol clip, he holstered the weapon as he hacked a lasgun being levelled at him in two with a backhand sweep of his chainsword. The sparking halves of the lasgun were ripped from the terrified soldier's hands, and as he staggered backwards in shock, Marduk cleaved him from shoulder to hip with a powerful two-handed blow with his chainsword.

There were no more living threats, and Borhg'ash revved its engine, expressing its desire for more blood. Seeing one soldier on the ground still living, though he was dying fast as his blood pumped from his severed leg, Marduk reversed his grip on his chainsword and drove it downwards into the man. The soldier shuddered as the sharp teeth of the weapon ripped apart his flesh, and Borhg'ash greedily sucked up the gore.

Marduk loaded a fresh sickle clip into his bolt pistol as he marched back out onto the main concourse. A frantic gun battle was still underway, with enemy soldiers high up on gantries sniping down at the Word Bearers below. Scores of white-armoured men were lying dead or dying throughout the area, some crawling vainly for the futile safety of cover.

Sabtec's 13th coterie was taking cover behind the bulk of the Land Raiders, positioned at corners and snapping off beams at the enemy soldiers. Lasgun shots impacted uselessly against the armoured hulls of the massive vehicles, and those few Word Bearers that were struck shrugged off the las-fire as if they were irritating mosquito bites.

One of the 13th dropped to one knee, aiming his stubby, daemon-headed missile launcher up high, and smoke billowed out the back of the missile tube as he fired. The missile screamed upwards and struck the underside of one of the gantries where a cluster of snipers was positioned, exploding in a billowing cloud of flame. The flesh of the soldiers was sliced apart as super-heated fragments of metal lacerated them, and the metal grid gave way. Those not killed by the explosion dropped ten metres to the next level of gantries, and were crushed as metal bracings were wrenched out of shape and pulled down in their wake.

Khalaxis and his warriors stormed across the gantries, unstoppable juggernauts of muscle and power armour that smashed through the enemy, throwing them over railings to fall fifteen metres to the ground, hacking limbs from bodies with sweeps of chainswords and killing everything in their path.

Three of the light armoured vehicles of the enemy were thrown upwards as a lascannon ignited fuel cells, and a mushroom of fierce orange flame billowed upwards, black, oily smoke licking at its edges. One of the vehicles spun end over end and slammed into a wall, while the other two came crushing down onto other unmanned vehicles behind which more enemy soldiers were hunkered down. They staggered back away from the inferno, and were dutifully gunned down by concentrated bolter fire.

Kol Badar strode through the firefight snapping off shots with his combi-bolter, his entourage of Anointed warriors walking steadily alongside him. They eschewed any attempt to take cover, the ancient, ceramite and adamantium plates of their Terminator armour offering them more protection than rockcrete or steel.

One of the Anointed swung the heavy twin barrels of his reaper autocannon before him like a scythe, laying down a withering hail of high-calibre fire that ripped everything apart indiscriminately: armour, men, vehicles and rockcrete.

A body landed in front of Marduk, having been hurled from a gantry above. The soldier's helmet was smashed, and his eyes stared blankly up at the First Acolyte. Marduk kicked the man in the head, splashing blood and brain matter across the floor.

More enemy soldiers were appearing, assailing the Word Bearers from all directions. They were caught in the middle of a crossfire, but were cutting the enemy down ruthlessly. Marduk saw that two Word Bearers had fallen, though their injuries were not mortal and they continued to fight on. At least fifty enemy soldiers had been slain, and the casualties were mounting.

Under Kol Badar's direction, Sabtec's 13th began advancing up through the hail of fire towards the gantries, while the Anointed laid down a hail of fire that kept the enemy's heads down. The Land Raiders pivoted on the spot, their lascannons destroying everything they targeted, and their heavy bolters ripping paths across the rock walls as they chased the enemy soldiers.

Marduk raced up a steel staircase, taking the steps four at a time. A las-blast struck him in the head, scorching his pristine alabaster skull helmet, and he snapped off a shot with his pistol in response, sending a man flying five metres backwards, a crater exploding from his back.

The enemy officers were shouting their commands, frantically attempting to rally their men and reposition them in the face of the relentless advance of the Word Bearers, but they were panicking, and their orders were not followed. Men crawled backwards, attempting to find any place to hide from the unholy fallen angels of death stalking towards them, firing off hasty shots with lasguns.

Marduk stomped onto one of the gantries and shot down two men, their blood misting the air. With a kick, he smashed aside a stand of barrels behind which three men were taking cover, and gunned the first two down. The other was torn apart by a concentrated burst of bolter fire from below, and Marduk moved on, his pistol raised before him as he fired more shots into the enemy arranged along the gantry.

One of the white-armoured soldiers raised a meltagun, and Marduk threw himself against the wall as the weapon fired. It scorched across his left shoulder pad, and warning symbols appeared within his helmet display. Namar-sin, coming up behind Marduk, hurled his axe, the weapon spinning end over end and slamming into the soldier, cleaving into his face and embedding itself deep in his skull.

Men screamed in agony as they were engulfed in flame, as Khalaxis's 17th coterie advanced opposite Marduk, trapping a score of soldiers on the gantry between them. The flamer roared again, and fire consumed half a dozen men, their flesh blistering as it burned. Several fell over the railing, plummeting to the floor where they smouldered and lay still.

The survivors were hacked apart as Khalaxis led the charge into their midst, his chainaxe screaming as it tore through bone and tendon. Marduk waded into the terrified soldiers from the other side, clubbing men to the ground and executing them without mercy.

Less than five minutes after the bastion gates had been breached, the echo of gunfire ceased. The Word Bearers moved among the enemy soldiers, dispatching any who still breathed with swift blows to the head.

Marduk came across one of the officers, his face awash with blood and his breath coming in short, sharp gasps. He looked up at Marduk's inscrutable skull-faced visage in terror.

'Emperor preserve me,' he gasped.

Marduk bent down and gripped the man, his massive hand closing around the soldier's face.

'The False Emperor as a deity is a lie,' he growled, squeezing, feeling the soldier's skull straining. 'No one will answer your prayers. Where is the commander of this facility?'

'The... the lift,' gasped the man. 'Top floor. Emperor save my soul.'

'The Corpse Emperor is not divine, and he does not care about the sanctity of your soul. You will see.'

Marduk crushed the man's skull effortlessly, blood bursting from the soldier's eyes, nose and mouth as he died. Standing up, he wiped his hand clean upon his tabard, and turned to face Kol Badar, down below in the main concourse.

'I grow tired of this world. It is time we ended this,' said Marduk, his voice booming across the open expanse. 'Bring forth the Enslaved One, and let us get what we came for.'

As THE FIRST alarms sounded, Guildmaster Pollo was taking a drink of his seventy-five year old vintage amasec. He almost choked on the fiery draught, and his adjutant, Leto, visibly paled. Pollo slammed his glass down onto his table and was up and moving instantly.

The portal slid open as he approached it, and he stormed out into the adjoining room.

'What in the name of Holy Terra is going on?' he barked at his personal guard, a group of five soldiers of the mercenary Skyllan Interdiction Force. 'Captain? This better not be another perimeter glitch.'

The captain of his guard, a tall, broad-shouldered soldier with a serious face, had his hand to his earpiece, his brow furrowed in concentration.

'No, sir,' he replied. 'The automated turrets have identified hostile targets on approach.'

'Hostile targets?' breathed Leto from behind the guildmaster.

'Have they been identified?' asked the guildmaster.

'No, sir, not as yet. Wait,' he said, raising his hand to forestall any response as he listened to incoming communications. The soldier's face turned grim. 'What?' he asked. 'Are you sure?'

'What is going on?' asked Guildmaster Pollo forcefully.

'Sir,' began the captain, 'the bastion has been breached.'

'Emperor preserve us,' said Leto.

'There must be some mistake,' said Pollo.

'No mistake, sir. A heavy firefight is underway on the garage concourse level.'

The captain swore, tapping at his earpiece as it went dead. The other soldiers of the guildmaster's guard looked uneasily at each other.

'We must get you out of here, sir,' the captain said, his face dark. 'The bastion is compromised.'

He strode towards the guildmaster and his adjutant, barking orders to his men. They responded instantly, and their lasguns hummed as they powered into life.

'I will not go,' said the guildmaster hotly. 'How many men do you have here?'

'Only three demi-legions, sir. The others are all out keeping the peace at the Phorcys starport, or aiding the evacuation efforts.'

'That is still, what, three hundred men?' asked Pollo.

'It will not be enough, sir,' said the captain softly.

Guildmaster Pollo glared at the captain. 'The Skyllan Interdiction Force is paid damn well to protect this fortress and hold the peace. You are not filling me with the confidence that the guild money is well-spent, captain.'

'My lord,' said the captain, his expression stoic in the face of the guildmaster's simmering anger, 'the enemy below are Astartes.'

'Space Marines?' breathed Leto. 'But we… we are loyal subjects of the Emperor. Aren't we?'

'Of course we are, Leto,' said Pollo.

'They are rebel Astartes, my lord, and I have lost all contact with the demi-legions. We leave, now,' he said, brooking no argument.

Pollo felt a sense of panic stab at him, though he was careful to maintain a calm exterior. He felt the flush of amasec clouding his mind, and he cursed himself for drinking so much. He licked his lips, and nodded to the captain.

With clipped commands, the soldiers fell in around the guildmaster, and the group marched back into the senior official's office. The captain was steering Pollo forcefully by the elbow, moving him quickly towards the reinforced door that led to his personal shuttle.

'My records,' protested the guildmaster.

'I'll get them, my lord,' said Leto.

'No,' snapped the Skyllan guard captain, 'we leave now.'

'My data-slate, Leto,' hissed the guildmaster, and his adjutant swept the book-sized piece of arcane technology up off his master's desk as he was hurried past.

The captain whispered the requisite prayer to the machine god as he entered the code sequence into the door, and the circular locks slid anti-clockwise with a hiss. The soldiers lowered their visors to cover their faces at a nod from their superior. Then the captain leant his weight against the door. It opened with a groan and snow billowed into the office, driven through the portal by the deafening gale outside.

Guildmaster Pollo covered his face with his arm as the biting chill struck him, and he took an involuntary step backwards.

Three soldiers moved out onto the landing platform, their lasguns panning left and right. Pointless, thought Pollo. No enemy could be up here.

His personal Aquila-class lander was perched some twenty metres away, covered in a thick layer of snow. The guard captain pulled an exquisite pistol of ornate design from his holster, and began guiding Pollo out onto the landing platform.

The cold was almost unbearable, and ice crystals formed instantly on his eyebrows and lips. His eyes stung from the cold, and even breathing was painful.

One of his guards, out in front, reached the shuttle and slammed his fist into an activation panel. Instantly, the embarkation ramp began to lower.

With his head down, Guildmaster Pollo allowed himself to be hurried towards the waiting shuttle, his boots slipping on the ice-slick landing pad. The captain supporting him shouted something, but he couldn't make it out over the roar of the wind.

BURIAS-DRAK'SHAL GRINNED IN feral anticipation as he stared down at the men ten metres below him, battling against the gale as they made their way towards the shuttle.

He dropped down amongst them and landed in a crouch, rockcrete cracking beneath the impact. A soldier was a step behind and to his left, and he swung around, taking the man in the head with one of his massive, fused talons. The force of the blow slammed the soldier into the rockcrete wall, his skull pulverised, Burias-Drak'shal's buried talon thirty centimetres into the rock.

Ripping the talon free, letting the soldier slump to the ground, he spun and lashed out with a backhanded blow that ripped across the throat of another soldier as he turned towards the possessed warrior, lasgun raised.

The man's throat was ripped open to the spine, and he spun, blood fountaining from the mortal wound.

SOMETHING HOT SPLASHED the back of Guildmaster Pollo's head, and he stumbled and fell to one knee. As the captain hauled him back to his feet, he reached up and touched a hand to his head. He stared blankly for a second at the fresh blood on his hands, before turning to look back the way he had come.

A daemonic beast from the deepest pits of hell had dropped down behind them.

Its bulk was immense, more than three times that of a normal man, and its lips curled back to expose the barbed teeth of the ultimate predator. Two men lay dead at its feet.

The captain saw the beast just as the guildmaster did, and he shouted a warning, pushing Pollo roughly towards the shuttle as he raised his pistol.

Another man died before the pistol fired, as the daemon punched a claw up through the soldier's sternum. The blow lifted the soldier off his feet, and the daemon's talons emerged from his back. With a dismissive sweep of its arm, the daemon hurled the man off the landing pad, disappearing in the gale to fall the three hundred metres to the base of the bastion.

The captain's pistol boomed, but Pollo did not wait to see if he had felled the beast. Terror coursing through him, he half-ran, half-stumbled towards the lowering ramp leading into his shuttle, his heart beating wildly.

The guard standing by the shuttle had his lasgun raised to his shoulder, and he fired past Pollo twice before running up the ramp to initiate the launch. Pollo heard several more shots as the other remaining guards brought their weapons to bear, and he paused at the foot of the embarkation ramp to look back. He saw his adjutant crawling towards him on all fours, blood splattered across his terrified face.

Without thinking of his own safety he ran to the young man. As he helped him up to his feet, Pollo looked back through the swirling snow.

Another man was down, his head ripped from his shoulders, and the captain was backing away from the daemonic beast stalking towards him. His pistol boomed, but the beast swayed its head to the side with preternatural speed, and the shot hissed past its face.

The captain risked a glance behind him, and his eyes locked onto the guildmaster's.

'Go!' shouted the captain, though his voice was lost in the roaring wind.

'Watch out!' roared Pollo at the same time, for the beast had sprung forwards as soon as the captain had taken his eyes off it.

Leto scrambled past his master, clambering up the ramp into the interior of the shuttle, but Pollo was locked in place, staring in horror at the daemon as it leapt at the captain of his guard.

The soldier staggered backwards and pumped three shots into the daemon as it bore down on him. The first shots hit the monster in the chest and the gorget, ricocheting uselessly off its blood-red armour, but the third shot struck it in the cheek, shattering bone.

It fell with a roar of anger before the captain, and the soldier levelled his pistol at the back of its horned head. Before he could squeeze the trigger, the beast was up and moving, and one of its immense clawed hands closed around the captain's arm. The pistol boomed, but its aim had been skewed, and the bullet glanced off the beast's skull.

The captain screamed in pain and fell to his knees as the bones in his arm were shattered, and the beast loomed over him, its visage twisted in fury. Blood dripped from its wounds, bubbling and hissing as it struck the snow.

Opening its mouth impossibly wide, it lunged down, its jaws clamping around either side of the captain's head.

His eyes wide with terror, Pollo staggered backwards. His movements attracted the attention of the beast, and it swung its burning gaze towards him, the captain's head still locked in its jaws. It clamped its mouth shut, and the soldier's head cracked like a nut in vice.

It dropped its lifeless prey to the ground and leapt towards Pollo, closing the distance with shocking swiftness, bounding towards him on all fours like an ape. Turning, Pollo ran.

The engines of the Aquila lander were roaring, and for a moment he thought he would make it. He saw Leto at the top of the ramp, frantically urging him on with beckoning waves of his hands, and he scrambled up the ramp into the shuttle.

A stink akin to rotting meat and the acrid stench of electricity reached his nostrils, and a hand closed around the back of his head. With a jerk, he was hurled backwards, skidding down the ramp to fall in a crumpled heap at its base.

One of his arms was broken, and he cried out as splinters of bone grated against each other. He saw Leto at the top of the ramp quaking before the immense daemon just before the adjutant was ripped in two by the beast.

Pollo tried to rise to his feet, the muscles and tendons of his back protesting, but he fell in a crumpled heap once more in the blood-splattered snow.

The daemon turned back towards him and stalked down the ramp, and Pollo scrambled back away from the monster, the heels of his boots slipping in the ice and snow.

BURIAS-DRAK'SHAL FELT THE terror of the Imperial official wash over him like an intoxicating wave, and he relished the sensation. He wanted to kill the man, slowly and excruciatingly, but the rational side of his mind knew that such a thing would anger Marduk, for his order had been clear.

He grinned as the man scrambled back away from him, a pathetic and futile attempt to escape. With sheer force of will, he pushed Drak'shal back, and his features were once again his own, pristine and unmarred, the bullet wound on his cheek already healed. Blood caked his mouth and chin, and he smiled at the man as he stepped towards him.

The engines of the shuttle roared behind him and the ramp began to close, and Burias swung his head around, Drak'shal instantly rearing within him once more.

'Let none escape,' Marduk had ordered.

Burias-Drak'shal turned and leapt onto the shuttle, his talons biting deep into the reinforced hull. He hauled himself hand over hand onto its top, and bounded across its fuselage until he was positioned above the cockpit.

The shuttle began to lift just as the pilot registered the shadow looming above him, and Burias-Drak'shal punched his fist through the glass, grabbing the man around his throat. With one swift motion he ripped the man's throat away.

The shuttle tilted suddenly to the side, its landing gear scraping against rock as the dying pilot fell across the controls. Burias-Drak'shal bounded across the top of the shuttle as it slid over the edge of the landing pad, its engines sending it into a death spin.

He hurled himself across the growing gap and landed in a crouch as the shuttle slammed into the body of the aquila eagle-structure thirty metres below, and erupted into a ball of fire.

He shook his head as he saw the wounded Imperial commander frantically punching a code into the reinforced door that led back into the building, and bounded after the man.

The commander was slamming the door when Burias-Drak'shal reached it, and he smashed it open with the palm of his hand.

The man, all hope of escape lost, collapsed on the floor of the office, staring up fearfully at him.

'Emperor curse you,' breathed the terrified man.

'Too late for that,' remarked Burias, slamming the door closed behind him.

CHAPTER SIX

LIKE A SLOWLY rolling fortress of steel, the ice-crawler moved across the ice flow, unaffected by the gale force winds ripping across the desolate landscape. Temperature gauges read that it was minus forty standard, though with wind chill it was closer to minus seventy. Banks of spotlights lit up the ice directly in front of the colossal vehicle. Fog rose from the moon's surface and the wind sent eddies of snow and ice particles ripping across the flows, rendering visibility almost non-existent.

The crawler was immense, over fifty metres long and almost twenty metres high. Its wedge-shaped hull sat upon eight sets of tracks, each more than five metres wide and powered by massive engines.

High up within the control booth of the crawler, Foreman Primaris Solon Marcabus reclined on his well-worn padded seat, his heavy boots up on the dash. He sucked in a long drag on his lho stick and closed his eyes.

'I've decided I don't much like people,' Cholos said, from the steering rig. 'Too much damn trouble. I'll take transporting ore yields over people any day.'

Solon grunted in response, exhaling a cloud of smoke. The expansive cargo holds below were filled to the brim with desperate evacuees. Perdus Skylla was being abandoned in the face of imminent xenos invasion, and it had fallen to the crews of the ice-crawlers to aid in the evacuation. In return, they would receive double pay for this run. Small comfort, thought Solon, if they didn't manage to secure a berth off-world.

The cabin was small and stuffy, and the stink of Solon's ashtray, brimming with lho stubs, was strong. He was jolted back and forth as the crawler continued to make its way through the darkness, but he was well used to that. Rosary beads hung above Cholos, and they swung back and forth wildly as the crawler drove slowly over an embankment.

'Guilders,' spat Cholos with a shake of his head, 'think they are so much better than us. Treat us like shit all these years, but who is it that comes to bail them out? Us. And do we get a word of thanks? Nope. Just complaints. "It's too cold, it's too hot, there's not enough room, the water tastes funny". You'd think the bastards would be thankful. Makes me sick.'

Solon grunted again.

'That sergeant, Folches, is the worst of 'em,' said Cholos. 'Left those people back there to die. That is one cold son of a bitch.'

'Nice to hear I made an impression,' said a voice.

Cholos visibly jumped. Solon sighed and slowly opened his eyes. He dropped his feet from the console dash and spun his chair around towards the door to the cabin, though he remained slouched. He blew out a puff of smoke.

Sergeant Folches stood in the doorway, big and imposing in his black and white Interdiction body plate. He had removed his helmet, and his thick-featured face glared down at Solon.

'This is a restricted area, sergeant. Rig personnel only,' said Solon. 'Be so kind as to get the hell out.'

'How long till we get to the Phorcys spaceport?' asked Folches.

'In this storm? Two and a half days, minimum,' said Solon.

The sergeant swore.

'The storm won't lift before then?' he asked.

'You haven't spent much time on the surface, have you?' asked Solon, taking another drag on his lho stick.

'What the hell does that have to do with anything?'

'Once a storm like this has set in, it might not clear for a month, maybe two,' said Solon, stubbing out his lho stick.

'You can't make this heap of crap go any faster?'

'No, sergeant, I can't.'

Folches swore and rubbed a hand across his head.

'Why don't you and your boys just settle down and enjoy the ride,' he said, 'and try to stop the guilders killing each other. They're only women and children, right?'

'Boss,' said Cholos. Solon felt the crawler begin to slow, but he didn't take his eyes of the sergeant.

'You ought to watch your tongue, you whoreson bastard,' said Folches, putting one hand on the autopistol holstered prominently at his hip.

'Easy, big fella,' said Solon. 'All I'm saying is that we are moving as quick as we can, and you coming up here to throw your weight around ain't gonna make us go any faster.'

Folches let out a tense breath and took his hand off his gun.

'What's the problem, anyway?' asked Solon. 'Three days and we'll be off this moon.'

'Something hit the access tunnels leading from Antithon guild to the spaceport.'

Solon frowned.

'Four demi-legions were gone, like that,' said the sergeant, clicking his fingers. 'And Emperor knows how many guilders.'

'Four demi-legions?'

'Four hundred soldiers. The enemy is not on its way to Perdus Skylla,' said the sergeant. 'It is already here.'

Solon bit his lip.

'Boss,' said Cholos, breaking the silence.

'What?' asked Solon in exasperation, turning to face his second in command.

'You better take a look at this.'

Solon spun his chair around, turning his back on the sergeant, and peered out of the small, ice-encased cabin window.

The wind was whipping across the landscape at over a hundred kilometres an hour, and virtually nothing could be seen except the glare of the crawler's spotlight reflected back at them by the snow and ice in the air.

'I don't see a damned thing, Cholos.'

Sergeant Folches leant down at Solon's side, looking out into the storm, and Solon felt his irritation rise.

'Damn it Cholos, what am I looking at?'

'Wait for the wind to drop,' said Cholos.

He slowed the crawler further and the three men looked intently out into the storm. At last the wind fell momentarily and Solon could see a dark, shadowy shape up ahead. It was another crawler, motionless and dark. Then it was hidden as the winds picked up again with a vengeance.

'That's Markham's rig,' said Solon.

'Looks like it, boss,' said Cholos.

'Hail them,' said Solon.

'You recognise it?' asked Folches as Cholos tried to make voice contact with the stationary crawler with the short-ranged vox-caster built into the dash console.

'Yeah,' said Solon. 'It should be at the starport by now. What the hell is it doing out here?'

'There's no response, boss,' said Cholos. The sound of static was hissing from the vox-caster. 'Might be the storm's interference though.'

Solon swore.

'Right, take us alongside it. If it still doesn't respond, then it looks like we'll be getting cold.'

'My squad will come with you,' said Folches.

'That would be appreciated,' said Solon.

* * *

THE LIFT HALTED its ascent and drew to a shuddering halt.

'Restricted access. Band XK privilege required,' croaked the robotic voice of the servitor built into one of the interior walls of the lift.

Marduk sighed in impatience.

A panel on one wall bore the symbol of the Adeptus Mechanicus, and the First Acolyte ripped it clear, his gauntlet wrenching the metal out of shape as if it were paper. Wires and cables spilt behind the panel like intestines, sparking and buzzing.

'Open it,' he ordered impatiently.

A mechadendrite tentacle stabbed into the open panel, and Darioq twisted it left and right.

'Access granted,' croaked the servitor as the magos retracted his metallic tentacle, and the lift doors hissed open.

Kol Badar stepped out of the lift in front of Marduk, swinging his combi-bolter from side to side. The lift rose a few centimetres as the Coryphaus's immense weight was removed from the straining winch mechanics.

'Clear,' the towering Coryphaus growled, raising his combi-bolter into a vertical position. Kol Badar held the sacred icon of the Host in the power talons of his left hand, the snarling daemon face of the Latros Sacrum in its centre, slamming the butt of the staff into the ground as Marduk stepped from the lift.

The First Acolyte took a moment to get his bearings before marching into the guildmaster's office.

'Stay, *Darioq-Grendh'al*,' he said over his shoulder, exerting the force of his will into his intonation, forcibly commanding the daemon within the corrupted magos.

Burias was leaning casually against a wall, drinking from a bottle that had had its neck smashed off. His mouth and chin were covered in blood, and a man lay shivering on the floor before him.

The icon bearer drained the fiery liquid from the bottle and smiled at Marduk, wiping his mouth with the back of one hand.

'Stand to attention when your seniors are present, warrior,' barked Kol Badar, the vox-amplifiers built into his quad-tusked helmet making his voice even more of an animalistic growl than usual.

Making no attempt to hurry, Burias languidly rose from his slouch and tossed the empty bottle away. It shattered on the floor.

'Consumption of all but necessary sustenance is a sin that leads to weakness, icon bearer,' snapped Marduk. 'You will submit yourself to three months of fasting and flagellation once we return to the *Infidus Diabolus*.'

'I am duly castigated, my master,' said Burias, bowing his head in a show of obeisance and mock remorse. Marduk's eyes narrowed.

Burias held a hand out to Kol Badar.

'My icon?' he said.

The Coryphaus flicked the heavy icon at the smaller Astartes warrior with far more force than was needed, but Burias caught it deftly in his hand.

'Enough,' said Marduk. 'This is the commander?' He motioned with his chin towards the man shivering on the ground.

'It is, my master,' said Burias, running his hands lovingly over the spiked length of his icon, as if he had been separated from it for years and was savouring being reunited. 'Alive, as you wished.'

Marduk knelt down before the man, who stared up at him fearfully, his face waxy and pale.

'You have something that I want, little man,' said Marduk, removing his skull-faced helmet and handing it to Burias, 'and you are going to tell me where it is.'

'Wha... wha... what is it you want?' managed the man, gritting his teeth in pain, gingerly cradling his left arm in his hand. He stared up at Marduk, a mixture of fear and defiance in his eyes.

'A person, if you could call it that,' said Marduk. 'Someone who was posted here, at this very facility: an adept of the weakling Machine-God.'

'What do you want with them?'

Marduk reached out towards the man, his movements slow and almost caring. The guildmaster recoiled from his grasp, but there was nowhere for him to run.

'You are injured, I see,' said Marduk, taking the man's arm carefully in his hands. 'This must hurt.'

With a slow twisting motion, Marduk turned the man's hand over, making the shattered bones grind against one another. The man screamed in agony and Marduk twisted it again. Then he stopped.

'Do not question me again, little man. This was punishment for doing so. Now, tell me, where is... What was its name?'

Marduk turned his head around, looking back towards the adjoining room and the lift.

'Darioq-Grendh'al,' he barked. 'Come.'

Like a hound coming to its master's call, Magos Darioq entered the room, his steps slow and mechanical. Having been allowed to recon-struct his servo-harness, four massive robotic arms emerged from his back, two coming around his sides, and two over his shoulders, like the stabbing tails of an insect. Black veins pulsed within the servo-arms as the lines between organic, mechanical and daemonic were increasingly blurred, and one of the arms twitched awkwardly as he walked.

The guildmaster's agonised eyes were locked on the magos, who wore a robe of black in place of his red Mechanicus garb. The red glow of Dar-ioq's augmented left eye gleamed malignly from within his deep cowl.

'What is the name of the target?' Marduk asked.

'Explorator First Class Daenae,' said Magos Darioq in his monotone voice, 'originally of the Konor Adeptus Mechanicus research world of

UL01.02, assigned to c14.8.87.i, Perdus Skylla, for recon/salvage of the Dvorak-class interstellar freighter *Flames of Perdition*, which reappeared within Segmentum Tempestus in 942.M41 and crashed onto the surface of c14.8.87.i, Perdus Skylla, in 944.M41 after being missing presumed lost in warp storm anomaly xi.024.396 in 432.M35.'

Marduk turned back towards the guildmaster with the hint of a smile on his face.

'How foolish of me to have forgotten its name,' he said. The smile dropped from his face. 'Where is this Explorator Daenae? Tell me now, or you shall be further punished. And I promise you, the pain you have already experienced will be but a fraction of what you will come to know should you displease me further.'

'I don't know who you mean,' hissed the man.

Marduk sighed.

'You are lying to me,' he said, and gave the man's arm a further twist. This time he did not relent quickly, and he ground the broken bones of the guildmaster's arm against each other with vigour.

Behind Marduk, Burias grinned at the man's pain.

'The explorator was assigned to this facility,' said Marduk over the guildmaster's screams of torment, 'therefore you know where it is. Tell me now, or your death will not be swift in coming to you.'

The guildmaster's eyes were shut tightly against the pain, and he passed out suddenly, going limp in Marduk's arms. The First Acolyte threw the man's arm down in disgust, the bones of the forearm bent almost at right angles.

'Permission to speak, Marduk, First Acolyte of the Word Bearers Legion of Astartes, genetic descendent of the glorified Primarch Lorgar,' said Darioq.

'*Glorified* Primarch Lorgar?' asked Marduk with a grin. 'You are learning, Enslaved. Permission to speak granted.'

'With the surgical removal of the inhibitor functions of my logic-engines, and the rearrangement of the frontal cortex of three of my brain-units, I find…' began Darioq-Grendh'al.

'Get to the point,' interrupted Marduk.

'Summary: it is not required that the location of Explorator First Class Daenae be obtained from the brain-unit of Guildmaster Pollo,' the magos intoned.

'What gibberish does it speak? Who is this Guildmaster Pollo?' growled Kol Badar.

'Guildmaster Pollo is the flesh unit whose radial and ulna bones of the left arm have been rendered inoperative and non-functioning by Marduk, First Acolyte of the Word Bearers Legion of Astartes, genetic descendent of the glorified Primarch Lorgar,' replied Darioq.

Burias snorted his amusement, though Kol Badar growled and took a step towards the black-robed magos, electricity coursing into life around his power talons. Marduk forestalled his advance with a raised hand, and looked at the magos intently.

'What do you mean, Darioq-Grendh'al? Speak simply,' he said.

'In order to garner the required information about the whereabouts of Explorator Daenae, all that is necessary is to gain access to the cortex hub of this bastion facility.'

Marduk turned to look at Burias. The icon bearer shrugged and Marduk turned back towards Darioq with a sigh.

'What do you need to find the location of the explorator?' asked Marduk, speaking in a slow and measured voice.

'In order to access the cortex hub of this bastion facility, a sub-retinal scan of the commanding officer must be made,' said Darioq.

A hint of a smile touched Marduk's lips, and he turned towards Burias.

'Fetch me his eyes, icon bearer.'

Burias grinned and flexed his fingers.

'As you wish, my master,' replied the icon bearer.

THE HEAVY CRAWLER doors slid aside with a sound like a mountain shifting, and snow and ice billowed into the cargo hold. The frightened refugees from Antithon Guild were huddled as best they could against the far wall, protecting their faces from the biting wind.

'Let's do this quickly,' shouted Solon over the wind. At his side, Cholos gave him the thumbs up. Solon looked towards Sergeant Folches, who stood with his soldiers. The soldier nodded.

'Keep her running,' shouted Solon to Cholos. 'The last thing we want out here is the engines seizing up.'

Solon pulled his mask and respirator over his face, obscuring his features, and turned around awkwardly in his bulky exposure suit. He grabbed the sides of the ice-encased metal ladder on the exterior of the crawler and began to climb down to the ground.

His breathing sounding heavy in his ears and he felt a momentary stab of claustrophobia. He hated these suits. The pair of circular synth-glass goggle-panes obscured his peripheral vision and the suit made all movement heavy and laboured. Still, they kept the cold out, and without one he wouldn't last more than an hour in these conditions.

He climbed down the eight metres from the cargo hold to the ground and stepped onto the ice. The wind threatened to knock him down, and he steadied himself with a hand on a massive wheel.

He turned around to look up at the bulk of Markham's lifeless crawler as the others descended. It reared, black and imposing, like an ancient monolith, dark and dead.

With his mask in place, he had no means to communicate with the others except by hand signals, and he pointed towards the front of the crawler. Sergeant Folches nodded his head and signalled for him and his men to take the lead.

'Be my guest, you bastard,' said Solon, gesturing his ascent.

The soldiers had their weapons in hand as they approached the derelict crawler. It was clear to Solon that its engines had not been running for some time, for there was a thick layer of snow across the crawler, including over its engine stack. Normally, a crawler's engineer maintained enough heat in the boilers that no snow would settle. Snow was banked up high against one side of the massive crawler, and Solon guessed that it must have been sitting dormant for at least five hours for such an amount of snow to have settled against it.

The white-armoured Skyllan Interdiction soldiers began moving towards the front of the crawler, their guns raised to their shoulders. With swift hand signals, the sergeant sent two men ahead on point, and they covered each other's blind spots as they moved forward. Solon and Cholos stomped through the snow behind the soldiers.

'Doesn't look like anyone is home,' Solon said to himself.

One of the crawler's immense tracks had been ripped loose, and it lay twisted and broken beneath the behemoth. This was no accident; nothing could tear a crawler's track loose except an immense mining detonation, or concentrated fire by a well-armed enemy.

Solon saw one of the soldiers gesture up at the side of the crawler, and he followed the direction of his hand. A hole had been blasted through the side of the immense transport, roughly the size of a man's head, scorch marks surrounding the strike.

Solon walked closer to the side of the crawler, peering at a line of smaller marks up the side of one of its wheels. Splinters of barbed metal were embedded in the steel rim of the wheel.

He peered closely at one of the splinters. It was viciously barbed, and he winced at its cruel design. Had it been embedded in a living body, the flesh would be torn to shreds in attempting to pull it free.

Solon jerked as a heavy hand slapped him on the shoulder, and he looked up into the faceless visor of one of the soldiers, who motioned for him to move on. Solon nodded his head, and began slogging through the snow and ice once more.

He stumbled as his foot caught on something, and fell awkwardly onto his front. A soldier helped him back to his feet and he looked to see what he had tripped over.

A hand, blue and frozen, was protruding from the snow.

Solon swore and staggered back, pointing frantically at the frozen hand. The soldier nodded grimly and motioned for him to keep moving.

Tearing his eyes from the grisly display, Solon hurried to catch up with the rest of the group. His breathing was coming in short, sharp gasps, sounding too loud in the enclosed space of his mask.

The group moved around the front of the crawler, and Solon saw that the reflective plasglass of the cabin had been shattered. Several holes had been punched through the front chassis of the crawler, and Solon marvelled at the immense power of the blasts. The front of the crawlers were heavily armoured, allowing them to push through ice, rock and snow if necessary, and he had been led to believe that even a lascannon would be unable to pierce its reinforced layers. Whatever had struck this crawler though had made a mockery of his teaching.

The soldiers moved warily around the side of the crawler, and Solon froze as the sergeant raised his hand. One of the soldiers dropped to one knee at the corner of the crawler and risked a quick glance around it before giving the all clear and moving on.

They were out of the worst of the wind behind the lee-side of the crawler, and Solon breathed a sigh of relief to be out of the relentless gale. The snow was not banked up so heavily here, and with a flurry of hand signals, the sergeant relayed his orders.

One of the cargo bay doors was wide open, and one of the soldiers warily climbed the icy ladder up to the cavernous opening. As he crouched below the lip of the cargo bay, he raised his lasgun and clicked on the powerful light under-slung below the barrel.

Rising up on the ladder, the soldier held his lasgun to his shoulder and swung the beam of his light around within the crawler's cargo hold. He signalled the all clear, and climbed up into the interior, disappearing from sight. The other soldiers moved towards the ladder, Solon being herded in the centre of the group.

Sergeant Folches and one of his men ascended quickly, while the other members of the squad covered them, and then Solon was signalled to climb up.

His bulky exposure suit made the climb difficult and he was breathing hard as he reached the top. Sergeant Folches grabbed him under one arm and hauled him over the edge, his pistol held at the ready in his other hand.

The sergeant held up a hand for Solon to stay put and his soldiers began advancing through the darkened cargo hold, the focused beams of their lights swinging left and right. They were swallowed by the darkness as they penetrated deeper into the stricken crawler, leaving Solon standing alone.

He turned around, the weak lights mounted on either shoulder of his exposure suit illuminating the area around him in their yellow glow. One of the lights flickered and buzzed, and Solon hit it with one hand. The flickering stopped, but then the light gave out all together, and he swore.

Feeling exposed and alone, he moved further into the cargo hold, trying to see the soldiers' lights. He couldn't see them, and the sound of his own breathing filled his ears. He also noticed evidence of fighting. Blackened scorch marks marred the sides of ore containers and severed cables hung limp from holes blasted in the walls.

The massive ore containers were loaded on top of each other and tightly packed, forming a maze of narrow corridors within the vast hold. The containers disappeared in the gloom above him, and Solon felt a rivulet of sweat run down his spine.

Turning a corner, he almost stepped on the corpse. It wore the uniform of a crawler orderly, and Solon recoiled in horror and disgust. The man looked as if he had died in absolute agony, his mouth wide in a scream, his eyes huge and staring, and his body frozen in a contorted death spasm. His hands were twisted like claws, and his legs were bent beneath him. It looked as though he had been writhing in agony as he had died. Solon saw a line of wicked splinters across his chest, embedded in his flesh.

Solon turned away, feeling his stomach heave. He ripped his mask away and vomited the contents of his stomach onto the floor. He pulled his canteen from one of the deep pockets of his exposure suit, and took a swig of the cold water, cleansing his mouth and spitting it out onto the floor.

He didn't look again at the corpse as he walked away, sucking in the cold air in deep breaths.

It felt like the soldiers had been gone for hours, though it was more likely just minutes, and Solon felt panic begin to rise within him. What had hit the crawler? What enemy was loose in the darkness? And was it still here?

The walls formed by the containers rearing up on either side of him seemed to close in, and Solon's breath was coming in shorter gasps.

'Stay here, he says. To hell with that,' said Solon, deciding to find Sergeant Folches and his soldiers. He might not like the man, but if there was still an enemy in the crawler, he would feel a lot more comfortable with the armed soldiers.

Thinking he heard a noise behind him, Solon spun around, his heart beating wildly. There was nothing there. The weak illumination given off by his sole functioning shoulder lamp made the shadows jump, and Solon's eyes darted around in fear.

'There's nothing here,' he said to himself.

He turned around to continue his search for the sergeant, and his lamp illuminated a pale face less than a metre behind him.

Solon staggered backwards, a strangled cry tearing from his throat and his heart lurching. His sudden movement made the light from his lamp swing wildly, making shadows dance in front of him, though his eyes were locked on the motionless figure.

He heard a shout, and boots pounded across the grilled flooring, coming closer, but still the face stared up at him.

It was a child, no more than ten years old by his reckoning, his face pale and gaunt. Solon stared at the boy in horror, as if the ghosts of his past had risen to haunt him; for a fraction of a second, the child was the spitting image of his son, dead these last eighteen years.

As the soldiers arrived, they shone their lights upon the child, and Solon saw that he was of flesh and blood, not some ethereal phantom come to haunt him, and his resemblance to his dead son faded. The boy's eyes were deeply ringed by shadow, and he recoiled from the bright lights, shielding his eyes.

The boy looked up in fright as Sergeant Folches and one of his soldiers appeared, their weapons levelled at the boy. In the cold light of the soldier's lights, his face took on a blue tinge. He must be half-frozen, thought Solon. He let out a long breath, and tried to force his pounding heart-rate to slow.

'Where in the hell did he come from?' barked Folches, sliding the visor of his helmet up.

'No idea,' said Solon, hardly able to take his eyes off the boy.

'You, boy,' said Folches. 'Are you the only one here?'

His face fearful, the boy merely stared up at the soldier.

'What happened here, boy?' asked Folches again, more forcefully. The boy backed away a step, looking as if he was going to bolt at any second.

'Ease up, sergeant,' said Solon, fumbling at one of his pockets. He pulled out a protein pack, and tore off its foil seal.

'You hungry?' he asked the boy, offering the food.

The boy merely stared back at him, and Solon took a small bite of the protein pack. It was bland and tasteless, but he nodded his head and made a show of enjoying it. He saw the boy lick his lips, and this time when Solon offered it to him he snatched it eagerly.

'You find any survivors?' Solon asked the sergeant in a low voice, though he kept his eyes on the boy.

'No,' said Folches. 'We found some… remains, but nowhere near as many as I would have expected.'

'Think they got away? Fled on foot, or something?' asked Solon.

'I don't think so,' said Folches. 'Whatever hit here, it hit hard and fast. I don't think anyone got away.'

'What then? They just disappeared? There must have been a couple of hundred folks onboard.'

'They were taken,' said the boy suddenly.

Solon and Folches exchanged a look.

'Who took them, son?' asked Solon.

'Ghosts,' said the boy, his eyes haunted.

BOOK TWO: GHOSTS

'Hate the xenos as you hate the infidel, as you hate the non-believer. Feel not mercy for them, for their very existence is profane. What right have they to live, those that are Other?'

– *Kor Phaeron, Master of the Faith*

CHAPTER SEVEN

THE FOUR LAND Raiders roared across the ice, passing the burnt-out shells of enemy vehicles. The bodies of men lay strewn around the smoking wrecks, their blood staining the snow beneath them.

'The last known location of the target is here,' said Kol Badar, indicating a position on the schematics that appeared in flickering green lines upon the data-slate. He was seated within the enclosed space of the second Land Raider, his hulking form filling the space around him, making the interior cramped. He had removed his tusked helmet, and the red lights of the interior of the tank gave his broad face a daemonic glow.

A passage from the Book of Lorgar was etched upon the skin of his right cheek, a gift cut from the face of Jarulek, back on the Imperial world of Tanakreg before the Dark Apostle fell.

Marduk too had borne a similar passage on his cheek, though it had been obliterated when the Dark Apostle had shot half his face off. He had removed his skull-faced helmet and stowed it in an arched niche above his head, alongside a pair of lit blood-candles, and the dark outline of the mark of Lorgar was clearly visible on his forehead.

Incense wafted from one of the daemon-headed braziers, filling the air with its cloying stench.

Marduk snatched the data-slate from the Coryphaus, and looked where Kol Badar had indicated.

'What is this structure?' he asked.

'A mining facility, a hundred and fifty kilometres to the east. But there is a problem.'

331

'Of course there is,' spat Marduk. 'Well?'

'The mining facility is located on the ocean floor. It is over ten thousand metres below the surface of the ice.'

'Lorgar's blood,' said Burias from the other side of the Land Raider. Blood still caked the icon bearer's lips and chin, and Marduk glared at him for a moment.

'On the ocean floor,' he said.

'That is correct, First Acolyte,' replied Kol Badar, 'if the information the magos extracted can be trusted.'

'It can,' said Marduk. He balled his right hand into a fist and slammed it down onto an armrest carved in the likeness of a spinal column.

He quickly recovered his composure, and quoted from the Epistles of Kor Phaeron, the revered Master of the Faith whom he had served under during the campaign on Calth fighting against the hated sons of Guilliman.

'Through our travails we journey further down the blessed spiral,' he quoted. *'Through pain and struggle and toil we prove ourselves before the true gods. Each new obstacle should be welcomed as a test of faith, for only the strong and true walk the Eightfold Path of Enlightenment.'*

'Indeed,' said Kol Badar dryly.

'You have formulated a battle order?' asked Marduk. They had been back within the Land Raiders for less than fifteen minutes, but he knew that Kol Badar's keen strategic mind would have already concocted a dozen plans to ensure victory for the Host, each one more complete than the last.

'There is an access tunnel beneath the ice here,' said the Coryphaus, indicating on the schematic map with one of his massive armoured fingers. 'It runs for two hundred kilometres, connecting this habitation base with a starport located to the west. Air recycling hubs connect the tunnel to the surface at intermittent positions,' he said, stabbing his finger into the data-slate at several points along the line of the access tunnel. 'This one is twenty-five kilometres from the habitation base. We proceed to that air-recycling hub by Land Raider, across these ice flows here, and here, and approach from the south. The wind will be behind us, and we should be able to approach without detection, or at least neutralise any resistance before a defence can be established.'

'The defences of this world are pitiful,' said Marduk. 'The majority of the standing defence force has already been vacated. Darioq-Grendh'al picked up an incoming transmission as he gathered the information. The xenos invasion is expected to make planetfall within the next sixty-three hours. Sixty-two hours now,' he corrected.

'Sixty-two hours,' said Kol Badar. 'This foolish mission cannot be achieved in sixty-two hours.'

'Find a way,' retorted Marduk.

'It cannot be done,' said Kol Badar hotly. 'It could not be done even were we to encounter zero opposition. I suggest that we vacate this place. There is nothing of value to our Legion here.'

'I am not asking for your council, Kol Badar,' said Marduk. 'You are the Coryphaus. You enact *my* will. I am giving you an order; make it happen.'

'The xenos will have commenced their invasion before we are back on the surface,' said Kol Badar.

'Explain to me how that changes anything?' snapped Marduk, losing patience. 'If they get in our way, we kill them. It is not complicated.'

'You wish to be here in the midst of a full-scale invasion? With less than thirty warriors?'

'That is the voice of cowardice, Kol Badar,' said Marduk, his voice low and dangerous. 'You shame the Legion and the position of Coryphaus with your fear.'

Kol Badar's eyes flashed, and he ground his teeth, clenching his power talons. Burias, sitting opposite, grinned.

'You go too far, you whoreson whelp,' said Kol Badar, his eyes blazing with fury.

'Learn your place, Kol Badar,' growled Marduk, leaning in to the bigger warrior and snarling in his face. 'Jarulek is dead. *I* am the power of the Host. Me! The Host is mine, and mine alone. *You* are mine, and I will discard you if you prove of no use to me.'

Kol Badar bared his teeth, and Marduk could see him fighting to restrain himself from lashing out. With the fall of Jarulek, there was no question as to who was next in line. Marduk, as First Acolyte, was rightfully the leader of the Host, at least until such a time as the Council of Sicarus deemed otherwise.

Marduk knew Kol Badar well. They had fought alongside each other in a thousand wars since the fall of the Warmaster Horus, and over that time he had come to understand, and despise, what he was. The Coryphaus was a deeply regimented warrior, who clung to ordained command structures and protocols with an almost holy fervour. Marduk had always seen it as a weakness, and had goaded the Coryphaus regarding it, many times.

'You should have been born into Guilliman's Legion,' he had said on more than one occasion, drawing a parallel between Kol Badar's stifling adherence to command structures and official stratagems of the puritanical weaklings of the Ultramarines.

Doubtless, there was a certain strength in Kol Badar's dogmatism. The Coryphaus had commanded the Host in battle thousands of times, and his understanding of the ebb and flow of combat, when to push forward and when to pull back, was second to none. In truth, Marduk had come to value the keen, perhaps brilliant, strategic mind of the Coryphaus, though his refusal to adopt more unconventional tactics was infuriating at times.

For all that, Marduk felt assured that if he pushed home his unquestionable position in the hierarchy of the Host, then the Coryphaus would back down. After ten thousand years of adherence to strict military hierarchy, Kol Badar would be lost to madness and insanity were he to abandon it.

Respect can wait, thought Marduk. For now, it is enough that he does what I wish.

'I am the leader of the Host,' continued Marduk, still staring into Kol Badar's eyes, 'and you will obey my will.'

Marduk felt the power of Chaos build within him, as if the gods of the immaterium were pleased. Things writhed painfully beneath the skin of his skull, and he smiled as he saw Kol Badar's eyes widen.

'Never question me, Kol Badar,' said Marduk evenly. 'Continue.'

Kol Badar's thick jaw tensed, but he lowered his gaze from Marduk's, and stabbed a finger towards the schematic in his hands.

'We use that hub to gain entry to the tunnel, and proceed along the access way into the heart of the hab-station. We secure one of the lifts located here,' he growled, pointing, 'which will take us to the mining facility on the ocean floor. This here,' he said, zooming in on the data-slate, through dozens of floors and focusing on a specific part of the mining facility, 'is the last recorded location of the explorator. The hulk crashed to the ocean floor around twelve kilometres distant from the facility. Here, the explorator boarded a maintenance submersible to investigate the wreck. He never returned. I would surmise that the explorator fool is still within the hulk, or dead.'

Marduk nodded.

'Fine,' he said.

'I still say this is a fool's errand,' said Kol Badar.

'Your opinion has been duly noted, Coryphaus,' said Marduk. 'Now, pass the word. We move on that air recycling hub.'

APPROACHING THE AIR recycling station unobserved had been pathetically easy. The armed forces of the moon were virtually non-existent, most of them having already been evacuated, and the one patrol they had encountered on the ice flows had been destroyed with consummate ease.

It was insulting, Kol Badar thought as he had killed.

Clouds of steam rose from the turbine vents that cycled air into the tunnels deep in the ice below, and the hub station had been protected merely by thick rockcrete walls and a reinforced door, half buried in the snow. There were no guards posted on its walls. There had been no sign of a living presence at all, cowering inside against the storm like frightened rodents, Kol Badar had correctly surmised.

He had ripped the door from its hinges and hurled it away, before stalking into the interior of the complex. The Land Raiders were situated half a kilometre away, hidden completely in the storm, where they would remain until this fool's errand of a task was completed.

He had been angry when the first shouts of warning from the Imperials within the complex had reached his ears, and he stormed into their midst, ripping them apart with concentrated bursts of his combi-bolter, tearing arms from sockets with his power talon.

It had taken only minutes to gain control of the facility.

It was strange, though; it appeared that the enemy had known they were coming, and prepared some hasty defences. No, that was not correct. They knew *something* was coming, but they had not barricaded the door out onto the ice, but rather, the entrance to the stairwell that led down to the access tunnel fifty metres below, as if they expected an attack from there.

'Don't try to understand them,' he reminded himself. 'They are heathen, blinded fools. Their ways are madness.'

Kol Badar levelled his combi-bolter at the last of the civilian workers. The man was breathing hard, staring up at the towering Terminator-armoured warrior in abject terror.

A waste of ammunition, the Coryphaus decided, and lifted the barrel of his weapon from the target. A flash of hope reared in the Imperial citizen's eyes, but that was extinguished quickly as Kol Badar stepped menacingly towards him.

'Please, no,' wailed the man, shaking his head as the Coryphaus loomed above him.

Kol Badar grabbed the man around one shoulder, power talons digging deep into flesh. Then he slammed the pistol-grip butt of his combi-bolter into his face, splintering his nose. The man's skull was caved inwards by the shocking blow, killing him instantly, but the Coryphaus continued to strike, until the man's face was an unrecognisable mash of blood and flesh.

He dropped the Imperial worker to the ground, feeling a small amount of satisfaction, though it did little to abate his simmering rage.

Why had Jarulek left him, allowing the whelp Marduk to assume control of the Host? For months, he had raged at Jarulek's failing. Long had he hated the First Acolyte, and long had he waited to kill him, just as Marduk had killed Kol Badar's blood brother so long ago.

He would have killed Marduk then and there had not Jarulek stayed his hand.

'Not now,' the Dark Apostle had said, though at that time he had been nothing more than a First Acolyte himself. 'He will be yours to kill, but not yet. He has a purpose yet to perform.'

It had been three hundred years into the Great Crusade, and Kol Badar had waited long and impatiently for his time to come, but waited he had, through all the long spanning millennia, until at last his time had come.

'If we both return, then you may kill Marduk, my Coryphaus. Your honour will be fulfilled,' Jarulek had said, just moments before he had descended into the heart of the xenos pyramid on Tanakreg. The pleasure of finally being given free rein to kill the whelp had been ecstatic. That had been shattered when only Marduk had returned.

'Damn you, Jarulek,' said Kol Badar to himself.

'YOU SHOULD DISPOSE of him,' said Burias in a voice low enough for none but Marduk to hear him. 'The insubordinate old bastard is long past his time. He is a weight hanging around the neck of the Host, and he will drag it down, slowly but surely.'

'You still hunger for power, Burias?' asked Marduk.

'Of course,' replied Burias sharply, his eyes flashing. 'Such is our teaching.'

'That is true, icon bearer,' said Marduk.

'He does not fear you,' said Burias.

'What?' asked Marduk.

'Kol Badar. He feared Jarulek, we all did, but he does not fear you.'

'Perhaps not yet,' agreed Marduk, 'but he will come to. I am changing, Burias. I feel the touch of the gods upon me.'

Burias sniffed, savouring the air. There was an electrical tang in the air that left an acrid taste upon his tongue, a sensation he had long come to embrace and recognise for what it was: Chaos.

Jarulek had exuded a potent aura so strong that it made those of lesser faith bleed from their ears, and this was the same, though admittedly less potent, force.

'If he does not learn his place,' said Marduk in a low voice, 'and soon, then I shall allow you to take him. I would enjoy watching you rend him limb from limb.'

Burias grinned savagely.

'But that time is not yet,' reminded Marduk.

'NO LIFE SIGNS detected, Coryphaus,' said one of the members of the 13th, looking at the gleaming red flashes on the blister-screen of his corrupted auspex, 'though there are cooling heat signatures ahead. Possible weapons discharge.'

'Understood,' growled the war leader.

Burias placed one hand upon the cold metal surface of the door and closed his eyes.

'The air within is rich with fear,' he said.

'Good. That will work in our favour,' said Kol Badar. 'Burias, take point. Go.'

Without ceremony, Burias kicked the door off its hinges, wrenching the reinforced steel out of shape and sending it smashing inwards.

A steel landing extended beyond, and Burias moved forward warily, his bolt pistol in one hand, the holy icon of the Host in his other. The landing was narrow, and a steel stairway descended from it. Moving swiftly and silently, elegant and perfectly balanced despite his bulk,

Burias stepped down the steel stairs that led into a corridor. The hallway extended ten metres ahead, before turning sharply to the right.

The walls, carved from solid ice, radiated cold, though he barely registered the sub-zero temperature. Moving swiftly forwards, his every daemonically enhanced sense alert, Burias rounded the corner and came up against a mesh-link fence that rose from floor to ceiling, barring the way forward. A chained gate was set into the fence, and a frozen corpse was slumped outside it.

Curious, Burias moved forwards. It was the body of a man, wearing the same white plas armour as the soldiers they had fought at the Imperial bastion. One hand was clutching at the locked gate. Clearly, the man had been shot down while attempting to flee, but the locked gate had barred his progress. Half a dozen dark splinters were embedded in his armoured back plate, and Burias frowned.

The icon bearer holstered his bolt pistol and grasped the heavy chain that secured the gate shut. With a sharp jerk, he snapped the heavy chain and dropped it to the ground. He wrenched the gate open and the corpse of the enemy soldier was dragged across the floor as it swung wide; frozen, dead fingers locked around the mesh-links.

Stepping over the corpse, Burias continued along the corridor. After several twisting turns and intersections, it opened out into an access tunnel at least fifty metres wide. Down the centre of the tunnel was a sunken carriageway, and two wide platforms ran alongside it.

Moving warily into the tunnel, Burias stepped over wreckage and debris, amongst which were sprawled a number of corpses. Their bodies had been slashed by blades and ripped apart by unfamiliar projectile weapons. Several burnt out vehicles were scattered throughout the tunnel, like the discarded toys of a giant. Several were upturned and leaning against the walls, while others had fallen into the sunken carriageway.

Climbing atop one of the ruined armoured vehicles, Burias squinted into the distance in each direction. There was no living soul in sight, though the gently curving tunnel ensured that the icon bearer could see no more than half a kilometre ahead.

He dropped onto the bonnet of the white-armoured APC, which buckled inwards beneath his weight, and stepped lightly to the floor.

'All clear,' he said into his vox-relay. 'Looks like someone got here before us.'

As the remainder of the Host moved on his position, he dropped to his haunches to inspect one of the corpses.

It was another of the white-armoured soldiers, whose face was purple and had swollen like a balloon. Burias plucked a long, barbed splinter from the corpse's neck, and studied it with interest. It was half the length of a finger, and so thin that if he turned it sideways it was all but invisible. He lifted it carefully to his lips, and his tongue flashed out to sample the serrated tip.

The taste was acrid, and he registered unknown toxic agents upon the splinter. He tasted blood as the barbed shard sliced his tongue.

Xenos toxins entered his bloodstream, and his limbs began to shudder. A slight sweat broke out on his brow, and he lifted a shaking hand in front of his eyes, attempting to keep it steady, but failing.

He felt the unknown serum coursing its way towards his twin hearts, but remained unconcerned. Indeed, as soon as the venom had entered his bloodstream, his bio-engineered defences had activated, and were even now isolating and breaking down the xenos poison. His heart rate increased as his body combated the threat, pumping his blood swiftly through his oolitic kidney implant, cleansing it of the deadly serum.

After less than a minute, Burias's heart rate had returned to normal and the shaking sickness had left him.

'Intriguing,' he said to himself.

THE COTERIES HAD been moving through the tunnel system for about an hour. They had encountered no sign of life, though there was evidence of furious firefights. The tunnels were as silent as tombs, and cold light blazed down upon them from the rows of strip lights overhead. The lights flickered abruptly and died.

'FIVE UNKNOWNS, MOVING on our position,' barked Namar-sin, breaking the silence. 'Coming fast. Very fast.'

Marduk and the Stetavoc Space Marines of Namar-sin's coterie were instantly moving for cover. A faint whine could be heard, approaching rapidly.

'Ware the north,' Marduk bellowed, just as five blurred shapes roared out of the darkness of the side tunnel, moving with impossible speed. They scythed through the air, skimming two metres above the ground and banked sharply into the access tunnel. They were as sleek and deadly as knives, and shot forward as their engines were gunned.

Khalaxis and his coterie were caught in the open, and before they could even raise their weapons to fire, three of their number were cut down beneath a hail of barbed projectiles.

Another was dropped as the jetbikes streaked through the coterie, a curved blade slicing off one of the warrior-brother's arms, severing it at the elbow.

Then the jetbikes were past, hurtling by the Word Bearers and jinking around the scattered debris.

Bolters coughed, lighting up the darkness, but they were too slow and the enemy too fast. One of the Anointed unleashed the fury of his reaper autocannon, and hundreds of high calibre rounds chased the jetbikes as they banked around in a wide circle, passing behind the wreckage of the derailed carriages of the rail conveyance. The autocannon tore through the carriages of the train and ripped out great chunks from the rockcrete walls, but even the enhanced targeting sensors built into the Anointed's

Terminator armour could not match the speed of the enemy.

Empty shell casings fell like rain from the mighty weapon, but the jet-bikes roared on through the darkness unscathed. A missile, launched by one of Namar-sin's Havoc Space Marines, streaked through the darkness towards one of the jetbikes as it rounded the debris. With preternatural reflexes, the jetbike's rider spun his vehicle around in a spiralling cork-screw roll, and the missile passed beneath it harmlessly, impacting in a fiery explosion against the wall.

Marduk fired his bolt pistol on semi-auto at the enemy silhouetted against the flames of the explosion, but even though he had compensated for their speed, still he was too slow.

Two more of Khalaxis's coterie were cut down as they scrambled for cover, and then the jetbikes were gone, disappearing up the tunnel that they had emerged from only seconds before.

Kol Badar was roaring orders, and the remains of Khalaxis's 17th coterie dragged their fallen brethren into cover.

The one-armed Namar-sin and his heavy weapon toting Havoc warriors rose from their position and ran forwards, half-dropping into cover behind a wrecked Imperial vehicle while others took up position behind rockcrete pillars. They readied their heavy weapons, hefting them to shoulders or bracing them in their arms, their stances wide as they sought targets.

'More hostiles inbound,' shouted Sabtec.

'Where?' snapped Kol Badar.

'Behind us,' replied Namar-sin, and Marduk swore.

'Sabtec, protect the rear. Enfilading fire,' ordered Kol Badar. The warriors of the 13th moved instantly into position, moving with practiced efficiency. All the warrior-brothers were in cover, with one line facing north, one west.

'Khalaxis, report,' ordered Marduk.

'One dead, one as good as,' growled the towering champion of the 17th.

The Anointed split, two moving to join the 13th in the rear, the other two standing with Kol Badar at the entrance to the north tunnel.

'Burias,' hissed Marduk, as he dropped in alongside Sabtec, watching the rear. He couldn't see anything moving in the distance, but, respectful of the speed of the enemy, he judged that that did not mean much.

'Yes, my lord?' came the silken response on the vox-net.

'Guard Darioq-Grendh'al.'

Burias was slow to respond, and Marduk read the resistance to his orders in the silence.

'Protect him, icon bearer,' snapped Marduk. 'He dies, and you die.'

BURIAS CROUCHED ATOP the wreckage of one of the train's carriages, sniffing the air. He sensed something nearby, but could not locate its whereabouts.

Movement out of the corner of his eye attracted his attention, and he snapped his head towards it, emitting a low growl. Even with his daemon-enhanced witch-sight, he could see nothing.

'Burias,' said Marduk, and the icon bearer hissed in frustration.

'Fine,' he replied, giving the area where he had sensed movement a final glare.

As he dropped down from the carriage to the cracked plascrete platform below, a whip-thin figure crawled forward across the top of the carriage behind him, its form vague as if it dragged the surrounding darkness around it like a shroud.

The icon bearer flicked a glance over his shoulder, and the shape melted into the shadows. In an instant, it was once more invisible, and Burias turned away, jogging towards Magos Darioq.

The stink of Chaos was strong around the magos, who was standing immobile behind the twisted wreckage of what may once have been an Imperial vehicle, oblivious to the preparations going on around him.

'Move there,' snapped Burias, giving the magos a shove. Darioq-Grendh'al walked mechanically forward, each slow step accompanied by the hiss and wheeze of servos.

'Here they come again,' said Kol Badar in his warning growl.

'Kill them, in Lorgar's name!' roared Marduk.

'Contact from the east,' said Sabtec, his voice calm and measured.

Marduk glanced around the twisted metal he was taking cover behind, and saw a number of lithe figures darting from cover to cover, heading towards them up the tunnel. Even with his advanced vision and the supplementary enhancements provided by his helmet, they were difficult to focus on, for they moved so quickly.

The First Acolyte narrowed his eyes, as he focused on one of the xenos humanoids. For a moment, it was clearly visible as it crouched, the long fingers of one hand splayed out on the floor.

Its slim body was encased in a form-fitting suit of reflective black armour that moulded to its movements; a far cry from the heavy, inflexible plate worn by the Word Bearers. Barbed ridges rose along its forearms and shoulders, and its head was completely encased within a sleek, backwards sweeping helmet. It carried a long, slim weapon of alien design, and elegantly curving blades protruded from the barrel and hand-grip.

Then the alien was moving once again, its movements sharp and precise as it darted into cover. Its speed was almost unnatural; one moment it was perfectly still, utterly balanced and focused, the next it was gone. There was a grace and fluidity to its movements that no human, however enhanced, could ever hope to match.

'Eldar,' spat Marduk.

CHAPTER EIGHT

SOLON SAT ALONE in the mess room. His tray vibrated slightly on the metal table from the reverberations of the crawler's engines, and the mugs hanging against the wall rattled. He still wore his bulky exposure suit, though he had slipped free of its upper half, which hung down behind him. He pushed away his half-eaten meal of bland synth-paste gruel as the door to the mess room was pushed open.

The foreman primaris tapped one of the nicotine sticks from his packet, and lit it with a deft flick of his butane lighter. He nodded to Cholos through the haze of blue-grey smoke as he sat down opposite.

The boy that they had found in the abandoned crawler unit moved forward from behind the door, his wide eyes wandering around the room.

'You gonna eat that?' asked Cholos, gesturing to the half-eaten meal.

Solon pushed the tray towards the orderly in response, blowing out another cloud of smoke.

Cholos coughed once and cleared his throat.

'Come on, kid. Get some food into you,' said Cholos, patting his hand on the seat of the vacant chair encouragingly. The boy moved forward warily, and his eyes locked on the food.

Solon stared at the boy, still seeing his son's dead face. The boy wore an exposure suit that was much too large for him, its hood drawn back away from his head. The sleeves hung well past his hands, and the cuffs of its legs were bunched up around his ankles. As he shuffled forward, trying not to trip, he would have made a comical sight were he not so clearly malnourished.

He'd spoken not a word since they had brought him aboard, except to say his name when questioned; Dios. The boy's words when they had found him still haunted Solon.

'They were taken,' the boy had said. There were some corpses aboard the crawler, but the vast majority of the people that had been onboard had apparently disappeared into thin air.

'By who?' Solon had asked.

'Ghosts,' the boy had replied, and the words had made Solon's skin crawl.

'There is no such thing as ghosts,' the Interdiction sergeant, Folches, had said, though there had been little conviction in his voice, and Solon wondered whether he had been trying to convince the boy, or himself.

Solon had to agree with Folches, though. He didn't believe in ghosts or spirits, but *something* had taken all those people. Fifteen hundred people do not just disappear.

Since bringing the boy onboard, the child had shadowed every step of Solon's second, Cholos. Solon was just glad that the boy had not latched onto him. For his part, Cholos seemed to be enjoying the attention, and had even suggested making the boy the crawler crew's mascot.

'That's the way,' said Cholos as the boy tucked into Solon's discarded food with gusto. 'Hungry, aren't you?'

'Find a woman amongst the refugees that has lost her son,' said Solon. 'Give the boy to her.'

'Oh, I don't mind lookin' after him,' said Cholos.

'We don't need a pet kid underfoot, Cholos,' said Solon. 'Foist him off on one of the refugees. There are plenty of women down below who would take him.'

Cholos glared at Solon for a moment.

'Don't listen to him, boy,' said Cholos. 'He's nothing but a mean old man.'

The boy, for his part, seemed oblivious to the conversation, focused on the meal before him. With a last lick of the standard issue spoon in his hands, he finished off the meal, smacking his lips loudly.

'Cholos,' began Solon, but his words were interrupted as the room shook violently. The crawler came to a shuddering halt, and warning lights began to flash. The wail of sirens blared from the hallway, and Solon was instantly up and moving.

'What the hell?' asked Cholos, knocking his chair over as he stood.

A second impact rocked the crawler, and mugs fell from their hooks to clatter on the floor. Solon clutched at the door-frame to steady himself.

'Ghosts,' murmured the boy, his eyes wide and fearful.

'Go, GO, GO!' shouted Folches as the crawler bay doors slid open.

The sergeant dropped to the ice and landed in a crouch, his laslock rifle humming as its charge powered up.

The storm had, if anything, become fiercer, and punishing winds lashed against the soldiers of the Skyllan Interdiction as they peered into the whitewash of billowing snow.

'Can't see a damn thing,' muttered one of Folches's men, the sound crackling through on the sergeant's micro-bead in his left ear.

'The crawler was hit from the north-east,' said Folches. 'Move out, dispersal formation.'

'How can we engage what we can't damn well see?' asked another of his team, his voice strained. Fear, Folches realised. He rounded on the man, and grabbed him by the shoulder, pulling him close.

'You done?' barked Folches into the man's face, and the soldier nodded curtly. With a shove, Folches pushed him away, and gestured for two of his men to move around the front of the crawler, and for the other two to proceed around its rear.

His men nodded their responses, and the sergeant began moving towards the rear of the hulking behemoth, loping along the length of the crawler with his body low and the butt of his laslock pressed into his shoulder. Behind him, the two soldiers loped through the snow and ice. The other two men, moving in the opposite direction, disappeared instantly into the storm.

Reaching the rear of the ice-crawler, Folches gestured for his men to halt, and risked a glance around the back of the immense vehicle. Smoke was billowing from the engine stacks, and hot oil was spilling out onto the ice. Steam rose from where the oil was pooling.

Crouched low, he signalled for his men to take cover.

One of the soldiers, Leon, dropped to his stomach and began crawling elbow over elbow through one of the deep depressions created by the crawler's track units, easing himself into position and sighting his long-barrelled lasgun out towards the north-east. The other ducked beneath the undercarriage of the crawler, and squirmed forward to take up a position looking out to the north-east.

Folches leant around the corner of the crawler, peering through the sight of his weapon. The scope rendered the landscape in shades of green, and though it lit up the darkness as if it were day, the fury of the storm was such that he could see no more than twenty metres ahead.

There was nothing to see, just a swirling blanket of snow and ice.

'Julius, you seeing anything out there?' he said into his micro-bead.

'Negative, sir,' came the response.

'Hold position,' he said.

The wind howled around Folches, and he remained motionless, waiting. Minutes dragged by, and the biting cold began to seep through his limbs.

He lifted his head away from his gunsight, and stared out into the blanketing white gale. A shadow of movement ghosted behind the veil of swirling ice.

He dropped his eye to his sight once more, straining to pick up the movement. He saw nothing, and swore under his breath.

'You see that, Leon?' he hissed into his micro-bead.

'Didn't see anything, sir,' said the soldier.

'Damn it. There's something out there. Julius, anything?'

There was no response from the other soldiers of his squad, just the relentless roaring of the wind.

'Julius, Marcab, come in,' said Folches, but again just silence answered him.

'Hell,' he swore.

The sergeant felt movement behind him, and he swung around, his heart thumping, bringing his laslock to bear on... nothing.

He was jumping at shadows, and he cursed himself. He forced his racing heart to slow, breathing in slowly.

'Calm yourself, man,' he said to himself as he resumed his position. He'd give anything for a blast of his stimm-inhaler around about now, but he had left the black market narcotics back onboard the crawler.

Trying to push the cravings away, Folches took a deep breath, and tried to contact his other soldiers once more.

'Marcab. Julius. Come in,' he whispered hoarsely into his vox-bead. 'Where the hell are you?'

Again, nothing but silence.

He flashed a glance towards Leon, lying concealed in the crawler tracks. The motionless soldier was face down, and blood was splattered out around his shattered head.

Folches pulled back from the corner of the crawler, and a flurry of projectiles impacted with the metal, centimetres from his face.

Several of the rounds sliced past the corner of the crawler, whistling sharply as they sped through the air.

A strangled grunt carried to Folches's ear on the wind, and he knew that the last of his squad, Remus, was dead.

Swearing, Folches leant out around the corner of the crawler, presenting the smallest target possible.

Half a dozen figures in glossy black armour were darting through the snow, and he saw larger, shadowy shapes gliding forwards behind them, several metres off the ground.

The sergeant snapped off a quick shot towards the closest of the figures, and ducked back into cover as return fire spat towards him. One of the enemy rounds struck him, slicing a neat cut through his body armour and scoring a wound across his forearm.

The cut was impossibly thin, and at first there was no pain, but then blood began to well and he cried out, clutching a hand to the deep wound.

Leaving a trail of blood drips that hissed and steamed as they struck the snow, the Skyllan Interdiction sergeant staggered away, dragging his laslock with him. He slipped in the hot oil pooling from the damaged engine block, and fell to his knees. Scrabbling through the sinking mire, Folches pushed himself back to his feet, and ran blindly around the corner of the immense ice-crawler, looking fearfully over his shoulder.

A thin, wickedly barbed blade entered his guts, sliding easily through his armour and flesh and halting him in his footsteps. His laslock dropped from his hands, and he stared up into the face of his killer. Nothing could be seen behind the cruelly slanted eyes of the blank helmet, and all Folches saw was his own face reflected back at him.

The figure was a good head taller than him, though it was inhumanly thin, and it cocked its head to the side, leaning into him as it twisted the blade embedded in his stomach, as if savouring every moment of the kill. Blood gushed from the wound as it opened up, and steam rose from the heat of his innards.

A hand, fingers like the black legs of a spider, clamped around Folches's neck, and he was pushed up against the crawler. The blade slid from his gut and was held poised in front of the sergeant's eyes, blood dripping from its elegantly curving tip.

The figure pressed almost intimately close to the dying sergeant, as if it wanted to experience every last dying sensation of the soldier. Then it pushed the blade into Folches's side, sliding it slowly up between his ribs to pierce the lungs.

Blood foamed up in the soldier's mouth as his lungs began to fill, and he gasped for breath as he slowly drowned on his own blood. The black fingers remained clasped around his neck almost lovingly until his heartbeat fluttered and stopped.

Then the black figure released its grip, and the sergeant slid to the ground.

SOLON RAN TOWARDS the control cabin of the ice-crawler, barging workers out of his way. The sirens in the claustrophobically narrow hallways were deafening, and he winced and clamped his hands over his ears as he ran past one of the blaring klaxons.

A burly orderly, his overalls covered in oil, ran into Solon as he rounded a corner, knocking him back into the wall.

'Sorry, boss,' said the man, helping him back to his feet, and Solon pushed past him.

He vaulted a steel banister, landed on the gantry below and ran on, turning to the right towards the control cabin. His boots rang out sharply as he climbed a short flight of stairs, and slammed the door to the control cabin open.

'What in the hell–' he began, but his words of reproach to the relief driver died in his throat.

A fist-sized hole had burned through the side window of the cabin and driven through the drive-mechanics on the wall opposite, leaving a smoking hole that dripped with molten metal. The driver was slumped back in his seat, half his head missing, the devastating blast having clearly passed through him when it had struck.

Solon gagged at the stink of burnt flesh, but moved into the cabin, trying not to look at the corpse, and failing. There was no blood. Whatever had struck him had cauterised the wound completely, forming a blackened crust. The blast had hit him in the temple, and everything in front of the line drawn between his ears was missing, down to his mouth, which was drawn in an almost comical expression of shock.

Tearing his gaze away from the corpse, Solon moved to the control console. It was dead, no lights flickering along the length of its panel at all, and he swore. He flicked a few switches, muttering an entreaty to the Omnissiah, but nothing happened. He balled his hand into a fist and stuck the console.

'Come on, damn you,' he swore.

Red warning lights flickered, the needles of the dials wavering back and forth, and Solon let out a surprised laugh of success.

His small victory was short-lived. A beam of solid darkness punched through the side of the control cabin, destroying the console in a shower of sparks. Cables and wires were fused by the lance strike and flames exploded outwards with immense force, shattering the already ruptured plasglass windows of the cabin and hurling Solon backwards through the cabin door.

Thrown backwards down the stairs leading to the cabin, the flesh of his face and arms blistering from the heat, Solon hit the deck hard. Frantically, he fought to rip his thermal undershirt off, for the synthetic material was melting onto his skin. Shaking the smoking, skin-tight shirt loose, he hurled it away from him, and began to stagger back.

The crawler, the closest thing he had to a home since he had been expelled from Sholto guild eighteen years ago, was beyond redemption. It was dead, and the vultures were circling outside to descend on its carcass.

He had to get away.

Rounding a corner, he almost ran headlong into Cholos, with the frightened boy Dios in tow.

'Solon,' began his second, his face panicked.

'Not that way,' he shouted, turning the man around and pushing him before him. 'The crawler's done. We have to get the hell out of here.'

Screams and shouts echoed up through the corridors, and Solon and Cholos fought their way through panicked workers. The crew looked to Solon for guidance.

'Get your exposure suits on,' the overseer bellowed. 'We stay here and we are all dead.'

Or as good as, he thought, thinking of the distinct lack of bodies aboard the crippled crawler they had come across just hours earlier.

'Damn,' swore Cholos. 'My suit.'

'Where is it?' asked Solon.

'In my locker,' answered his second. 'But Solon, the refugees... there are not enough suits for them all. We can't leave them.'

'We stay here and we die.'

'But all those people?'

Solon swore and punched the wall, bruising his knuckles.

'What do you want me to do, Cholos? I can't save them, and with the generators down, they're going to freeze to death as surely in the cargo bays as out on the ice.'

'There must be something we can do,' said Cholos.

'Well, if you come up with something, I'm all ears. Maybe that bastard Folches can call in support from the Skyllan Interdiction, or something. I don't know.'

Cholos let out a long breath, and rubbed a hand across his face.

'Take Dios, Solon,' he said. 'I'll meet you down below. I'll be quick'

Solon looked down at the boy, who was staring up at him with wide eyes, and swore. Cholos dropped to his knees.

'Go with Solon,' he said slowly to the boy. 'He'll see you safe. You understand?'

Dios nodded solemnly.

'That's the way,' said Cholos, ruffling the boy's short-cropped hair as he stood once more. 'I won't be long.'

'I'll meet you on deck three,' said Solon.

'I'll be there, boss,' replied Cholos, giving Solon a tense smile.

'You'd better be,' said Solon, and slapped his second heavily on the shoulder, urging him to move. 'Go.'

Cholos ducked through a side hatch, and Solon glanced down at Dios once more.

'Come on, boy. Move,' he said, gruffly.

The boy gave him a salute, his face serious, and the two of them set off towards the cargo bays. It took them the better part of five minutes to move from the crew area to the cargo holds, passing through twisting corridors and past dozens of panicked crewmen.

Punching the locking plate of cargo bay three, the door hissed open and swirling wind struck him. Screams were lost in the gale roaring through the cargo hold, and Solon saw that one of the cargo bay hold doors was wide open.

Through the blinding snow and ice, Solon saw a dark shape hanging in the air outside, hovering four metres above the ground. It was sleek and black, with wicked blades and spikes protruding along its sides, and it rocked slightly as the winds buffeted it, like a ship rolling on the open sea.

Black figures, taller and slimmer than a man were dragging people kicking and screaming towards the skiff hanging in the air outside. As he stood frozen on the spot, transfixed by the horror of what he was seeing, a struggling woman was knocked to the ground by a backhanded slap, and hauled towards the gaping cargo bay door by her hair.

A score of people were already trussed up on the mid-deck of the skiff, lying in a moaning pile, their hands bound behind their backs.

One of the black figures turned its faceless helmet towards Solon, and he felt a fear that he had never before experienced as the reflective eye lenses bore into him.

The figure barked a word in a language that Solon could not understand, spun on its heels like a dancer and swung something up from its side. With a flick of its arm it hurled the object towards him, spinning it end over end.

Even as the dark figure cast its weapon, Solon was backing away, and he tripped over the boy, Dios, who was clinging to one of his legs. Solon fell, swearing, and the spinning weapon scythed above him to strike one of his crewmen who had come up behind him.

The man fell, gagging, his hands clutching at the weighted wires wrapped around his neck. A flicker of energy coursed along those constricting wires and the man fell, convulsing violently, to the ground.

Scooping the boy up in his arms, Solon punched the door panel, bringing the hatch slamming back down, and turned and ran, leaping over the twitching figure on the ground.

The other cargo bays were to the left, the engines to the right, and Solon paused for a second, not knowing where to go. The boy wrapped his arms around Solon's neck, burying his face against his chest, and a pair of Solon's crew came running down the stairs towards him, their faces fearful.

'Run,' shouted Solon, and as he heard the hatch behind him slide open he made his decision, turning and bolting to the right.

The pair of crewmen stood staring behind Solon, firstly in incomprehension, then in dawning horror. There was a rapid sound like air being expelled, and one of the men collapsed, his left leg peppered with tiny splinters that tore through his overalls and the flesh beneath. The other man turned to run, but he was too slow and splinters shredded his legs from under him. His agonised scream followed Solon as he ran into the engine room, slamming his shoulder against the wall as he rounded a sharp corner.

The massive twin-engines were silent, and he raced between them, his heavy boots echoing loudly. Steam billowed up from beneath the walkway grid, where the massive drive shafts and gears of the crawler lay dormant and motionless. He swung around to the right, and grabbed the metal rungs of a narrow ladder that climbed one of the inner-hull walls.

'Hold on, boy,' he said, and the child tightened his grip, clinging to Solon like a limpet. With his arms free, Solon pulled himself up the ladder, expecting at any moment to be cut to shreds by the enemy.

Half way up, he leant out from the ladder and tried to loosen the access hatch that led out to the exhaust stacks. The circular wheel-lock wouldn't budge.

'Come on, damn you,' Solon hissed, casting a quick glance towards the entrance to the engine room as another strangled cry echoed down the hall. His hands were slipping on the wheel, and he strained with all his might to turn it. His face was red with exertion, and he had almost given up hope when he felt the hatch lock give a little. With renewed strength, he yanked the wheel into the unlocked position, and pushed it outwards.

Snow billowed in through the hatch, blinding him for a second, before Solon urged the boy through the hole.

'Go, boy. Now! I'll be right behind you,' he said in a hoarse whisper, casting a quick glance behind him. A shadow was stalking into the engine room, a bladed pistol of alien design in its hand.

Solon pushed the boy through the hatch, receiving a kick in his face for his troubles, almost making him lose his grip on the ladder. With a shove, he pushed the boy clear, and scrambled his way through the hatch. His hands slipped on the ice-encased metal exterior of the crawler, and he could not get any purchase. He kicked his legs awkwardly, half in the hatch and half out, expecting a hand to grab him at any moment and drag him back inside. The boy tugged at his arm ineffectually.

Awkwardly, he managed to squirm through the hatch onto the small balcony outside from where running repairs could be made to the exhausts. He cast a glance back through the open hatch to see a lithe figure looking up at him. In an instant, it raised its pistol, and Solon threw himself to the side, dragging the boy with him.

Splinters of rapidly propelled metal hissed through the open hatch and sliced through the steel exhausts as if they were made of synthpaper. Lifting the boy, Solon threw him over the edge of the crawler, and vaulted the balcony railing, praying he wouldn't crush the boy.

He hit the ground hard, and winced as shooting pain lanced up his left leg. He could hear screams on the wind, and he dragged the boy with him as he ducked beneath the crawler, squeezing himself between its massive tracked units.

He was already shivering uncontrollably, having discarded his thermal undershirt. There was little room in the cramped space beneath the crawler, but he managed to struggle his exposure suit up over his body, and he pulled its hood down low, securing it over his face. The boy too had pulled his exposure suit hood over his head, and he stared back at Solon through its two circular goggle-lenses.

Together, they crawled beneath the massive undercarriage of the tracked hauler. Solon saw the slumped form of one of the Skyllan Interdiction soldiers and his hopes were raised for a moment before he saw the blood.

Drawing the boy away from the grisly sight, Solon squirmed further beneath the hulking vehicle, moving towards the darkest recesses, the boy crawling silently behind him.

They froze as a weight crunched down into the snow nearby, and Solon looked into Cholos's terrified face. The crewman had landed on his hands and knees, and his exposure suit hung half off down his back. Solon gestured swiftly for him to crawl under. Clearly not having seen them in the darkness beneath the crawler, Cholos scrambled to his feet, and began running blindly into the storm.

Solon almost shouted out to him, but a pair of slender shapes dropped down into the snow, silent and deadly. They landed lightly, and took a few unhurried steps towards the fleeing man. Their glossy black legs were all that was visible, but Solon stared at them in horrified fascination. The spiked, overlaying plates of armour flexed as easily as synth-fabric, moulding to the contours and muscles of the figure's legs.

Cholos continued his mad flight into the storm, but Solon knew that he would not escape, and his heart wrenched as he heard the cruel laughter of the black-clad raiders as they watched his plight. They will gun him down any second, Solon thought.

They didn't.

Instead, a sleek shape hurtled out of the darkness, its form blurred by speed and the howling gale. A missile, was Solon's first thought, but then he saw that there was a figure hunched upon the rapidly moving object, and he realised that it was a bike propelled by anti-grav technology.

The rider leant down and slashed with a blade as the jetbike streaked past.

Cholos was spun by the impact, blood spraying out onto the snow. Still, the wound was not fatal, and he leapt back to his feet, a hand clutching at his shoulder. His assailant was nowhere to be seen, lost in the darkness and the storm, and Cholos turned around on the spot, eyes wide. Solon felt sick as the raiders laughed once more, the sound making his skin crawl with its cruelty.

The bike roared out of the darkness behind Cholos, streaking past him, knocking him down before being once again swallowed up in the storm.

Cholos was slower to rise this time, and blood gushed from his arm. Solon didn't want to watch any more, for the raiders were toying with the man, but he found that he couldn't look away.

Again, the bike came out of nowhere, and Cholos fell with a scream as one of his hamstrings was slashed. He couldn't rise from that blow, but still he tried to escape, crawling forward desperately, leaving a trail of blood in the snow.

Once more, the bike appeared, but this time it slowed as it approached him, dropping its speed with remarkable swiftness. It hovered in the air alongside Cholos as he tried vainly to stand. The rider of the anti-grav vehicle was garbed in a skin-tight glossy black suit with bladed plates of armour over its chest and shoulders, and a long topknot of blood-red hair streamed from the back of its elongated helmet.

The gleaming, blade-like bike sank towards the ground, and the rider reached out and grabbed Cholos by the scruff of his undershirt. Then the bike accelerated sharply, and Cholos was dragged behind it, his legs smacking into the ground every ten metres. He was dropped unceremoniously in front of the waiting pair of reavers, and the bike zoomed off into the storm once more.

The pair of reavers laughed again, and dragged Cholos away. It was the last time that Solon would ever see him, and he knew that the image of the terrified man, covered in blood and with both legs twisted horribly beneath him would be ingrained in his mind until his dying day.

Horrified and sick to his stomach, Solon slunk backwards into the concealing darkness, dragging the boy Dios with him. They cowered in the darkness behind the shadow of one of the main drive-wheels of the tracked crawler. Solon didn't know how long they hid there, but for the first time since he was a child he prayed.

MARDUK GRUNTED AS a line of splinters struck his left shoulder plate, embedding deep into the ceramite-plasteel alloy, but not penetrating. He replied with three quick shots of his bolt pistol before ducking back into cover as more fire was directed towards him. With a practiced flick, he discarded the spent sickle-clip, and rammed another into place.

'Jetbikes,' warned Kol Badar, and again the rapidly moving vehicles screamed out of the darkness of the north passage. The heavy weapons of Namar-sin's Havocs roared, and two of the accelerating bikes were taken down, one as a gout of hot plasma turned its elongated faring molten, and another as heavy bolter rounds ripped through its drive mechanics. The bike struck by the heavy plasma gun struck the floor, nose first, and flipped end over end, sending its rider flying. The other bike veered sharply to the left, spinning uncontrollably and impacted with the tunnel wall, disintegrating in a shower of sparks and flame.

Then the other bikes were screaming through the main access tunnel, banking sharply as they roared overhead. A shower of splinter-fire raced along the floor and peppered one of the Anointed, but the Terminator-armoured warrior-brother stood against the fire pelting him like a man bracing himself against the wind. His twin-linked bolters roared, ripping head-sized chunks from the front of one of the bikes, but it did not fall, and continued to slice through the air in tight formation with its peers.

Marduk and the warrior-brothers of the 13th were caught with their backs vulnerable to attack from the bikes, and they spun around and unleashed the fury of their bolters.

One of Sabtec's warriors was caught in the fire of two bikes, and though the splinters could not fully penetrate his thick armour, dozens of the cruel barbs sank through the gaps between the plates of his Mark IV armour, and he fell without a sound. Splinters had pierced the small gap between his breastplate and his helmet, filling his throat with slivers of metal, and two other splinters shattered his left eye lens, driving into his brain.

Another bike was brought crashing down by the combined fire of the 13th, and Marduk blew the head off another rider with a carefully aimed shot of his bolt pistol. The headless rider was ripped from the saddle of his bike and hurled backwards, and Marduk threw himself into a roll as the rider-less bike speared towards him, skimming across the surface of the floor like a stone hurled across still water.

The bike smashed into the remnants of the ruined Imperial armoured vehicle that Marduk had been crouching behind, the force of the impact spinning it sideways. The last bike was gone, screaming away into the distance as its rider accelerated.

A flurry of splinters struck him in the back, and Marduk was knocked forwards as he rose. He cursed, and pushed himself to his feet, swinging around and firing in one motion. With satisfaction, he saw the frail chest of one of the advancing black armoured eldar explode as the mass-reactive tip of the bolt-round detonated.

'Thirteenth, advance on me,' roared Marduk, having had enough of cowering in cover.

BURIAS HISSED IN hatred as the last remaining jetbike banked around once more, chased by bolter rounds that pinged off the debris scattered around the access tunnel. It moved so fast that it was little more than a shadowy blur, and he narrowed his eyes and allowed the daemon Drak'shal to rear up within him.

The eldar vehicle speared through the air like a dart, jinking around the burnt-out hulls of Imperial vehicles, dodging the blanket of incoming fire.

It straightened and gunned its engines, accelerating directly towards Burias-Drak'shal and Magos Darioq, who stood immobile behind him, apparently unconcerned by the carnage.

The cannons, under-slung beneath the chassis of the jetbike, roared, spitting a stream of splinters towards the possessed warrior, but he was already moving, springing into the air, the heavy icon of the Host held in one hand as if it weighed nothing at all.

The fire of the jetbike's cannons flashed towards Darioq, but a glowing sphere of light surrounded him, and they rebounded off the energy barrier to leave him unscathed.

Burias-Drak'shal leapt over the elegantly tapering faring of the jetbike, his taloned hand locking around the eldar rider's throat and ripping him from his saddle. The rider-less bike veered sharply and flipped, exploding against the tunnel wall as Burias-Drak'shal landed in a crouch, the eldar warrior helpless in his grasp.

Lifting the eldar as if he was a child, Burias-Drak'shal slammed its head into a corner of scrap metal, once part of an Imperial vehicle. Its head splattered, the frail skull splintering like porcelain.

'Weakling thing,' commented Burias-Drak'shal, flicking the corpse away from him.

A blade rammed into his back, and Burias-Drak'shal roared in anger and pain. The blade was wrenched agonisingly against his spine and he twisted, swinging the icon around in a lethal arc.

The blow didn't hit anything, indeed, there did not seem to *be* anything behind him. With his witch-sight, he registered a shadowy shape in the corner of his vision, and then twisted away as a blade stabbed towards him once again, putting some space between him and his nigh-on invisible assailant.

His eyes narrowed as they locked on a lean, ghostlike figure. It became visible for a second, taunting him, and he saw a slim figure, its skin as black as pitch, with arcane sigils cut into its flesh. Its eyes were milky white, with no pupils, and it snarled at him, exposing a maw filled with tiny, barbed teeth.

Then the figure was nothing more than a shadow again, a vague ghostly shape that surged towards him in a blur of motion. Burias-Drak'shal swung his icon like a hammer, the spiked tip humming as it arced through the air. The shadow-creature ducked beneath the blow and came up inside his guard, and Burias-Drak'shal hissed in pain as a blade rammed into his side.

Burias-Drak'shal connected with a heavy backhand blow that sent the shadow-creature tumbling backwards. It came to rest on all fours, and its form once more became visible as it snarled up at him in hatred. Then it was gone, disappearing into thin air as if a veil had been drawn over it.

Burias-Drak'shal experienced an unfamiliar emotion: unease.

The creature had seemed at once familiar and alien. He thought he had scented the power of the warp within its being, but the creature had been no daemon, nor truly one of the possessed.

His slit eyes flicked from side to side, wary for another sudden attack, but none came. He slammed the butt of his icon into the floor, cracking the plascrete platform, and roared his defiance.

MARDUK HEARD THE roar, but pushed it out of his mind as he drew his chainsword, feeling the ecstatic bond as the daemon weapon melded with him. Thorns in the hilt burrowed into the flesh of his palm through the plugs in his gauntlet, and he surged towards the eldar warriors.

The disciplined warriors of the 13th coterie responded instantly to his rallying cry, rising from cover with bolters thumping. They began to advance on the enemy, bearing down on them, moving in two unstoppable phalanxes, the zones of their fire-arcs overlapping.

Each of the coteries had been joined by one of the Anointed, and these behemoths of muscle and metal stomped forwards, shaking off the fire directed against them and snapping off bursts from their twin-linked bolters.

The closest enemy was less than twenty metres away, and still, foolishly Marduk thought, advancing towards the Word Bearers.

'Slaughter the unbelievers!' roared Marduk, breaking into a run, his bolt pistol bucking in his hands as he fired.

The warriors of the 13th moved up in support, snapping off shots as they bore down on the enemy.

Marduk saw two of the enemy ripped apart by bolt fire. One-bolt round detonated in the shoulder of one of the eldar figures, ripping its arm clear in a spray of blood, and another was torn in two as a burst of fire caught it in its slender midsection.

A spray of splinters embedded themselves in Marduk's chest plate, but he did not slow his charge, and pumped another burst of shots towards a pair of eldar raiders. Displaying inhuman speed, they darted to the side and his shots went wide, ripping chunks out of the wall.

He roared his hatred as he closed on one of the eldar, and swung his chainsword in a murderous arc that would have cleaved the frail warrior in two had it connected. The eldar swayed under the blow with a speed that, for all his Astartes genetic coding and training, made Marduk feel slow and awkward, and slashed a groove across Marduk's thigh with the curving bayonet blade beneath the barrel of its rifle.

The blade bit into his flesh, and Marduk hissed in anger. He threw a backhanded slash towards the eldar's midsection, the hungry teeth of his chainsword whirring madly. The black-armoured figure dodged backwards, the very tip of the chainsword scant centimetres from its belly, and stabbed with the tip of its blade towards Marduk's throat.

The First Acolyte twisted his body as the blade darted towards him, and its length sank into his shoulder plate. Punching with his right hand, which held his bolt pistol, Marduk snapped the blade off, leaving the tip embedded in his armour. Dropping his shoulder, he threw himself forward, slamming into the frail xenos warrior even as it tried to sidestep.

The force of the blow shattered the eldar's chest, and Marduk bore it to the ground. He smashed the pommel of his chainsword into the raider's face, driving it downwards like a blunt dagger, smashing the faceplate of its helmet into splinters and pulverising its skull.

Rising, his chest heaving, Marduk grunted as a blade stabbed into his side, sliding between his armour plates and burying itself deep in his flesh. Dropping his bolt pistol, he grabbed the arm of his attacker, crushing the slender bones of its forearm. It struggled to get away from him, but his grip was like iron, keeping it pinned in place, and he hacked his chainsword into its neck.

Whirring teeth shredded through black armour and blood began to spray as Marduk forced the weapon into the alien's body. It ripped through tightly bound muscle and sinew, and tore apart the delicate vertebrae of the eldar's neck. With a heavy kick, Marduk sent the dead eldar flying away from him, and dropped to one knee to retrieve his bolt pistol.

Hefting the pistol, Marduk found no new target to unleash his wrath upon. The eldar slipped away into the shadows with ungodly speed, moving like shadows being dispelled by the appearance of a lantern. They were gone in an instant, and Marduk stood breathing heavily as he surveyed the carnage of the frantic battle.

The fight had lasted less than a minute, all told, but the savagery, swiftness and effectiveness of the attack was staggering.

Three members of the 13th were down, one of them not moving as blood poured from a wound to his head, too severe for the potent larraman cells of his Astartes make-up to seal. Two members of Khalaxis's 17th coterie were dead, two more injured. Nine eldar had been slain, and three more had been injured and callously abandoned by their brethren.

Marduk strode towards one of the injured lean warriors. Its left leg had been blown off at the knee, and it was trying to crawl away, leaving a bloody smear on the floor beneath it.

Marduk placed his foot on the lower back of the wounded eldar, pinning it in place as Kol Badar stalked to his side. The black armour was curiously soft and pliable beneath his foot, but as he exerted more pressure he felt it strengthen and grow rigid, resisting him. He kicked the eldar over onto its back, and it stared up at him through elongated eye lenses. Its hatred of him was palpable, and its hand flashed down to its thigh, reaching for a jagged blade strapped around its lean limb.

Its movement was crisp and precise, and the blade was flashing towards Marduk's throat. He caught the eldar's wrist and gave it a wrench, breaking its slender bones with a snap, and it dropped the blade to the ground, hissing.

'I've never seen their faces,' said Marduk, pinning the eldar's broken arm beneath his knee and reaching for its helmet, ignoring the feeble attempts by the xenos humanoid to fight him off as he tried to work out the best way to remove it. Growing quickly frustrated, he simply hooked the fingers of both hands under the lip of the helmet around the eldar's scrawny neck and pulled. With a wrench, he ripped the helmet in two, almost breaking the alien's neck in the process.

The First Acolyte tossed the ruptured helmet aside as he stared down at the revealed face.

It was unnaturally long and thin, ethereal and otherworldly. High cheekbones and a pointed chin gave it a severe, angular shape that was at once delicate and darkly handsome, yet utterly alien. Its head was bereft of hair, and sharp, jagged runes or glyphs of xenos origin, similar in shape to the elegant blades of the eldar, were tattooed across the left half of its face. Its lips were thin and sneering, and its eyes were shaped like almonds, elegant, alien and filled with hate.

'It's a frail as a woman,' said Marduk. 'Reminds me of Fulgrim's Legionaries.'

Kol Badar snorted.

Although the III Legion, the Emperor's Children, were mighty warriors and had wisely thrown their weight in behind the Warmaster and embraced Chaos, there was no love lost between the Word Bearers and the Emperor's Children.

Where the Word Bearers were severe, their lives dominated by ritual, prayer and penance, the Emperor's Children were renowned for their flamboyant decadence, embracing excess in all its guises. Where the Word Bearers worshipped Chaos in all its varied manifestations, the Emperor's Children dedicated themselves solely to the darkling prince of Chaos: Slaanesh.

The eldar glared up at Marduk hatefully.

'I agree, yet they are a worthy foe,' said Kol Badar.

'Worthy? They are xenos. They deserve nothing more than extermination,' replied Marduk.

'I do not disagree,' said Kol Badar, 'but it does my soul good to fight against an enemy that can at least test us.'

'Their tainted, alien weaponry is potent,' agreed Marduk, reluctantly, gripping the eldar roughly behind its neck with one hand. He raised his fist.

'And they are certainly quick,' said Marduk. slamming his fist down, punching through the eldar's face, 'but they break easily enough once you get a hold of them.' Marduk shook blood, brain matter and shards of skull across the floor.

CHAPTER NINE

IKORUS BARANOV WAS an optimist. When he first heard of the plight of the worlds being evacuated in the face of the tyranid menace, he had smiled.

Hundreds of inhabited worlds were being abandoned. Countless millions had already perished, either consumed to feed the insatiable hunger of the xenos hive fleet, or utterly destroyed by the zealous policy of Exterminatus employed by the Imperium. Any world not fully evacuated before the tyranid ground invasion began was stricken from the Imperial records and bombarded from high orbit. Already a score of colonised planets had been put to the sword, every living thing – tyranid, human, animal, vegetable – utterly consumed in purifying flame.

Baranov cared nothing for the millions of destroyed lives. He saw the positive flip-side of every ill turn, and while others regarded this time as one of terror and darkness, he saw it as a time to make himself filthy rich.

His ship, the *Rapture*, was docked at landing zone CXVI, a privately-owned docking pad of the Phorcys starport. Only those wealthy few with the required access privileges were allowed entrance onto this private dock.

Baranov had heard that the regular docks were overrun with tens of thousands of frantic guild workers and their families, desperate to secure passage off-world. In contrast to that mayhem, landing zone CXVI was a veritable utopia of peace and tranquillity.

The private lounge adjacent to the dock was opulently decorated with extravagant off-world flora, for it had been designed to mimic a fecund, semi-tropical rainforest. Paths of fine gravel wove through the undergrowth, and ferns and broad-leafed plants grew up overhead, hiding the strip lights in the high domed ceiling. A waterfall crashed down over rocks imported from a distant feral world, creating a mist of warm water vapour in the air, and butterflies, with wingspans as wide as a man's forearm is long, bobbed lazily through the air.

Baranov shook his head in amazement and envy. Perdus Skylla was a desolate wasteland of frozen, wind-swept plains, the crude worker class living beneath the ice, and yet there were those with enough wealth to create an oasis of life like this in its midst.

The pursuit of wealth had dominated Ikorus Baranov's life, and he liked to think that he had achieved much from his humble beginnings, but it was at times like these that he was reminded that his wealth was not so great. *This* was the wealth that he desired. He wanted to be able to build a sub-tropical rainforest in the middle of an ice-locked ocean world just because he could. Of course he didn't literally want to build a rainforest – he found this place with its high humidity and crawling things quite unsettling – but he wanted the wealth to be able to do so at a whim had he desired it.

These were the people to lift him to that stage of wealth.

There were thirty-two men here, most with young, surgically enhanced women clinging to their arms like leeches. Some were accompanied by older women, fierce beasts that clearly dominated their husbands or lovers, but they were few in comparison to the glittering array of nubile young women, bedecked in fine jewels and headdresses.

Baranov smirked. Clearly many of these high-ranking guild officials had chosen to bring their courtesans along with them rather than their wives. If he had not been a callous man he might have been offended by how easily these men cast off their wives, abandoning them to their fate while they fled for safety. A few had brought both wife and courtesan with them, but that was rare. The price that Baranov was charging for a berth on his ship was nothing short of extortionate, even for this upper echelon of the truly elite.

'Lords and ladies,' began Baranov, his voice silken, 'may I please have your attention.'

The group was gathered upon a decked clearing in the middle of the rainforest façade, seated on cane high-backed chairs. The hum of conversation died as the gathered social elite turned to regard Baranov. Baranov saw fear in their eyes, which was understandable for their world was being abandoned in the face of an alien menace that would destroy and kill everything in its path. But even so, they regarded him with considerable distaste, as if he were common vermin that had somehow infiltrated into their elite company.

Baranov suppressed a grin. In truth he *was* vermin, but he was vermin that was about to get seriously wealthy.

He gave a mock bow, waving his hand in a flourish. He was a short man of middling build, and he wore a long-tailed coat of regal blue with overly prominent gold buttons. His hair was pulled back in a pony-tail that hung down his back, and his fingers were bedecked with rings. He knew that to these rich guilders who were born to their wealth, he looked like a rogue or a pirate, an individual who had some wealth but not the class to know what to do with it, but he didn't give a damn what they thought of him. Right now, he was their only ticket off this cursed world, and he fully intended to milk that for all it was worth.

'Thank you for your patience, my esteemed friends,' said Baranov. 'My ship, the *Rapture*, is refuelled and provisioned, and is now ready for embarkation.'

'About time,' stated one of the guilders, a scowling, porcine individual pawing at a girl who looked little more than a child, though she was clearly his mistress. Other men muttered and huffed impatiently. These people were not used to having to wait for anything.

'I regret to have kept you waiting, noble lords, but I assure you that the *Rapture* is now ready to receive your esteemed selves. She is a humble craft, but I trust that you will find her suitable for your use.'

'Get on with it, man,' snapped another man, an imposingly tall individual with a hooked nose.

'I shall forestall you no longer, my lords,' said Baranov, holding up a hand. 'However,' he added with a rakish grin, 'there is just the small matter of my compensation.'

With a snap of his fingers, four of Baranov's crewmen stepped out of the shadows of the foliage to join him. Two of them guided a container forward, which hovered just above the ground, held aloft by anti-grav technology. They were rough sorts, and Baranov saw the noses of the lords and ladies crinkle as they stared disdainfully at them. He grinned again.

One of the crew, sat down at a desk facing the nobles, a data-slate and stylus in his hands. An immense brute with a shaved head took his place behind him, standing with his thick arms folded across his chest.

'If you would be so kind as to make your monies ready, my associates will collect your dues,' he said. 'Step forward if you will, and make a line behind Lord Palantus. This will be as quick and painless as possible, and we shall all be on our way shortly.'

The nobles shuffled into line, huffing and muttering, angry at being treated like commoners. The first in line, Lord Palantus, Prime Magnate of Antithon Guild, stepped forward and slid a slim hand-case onto the desk.

'Name?' said the seated crewman, tapping at the data-slate.

'Oh, for the love of the Emperor,' said Lord Palantus, outraged at having to commune with such a lowborn cur. The seated man looked up at him, eyebrows raised.

'Get on with it, Antithon,' muttered one of the other nobles.

'Palantus,' the lord spat, glaring down at the man before him as if he were a bug that he had just found in his food.

'Open it,' said the seated man, indicating the hand-case with the tip of his stylus.

'You are going to check it's all there, Baranov?' asked the noble imperiously. 'I am a noble of Antithon Guild, and my word is my honour. It is all there, as agreed.'

'My dear lord, of course I trust your esteemed word,' said Baranov smoothly, 'but please, indulge my men. They are unused to dealing with such luminaries. Please, open it.'

The prime magnate huffed and folded his arms, looking away. He nodded to his mistress at his side. She clicked the release nodules of the case with her thumbs and it opened with a hiss.

With a nod, the seated man made a mark on his data-slate. The heavily muscled crewman standing behind the desk sealed the case, and it was placed inside the hovering container.

'Now, my dear Lord Palantus,' said Baranov, guiding the man to the side with his hand on his elbow, 'if you would please go with my associates, they will see you safely onboard.'

The lord looked outraged that Baranov dared lay a hand on him, but allowed himself to be guided away.

'Next,' said the seated man, tapping with his stylus.

WITH ALL PAYING customers aboard the *Rapture*, Baranov smiled and let out a slow breath. He had made an absolute killing today, and he couldn't keep the smile from his face. The engines of his ship roared, and he gave a last look around the starport before climbing the embarkation steps.

'A good day's work,' he said. Keying a sequence of buttons, he sealed the hatch behind him.

Minutes later, the *Rapture* was cleared for take-off. The wedged segments of the dome far overhead peeled back like the petals of an immense flower, opening up the landing pad to the fury of the elements outside. Wind swirled furiously, ice and snow spiralling in mad eddies as the *Rapture's* engines roared into life, flames gushing from the powerful downward-angled thrusters. The ship lifted, rising vertically out of the landing dock, and as the petal segments of the dome began to close once more, the *Rapture's* thrusters rotated backwards, and it screamed up towards the heavens, leaving the doomed ice-world of Perdus Skylla behind it.

MARDUK SHOT AN Imperial soldier in the face, and the back of the man's head exploded outwards, spraying blood and brain matter across the wall.

'That the last of them?' he growled, kicking the corpse out of his way.

'There are a few survivors,' said Kol Badar. 'They are being executed as we speak.'

'Move in, secure the area,' ordered Marduk.

The Coryphaus barked his orders, and the warriors of the Host closed in.

For three hours they had proceeded along the access tunnel, homing in on the location pinpointed by Magos Darioq-Grendh'al as the access lift that would take them down to the mining facility below, to the last known whereabouts of the Adeptus Mechanicus explorator.

They had encountered little resistance en route.

One Imperial patrol of soldiers had been encountered, escorting some two thousand civilians, and they had engaged and neutralised the foe for no losses. Not all of the civilians had been killed in the resultant slaughter, for it would have been a waste of ammunition to gun them down. Almost three hundred had been killed, caught in the middle of the firefight or hacked down in close combat, but the remainder had been allowed to flee, running wildly back the way they had come, though there was evidence to suggest that most of them had been subsequently taken by the dark eldar.

Of the eldar themselves, the Word Bearers had seen no sign since their first, frantic encounter. On several occasions, the whine of their jetbikes had been heard in the distance, accompanied by the echoing screams of Imperial citizens from further along the tunnels, but no bodies had been discovered that spoke of battle.

'They are a piratical race,' Kol Badar had said to Burias, who had never encountered the eldar before and seemed, Marduk noted curiously, to have been somewhat unnerved by his first encounter.

'What are they doing here? What purpose could they possibly have on this gods-forsaken Imperial moon?' asked Burias.

'Certain eldar sects have been observed taking captives, though for what purpose has not been ascertained,' growled Kol Badar. 'I assume that the eldar on this world are such a sect, taking advantage of the confusion of the evacuations to reap a tally of slaves.'

'It doesn't matter why they are here,' said Marduk. 'The only thing that need be understood is that they are xenos, and therefore the enemy.'

'Had the Great Crusade been allowed to fulfil its purpose,' Kol Badar added bitterly, 'with the Warmaster at its head, then the foul race of witches and sorcerers would have been eradicated from the galaxy long ago. But they remain a cunning foe, swift and deadly. They are not to be underestimated.'

'Overestimation of the foe reeks of fear and weakness,' snapped Marduk. 'The eldar are nothing more than the last fragmented strands of a dying race. We are the chosen bearers of the great truth, the favoured sons of Chaos. We are the greatest warriors the universe has ever seen, and will ever see. We need not be concerned with the appearance of a handful of xenos pirates.'

Marduk felt pride surge through the warriors of the Host in response to his words, and he knew that they would fight even harder against the eldar if they appeared again. He doubted that they would, in truth, for he believed that Kol Badar was correct in his assumptions: that they had encountered a dark eldar sect engaged in slave raids upon this doomed world, and that they expected little resistance. Certainly, they had not expected to encounter members of an Astartes Legion. Marduk knew that the eldar were a long-lived race, and one that was on the brink of dying out altogether. He was certain that the eldar would rue the day that they had attacked the revered XVII Legion. They would move on, avoiding the warriors of the Host, to find easier pickings elsewhere.

Nevertheless, the progress of the Word Bearers was slowed, for it would be foolishness not to show caution after the lightning attack of the dark eldar. Though it defied logic for the eldar to attack them again, he knew that they were xenos, and so could not be understood. He had studied reports of engagements against the eldar, and everything that he had read spoke of their unpredictability.

The priority target was an access lift that linked one of the dozens of sub-ice hab-cities with its mining facility on the ocean floor far below, and it was towards this location that they were moving. On the approach to one of the many entrances to this guilder hab-city, they had come upon a blockade of enemy soldiers, accompanied by sentry guns with servitors hard-wired into their targeting systems and lightly armoured vehicles similar to those they had encountered on the ice above, though modified for use on man-made surfaces rather than the nebulous ice-flows. The soldiers had been ready for them, either having received warning of the Word Bearers approach or merely prepared for a dark eldar attack, but it mattered little.

The Anointed had led the attack, marching resolutely through the weight of fire while Namar-sin moved the Havocs of the 217th coterie up in support, targeting and neutralising the enemy sentry guns. With the Anointed still weathering the brunt of the enemy fusillade, Sabtec's veteran squad took up position on the left flank, laying down a blanket of fire that allowed Khalaxis and his warriors to charge up the middle, with Marduk at their forefront roaring catechisms of vengeance and hate.

Every carefully targeted burst of fire from the Anointed had ripped another of the enemy soldiers apart, but it was Marduk's charge that signalled the commencement of the real slaughter. Up close, the enemy had no hope of survival. Hastily fired point blank lasgun shots had seared burning furrows across power armour plates as Marduk and Khalaxis entered the fray, chainsword and axe cutting and ripping. Bolt pistols created gory craters of flesh in chests, and limbs were ripped from their sockets as Khalaxis's warriors tore through the heart of the enemy defence.

Those cowards that had turned to run were hacked down without mercy, chainswords and heavy axes severing spines and cutting arms away at the shoulder. Kol Badar and his Anointed moved through the mayhem, ripping apart the remnants of the Imperial defenders, gunning them down with combi-bolters and heavy reaper autocannon fire. The Coryphaus smashed the scorpion-legged rapier sentry-guns aside with backhand blows of his power talons, sending them crashing into cowering defenders, crushing limbs and breaking bones.

As the last enemies were brutally butchered, and as Sabtec's squad moved forward to secure the area, Darioq-Grendh'al stamped mechanically forward, each heavy step accompanied by a whine of servos.

The magos, Marduk noted with a smile of satisfaction, was now truly a being of Chaos. The four powerful arms of his servo-harness were as much organic as metal, and bony protuberances, serrated thorns and hooked spines ridged the once pristine metal limbs. Fleshy lumps of muscle had grown around the servo-bundles and coupling links that joined the servo-limbs to his body, and a large curving horn emerged from the left side of the magos's head, bursting through the blood-stained fabric of the low cowl that hid his face in shadow.

Waving mechadendrite tentacles sprouted from his spine, and where before they were tipped with mechanical claws, sensory apparatus and data-spikes, now several of them ended in gaping lamprey mouths, filled with rings of barbed teeth, from which ropes of oily saliva dripped. The surface of many of the tentacles too had changed, their metal bands morphing into smooth, black skin, wet and slick like the body of an eel.

The insignia of the Adeptus Mechanicus had been altered and corrupted, for such a reminder of the false machine faith was offensive to the fundamentalist Word Bearers. The cogged wheel of the Mechanicus had been overlaid with the holy eight-pointed star of Chaos, and the black and white skull motif of the machine cult had been corrupted, now bearing daemonic horns and wreathed in flames so that it mirrored the sacred Latros Sacrum borne upon the left shoulder of every warrior-brother of the XVII Legion.

As if to emphasise the corrupted nature of the magos, Darioq-Grendh'al paused beside a dying Imperial soldier, who stared up at him in horror, face awash in blood. The magos peered down at the man, his unfathomable red glowing right eye boring into the soldier. Four of the lamprey mouths of the semi-organic mechadendrites waved towards the fallen man, who recoiled away from them in horror. The tentacles were drawn to him as if they tasted his blood in the air, and latched onto him, attaching to his neck, his chest and his face.

The man screamed in horror and pain as the tentacles twisted back and forth, burrowing into his flesh and began sucking away his vital fluids. The man died in torment, and as the feeder mouths pulled away from the corpse with a wet sucking sound, blood dripping from their gaping apertures, the magos tilted his head to one side and, with an almost tender, tentative movement, lifted one of the man's limp arms with one of his own mechanical power lifters. Releasing the man's arm, it flopped back to the ground, and Darioq-Grendh'al stared down at it in incomprehension.

Amused, Marduk watched as the magos tried to raise the man to his feet, lifting him up gently in his mechanical claws, careful not to crush him in his powerful grip, but the body collapsed to the ground as soon as it was released.

'The life-systems of this flesh-unit have failed,' said the magos. 'Already its body temperature has dropped 1.045 degrees, and its cellular make-up is entering corporal decay.'

'He's dead, magos,' said Marduk softly. 'You killed him.'

The magos looked at Marduk, and then back down at the corpse. Then, slowly, he raised his head once more to meet Marduk's gaze.

'Feels good, doesn't it?' said Marduk.

The magos paused, looking down at the corpse at its feet in incomprehension. Then the corrupted once-priest of the Machine-God straightened.

'I wish to do that again,' he said.

'Oh you will, Darioq-Grendh'al,' promised Marduk.

HAVING BREACHED THE defences of the guild hab-city, the Word Bearers made swift progress through the tunnelled streets and boulevards, encountering no resistance and sighting few living beings. The citizens that still remained in the city fled before the advance of the enclave, scurrying like vermin into the darkness of side-tunnels and alleys.

Marduk gave them no mind. He cared not for the fate that awaited them once the tyranids had descended on the planet. They would all be slaughtered, their bodies consumed to feed the growth of the hive fleet.

They descended deeper into the guild city, guided inexorably onward by schematic maps that flickered across auspex screens, uploaded from the data-banks of the guild bastion. They marched through what must have been the mercantile district of the sub-surface city, which was rife with detritus and evidence of looting. Doors were smashed from hinges, and goods and foodstuffs lay scattered across the tunnel floor, along with the occasional corpse.

'Trampled to death in the exodus,' said Sabtec evenly as he knelt by one of the bodies.

'The cowards won't even stand to fight for their own world,' said Khalaxis, a fresh array of scalps and death-skulls hanging from his belt, 'and they kill each other in their panic to escape. These are not worthy foes.'

'Rejoice at the weakness of the Imperium,' said Marduk. 'Namar-sin, which direction?'

'East, two kilometres,' said the champion of the Havoc squad, consulting the throbbing blister display of his auspex. 'There, we must rise four levels towards the surface, and proceed a further kilometre to the north-east before we get to the ore docks. That is where the lift rises from the ocean floor.'

'Burias, take point,' rumbled Kol Badar. 'Khalaxis, move in support of the icon bearer. Let's move.'

DRACON ALITH DRAZJAER raised one thin eyebrow a fraction, his almond-shaped eyes glinting dangerously. That one small movement would have been all but unseen by a human, but to the keen eyes of the eldar, the subtle nuance spoke volumes.

The dracon reclined languidly on his command throne, his thin chin supported by the slender fingers of one hand as he stared down at the supplicant kneeling before him. He was bedecked from neck to toe in tight fitting segmented armour, like the scaled skin of a serpent, glossy and black. A mask covered the left half of his face, its barbed blades, like the legs of spiders, pressing against his flesh. A pair of blood-red tattoos extended down his pale cheeks from his eyelids, like bloody tears.

'How many?' Dracon Alith Drazjaer said, his voice a soft purr.

The sybarite supplicant, Keelan, paled and licked his thin lips. Unable to hold his master's gaze, his eyes moved to the figures behind the throne. A pair of the dracon's incubi guards stood there, but there was no hope of support from them. They were as still as statues, their faces hidden beneath tall helmets, and they held curving halberds in their gauntleted hands. Keelan's eyes flicked to the other two figures standing by the dracon's side.

On the left stood the firebrand, Atherak, her tautly muscled body covered in swirling tattoos and wych cult markings. The sides of her head were shaved to the scalp and tattooed, and a ridge of back-swept hair ran along her crown like a crest, falling down her back past her slim waist. A myriad of weapons were strapped to her limbs, and she sneered at Keelan.

On the right was the haemonculus, Rhakaeth, unnaturally tall and thin even by eldar standards, his cheeks sunken. He looked like nothing more than a walking corpse, and his eyes burnt feverishly hot with the soul-hunger. Keelan quickly averted his gaze, looking at the floor.

'How many?' Drazjaer asked again, a subtle change in his inflection registering his displeasure, and the sybarite knew that he would not escape without punishment. Dracon Alith Drazjaer of the Black Heart Kabal was not a forgiving master. Doubtless he would experience torment beyond imagining at the hands of the haemonculus, Rhakaeth, but not death. No, he would not be allowed death.

'We lost twelve of our number, my lord,' Keelan said finally.

'Twelve,' repeated his master, his voice expressionless.

'It was not the regular mon-keigh forces that we faced, my lord,' said the sybarite, desperation in his voice. 'The… augmented ones were there.'

A line furrowed the dracon's brow for a second, and the haemonculus, Rhakaeth, leant forwards hungrily.

'You are sure?' asked the dracon.

'Yes, my lord,' said Keelan. 'It was not my fault; it was Ja'harael. He is to blame. He drew us in, and we had no warning that we faced anything but the regular mon-keigh forces.'

'We should not have sought the service of the half-breed and its kin in the first place,' spat Atherak, her cruel features sharpening. Her muscles tightened, her hands clenching and unclenching into fists, and beads of sweat ran down her long limbs.

'The mandrake half-breeds serve us well,' said Drazjaer evenly, dismissing the wych's words. 'How many slaves did you take, sybarite?'

Keelan licked his lips again. The dracon doubtless already knew the answer to his question. He looked up, feeling eyes upon him. The haemonculus, Rhakaeth, was staring at him hungrily, a slight smile upon his lips. He looked like a grinning corpse, and Keelan swallowed thickly.

'None, my lord,' he said, his voice little more than a whisper.

'None,' said Drazjaer flatly, 'for the loss of twelve of my warriors.'

'Ja'harael is to blame, my lord,' protested Keelan. 'If anyone is to be punished, it should be him.'

'What have you to say on the matter, mandrake?' asked the dracon, and Keelan stiffened. Ja'harael materialised out of the shadows next to him, darkness clinging to him like a shroud. His milky eyes stared into Keelan's for a moment, and the sybarite recoiled at the half-breed's presence. He was an abomination, a thing that should not be, and his mouth went dry.

The mandrake's skin was as black as pitch, and sigils were cut into his flesh, marking his damnation. The mandrakes were shadow-creatures. Once, they had been eldar, but they had long ago given themselves up to darkness, inviting the foul presence of *others* into their souls. Now they were something altogether different, living apart from the eldar race, preying on their own in the darkness of Commorragh and the webway. They existed in three planes – the real, the webway, and the warp – and were able to slip between the realms at will.

'I did not realise that I was employed to safeguard your warriors from harm, Drazjaer,' hissed Ja'harael.

'You are not,' said the dracon. If he was offended by the casual use of his name, he gave no indication.

'Their failure shames you, Drazjaer,' hissed the mandrake. 'They make you look weak.'

The dracon smiled coldly.

'Do not seek to goad me, half-breed,' said the dracon stroking his chin thoughtfully. The haemonculus leant over the dracon, whispering. Drazjaer nodded, and leant back in his throne, stretching his back languidly.

'The presence of the mon-keigh elite intrigues me,' he said finally. 'Their souls are much sought after in Commorragh, and will garner much favour.'

'And perhaps offset a certain amount of your Lord Vect's displeasure,' hissed Ja'harael.

Drazjaer's eyes flashed angrily, but the mandrake continued regardless.

'Perhaps you see your time running out, Drazjaer, and your quota not yet achieved.'

A blade appeared to materialise in Atherak's left hand so fast did she draw it, and in her right she flicked her long whip, its barbed tips writhing like serpents across the floor at her feet. Her muscles quivered with anticipation, and Ja'harael smiled at her, exposing his array of teeth, flexing his fingers. The wych cracked her whip and took a step towards the mandrake, but was halted by a sharp word from the dracon. Drazjaer's anger was gone, and he smiled coldly.

'It seems you know much, half-breed,' he said, 'but be careful, knowledge can be dangerous, and my patience can be stretched only so far.'

The mandrake spread his arms wide and gave a mocking bow.

'The souls of the enhanced ones will offset any shortfall in the quota, it is true, and Rhakaeth desires to work upon one of the enhanced mon-keigh creatures,' said the dracon, indicating the haemonculus with one languid gesture, 'though why he would wish to perform his art upon their brutish forms is beyond my understanding. However, he has pleased me of late, and I shall indulge his whim. Bring him some specimens, Ja'harael.'

'You would honour the half-breed abomination with this hunt?' sneered Atherak. 'Let me lead my wyches in. You owe me that honour.'

'You would make demands of me now, wych?' asked the dracon. He did not look at Atherak, and the words were said casually, but Keelan could feel the underlying threat in his voice.

'I make no demands, lord,' said Atherak, 'merely a request.'

'Ah, a request,' said Drazjaer. 'I refuse, then. Ja'harael will go. He and his kin are being well compensated for their service, and it is high time that they began earning it. We shall see how well he fares, since my warriors have failed me so. Go, half-breed. Get out of my sight, for your presence is beginning to offend me.'

The mandrake grinned and then was gone, as if he had never been there in the first place.

'I'd like to gut the filthy creature,' hissed Atherak, and the dracon smiled.

'All in good time,' he said, stroking his chin. Then his gaze dropped once more to Keelan, who was trying to remain inconspicuous on his knees, praying that his lord and master might have forgotten about him.

'Take him,' said the dracon, banishing any hope that Keelan had of escaping punishment. 'Rhakaeth, see that he is suitably chastised for his failure. I leave the level of his punishment to your discretion.'

Keelan felt his heart sink as he saw the hungry light in the haemonculus's dead eyes.

'Thank you, my lord,' said the haemonculus, and Keelan was dragged away.

MARDUK STOOD GAZING down into the gaping hexagonal shaft that descended into darkness below. Yellow and black hazard stripes lined the edge of the impossibly deep drop-off, and a steel barrier stood along its rim to protect the unwary or the clumsy from falling.

It had been time-consuming but not difficult to breach the guild city, nor to penetrate to its heart.

Warning lights were flashing, and the immense cable that descended down the centre of the shaft vibrated as the lift rose from the stygian darkness. The cable was over five metres in diameter, and was formed of thousands of tightly bound ropes of metal. It connected the guild city to the mining facility on the bottom of the ocean far below, and it shuddered as the lift ascended.

The surrounding loading area was vast, easily the size of one of the embarkation decks of the *Infidus Diabolus*. Scores of loading vehicles lay dormant in neat rows, as if in readiness to unload the next shipment of the ore transported up from the mining facility below. Over a hundred servitor units stood immobile within the arched alcoves lining the loading dock walls, their arms replaced with immense power lifters. Massive hooks and clamp-mouthed lifters hung from thick chains linked to heavy machines overhead that would come to life to lift the heavy containers of mining ore onto waiting transport pallets when a fully laden lift ascended from below.

The lift rose from the shaft, water streaming from its sloping sides. It was shaped like a diamond, with powerful engines positioned in either tip that hauled it up the thick cable. It came to a grinding rest, and steam and smoke spewed from the engines as they powered down. The sides of the pressurised, octagonal lift hissed as they slid upwards, exposing the expansive interior.

The lift was spartan, consisting of a single grilled, open floor-space where cargo could be loaded, with a barricaded area around the thick cable that spooled through its centre. In effect, the lift was like a massive bead through which the thick cable was threaded, and its interior, though the ceiling was low, was large enough to house half a tank company. Its sides were thickly armoured to withstand the intense pressure of deep sea

'Sabtec, Namar-sin,' said Marduk. The two named champions snapped to attention. 'You and your squads are to stay behind, to hold this position. Khalaxis, you and your brethren will join me, Burias and the Anointed for the descent.'

'You heard the First Acolyte,' barked Kol Badar. 'Let's get this done. Move out.'

The chosen warriors stamped forward into the expansive interior of the lift. Buzzing strips of glow lights hung from the roof of the lift. More than half of them were dark, but the flickering remainder lit the space with a dim, unnatural light.

'Darioq-Grendh'al,' said Marduk, his voice commanding, 'come.'

Impelled by the power in the First Acolyte's voice, the magos stepped forward obediently.

Marduk slammed his fist down onto a large button on the lift's command console, and the sides of the lift began to close, venting steam.

'May the gods be with you,' said Sabtec, bowing his head as the doors slid shut.

'Oh, but they are,' said Marduk.

Burias tensed, sniffing the air as an unusual scent reached his nostrils. It was the same odd scent that he had registered just before the dark eldar attack in the tunnels. His every sense alert for danger, he registered a flicker of movement outside the lift.

He roared a warning, but his cry was lost as the lift doors sealed shut.

CHAPTER TEN

Sabtec and Namar-sin watched as the lift descended into darkness down the abyssal shaft in the floor. Neither of them had heard Burias's cry of warning, and neither of them noticed the shadowy figure crawling headfirst down one of the hanging chains ten metres above their heads.

The black figure dropped soundlessly from above, twisting in the air like a gymnast and landing in a crouch, with one foot on each of Namar-sin's shoulders and one hand steadying itself on the top of his helmet. Before the sergeant-champion could react, the shadowy creature punched a blade through the back of his neck, severing the vertebrae. Its serrated tip emerged from the front of his throat, the monomolecular blade sliding through his gorget as if it were made of paper.

The Word Bearer champion fell soundlessly, blood spurting from the fatal wound as the blade was retracted. Sabtec bellowed a warning as he lifted his bolter. The shadowy creature, its skin as black as pitch and with glowing runes cut into its flesh, sprung from the dying Word Bearers champion's shoulders, throwing itself into a back flip even as Sabtec began to fire.

The explosive-tipped bolt-rounds passed straight through the creature as it became as ethereal as smoke, even as Namar-sin fell face-first to the floor, dead.

Sabtec lost sight of the murderous eldar and threw himself into a roll as he felt a second presence materialise behind him. A blade slashed the air where he had been standing a fraction of a second earlier, and he came up firing. Again, his bolt-rounds found no target.

Shouts and screams echoed through the lift bay, accompanied by the percussive barking of bolt weapons as more of the ghostly attackers materialised, dropping from overhead and emerging from shadows that had been empty moments before.

Moving faster than he could track, one of the insubstantial attackers darted around Sabtec, a fraction of a second in front of his coughing bolter, and the Word Bearer backed up a step, attempting to put some extra space between him and his ethereal attacker.

The creature darted forwards, dissipating into mist as Sabtec fired upon it. It re-formed just to his left, and he swung his bolter towards it. A blade slashed down in a diagonal arc, slicing the holy weapon in two, and a second blade stabbed towards Sabtec's throat. He swayed aside from the attack, but such was its speed that it still gouged a line across the faceplate of his helmet. Dropping his useless bolter, he grabbed his attacker's slim arm. Feeling solid armour and flesh beneath his grasp, he hurled his attacker away from him, sending it spinning through the air, and drew his sword from his scabbard.

'Thirteen!' he roared, bellowing the rallying cry that would bring the warriors of his coterie together.

Thumbing its activation glyph, Sabtec brought his sword humming to life. The metre-and-a-half blade gleamed as a sudden wave of energy raced up its length, and he swung it around in a glittering arc to deflect a dark blade that sang towards his groin. The blade severed the attacker's hand at the wrist, and the eldar warrior gave out a hiss of pain before becoming one with the shadows once more.

'Thirteen!' roared Sabtec again, breaking into a run towards the bulk of his coterie, which was fighting its way towards him through the confusing blur of darting shadows.

'Twenty-third, form up on me,' he roared, seeing Namar-sin's warriors becoming isolated and surrounded.

Even as he closed with his warriors of the 13th coterie, he saw one of them hamstrung by a slashing blade from behind and fall. Instantly, a trio of shadows materialised around the fallen warrior, looming like shades of death over him, and they dragged him backwards.

One of the black-skinned eldar warriors made a slashing motion with its hand that parted the substance of the air, cutting aside the veil between real space and beyond. In an instant, the fallen warrior was bundled through the rent in reality, which sealed up behind him as if it had never been.

Sabtec slashed with his blade, keeping the darting shadows around him at bay. He focused on one of the creatures as it materialised behind another of his squad brothers, its slanted, milky white eyes focused on its prey.

Sabtec roared as he launched himself forwards and impaled the shadow eldar on his power sword, plunging the weapon into its throat.

Its blood danced upon the energised blade, spitting and jumping. Sabtec freed his weapon, slicing it out through the side of the eldar's neck. Its head flopped to the side, and it dropped to the ground. The glowing runes across its body blazed with sudden light, and then faded, smoking slightly, leaving just a shattered eldar corpse lying on the floor.

Having formed up, the 13th coterie fought back to back, protecting each other's vulnerable flanks. The enemy was coming at them from all directions, yet the warrior-brothers had fought alongside each other for countless centuries, and each could predict his brothers' movements with the understanding that came from a lifetime of shared battle.

Heavy bolter-rounds from one of the Havoc Space Marines of the 217th ripped a swathe through the shadows, tearing two of the eldar apart. A pair of blades punched into his back and he was dragged into another dark rift that swallowed him, closing off behind him.

Sabtec's 13th blazed away at the shadows, most of their shots missing their targets, but a few striking their attackers, blasting bloody chunks out of armour and flesh.

The attack ceased as quickly as it had started as first one of the mandrakes stepped into shadow and was gone, and then another and another, until the Word Bearers were alone, smoke rising from the barrels of their boltguns, and steam venting from the cooling chambers of plasma weapons. The sudden silence was eerie, and Sabtec's breathing sounded loud in the confines of his helmet. The warriors of the 13th took the moment's respite to load their bolters, dropping empty clips to the floor.

Sabtec turned his head left and right, seeking the enemy, but it seemed they had truly gone. Still wary, he broke from the circle of his squad, and moved cautiously forward.

'Report,' he snapped.

Of 13th coterie, two members were dead and one was missing, taken by the dark eldar. Three of the surviving members were wounded, but not seriously. The 217th Havoc coterie had fared even worse, with three members dead, Namar-sin included, and two of their squad missing, leaving only three members remaining.

Sabtec swore.

'You three,' he said, stabbing a finger towards the remaining warriors of Namar-sin's coterie, 'you are 13th now. 217th is dead.'

The brother warriors bowed their heads in assent. It was a great honour to be taken into the hallowed 13th coterie, but they had fought as part of the 217th under Namar-sin for centuries.

Ammunition was running low, and the Word Bearers moved amongst their deceased kin, stripping them of weapons, grenades and clips. Sabtec knelt alongside each of the fallen warriors, speaking the oath of the departed over each in turn. With his combat knife, he carved an eight-pointed star into the forehead of each warrior, solemnly intoning the ritualised words, and daubed their eyelids with blood.

Kneeling over the corpse of Namar-sin, Sabtec removed his helmet, and placed it on the floor alongside his fallen brother. Then, he reverently lifted one of the champion's hands up, and stripped it of its gauntlet. Cradling the warrior's meaty fist in one hand, he reached again for his knife, and began to saw through the champion's fingers, using the serrated edge of his blade.

After hacking through each of the digits in turn, he tossed a severed finger to each of the members of Namar-sin's coterie. He kept one for himself, for Namar-sin had been his battle-brother since the Great Crusade, and he had respected the warrior greatly, and valued his comradeship.

He began to strip his battle-brother's body, removing his shoulder plates and placing them carefully at his side, before moving onto his gorget and outer chest plates, removing each piece carefully and reverently. The other members of his squad stood by solemnly.

He pulled the breastplate away with a sucking sound, taking with it the outer layer of skin that had long fused with the armour.

The flesh of Namar-sin's broad torso was heavily muscled, and the tissue of that muscle glistened wetly. With a deft movement, Sabtec sliced a deep cut from the breastbone to the navel. Inserting his hand into the cut, he searched around in the chest cavity, groping behind the thick, fused ribcage. Grasping Namar-sin's motionless primary heart, he pulled it free, cutting it loose with his knife.

Sabtec stood and lifted the heart up in his bloody hands.

'Namar-sin was a mighty warrior and devoted brother of the true word,' said Sabtec. 'We mourn his passing, yet rejoice, for his soul has become as one with Chaos. In honour of his service in the name of Lorgar, we eat of his flesh, that he may live on with us as we continue the Long War without him, and that we may carry his strength with us, always.'

Lifting the heart to his mouth, Sabtec took a bite, ripping the flesh away with his teeth. Blood covered his chin, and he chewed the lump of flesh briefly before swallowing it. Then he stepped in front of the first of the three remaining warriors that had belonged to Namar-sin's coterie, offering the heart.

MARDUK STARED THROUGH the thirty-centimetre thick porthole into the inky blackness beyond as the lift continued to power its way down into the stygian depths of the ocean. Little could be seen apart from occasional bubbles of expanding gas, and the visage of his skull helmet was reflected back at him, distorted in the curved therma-glass.

'There is no going back now; we have not the time. I feel the threads of fate weaving together. The time of the completion of this... necessary task, draws close,' said Marduk with a hint of impatience and irritation.

'Sabtec and Namar-sin are veterans. They can look after themselves.'

The lift strained and creaked alarmingly as the building pressure of the water outside pressed in. The thick metal plates of the hull, supported by countless brackets and thick bolted girders, flexed inwards, groaning like a beast in torment.

The lift had descended at a steady rate, down the shaft carved from solid ice. The rate of descent slowed as they reached the lower crust of the ice and plunged into the sea, before increasing in speed once more as they sank further into the icy depths. They were some four thousand metres below the surface, nearing halfway to the ocean floor.

Burias was pacing back and forth like a caged animal, glaring hatefully at the bulging hull as if daring it to give way.

'Be calm, icon bearer,' snapped Marduk, turning away from the porthole. 'Your restlessness is distracting.'

Marduk could feel Burias's impatience like a living thing, intruding on his spirit.

'What is the matter with you?' asked Marduk in irritation.

'I am envious,' said Burias, pausing in his pacing for a moment, flashing Marduk a dark glance. 'I had wished to fight the eldar again. I wish to test my speed against them.'

'You sound like a spoilt child,' spat Marduk. 'Recite the Lacrimosa. Begin at verse eighty-nine. It will calm your nerves.'

Burias glowered at Marduk.

'Eighty-nine?' he said, furrowing his brow.

'*And when the accused are confounded and confined to flames of woe, rejoice and call upon Me, your saviour,*' he quoted.

'The Lacrimosa has always been a favourite of yours, hasn't it, brother?' asked Burias.

Marduk smiled. Alone amongst all the warriors of the Host, he tolerated Burias referring to him as brother, in honour of the blood-oaths that the pair had sworn aeons past, when they were both idealistic young pups, freshly blooded in battle. Nevertheless, Marduk allowed the icon bearer the honour only when they were alone, or out of earshot of the other warrior-brothers of the Host, for such familiarity was unfavourable, especially now that he was certain that his ambitions of becoming Dark Apostle were fated to be, at last, fulfilled.

A Dark Apostle must be aloof from his flock, a symbol of the undying faith of the holy word. He had learnt that from Jarulek, and it was, his arrogant master had taught him, part of the reason why the role of the Coryphaus was important. The Dark Apostle must be more than a warrior... he must be an inspiration, a saint, the holiest of disciples. He must be raised above the warriors of the Host, for the gods spoke through him. A Dark Apostle had no brothers except others of his rank, for it was deemed that familial relations within the Host humanised him too much, weakening the awe he was held in by his warriors. Such a thing led to a weakening of the strength of the Host, and a lessening of the faith.

'A Dark Apostle,' Jarulek had lectured him condescendingly, 'must be above reproach, above question. He cannot have close ties with the warriors of his flock. Your Coryphaus is your closest confidant, and your will is enacted through him. He is the bridge that spans the gap between the Dark Apostle and the Host.'

Marduk pushed the distracting, errant thoughts back, his mood darkening.

'The Lacrimosa brings me great calm,' said Marduk. 'It at once soothes my soul and rekindles my hatred.'

'I shall do as you suggest, brother,' said Burias. 'So long as Sabtec leaves a few for me, I guess I can wait.'

Another loud groan shuddered the lift, and Burias scowled.

Kol Badar stamped towards them, and the cordial companionship between Marduk and Burias evaporated. At once, they were no longer long-time friends and blood brothers; now they were once again First Acolyte and icon bearer.

'This lift is a relic,' remarked Kol Badar. 'If a fault in the hull appears, we will all be crushed to death. This is a foolish endeavour, an unnecessary risk.'

'Are you going senile in your dotage Coryphaus?' snapped Marduk. Burias sniggered. 'You are repeating yourself. Your protestations have been heard before, and duly noted. I don't care what you think. I am your leader now, and you will do as I wish.'

The Coryphaus's brow creased in anger.

'If a fault appears, then we are dead,' Marduk said, more calmly. 'Such would be the will of the gods, but I do not believe it will be so.'

'How can you be so sure?' asked Kol Badar.

'Have faith, Coryphaus,' said Marduk. 'Each of us is in our allotted place, as per the will of the gods. If it is our time to die, then so be it, but I do not think that it is. The gods have much more in store for me, of that I am certain.'

'And for me?' asked Burias.

Marduk shrugged.

'You speak as if all our actions are already predetermined,' growled Kol Badar.

'Are you so sure they are not?' countered Marduk. 'I have seen things in dream visions that have come to pass. Many amongst the Host have. Does such a thing not suggest that every decision that we think we make has not already been determined beforehand? A path set in front of us that we, try as we might to avoid our fate, are condemned to walk?'

'By that rationale, why should we strive for anything? Why should we seek to destroy our enemies, if the outcome has already been decided?' asked Burias.

'Don't be a fool, Burias,' said Marduk sharply. 'The gods help those that help themselves. If you were not going to try to defeat your enemies, then you were already fated to lose.'

'If what you suggest is correct, then this,' said Kol Badar, levelling his combi-bolter at Marduk's head, 'is the will of the gods?'

The Coryphaus's weapon system whined and clicked as fresh bolts were loaded into the firing chambers. Burias licked his lips, glancing between the First Acolyte and Kol Badar.

Behind them, kneeling in a tight circle with his squad, Khalaxis half-rose to his feet, but the heavy hand of one of the Anointed held him in place.

The sergeant-champion glowered up at the Terminator-armoured warrior, his rage building, but he relented and remained kneeling, watching the outcome of the confrontation.

Marduk took a step forward so that the twin barrels of the Coryphaus's weapon pressed against his forehead.

'Pull the trigger and find out,' said Marduk.

After a tense moment, Kol Badar bent his arm, removing the weapon from his superior's head, and stalked away angrily.

'What if he had pulled the trigger?' asked Burias quietly.

'Then I'd be dead,' said Marduk.

SINKING EVER DEEPER, the lift continued descending through the inky-black water. This was more of an abyss than the depths of deep space, thought Burias. At least there pin-pricks of light could be glimpsed, distant stars and coronas a hundred million light years distant. Here, the darkness was complete and all-consuming.

Still they descended. It felt like they had been descending for days, though it had been less than an hour, and Burias continued his restless pacing, stalking back and forth, clenching and unclenching his fists.

Khalaxis's squad knelt in a close circle around Marduk, who was in a half-trance, intoning from the unholy scriptures. The warriors of the Anointed stood in a second circle around the kneeling figures, the Coryphaus leading a morose counter-chant.

Of the warrior brethren, only Burias stood apart, for he could not calm his mind enough to be part of the communion.

Impatience knotted his stomach, and he snarled in frustration.

Burias stamped around the interior of the lift, slamming the butt of his icon into the grilled flooring with each step. The flickering lights above were irritating him with their incessant buzzing and for a moment he toyed with the notion of smashing them.

While other Astartes warriors within the Host took pleasure in creation, painstakingly copying the illuminated volumes of the Books of Lorgar into new volumes, labouring for weeks on end over each page, Burias had not the patience for such pursuits. He took pleasure in destruction, whether it was ripping apart a living creature and watching its life fade, or smashing apart the profane statues of the Imperium.

What worth was a hundred years of toil if a man could destroy it in seconds?

Thankfully, the Host was almost constantly at war. It was at times like these, however, when the enemy was so close, yet the thrill of battle was denied him, that his fury rose, clouding his mind and shattering his concentration.

He paced around the extent of the lift, until finally he saw a soft glow permeating up from below through the porthole windows.

In the distance below, the lights from the mining station were radiating up from the ocean floor.

It looked like some outpost station on a desolate asteroid or moon, with the blackness of space all around it. A broad, domed central hub, roughly the size of the largest galactic battleship, was rooted in the rock bed, surrounded by dozens of bulbous satellite outbuildings. Cylindrical, transparent corridors connected all the sub-structures to the main hub. Light, harsh and unnatural, spilled from the arterial tubes, and peering closely, Burias thought he could see vehicles and people moving through them, like tiny insects within an artificial environ-farm.

Burias rolled his shoulders and stretched the muscles of his neck.

'Finally,' he muttered.

PRESSURE GAUGES VENTED, equalising the compressed air within the lift with that of the mining facility. The sides of the lift slid aside with a clatter and water gushed down from above, slipping off the angled surfaces of the lift's hull, and draining away through the grates set in the floor. Darkness greeted them inside the mining facility, though an infrequent strobe of light sparked from severed cables hanging loose from the low ceiling.

The Word Bearers walked cautiously forward, stepping through the dripping water, weapons seeking targets. There were none.

Kol Badar's Anointed led the way, combi-bolters and repeater autocannon tracking from side to side.

The air was hot and humid, a far cry from the dry, gelid atmosphere on the planet's frozen surface.

'There is no one down here,' growled Kol Badar.

'There *are* people here,' said Burias. 'I saw them on the descent.'

The warriors drew towards the main entrance into the mining facility, an immense arched processional that led from the lift base to the main hub of the structure.

Marduk's eyes were drawn up above the archway. A massive figure had been roughly painted onto the plascrete wall, like a mural, though its workmanship was crude to say the least. A low hiss escaped his lips.

'What is it?' asked Burias, his eyes wide. 'A daemon? Are these miners cult worshippers?'

'No, it's not a daemon,' said Marduk, not taking his eyes from the primitive mural.

'You are sure?' asked Kol Badar, glowering upwards.

'I feel no touch of the warp here,' said Marduk. 'Worship of the great gods of the immaterium would leave a palpable trace, a lingering presence, but there is none. No, this is no daemon. I could command a daemon. There is no commanding *that*.'

The warriors of the Host shuffled uneasily.

A four-armed figure was daubed on the wall above the archway, painted in garish blues and purples. Two of its arms ended in claws, while the others ended in human-like hands. Its eyes were yellow and its mouth was wide, exposing a caricature of sharp teeth, painted as simple triangles and dripping with garish red paint representing blood. A long, stabbing tongue protruded from the toothy maw.

'I think your battle-lust will soon be sated, Burias,' said Marduk in a soft voice.

CHAPTER ELEVEN

'You want us to go in there?' asked Kol Badar flatly, looking in disdain at the maintenance submersibles bobbing slightly on the surface of the dark pool of water.

'This is the way that the explorator came; we must follow in his footsteps,' said Marduk evenly.

'That statement is categorically false, Marduk, First Acolyte of the Word Bearers Legion of Astartes, genetic descendant of the glorified Primarch Lorgar,' intoned Darioq-Grendh'al.

Marduk turned slowly towards the daemonically infused magos, glowering within his skull-faced helmet.

'What?' he said in a low, dangerous voice.

'Repeat: "This is the way that the explorator came; we must follow in his footsteps" is categorically false,' said the magos.

Marduk licked his lips. If he did not feel like he had such control over the daemon inhabiting Darioq's body, he would think that the magos was being wilfully obtuse.

'What is incorrect about that statement?' asked Marduk slowly.

'Explorator First Class Daenae,' said Magos Darioq in his monotone voice, 'originally of the Konor Adeptus Mechanicus research world of UL01.02, assigned to c14.8.87.i, Perdus Skylla, for recon/salvage of the Dvorak-class interstellar freighter *Flames of Perdition*, which reappeared within Segmentum Tempestus in 942.M41 and crashed onto the surface of c14.8.87.i, Perdus Skylla, in 944.M41 after being missing presumed lost in a warp storm anomaly xi.024.396 in 432.M35, is of the female gender.'

Marduk blinked.

'Well I am certainly glad that we got that cleared up,' he said in a deadpan voice.

'I am pleased to have caused you gratification, Marduk, First–' began the magos, but Marduk held up a hand to stop him.

'Enough,' he impelled, the word laced with the power of the warp, and the magos fell silent mid-sentence.

'Why don't we rip out his tongue?' suggested Burias. 'Or his speaker box, or whatever.'

'The thought had crossed my mind,' said Marduk, before turning back towards the line of docked submersibles.

'We are going in those,' he said to Kol Badar. 'No discussion.'

Though wary of possible attack and on edge having witnessed the profane mural upon entering the mining facility, they had encountered no resistance as they penetrated deeper into the complex. They had come across several shrines that appeared to venerate the four-armed creature that Marduk recognised as xenos in origin, with crudely scrawled images of the beast in alcoves surrounded by offerings of tokens, charms and coins. He ordered these fanes destroyed, and the walls cleansed with bursts of promethium from flamer units.

Though they faced no resistance, a growing crowd of humans, miners it would seem, were shadowing their progress. At first, just a few figures were seen ghosting their steps, ducking into the shadows whenever warrior-brothers looked in their direction. As they continued onward they attracted more of a following, until hundreds of miners were following in their footsteps, though they still maintained a wary distance. Marduk felt their anger as the shrines were obliterated but, wisely, they did not dare to attempt to stop the actions of the Word Bearers.

Not wishing to be slowed, Marduk ordered the warrior-brothers to ignore the growing crowd that shadowed their progress, pressing on with an increasing sense of urgency.

The interstellar freighter *Flames of Perdition* had settled on the ocean bed some eight kilometres from the mining complex, and the last recorded location of the explorator he sought had been a docking station of submersible maintenance vehicles. Presumably, the explorator and her team had commandeered a flotilla of the craft to investigate the submerged ship, and so Marduk's progress had led here, to the very same dock.

Half a dozen submersibles were docked here, held in place by massive locking clamps that looked like giant, mechanical crab claws. Each of the submersibles was the size of a Land Raider and roughly spherical in shape, with an array of sensors protruding from forward hulls like the antennae of insects. A pair of mechanical arms were under-slung beneath their bulbous chassis, just visible in the dark water, and the monstrous insectoid limbs ended in powerful claws, industrial-sized welding tools and drills the length of two men.

Hundreds of onlookers watched from the shadows, crowding in around the gantries overlooking the holding pool of the dock. Marduk glimpsed hooded faces, eyes gleaming with feverish light and their skin an unhealthy, blue-tinged pallor. The tension in the crowd was palpable, and the warriors of the Host kept their weapons ready, yet the miners made no move to obstruct them.

Four-armed stick figures had been scratched into the circular boarding hatches in the sides of the submersibles, as well as phrases scrawled in what must have been the local Low Gothic dialect. It made little sense to Marduk, though he was schooled in dozens of Imperial dialects, but the general message could be understood. The scratching seemed to indicate that the submersibles were the 'carriages of the earthly gods', and that to enter them would bring enlightenment.

Marduk was repulsed by the idolatrous pseudo-religious sentiments, but he had not the time nor the inclination to 'educate' these wretches of their misguided beliefs. They would all be dead soon enough anyway.

'You still maintain these people are not daemon worshippers?' asked Kol Badar, tracing his finger along the deep gouges that formed the stick figure of a four-armed monster. It certainly did look daemonic, but Marduk was certain.

'I believe these people are held in the sway of xenos creatures,' he stated. 'A tyranid vanguard species, perhaps. I feel that there is some form of psychic control over these miners that draws the hive fleet like a lure. These deluded fools are worshipping a xenos creature, or a host of them, that will be the death of them.'

'Worshipping xenos as gods?' asked Khalaxis, his voice expressing his disgust.

Marduk nodded.

'A powerful foe, then,' said Burias with relish.

'Oh yes,' agreed Marduk. 'A powerful foe.'

MARDUK PEERED AT the small viewscreen. The submersible had no viewing portal; it was built to traverse the deepest abyssal channels of the ocean floor, and at extreme depths even the most heavily reinforced window would crumple beneath the tremendous pressure. In its stead, the grainy, black and white pict screen fed visual information from the sensor arrays on the exterior of the deep-sea vessel.

The interior of the submersible was cramped and hot, and the Word Bearers had needed to commandeer four of them to fit all of the warriors accompanying Marduk. The secondary locking gate on the underside of the sub-docks slid aside, and the four mining craft descended into the open water, powerful impeller motors whirring.

Burias sat at the controls of the craft, looking ludicrously large hunched over the dials and levers that controlled the pitch, speed, depth, direction and roll of the submersible. It was a simple control system akin to that of a shuttle, and he had little trouble becoming familiar with it. He grinned like a madman as he discovered the controls of the exterior robotic arms, and in the viewscreen Marduk could see the massive power-claw snapping, and the huge drill spinning, creating a small whirlpool of turbulence.

'Burias, it is not a toy,' said Marduk.

The submersible struck one of the underside legs of the mining facility, and Burias looked around at Marduk guiltily.

'Sorry,' he said, and stopped fooling around with the robotic arms to concentrate on piloting the craft. It wanted to turn to the left all the time, and he struggled with the controls to keep it steady.

It levelled out abruptly and swung around smoothly to port, its impeller motors whining as the submersible powered forwards. Burias swore.

'You seem to have got the hang of it,' said Marduk.

Burias held his hands up, removing them from the controls.

'I'm not controlling it,' he said. 'It is following an automated piloting route.'

He consulted the stream of data on a side-screen.

'It's taking us to the downed ship.'

They could do little but watch the grainy pict screens as the submersible carried them away from the mining facility, following its pre-determined route.

The ocean floor was jagged and uneven, and jutting spears of rock reared up before them, but the submersible traversed the terrain carefully, rising above the smaller outcrops, and accelerating beneath vast bridges of rock.

The undersea landscape was breathtaking, with vast cathedral-like spires of rock rising thousands of metres up into the dark water. Their vision slowly diminished the further they got away from the glow of the mining facility, until they could see only what was lit by the powerful spotlights on the prow of the submersible.

The lights of the other craft blinked, as all four of the submersibles travelled along the same line. As they passed beneath yet another towering arched causeway, they came upon a sheer drop-off, an undersea cliff that plunged down into blackness. It was down this vertical wall that the submersibles dropped, leaving trails of bubbles in their wake.

The sheer drop seemed to have no bottom. The chasm must have been over two kilometres in width, and it dropped away into utter darkness.

At last, something came into view, something immense.

'Gods of the ether,' swore Burias as they came upon the wreckage of the *Flame of Perdition*.

The Dvorak-class freighter was wedged between the walls of the chasm, its prow and stern ground into the sheer walls of the drop-off, bridging the bottomless gap.

As the submersibles ploughed on through the clear water, impeller engines whirring, the sheer size of the ship became apparent. It was one thing to see battle cruisers hanging in space where there were few reference points to give an indication of their sheer scale, but seeing this ship wedged firmly between the two distant sides of the chasm was breathtaking.

A portion of the lower stern looked as though it had been sheared away. It might have suffered the damage as it struck the mouth of the chasm, or it might have occurred thousands of years before the ship entered this sub-system, long before it had smashed through the ice crust of Perdus Skylla. According to Darioq-Grendh'al, the ship had been lost in a warp storm anomaly for some six and a half thousand years. Anything could have happened to it in that time.

Warp storms were notoriously unpredictable, and time and distance became blurred within their bounds. The *Flame of Perdition* might have been drifting through the nebulous warp storms for fifteen thousand years, twenty thousand years, thrown like a leaf on the wind through the ether. Or, equally as likely, it might have seemed to its crew to have been gone only a fraction of a second before it struck the surface of the frozen moon, and plunged into the oceanic depths.

During its time in the warp, and wherever else it may have emerged, the ship may have encountered any number of daemonic and xenos entities, and it was highly possible that some of the creatures remained onboard.

Apart from the shattered stern, the ship appeared to be in a remarkably complete state, and though Marduk feared that its interior had been flooded, there was every likelihood that at least the upper decks might still contain breathable air.

At such depth, and with its integrity compromised, what air did remain within the ship would have shrunk to a tiny fraction of its previous volume, but if any man-made structure could withstand the immense pressure as deep as this, it was a space-faring cruiser.

The submersibles ploughed inexorably towards the ship that grew ever larger in the small pict screen. As they drew closer, Marduk could see that the sides of the ship were scarred. Entire sections of its thick armour had bubbled, and other portions looked unnaturally smooth, like the skin of a burn victim, or as if they had been splashed with corrosive, high-grade acid.

The four submersibles drew towards the immense freighter, dipping down towards one of its gaping, water-filled hangar bays, still following an automated route.

'At least they seem to know where they are going,' said Marduk.

'Or they are leading us into a trap,' said Burias, angrily flicking switches and yanking on the controls.

The four deep-sea craft, dwarfed to insignificance by the sheer size of the *Flame of Perdition*, entered the cavernous hangar bay. It was a surreal experience to drift through the submerged bay, to pass by upturned shuttles that had clearly been tossed around the expansive hangar bay by the force of the impact with the ice, or the chasm sides. The four submersibles ghosted through the massive open space, leaving a swirling wake of turbulence behind them that blurred the water.

They began to ascend vertically, climbing up through the flooded levels of the ship, the automated controls carefully navigating them safely through the tangle of shattered girders and twisted metal.

The corpse of a man dressed in naval fatigues reared up in front of the submersible, filling the pict screen with its cadaverous rictus grin. The flesh was almost completely rotted from its bones and as the submersible bumped the corpse out of the way, one of its arms came loose. A host of wriggling eel-creatures squirmed from the cavity, thrashing madly, and then the corpse drifted out of sight.

As they continued to ascend, passing through flooded cargo bays and freight holds, they passed more corpses, all being slowly devoured. They powered along a wide corridor, the tilt that the ship had come to rest at forcing the submersible to travel at an obtuse angle.

They entered another area of the ship, and the submersibles bobbed to the surface of the water like corks. Automated pressurisation systems kicked into gear, slowly equalising with the outside pressure, and once the dials began to flash green, the access hatch began to release. It swung wide with a slight vacuum hiss, and Marduk stepped out into knee-deep water. The submersible had brought itself up to a raised gantry twenty metres above what appeared to be a holding area. Evidently, the upper portion of the ship was still structurally sound, and air had been trapped within it.

Marduk's helmet readouts gave him a flood of information and he saw that the air was unsafe for an unprotected human to breathe. Astartes warriors, with their superior, genhanced physiology, would probably last around an hour before they expired.

Marduk saw that the submersible he had emerged from was drawn up alongside half a dozen others.

'The explorer and her team's vessels, presumably,' said Kol Badar, stamping through the water to Marduk's side.

A massive doorway yawned behind them, leading further into the Imperial freighter. With no other obvious way of proceeding, Marduk led the warriors through its arched expanse.

They came upon a series of bulkheads, part of the latticework that subdivided the ship into distinct sections, adding strength to the whole and allowing areas of the ship to be isolated from each other in the event of hull breach.

Though there was no power within the ship – its plasma core reactors were clearly dead, or at least dormant – the bulkheads could be accessed manually. Kol Badar ripped one of them open with a wrench, half-expecting to be washed away by a flood of water. Once all the warriors had passed the bulkhead it was sealed behind them once more, and the next bulkhead opened. The ship beyond was dark, but the air was breathable without danger, and Marduk felt certain that this was the way that the explorator had taken.

He grinned within his helmet. He could almost feel the presence of the wretched devotee of the Machine-God. He had but to reach out to possess her.

'She is here, somewhere,' said Marduk. 'I know it.'

'She'd better be,' growled Kol Badar.

Warily, the warriors of the Host began to move further into the wrecked hulk that was the *Flame of Perdition*, weapons at the ready.

THEY HAD ADVANCED for over three hours, though in that time that had been forced to retrace their steps a dozen times as their way was blocked by shattered sections of the ship, or by bulkheads that led back into the flooded lower sections.

Burias's mood, previously buoyed by Marduk's optimism, had slowly soured as the sheer improbability of finding the explorator within this confusing maze was driven home. Kol Badar was right. The cursed worshipper of the profane Machine-God could be anywhere within the ship, *if* she were here at all. The ship was over two kilometres in length and consisted of almost fifty deck levels, depending on where within the ship one was located. In addition, a myriad of air ducts, sub-floor tunnels and inter-deck stowage vaults made the *Flame of Perdition* a veritable labyrinth, and despite the fact that perhaps seventy per cent of it was flooded and impassable, it would take a Herculean effort and incredible luck to locate a single individual within its confines.

'There is no such thing as luck,' Marduk snapped angrily, picking up the vagaries of the icon bearer's unfocused thoughts. This was a test of his faith, the First Acolyte reminded himself, ridding his thoughts of any shadow of doubt. The explorator would be delivered to him; it was the will of the gods. He had only to open himself up to the powers of the ether, and allow his earthly flesh to be guided.

'Keep moving,' said Marduk.

Kol Badar and two of his Anointed warriors were leading the advance, walking in single file, their massive shoulders sometimes scraping along the walls of the narrow, dark corridors.

Terminator armour had been originally constructed with brutal ship-to-ship boarding actions in mind, where the immense protection its heavy plates provided far outweighed its lack of speed and manoeuvrability. Within the flooded hulk, they were the obvious choice to lead the advance.

Khalaxis walked a pace behind them, a blinking auspex held before him, scanning for movement. The amount of interference from the ship was playing havoc with its accuracy, limiting its range to less than fifty metres. Anything moving within the range of its sweeps would appear as a blinking icon, but thus far only the other members of the Host had appeared on its blister screen.

Marduk walked with Burias in the centre of the group, along with the hulking form of Darioq-Grendh'al. Members of Khalaxis's coterie surrounded them, and the other two members of the Anointed brought up the rear.

They moved with well-practiced discipline. Despite no movement or heat signatures being picked up by the auspex, individual warriors peeled off to lay fields of over-watch down side corridors and into darkened rooms. Those behind moved past the sentinels, which filed back into line towards the rear. At the very back of the formation, the Anointed ensured that no enemy was able to approach unannounced. The formation was in constant movement, each warrior providing cover for his brethren before moving on, and though their progress was slow, they moved inexorably deeper into the hulk. It was standard practice in unknown, tight confines such as these, and centuries of drilled combat doctrine ensured that everyone knew his place.

The air within the ship was perfectly still, like the inside of a mausoleum, and the silence was oppressive. The darkness was all consuming, and with the utter absence of any form of light, even the enhanced vision of the Word Bearers was impaired. Their footsteps echoed painfully loudly along the empty corridors, and Marduk ground his sharp teeth in frustration, drawing blood. In the desolate silence of the hulk, sound travelled easily, and their quarry may already have heard their advance and moved deeper into the freighter.

The line of warriors emerged from a branching corridor into a room that might once have been a thriving workshop. Piles of mechanics and engine parts were strewn across the grilled, uneven flooring, and heavy machinery that would have taken a dozen power-lifter equipped servitors to shift lay overturned, like the discarded toys of an infant.

Half a dozen dark, uninviting corridors led from the room, as well as at least four closed, powered doors. Warriors had taken up position at each entrance, auto-sensors straining to locate any threat.

'Which way?' asked Kol Badar.

The Coryphaus's tone conveyed the warlord's thoughts clearly, without need for words, that this was a hopeless venture, but Marduk ignored his inference and paused, calming his breathing and closing his eyes.

He had entered this half-trance a dozen times already within the ship, searching for any residual warp trace that might suggest the explorator had come this way, but so far had found nothing. The soul of every living creature in the universe was a flaring beacon within the warp – those individuals who manifested latent psychic powers burning the most fiercely – and to those schooled in the occult teachings of the Word Bearer's priesthood, it was possible to perceive this soul glow in the material realm, sensing it even at distance.

Marduk strained to pick up anything, and had almost resigned himself to failure once more when he felt… something. It was very faint, like the fading heat image that surrounded a body an hour dead, but it was definitely there.

His eyes snapped open.

'There,' he said, pointing towards one of the corridors.

Without a word, the Word Bearers continued deeper into the *Flame of Perdition*.

Somewhere in the distance there was an echoing clang. It was impossible to gauge the distance of the sound, but to Marduk he felt it was confirmation of the whereabouts of the explorator.

'Quickly,' he urged.

THE ANOINTED WERE leading the way, their combi-bolters tracking for movement. Khalaxis's auspex throbbed with its steady light.

The remainder of the warriors followed single-file, weapons held at the ready.

They had been moving within the *Flame of Perdition* for over an hour, time enough to have walked its length twice over had their path not been so circuitous and slow. No further sound had been heard other than that one, distant echo, but Marduk was confident that his quarry was near.

The First Acolyte was lost in his thoughts when it happened.

A sheet metal wall panel punched inwards, crumpling like synthboard, and a blurred, dark shape leapt from the gaping hole in the wall. A clawed limb smashed into a warrior-brother's helmet, crumpling it like paper, and hot blood spurted, splashing across the wall.

Marduk saw a blur of limbs, an exoskeleton of dark chitin, and another warrior-brother was dead, claws tearing an arm from its socket and punching through a breastplate.

In the tight confines of the corridor, all was suddenly chaos, with warriors shouting and bolters barking.

The warrior in front of Marduk staggered backwards as the xenos creature turned its attention towards him, claws flashing. In an instant, his hand was severed at the wrist by the flashing claws, the bolt pistol in his hand still firing as it hit the ground, and Marduk stared into the venomous eyes of the deadly killer.

The creature was bipedal and hunched, its four arms hanging low from its armoured carapace, and its hypnotic eyes, glinting yellow slashes, set deep into a wide, pallid face. Marduk found himself ensnared by the power in those golden orbs, and for a second he was frozen in place, staring dumbly at the alien.

It pulled the disarmed warrior into a tight embrace, and its jaws closed around the Word Bearer's helmet.

Bolter fire struck the xenos creature from behind and a high-pitched, inhuman scream was ripped from its throat as chunks of chitin were blasted from its body, splattering Marduk with its vile, xenos blood.

The splatter of blood upon the skull-face of his helmet broke his hypnotic reverie, and Marduk lifted his bolt pistol. Even as his finger was squeezing the trigger, the xenos creature spun towards its assailant.

Marduk's shots took the creature in the back of the head, and its forehead exploded like a ruptured egg, spraying brain matter, blood and shards of skull, and it fell to the ground, dead, a tangle of alien limbs.

Khalaxis gave a warning shout as his auspex suddenly lit up with movement.

'Contact,' he shouted.

'Where?' bellowed Kol Badar.

'Everywhere!' came the frantic response.

Marduk swore, and stared down in disgusted fascination at the lifeless corpse of the xenos creature on the ground.

The exposed flesh of its head and hands was pallid, tinged slightly purple-blue, and its chitinous shell, like that of an insect's, was the colour of the night sky. It had been monstrously fast and strong, and the fact that one creature had managed to kill two veteran Astartes and injure another in mere seconds meant that this corridor was not a place Marduk wanted to be when more of them appeared.

'Move!' he hollered.

With a nod from the Coryphaus, the Anointed at the forefront of the group began advancing.

The Anointed in the rear began firing, their combi-bolters barking loudly as they fired at the wave of creatures surging at them from behind. Passing a side passage, Marduk looked to the left and began firing, seeing another of the creatures scuttling up the corridor towards him with sickening speed. He dropped it with a controlled burst from his bolt pistol.

The warriors at the front of the group halted, opening up with their weapon systems as more of the xenos creatures appeared.

'A powerful foe,' growled Burias-Drak'shal with relish, forming the words with some difficulty now that his mouth was filled with daemonic tusks and teeth.

Marduk shook his head, and swung to his right, blasting another of the xenos creatures.

A sheet of metal in the shadowy ceiling overhead smashed down in front of him, and another of the creature's leapt towards him, murderous claws flashing for his face.

Burias-Drak'shal leapt past Marduk and hit the creature in mid-air, driving it into the reinforced steel wall, which buckled inwards at the force of the blow. The possessed warrior and the deadly xenos creature were locked together as they slid to the floor, thrashing frantically, limbs entangled.

After a few frantic seconds of combat, the fight ended, Burias-Drak'shal pinning the creature's head to the wall with one of his thick talons. Pulling his talon free, the creature slumped to the ground. Burias looked up at Marduk, a feral grin plastered across his daemonic visage. His armour was hanging loose from his body in half a dozen places, and strips of flesh had been torn from him, but his pleasure was palpable.

'Good fight,' he said with some difficulty.

'Good fight,' said Marduk, with somewhat less enthusiasm.

The Anointed had picked up their pace again, blasting with their combi-bolters as they stamped forwards. Marduk heard the roar of a reaper autocannon firing on full auto, and the alien screams of dying xenos.

To Marduk's right, one of the 17th coterie was standing braced in an open doorway. A dozen xenos creatures were hurtling up the side-corridor towards him, their claws clicking like the legs of an insect scuttling along a metal table. The warrior's flamer roared, and they screamed and thrashed as they were engulfed in flaming promethium.

One of the creatures, its body wreathed in flame, leapt through the inferno, and ripped the warrior's head from his shoulders with one sweep of its claws. Marduk hacked his chainsword into the alien's neck, the teeth of the weapon whirring madly as they ripped through chitin and flesh, spraying blood in all directions, and the creature fell twitching to the ground, tongues of fire still burning across its body.

The corridor was a charnel house, promethium burning fiercely across the walls and floor, and the blackened corpses of the aliens were smoking ruins. Still, more of the creatures were leaping forwards, throwing themselves towards Marduk along the blackened hallway.

Snatching up the flamer from the lifeless hands of the headless warrior at his feet, Marduk squeezed the trigger, sending a wall of flame roaring down the corridor, lighting up the darkness and engulfing the wave of xenos creatures. They screamed as they died, chitin melting and eyes dripping down their blackened faces. Still, several of the creatures continued to claw their way towards him, and he sent another burst of flame shooting down the corridor.

The warriors of the Legion continued their advance for five minutes, being attacked by wave after wave of xenos assailants that hurtled headlong into their gunfire. They must have killed somewhere in the realms of thirty of the deadly creatures, ripping them apart with concentrated bursts of bolter fire and flame, though it was clear that they could not endure such a furious assault indefinitely.

It was impossible to gauge the number of the enemy in the shadowy confines, but the Word Bearers were already running low on ammunition.

Firing a final burst of flame behind them, Marduk discarded the flamer unit, dropping it to the ground, its promethium canister expended.

'Keep moving,' he barked as he drew his bolt pistol once more.

KOL BADAR HISSED as the claws of a xenos creatures sheared through one of his immense shoulder plates, gouging a deep wound in his flesh. Firing his combi-bolter at point blank range, explosive rounds tore through the thorax of the creature, ripping it in two. He smashed another alien predator away with a backhand sweep of his fist, the blow crushing bone and sending it reeling into the wall. Another creature leapt upon him, claws scraping deep furrows through his Terminator armour, and its jaws opened wide as its thick, muscular tongue darted towards his throat.

The Coryphaus closed his power talons around his xenos attacker's head, coruscating energy rippling up the long blades. With a twist, he ripped the alien's head from its shoulders, half a metre of its spinal column still attached, and flung it away from him before unloading with his combi-bolter once more, tearing another two aliens apart with concentrated bursts of fire. Warning icons flickered before his eyes as the chambers of his weapon emptied.

'Swap,' ordered the hulking Coryphaus, and he stepped to the side to allow the Anointed warrior behind him to pass.

The massive warrior stamped forwards to take up the position at the front of the formation, and his freshly loaded weapon roared.

'Keep moving,' ordered Kol Badar as he reloaded, feeding a fresh pair of ammunition belts into his weapon system and locking them into position. His weapon whined and pulled the first bolts into the firing chambers, and the warning icon within his helmet flashed green and disappeared.

The formation approached a cross-junction, the side-passages hidden from view by the dull metal corners.

'Khalaxis,' said Kol Badar. 'Grenades.'

The column paused briefly as the sergeant-champion of the 17th primed a pair of frag grenades.

'Fire in the hole!' he shouted, tossing the grenades forward. Kol Badar's optic stabilisers compensated for the sudden flash as the grenades exploded, dimming his vision so that the sudden flash did not blind him, and instantly the column was moving once more, the lead warriors stepping around the blind corners.

Lumps of flesh and severed xenos limbs had been scattered by the explosions, and Kol Badar began to fire as he picked up movement. The creatures had been lying in ambush for them, and he gunned a pair of them down as his auto-sensors flashed up targeting cross-hairs before his eyes.

Too late, he registered a flash of movement to his flank, and tried to bring his weapon to bear on the alien leaping towards him from the side, but the bulk of his Terminator armour slowed his movements.

A chainaxe slammed the creature into the ground, whirring teeth ripping it almost in two, its hot blood steaming as it poured over the floor panels, dripping down between the metal grid. Khalaxis kicked the corpse off the blade of his axe, his bolt pistol making another alien's head disappear in a red mist, and Kol Badar nodded his thanks to the veteran berserker.

'Advance to the east,' said Marduk through the vox network. 'Our quarry is near.'

Kol Badar took up the lead once more, stamping forward down the long corridor leading to the east, wary of attacks, but sighting no enemies. The corridor was a hundred metres long, and he felt a growing unease as he led the advance.

Behind him, the rest of the formation was following in his footsteps, the Anointed warrior in the rear walking backwards steadily, his combi-bolter firing almost constantly.

Stepping over ribbed pipes and cables that made his footing uneven, Kol Badar came upon a closed room, its walls thick with a tangle of pipes and insulated wiring. His combi-bolter tracked around the enclosed space, registering no threats, but he saw that there was no exit from the room bar a heavy blast-door on the far side.

Cursing, he moved swiftly towards the blast-door, but it was sealed shut. It had been welded fast, and deep gouges in its thick surface attested to its strength. Clearly, the xenos creatures had attempted to gain access through the door, but even their deadly claws, which had torn through power armour and even the vaunted suits of Terminator armour with contemptible ease seemed incapable of penetrating this thick bulkhead.

A chainfist would make short work of the bulkhead, but of his Anointed warriors, only Elimkhar was equipped with one of the weapons, and he was bringing up the rear.

Swinging his heavy, quad-tusked helmet around, the Coryphaus saw that the bulk of the warriors had already entered the room. Only two of Khalaxis's 17th coterie still stood, and he cursed again.

'You have led us into a dead end, First Acolyte,' barked Kol Badar.

'She is there,' said Marduk, staring resolutely towards the sealed bulkhead door.

Only Elimkhar was still moving down the long corridor, walking steadily backwards, his combi-bolter firing almost constantly. The corridor was filling with the xenos dead, but still more of the creatures were surging forwards, throwing themselves uncaring into the deadly fire.

'Brother Elimkhar, keep moving, we need your chainfist,' ordered Kol Badar, urging the Anointed warrior to hurry. 'Brother Akkar, be ready to clear the corridor.'

Brother Akkar nodded his acknowledgement of the order, and stepped towards the corridor, the heavy barrels of his reaper autocannon extending forwards beneath his arm.

Abruptly, Brother Elimkhar's weapon jammed, and he stared down at the suddenly silent, overheated bolter.

'Move!' roared Kol Badar, but the strength and speed of the xenos creatures was staggering, and the Anointed disappeared as a wave of enemies smashed over him, claws stabbing and rending. He was dead in an instant, and Kol Badar swore again.

The reaper autocannnon of the Anointed warrior-brother, Akkar, roared into life, the flame of the mighty weapon's muzzle flash lighting up the dark room as if it were daylight. Hundreds of shell casings poured from the heavy weapon as it unleashed its full power, and a constant stream of high calibre rounds ripped up the length of the corridor, shredding everything that they struck.

Scores of the aliens were ripped apart as the shells tore through them, the high-pitched screams of the dying aliens all but lost beneath the roaring of the autocannon's twin barrels.

'We must go back,' shouted Kol Badar over the roar of the heavy weapon. 'There is no way through here.'

'She is in there, I know it,' said Marduk hotly. 'There is no going back.'

'How do you propose to get through that?' snapped Kol Badar, gesturing with one of his powered talons towards the bulkhead.

Marduk stared at the door for a moment.

'Darioq-Grendh'al,' he ordered. 'Open it.'

'As you wish, Marduk, First Acolyte of the Word Bearers Legion, genetic descendant of the glorified Primarch Lorgar,' said the hulking figure of the magos, stepping forwards, his four mechanical servo arms unfolding from his back.

CHAPTER TWELVE

SOLON MARCABUS TRUDGED through the blinding snowstorm, leaning into the relentless winds that threatened to knock him to the ground with every gust. He stumbled as he stepped into a small drift, sinking up to his knees. It took all his effort to haul himself out, and he lay on his back for a moment, catching his breath.

His eyelids flickered and closed as his breathing steadied. It would be so easy just to drift away, to give in to exhaustion. He knew that to fall asleep out here unprotected was to die, but he almost didn't care anymore. He would just close his eyes for a few minutes.

It had been almost a full day since they had left the dead husk of the crawler behind. It had not been an easy decision to try to make the starport on foot, for their chance of success was minimal, but it was better than waiting for what the boy called *ghosts* to return. He was jolted from his micro-sleep as he felt a hand on his shoulder, shaking him, and he looked up at the boy, Dios, who was kneeling over him. Through the circular goggles set into the boy's oversized exposure suit hood, he saw the concern in Dios's eyes.

The boy's face was an unhealthy blue, and his eyes gleamed feverishly. Solon was impressed with the boy's stamina, and he realised that if he succumbed to the lure of sleep, he would not only be condemning himself to death; out here, lost in the wilderness of swirling snow, the boy would not last a day.

Nodding to the boy, Solon pushed himself painfully to his feet and continued to trudge on. Dios followed in his wake, walking through the furrow that Solon's feet made, one hand holding onto Solon's belt.

The boy's determination was driving Solon on, and he drew strength from Dios's indefatigable will to live. He gritted his teeth and cursed his momentary weakness. He knew that if the boy had not been with him, he would not have woken. He would have died out here but for the strength of a boy no more than ten years of age. Perhaps his body would have been buried beneath the snow, entombed within the ice of Perdus Skylla. Perhaps in a thousand years, erosion and wind may have exposed his preserved corpse, and someone would have wondered what had become of him. Why had this man been wandering the wastes, they might have asked.

Pushing such morbid thoughts from his mind, Solon concentrated on keeping moving, each painful step a challenge, but also a minor victory. *Just keep moving*, he told himself, and he repeated the phrase under his breath, like a mantra. *Just keep moving. One step at a time.*

Solon had no idea how long he had been walking when he realised that there was no longer a small hand grasping his belt. He turned around as quickly as the bulky exposure suit allowed him. Dios was no longer walking in his footsteps. The boy was nowhere in sight.

Cursing himself, Solon turned around in every direction, eyes straining to pierce the whitewash of billowing snow and fog all around him, desperately trying to sight the boy. He saw nothing.

Throwing his fatigue off, Solon began to backtrack, following the path he had cleared through the snow. It was not hard to follow, though the falling snow was already beginning to fill in his footsteps. In an hour, they would be gone.

He hurried back along his path, jogging heavily through the snow, stumbling several times, but pushing himself back to his feet, his fear for the boy's safety allowing him to plumb reserves of strength that he didn't know he had.

He had failed the boy, just as he had failed his son.

Despair lent him strength, and he pushed on, slogging through the mire of snow and ice, desperately squinting through the blinding blizzard.

At last, he saw a small, dark shape slumped in the snow, and he broke into a run as he drew towards it. It was covered in a light dusting of snow, and Solon prayed that he was not too late.

'You can't be dead,' said Solon desperately, and drawing near, he dropped to his knees before the figure of the boy. Rolling Dios over onto his front, he looked down into eyes that were half open and unfocused. Dark circles surrounded the boy's eyes, and his flesh was a sickly blue colour.

'No, no, no, no, no,' said Solon, feeling panicked and desperate.

He quickly erected his survival tent, pulling it loose from his thigh-pocket and unravelling it before turning it into the wind, which expanded it like a balloon. He dragged Dios's lifeless body into the cramped interior and ran a finger down the tent-flap, sealing it, before ripping loose the seals of the boy's hood, pulling it down away from his face.

Tearing his own suit away from his upper body, Solon pressed his fingers to the boy's throat. There was a pulse there, though it was weak and irregular, and he groaned in relief. Solon pulled off the insulating inner gloves from Dios's hands, and pulled off his own gloves with his teeth.

Ignoring the throbbing pain as feeling began to return to his fingers, Solon began rubbing warmth into Dios's hands. Blood was not circulating properly and the boy's fingertips were icy to the touch.

For an hour, Solon rubbed life back into the boy's hands and feet, until colour had returned to the digits, and his breathing had become steady. The temperature in the tent had risen sharply from their body-heat, and condensation had formed on its translucent walls.

Solon had set up his water distiller, and the trickle of purified water was now constant. He had filled both his water flasks, and the taste of the cold, fresh water on his tongue was like divine nectar. He had dribbled water into Dios's mouth, and had felt his spirits soar as the boy swallowed greedily.

At last, the boy had woken, and smiled weakly at Solon. Finally satisfied that the boy was out of immediate danger, Solon had allowed himself to fall into an exhausted slumber, as the wind battered the fragile tent outside.

Dios appeared as strong as ever when Solon woke, and the pair shared a small portion of the emergency ration bar that every exposure suit was equipped with. The dry protein ration was stale and old, but it tasted as fine as any meal Solon had ever eaten, though he was stringent in how much he allowed them to eat.

Water was not a problem. With his water distiller, and the amount of ice and snow around, they had an abundant supply. Food was another matter, however. This one ration bar was all they had, and though he portioned it out only sparingly, he knew that it would not last more than two days. Without food, they would become increasingly tired and sluggish, and they needed all the energy they had to make the long walk to the Phorcys starport.

In his heart, Solon knew that it was impossible, but as he saw Dios smile, the first smile he had seen on the boy, he felt rejuvenated and refreshed.

They had to dig themselves out of the tent, which was buried beneath five feet of snow, and Solon was exhausted as they clambered out onto the moon's icy surface, but his spirits were strangely high. He felt almost euphoric, and though he assumed it was a side effect of exhaustion and lack of nourishment, he didn't care at that moment.

Lifting the smiling Dios onto his shoulders, determined not to let the child out of sight, Solon began a new day of walking.

He would be damned if he allowed himself to succumb to fatigue before he saw the boy to safety.

'AMMUNITION THIRTY PER cent,' growled the Anointed warrior Akkar, registering the blinking icon that flashed before his eyes. Smoke rose from the twin barrels of the weapon, and he swung them before him, seeking a target.

Another wave of enemy creatures surged down the corridor, leaping the shattered remains of their kind, and Akkar depressed the thumb trigger of his heavy reaper autocannon once more, sending hundreds of high-calibre rounds into their line, ripping them apart without remorse.

'Weapon temperature peaking,' said Akkar.

'Understood,' said Kol Badar. Indicating with one of his glowing power talons, he organised the remaining warriors into a semicircle facing the corridor, and with a curt command ordered Akkar back from the corridor entrance.

The Anointed warrior stepped slowly backwards, still firing, the barrels of his high-velocity weapon glowing hot.

'Hold,' said Kol Badar, as Akkar's reaper fell silent. The hissing of the aliens was clearly audible in the sudden silence and clawed limbs clicked loudly on the corridor floor and walls.

'Hold,' repeated Kol Badar. The reaper autocannon's killing range was far in excess of the bolters and combi-bolters wielded by the other warriors, and conserving ammunition was becoming a serious issue.

'Now!' roared the Coryphaus as the first xenos creatures spilled from the corridor into the room, bounding forwards with inhuman speed. At his order, the warriors began firing, ripping the aliens apart. Within twenty seconds a score of the aliens were dead, and gore and blood splashed across the walls.

Marduk risked a glance behind him, seeing the hulking form of Darioq-Grendh'al working on the bulkhead. The lascutter on the tip of one of his servo-arms burned white hot as it seared through the reinforced, thirty-centimetre structure, but the magos was only half way around the bulkhead's circumference, and he growled in frustration before turning away and burying a bolt in another alien's brainpan.

The xenos attacked their position furiously, racing headlong towards the Word Bearers only to be shredded by the concentrated weight of fire. Still more of them poured into the room, and the pile of dead at the corridor entrance was growing.

'Have your Mechanicus lapdog hurry it up,' rumbled Kol Badar to Marduk. 'Our ammunition will not last forever.'

Marduk did not answer. No words would have hurried the methodical work of the magos, but he knew that the Coryphaus was right; if the enemy maintained this intensity in attack, they could not hold.

Even as the thought formed, one of the aliens reached the semicircular line of the Legion warriors, despite the weight of fire. Two of its arms were blown clear of its body by percussive blasts, but it did not drop, and it leapt forwards and drove its claws through the faceplate of a brother Space Marine's helmet, popping his skull like an overripe fruit.

The alien was cut from shoulder to hip by Khalaxis's roaring chainaxe, and then in half by the veteran's chainsword, retrieved from one of his fallen warriors, which he wielded in his other hand.

'Hold the line,' roared Kol Badar, but Marduk had seen Khalaxis's bloodlust dozens of times, and knew that the words would probably not penetrate the red haze that had descended over the warrior.

Alien blood splattered across his armour, Khalaxis roared as he leapt forwards into the no-man's land, spinning the pair of chain weapons around in a brutal arc that tore through the body of another alien as it was forced backwards by explosive bolt rounds.

Not wishing to be outdone by the blood-frenzied champion, Burias-Drak'shal leapt into the fray, slamming another of the aliens into the wall with a swing of his icon, his talons shearing the face from another.

The killing ground was gone, and firing into the melee risked hitting Khalaxis and the Icon Bearer, and so Marduk roared a deafening cry and hurled himself into the fray, his daemonic, heavy-bladed chainsword roaring.

The other warriors reacted instantly, throwing themselves forwards without thought for their own safety, firing their bolt pistols at point blank range into the melee and swinging their chainblades in murderous arcs.

Kol Badar stalked forwards, gunning down one of the creatures before swatting the head of another from its shoulders with a backhand sweep of his power talons. The Anointed advanced alongside the Coryphaus, power weapons humming with energy. One of them sent a white-hot gout of plasma shooting from his combi-weapon into the face of one genestealer, liquefying its flesh and rendering its bones to powder.

Still, the xenos creatures were fast beyond belief, and their strength was inhuman. Marduk fought with controlled rage, all the anger and tension of the last months fuelling every murderous stroke of his chainsword.

'This is not my time!' he roared. His bolt pistol clicked impotently as his last bolts were expended, and he threw it to the floor in disgust. Claws slashed across his chest plate, gouging deep rents through the ceramite armour, and tearing through his flesh. He grasped the daemon chainsword with two hands, allowing the daemon's hunger for blood to flow through him, and hacked the blade into the widespread maw of the alien as it lunged towards him.

Marduk carved the daemon weapon through alien teeth, muscle and flesh, spraying blood and fang-shards in all directions, and the creature's lower jaw was torn away as he wrenched the chainblade clear. Inhuman, gargling screams burst from its throat, and it thrashed around madly, spraying blood left and right, slashing and tearing at Marduk's armour.

His left shoulder plate was ripped away, shorn almost in two, and a tri-clawed talon dug into his neck, punching through his armour and flesh, grinding against his hyper-strengthened vertebrae. Blood pumped from the wound, and he reeled backwards from the pain-fuelled, frenzied attack of the alien. It came after him, but was driven into the ground by a hammer-blow from Kol Badar's power talons. The Coryphaus silenced its screams, crushing its skull with a heavy stamp of his foot.

Khalaxis booted another in the face with the flat of his foot, cracking its skull before shearing a pair of its arms away with a downward sweep of his chainaxe. The claws of its remaining arms ripped across his chest, crumpling his breastplate like paper and gouging a deep wound through his fused breastplate, but his blood frenzy drove him on, and he rammed his chainsword into its midsection, disembowelling it. Sickly purple and pinkish steaming organs flopped from the wound.

Brother Akkar swung his reaper autocannon like a club, smashing an alien away from him as it hurled itself at him, sending it crashing into a wall. As it struggled to right itself, sinuous limbs thrashing, the Anointed warrior tore it to shreds with a burst of fire from his heavy weapon, the high calibre rounds ripping through its body and puncturing the pipes and cables behind, which spewed steam into the blood-soaked room.

A genestealer hit the Anointed brother from behind, driving claws into either side of his helmet, and his skull was crushed to pulp.

Burias-Drak'shal gripped the writhing alien in his arms, pulling it away from Akkar, who was already dead and falling to his knees, and bit down on its elongated cranium, his fangs piercing its skull. Black blood squirted into his mouth as the creature died, and the possessed warrior hurled it away, his forked daemon-tongue lapping at the blood covering his lips and chin.

The attack was repulsed abruptly, though the throbbing auspex showed that another wave of the aliens was gathering further along the corridor. The remaining Word Bearers hastily reloaded their weapons and began to fire once more.

Pulling his hand away from his neck, Marduk stared at the bright red blood on his fingers and palm, and his anger surged. The blood began to bubble and spit on his gauntlet, and inside his helmet, Marduk's eyes turned black as the power of the warp surged through him, fuelled by the bloodshed and the fury of the warriors around him, and jolting his body with its suddenness and its power.

Feeling the building power, Burias-Drak'shal was driven to his knees, clasping his icon in both clawed hands, his head lowered. Blood ran from his ears, and his hands shook as infernal power coursed through the icon, which began to vibrate and smoke, giving off an acrid, sulphur-ous stench.

The sounds of weapons firing and Kol Badar bellowing orders faded from Marduk's consciousness as the fury of the Lord of Skulls entered him, and he struggled to contain the unrelenting waves of insane anger coursing through his body.

His muscles tensed to the point of bursting, veins bulging in his neck and arms, and he struggled to maintain control over the bloodthirsty urges that assailed him, urging him to lash out, unmindful of who he killed so long as the blood flowed. Blood pumped loudly through his veins, drowning out all sounds, and his vision was red and hazy. Slowly, he gained mastery over the surge of diabolic power, forcing it to submit to his will.

'Darr'kazar, Khor'Rhakath, Borr'mordhlal, Forgh'gazz'ar,' intoned Marduk, speaking the true names as they formed in his mind's eye. Daemonic voices roared in rage and hatred at his command over them, but Marduk cared not, and continued to recite the names as they came to him.

'Borgh'a'teth, Rhazazel, Skaman'dhor, Katharr'bosch,' said Marduk, completing the eight names that burnt red-hot within his mind's eye. He dropped to his knees and spread his arms out wide, throwing his head back as he spoke the words of summoning and binding.

Akkar's body, lying on the floor with its skull a bloody ruin, began to bloat, as if his innards were expanding exponentially, like a balloon filling with gas. His hermetically sealed Terminator armour groaned and strained, threatening to rupture like a canister of promethium hurled into hot coals. A tiny hairline fracture appeared in the centre of the breastplate and it quickly expanded outwards, until, with the sickening sound of cracking bone and tendon, the armour ripped apart, like the shell being peeled from a crustacean.

A shapeless blood-bag swelled from the fissure, flopping down onto the floor alongside the ruptured corpse. The veined skin of the amorphous mass pulsed and heaved as something struggled to be released from within, and the whole mass swelled as it increased in volume, growing larger with every passing moment.

A blade pierced the birth-sac, its surface blackened as if by fire and with glowing, infernal runes carved upon its surface. A daemon rose to its clawed feet as the skin of the blood-bag sloughed from its body.

The daemon was one of Khorne's minions, a foot soldier of the Lord of the Brazen Skull Throne, and its flesh was the colour of congealed blood. It uncurled from its hunched, foetal position as the last vestiges of its birth-sac dropped away, and it sucked in a deep breath, its first in the material realm.

Its limbs were long and scaled, and they rippled with sinuous muscle. Its head was elongated and bestial, and the fires of hell burned in its hate-filled serpent eyes. It hefted its immense blade in one hand as it staggered drunkenly for a moment, getting a feel for its new, physical incarnation. The runes upon the hellblade's blackened surface glowed with the heat of an inferno, and as the daemon steadied itself, becoming instantly accustomed to its new-found body and the rules of the material plane, it exhaled, breathing out a blast of sulphurous black smoke.

Then it roared, throwing its horned head back, the infernal sound ripping forth from deep within its tautly muscled chest with all the fury of its patron deity. It clenched its tall hellblade tightly, quivering in anticipation of the slaughter, and took in its surroundings with malevolent eyes.

It snarled, eyes narrowing as it looked upon the red-armoured figures of the Word Bearers. Its gaze met Burias-Drak'shal's, and its muscles tensed as it prepared to hurl itself at the possessed warrior, the runes upon its brazen hellblade glowing like lava.

Marduk's carefully weighted words stabbed at the daemon like intangible blades and it recoiled, swinging its heavy head towards the First Acolyte in hatred. It bared its teeth at its summoner, but Marduk's mastery over it was complete, his will binding it more effectively than chains, and though it fought against him with every fibre of its being, muscles straining, it was powerless against him.

There was always an element of risk involved in summoning the infernal denizens of the ether, and Marduk would normally only beseech the warp for aid when he had the time to prepare the correct rituals. The tiniest mispronunciation, a slip of concentration, could have catastrophic and eternally damning results, and yet, the rewards were often worth the risk.

Eight of these bloodletters stood over the shattered corpses that had borne them. Eight was the sacred number of the blood god Khorne, and the muscles of the daemons in echo of their patson twitched with barely restrained rage as they waited for a command.

'Well?' asked Marduk, his voice infused with power. 'Go.'

As one, the eight lesser daemons of Khorne threw themselves into the corridor, like rabid pack-dogs unleashed from their tethers. They roared their daemonic fury as they charged into the massing genestealers, their hellblades carving burning arcs through the air.

The aliens leapt to meet the daemons head on, talons ripping and tearing at bodies formed of the stuff of Chaos, alien speed and strength pitted against the diabolical fury of the god of battle and murder.

His limbs quivering with the residual power of the summoning, Marduk swung around and stalked towards Darioq-Grendh'al, who had almost completed cutting his way through the bulkhead.

With a barked order, infused with the essence of the immaterium, Marduk forced the defiled magos aside and slammed the flat of his boot into the bulkhead. It buckled under the blow, and another kick sent it smashing inwards.

Marduk's blood was up, and he stepped through the portal, brandishing his daemon blade, ready for anything.

A robed figure sat cross-legged on the floor, and it looked up as the First Acolyte stormed into the enclosed, darkened room.

Marduk crossed the distance in three steps, and grabbed the figure by the neck, lifting it a metre off the ground and slamming it back against the far wall.

'Tell me you are the one I seek, and you shall live to draw another breath,' said Marduk.

The figure's legs kicked uselessly in the air, and Marduk peered closely into its round, hairless face. Neural implants bedecked its bald head like feral ornamentation, and a fist-sized, cog-shaped badge of the Adeptus Mechanicus was fused to its forehead, puckering the skin.

The figure struggled to draw breath.

'Speak,' commanded Marduk. 'What is your name, dog?'

'Daenae,' came the gasped reply.

Marduk grinned within his skull-faced helmet. The figure's kohl rimmed eyes bulged, and feminine lips grimaced beneath his torturous grip. Marduk released his crushing hold, and the explorator crumpled to the floor at his feet.

'I do not know who you seek,' gasped the woman, her voice hoarse, 'but my name is Daenae, Explorator First Class Daenae of the Adeptus Mechanicus, and you are a traitor of the Imperium.'

'You have no idea how pleased I am to have found you, woman,' said Marduk.

EXPLORATOR DAENAE WAS of stocky build and considerable girth. Her waist was thick and strong, and her bosom heavy. Even had Marduk been more familiar with mortals, or cared, he would have been unable to gauge her age, for she had been extensively altered by juvenat surgery, one of the only vanities in which she indulged.

Her body was not augmented to nearly the degree of Darioq's, and what augmentation she had was relatively subtle. Both arms had been enhanced with mechanical bionics, though they had been fashioned such that their mechanised nature was not initially obvious, and she bore a slim-line power source on her back that was a fraction of the size and weight of the immense generator that Darioq required to power his servo-harness and largely mechanised frame.

Power couplings linked her backpack to her bulky forearm bracers, within which were stored her tools. Neural implants allowed her to access these tools with a thought, extending lascutters, data-spikes or power drills behind her fist as required.

Her eyes opened wide as the bulky form of Darioq-Grendh'al entered the room.

'Darioq?' she whispered hoarsely. 'By the blessings of the Omnissiah, is that you?'

'Darioq is still here,' said the magos, and Marduk smiled to see the explorator recoil from the voice, interlaced with the voice of the daemon Grendh'al.

'He is pleased to see you, Explorator First Class Daenae,' continued Darioq-Grendh'al, 'originally of the Konor Adeptus Mechanicus research world of UL01.02, assigned to c14.8.87.i, Perdus Skylla, for recon/salvage of the Dvorak-class interstellar freighter *Flames of Perdition*, which reappeared within Segmentum Tempestus in 942.M41 and crashed onto the surface of c14.8.87.i, Perdus Skylla, in 944.M41 after being missing presumed lost in warp storm anomaly xi.024.396 in 432.M35.'

'What have they done to you?' asked the explorator in revulsion.

'Enough,' interjected Marduk. 'I have it on the authority of the magos that you are in possession of knowledge that I would own.'

'What?' asked the explorator. 'Me? You think I have knowledge that great Darioq, my *master*, does not possess? Surely you are mistaken.'

Her voice fairly dripped with scorn.

'The knowledge I seek is in regard to a xenos artefact, an artefact taken from the necrontyr.'

'I know nothing about any xenos tech,' said the explorator emphatically. '*Nothing*.'

Marduk glowered at her, and then looked up at Darioq-Grendh'al.

'A direct answer, magos,' said the First Acolyte, empowering his voice with command. 'Does she have the key to unlock the device?

'She does,' said Darioq-Grendh'al.

'What?' asked the explorator. 'I don't know anything! He lies!'

'He cannot lie, not to me,' said Marduk. 'You are coming with us. Your secrets will be revealed. My chirurgeons can be *very* convincing when I need them to be.'

'I do not lie! I know nothing!' said the explorator fiercely as Marduk yanked her to her feet.

'We have to move,' said Kol Badar from the doorway.

'You are certain that she has what we need?' hissed Marduk to Darioq, shaking the explorator like a rag doll. 'I sense no lie in her words.'

'I am not lying,' said the explorator emphatically.

'Quiet,' said Marduk, twisting her arm sharply, snapping the bone.

'I am certain,' said Darioq-Grendh'al, 'but she speaks the truth.'

'You dare speak in riddles to me, magos?' growled Marduk.

'Explorator Daenae speaks the truth because she does not *know* that the knowledge is locked within her brain unit. Magos Darioq implanted it within her sub-dermal cortex without her knowledge, for safe-keeping, before he ejected her from his service, and we do not need to take her with us to extract it.'

Marduk's scowl changed to a smile.

'Ah, Darioq-Grendh'al,' he said, 'I think I might be starting to like you.'

CHAPTER THIRTEEN

THE BODY OF Explorator Daenae lay face down on the floor, in a pool of tepid blood. The top half of her head had been removed and cast aside and her skull cavity was empty.

'You are done?' asked Marduk impatiently.

Darioq-Grendh'al sealed the bell jar, which now held the explorator's brain, joining the others that emerged from the back of his hunched, perverted body. Viscous, purple-hued liquid filled the receptacle, and dozens of needle-like proboscis connectors pierced the brain.

'One moment, while the neural pathways connect,' said Darioq-Grendh'al. The gently waving mechadendrite tentacles attached to the corrupted magos's spine quivered, and the magos's head twitched to one side. Darioq-Grendh'al uttered a low, mechanical groan, and a shiver ran along what flesh remained of his once-human body as the explorator's brain connected.

A veritable tidal wave of information flooded through Darioq's consciousness as the neural connections fired. Memories, emotions and thoughts that were not his own flickered through his consciousness.

Neural pathways in the explorator's brain that had been dead for almost forty seconds during the transplant reconnected, and Darioq-Grendh'al plumbed their depths, driving towards the secrets that he had locked there decades earlier. Daemonic tendrils burrowed through the brain, re-forging the severed brainstem, and the knowledge was released in a wave of data.

Eight hundred years of knowledge deemed unfit for study by the

High-Magi of the Cult Mechanicus: necrontyr, hrudd, eldar, borrlean. Knowledge of xenos tech that had been lost for eight hundred years was recovered in an instant.

Unannounced, a yearning dredged from the locked away depths of his brain-core resurfaced, dragged from beyond self-imposed restraints: a yearning, a thirst, a *need* for knowledge, a yearning that had long been restrained, castigated and repressed within the constrictive bounds of the Adeptus Mechanicus.

The quest for knowledge and understanding would begin afresh, this time with willing, supportive patrons that would not tether him/them with rules, regulations, outdated morals and archaic beliefs.

'It is done,' said Darioq-Grendh'al.

'Good. You have what you need to continue your study of the Nexus Arrangement?' asked Marduk hungrily.

'It has all become clear to us,' agreed Darioq-Grendh'al. 'We have what is needed to unlock the xenos tech device.'

'Then let us get the hell off this damnable moon,' said Marduk.

KOL BADAR TOOK point, leading the bloodied warriors through the labyrinthine corridors of the *Flames of Perdition* towards their submersibles. The Word Bearers moved swiftly, not wishing to linger within the xenos-haunted wreck any longer than necessary.

Distant daemonic roars filtered through the darkened hallways as the bloodletters continued their frenzied rampage. Such summoned daemons had only a finite existence in the material plane. If their physical bodies were not killed, they might last a day before their substance unravelled. They were tools for the First Acolyte to use and discard as he saw fit, and they had served their purpose.

Twice, the Word Bearers were ambushed en route, genestealers launching blinding attacks that saw two more warriors injured, one sustaining a deep wound in his side that would have killed a mortal man, and the other, one of the last members of Khalaxis's coterie, had half his face ripped off. He stoically continued on, hurling aside his sundered helmet and gritting his teeth, refusing to succumb to the pain in front of such vaunted warriors as his champion, the Coryphaus and the First Acolyte. Marduk had nodded his respect to the warrior, who had puffed out his chest and struggled on, pushing through the pain, at the unexpected acknowledgement.

They had not encountered any enemy for more than fifteen minutes, and they picked up the pace as they closed on the location of the submersibles, keeping a wary eye on the throbbing blister-screen of their tainted auspex.

The *Flames of Perdition* shifted suddenly, the prow of the massive ship dropping as it tore loose from the submerged cliff. The entire ship tilted, and Marduk lost his footing as the floor tipped beneath him.

The Word Bearers were thrown to their left, smashing into the side wall of the passage as the immense freighter lurched. One of them tumbled down a side-corridor that was more like a vertical shaft, fingers scrabbling vainly for purchase. Marduk flailed for a handhold amidst the piping on the left wall, but found none, and began to slide down the corridor-shaft behind the power armoured brother Space Marine.

Burias-Drak'shal held out his icon, his other hand grasping onto a side-rail as other Word Bearers tumbled past. Marduk reached and grabbed the proffered icon, fingers locking around its barbed haft, and Burias-Drak'shal hauled him to safety. With a nod of thanks, Marduk pulled his body over the lip of the shaft, dragging himself forward on his belly.

The ship rolled onto its side, its nose still tipping, before it finally came to rest, settling into its new position.

Outside, rocks dislodged from the chasm walls by the immense weight of the freighter dropped down into the abyss, tumbling down into the darkness.

'Who have we lost?' growled Kol Badar, picking himself up from the ground, ripping his power talons from the wall, which had been the ceiling.

'Darioq-Grendh'al?' said Marduk in concern.

'He's here,' said Burias, pushing the daemon back within him as he picked himself up.

The corrupted magos's mechadendrites had shot outwards, clamping to walls like the legs of a spider, halting his fall.

'Rhamel is gone,' growled Khalaxis.

'Is he the only one?' asked Marduk.

'Yes,' said Kol Badar, looking around, 'but the ship could fall at any moment. We have to get out of here.'

'Where is he?' asked Marduk, looking down over the lip of the corridor-shaft. It extended some fifty metres before disappearing into the gloom that even his augmented sight could not penetrate.

Khalaxis cursed. 'The auspex is gone,' he said.

'Brother Rhamel?' asked Kol Badar through the inter-vox.

A static-filled voice came back, though it was distorted and patchy.

'...amel... broken arm... faulty...' came the response.

'His vox is damaged,' said Marduk.

'He is not getting up there with a broken arm,' said Burias, assessing the climb. 'You want me to go get him?'

'We don't have the time,' snapped Kol Badar.

Burias looked over at Marduk, who reluctantly nodded his head in agreement. Khalaxis stared down the vertical corridor, his hands clenched around the hilt of his chainaxe. Rhamel was Khalaxis's blood-brother, having come from the same cult-gang on Colchis before the hated Ultramarines' cyclonic torpedoes had destroyed the Word Bearers' home world ten thousand years earlier. Together, they had been amongst the last batch of aspirants taken from the obliterated world.

'Brother Rhamel,' said Kol Badar, 'proceed to the rendezvous point. We will meet you there. Repeat, proceed to the rendezvous point.'

'…cknowledged… phaus,' came the stilted reply.

'Come,' said Kol Badar to the rest of the dwindling group of warrior-brothers. 'If he makes it, he makes it. If not, then it is the will of the gods,' he said mockingly, with a nod towards Marduk.

Khalaxis stood stone still, looking down into the darkness.

'May the gods be with you, my brother,' said Khalaxis, before turning away.

The Word Bearers renewed their advance. With the ship on its side, the way they had come was foreign. What had been familiar was now strange, and where before they had advanced easily, they were now forced to half-climb through doorways that were horizontal, and half-leap across vertical corridors shafts that fell away below them.

The power armoured warrior-brothers leapt these expanses with ease, but the progress was not so easy for the bulky Terminator-armoured Anointed warriors, and Marduk ground his sharp teeth in frustration at their slow progress, drawing blood.

Burias ripped a pair of thick support girders from the walls, and dropped them over one of the expanses, and Kol Badar and his Anointed shuffled across them, though the girders strained beneath their weight.

Last to come was Darioq-Grendh'al, and Marduk swore.

'They will not take his weight,' hissed Kol Badar.

The corrupted magos, with his full servo-harness and plasma-core generator attached to his back, weighed almost twice as much as one of the Terminator-armoured Anointed warriors, and Marduk swore again, knowing that the Coryphaus was correct.

'We'll have to find another way round,' said Marduk, his voice terse with frustration.

'Wait,' said Burias, a smile playing on his lean face.

Marduk looked up to see the magos traversing the gap, his mechanical legs hanging beneath him in mid-air. Half-mechanical, half-fleshy mechadendrite tentacles punched through the panels in the ceiling, gripping tight as the corrupted magos's four immense servo-arms extended out to either side at full stretch, gripping the girders there. With a surprised barking laugh, Marduk watched as two of the servo-arms released their grips and reached forwards to grasp the girders further along, before releasing its other arms, and repeating the manoeuvre. Mechadendrites pulled free overhead before punching through the ceiling panels further along.

It was like watching some multi-armed, mechanical ape making its way through the treetops, and even Kol Badar was taken aback by the bizarre spectacle. The magos lowered himself safely to the floor once more, his daemon-eye glinting.

'Full of surprises,' said Marduk.

In the distance, they heard the percussive echoes of boltgun fire, and knew that the enemy had found Brother Rhamel. Khalaxis was tense and brooding, and the other warriors kept a respectful distance from the champion.

Marduk patted Khalaxis on the shoulder, and the Word Bearers pressed on in silence.

BROTHER RHAMEL PUMPED shot after shot into the never ending swarm of genestealers coming at him. He had five confirmed kills, the bodies of the xenos creatures lying motionless on the ground, but they were coming at him from two directions, and he knew that it was just a matter of time before they overwhelmed him. The red icon warning him of low ammunition had been flashing before his eyes for some time, and he watched with grim finality as the icons displaying his last rounds were slowly depleted.

His left arm hung useless at his side, broken in three places. Turning to the left, he shot another genestealer in the head, before swinging back to the right and taking another one high in the chest, the percussive blast hurling it backwards.

Squeezing the trigger once more, he fired the last of his bolts, and dropped his useless weapon to the ground. He tossed the last of his frag grenades down one of the corridors, turning his back to the resultant blast and unslinging his heavy blade from his waist.

The blast of the grenade knocked him forwards a step as flame rolled up the corridor at his back. Steadying himself, he passed the wide blade before him, knowing that the end was near.

A handful of genestealers were stalking towards him, their backs hunched and their eyes glittering hatefully. They moved slowly, readying to pounce, as if knowing that their prey was all but defenceless.

'Come on, you whoresons!' Rhamel roared as a fresh batch of combat drugs was injected into his body.

One of the xenos creatures hissed in response, ropes of saliva dripping from its fangs. Feeling movement behind him, Rhamel flicked a glance around, and saw another half a dozen of the genestealers creeping forwards at his flank.

'Come on! Finish me!' Rhamel bellowed, keeping both groups of aliens in his field of vision.

At some unspoken command, both groups leapt forwards, covering the distance with horrifying speed.

Rhamel swung in towards the first creature, his blade biting deep into its snarling face, cracking its skull. The genestealer wrenched its head to the side, almost dragging the blade from Rhamel's hand, but the Word Bearer ripped his sword clear and stabbed it into the open mouth of another genestealer as it lunged towards him.

He buried the blade deep in the creature's throat, and hot xenos blood bubbled from the wound. He had no time to drag his sword clear, however, before he was overwhelmed. He was smashed to the ground, losing his grip on his weapon, and he bellowed at the pain that shot through his broken arm.

Gritting his teeth, murmuring a final prayer to the gods of the ether, he waited for the killing blow to fall.

It never came.

One of the creatures was crouching over him, pinning him to the floor. Rhamel strained within its grasp, powerless against its strength. Its hot breath fogged the eye lenses of his helmet.

'Do it,' he roared in the genestealer's face. 'Kill me!'

The alien leant forward and a thick rope of drool dripped from its maw onto Rhamel's helmet. With a darting movement, the xenos creature stabbed its tongue towards his neck. The powerful proboscis punched through his armour and sank into his neck. It stung painfully, and Rhamel roared.

Then the creature pushed off him, scuttling backwards.

Rhamel staggered to his feet, scrabbling for his blade. He stood in a fighting crouch, ready for the creatures to revert back to their murderous nature and come at him once more, to rend him limb from limb, but they continued to back away from him, slipping into the darkness.

In an instant, they were gone, and Rhamel was left alone.

His vision swam, and the throbbing pain of his neck wound made him wince. He presumed that his body's enhanced metabolism was working hard to overcome whatever foul poison had been injected into him, and he fought the sudden lethargy that assailed him.

Whatever had been done to him, he felt certain that his enhanced metabolism would combat it. No poison could kill one of the Legion, and he was confident that the discomfort he was feeling would pass with time.

Giving no more thought to the genestealer's bizarre behaviour, Rhamel set off, loping down the eerily silent corridors at a kilometre-eating pace, working his way towards the rendezvous point.

MARDUK HEARD THE distant gunfire cease abruptly.

'He has become one with Chaos,' he said to Khalaxis, whose anger was palpable. 'He was a fine warrior. Honour his memory.'

Khalaxis nodded his head, though his anger still seethed within him like a living thing.

It took them the better part of an hour to reach the submersibles, for they were forced to take a different path than they had travelled before, clambering up steep inclines, sliding down others, and navigating vertical shafts.

The holding deck where they had left the submersibles had been tipped onto its side when the ship had slipped, and the interior was only vaguely familiar. Only the bobbing shapes of the submersibles confirmed that they had reached their goal, though the aquatic vessels had been tossed around when the ship had shifted. One of them was stranded out of the water, like a beached deep-sea mammal, lying on its side on a gantry that had buckled beneath its weight.

With a clipped order, Kol Badar sent Burias clambering over the wreckage, and he leapt into the air to grab a ladder that was positioned horizontally above them. The icon bearer climbed hand over hand across the expanse of dark water before dropping down onto the top of one of the submersibles. He landed in a steady crouch, and grinned across the open water towards the others before unscrewing its top hatch and dropping down into its interior.

Within moments, Burias had powered the vessel to life, its twin spotlights piercing the dark water like a pair of glowing eyes, and manoeuvred it towards the waiting warriors of the Host, its impeller engines creating a whirlpool of turbulence.

One by one, the warriors stepped onto the submersible, clambering into its belly, until just Marduk, Khalaxis and Darioq-Grendh'al remained.

'You next,' said Marduk, nodding towards the corrupted magos.

'A biological entity approaches,' said Darioq-Grendh'al, and both Marduk and Khalaxis were instantly alert, weapons raised as they sought a target.

'I see nothing,' hissed Khalaxis.

'There,' said Marduk, nodding towards a darkened side-passage. His finger tensed on the trigger of his bolt pistol, before he relaxed and holstered the weapon.

A shape solidified out of the darkness, staggering towards them.

'Rhamel,' laughed Khalaxis, 'you whoreson! You had me worried for a moment there.'

'Fine, brother,' replied Rhamel, his voice strained. 'I don't die easily.'

Khalaxis laughed and slapped his blood-brother on the shoulder, knocking him forward a step.

'Are you well, warrior-brother?' asked Marduk, eyes narrowing.

'I will be fine, First Acolyte,' Rhamel replied fiercely.

'Remove your helmet, warrior of Lorgar,' commanded Marduk.

Rhamel pulled his helmet clear, standing to attention before the First Acolyte. The flesh of his broad, ritually scarred face was pale and waxy, and deep rings circled eyes that glinted with a feverish light. A scabbed wound was located on his neck , and the skin around the puncture was tinged vaguely blue.

'You are… unwell?' asked Marduk. 'Poison?'

'Ovipositor impregnation,' intoned Darioq-Grendh'al.

'What is the machine speaking of?' asked Khalaxis.

'I don't know,' replied Marduk.

'Source: Magos Biologis Atticus Fane, Lectures of Xenos Bioligae, 872.M40, Consultation of Nicae, Tenebria, Q.389.V.IX. Ref.MBim274. ch.impttck. The xenos subject species, genus *Corporaptor*, observed implanting gene-template into body of host,' said Darioq-Grendh'al. 'Override of genetic coding documented. Bio-gene-splicing observed. Conclusion: *Corporaptor Hominis* overrides genetic makeup of host species, dominating upper cerebral cortex functions. Speculation: *Corporaptor Hominis* a vanguard species, locating and suppressing indigenous populations. Genetic corruption of local species suspected as a method of drawing a hive fleet to suitable prey-worlds.'

The three Word Bearers looked blankly at the corrupted magos.

'Potential reversal of implanted host species' gene-corruption: nil,' concluded Darioq-Grendh'al.

'Gene-corruption,' murmured Marduk.

'The machine babbles nonsense,' growled Khalaxis.

'Speak more clearly, Darioq-Grendh'al,' said Marduk, 'perhaps in words that we might understand.'

'It is believed that the genestealers infiltrate potential prey-worlds for the tyranid xenos species to feed upon,' intoned the magos. 'They infect the populace, and some believe that the collective control they exert over those bearing their genetic coding acts as a psychic beacon, drawing the organic hive fleets to those worlds where the beacon burns strongest.'

'And you say this… implant attack that Rhamel has suffered is altering his genetic coding?' asked Marduk.

'That is correct, master.'

'The bodies of the warriors of Lorgar are sacred temples, for in them we bear the mark of Lorgar. From his genome were we created,' said Marduk, 'and such a… corruption is an abomination.'

The First Acolyte looked at Rhamel, who grimaced as another wave of pain shot through him.

'You understand what must be done, Brother Rhamel,' said Marduk. It was a statement, not a question.

'I understand, my lord,' said Rhamel through gritted teeth, and the warrior dropped to his knees before the First Acolyte.

'What if the machine is wrong?' asked Khalaxis. 'Could not the chirurgeons on the *Infidus Diabolus* reverse this corruption?'

'The machine is not wrong, brother,' said Rhamel. 'I can feel it working within me, changing me. Let me pass with honour, my brother.'

The warrior closed his eyes tightly against the pain.

'I would ask that you do it, Khalaxis,' he hissed, pleadingly. 'Do this for me, my brother. Please.'

Khalaxis looked at Marduk, and the First Acolyte nodded his head grimly.

'It is only fitting,' said the First Acolyte.

'As you wish, my brother,' said Khalaxis, moving in front of the kneeling warrior.

Marduk passed the champion of the almost obliterated 17th coterie his bolt pistol, and the taller warrior took it in his hands with great reverence. Then he raised the bolt pistol and placed it against Rhamel's forehead.

'Into the darkness he strode,' quoted Marduk, from the Trials of the Covenant, 'into the flames of hell, with his head held high, and he smiled.'

'Be at peace,' said Khalaxis.

Rhamel smiled, looking up at Khalaxis with eyes shining with belief.

'I'll see you on the other side, my brother,' he said.

Then the bolt pistol bucked in Khalaxis's hand, and the back of Rhamel's head was obliterated, exploding outwards in a shower of gore.

Marduk dipped a finger in the blood and drew an eight-pointed star on Rhamel's forehead, the hole of the entry wound at its centre.

'What was that all about?' Burias asked in a low voice as they climbed into the submersible, eyeing the brooding Khalaxis.

'Nothing,' said Marduk. 'A brave warrior is dead. He will be mourned.'

CHAPTER FOURTEEN

A CROWD OF hooded cultists was waiting for them as the submersible entered the docking pool within the mining station, pushing in as Burias climbed out onto the wharf. Nevertheless, they kept their distance, wary of the immense red-armoured warrior and the potent aura of savagery around him.

The icon bearer snarled as he looked upon the press of humanity, and dropped onto the docking wharf, eyeing the crowd darkly. He allowed the change to come over him and took a menacing step forwards, enjoying the fear that made the people recoil. They did not run, however, and there were shouts and jeers from the masses. It was curious behaviour for mortals, and Burias could not understand it. Lesser beings always reacted to his presence with abject terror, so why did these ones not flee?

As the other Word Bearers emerged from the deep-sea scout/maintenance vehicle, one man pushed to the front of the crowd. His pale face was cowled and thin, and a servo-skull hovered near his shoulder. His eyes gleamed with feverish light.

This man studied the Word Bearers as they disembarked, an expression of outrage upon his face. The anger twisted his features so that he looked barely human at all.

'They have spilt the blood of our brood-fathers!' he bellowed, holding his arms up high. The billowing sleeves of his robe fell back at the movement, exposing pale arms pitted with plugs. Spiralling tattoos covered his flesh, oddly alien embryonic shapes that wrapped around his forearms. An angry roar rose from the gathered crowd that stepped forwards, faces twisting into visages of hatred.

'Someone shut him up,' said Marduk.

Kol Badar stepped towards the man, who stood defiant before him even though the people around him shrunk back from the Coryphaus's titanic frame.

'You have befouled the inner sanctum of the brood-fathers,' howled the man at Kol Badar as he approached. He came up barely to the Coryphaus's chest, but held his ground defiantly. 'And for that grave insult, you will be punished.'

'Who is going to punish me, little man?' asked Kol Badar. 'You?'

The man quivered in rage, and with a scream of hatred hurled himself at Kol Badar's immense figure, hands outstretched like claws.

Kol Badar wrapped his power talons around the man's head, and lifted him off his feet, which kicked uselessly a metre off the ground.

The crowd surged forwards, many drawing laspistols and cudgels from their robes, screaming in outrage.

Bemused, Kol Badar clenched his fist and there was an audible wet crunch as the man's skull was crushed. He hurled the body into the crowd.

There were hundreds of the frenzied cultists, but they were as nothing next to the warriors of the XVII Legion. None of the Word Bearers deigned to expend any of their precious ammunition upon the crowd, and they weighed in with chainswords and fists as the crowd surged in to surround them.

It was as if the crowd was in the grip of some kind of group hysteria, thought Marduk, eliminating all fear, and replacing it with this frenzied hatred. That was exactly what this was, he realised these people were the dupes of the xenos hive mind.

The butchery was over in minutes. Bodies lay sprawled across the floor, many of them maimed and brutalised almost beyond recognition, life fluids smearing the metal flooring with a thick gruel.

Pulling his blood-smeared helmet from his head, Marduk sucked in a deep breath, inhaling the hot, heady scent of death.

'Glory be,' he said, a rapturous smile upon his face.

GEARS GROANED AS the giant lift rose from the shaft, powerful engines hauling it up the immense chain connected to the mining station eight kilometres below. It came to a clanking rest, and steam vented from its engines. The sides of the diamond-shaped lift crashed open, and Sabtec bowed his head as the First Acolyte stepped from within, his armour caked in blood.

The champion lifted his gaze once more, eyes flicking over the blood-drenched warriors marching from within the lift. He raised an eyebrow as he saw that only half of the warriors that had accompanied Marduk returned.

The First Acolyte's gaze wandered, coming to rest on the corpse of a Legion warrior, lying on its back and with its arms crossed over his chest.

'Namar-sin?' asked Marduk.

Sabtec nodded his head.

'Report,' said Kol Badar as he stalked out of the lift.

'Dark eldar,' said Sabtec, 'though ones we have not fought before. They were shadow creatures, here and yet not here. Two brother warriors fell along with Namar-sin.'

'I do not see their bodies,' said Marduk.

'They were... taken, my lord,' said Sabtec.

'They were taken,' said Marduk flatly.

Sabtec stood with his head held high, looking resolutely forward.

'Yes, my lord,' he said.

'You allowed two warrior-brothers of Lorgar to be taken by eldar slavers?' snarled Kol Badar.

'They were taken while under my command, my lord, yes,' said Sabtec, 'and I will accept any punishment that my shame requires.'

'You offer no excuses, Sabtec?' asked Kol Badar.

'None, my lord,' said Sabtec. His voice betrayed no fear. He moved his gaze towards Marduk. 'If it would please you, First Acolyte, I shall take my own life for the shame I have brought upon the Host.'

'That will not be necessary, Sabtec,' said Marduk smoothly, 'though I am pleased at your devotion to the great cause. I shall have need of loyal warriors in the days to come.'

'The tyranid invasion could begin at any moment,' said Kol Badar. 'It might already be under way. We move out, now.'

Marduk was left alone with Kol Badar as the warriors of the Legion made ready to move out once more, their movements crisp and full of purpose.

'This world has claimed many warrior's lives,' said Kol Badar. 'Six Havocs of the 217th, including their champion, Namar-sin; two warriors of the 13th; six of Khalaxis's 17th, and two of my Anointed, all dead to secure the mind of a single mortal. I hope that it was worth it.'

'It will be,' said the First Acolyte.

'For the glory of Marduk?' sneered Kol Badar.

'For the glory of Lorgar. For the glory of the XVII Legion,' said Marduk, keeping his anger in check, though he felt the powers of Chaos stirring within him, feeding his desire to strike down the insubordinate Coryphaus.

Thoughts of blood filled his mind, and Marduk reached involuntarily for his blade. He saw Kol Badar's power talons twitch. With all his strength, Marduk pushed the hatred deep inside, where it would fester and grow strong, but where he could control it.

'Lead forth, oh mighty Kol Badar,' said Marduk, his voice thick with sarcasm.

* * *

THE WORD BEARERS moved out onto the ice, leaving the guild city, with its subterranean tunnels and claustrophobic chambers behind. They had not seen any further sign of the enemy, either Imperial or eldar. The storms wracking the landscape had not abated. If anything, it seemed that they had increased in intensity, furiously whipping ice and snow across the flows.

'How long?' asked Marduk. He spoke using his inter-vox rather than attempting to roar over the howling winds.

'Ten minutes,' said Kol Badar. 'Thirteenth, form a perimeter.'

Under Sabtec's crisp orders, the warriors of the 13th coterie, both old and new members, moved into position, weapons at the ready. It was probably an unnecessary precaution, for the chance of attack within the next ten minutes was unlikely, but having heard the reports of the dark eldar attacks from Sabtec, Kol Badar was taking no chances. Marduk also knew that it did the warriors good to have a duty, something to occupy them.

'The only certainty in a warrior's life is death,' was an old adage, though Marduk knew that such a statement was inherently false. For mortals, yes, death came for every soul eventually, but for one of the blessed warriors of Chaos, death was no certainty. Likely, but not certain. One could always be raised to daemonhood, and then one might live for all eternity, a demi-god worshipped in one's own right.

Something stirred within Marduk, and he felt the presence of Chaos writhing within him. He had long become used to the bizarre sensation, and it gave him comfort to know that he was not alone.

'Incoming!' roared Sabtec suddenly, his crusade-era helmet angled skywards.

There came a whistling sound overhead, and the warriors scattered as something large came hurtling down through the gale.

Marduk threw himself to the side as it came smashing down and struck the moon's surface just metres away, sending snow and chunks of ice flying into the air, and sending warriors of the Legion sprawling. The First Acolyte rolled smoothly, coming up to one knee with his bolt pistol in his hand.

Had it been an explosive shell, he would be dead, but the thing that had struck the ice was no shell, nor was it an orbital strike… at least not one of Imperial origins.

At first, Marduk thought it was an asteroid, but now he saw it was something fleshy, something organic.

It was like the giant seed pod of some fleshy fruit, and it had smashed a crater four metres deep and eight metres in diameter. Steam rose from it, and even as he watched, the tip of the roughly spherical shape peeled back, flopping down onto the ice, revealing a shapeless, quivering skin-sac the size of a Dreadnought.

Veins branched across this lump of living flesh, and shapes within strained to be released.

'What in the name of the true gods is that?' asked Burias curiously, stepping carefully towards the pulsating shape.

'Careful, icon bearer,' said Kol Badar.

The skin of the shape bulged and Marduk could make out the shape of a xenos head straining to escape.

'Tyranid,' he hissed, just as the first of the hive creatures burst from its embryonic birth sack. The death of the world has arrived, he thought.

Claws ripped through the film of skin and foul waters erupted from within, bio-fluids gushing out. Clouds of fog rose as the warm liquid melted through ice and snow.

Bolters began to fire, tearing gaping rents in the sac that gushed hot liquid. These amniotic fluids were pinkish and thick, like glutinous syrup. Inhuman screams burst from the spore as the bolts ripped through it.

Then the first of the creatures leapt from within, launching itself directly at Burias, four slender, bladed limbs poised to impale him. The blades of its two forelimbs were the length of swords, and though the creature was smaller than the genestealers they had encountered in the hulk on the ocean floor, the similarities were marked.

Burias swatted the creature aside with the holy icon of the Host, breaking its back, and it slid through the ice and snow, carving a furrow, until it came to a halt at Kol Badar's feet. It snarled up at the Coryphaus, struggling to stand on its powerful hind legs, which would not respond. It hissed, and tried to stab at Kol Badar, but the Coryphaus planted a bolt in its head that ended its struggles.

Marduk fired, his round screaming less than half a metre past Burias's head to detonate in the chest of another of the creatures as it scrambled from the crater. The rest of the Host opened fire as more of the creatures leapt from the spore, their weapons ripping the creatures apart, spraying sickly ichor across the snow.

Another mycetic spore screamed from the heavens and smashed into the ground ten metres away, and then another.

'How long?' asked Marduk, his bolt pistol bucking in his hands as he killed another of the leaping tyranid creatures.

'Five minutes,' said Kol Badar.

More of the creatures ripped free from their birth-sac as the sides of the spores flopped open, and they launched themselves at the Word Bearers, covering the distance over the snow in powerful leaps.

'Close ranks,' roared Kol Badar, and the Word Bearers formed a tight circle facing outwards, with Darioq-Grendh'al in the centre. Weapons barking, ripping the first of the leaping tyranids out of the air, smashing them backwards as their flesh and chitin was torn apart.

Another spore crashed down nearby, its impact spraying Marduk with snow and ice. One of the warrior-brothers sent a missile screaming from the launcher braced against his shoulder into the fleshy pod as its sides flopped heavily to the snow. The missile detonated inside the convulsing birth-sac, lighting it up from within for a moment, and the mass of creatures inside could be seen clearly through the skin of the sac enclosing them. Then the sides of the pod were ripped apart, and the high-pitched screams of the dying tyranids echoed through the gale as they were consumed in flame and shrapnel.

The missile launcher was tossed aside, its ammunition spent, and the warrior drew his bolt pistol and combat knife.

Marduk blasted the head of another creature into pulp and tracked his pistol skywards as one of the xenos creatures leapt high into the air. It descended towards him, sword-bladed arms lancing at him, and he fired. The bolt took the creature in the chest, passing through its chitinous exoskeleton before detonating, creating a head-sized crater of ruined flesh. Still it fell towards him, its brain not yet registering that it was dead, its every instinct willing it on to kill.

Marduk swiped it out of the air with his chainsword, ripping the toothed blade through the creature from neck to sternum, but one of its arms stabbed into his chest, biting through his power armour and embedding itself in his fused ribcage.

Slashing with his chainsword, Marduk sheared through the tyranid's elbow joint and it fell dead at his feet, its forelimb still protruding from his chest. He had no time to remove it, as a wave of the tyranids swarmed out of the storm.

Shouting a warning, Marduk held his fire until the tyranids were closer. The creatures from several of the spore-pods must have banded together, for this brood numbered perhaps thirty individual aliens. However, they did not move as individuals; they moved as one single living organism, with synchronicity that could never have been matched by even the best drilled veteran coterie of the Legion.

Without any obvious form of communication, the swarm of aliens turned as one, angling towards the Word Bearers, their movements precise and almost robotic. Marduk saw that these were a different sub-species from the leaping aliens, though they were similar.

More hunched, these ones scuttled forwards bearing what might have been projectile weapons in their forelimbs, though in truth the weapons were merely extensions of their limbs, fused to them, as much a part of the creature as the rest of their vile bodies.

Bolters and heavy weapons roared, ripping the first of the creatures apart in bloody explosions, but they continued scuttling forwards, oblivious or uncaring of their fallen. Their bio-weapons pulsed, the fleshy projectile tubes contracting sharply with peristalsis. Marduk felt something splatter across his left arm plates, and hissed in pain.

Looking down, he saw a mass of fleshy grubs boring through his ceramite vambrace and into his flesh, and he swatted frantically at them, trying to dislodge them. He squashed dozens of them as they scrabbled for purchase on his armour, but several of them were already too deep for him to easily remove, burrowing into the muscle of his forearm, squirming within his body as they feasted on his flesh.

Focusing his mind, he pushed away the pain and discomfort, and killed two of the tyranids with his pistol. He saw one of the 13th coterie fall to the ground, screaming in agony as a mass of writhing flesh-worms burrowed through his helmet, clogging his respirator and boring through the lenses covering his eyes, gnawing their way through his skull and into his brain.

A flamer roared, bathing the tyranid brood in burning promethium, and they screamed in inhuman torment as their bodies were consumed. Bolters tore through the survivors, but still more clambered over the bodies of the dead to fire their living ammunition into the tight circle of Word Bearers. More snow was kicked up as another spore slammed down into the ice.

Marduk ducked his head as a stream of beetles was spat towards him. Several wriggling bugs struck his right shoulder pad, painted black in mourning for Jarulek, but he squashed the voracious feeder creatures before they could bury themselves in his armour and flesh.

A second putrid stream of voracious organisms spat past Marduk to engulf Darioq-Grendh'al. An orb of energy appeared around the corrupted magos, and the coruscating electricity of the potent conversion field fried the tiny creatures.

The magos turned heavily towards its attacker as the flickering energy field disappeared, and Marduk sensed anger surge through the daemon inhabiting the ex-priest's flesh. Darioq-Grendh'al planted his feet, bracing himself as the two servo-arms over his back stabbed forwards, their forms blurring as they were altered by the power of the warp. Metal re-formed and a pair of fleshy tentacles joined with the servo-arms, forming a cable, part organic and part mineral, pulsing with energy.

A pair of incandescent beams roared from the re-formed servo-arms, and the power of Chaos screamed in Marduk's ears.

The beams struck the tyranids, and half a dozen of them were engulfed in an inferno, hissing and writhing as their flesh mutated. Tentacles tipped with chitinous barbs burst from within the tyranids, ripping through their flesh and thrashing out through eye-sockets and mouths, turning the xenos beings inside out. Within moments, all that remained of the tyranids struck by Darioq-Grendh'al's fire was a thrashing mass of tentacles.

'Impressive,' said Marduk with a smile as Darioq-Grendh'al's servo-arms moulded back to their usual form.

'Two minutes,' shouted Kol Badar as yet another spore-pod slammed down, crushing a handful of tyranids beneath its impact. This pod was much larger than the others, and powerful forms larger even than an Astartes warrior struggled to free themselves from within it.

'To the north-west, move!' roared Kol Badar as a trio of giant tyranid beasts ripped free of the skin of the large spore-pod and reared up to their full height – easily twice that of a normal man – and another brood of smaller creatures swarmed from the howling winds, angling towards the Word Bearers. More pods slammed down from the heavens.

'Move, Grendh'al,' said Marduk, impelling the creature with his voice of command, and though the daemon resisted him, its will was overpowered, and it reluctantly turned to do as it was bid.

The Word Bearers carved through the hordes of lesser tyranids like a spear through water, smashing them aside as they drove forwards. A warrior stumbled as maggot-like organisms splattered across his armour, acidic life-fluids melting through his armour plates and burning into his flesh. Marduk lifted the warrior back to his feet, supporting him with one arm as he fired.

Spotlights tore through the darkness and the swirling snow, and the hulking shapes of Land Raiders appeared through the whitewash of fog and ice. Incandescent lascannon beams stabbed from side-sponsons, scything through tyranid organisms that hurled themselves at the Word Bearers, symbiotic bio-weapons spitting. Heavy bolters scythed through dozens of the xenos beasts, ripping them apart with their high calibre rounds.

The Land Raiders came to a grinding halt before the warriors of the XVII Legion, growling like daemonic beasts, their hot breath steaming from exhaust stacks. The frontal assault ramps smashed down onto the ice, and the warriors of the XVII Legion stormed inside the gaping interiors of the immense steel beasts.

Sabtec relieved Marduk of the wounded warrior he was supporting. The warrior was reciting the Doxology of Revilement, focusing on the words to alleviate the pain of the bio-acid melting through his armour and flesh. As he passed the warrior into Sabtec's care, Marduk spun around standing in the door of the Land Raider as the last of the warriors of the Host stamped forwards.

The larger tyranid creatures they had seen clawing their way free of their spore-pod were stalking towards the Land Raiders, their tails thrashing. Each pair of upper arms ended in scything blades, and their secondary pairs of arms moulded into long-barrelled bio-cannons. A swarm of the lesser tyranids raced towards Marduk as the assault ramp began to close, and he fired into the pack, dropping two of them.

Lascannon beams made the air crackle with electrical energy as the twin-linked side-sponsons of the mighty Land Raiders fired, and one of the large tyranid creatures was vaporised. The other two lurched forwards, discharging their long-barrelled bio-weapons towards Marduk even as the swarming horde of lesser xenos raced towards him.

The bio-weapons ammunition splattered onto the assault ramp of the Land Raider as it rose, spraying acid across the thick metal that began to hiss and bubble. A drop splashed onto Marduk's chest plate, burning a hole through his armour and searing his flesh, but he ignored the wound and slashed with his chainsword as the lesser tyranids launched themselves onto the Land Raider's chassis.

Heavy bolter fire ripped two of them to shreds as the Land Raider lurched into reverse, but two of them hurled themselves through the closing aperture as the assault ramp hissed closed, and Marduk killed the first, impaling its head on his chainblade, the whirring teeth ripping its skull apart. Sabtec killed the second creature, slamming its bestial, xenos face into the side of the Land Raider again and again until it was an unrecognisable, bloody pulp.

More of the small tyranids scrabbled at the assault ramp as it closed, but then the assault ramp was sealed, severing several stabbing blade-arms that fell to the floor inside, leaking foul-smelling fluids.

Marduk slumped down into one of the seats, breathing hard.

Only then did he realise that he still had the bony blade-arm of one of the creatures protruding from his chest. He ripped it clear with a sharp movement, and tossed it to the floor alongside the pair of tyranid corpses.

The Doxology of Revilement was still being recited as Sabtec tore the melting breastplate from the warrior of his coterie who had been splashed with bio-acid, and the champion sprayed a black film over the wounds.

'First Acolyte,' said Kol Badar over a closed channel from the other Land Raider.

'Go ahead,' said Marduk.

'The tyranid invasion may have covered half this world already,' said the Coryphaus. 'I feel that it would be inadvisable to proceed to the drop-ship's location overland. We do not know the numbers of the xenos between here and there.'

'Agreed,' said Marduk.

'I suggest that we order the ship to launch, to meet us half way.'

'Understood. See that it is done,' said Marduk severing the connection.

Bloody and battered, Marduk pulled his helmet from his head and stowed it in the alcove above him.

At last they were leaving this doomed Imperial backwater planet, he thought, and he smiled, exposing his sharp teeth.

A month, maybe two, and he would be back on Sicarus, returning in glory.

The Land Raider rocked as tyranid bio-weapons struck its armoured hide, but still Marduk grinned.

Glory would be his.

CHAPTER FIFTEEN

DRACON ALITH DRAZJAER of the Black Heart Cabal strode down the dark corridor, his thin lips curled in distaste. He moved with the supple, arrogant grace of a born warrior. A pair of heavily armoured incubi bodyguards walked warily on either side of him, the sweeping blades of their punisher glaives lowered.

They passed dozens of cells, all crammed with wailing, wretched slaves, many of whom had already felt the ministrations of the haemonculus Rhakaeth, or soon would.

The wretched creatures were mostly human, but there were other lesser species packed into the crowded cells as well: tall, reptilian k'ith; kroot mercenaries; stony-faced demiurg; as well as eldar, either those of Drazjaer's dark kin that had fallen from his grace, warriors of his rivals, or his deluded craftworld cousins.

The cells closest to the haemonculus's operation chambers were filled with his experiments, and these blighted creatures filled the corridor with their sickly cries. Humans with their spines removed flopped impotently on the floors of cells, while others that had had their legs replaced with muscular arms whooped in insane rage, hurling themselves against the invisible barrier separating them from Drazjaer. They were thrown backwards as energy arced across the barrier, accompanied by the stink of ozone.

Other twisted monstrosities had insect-like eyes, more than one head, or random limbs sprouting from their bulbous stomachs. Some had leathery wings grafted to their backs, and others pulled themselves across the floor of their cells with flipper-like appendages where human hands had once been, their lower bodies shrunken and wasted, like the malformed legs of a foetus not yet reached its term.

421

Some of the abominations scratched at faces that were already torn to bloody ribbons, and all cried out for death. Still others flexed overgrown muscles, fan-like webs of skin opening up beneath their arms, while others appeared almost normal, with just minor enhancements, such as arms that ended in glittering blades, or had sharp ridges of bone running down their craniums.

A pair of Rhakaeth's grotesques guarded the door to the haemonculus's chambers: his altered ones, his companions, his twisted cortege; his more successful experiments. These eldar had come to the haemonculus willingly, desperate to experience new and varied sensations, and they had begged and backstabbed their way into Rhakaeth's favour in order to feel the touch of his razors.

One of the grotesques stood taller even than Drazjaer. Hundreds of quill-like spines had been surgically inserted into his flesh, running down his spine and across the backs of his arms. His mouth had been cut into a new form, a vertical slash bisecting his horizontal lips, and additional musculature added so that when it opened, its four corners peeled back independently. The abomination's eyes were those of some serpentine, alien species, and a dual pair of eyelids blinked as the grotesque looked towards the approaching dracon and his incubi. Its quills stood on end and began to shiver noisily. More spines flicked from within his forearms, and others slid forwards from the base of its palms.

The second of Rhakaeth's guards, a female eldar, was completely naked, though her flesh was covered in small metallic blue scales that shimmered and turned a dusky red as Drazjaer drew near. Her luscious, ruby lips parted and a forked tongue, pierced in a dozen places with metal studs, flicked out past sharpened teeth. The fingers of her left hand had been replaced with long knives, and parts of her body – and her companion's – bore scars and fresh wounds that had clearly been the result of her caresses.

Neither of the altered eldar warriors bore weapons, their enhanced bodies their instruments of death.

The incubi at Drazjaer's side levelled their glaives at the pair, and runes flickered with witch-light upon the blasters built into their sweeping tormentor helms. The potent weapons were neurally linked to the incubi's brain waves, and could be fired with a mere thought, leaving the warrior's hands free to wield their punisher glaives.

The grotesques hissed at the powerfully armoured incubi, the female creature flexing her fingers, and her male counterpart turning his upturned hands towards them. Drazjaer had seen that one fight before. It was capable of firing the spines from its palms, and the merest scratch of one of the quills would cause a slow and painful death. The haemonculus Rhakaeth had been particularly proud of that creation.

Drazjaer waved them aside with a languid, dismissive motion, and the pair of grotesques backed away from the portal, still hissing at the incubi.

'Stay here,' Drazjaer said to his bodyguards, in his soft, dangerous voice. The incubi bowed their helmeted heads in respect of his wishes and stood to attention, taking up a position opposite the grotesque bodyguards, the ruby-red crystal lenses, hiding their eyes, glittering menacingly.

Drazjaer strode into Rhakaeth's chambers, the bladed arcs of the door slicing closed behind him, and gazed around.

He avoided the haemonculus's private chambers whenever possible, and it had been some years since he had last set foot in this part of his ship.

The only light within the room was a dull, pulsing glow that emanated from the floor and ceiling, throbbing like the beat of Khaine's heart; Rhakaeth's eyes were particularly sensitive to bright lights. The walls of the circular chamber were smooth and the colour of dried blood and bladed stands atop which was spread a veritable cornucopia of curios and torturous implements hovered above the floor.

There was no obvious order to the mess of objects strewn across the levitating stands. The hollowed skulls of eldar, carved with runes, lay alongside blades covered in rust-like flecks of dried blood, jars filled with blinking organic creatures that squirmed within their confinement, and decomposing severed limbs and organs left to rot.

Drazjaer moved to one of the hovering stands and lifted up a cube the size of a child's skull. Its sides were covered in stretched, flayed eldar skin, and as he held it, faces began to push from within, straining to escape. They opened their mouths wide in silent cries of torment.

'That was a gift to me from my old master,' said a hollow voice, and Drazjaer turned to see his haemonculus, Rhakaeth, ghost into the room, his impossibly thin, skeletal frame seeming to glide across the floor. Blood was splashed across one emaciated cheek, shockingly bright on his monotone countenance.

The haemonculus folded his wasted arms across his chest, skeletal fingers covered in blood scratching idly at the emaciated flesh of his upper arms.

'Before you killed him?' asked Drazjaer.

'Indeed. It is a crucible. The soul-spirits of an entire seer-council of our brothers of Ulthwé are housed within it,' said Rhakaeth.

'It's very nice,' said Drazjaer, placing the cube back upon the hovering stand.

'But you did not come here to admire my collection,' said the haemonculus, 'you came here to pay witness to my work. Please, my lord, come through.'

Drazjaer followed him through to a side room and gazed upon the two bloodied bodies that were held aloft by a multi-legged mechanism, their limbs pierced by the blade-arms of the machine.

The two figures were immense, as tall as eldar, but easily three times the weight, their bodies bulked out with thick slabs of muscle. Blood was everywhere in the circular room. It had sprayed across the walls and ceiling, was pooling on the floor, and covered the bodies and the mechanical arms that pinned them in place.

The dark red armour plates of the mon-keigh were scattered across the floor. Drazjaer moved one of them with his foot. It was heavy and inflexible, a brutal and crude form of armour for a brutal and crude race.

Returning his gaze to the two human bodies impaled upon the bladed arms of the mechanical apparatus that held them, Drazjaer saw that one of them was clearly lifeless, and anger blossomed within him. What good were they to him if they were dead?

As if feeling his master's anger bloom, Rhakaeth stepped away from the dracon, putting the bodies between them. The eyes of the still living human flicked towards the dracon, fires of rage in his lidless orbs. The man's flesh had been stripped from his body, and his chest cavity was open to the air, organs pulsing within.

'My lord dracon–' Rhakaeth began in his deep, hollow voice, but Drazjaer cut him off.

'I told you to keep them alive,' the dracon said, his voice low and deadly.

'This one did not die as a result of my ministrations, my lord dracon,' said Rhakaeth. 'The mandrake, Ja'harael, delivered it half-dead. It was all that I could do to keep it alive for as long as I did.'

'Ja'harael. It's all Ja'harael's fault,' said Drazjaer, sneering. 'I've heard that before, from the snivelling sybarite rotting in your cells. I do not wish to hear any of your excuses, haemonculus.'

'Whether you wish to hear me or not, my lord dracon, I speak the truth,' said the haemonculus, his voice devoid of fear. Indeed, Drazjaer had rarely heard any emotion in his servant's voice.

'And this one?' asked Drazjaer, leaning over the massive form of the still living human creature. It pulled at its restraints, massive muscles bulging as it stared at him in hatred. The dracon was unmoved, and peered with interest inside the figure's exposed torso.

'Living, and strong, my lord dracon. The potency of its soul-essence is worth a hundred, a thousand of the lesser mon-keigh breed.'

Drazjaer licked his thin lips. He had already gathered almost ten thousand souls for his lord and master, the dark lord Asdrubael Vect, but this did not yet meet the extortionate tribute the high lord of the Black Heart cabal had demanded of his vassal.

When Vect had butchered the cabal leaders of the Bleeding Talons, the Vipers and the Void Serpents in one dark night, Drazjaer had been cast adrift, vulnerable, now that his lord had been slaughtered in the murderous plot. He had been forced to kneel before Asdrubael Vect in chains, and had been asked if he would submit to his rule, if he would join the Black Heart. Only once he had sworn his warriors to the Black Heart over the soulfires of *Gaggamel* did Vect lay down his terms.

Drazjaer's time was running short. The Great Devourer hive fleet would overrun the system within the day, and his harvest would be over, his tribute not yet fulfilled. There was no running from Asdrubael Vect. No matter where Drazjaer went, no matter how far from Commorragh he fled, Vect would find him.

However, if he could gather more of these enhanced mon-keigh, these *Space Marines*, he mighty yet gain Vect's favour. Perhaps the dark lord would even raise him to the exalted status of archon, in command of an entire slave-fleet.

'Their physical makeup is interesting,' the haemonculus was saying, 'clearly the result of gene-conditioning and surgical enhancement. It is offensively crude work, with little subtlety or grace, but I feel that I could harvest their organs to create a superior blend of eldar warrior.'

Drazjaer barely heard the sibilant hiss of Rhakaeth's voice, lost in his own thoughts of greed and desire.

'Do whatever pleases you, Rhakaeth,' he said. 'Just see that that one does not die. I believe that it is time to unleash Atherak and her wych cult upon the Imperial world.'

'The bitch's arrogance knows no bounds,' said the haemonculus.

'Indeed,' agreed Drazjaer. 'Let us see if her boastfulness is founded. Let us see if *she* can bring back more than two of these mon-keigh.'

'I will look forward to working upon more of these,' said the Rhakaeth, indicating the pair of altered humans strung up before him.

'Fine,' said Drazjaer, turning and striding from the haemonculus's chambers.

Outside, his incubi were still eyeing up the grotesque guards, and a third warrior had joined them, another of his sybarite captains.

'What is it?' asked Drazjaer.

'My lord dracon,' said the warrior, bowing. 'The traitor returns.'

SOLON MARCABUS KNEW that the end was near. They were running low on food, down to the last protein bar, and his strength was fading.

Dios seemed neither to tire nor despair, and he pressed on through the snow with grim determination while Solon often lagged behind, and it was Dios who rubbed warmth into Solon's frostbitten fingers and toes whenever they set up camp.

He was determined to see Dios on a shuttle away from Perdus Skylla, and though he had never been a pious man, Solon swore that he would devote his life to the Emperor if he only allowed the boy to survive this nightmare. Dios would have a future somewhere, on some distant planet, far from the threat of xenos incursions. Solon was fixated on the completion of what had become an epic pilgrimage towards the Phorcys spaceport, and he would fight to his dying breath to see the boy safely off-planet.

Dios could have the life that Solon's son had been denied.

The ice crunched beneath his laboured steps. He could barely feel his arm, and though it was a relief to be free of the throbbing pain of his wound, he knew that it was a bad sign.

He heard a sound like thunder rolling towards them, over the blinding gale, but he gave it little thought; just more bad weather heading in their direction he thought grimly. He kept plodding along through the snow, putting one foot in front of the other.

The sound got louder, and Dios cried out. Solon lifted his head to see the boy gesturing wildly into the air.

A shuttle roared out of the banks of billowing snow and ice, flying low and fast through the storm. It was hit with a blast of wind and dropped metres through the air as it was buffeted to the side, and for a moment Solon thought it was going to crash, but the pilot compensated and the shuttle righted itself, engines screaming. Solon waved his arms above his head, attempting vainly to get the attention of the pilot, hoping and praying that the shuttle would stop. It passed low overhead, blocking out all sounds of the wind, and Solon stared up in awe and amazement as the shuttle screamed past, making the ground shudder with the power of its engines.

Then the shuttle was past them, its retro-burners blazing with blue flame. Solon whipped his head around as the shuttle roared over their heads. He could feel the heat from the plasma-core engines even through his exposure suit, and he relished the almost forgotten sensation. Stabiliser burners fired on the underside of the shuttle, lifting it over an outcrop of ice. Dios was standing, staring, his eyes filled with wonder as he watched the shuttle disappear once more into the concealing storm.

Solon felt a sudden surge of hope. They had come for them! They *had* come looking for survivors! He was certain that he had sensed the shuttle slowing down. The pilot must have seen them!

'Hurry, Dios!' he shouted, filled with a sudden surge of energy, and he set off in pursuit of the shuttle, pounding through the snow and ice, his fatigue forgotten. They had come for them! They must have picked up the blinking distress beacon in Solon's exposure suit that he had activated as soon as the raiders, the ones that Dios called the ghosts, had departed.

Dios was falling behind, and Solon paused to wait for the boy to catch up, his heart thumping. Scooping the boy up in his arms, who whooped in excitement, Solon set off, pounding through the snow, running madly towards where the shuttle had disappeared.

Reality hit home like a punch in the guts. No one would be coming back. The shuttle was probably heading to Sholto guild to pick up rich merchants, or other high guilders of influence. No one would be coming to find an orphan and a lowly crawler mule.

He slowed his pace, feeling suddenly exhausted, and dropped Dios back down to the ground. The boy looked up at him in confusion. Solon avoided the boy's eye contact, hanging his head and putting his hands on his thighs, leaning forward as he strained to catch his breath.

Dios reached out to him, taking hold of his hand and urging him on. Solon angrily shook his hand free. Again, the boy reached for him, and Solon swatted his hand away.

'It's over, boy!' he shouted, suddenly enraged. 'Don't you get it? There is no salvation. No one is coming to help us! We are going to die out here, and no one is going to know. No one is going to care!'

Dios stared back at Solon blankly, and Solon fell forward to his hands and knees, tears welling in his eyes.

'No one is coming,' he said again, this time more softly as despair washed over him. 'No one is coming.'

Dios stepped alongside him, putting his arm around Solon's shoulders, and he felt all the tension and fear within him well up. The tears ran freely, and Solon was glad that the hood of his exposure suit hid them from the boy. After a few minutes, a calmness descended over Solon, and he took a deep breath.

He looked up at Dios, who was peering at him in concern, and he gave the boy a smile.

Solon pushed himself wearily to his feet and checked the digi-compass beneath a flap of canvas on his left arm, realigning himself with the direction of the Phorcys starport, which he guessed was still a day and half's hike away. Nodding to Dios, he set off again in that direction, but a tugging at his belt gave him pause.

Dios was gesturing in the direction that the shuttle had taken.

'No, Dios. It wasn't coming for us. I'm sorry, boy.'

Still, the orphan was insistent, gesturing more emphatically in the opposite direction that Solon had set off in.

With a sigh, he gave in, and turned back. Dios leapt forwards enthusiastically, grabbing hold of his hand and dragging him through the snow, into the billowing ice storm.

They had moved perhaps a kilometre through the snow when the wind changed direction, blowing the banks of fog and ice away to the west, leaving the view out in front suddenly clear. Solon could see further than he had done for months, and he marvelled at the display of colour that danced across the heavens.

It was called the Aurealis Skyllian, and it was said that the phenomenon occurred only under specific atmospheric conditions. Solon had seen it only twice before in his lifetime, once when he was a boy, a week after his father had died in a mining accident, and again on the first night he had spent on the foreign and terrifying ice crawlers, just after he had been expelled from the guild. Both times had been momentous occasions in his life, and this one would prove likewise, for there, on the ice, a kilometre away, lit up by the eerie, heavenly light in the dark sky overhead, was the shuttle.

It was settling on the ice flow, and Solon again felt his spirits soar. They *were* stopping for them! Even if they had not actually seen the two refugees tramping across the ice, it didn't matter. What mattered was that the shuttle was landing, and it was within their reach.

A desperate fear that the shuttle would leave again before they reached it filled Solon, and again he scooped up Dios in his arms, and began to plough his way through the snow.

Salvation had come, at last.

Thank the Emperor, thought Solon.

'The Idolator is inbound,' said Kol Badar's voice, 'touching down over the ridge to the north.'

'Good,' said Marduk.

The Land Raiders had outrun the downpour of xenos spores, and there had been no enemy contact for almost an hour. Nevertheless, sensors indicated that the waves of inbound spores were intensifying, and their spread widening.

'Be ready for disembarkation,' Marduk snapped at the warriors in the Land Raider. 'Two minutes and counting.'

CHAPTER SIXTEEN

'BARANOV,' SAID EUSTENOV, the pilot of the *Rapture*, 'they are pulling us in. Five minutes.'

The smuggler, rogue trader and sometimes blockade-runner leant forward over the back of his pilot, peering into the blackness of space ahead, on the shadow-side of the doomed planet Perdus Skylla. The sleek shape of the ship that the *Rapture* was to dock with could barely be seen, even at this distance, and he shook his head, marvelling at the technology that concealed it. It was merely a part of the surrounding darkness, though the bladed vales that protruded from its length like the fins of a fish gleamed sharply as the forward lights of the *Rapture* swept across them.

Patting the clearly nervous pilot on the shoulder, Baranov turned and stalked towards the rear compartment of his trading vessel, where members of the wealthy elite of Perdus Skylla were housed. He took a deep breath, gathering himself, and wiped the sweat from his brow. Then, with a casual, relaxed smile on his face, he placed his palm on the register panel beside the doorframe. The portal slid silently aside and he strode confidently through.

The gathered nobles and upper guild officials were lounging on the low, cushioned couches within, sipping from glasses filled with the finest amasec that Baranov could obtain. Each bottle had cost him a small fortune, but it mattered not when compared with the price the Perdus Skyllans had already paid him, and the wealth that he was promised from his employers.

Surgically enhanced beauties, the courtesans and mistresses of these fine, upstanding gentlemen, were laughing gaily as they sipped from their high glasses, and gave each other venomous glances behind their masters' backs. The men were gathered in small groups, talking earnestly about whatever they talked about, probably their latest guild takeover moves, or their strategies for the future.

No one paid any mind to Baranov as he stood before them. He was as invisible as a servant, and he cleared his throat to gain their attention.

'How far are we from the Imperial fleet, Baranov?' huffed a heavily jowled guild senator, and the rogue trader held up a hand to forestall him.

'My most esteemed companions,' he said with a broad smile, his voice raised over the din of chatter, 'I come to inform you that we are nearing our destination. I hope that you have been comfortable on your journey, and I apologise for any inconvenience that the turbulence we experienced earlier caused you. Alas, it was a necessary inconvenience. It was as if the loathsome xenos were determined to make your lives less comfortable, abominable creatures, all of them.'

Baranov raised a hand as murmuring rippled across the gathered group, and gasps came from several of the courtesans.

'Have no fear, ladies and gentlemen, the bulk of the xenos fleet is attacking Perdus Skylla from galactic east, on the far side of the planet. You were in little real danger, and my pilot, dear Eustenov, is the finest pilot in the eastern quadrant. Only the best for such vaunted company,' he said, bowing with a flourish.

The lie came easily to Baranov's lips. In truth, the *Rapture* was lucky to have avoided destruction, as several of the spores launched from the still distant tyranid hive fleets had come perilously close to colliding with his ship. It had taken more luck than skill to avoid them.

'We will be docking in around two minutes,' said Baranov, checking the time on his wrist-piece. 'It has been a pleasure to have such esteemed guests aboard the *Rapture*. Never before has such a fine group of individuals graced its humble decks, and I shall look back upon the service I was able to perform with pleasure for many years to come.'

Many of the nobles refused even to look at him, but Baranov didn't care.

'Many years to come indeed,' he said again, more softly, and bowing with a flourish, he returned to the shuttle's cockpit, thinking of what he would do with his new-found wealth.

'Hurry, Dios,' said Solon as he raced through the snow towards the landed shuttle. The effort of carrying the boy had all but exhausted him, and now the boy was running along behind him, his eyes wide with excitement and hope.

They were no more than fifty metres from the shuttle, and he could see the embarkation deck at the rear of the fuselage lowering to the ground, beckoning him.

Salvation!

With a burst of speed, Dios overtook him, laughing as he ran, but then the boy stopped short, freezing in place. Laughing, Solon drew to a halt next to the boy, a smile on his lips.

'Isn't it the most wonderful sight you've ever seen?' he breathed, his heart pumping from the exertion.

Dios's eyes were locked on something in the distance, something moving fast. Squinting through the darkness, Solon could see four shapes moving rapidly across the ice flow, a white backwash kicking up behind them.

'Interdiction forces?' said Solon, but the vehicles were not the uniform white of the moon's military forces. They were the colour of congealed blood, and a shiver ran down Solon's spine as he looked upon them. They were larger than any Interdiction vehicle he had ever seen, for even without landmarks for reference to give the vehicles scale, he could see that they were massive.

Solon began to walk slowly towards the waiting shuttle, but a sudden wave of fear struck him, and he dropped to his belly, dragging Dios down into the snow with him. Sponson-mounted weaponry on the vehicles, which could only have been battle tanks, turned in their direction.

Solon and Dios watched with growing panic as the four battle tanks drew nearer, and they could see that their hulls were covered in chains, spikes and blasphemous runes. Skulls were rammed onto sharpened metal stakes that ran in ridges down the flanks of the massive machines, and strips of parchment were plastered to their sides, half obscured by snow and ice.

The first of the tanks ground to a halt before the shuttle, and dark smoke rose from its exhaust stacks. An assault ramp at the front of the vehicle slammed down on to the ice, and giants dressed in red plate armour emerged.

Solon had only heard stories about the blessed Space Marines that protected humanity, and he had never dreamed in his wildest fantasies that he would ever get a chance to lay eyes on the nigh-on mythical warriors of the Emperor. They were the Emperor's chosen, biologically enhanced warriors that were as strong as ten men, armed with the most advanced weaponry the Adeptus Mechanicus could provide, and armoured in heavy plate that could withstand a direct hit from a Leman Russ battle tank, so it was said. They were the finest fighting force that the galaxy had ever seen, and it was said that nothing could stand against them. Looking upon the divine warriors, Solon could well believe it, though these warriors looked more like bloodthirsty butchers than holy protectors of humanity.

'Angels of death,' he whispered.

In his childhood dreams he had pictured them armoured in faultless golden plate, with angelic countenances and noble bearing. While such beliefs were clearly childish, Solon knew that there was something horribly wrong here. He was desperate to believe that salvation had come to Perdus Skylla, that the Emperor had dispatched his finest warriors to free the moon from alien invasion, but these Space Marines filled him with dread.

The other monstrous tanks disgorged their cargo of Space Marines, and two of the massive vehicles backed under the shuttle's stubby wings. Locking clamps descended like umbilical cords, latching onto the immense tanks and lifting them up beneath its wings while the other pair manoeuvred into position behind.

The first warriors stamped up the embarkation deck into the belly of the shuttle. One of them paused on the ramp, consulting a handheld tech-device. It turned in their direction, and Solon sank down lower into the snow, barely daring to breathe.

A warrior with a helmet fashioned like a grinning death's head spun to face them, and a fresh wave of panic gripped Solon as he realised that they had been spotted. Other warriors turned in their direction, and, raising their weapons before them, they began to march towards their position.

Sick with panic, Solon staggered to his feet, his heart thumping. He lifted his hands up before him, to show that he was unarmed.

The Space Marines halted, though they did not lower their weapons. One of them, a lean warrior whose head was bare to the elements, turned to the skull-helmed one, speaking something that Solon could not hear. The warrior appeared to approve, nodding his head almost imperceptibly before turning away and striding up the embarkation ramp towards the interior of the shuttle.

The barefaced warrior turned back towards Solon with a cold smile upon his noble face, and Solon licked his lips uneasily. The other Space Marines turned away, but this one warrior remained staring at them. Solon felt as if he was transfixed by the Space Marine's gaze.

Then the man turned into a monster, and Solon felt his sanity fray.

'No,' he whispered, as the warrior grew, his shoulders bulking out and his hands extending into talons. The warrior's image flickered like a faulty pict screen, and for a moment Solon could see the image of two beings overlapping each other, both inhabiting the same space. Although he knew such a thing was impossible, and his rational mind baulked at what he was seeing, he could not refute what he saw with his own eyes. The warrior was still there, lean and striding towards them with an easy, relaxed grace, but there was something else... something horrific.

It was a hulking daemon from the pits of hell, and its hateful features overlaid the classically handsome face of the Space Marine. Its eyes burnt with malice and the promise of pain, and its lips curled back to expose hundreds of sharp teeth, arrayed in serried layers, one behind the other, all the way to the back of its throat. Tall horns rose from its brow, and the air was thick and cloying where it exhaled.

The two images became one, a bastard hybrid, and Solon, horrified beyond reason, began to back away even as the daemonic hybrid creature began loping towards them.

'Run!' Solon roared, his paralysis giving way to abject terror.

Glancing over his shoulder, Solon saw that the hellish creature was gaining on them rapidly, covering the ground with tremendous leaps, using its arms to steady itself with each landing.

These were not the Emperor's divine angels, he thought; they couldn't be. They were the flip side of everything he had ever heard about them, and they were going to butcher him and Dios, after all they had struggled through.

Solon glanced back to see the daemon close behind them, its powerful legs bunched beneath it as it prepared to launch itself upon them. Solon shoved Dios to the side as the creature leapt. It would not get them both at once, but he knew that he was only delaying the inevitable, for neither of them could hope to stand against such a creature.

Solon spun around to face the monster as it lunged towards him, staggering backwards in the snow, raising his hands futilely to ward off its attacks.

A beam of pure darkness stabbed through the air and slammed into the daemon's body, smashing it to the ice, and it roared in fury and pain.

The daemon writhed on the ground. A searing hole had punched through its side just above the hip, passing clean through its body, and as it thrashed around, hot blood splashed across the ice and snow, causing steam to rise where it landed.

Solon spun to see where the blast had come from, and blinked as he saw several dark vehicles gliding smoothly across the ice. They looked similar to the skiffs that the first colonists on Perdus Skylla were said to have used, long thin boats with blades on their undersides that had used the power of the winds to propel them across the ice flow. These were not touching the ground at all, but hovered two metres above the ground, and slid forward with phenomenal speed.

Another lance of dark light stabbed from one of the vehicles, striking one of the daemonic Space Marines' battle tanks, which exploded spectacularly, the immense fireball throwing the shattered vehicle high into the air.

Dark figures leapt from the sides of the skiffs. Somersaulting from the decks and landing effortlessly on the ground, they began running lightly towards the Space Marines.

'Ghosts,' breathed Dios, his eyes wide with fear and panic.

Grabbing the boy around the waist, Solon lifted him and ran.

BURIAS-DRAK'SHAL PUSHED HIMSELF to his knees, growling and spitting. The shot had gone clear through him, passing between his hip and the base of his fused ribcage, leaving a gaping aperture of weeping flesh and internal organs exposed to the air. Already his enhanced, daemonically infused physiology was sealing the wound, his blood flow clotting and his flesh beginning to re-knit, but it would take some time before he was fully healed, and no amount of healing could repair his sundered power armour.

Pushing himself to his feet, Burias-Drak'shal hissed in pain and staggered, falling back to his knees before once again rising. All thought of the pair of humans was gone, and he scanned the landscape, focusing on the dark shapes of the eldar as they darted towards his comrades.

Wincing in pain, the icon bearer began to stagger back towards the shuttle, when his enhanced senses picked up a familiar scent on the air. He threw himself forward into a roll as he registered the appearance of the shadow-eldar behind him, and came up facing the being, teeth bared.

That the creature was of eldar origin was clear, for its frame was tall and slight, its limbs long and elegant, but that was where the similarities ended. Its skin was as black as the night, and runes of twisted eldar design were inscribed into its flesh. These runes glowed with cold light, pulsing brightly as the creature entered fully into the material realm.

Burias-Drak'shal felt the power of the warp within the creature, but it was not possessed in the same manner as he was. It was almost as if the daemon within the eldar shade was at once there and not there, its will and individuality gone, but its strength tapped.

The shadow-eldar hissed at him, elegant, alien features contorting to reveal an array of small, sharp teeth, and its milky, elongated eyes, shockingly white against its black skin, flashed its murderous intent a fraction before it moved.

The creature disappeared, leaving a smoky outline in its wake, before it reappeared beside Burias-Drak'shal, the blades emerging from the back of its forearms slashing towards his wounded side.

Burias-Drak'shal was ready for it this time, swinging his arm around in a brutal arc that would have decapitated the slender eldar had its reflexes been less than preternatural. It swayed backwards from the blow, the possessed Word Bearer's talons passing just centimetres from its face.

Burias-Drak'shal pushed his advantage, throwing a stabbing blow towards the eldar's torso, seeking to rip its heart from its chest. The shade threw itself backwards and disappeared again, only to reappear to the icon bearer's left, and the twin blades protruding from the back of its arm stabbed deep into his body. The blades of its other arm slashed across his pauldron, slicing monomolecular cuts through his power armour and drawing blood from his bicep.

Burias-Drak'shal snarled and spun, lashing out at the shadow-eldar, but his claws merely passed through a dark mist as the creature leapt away once more. It re-entered the material plane to his other side, its blades flashing again, and the icon bearer felt hot blood begin to flow from another trio of wounds.

His anger grew as the eldar continued to prey upon him, taunting him with its speed, and Burias-Drak'shal roared in frustration as once again his claws found nothing but air.

For all his anger he could sense that there was a pattern forming in the creature's attacks. It attacked and jumped away, always moving, and always attacking from a different angle.

As the shade disappeared once more, Burias-Drak'shal spun around on the spot, anticipating where its next attack would come from and lashing out. The eldar appeared where he had expected, and even its alien speed and reflexes were not up to avoiding the icon bearer's pre-emptive strike.

Burias-Drak'shal's talons closed around the slender eldar neck, and he pulled the creature sharply towards him, throwing it off balance.

'Got you,' growled Burias-Drak'shal, pulling the alien straight onto his rising knee, which thundered into the creature's sternum.

Burias-Drak'shal grinned as he felt the bones and tendons under his grip strain, and he clubbed the creature in the back of its head as it bent over double. It was slammed to the ground, and Burias-Drak'shal followed it down, driving his knee into the small of the eldar's back.

Burias-Drak'shal pulled his right hand back, and thrust down with all his enhanced might, seeking to drive his talons through the back of the creature's skull.

It disappeared from beneath him, his talons spearing deep into the ice, and the icon bearer snarled in frustration.

Flicking his head to the side, he saw that his brother warriors had been engaged by the bulk of the eldar raiding force, and with a hiss he began loping painfully towards the escalating battle.

BARANOV COULD BARELY contain his satisfaction as he hauled the bay doors of the *Rapture* open and the pompous, condescending elite of Perdus Skylla gaped in horror.

Eldar warriors were standing just outside the bay doors of the *Rapture*. Several of the courtesans screamed, while others whimpered in terror or merely gaped and soiled themselves. Baranov grinned, and stepped to the side.

A screaming woman was dragged from the shuttle by her hair, and the remaining high-ranking guilders shrank back, only to be pushed forward by Baranov's burly crew members.

Chuckling, Baranov swung away from the spectacle. For a moment, his gaze was drawn towards the shimmering integrity field that covered the yawning docking bay. It was almost imperceptible to the naked eye, looking as though nothing separated the inside of the ship and the vacuum of space, and it always made him feel slightly uneasy, as if he would be sucked out into the void at any moment.

Ikorus Baranov stepped back alongside the dark eldar lord's proxy, his arms folded across his chest as the wailing, weeping guilders and their lovers were led away in glimmering manacles that crackled with energy. He had never learnt the name of the eldar pirate, nor that of his representative. Not that it mattered, he thought. He would be unlikely to be able to pronounce it anyway.

'You have done well for me these past months,' said the eldar, his voice as smooth as velvet. The eldar spoke a curious form of Low Gothic, his pronunciation pitch perfect, but with a strangely singsong inflection.

'I am glad that your lord has been pleased with my deliveries,' replied Baranov, trying to keep his voice calm. In truth, the eldar terrified him, but they paid well. 'That will be the last of them, I'm afraid. I won't risk another run, not with the tyranids so close.'

Baranov flashed a glance at the eldar's face, trying to read him. Normally a good judge of character, he found it galling that he could not gauge the eldar's emotions in the slightest. Never again will I work with xenos, he thought, though he knew as soon as he thought it that it was a lie.

'The… what do you call them? Tyranids?' said the eldar. Baranov nodded.

'Your pronunciation is perfect,' commented Baranov. The eldar stared at him for a moment, and he felt himself shrink under his unfathomable gaze.

'The *tyranids* might well exterminate all of the lesser races, in time,' said the eldar casually.

'They are a menace,' agreed Baranov, unsure where the conversation was leading, and uncomfortable making small talk with the deadly eldar lord.

'If all of your kind are eradicated, where then will my lord find such slaves?' asked the eldar, gesturing towards the guilders being dragged away. 'Your race breeds like vermin. Your race *is* vermin, but you have your uses, don't you, Ikorus Baranov?'

'I… I believe we do, my lord. Or at least some of us do.'

'I am glad that you believe so,' said the eldar. He gestured more of his warriors forward, and they began to surround Baranov and his crewmembers.

'Ah,' said Baranov, 'I think we should part ways now, honoured lord. I won't press you for the payment for this last group. Consider it a gift, a gift to honour the friendship between us.'

'Friendship?' said the eldar slowly, as if savouring the word. 'A curious, irrelevant mon-keigh concept. And honour? Where is the honour in betraying your own kind? Delivering them to an enemy, albeit superior, race? That is honourable in your eyes?'

Baranov felt the sweat running down his back, and his throat was suddenly dry. He flinched as the eldar walked behind him, but he felt rooted to the spot, unable to think, unable to move.

'You are a detestable race,' said the eldar. 'Your very stench offends me, and yet, you have your uses. Your soul-fires burn so bright, and your fear... your fear is delectable.'

The eldar spun away from the petrified mon-keigh worm.

'Enslave them,' he said in the eldar tongue.

MARDUK TOOK CAREFUL aim at one of the frenzied eldar wyches as it darted towards him. Squeezing the trigger, the eldar's head disappeared in a mist of blood. The eldar warriors were almost naked, their flesh covered only by totemic war paint and ritual piercings, and they moved like deadly dancers as they cut into the warriors of the XVII Legion. Their strangely fashioned weapons wove dazzling patterns through the air, their movements at once enthralling and deadly.

A score of them had died as they approached, ripped apart by the murderous swathe of fire that the Word Bearers had laid down. More had perished when one of their hovering skiffs had been shot from the air, the fragile vehicle tipping onto its side, throwing its occupants onto the ice before it smashed down upon them, impaling several on its bladed sides and crushing more beneath its weight.

Now the wyches had engaged them in melee combat, and the odds were tipping towards the greater numbers of the eldar warriors.

Parallel beams of incandescent light speared through the night as a Land Raider fired upon the knife-like shapes of the dark skiffs that circled the battle, searing a pair of holes through one of its barbed, sail-like uprights. The raider vehicle veered to the side, moving with remarkable speed and grace as it avoided another pair of shots directed towards it, and another of the vehicles returned fire, a beam of darkness stabbing into the front of the Land Raider, which was rocked by the blow.

Jetbikes streamed out of the night, screaming low through the fight, peppering the Word Bearers with splinter fire. Marduk spun, his chainsword roaring, and cut the arm from one of the jetbikers as the vehicle screamed past him. Blood pumped from the wound and the rider lost control of his jetbike, which flipped into a sudden dive, skidding into the ice and smashing headlong into Kol Badar.

The Coryphaus saw it coming out of the corner of his vision and braced himself, leaning his shoulder into the careering jetbike. It shattered against him, breaking apart as it knocked him back a step, and the rider was catapulted over the handlebars, blood spraying in a wide arc from the stump of his arm.

Marduk fired his pistol into the chest of another of the wyches as it closed on him, and the painted figure was hurled backwards by the force of the shot. He spun, targeting matrices lighting up around him, and saw another of the wyches, her gaudy dyed red hair swinging behind her as she ducked under a swinging blow from one of Sabtec's coterie brothers and slashed a blade through the warrior's leg, cutting it off at the knee.

Marduk judged that this was the leader of the wych troop. She moved with exquisite, savage grace, her serpentine whip writhing with a life of its own. The whip cracked out, and its multiple barbed tips lashed around the arm of another warrior-brother. Energy coursed up the length of the whip and the warrior of the XVII Legion dropped to the ground, his body convulsing.

Marduk levelled his bolt pistol at the wych's head, but before he could fire, a net of fine, razor-sharp wire wrapped around his arm, pulling his aim off target and slicing through his vambraces. A tri-forked spear stabbed towards Marduk's chest, but the First Acolyte swatted it aside with his chainsword and hacked into the eldar's neck, ripping his chain-blade through flesh.

Untangling himself from the wire net that had cut half-through his vambrace, Marduk turned and staggered back from the furious assault of another of the wyches. It danced towards him with a pair of long-bladed swords weaving before it. Each of the swords had a guard that protected the wielder's hands, and they had curving blades for pommels.

The blades moved faster than Marduk could follow, and he was losing ground before their flashing advance. Snarling, he leapt forwards, his hatred fuelling his servo-enhanced strength.

One of the blades slashed for his neck, and Marduk blocked the attack with his forearm, while the other sword slashed up towards his groin. He met the blow with one of his own, and for a moment the two combatants were locked together. Then the eldar flipped backwards, first one foot and then the other cannoning into the base of Marduk's helmet, snapping his head backwards.

The two blades stabbed towards Marduk's heart, but he twisted at the last moment, and they scraped a pair of furrows across his chest. The First Acolyte grabbed one of the eldar's wrists, pinning it in place, and smashed the spiked guard of his chainsword into the wych's face, pulverising its skull.

Dropping the lifeless corpse to the ground, Marduk surveyed the battle. The eldar were everywhere, darting in and out of the melee, blades flashing and pistols spitting razor-sharp splinters. Another of the Land Raiders was destroyed, its blackened hull smoking and lifeless, and jet-bikes screamed around the outside of the battle, banking sharply before gunning their engines and cutting like knives through the combat. Shadowy figures appeared on the outskirts, preying upon the unwary, blinking into existence behind warrior-brothers engaged in combat, and cutting them down.

His warriors were acquitting themselves well, and the ice was strewn with the eldar dead, but he knew instinctively that this was not a battle he could win. The notion of retreating was repellent to him, but he had to keep things in perspective. He had what he needed. The knowledge was locked inside the explorator's brain, housed in the body of Darioq-Grendh'al. He had only to get away from this damnable moon, and return to Sicarus. Everything else was meaningless.

Marduk had ordered the warriors of the Host to protect Darioq-Grendh'al, but he saw now that such precautions were unnecessary. The corrupted magos was killing anything that came near him, and the first Acolyte smiled at the daemon's bloodlust as it overcame any resistance left within its host body.

A mass of writhing, daemonic tentacles, black and oily, burst from the magos's body to join his mechadendrites, each appearing to move with their own will and sentience. They coiled around the legs of those eldar that closed in around the magos, effortlessly hurling them through the air, while other sucker-tipped tentacles drew victims in close, where they were dismembered by Darioq's toothed servo-arms.

Snapping mouths upon the tips of mechadendrites burrowed into xenos bodies, and fresh mutations appeared upon the magos's flesh. More spines and horny protrusions pushed out along the ridges of his servo-arms, and from his knee-joints, metal merged seamlessly into bone and horn.

'We are leaving!' roared Marduk, and Kol Badar instantly set about ordering the evacuation.

An arc of black light struck the side of the shuttle, and Marduk felt a stab of unease. It was not a feeling that he was used to, and it served only to feed his anger. If the eldar immobilised the shuttle, there would be no getting off the moon.

'Move!' roared Marduk, stepping back towards the embarkation ramp of the *Idolator*, holding his chainsword in both hands. His bolt pistol was gone, but it mattered not. All that mattered now was getting off this cursed world.

The Word Bearers formed a retreating arc, closing together and backing towards the shuttle, bolters blazing and chainswords roaring, and the engines of the *Idolator* roared to life.

MARDUK STOOD WITH Kol Badar and Sabtec at the top of the embarkation ramp as the engines of the *Idolator* fired.

'Here he comes,' remarked Kol Badar as Burias-Drak'shal leapt through the press of dark eldar, crushing the skull of one of the wyches as he came. He was bleeding from dozens of wounds, the largest a gaping hole in his side, and his armour was peppered with splinters that protruded from his armoured plates like bizarre decorations.

The icon bearer staggered up the ramp, and Marduk stepped aside to let him pass.

'One minute more and we would have left,' barked Kol Badar, snapping off shots with his combi-bolter.

The daemon left Burias, his natural form returning, and he slumped forward unconscious, sprawling face first out on the deck, blood running freely from his wounds.

'Somebody see to him,' barked Marduk.

The engines roared as the plasma core came into full power, and the ramp began to close. Splinters spat up at the trio standing guard atop the ramp, and Sabtec and Marduk ducked back to avoid the deadly projectiles. A line of the fine shards struck Marduk across the side of his helmet, their tips just penetrating far enough to graze his cheek. He ripped his helmet off and tossed it into the shuttle's interior. Kol Badar merely endured the barrage of fire, for the splinters had not the power to penetrate his thick Terminator armour.

The eldar wyches made a last charge, leaping lightly onto the ramp as it rose past horizontal. Kol Badar killed three of them, firing his combi-bolter on full auto, and Sabtec took down another two, his bolter ripping the slender warriors in half. Marduk's chainsword killed another, the toothed blade ripping it from groin to heart.

Behind them was another wych, the tall, elegant and sneering female with flowing hair that Marduk had seen take down at least three of his warriors, and as Kol Badar and Sabtec gunned down her companions, her sinuous, serpent-like whip lashed out, its barbed tips whipping around Marduk's throat.

Debilitating energy coursed through the length of the whip, rendering Marduk's enhanced physiology all put paralysed, and his muscles twitched spasmodically. Fighting the energy coursing through him, Marduk dropped his chainsword and reached up to the strangling whip wrapped around his neck, trying to pry it loose. With a powerful wrench, the eldar warrior hauled Marduk towards her.

Sabtec cried out and reached for the First Acolyte, but Marduk was already falling. Kol Badar's combi-bolter roared, but the wych back-flipped from the ramp that was now more vertical than horizontal, and the bolts missed their mark. Marduk was dragged from the ramp behind the wych.

Kol Badar's power talons lashed out, grabbing Marduk around the wrist as he fell. The Coryphaus leant his shoulder against the closing ramp, and its motors strained against him as he held it open.

Debilitating energy was coursing through Marduk's body from the whip lashed around his neck, but he looked up at Kol Badar with fiery eyes.

'Don't… let… go,' he hissed.

Kol Badar stared into the First Acolyte's eyes, his entire body straining to hold the shuttle's ramp open.

Then the Coryphaus's talons opened, and Marduk fell to the ground below.

'No!' gasped Sabtec as the ramp slammed closed and the shuttle lifted from the ice. 'We must go back!'

'Be silent,' barked Kol Badar. 'He's gone.'

BOOK THREE: SHE WHO THIRSTS

'And so from decadence, wantonness and depravity a new power was birthed into the darkness. In darkness it resides and in darkness it hungers, now and for all time.'

– *Ravings of the Shalleigha, Flagellantaie Diabolicus*

CHAPTER SEVENTEEN

MARDUK OPENED HIS right eye groggily as he regained consciousness. His left daemonic eye was lidless, but he could see nothing with it. Perhaps it had been ripped from his socket while he was unconscious, he thought, before he remembered the needle that had been pushed into the eye. He tried to move his limbs, but they were held fast, and he gritted his sharpened teeth as pain coursed through his body.

With the pain, his memories came flooding back to him. Again, he felt the paralysing length of the whip wrapped around his neck and the jolt as he hit the ice. He felt the Coryphaus's grip on him slip, and saw again the blue engines of the *Idolator* as it roared up into the heavens away from him. Rage had blossomed as he had realised that it was not turning back.

He had been bound with manacles that coursed with energy, sending shooting pain through his nervous system, and had endured the humiliation of being bundled from the battlefield, hovering a metre above the ground, held aloft by the vile sorceries of the eldar. He had been raised to the back of one of the eldar skiffs, and he saw that other warrior-brothers had been captured. They were prodded and kicked into low cages beneath the deck of the skiff, while the hateful xenos laughed.

Marduk had stared hatefully at the female wych that had disabled him, her long, fiery hair flowing down her back. She sneered at him and slammed the solid cage door closed.

The vehicle had reached incredible speed, and at some point Marduk had felt a subtle change in the air, as if the skiff had been transported somewhere else entirely, and its speed increased tenfold. At some point he had passed out, and he had come to again only when the skiff screamed to a smooth halt. Once again, the air tasted subtly different, more cloying and close.

Marduk and the other captives had been dragged from the hold beneath the deck of the skiffs, and had looked around them angrily. They were inside a cavernous, expansive dome, with bladed ribs arching up above them, and Marduk saw scores of alien skiffs and jetbikes lined up around its sides, hovering at rest above the floor, lined up one above another. Hundreds of eldar soldiers moved through the lair, and Marduk glowered at them hatefully.

A gateway of crackling darkness hung in mid-air in the centre of the dome, enclosed by elegant bladed arches. Even as he watched, Marduk had seen a skiff emerge from the portal, appearing from the wafer-thin, vertical pool of darkness and gliding effortlessly several metres above the ground, the warriors upon its decks leaping to the floor.

Then searing pain exploded through Marduk's body, his every nerve ending on fire as needles stabbed into his flesh. He resisted it as long as he was able, and a further set of needles stabbed into him. Still, he fought his captors, struggling and roaring his anger. A third set of needles plunged into his neck, and at last he was overcome, and everything had gone black.

Glancing down, Marduk saw that his arms and legs were spread-eagled out to either side. His blessed armour had been stripped from his upper body, and his pallid skin was puckered with tens of thousands of tiny pinpricks of dried blood. His armour had been slowly fusing to his body, and the inside of their plates were covered with thousands of tiny barbs that were growing into his flesh. Removing the armour plating was a painful and oddly distressing procedure, for it was as much a part of him as his limbs, and he had only twice removed his breastplate since the blessed Warmaster had perished.

That was an age ago, a lifetime in the past. Once his armour had been granite grey, as had the armour of all the warriors of the XVII Legion, the colour they had worn since the Legion's inception, but he had long ago stained it the deep red adopted by all of his brethren at Lorgar's decree.

Marduk gazed blearily down upon his naked torso for the first time in untold millennia. It looked like the body of a stranger. His pectorals were thick and slab-like, and the muscles of his abdomen rippled as he strained against his restraints. Dozens of scars marred his perfect form and blue veins could be seen clearly through his translucent, pale flesh.

Marduk turned his head groggily to the side, looking along the length of his outstretched arms. His powerful limbs had been stripped of his power armour, exposing passages from the *Book of Lorgar* that ran in spirals of tiny script around his forearms. Just looking upon the tiny, archaic script gave him comfort, even though his eyes still could not focus on the individual words and characters.

Casting his gaze further along his arms, Marduk saw what was constricting his movements. A slender, tapering blade had pierced his wrists, passing through his flesh and between his bones, protruding a metre out the other side.

Marduk pulled against the restraints, trying to slide his limbs off the impaling blades, but jolting pain accompanied his efforts, making his body shudder and contort in agony. He could feel the needles, the long shards of metal that had been inserted between his vertebrae, piercing his central nervous system. They ran from the base of his spine to his skull, a slender needle inserted into every gap between the bones. Marduk ceased his struggles, and the pain instantly receded.

He was suspended, upright and hanging upon the blades piercing his wrists and lower legs. The blades shifted slightly, angling upwards, and Marduk hissed in pain as he slid further back along their lengths, the spikes grinding against bone.

As his vision cleared, Marduk took in the details of the room. It was circular in shape, and the ceiling was low. It was dim, the only light coming from the featureless floor and low roof, fading in and out in rhythmic pulses. There was a single exit from the room, semi-transparent strips of plas-like material blocking his vision of the room beyond.

Marduk registered the presence of another being in the centre of the room. He had thought he was alone, but his vision focused on the back of a tall, unearthly thin individual. Marduk glared at the creature hatefully, remembering its touch.

Its emaciated upper body was garbed in a tight-fitting, glossy black bodysuit, and its legs were concealed beneath an apron of similar material. The figure was leaning over something, a body perhaps, and appeared engrossed in its work. Dozens of blades, hooks and other less easily recognisable implements hung from its waist, and its hairless head was strangely elongated, its skull extending back further than was normal. Dozens of needles and tubes entered the flesh of its skull, flowing backwards like a mockery of hair.

Hovering above the table on which the death-like eldar worked was an immense spider, a dozen slim limbs extending from its body. The long, multi-jointed limbs were akin to the blades that pierced his own body, their surface black and reflective, and he wondered if it was a similar creature that held him. Its legs moved with swift, precise movements, each one easily four metres long and elongated to sharp points. Marduk decided that his first impression had been wrong. This was not a living creature at all. It was a machine.

As the machine spider rotated slightly in the air, its long legs moving rapidly and independent of each other, Marduk saw that his assumption was not quite correct. The thing *was* alive, or at least part of it was. In the dull light that pulsed from the ceiling and floor, he could see that there was an eldar figure at the heart of the spider-machine, or at least what must have once been one of the decadent xenos beings. Its face was obscured beneath a shiny black, featureless mask, and the spider-like limbs were attached to its torso, protruding from its spine. The eldar's humanoid upper arms merged into another pair of long spider limbs, though they were shorter than the others and ended in cruel barbs. Where its two legs ought to have been there was instead a bulbous, glossy black abdomen that hung low, bloated and obscene. From the tip of this abdomen, a pair of spinnerets exuded a sticky substance.

As Marduk's eyes became used to the dim lighting, he saw that the spider-eldar was not hovering at all, but was attached to the ceiling via a series of coiled cables. A black substance moved within those cables in rhythmic spurts, like blood pumped through arteries by a beating heart.

The tall, black-clad humanoid, that Marduk took to be a sub-species of the eldar race, was talking to itself in a hissing voice. The First Acolyte could not understand its words, for it spoke in the foul eldar tongue, but he sensed that the creature was pleased. As it moved to the side, he saw what was occupying the creature's attention. A fellow warrior of the XVII Legion; Sarondel, one of the 13th coterie was pinned down upon a bladed slab, his chest sliced open to expose his internal organs.

Anger roiled up within Marduk to see one of his sacred brothers of the Word so violated. The tall, skeletally thin eldar was removing the warrior's organs one by one, and placing them in shallow dishes that hovered alongside the slab. The eldar's long fingers ended in scalpel blades, and he saw a cruel smile on the creature's face as he got his first look at his captor's visage.

Its cheeks were hollow and sunken, emphasising its sharp, high cheekbones and thin mouth, and its almond-shaped eyes were black and dead. Its movements were crisp and sure as at sliced through Sarondel's flesh, and the warrior growled, gritting his teeth against the pain as his blood began to flow anew.

Marduk felt savage pride as the warrior of the 13th coterie spat a wad of blood and phlegm up into the twisted surgeon's face. The eldar was unconcerned, and wiped its face with the back of one hand.

'The dark gods of Chaos will feast on your soul come the end,' said Marduk. 'You are already lost, you just don't know it yet.'

The eldar straightened, dead eyes fixing on Marduk. It ghosted across the floor to stand before him.

'In the end we are all lost,' it said, lifting a bladed fingertip to Marduk's cheek.

The First Acolyte did not flinch beneath its touch, though he felt hot blood running down his face. Instead, he grinned, his blazing eyes holding the eldar's gaze.

'Your time will come sooner than you think,' he said.

'That is your prediction? You are a prophet then, human?'

'I am far beyond humanity. I am Marduk, First Acolyte of the 34th Grand Host of the XVII Legion, the Word Bearers, blessed of Lorgar. I make no predictions, xenos filth. I make you a promise.'

Marduk's eyes rolled back into his head as he sought to draw the power of the warp into his body, to call the daemons of the immaterium to him and unleash their fury upon this wretch that dared to defile the sacred forms of Lorgar's angels of the Word… but nothing happened. Silence and emptiness was all that greeted him, vast, cold and empty, and he screamed his fury.

Marduk tried to fly free of his mortal body, to rise above his earthly shell and become as one with the blessed ether, but it felt as if shackles held him locked into his body, imprisoning him within the cage of his flesh.

Had the gods of the ether forsaken him? Had they withdrawn their favour from him? The thought was more terrifying than any pain or horror that this being could ever heap upon him.

The eldar sneered at him, dead eyes watching him with keen interest.

'You can bring none of your taint here, slave,' it said, its voice mocking. 'Your gods have turned their backs on you.'

Marduk gritted his teeth and threw himself forward, muscles straining as he sought to rip the eldar limb from limb, but he was jerked backwards. The bladed limbs that impaled him hauled him back, and shooting pain blossomed up his spine.

Marduk thrashed and roared, and fresh blood began to run from his wounds as he fought to tear himself loose. The eldar merely gave a dry, cruel laugh, and turned away from him, and Marduk stared venomously at the retreating figure as it strode from the room, parting the hanging partition with a wave of its hand.

You can bring none of your taint here, slave, his captor had said, and Marduk could well believe the truth in the words. The feeling of isolation was staggering.

Did a null field containment force keep his link with the warp at bay? Or had the gods truly forsaken him?

He had experienced a similar sensation of being cut off from the powers that be, once before, deep within the xenos pyramid on the Imperial world of Tanakreg, in that hellish otherworld that was not truly part of the material universe, but something else entirely. He had experienced a similar sensation there, and there he had won out, defeating his former master and escaping with his prize.

Escaping? The doubt came unbidden to his mind. Had he truly escaped? Or had he merely been *allowed* to escape? Surely such a being as powerful as the Undying One would never had allowed him to flee its realm had it not wished it to be so.

'My lord,' said a cracked voice, and Marduk glanced over towards the mutilated figure of Sarondel, stretched backwards upon the surgeon's slab, his chest ripped open. The monstrous spider creature was still poised over him, and it sprayed a liquid film over the exposed organs from the tip of its vile, bulbous, segmented abdomen.

'The gods… have they deserted us?' breathed Sarondel, echoing Marduk's thoughts. 'I cannot feel their touch.'

'Speak not such heresies,' growled Marduk. 'This is a test of our faith. The xenos filth will be punished for what they have done to you, brother. I promise you that.'

Sarondel groaned something indecipherable in response, and Marduk strained again to pull his limbs from the spikes impaling them. His efforts were hopeless. His muscles bulged with all his hyper-enhanced strength, but he was powerless against the slender blades that held his crucified form.

What if the gods *had* deserted them, thought Marduk with a stab of terror?

Silence such thoughts, Marduk raged. Such doubts are poison. Fortify your soul, he reminded himself, your faith will be rewarded.

Patience, he told himself.

His time would come, and he would be ready.

'You LEFT HIM behind,' said Burias flatly, his eyes glinting dangerously.

'Am I going to have a problem with you, Burias?' growled Kol Badar.

Burias pursed his lips, not taking his eyes off the Coryphaus. He took a deep breath, repressing his violent urge to leap across the shuttle's cabin and tear the older warrior's head from his shoulders.

He had always fought at Marduk's side. Even as an acolyte, Burias had recognised that Marduk was destined for great things, and he was honest enough to admit that he had befriended him in the hope that he would be dragged up the chain of command with him. Burias had never made any secret of this fact, and he had enjoyed the success he had achieved, and the privilege he had gained, as Marduk had risen to First Acolyte. With Jarulek dead and gone, it was surely just a formality before Marduk became a Dark Apostle, and then Burias's position would become even more influential. He was Marduk's confidant, his brother, his friend, and he would have had the ear of a Dark Apostle at his disposal.

In one swift, opportunistic move, Kol Badar had eliminated that future, and for that Burias would dearly love to rip his hearts from his chest.

'You think he is dead?' asked Burias in a low voice.

'He's gone,' said Kol Badar. 'The dark eldar took him. There is no coming back.'

Burias scowled, all his years of comradeship with Marduk, wasted. Once again, he let his eyes roll back into his head and the deafening tumult that was the immaterium screamed into him. Drak'shal had a bond with the First Acolyte, stronger than any bond between Burias and

Marduk, a bond of servitude, a bond of command. It was, after all, Marduk who had first summoned Drak'shal into the icon bearer's flesh.

Drak'shal reached out at Burias's urging, searching for Marduk's soul-fire, for some hint of its existence. The daemon found nothing. Of course, it would take days, weeks even, to properly scour the turbulence of the empyrean, despite the bond the First Acolyte and the daemon shared, but a shadow presence should have been simple to locate. It was as if everything that Marduk was had been snuffed out. Slowly, Burias opened his eyes.

'He is truly gone,' he muttered in disbelief.

'As I said,' said Kol Badar.

This changed everything. If Marduk truly was dead, and what other explanation could there be, then Burias would have to quickly reassess his position. Without the First Acolyte's backing and favour, his position within the Host was tenuous. Kol Badar, as Coryphaus, was the most powerful individual within the Host, and would, as protocol demanded, take over the leadership role. Burias would be foolish to take that lightly. Without the First Acolyte to shield him, Kol Badar could do with him as his wished with impunity.

'What of the Council?' asked Burias, his mind whirring. 'The life of a Coryphaus that has allowed his Dark Apostle to die is a tenuous thing, but a Coryphaus that has allowed his Dark Apostle *and* First Acolyte to fall? You'll be made to suffer, and I have no wish to fall with you.'

'Walk with me,' commanded the Coryphaus, releasing the harness clamping him into his seat, and making his way towards the control cabin of the *Idolator*, fighting the angle of the ship's assent and the G-forces that pushed against his massive frame. Clearly, Kol Badar wished to continue the discussion out of the earshot of the other warrior-brothers of the Host, which made Burias at once both suspicious and intrigued.

Burias threw off his harness and stood up unsteadily. Using the rail-holds above his head he hauled himself hand over hand towards the front of the shuttle. Once inside the control cabin, Kol Badar punched a blister-rune and the hatch was sealed behind them.

The crew of the *Idolator* had long been fused with their controls, and what remained of their flesh was covered in runes and sigils of binding. They stared ahead with sightless eyes, their entire existence dedicated to serving their infernal masters. They would not repeat what words were spoken in their presence even were they capable of speech.

'The Council need not know all the details,' said Kol Badar slowly, his eyes intense.

'They will need to be told something,' Burias hissed, 'unless we do not return to Sicarus at all.'

'No, that is not an option. No warrior of Lorgar has ever turned from the XVII Legion. No, we tell the Council the truth.'

'The truth?' asked Burias.

'Yes, that the Dark Apostle Jarulek was treacherously cut down by the traitor Marduk, who was envious and covetous of his hallowed role,' said Kol Badar, 'and that Marduk was subsequently slain for his misdeed.'

'You wish to lie to the Council?' asked Burias, his voice incredulous.

Kol Badar did not have a chance to answer, as warning lights lit up across the consoles of the shuttle. The Coryphaus moved swiftly towards the pict screens flashing with a stream of data, and swore.

'What is it?' asked Burias in alarm.

'A tyranid spore shower,' answered the Coryphaus.

It was heading right towards them.

'ADMIRAL,' SAID GIDEON Cortez, flag lieutenant of the *Hammer of Righteousness.* 'The master of ordnance has a firing solution. Request approval to launch torpedoes.'

'Approved,' said Admiral Rutger Augustine.

He was standing at the forward observation deck with his hands on his hips, watching the battle unfold before him. The strategy of maintaining a blockade in front of the encroaching tyranid menace and decimating any world, inhabited or not, in its path still rankled with Augustine, but such were his orders.

Most of the enemy hive ships were still tens of thousands of kilometres away, but he could see them: immense, sentient creatures kilometres long with skin thick enough to endure living in deep space, their vile bodies armoured in segmented carapace easily as strong as the hull of the mighty Retribution-class battleship he stood in. It almost defied logic that creatures as large as this could exist in the universe. The largest of the bio-ships was easily a match for the *Hammer of Righteousness*, and rivalled her for size, and there were hundreds of smaller living ships that shoaled around the largest organisms. The smaller creatures ranged from the size of light cruisers all the way down to the size of attack craft and interceptors. The smallest bio-ships flew in dense clouds around the large hive ships, like swarms of angry bees around their mother-hive, and several Cobra-class escorts had already been destroyed by them when they had ventured too close.

The tyranid fleet was a terrifying prospect to face at close range, and Augustine had decreed that no Imperial vessel approach within six thousand kilometres of it. Even so, the xenos bio-ships were capable of startling bursts of speed that had at first taken the Imperials by surprise, and Augustine had lost the light cruiser *Dominae Noctus* and its entourage of frigates and escorts due to this unexpected trait.

A pair of hive ships had swung towards the Dauntless-class light cruiser as she had been turning to starboard to make a strafing run across the flank of the hive fleet, breaking from the formation of bio-ships.

Though the commander of the *Dominae Noctus* had seen the danger, he had been powerless to pull away fast enough. The cruiser had desperately unleashed the fury of a full broadside into the two bio-ships training in on him. Augustine had watched the destruction unleashed on the living organisms on one of his flickering pict screens, and had seen the carapaced hides of the beasts rupture beneath the barrage, spilling bio-fluids into space. Still, the bio-ships had continued on, spitting streams of acid that melted the side of the Dauntless light cruiser and launching swarms of smaller creatures, exhaling them from gill-like rents in their sides.

A trio of Sword frigates had nobly moved into the path of the behemoths, seeking to draw them away from the floundering light cruiser, and two of them were overwhelmed as boarding chrysalides were excreted from the hive ships, clamping onto and cutting through their hulls before overrunning their decks with swarms of warrior organisms.

One of the bio-ships was drawn by the bait, and turned on the last remaining Sword frigate, while its twin closed on the doomed *Dominae Noctus*. The rest of the fleet had watched in growing horror as immense hooked tentacles shot forth from the prow of the bio-ships, locking onto the hulls of the light cruiser and the frigate, drawing them into the immense living beasts. More tentacles wrapped around their hulls. The Sword frigate was crushed utterly beneath the pressure and ripped in half. The *Dominae Noctus* lasted little longer, for the tentacles drew it in close to the hive ship, and its hull was rent by the immense, bony beak concealed at the heart of the mass of tentacles. For an hour, the creature gorged upon the light cruiser, its hull almost entirely obscured by the tentacles that wrapped around it, and Augustine had listened in stoic silence to the screams of the dying as bio-acid and feeder organisms had been spewed into the interior of the compromised ship.

Augustine had no intention of losing any more of his fleet to the xenos fleet, and the Imperials were engaging the tyranids only at medium to long range.

The *Hammer of Righteousness's* dorsal lance batteries had taken a heavy toll on the advancing tyranid fleet, but the xenos ships continued on relentlessly, absorbing the casualties they suffered and pushing ever forwards. The bio-ships mortally wounded by the long distance barrages were devoured by the other hive-ships, who would doubtless use the genetic material to spawn more of their foul kind.

Augustine felt a shudder beneath his feet as the prow torpedo tubes fired, and he watched with satisfaction as the six immense, plasma-core projectiles, each almost eighty metres long, powered through the gulf of space towards the largest of the hive organisms.

Lance batteries from the rest of the fleet stabbed into the closest bio-ships, and other torpedoes impacted with fleshy bodies several kilometres in length. Tentacles flailed in death-spasms, and thousands of tiny organisms flew into the mighty wounds in the hides of the immense beasts, latching onto flesh and each other and excreting a cement-like substance over themselves to form a living bandage, sealing up wounds even as they were caused.

The largest of the hive ships veered to avoid the flagship's torpedoes, but its immense bulk turned slowly, and it was clear that it could not avoid the impacts. Smaller bio-ships interposed themselves, and three torpedoes exploded prematurely as they slammed into the sides of the lesser vessels. The last three plasma torpedoes hit their target, and gobbets of flesh the size of city blocks were blasted from the behemoth's flank.

'Order the *Valkyrie* to pull back,' said Augustine to one of his aides. 'She is getting too close.'

'Yes, admiral,' came the response, and the order was quickly passed on.

'Ground invasions have commenced on both the Perdus moons,' said Gideon Cortez, Augustine's trusty flag lieutenant, his face grim.

Augustine sighed wearily. He didn't know how long it had been since he had slept. *Plenty of time to sleep when you are dead*, he thought.

He had already ordered the destruction of six inhabited Imperial worlds in this sector, but at least those worlds had been successfully evacuated before he had been forced to order their destruction.

Trying to give the citizens of the two moons as much time to evacuate as possible, Augustine had moved the blockade forward, so that the fleet could hold back the tyranid advance for as long as possible. Now, he looked down upon the twin moons, orbiting the gaseous giant nearby, and he cursed that he could buy them little time.

'Percentage of the populations evacuated?' he asked, already dreading the answer.

It had been estimated that the twin moons of Perdus Skylla and Perdus Kharybdis would require three journeys of the bulk transport ships available, at the minimum, for a complete evacuation. As far as he was aware, only one journey had been completed.

'Less than thirty per cent,' replied Gideon.

'How many are left?' asked Augustine. He didn't really want to know the answer, but felt that he ought to know how many people he was condemning to death.

'On Perdus Kharybdis, around eighty million,' said Gideon in a quiet voice.

'Eighty million,' said Admiral Augustine in a weary voice, 'and Perdus Skylla?'

'No more than twenty million.'

'The evacuations were more successful there?'

'No,' admitted Gideon Cortez, shaking his head. 'The population of Perdus Skylla is but a fraction of its twin, mostly labourers and mine workers.'

'One hundred million loyal souls, and we are going to eradicate them, like that,' said Augustine, *clicking* his fingers together.

'Some might say it is a blessing, sir,' said Gideon, 'better than being devoured by the xenos.'

'Yes, you are quite right,' snapped Augustine. 'They should be thanking us.'

Gideon gave him a hurt look, and the admiral sighed.

'I'm sorry, Gideon,' he said quickly, 'that was unfair. How long would it take to do one final evacuation run?'

'The carriers are already en route for a final pickup,' said Gideon, 'though they will need an escort. Six hours, they'll need, according to the logistics reports.'

'Order the left flanks to close up, with the *Cypra Mordatis* at the fore,' said Augustine after a moment of deliberation. 'We can buy them six hours.'

Feeling Gideon still hovering behind him, Augustine turned to face his flag lieutenant, one eyebrow raised.

'You have something to say, Gideon?'

'Can we really hold them for another six hours?' asked the flag lieutenant, his voice low to avoid any of the other crew members overhearing his words.

'I don't know,' admitted Augustine, 'but we owe it to those people to try.'

Gideon still did not look happy.

'You can't save them all,' he said.

'No,' agreed Augustine, shaking his head, 'I cannot.'

THE IDOLATOR BANKED and jinked from side to side as hundreds of mycetic spores, fired by the hive fleet still some ten thousand kilometres from Perdus Skylla streamed down towards the surface of the moon. Each of the cyst-like chrysalis organisms was filled with a deadly warrior cargo, which would scour all life from the doomed world. They fell like a meteor shower through the atmosphere, their shell-like exteriors glowing hot as they descended at phenomenal speeds.

One of the spores passed within metres of the shuttle, which was pulled to the side by the rush of air, but the guidance systems of the ship hauled it back on course, narrowly being struck by another pair of mycetic spores as they roared down towards the surface of Perdus Skylla.

Each of the spores was the size of a Rhino transport vehicle, and a direct hit would cause tremendous damage to the unshielded *Idolator*. Engines roared as the shuttle veered sharply to avoid a collision, but its movement took it into the path of another descending spore, which clipped the side of the ship, sending it into a spin.

The *Idolator* rolled through the air, dropping hundreds of metres and narrowly avoiding being struck by more of the spores, but it came back under control, pulling out of its death spin and shooting once more skywards, pulling free of the descending shower of ohrysalides.

Burias and Kol Badar picked themselves up, the Coryphaus reading the damage reports that spewed from the mouth of a graven, daemonic face. He swore.

'We are not going to make it to the *Infidus Diabolus*,' he said, scrunching the thin strips of mnemo-paper in his fist. 'Guidance systems are damaged, and the aft engines are at quarter power.'

Burias was silent while the Coryphaus muttered, his strategic mind working to solve the problem.

'Do we have enough power to break from the moon's gravity?' he ventured.

'Yes,' snapped the Coryphaus, 'but we'd be drifting. We'll conserve our power once we have broken the atmosphere, and fire the engines to take us past the Imperial blockade. We'll order the *Infidus Diabolus* to break from its mooring and come to meet us half way.'

'The Imperial fleet will be aware of its presence as soon as it pulls out of the radiation of the sun,' said Burias. 'If they turn their fleet…'

'Then we must pray that they do not. Let us hope that the cursed Imperials are too occupied by the xenos to swing their blockade.'

'And if they don't?'

'Then we are dead.'

CHAPTER EIGHTEEN

'YOU ARE WASTING your time,' growled Marduk, blood and spittle dripping from his lips. His head was held immobile by bladed callipers that had emerged from the floating slab on which he lay, making any movement of his head or neck impossible. He glared at the eldar tormentor out of the corner of his left eye, his daemonic right eye rendered useless.

'I won't break,' snarled Marduk. 'You will have to kill me first.'

His torturer did not look up, his utterly black eyes focused on the incisions that he had cut into Marduk's neck. He was gazing into them, prodding and poking around the area where one of his progenoid glands, those sacred glands that contained the essence of his enhanced gene-seed, had been surgically removed thousands of years previously. As if satisfied, the eldar closed up the wound, and lifted what looked like a spike-tipped handgun from a pad that hovered at his side.

Marduk tensed, thinking momentarily that perhaps the eldar *was* going to kill him. The eldar ran the spiked tip of the pistol along the edge of the incision at his neck, and Marduk hissed in pain, feeling a searing laser melting his flesh. The eldar replaced the strange implement back on its floating platform, and Marduk realised that the wound in his neck was sealed.

The First Acolyte stared at the spiked pistol-like piece of apparatus for a moment, and then flexed his neck from side to side as the callipers retracted from their clamped position around his cranium. The bladed lengths slid away soundlessly, and came to rest around his head like a razor-sharp halo, leaving him free of their constriction, but still protruding from the hovering slab, just centimetres from his head.

Marduk hissed as fresh pain seared across his abdomen. Two long cuts bisected his flesh, and snarling, he leant forwards to watch the monstrous eldar surgeon at work. Doubtless that was the reason his head restraints had been retracted, so that he could witness the surgery being performed upon him. His skin was sliced, and the thick black carapace beneath, the implant that allowed his holy armour to be plugged directly into his body, was cut open with laser-tipped tools.

The bio-mechanical creature hovering on the pulsing ceiling reached out with four slender limbs, each of them piercing one corner of his flesh, painfully drawing his sliced black carapace apart to expose the stomach cavity. The wraith-like eldar began to probe his organs with his slender fingers. Marduk's chest had not yet been cut open, but he knew that it was just a matter of time. He had witnessed two of his brother Space Marines have their organs removed, though Marduk had noted that the eldar was careful to leave his victims alive, using inferior substitute organs to keep them going. It had taken some time to cut through the black carapace beneath the flesh of the warriors' chests, but the tools of the twisted creature were powerful.

'I have no interest in your death,' intoned his torturer, still engrossed in his work. Marduk could feel the fingers probing within him, handling his enhanced organs. The feeling was uncomfortable, but he pushed the sensation away, focusing his mind.

'If your intention is not to kill me, what then is to be my fate?' asked Marduk, feigning weakness in his voice.

The twisted surgeon did not pause in his work, and for a moment Marduk thought he would not get an answer, but at last the eldar spoke.

'Upon reaching Commorragh,' said the eldar, though Marduk did not recognise the word, 'your s*avayaethoth*, your… soul-flame… will be drained from your body. This soul-essence will be delivered to Lord Vect, for him to do with as he pleases. Your s*avayaethoth* burns brighter than those of your comrades. Most likely, the Lord Vect will take it into himself. All that you are will be consumed, utterly and completely, and She Who Thirsts will be denied her claim upon him a little longer.

'The soul-extraction,' continued the eldar torturer, 'is excruciatingly painful. What you have experienced thus far is nothing beside it, and I have been known to prolong the process for a week or more.'

'What will happen to you if I die beneath your scalpel before then?' asked Marduk.

'My master would be displeased,' said the eldar simply, as if he were talking to an imbecile.

'Your master is going to be very displeased, then,' said Marduk, and his primary heart stopped beating.

* * *

ADMIRAL RUTGER AUGUSTINE stared at the blinking icon in disbelief. Scans had picked up the telltale sign of a ship moving towards the rear of the Imperial blockade, emerging from within the radiation field of the system's dying sun.

'It's an Adeptus Astartes cruiser, sir,' said his aide in awe. 'And it's big.'

'Yes, I can see that,' snapped Augustine, 'but is it friend or foe?'

'You think it may be renegade, sir?' asked the man, looking at him in shock.

'I don't know. I have received no information of a Chapter of Astartes coming to our aid, though it would be welcome. That they have not intervened thus far does not bode well.'

'Initial hails have been ignored,' said the aide. 'The archives are being scoured as we speak to identify the vessel.'

'Fine,' snapped Augustine, waving the man away.

'Trouble?' asked his flag lieutenant, Gideon Cortez, as he strode to the admiral's side.

'Possibly,' replied Augustine. 'Damn it, I need more ships.'

'We could always order the Exterminatus of the Perdus moons now,' said Gideon in a low voice. 'Pull back, and swing to face this strike cruiser.'

'No,' said Augustine. 'I want that last convoy secured before I make the order.'

'Are the lives of those people down there worth risking the fleet for?' asked Gideon.

Augustine clenched his fists. Then he sighed.

'I'll give it one hour,' he said. 'Order the *Implacable* to disengage and swing around to the rear, with its full escort. Order them to stand off, though. Let the Astartes make their move.'

GLOWING RUNES FLASHED, appearing in the air above Marduk's still chest, and the haemonculus's pitch-black eyes flashed towards them in alarm.

With a flick of his bloody fingers he banished the runes and brought another set up before him, swiftly acknowledging the diagnostic reports. The mon-keigh's secondary heart had failed to pick up where its larger organ had failed. His subject was dead.

No! This could not be, he railed. There was no possible way that the subject's heart could have stopped, unless the creature had control of its functions, but such a thing was surely impossible in one as lowly as this lesser being.

More glowing runes appeared, hovering in the air above the mon-keigh's body, and Rhakaeth frowned deeply as he pulsed a swift mnemo-command to the lesser talos-artifice hovering above him. The creature's spider limbs were twitching nervously, sensing the displeasure of its master. His subject was not breathing.

Rhakaeth stabbed a needle into the Space Marine's neck before dropping the syringe to a waiting hover-pad, and summoning a breath-regulator to his side with a wave of his hand. Above, the lesser talos-artifice sank low above the table at Rhakaeth's mnemo-command, rubbing its forelegs together. Blue electricity jumped between the two bladed limbs, and at Rhakaeth's command, it touched the tips of the blades to the subject's chest.

The subject jolted, his body arching as power surged through him, and the runic projectors informed Rhakaeth that its twin hearts had recommenced their regular beat. Two heartbeats later, they had stopped again, however, and the haemonculus realised that the being was resisting his attempts to revive it.

Rhakaeth gestured, and additional hardware emerged from the underside of the operating slab, hovering up to his side. It mattered not that the creature was attempting to kill itself. It had no choice in the matter. He would keep it alive whether it wished it or not.

Leaning down low over the subject's lifeless face, Rhakaeth hissed in the crude, human tongue.

'You will not escape me so easily,' he hissed, 'and I shall make you pay for such disrespect.'

The subject's dead eyes flickered suddenly, its primary heart lurching back into life. Rhakaeth tried to pull back, realising that he had been tricked, but he was too slow, and the subject's teeth flashed for his throat.

IT HAD NOT been hard to fool his torturer. The eldar were an arrogant race and Marduk had guessed, correctly, that his captor would have no real understanding of Astartes physiology or what it was capable of.

It had been a simple matter to activate his sus-an membrane and begin the process of entering suspended animation, though it had taken more control to halt his primary heart completely.

Marduk bit into the eldar's neck, his teeth gripping the jugular tight. The eldar's flesh was dry, like a desiccated cadaver's. It would have been so easy to rip out its throat in one sharp movement, but that would achieve nothing other than fleeting satisfaction. Instead, he turned his head to the side, pulling the eldar across him, dragging its face towards one of the recurved, protruding calliper blades positioned to the side of his face.

Bladed spider limbs stabbed into his flesh, straining to pull its master free, and he felt the scalpel fingers of the eldar slashing frantically against his face and neck, but Marduk had no intention of relinquishing his hold. With relentless strength, he pulled the eldar towards the blade, careful not to tear its throat out. Still, the eldar resisted, but its body was weak in comparison to Marduk's, even restrained as he was, and the thick muscles of his neck bulged as he pulled the haemonculus onto the point of the blade. The tip of the calliper pierced the dry, wasted skin of its cheek, and a trickle of blood ran from the wound down the blade.

The eldar uttered something in its sharp language, and the blade-restraints were instantly retracted, ensuring that the torturer was not impaled, but also freeing Marduk's limbs.

The First Acolyte surged upright, tearing a chunk of dry flesh from the eldar's throat. The haemonculus fell backwards, gasping, hands trying to stem the blood flow gushing from the wound, and Marduk swung his legs from the bladed slab hovering just off the floor.

His stomach was still sliced open, and four of the spider-like legs of the eldar-machine hovering above him still pierced his skin. They slid from his flesh, and all twelve of the slender, powerful limbs descended towards him, stabbing and cutting. Marduk grabbed the spiked, gun-like instrument from the floating tray to his side, and with one hand holding his organs in place, he rolled himself off the bladed slab.

Marduk hit the ground hard, his intestines bulging from between his fingers. He rolled under the hovering slab, narrowly avoiding the stabbing legs of the spider-being that smashed down to impale him.

The haemonculus was crawling away, one hand clasped to his throat, blood gushing across the floor. He was trying to call for aid, but all that came from his mouth was a gargle of blood and froth.

Praying to the gods of Chaos that it would work, Marduk pulled the flaps of skin across his abdomen and pressed the bladed tip of the surgical instrument against the join. Its trigger was too small for his large fingers to easily operate, and they slipped off the slender trigger rune twice. The spider-creature wrapped its limbs around the bladed, hovering slab under which Marduk lay, and with a surge of power it hurled the table aside, throwing it into the wall, which shuddered and cracked beneath the impact.

Marduk managed finally to squeeze the trigger, and with a swift, painful movement, he roughly sealed the incisions. A pair of glossy black spider-limbs stabbed into his shoulders, and he howled with pain as the slender limbs passed through him, impaling his body on their lengths, and the wound-sealing implement fell with a clatter from his hands.

The First Acolyte was lifted into the air, still impaled on the two limbs, and was hurled away from the frenzied spider-creature. He struck the wall heavily, sending a ripple of cracks arcing out across its surface, and slid to the ground.

The spider-being disengaged from the ceiling, dragging its cabling and wires with it, and hit the ground, its bladed, slender limbs scrabbling for purchase. It launched itself at the First Acolyte, its forelegs rising to impale him once again.

Rolling beneath the stabbing limbs, which smacked into the wall behind him with colossal force, Marduk came up underneath the vile creature. He threw his body against the joint of one of the beast's back legs, which buckled under his sudden weight, and it stumbled.

Marduk grasped the slender limb with both hands and pushed his knee against the joint, grunting with the effort. The muscles of his arms and back strained, and he felt the limb bending beneath his force, until with a final, sickening crack, he sheared the limb in two.

Black fluid ran from the hollow limb, and the creature sprang away from him, scrabbling and sliding on the smooth floor.

Holding the bladed limb in both hands like a sword, Marduk waited for the creature to spring. He risked a glance behind him, and could see no sight of the haemonculus, though a telltale trail of blood was smeared across the floor and past the strips that led into an adjoining room.

Sensing movement, Marduk ducked and rolled to his right, narrowly avoiding being impaled on two barbed forelimbs. He slashed with the hollow limb, shearing through two of the creature's legs, which dropped to the floor, and more hissing, black fluid seeped from the creature's wounds. It spun to face him and thrust the rear of its bloated abdomen forwards, stabbing it towards him from beneath its body. Liquid squirted from its grotesque spinnerets, and although Marduk managed to avoid the worst of it, a line of the foul substance sprayed across his right shoulder. His flesh began to hiss and bubble, but he stood before the creature with his makeshift blade in both hands, ignoring the pain.

The creature's eldar torso writhed in obvious torment as ichor dripped from its severed limbs. Its blank face snapped towards Marduk, and it launched itself at him once more, bladed limbs flailing frenziedly.

The First Acolyte leapt to meet the beast, spinning the bladed limb around in his grasp so that he held it over his head like a spear. With a roar of animalistic fury, Marduk slammed the blade into the twisted eldar, the tip of the weapon piercing the flesh of its throat and driving on into its body behind its ribcage.

Bladed limbs hacked at his arms, tearing bloody strips of flesh from his bones, but the force of the creature's momentum was its death, for it continued to push forward, impaling itself further onto its own bladed limb.

Its front legs collapsed beneath it, and Marduk stepped back, breathing heavily, blood running down his arms. The loathsome creature fell headfirst into the floor, its greyish lifeblood running from its wounds. It tried piteously to lift itself up again, but its legs gave way beneath it, and it crumpled in a heap on the floor at Marduk's feet. He spat down onto the dying beast, and wrenched the bladed limb from its neck. Reaching down, he retrieved another of the creature's severed, razor sharp limbs from the floor, and so armed, he followed the trail of blood left by the haemonculus.

With the tip of one blade, Marduk parted the strips of heavy, semi-transparent material that hung from the doorway leading from the circular room that had been his entire world for the gods knew how long. He moved cautiously forwards, eyes darting around him, seeking any threat or movement.

This room was larger than the first, and circular, and half a dozen chambers led off it, each partially hidden behind hanging, translucent strips. He could hear groans and muffled shouts from within those rooms, voices crying out from raw throats whose owners had clearly heard the sound of Marduk's escape. Some of them sounded familiar, but Marduk ignored them, focusing his senses on finding the whereabouts of his twisted captor.

The centre of the room was bare except for a torturous bladed slab akin to the one he had just escaped from, with pale, thin lights shining down upon it. This table had a score of bladed arms extending from beneath it, but they appeared lifeless, or at least dormant. The room had dozens of hovering shelves and tables around its circumference, each one with strange perverse implements and objects arrayed upon it. The light was dim, pulsing faintly from the floor and the ceiling, but he could see the trail of blood on the floor clearly, and he quickly saw his wasted torturer crawling away from him, one hand still clamped around its bloody throat.

With a roar, Marduk leapt forwards, ignoring the pain in his tortured limbs. One of the eldar's wasted, skeletal hands was reaching up towards a flickering rune that hovered before what Marduk took to be a sealed, circular portal, but before it could activate the doorway, Marduk stabbed one of the slender blades down into the back of its thigh and dragged it backwards. It gave a wet, gargling cry of pain as it struggled futilely against him.

Marduk knelt over his eldar tormentor, twisting the blade ruthlessly, feeling it grinding against the bone, and smiled.

'How do you like the feel of that, xenos filth?' he snarled.

The eldar did not answer, but the bladed arcs of the circular portal slid aside soundlessly, and Marduk shifted his attention to the new threat, leaping forwards and spinning the twin blades in his hands before he even saw what was coming.

There were two creatures, vaguely eldar in appearance but altered, like mutant versions of the slender xenos. One was a woman, her body covered in tiny scales that flushed an angry red, and the other was almost reptilian in appearance, with hundreds of shivering quills inserted into its flesh.

The first blade struck the woman in the side of the neck before she could react, nigh on decapitating her, and his second blade stabbed towards the other creature's gut. Spines emerged from its wrists and it deflected the blow with a circular sweep of its arms. Then it threw its arms towards Marduk.

The First Acolyte swayed backwards, moving his body out of range of the creature's touch, but the spines in its wrists shot forward. Marduk twisted, but even so one of the spines sliced a shallow graze across his side, shooting pain blossoming from the scratch.

The female creature was on its knees, holding its head in place so that it did not flop to the side. Its scaled body was covered in rich, hot blood.

Marduk backed towards the centre of the room, stepping over the prone form of the haemonculus, which had managed to knock a surgical implant to the floor and seal its neck wound with a spray of a synthetic skin.

The spined abomination, enraged by the harm done to what Marduk guessed was its mate, threw itself towards him wildly. Marduk's blade swung up, swatting aside a pair of spines that were shot towards him. He rammed his weapon deep into the creature's side, wrenching the blade up under the ribs to pierce the heart. It slumped to the ground, hissing in hatred and scrabbling at his flesh as it died.

Moving to his torturer, which stared up at him venomously, Marduk hauled it to its feet. Holding it upright by the scruff of its thin neck, Marduk moved towards the circular portal, intending to step into the corridor beyond.

Claws dug into his shoulders as the female creature, its horrific neck wound all but healed with astonishing swiftness, landed on his back. It bit deeply into his neck, and Marduk dropped both his captor and his weapon.

Reaching over his back, his hands brushing past something cold and smooth attached to the back of his neck, he grabbed the feral creature in his crushing grip, and threw it over his head towards the wall. It tore a chunk from his neck as he hurled it away from him, and he cursed as blood gushed from the wound. The creature spun in the air like a cat, and landed on the circular wall on all fours. It did not fall, but rather remained stuck there, staring at him with hate-filled eyes.

It skittered up the sheer wall and onto the ceiling, and raced across it towards him. When it was three metres from him it launched itself from the ceiling, reaching for him with outstretched claws.

Marduk stepped into the creature as it flew towards him, and slammed his fist square into its face. Its skull crumpled beneath the blow, and its limbs went limp as it flopped to the ground. Having seen its regenerative powers already, Marduk gave it no chance to recover, and ripping the blade from the gut of its dying companion, he hacked completely through the creature's neck and tossed its head to the far corner of the room.

Swaying with blood-loss that his enhanced physiology struggled to stem, the result of the torturous wounds covering his body, Marduk dropped to one knee. His hands reached up behind his neck, towards the alien device that he had felt attached to the base of his skull when he had hurled the she-bitch monstrosity from his back.

His hands closed around a smooth, coldly metallic artifice embedded in his flesh. His fingers gripped the device around its edges, and his agonised muscles strained as he sought to rip it away from his flesh. The pain was intense, and it felt as if he might rip a part of his mind away with it, but Marduk ripped the alien device from his neck with a powerful surge of adrenaline.

The force of Chaos hit Marduk like a roaring tidal wave, staggering in its power. The full force of the warp rushed to fill the emptiness of his soul as the null field generator that kept the power of the immaterium at bay was ripped clear, and his body was suffused with the power of the dark gods once more.

His vision swam, and blood dripped down his back as Marduk stared dumbly at the black thing in his hands. Synthetic claws with patches of skin and hair still clinging to them rimmed the ovular shape.

Understanding came to him. The gods had not deserted him. This foul device had merely cut him off from its blessed presence. It was a form of null field generator. Marduk hurled it away in disgust.

BURIAS STOOD ALONGSIDE the Coryphaus, Kol Badar, on the foredeck of the *Infidus Diabolus*. The *Idolator* had docked with the mighty strike cruiser less than twenty minutes earlier, and Kol Badar had straight away ordered the warp engines of the ancient ship fired up, preparing to jump into the roiling ether and leave this cursed system behind.

It had been a tense flight from Perdus Skylla, for the damage done to the *Idolator* had meant that they had drifted, powerless, through the Imperial armada. At any moment, Burias had expected them to drift into the path of a broadside, and for the fragile shuttle to have been blasted to smithereens. Once clear of the blockade, they had drifted for tens of thousands of kilometres, until at last they had been drawn into one of the strike cruiser's immense docking bays.

There had been unease as they had disembarked from the shuttle and it became clear to the waiting warriors that Marduk was not accompanying them. Refusing to address the Host yet, Kol Badar had ordered Darioq-Grendh'al confined to his spartan quarters, and stalked to the strike cruiser's foredeck in preparation for warp jump.

Flickering screens of red light showed the relative position of the Imperial and tyranid fleets, and though the Imperials must have been aware of their presence, for the *Infidus Diabolus* had left the surging radiation of the system's sun to come to meet the damaged *Idolator*, they had made little move to break their blockade to intercept them. A single cruiser with a host of escorts had formed a rearguard behind the bulk of the cordon, though it had made no hostile move towards them as yet.

Indeed, there was only one ship nearing weapon range, but the blinking screens relayed that this was nothing more than a passenger freighter, and scans had come back negative for weapon sweeps. It was of no consequence to the powerful strike cruiser.

Burias felt Drak'shal stir within him, and his eyes rolled back as he ventured inwards, to witness what had roused the daemon from its slumber.

'Jump on my mark,' said Kol Badar, instructing the daemon-symbiotes that acted as the strike cruiser's command personnel.

Burias blinked as he came back to himself, and turned towards the Coryphaus, disbelief and dawning horror plastered on his face.

'What is it?' asked Kol Badar, seeing the icon bearer's face pale.

'Marduk,' gasped Burias. 'He is alive!'

'Where?' growled Kol Badar.

Burias's eyes settled on the insignificant Imperial freighter.

'There,' he said, stabbing a finger towards the blip.

Kol Badar swore. The bladed fingers of his power talons clenched.

'Hold jump routine,' the Coryphaus said at last.

'What are you going to do?' asked Burias in a neutral tone. Kol Badar stared at him.

'Bring us to heading L4.86,' said the Coryphaus, holding the gaze of the icon bearer. 'Order the starboard gunnery crew to prepare weapons for firing.'

Burias raised an eyebrow

'Is there a problem, icon bearer?' rumbled the Coryphaus.

Burias licked his lips.

'No problem, my Coryphaus,' he said at last.

WITH FRESH ENERGY coursing through his body, Marduk rose to his feet, his eyes burning with the fire of devotion and belief. He stalked towards the pathetic figure of his torturer, who was vainly trying to crawl to safety, and lifted the skeletal eldar into the air.

Hefting him like a rag doll, Marduk stepped through the bladed portal doors.

The corridor was long and lined with hundreds upon hundreds of cells, each filled with piteous slaves. Many of them lay on their backs, with blank masks pulled over their heads that plugged into sockets in the walls behind them. They groaned and twitched as a barrage of terror was sent into their brains, while others were hooked up to all manner of torturous devices, while their cellmates looked on in horror. Marduk saw a naked human stretched backwards across a rotating wheel-like device, his hands and ankles bound and a slender blade poised in the air above. With each turn of the wheel, the man was brought fractionally closer to the blade, cutting into his flesh in a line from chin to groin. Other figures hung from insubstantial chains of light, bizarre apparatus attached to their heads by biting metal claws and their eyelids held forcibly open by tiny, black legs. A parade of horror passed before their eyes, and they thrashed around trying to escape their torment, but unable to look away as every debauched and horrific act imaginable was flashed directly into their retinas.

None of the cells appeared to have bars. Indeed, nothing appeared to hold them within their confinement at all, and Marduk moved warily along the corridor, eyeing the tortured humanoid forms to either side of him. Few registered his passing, and those that did stared at him with hollow, despairing eyes.

Marduk saw other cells filled with what could only have been the haemonculus's experiments, wretched eldar grotesques that had been twisted and surgically altered into whatever form pleased the perverted creature. He saw some with additional limbs grafted to their bodies, others with feathers that protruded where hair ought to have grown, and others bent over backwards and walking on all fours. One of them saw him holding the torturer before him, and it screeched in outrage, frill-like flaps of skin flaring up on either sides of its neck and a tri-pronged tongue darting from its mouth. Others turned to see what had enraged it, and as one they wailed, gnashed their teeth and whimpered to see their master laid low.

One monstrous grotesque opened its gaping mouth, the aperture spreading in four quarters that peeled back from its neck to its cheeks. It threw itself at Marduk, who spun towards it, but it slammed into an invisible barrier of energy that let off a stink of ozone and hurled it backwards.

More of the inmates began to turn in Marduk's direction, and he saw the hatred in the eyes of many of them as they looked upon the skeletal form of the haemonculus, helpless in Marduk's grasp. They rose to their feet to witness his passing, lining up to form a twisted honour guard for him.

One of the inmates, a human male, started calling to him, but Marduk ignored its cries, even as more of the wretched slaves began to holler, whoop and cheer, speaking a thousand tongues, both human and xenos.

This one human was particularly insistent, running alongside Marduk within the confines of his dark cell, begging and pleading.

Marduk paused, seeing a troop of eldar warriors moving towards him in the distance, clearly alerted by the ruckus.

'Release me, I beg you, my lord,' cried the man, no more than a metre from Marduk, but separated by the invisible wall of power. Marduk glanced down at the wretch. The man had obviously not been in his confinement for long. He bore no obvious injuries, and his skin was relatively clean, in stark contrast to the filth-encrusted masses. More than that, his eyes did not yet have the hollow look of hopelessness within them.

'Why?' asked Marduk simply, which gave the man pause. He licked his lips, and Marduk swung his head back the way he had come, seeing another troop of dark eldar warriors running lightly towards him.

'I have a ship docked on this vessel! We could escape, you and I together!' cried the man as Marduk made to move on. He paused, and swung back towards the wretch.

'What guarantee do you have that your ship is still here?' he asked quickly.

'None,' admitted the man, matching Marduk's fearsome gaze without faltering, 'but how were you planning on getting off-ship?'

Marduk swung his gaze around once more, seeing the eldar warriors drawing nearer from both quarters. The ones to his right were closer, and he saw several of them drop to their knees, raising weapons to their shoulders. Marduk lifted the haemonculus up in front of him for them to see, placing the blade of the spider-eldar's limb upon its already blood-drenched throat. That gave the warriors pause, though they did not lower their weapons.

'Things are not looking so good for you, friend,' said the man in the cell.

'I am not the one in a cell,' said Marduk.

'True,' said the man. 'The cell controls for this section are behind you.'

Marduk swung his head around to see a blank wall panel, though even as he looked upon it, glimmering runes of xenos origin flickered into being, hovering in the air a few centimetres from the wall.

'Touch the middle one, the one that looks like a serpent,' said the man. 'No, not that one, the one next to it. That's the door release. I've seen the guards use it.'

Marduk paused, indecision staying his hand. The man might be lying.

'What have you got to lose?' asked the man, as if reading his mind.

Marduk backed up to the control panel, his eyes flicking between the two groups of eldar warriors that had begun to edge forwards once more, just waiting for an opportunity to fire without hitting the haemonculus. His eyes drifted down to the eldar runes flickering in the air in front of the panel.

'Release him,' Marduk growled into the haemonculus's ear, tightening his grip on the skeletal creature. The eldar made no move, and Marduk pushed the blade more forcefully against its throat, drawing blood.

The eldar reached out a long, bony finger, moving it towards the glowing runes.

'No tricks,' said Marduk, 'or I'll have my own torture fun with you before anybody comes to save you.'

The haemonculus's finger paused just before it pierced the holographic image of a rune that resembled a jagged blade. Then it moved to the side and passed through the serpent-like rune, the one that the man had indicated.

There was a descending hum, and the man reached out a tentative hand. There was no surge of power and no stink of ozone, and the man exhaled deeply, flashing Marduk a grin.

'Thank you friend,' said the man. 'My name is Ikorus Baranov.'

Marduk ignored him. He was less than nothing to him, but the puny human's words were enticing. *How were you planning on getting off-ship?*

'Now the rest of them,' said Marduk. The haemonculus faltered, gargling something from its shattered throat, and Marduk pushed the blade deeper.

Instantly, the haemonculus's hand flickered over a series of rune images, and all the cell doors in the section powered down.

At first, nothing happened. Then a hulking two-metre beast covered in matted fur staggered into the corridor. Throwing its head back, it gave a blood-curdling roar. The dark eldar guards fired, knocking it back a step. It roared again, and lurched towards the group of warriors. Barbed prongs that shimmered with arcane powers were fired into its flesh, and it fell to its knees as agony seared through its body.

More and more of the slaves staggered from their cells, blinking their eyes heavily, as if believing that this was just another part of their torture. A broad shouldered, four-legged, centaur-like creature with a reptilian head lurched from its cell, which was barely large enough to hold its massive form. It hurled itself into one of the groups of eldar warriors, and two of them died instantly as it slammed their heads together, crushing their fragile skulls.

Eldar warriors began firing as more slaves spilled from their confinement, and crackling electro-whips lashed out. Slaves shuddered and screamed as the whips struck them, sending shooting pains through their nervous systems, and others fell, their fears, terrors and nightmares coming to life before their eyes as hallucinatory venom surged through their veins.

Other slaves fell upon each other, fists cracking against skulls and hands wrapping around throats as racial enmities surged to the fore and individuals driven out of their minds by their torments sought to slake their insane bloodlust.

All was chaos along the corridor, and Marduk smiled broadly, relishing the surge of hatred, fear and anger that washed over him.

'Which way?' he said.

CHAPTER NINETEEN

Dracon Alith Drazjaer stared at the curved, three-dimensional observation screen projected before him, watching as the hive fleet of the Great Devourer drew ever nearer. The bridge of his corsair flagship was dark. Reclining upon his throne, with its razor-sharp barbs rising around him, he scowled at the holographic images appearing before him.

He saw the twin moons orbiting the giant gas planet, with the flickering ghost-image of his bladed ship pulling away from them. His ship was as one with the darkness, and had the voracious organism-ships of the Great Devourer not been encroaching, Drazjaer was confident that he could have preyed upon this system for years to come without detection.

As the moons had finally completed their long arc around the gas giant and emerged into the light of the system's dying star, the dark eldar ship had slipped unseen through the mon-keigh blockade. It was likely that none had even registered his ship's presence, and those that had would have seen nothing more suspicious than a passenger freighter of their own design.

He had plied his trade in this system for two months, relying on the mimic engines and shadow fields of his slave-ship to confuse the mon-keigh scanners, while his warriors raided the evacuating populations. Within visual range, the mimic engines would no longer be able to fool even the pitiful scanners of the mon-keigh, but still his ship would be almost impossible to pinpoint, thanks to the shadow fields that cloaked its presence, and it was easy to keep out of the visual range of the lumbering mon-keigh ships.

It had proved a profitable and successful hunt, and thousands of souls were held in the torture decks below, ready for delivery to Commorragh. Still, it was not enough, and for the thousandth time Drazjaer cursed the very existence of the black-hearted lord of the Black Heart cabal, Asdrubael Vect. The tribute he demanded was extortionate. Drazjaer had hoped that raiding this one sector would have provided enough souls to please the vicious lord, and it had come close, but his time here was done.

Within the day, the tyranids would have overrun the prey-moons. The mimic engines would not fool the hive-mind. It was time to move on, to continue his raids elsewhere, for to return to Commorragh without his full tribute was out of the question.

Dismissing the observation screen with a thought, Drazjaer swung away from the console, which retracted smoothly into the floor behind him. He saw one of his Incubi guards waiting for him, head bowed.

'What is it?' the dracon asked.

'There is a problem on *antitherea* deck, lord dracon,' murmured one of the incubi, his voice distorted by his tormentor helm.

With his screens down and completely confident that his mimic engines and shadow fields would be able to fool any of the mon-keigh vessels, Drazjaer did not see the Astartes strike cruiser turning towards his ship.

MARDUK HACKED A path through the press of inmates, slashing with the blade-limb and sending them reeling away from him, blood pumping from severed limbs. Those who fell were crushed in the rush to escape, and the man, Baranov, kept close behind him.

The First Acolyte had the skeletal form of the haemonculus in a headlock, using his body as a shield in front of him, and he hacked the blade through the neck of another inmate, who turned towards him, froth spilling from his mouth. The guards were being overwhelmed by the surge of slaves and paid Marduk no mind as they fought for their lives, weapons spitting and torturous electro-whips snapping.

'This way, I'm sure of it!' shouted Baranov, directing Marduk down a side corridor. The slave deck was a labyrinth of side-tunnels and holding cells, and everywhere was chaos as the slaves set upon their captors and each other with insane fury. Marduk had sworn that he would make the xenos scum suffer for the ignoble sufferings that had been committed upon his flesh, and he smiled to see the mayhem he had wrought.

Marduk moved past dozens of cells. The wretched inmates still cowered within many of them, crouching in the corners, rocking back and forth, their heads in their hands, but it did not matter. Enough of the slaves were hell-bent on overcoming their captors to provide an adequate distraction.

'There!' shouted Baranov, pointing towards what looked like a dead end. 'That is where they brought me from.'

Marduk swung down the corridor. A group of eldar warriors was backed up against its end, a circular, closed aperture behind them. A slave, a human, launched itself at Marduk, hands clawing for him, but the First Acolyte slashed his blade across its face.

With the haemonculus held in a brutal headlock, Marduk broke into a run, dropping his shoulder and barging his way through the crowd towards the far end of the corridor. Baranov struggled to keep up, running in his destructive wake.

With a swat of his arm, Marduk slammed the first of the guards back into the wall, and slashed his blade across the neck of the second, blood gushing from the wound.

Something stabbed into Marduk's unarmoured back, and his body was jolted as his pain receptors flared, and his muscles twitched uncontrollably. He lost his grip on the haemonculus, who slumped to the ground in a bloody heap, and twisted around to see a trident sparking with energy jabbed into his flesh, held in the grasp of a blade-helmeted dark eldar warrior. He grabbed the haft of the weapon, sending flaring pain up his arm, and swung it upwards, sending the warrior wielding the weapon smashing into the low roof. The warrior released its hold on the trident, and Marduk turned and impaled another of its dark kin on its points.

'Get the doors open,' he barked, spinning and decapitating another warrior with a sweep of his blade.

'I'm trying,' shouted Baranov, his fingers flickering over the glowing rune of a side-panel.

'Try harder,' roared Marduk, just before he was slammed back against the wall as a coruscating arc of dark energy struck him square in the chest, fired from the snub-nosed rifle of another enemy.

The eldar warrior was about to fire on him again, but stumbled as another slave slammed into his back, knocking the eldar off-balance and towards Marduk. The First Acolyte reared up with a growl, the flesh of his chest blistered and smoking, and slammed his fist up into the eldar's chin, throwing his full force behind the blow.

The warrior's neck snapped backwards with an audible crack, and Marduk positioned himself in a protective position in front of Baranov, ensuring that no one came near him. He saw the haemonculus clawing away from him on the floor, and at a whim he placed his still-armoured foot upon the skeletal eldar's elongated cranium, pinning it to the floor.

'It's not opening,' said Baranov desperately. 'It's been locked down, or something.'

'You can open it for me,' Marduk said to the haemonculus, exerting more pressure on the creature's skull. It gurgled something, and Marduk bent down and picked it up by the scruff of its neck. His fingers completely encircling its neck, he held it half a metre above the ground. He pushed Baranov roughly aside.

'Open it,' Marduk growled, and slammed the haemonculus's head into the control panel for emphasis. Its nose broke, and blood splattered across the black panel.

The eldar gargled something, but its voice was unintelligible, and Marduk slammed its face into the panel again.

'Open it,' he hissed again, before slamming its head into the panel once more. Its face was a bloody ruin, its nose smashed, and blood and mucus was smeared across the deathly visage.

'You'll kill it,' warned Baranov, but the haemonculus lifted one of its claw-like hands, reaching blearily towards the panel.

The eldar's fingers stabbed at a series of runes and blade-arcs of the circular door slid open.

An armed group of eldar warriors stood beyond the doors, a hundred slender rifles lowered towards him. At the centre stood a tall figure in glistening black, barbed and segmented armour, its pale xenos face staring at him with noble arrogance. He saw the long-haired bitch that had ensnared him at its side, and a milky-eyed creature, glowing blue runes carved upon its ebony flesh.

'You... lose,' gargled the haemonculus, looking up at him in triumph.

'I don't think so,' said Marduk, and slammed the haemonculus's head into the control panel once more, this time with fatal force. Its skull crumpled.

He flicked his glance towards Baranov, whose face was pale as he stared out at the horde of enemy warriors before them.

'Stay close to me,' hissed Marduk.

Letting the dead figure of the haemonculus slump to the ground, leaving a smear of brainmatter across the control panel's surface, Marduk lifted his head high and stared defiantly at the eldar, awaiting his fate as a warrior of Lorgar.

Blood covering his heavily scarred, naked torso, Marduk locked his eyes on the central eldar figure. This one was clearly the leader of the dark kin, and if he had any hope of escape, it lay in him. The arrogant bastard stood with his arms folded across his chest, blades gleaming down its forearms, a look of utter contempt and sardonic humour on his xenos face. Surrounded by over a hundred of his warriors, all with weapons lowered, the haughty eldar lord sneered down his nose at Marduk.

'This is the prey-slave that has caused all this disturbance?' he asked, enunciating the words in a perfect, old form of Low Gothic. 'I am disappointed. It does not look like much.'

'I've still got the strength to rip your heathen head from its shoulders, xenos filth,' growled Marduk. 'Come, face me alone, if you have the nerve.'

'Face you alone?' laughed the dark eldar lord. 'We are far beyond any mon-keigh notions of honour, fool.'

'Coward,' snapped Marduk. 'Even unarmoured you fear to face one of the blessed warriors of Lorgar.'

The fiery-haired wych that had ensnared Marduk stood alongside the eldar lord, and said something sharp in the twisted eldar tongue, her eyes flashing and her hand darting towards one of the blades strapped to her slim waist. Her intent was clear; she wished to face Marduk in her lord's stead.

'Let your lapdog bitch fight,' urged Marduk, fixing his hate-filled gaze upon the wych. 'I'll tear her beating heart from her chest and laugh as I watch the life drain from her eyes.'

The dark lord snapped something sharp as the wych took a step towards him, sneering, and she paused.

'I have no wish to see you dead, prey-slave,' said the dark lord, 'and I fear that Atherak will not hold a killing blow. You are less than nothing to me, one of a race that exists merely to be preyed upon. You have no right of challenge.'

Marduk's muscles tensed in anger.

Having been stripped of his blessed armour, and with his flesh covered in the hellish wounds inflicted on him by the ministrations of the haemonculus, Marduk was but a shadow of his former self, but still his bulk and strength were impressive to behold. He advanced towards the arc of enemy warriors with his head held high, determined to face his fate defiant and proud to the end.

Marduk grinned, as he called the darkness forth.

NEVER BEFORE HAD Marduk felt such power as coursed through him now, and he felt the presence of the darkling god of Chaos, Slaanesh, surge into his being, almost shattering Marduk's sanity with the full force of its potency.

Marduk had always honoured Chaos in all its guises, and had reproached those within his flock who had strayed too close to the worship of any of the infinitesimal deities of the immaterium in isolation. He had never felt the attentions of any single god upon him like he did now, and he struggled to maintain control as the Prince of Pleasure exerted its will upon him. He fell to one knee, clenching his eyes closed tightly, struggling not to be overwhelmed by the surging power that threatened to tear him apart.

Do not fight me, whispered a seductive voice in his mind, its power staggering. The voice was silken, though behind its whisper Marduk could hear a billion souls screaming in torment and ecstasy. The power of the words ripped through his soul, and a tortured groan escaped his lips.

It is not for you that I come.

In an instant, Marduk lowered his defences, allowing the full potency of Slaanesh to manifest within him.

'Get it out of my sight,' said the dark eldar lord, unaware of the power growing within Marduk. Arrogant fool, thought the First Acolyte, he still believes me to be contained by the null field device.

Marduk's face snapped up, his eyes a milky, pale blue with narrow slits in place of his pupils.

'*I know what it is that you fear,*' Marduk hissed in a voice that was not his own, and the dark eldar lord recoiled as if physically struck. '*Your souls are mine!*'

'The Great Enemy,' breathed the dracon in horror, speaking in the eldar tongue, though Marduk found that he could understand its words.

The First Acolyte pushed himself to his feet, feeling immeasurable power suffusing his body, and he lifted his arms out wide to either side, palms upwards. He could feel the panic and fear flow from the gathered eldar warriors, washing over him in a tantalising, delicious wave.

Marduk exhaled, and a pink mist rolled from his throat, filling the air with its heady, musky aroma.

'Kill it! Kill it now!' screamed the eldar lord, and a hundred weapons fired, as if his words had snapped his warriors from their horrified paralysis.

The air was filled with thousands of barbed splinters, lances of dark matter and coruscating arcs of energy.

None of the shots struck his flesh as Marduk continued to exhale, the mist curling and billowing from his mouth. Splinters slowed as they came within centimetres of his flesh, dropping to the floor in their hundreds with a musical ring, and beams of dark matter fizzled and dissipated as they seared towards him. Arcs of energy flowed around his body, leaving his flesh unscathed.

The pale mist rolled across the floor, and the eldar recoiled, continuing to fire their weapons as they backed away.

'*Come to me, my handmaidens,*' hissed the voice speaking through Marduk.

CHAPTER TWENTY

BARANOV THREW HIMSELF backwards as the eldar began to fire, and stray shots sliced through the air around him as he scrambled back behind the doors leading into the slave deck. His heart beating wildly, he pushed himself backwards with his feet, so that he came to rest with his back up against the wall alongside the dead figure of the haemonculus. He stared down at the crumpled, unrecognisable face of the eldar.

Several slaves had been cut down by stray fire, and lay bleeding on the floor. One of them, a young woman, reached piteously towards Baranov for help, blood bubbling from her mouth like foam. Baranov kicked at her hand to keep her away. Behind her, the other slaves were streaming away from the open portal as more stray shots pinged off the walls. A splinter ricocheted off a wall panel and struck the woman in the eye, killing her instantly.

The Space Marine spoke, and Baranov reeled in horror, doubling over in pain. It felt like *things* were clawing inside him, and an intrusive stabbing pain gripped his guts. He vomited, emptying his stomach as the utter *wrongness* of the voice clawed at his sanity, and tears ran down his face as he spat yellow bile onto the floor.

Baranov sank to the floor, oblivious to the vomit and drool on his chin and down the front of his chest, his limbs shaking. The Space Marine spoke with the voice of a daemon, a voice of madness. Its words were alien and horrific to Baranov, like a deafening cacophony of screams and guttural snarls.

A sudden compulsion made him crawl forwards on his hands and knees to peer around the corner of the circular doorway, and though he fought the urge, his soul screaming, he could no more stop his movements than he could stop his heart from beating. With tears running down his face, and shaking his head in denial, Baranov looked around the corner.

The Space Marine was standing with his arms spread wide, his head thrown back, and pink mist was seeping from within him, billowing from the cuts upon his body and spilling from his eyes, nostrils and mouth. The mist rolled out across the floor before him, and the black-armoured xenos warriors continued to blaze away at the daemonic figure as they backed away from its touch, though their weapons did nothing.

Baranov thought he saw shapes within the mist, sensuous bodies wrapped around each other in ecstasy, but he blinked his eyes and they were gone, nothing but contorting shapes formed by the roiling, pink smoke.

The mist coiled around Baranov's legs, and he felt hands caressing his skin, which was at once arousing and repulsive. The musk entered his lungs and he felt instantly light-headed, as if his mind was addled with opiates, and his flesh tingled with sensation.

He saw that his first impression had been correct. There *were* figures in the mist, and they were rising like serpents, their bodies unfurling as they stood, their every movement fluid and supple beyond human capacity.

There were dozens of them: tall, slender figures not unlike the eldar in proportion, though the similarities ended there. They were neither male nor female, or rather, they were both simultaneously, and they moved with inhuman grace and suppleness, their bodies twisting and writhing. Baranov found that his breath was coming in husky gasps as he looked upon their unnatural forms.

The figures solidified, and Baranov was paralysed in horrified rapture. His soul screamed within him of the utter wrongness of what he was seeing, yet his body was responding to the hellish allure of the figures. He saw their faces, and they were angels, beings of incomparable beauty. Their hair writhed like nests of vipers, and their eyes gleamed with the promise of pleasure… and pain.

The daemon's faces changed suddenly, the facade of beauty sloughing off as they opened luscious mouths, exposing needle-like teeth. Their eyes were as black as night and too large for their hellish faces, and Baranov realised that the daemon's slender arms ended not in hands, but in elongated, serrated claws.

Then the killing began.

The daemonettes moved with impossible grace, matching and surpassing that of the eldar. Every sharp movement of the daemons ended in a spurt of blood, a killing thrust, a severed limb. Bladed arms slashed across jugulars, and slender claws snapped bones. Elongated, tri-forked tongues lapped lasciviously at spilled blood, and the daemonettes spun and pirouetted through the carnage, killing with every graceful, savage movement.

Baranov breathed deeply of the intoxicating musk as he began to hyperventilate, and his irises swelled into wide, staring discs.

A daemonette appeared out of the mist alongside him, running a slender claw along the inside of his thigh, drawing blood. A stinging tongue caressed his neck, and Baranov moaned.

MARDUK LAUGHED ALOUD, hacking left and right with his blade, severing limbs from bodies and relishing the unabashed terror of the eldar.

The daemonettes were tearing through the eldar, carving a bloody swathe through their panicked ranks. Dozens of the daemons were snuffed out of existence as their physical bodies were torn apart by the frantically fired weapons of the eldar, but more of them continued to appear from the heady musk, taking shape even as their sisters were cut down.

Marduk fought his way towards the eldar lord, who was backing away frantically, his guards closing around him in a tight-knit circle. The heavily armoured warriors slashed around them with curved-bladed glaives, scything through daemonettes screeching like banshees, their voices raised in piercing cries that were at once hauntingly beautiful and horrific.

One of the incubi was dragged down, bladed arms stabbing into its stomach and head simultaneously, and a pair of daemonettes danced towards the dark eldar lord, claws slashing towards him.

The dark eldar lord moved with blinding speed, catching the blows on his bladed forearms, turning them aside and snapping one of the claws clean off with a deft twist. The daemonette hissed as milky ichor dripped from the wound, and the eldar lord stepped in close, slashing the blades across its face, tearing its unholy flesh from ear to ear.

The eldar lord swayed back from a sweeping blow from the other daemonette, before leaping into the air, spinning, and slamming first one foot and then the other into the daemonette's face. Blades in his boots sliced through infernal skin, spilling more steaming ichor, and the lord stepped back as his incubi bodyguards finished the injured creatures, ripping them in two with powerful blows of their punisher glaives.

'*I come for you!*' roared Marduk, his voice still that of the daemon, as he slashed a path towards the dark eldar lord.

'IT'S MOVING A little fast for a freighter, don't you think?' commented Burias, looking with narrowed eyes at the flickering vid-screens on which the positions of the fleets blinked.

The Imperial vessel that Marduk was located aboard had moved swiftly as the *Infidus Diabolus* had swung towards it, altering its trajectory with a speed and manoeuvrability that seemed far beyond that of a simple freighter; indeed it came about to a new heading with a swiftness that was far beyond any Imperial ship. Despite its surprising swiftness, the sudden movement of the *Infidus Diabolus* would surely allow at least one barrage upon it before it slipped out of range.

'Targeting matrices locked on,' croaked seven daemon-servitor symbiotes in unison.

'Fire,' barked Kol Badar.

A moment later, Burias felt the reverberations through the *Infidus Diabolus* as a full broadside salvo was launched upon the curious Imperial freighter.

THE ELDAR VESSEL veered to starboard as hundreds of cannon batteries unleashed their devastating fusillade, displaying a speed of manoeuvrability that a strike craft a tenth of its size would have envied. That brutal salvo would have torn through the void shields of any Imperial ship in seconds, and smashed apart its hull armour within moments, but the bulk of the shots went screaming past the shadowy outline of the dark eldar ship. Its mimic engines projected an outline that was vastly different to its actual proportions, fooling the targeting arrays of the *Infidus Diabolus*, and hundreds of tonnes of heavy duty ordnance roared past the ship, screaming wide of the mark.

Even with the naked eye, its exact position was impossible to discern thanks to its shadow fields, all light refracting and curving around its hull so that it seemed barely there at all.

Still, the weight of cannon fire was heavy and indiscriminate, and it tore through the bladed membranes of the back-swept vanes that rose like a ridge across the back of the dark eldar ship. Several barrages also slammed into its hull proper, wreaking terrible damage.

Even as the ship dived away from the *Infidus Diabolus*, slicing through the void like a knife, it returned fire, and stabbing lances of dark matter slammed into the Word Bearers' strike cruiser.

A dozen broadside cannon batteries were destroyed instantly, and tens of hundreds of indentured slaves, chained together in long worker gangs, whose sole existence was to load and prepare the mighty weapons for firing, were dragged into the emptiness of space, where their organs imploded. Fire blossomed across the strike cruiser as its hull was compromised in a handful of places, though the flames almost instantly died as bulkheads isolated the crippled areas and the air within was sucked into space.

The Astartes cruiser fired again, correcting its aim now that the mimic engines of the dark eldar vessel had been nullified.

'ADMIRAL!' SHOUTED THE flag-captain of the *Hammer of Righteousness*.

'What?' snapped Admiral Rutger Augustine. His knuckles were white as he clenched the railing before his viewscreen on the bridge of his flag-ship.

'That rogue freighter…' began his second in command, Gideon Cortez.

'What about it, Gideon? We are fighting a damn engagement here.'

'It's… it's not an Imperial vessel, lord.'

'What are you talking about?'

'The scans, they've been wrong. It's a xenos vessel, sir. Eldar. They must have been transmitting a false signal that's been fooling our sensors.'

Augustine swore. He had his hands full already with more than half his fleet engaged with the tyranids. The last thing he needed was for an eldar fleet to turn up. One never knew what their intentions were. Were they here to fight the tyranids for their own benefit? Or would they attack the Imperial fleet while it was engaged with the xenos foe?

'Is its disposition hostile?' he asked.

'Negative, sir, it is moving away from the fleet.'

'Well that is something at least. Ignore it. I have no wish to incur the wrath of the eldar. Not here.'

'There is something else, Rutger,' said Gideon, and Augustine could hear the reticence in his friend's voice. It must be bad, he thought with a sigh.

'Go ahead,' he said wearily.

'The Adeptus Astartes cruiser has been identified. Its signature has been pulled from the archive banks of command central. It is the *Infidus Diabolus*, lord. Word Bearers Legion.'

'Traitors,' said Augustine. He cast his gaze heavenwards, and barked a humourless laugh. 'Tyranids, eldar, and now traitor Space Marines. Perfect.'

'There is some good news, sir,' said Gideon.

'Oh?' replied Augustine.

'It would appear that the eldar and Chaos ships are engaging each other.'

Augustine shook his head.

'The Emperor works in mysterious ways,' he said.

Eldar were one thing, as often friends as foes, but a cruiser of traitor Space Marines? They were the enemy, and must be eliminated.

'Order the *Implacable* to move up in support of the eldar vessel,' ordered Augustine. 'Order them to engage and destroy the *Infidus Diabolus*.'

MARDUK STUMBLED AS the entire xenos ship was rocked by a second series of impacts, and he cursed. He had to get off the ship.

He saw the female, flame-haired wych that had captured him cart-wheel through the melee, her whip crackling through the air behind her, and three of the daemonettes screamed in fury as their earthly bodies were slain, disappearing into mist.

Another daemonette reared up behind her and rammed its claws through her slender, tattooed body. Marduk plunged his blade into the wych's face, spitting her head on its length. Face to face with the daemonette, Marduk grinned. The daemon licked its teeth at him in response, and ripping its claws from the wych's body, it spun lightly on its heel, claws singing through the air to decapitate another eldar, sending its head flying.

Marduk whipped the blade free, spraying blood in a wide arc and spun to his right, slashing it across the helmet of another warrior, the slender xenos limb slicing through the armour with consummate ease.

Another barrage struck the eldar ship and Marduk stumbled again, cursing.

Darts spat into Marduk's chest, and he hissed as debilitating pain wracked his body for a moment, before the power of the warp within him surged, and he felt the pain recede. One of the dark lord's guardians stood before him, and more darts were fired from the tip of its backwards-curving helmet, which resembled a scorpion's tail.

Marduk lifted a hand, the movement guided by the power of Slaanesh surging within him, and the darts were halted in mid-air. With a quick motion, Marduk sent them slicing off to the side, where they took an eldar in the face.

The bodyguard darted towards Marduk, swinging its glaive with surprising swiftness, forcing him to leap backwards to avoid being cut in two. There was no time to launch a riposte, for the eldar danced after him, its return blow striking towards his neck.

Marduk met the blow with one of his own, but the glaive sheared through his blade as if it were not there, and though Marduk swayed to the side at the last moment to avoid the killing blow, the blade smashed into his shoulder, sinking deep into his flesh.

Grabbing the blade with one hand, keeping the eldar from pulling it clear, the First Acolyte and the eldar were momentarily locked together. Marduk stood half a head taller than the slender warrior, and over twice his weight, but the eldar was swift, despite its heavy armour.

The eldar's foot snapped out, hitting Marduk squarely in the throat. Again, the eldar snapped a kick to his neck, but this time the Word Bearer met its force with his arm, clubbing down hard on the leg as it rose towards him.

The eldar gave a reptilian hiss of pain as its leg was broken, its armour crushed beneath the blow. Instantly, Marduk ripped the glaive from his shoulder and whirled it through the air. He hit the eldar in the back as it fell away from him, severing its spinal column.

The weapon was phenomenally light in his hands, and he slashed it to the right, cleaving the arm from another of the eldar lord's bodyguard as it despatched another daemonette.

There was no order to the battle. The eldar were completely overrun by the daemons of Slaanesh. The musk had a powerful, intoxicating effect, and everything was brighter, more alive, and more intense than in any battle Marduk had experienced before. He heard every groan, scream and gasp, and every splatter of blood as it struck the flooring. The blood being spilled was the most entrancing, vivid colour imaginable, and he felt a savage joy at the play of light across the armour of the eldar warriors, the alluring smell of death, and the feel of the xenos weapon beneath his hands.

He saw the guards of the eldar lord fall one by one, dragged down into the mist, until the black-armoured figure stood alone, defiant and savage, yet hopelessly overwhelmed. This one moved well, and Marduk longed to test his strength against him, but it was not to be.

The daemonettes circled in around the eldar lord, snarling and hissing, closing off any chance of escape, and Marduk had no wish to come between the daemons and their prey.

Another series of detonations rocked the eldar ship, and Marduk swung away from the doomed eldar lord, leaving him to his fate.

'THAT ONE IS MINE,' said a voice, and Baranov looked up to see the Space Marine that had released him from his imprisonment striding towards him through the pink mist, eyes blazing with dominating power as he glared at the daemonette that held Baranov in its thrall.

The daemonette hissed in anger, but obediently spun away from Baranov, who cried out in desire and pain as it relinquished its hold on him. Bloody, stinging welts covered Baranov's body, and his eyes lingered on the fey creature as it spun away on one clawed foot and slashed its arm across the neck of a slave, who was standing nearby, mouth agape. Blood fountained from the mortal wound, yet the man moaned in pleasure, and the daemonette bore it to the ground in its embrace, the pair disappearing into the knee-high mist.

Baranov was insensible, shaking and gibbering from the horrors he had witnessed as the Space Marine hauled him brutally to his feet.

'Take me to your ship,' growled the immense figure, eyes blazing with fury and power.

'My ship,' muttered Baranov, his sanity in tatters, but he was brought back into reality as the Space Marine slapped him across the side of the head. His brain was rattled inside his skull by the force of the blow. The immense figure grabbed Baranov by the front of his shirt and pulled him towards his snarling, bloody face.

'Take me to your ship, or I'll gut you here,' he growled.

DRACON ALITH DRAZJAER turned on the spot, his eyes darting between the encircling daemonettes. All his long centuries of decadent life, avoiding the claim that She Who Thirsts had over his soul, and it had come to this. Anger, bitterness, desperation and fathomless terror flowed through him in equal measure, but his body had been well trained in the death-cult temples of Commorragh, and he reacted instinctively as the daemonettes closed in on him.

He spun towards one of them, catching the daemonette's blow in one hand and slashing his bladed forearm across its neck with his other arm. He spun the daemonette into the path of one of its companions, and ducked beneath the slashing claws of the third daemonette, coming up inside its guard and ripping its abhorrent body apart with twin swipes of his arms.

Turning swiftly, he swayed beneath a swinging claw that would have ripped his head from his shoulders, and slammed a kick into the daemonette's perverted, backwards jointed knee, shattering it. As it fell, he rammed his elbow into its face, spitting it on the blade that jutted from his armoured plates.

He caught a blade on one forearm, and then another on his other arm, and snapped a kick into the daemonette's leering face. Blades snapped forwards from his knuckles and he stepped in close and punched the bitch daemon in the throat twice, hissing fluid spraying from the wound even as the infernal lesser daemon returned to smoke.

Drazjaer felt the presence of the mandrake, Ja'harael, materialise at his side.

'Save me, half-breed, and all that is mine will be yours,' Drazjaer hissed in desperation.

The mandrake stepped in close behind him and rammed blades into the dracon's unprotected back.

'You have failed Lord Vect, dracon,' hissed the mandrake in his ear. 'Your path is your own.'

The daemonettes closed in once more, licking their lips seductively.

'Goodbye, lord dracon,' said Ja'harael, and his form turned to shadow, even as the graceful claws of a daemonette slashed towards him. The daemonic blade-limbs sliced harmlessly through his insubstantial body, and he disappeared, retreating into the refuge of the webway.

Drazjaer screamed, his earthly voice and that of his damned soul joined together in union.

Delicate claws snapped closed, and Drazjaer's body was shorn into a dozen pieces. His soul was sent screaming to feed the insatiable hunger of the daemonettes' master.

Screams and screeching inhuman cries echoed in the distance, and Baranov was pulled sharply into the darkness of a side-passage as yet another troop of eldar soldiers ran past, heading towards the escalating mayhem of the battle underway within the heart of the eldar vessel.

'There,' whispered Baranov, unable to stop his body shaking. He pointed across the open dock towards his ship, the *Rapture*, which was, thankfully, still where he had left it. The yawning expanse of space could be seen beyond, held at bay by an invisible integrity field.

Another explosion rocked the ship, and Baranov fell to his knees, though his companion yanked him back to his feet instantly.

'Keep behind me,' boomed his immense, bloodied benefactor, who broke into a run towards the *Rapture*. Baranov had no time to think, and he bolted from cover after the towering, terrifying Space Marine.

There was a shout, and Baranov saw a pair of eldar move to intercept the hulking Space Marine. Pistols spat shards of death towards the immense figure, but they barely slowed him, and he thundered into the pair, his halberd swinging in lethal arcs. Two slices and the fight was over, and two eldar bodies fell to the floor with mortal wounds.

The Space Marine reached the *Rapture* some ten paces ahead of Baranov, and swung around, his hellish eyes scanning for the enemy. Baranov ran underneath the landing gear of his prized shuttle and keyed the entrance code. The gangway ramp lowered towards the floor with a satisfying hiss. He ran up the ramp and bolted towards the control cabin, throwing himself into the pilot's seat. Flicking levers and turning dials, the *Rapture's* engines roared as they made ready for flight, and Baranov ran through a hasty diagnostics check.

'Are you in?' he called out over his shoulder.

'Go,' came the roared reply, and Baranov heard the sound of weapons fire.

'Hold on,' he shouted, and he gunned the engines.

The *Rapture* lifted from the deck, and her landing gear folded up beneath her as she turned on the spot, aiming towards the gaping docking bay doors and the refuge of space beyond. Weapon fire struck the hull, and Baranov swore as he saw a flashing damage report register on one of his pict screens. Then he slammed the two propulsion levers flat to the console, and the *Rapture* filled the dock with the flames of her engines. The rogue trader vessel speared out through the gaping bay doors, shooting free of the eldar vessel that had so nearly claimed his life and soul.

CHAPTER TWENTY-ONE

SOLON PUSHED THROUGH the bustling crowds with growing desperation and fierceness, shoving people brutally out his way, ignoring their curses and cries of anger as he fought his way towards gate D5, one of more than fifty that was still taking passengers. He dragged Dios through the press, determined not to release his grip on the boy now that they were so close.

They had seen the mass transport from some two kilometres distance as it descended through the atmosphere, hundreds of massive retro engines roaring to slow its vertical descent. The storms that had raged over the moon had been rolling away to the south for the past six hours, and for the first time in almost three months Solon had seen the stars overhead from horizon to horizon.

The angry red glow of the Eye of Terror dominated the sky, a circular corona of hellish light that peered down on Perdus Skylla with evil intent, gloating over its fate. Flashes of light sparked in the heavens, like a hundred stars being born and dying again instantly, and it took Solon some time to realise what the flashes were.

'An Imperial armada is fighting for us, Dios,' he had said in awe when realisation had finally come to him, and he marvelled at the spectacle, trying to imagine the colossal battle raging overhead.

It had taken them almost four days to close towards the Phorcys starport, and they had met thousands of refugees, joining their convoys as they gravitated towards their last hope of salvation. Burning streaks of fire could be seen in the distance as hundreds of alien spores descended on the ice-world, each one filled with xenos warriors intent on slaughter, and Solon knew that the final death of the world drew near.

With grim determination he pushed on through the crowd, elbowing his way forward, struggling along with more than a hundred thousand other desperate souls to pass through gate D5 and secure a berth upon the last of the mass transports.

It was like a form of hell, with so many thousands of people straining to push into the narrow defile leading to the boarding gate, and the stink of humanity was heavy. People screamed as the breath was crushed from their lungs by the press, and others cried out as they fell, to be trampled to death underfoot.

Women wailed as children were swept away from them in the surging crowd, and thousands of voices rose, yelling out in desperation to loved ones lost in the press. Other voices lifted desperate pleas to the Emperor, crying out for aid, for salvation, for forgiveness.

Wild-eyed priests had climbed up radial spires along with gaggles of frenzied supporters, and they raved and screamed their sermons over the heads of the crowds that rippled like a living sea beneath them.

A form of mass hysteria and mania gripped the flood of humanity, and fights broke out in isolated pockets of madness within the sea of bodies, with men clubbing each other to the ground, their faces twisted in rage and fear, only to be trampled en masse as the crowds surged back and forth.

A woman that had scratched a bloody aquila into her forehead screamed that the time of repentance had come, calling out for others to join her in joyous suicide, so that their souls might join with the Emperor in glory. She grabbed Dios by the arm, pulling him towards her, but Solon smashed his fist into her face, and she disappeared into the crowd once more.

Other desperate Imperial citizens, knowing that they had no chance of getting on board the mass transport and driven mad with despair and terror, hurled themselves to their deaths from the upper levels of the starport, screaming for the Emperor to draw their souls to Him. They plummeted down into the crowds, creating momentary gaps as they crushed those beneath them, before the gaps were instantly filled with more desperate people, clambering over each other towards the boarding gate.

Solon was nearing the vast gateway that led towards the immense transport ship, and was being carried along with the crowd down the centre of the vestibule area that angled into the gate. Those on the outer edges of the crowd were pressed against the rockcrete walls as they angled inwards, the weight of bodies behind them surging into the narrowing defile crushing the life out of them.

Someone stumbled in front of Solon, and soon dozens of citizens were pulled down, screaming and roaring. Dragging Dios behind him,

Solon clambered over the morass of bodies, uncaring of who he stamped underfoot in his desperation to get to the gates.

A wailing roar rose from the crowd as the immense gates began to close, grinding in from either side, and Solon pushed on with added fury, smashing people aside as he strove towards the front.

He was only fifteen metres from the gates, and he surged forwards, pulling those in front down and clambering over them in desperation. Skyllan Interdiction Forces were screaming out over the crowd on loudhailers, ordering them back, but no one listened to their words. The gates continued to close, the press unbearable, and Solon was pushed back further from the gates, crying in anguish.

Once again, the crowd surged, and more people fell to the ground. A gap opened up, and Solon stumbled forwards, pulling Dios behind him, towards the closing gate.

The Skyllan Interdiction soldiers opened fire into the crowd to force them back, laslocks stabbing into the crowd. People screamed, but there was nowhere to flee, and the sickening stink of burnt human flesh caught in the back of Solon's throat, making him gag. Soldiers roared, ordering the crowd back, but it was an impossibility, and again they fired into the crowd, indiscriminately spraying las-fire into the mass of humanity.

Solon was struck a glancing blow high in the shoulder that spun him around, and he almost fell. Dios shouted something that was lost in the deafening roar around them and leapt forwards, trying to pull him to his feet. Knowing that to fall was to die, Solon grabbed at those around him, scrabbling for purchase. Hands punched down at him, trying to dislodge his grip, and boots kicked him in the ribs, and trampled on his legs. With a burst of energy, he dragged one man down, scrambling to his feet as he condemned the man to death, crushed to pulp beneath the surging crowd.

Five metres.

The gates were grinding closed, but Solon was so close it was painful. He pressed forward once more, and made good progress, battling his way towards the gates. He reached the front just as the gates slammed shut with a resounding crash. The sound struck Solon like a death knell, and he reached forwards and grabbed the bars of the gate, crying out in anguish.

The soldiers on the other side of the gates were backing away, eyeing the crowd nervously.

Hundreds of people threw themselves on the barred gates, clambering up onto support struts, calling after the soldiers or the last citizens that had made it through.

'Open the gates,' shouted scores of voices. Those behind, not yet realising that the gates had been sealed, that all hope had evaporated, continued to press forwards, crushing those at the front against the thick bars.

'Just take the boy!' roared Solon, his voice hoarse. One of the soldiers heard him, but shrugged his shoulders and turned away.

'Squeeze through, Dios,' urged Solon as they were hammered from behind and drove into the gate with crushing force. Dios cried out as his small body was pressed against the bars.

'Push through, damn it!' shouted Solon, and Dios squeezed one arm and leg through the narrow gap between the bars. He cried out as he got stuck, and looked around frantically for Solon.

'Breathe out, boy,' said Solon. 'You can make it.'

Dios exhaled all his breath, and Solon gave him a push. The boy was stuck tight, and he feared that his skull or hipbones would break if he pushed any harder, but the alternative was no more appealing. Another few minutes in this crush and the boy would be dead anyway.

'Breathe out, Dios!' he shouted again and gave the boy another shove. Dios cried out in obvious pain, but then his head passed through the bars and he fell to his knees on the other side. His head was bloody, and Solon realised that it was the blood that had saved the boy's life, for it had probably made the bars more slippery.

Dios picked himself up, and looked through the bars at Solon, his face fearful.

'Go!' screamed Solon, pointing behind Dios, where the lucky ones who had managed to pass through the gates were streaming into the expansive open holds of the mass transport, being herded by soldiers.

Dios turned and looked towards the ship, and then back at Solon. Solon saw that his face was an even more unhealthy shade of blue, and his eyes still burned with feverish light.

'Go, Dios!' Solon roared. The press behind him was intolerable, and he clambered up the bars, stamping on faces behind him.

'Go!' shouted Solon again, and the boy gave him one last look before he turned and ran towards the waiting mass transport.

Solon remained clinging to the bars until he saw Dios board the ship safely, and the transport's massive bay doors were locked and closed behind him. He felt strangely numb, and impossibly weary. The crowds were dissipating, wandering aimlessly, staring around with hollow eyes. Some sat down, numb with shock, while others gathered in small groups to pray. Others set about looting and destroying anything that they could, while some merely lay down on the ground to wait for the end.

Solon walked through the crowd, feeling hollow and empty. He took comfort in the fact that he had got Dios to safety, though he knew it was but a displacement of the guilt he harboured for not having been able to save his son.

He avoided the frenzied priests screaming of the end times, though hundreds flocked to hear their impassioned, doom-laden sermons.

With no real destination in mind, Solon wandered through the spaceport, seeing misery, fear and resignation everywhere he looked. After perhaps an hour he found himself at the windows of a viewing station, and watched the mass transport rise from its dock, as the flower-petal segments of the dome overhead parted to the heavens.

Solon watched the mass transport as it lifted up and rose from the dome, and he breathed out deeply, content in the knowledge that Dios was safely aboard.

He had no way of knowing that the boy had been infected by a gene-stealer and was, even now, taking that taint further into the heart of the Imperium.

Solon found a place that overlooked the ice flows, and settled down to watch the world die.

'ENEMY FIGHTERS LAUNCHED,' croaked the daemon-servitor, and Kol Badar glared at the pict screens that showed the flock of Fury interceptors and Starhawk bombers being disgorged by the closing Imperial Dictator-class cruiser. Sword frigates and destroyers were moving towards the *Infidus Diabolus* in a flanking formation, and the Coryphaus slammed his fist down on the pict screen. The plasglass screen shattered, its image distorting as hundreds of spider-web cracks appeared across its surface.

The eldar ship was slipping out of range of the *Infidus Diabolus's* batteries, and Kol Badar reluctantly ordered the Word Bearers' ship to pull off its pursuit, and to swing around to face the new threats. He watched with angry eyes as the eldar vessel darted away, taking the whoreson bastard Marduk with it. He would have felt much more comfortable knowing that the First Acolyte was dead, but he would have to content himself with the fact that the eldar had probably already killed him.

'Launch Thunderhawks and Stormbirds to intercept the enemy fighters,' said Kol Badar, 'and come to new heading, CV19. This is not a fight we can win.'

IKORUS BARANOV THREW the *Rapture* into a spiral as a formation of Imperial attack craft screamed past the front of the shuttle, their forward-mounted lascannons stabbing through the darkness.

The boxy shapes of larger assault craft the colour of congealed blood roared into view, battle cannons blasting at the swiftly moving formations of Imperial ships. As Baranov hauled on his controls, he saw several of the Fury interceptors explode beneath the barrage while those caught on the edge of the detonations spun crazily, wing thrusters destroyed.

Larger vessels that resembled immense birds of prey swept through the chaotic space battle, weapons flashing, and more of the interceptors were destroyed. The birds of prey were slower than the darting Furies, however, and as Baranov threw the *Rapture* to starboard to avoid a flurry of lascannon fire, he saw one of them explode in a fireball as numerous strafing runs from the smaller fighters peppered its dark red hull.

Behind the streaking, smaller ships, Baranov saw the distinctive, heavily armoured prow of an Imperial cruiser in the distance, a flotilla of frigates and destroyers fanning out to its sides. Swearing, Baranov dragged on the controls of his labouring ship, and an immense shape hove into view.

This ship was far closer than the Imperial vessels, and its deep red hull was powerful and bristling with weaponry and launch bays. It lurched as it turned to face the Imperial battle group, and Baranov dragged on his controls, not wanting to be caught between them when they began firing.

'THERE,' SAID MARDUK, stabbing a finger towards the familiar shape of the *Infidus Diabolus*. 'Take us there.'

He saw the human wretch, Baranov, give him a sidelong glance, and bared his sharpened teeth at the man. Baranov paled, and dutifully swung the *Rapture* towards the mighty vessel.

Attack craft sliced across the nose of the rogue trader's ship, pursued by the powerful, boxy forms of Thunderhawks, and defence turrets on the sides of the *Infidus Diabolus* spread a blanket of fire out towards the slower moving enemy bombers as they began an attack run against the strike cruiser.

Baranov dived the *Rapture* down towards the underside of the *Infidus Diabolus*, taking them out of the danger zone as the defence turrets increased the weight of their fire against the incoming bombers.

'Towards the lower launch decks,' said Marduk, pointing. 'There are fewer defence batteries there, and they have already locked onto the Sunfires. We should be able to enter the hangar bays unmolested.'

Marduk knew that the enemy bombers and interceptors would take precedence over an unarmed shuttle, and that the automated guidance systems of the *Infidus Diabolus* would probably not fire upon them while being assailed by other more pressing targets.

'That's it,' said Marduk as they drew ever closer.

A Fury wove across their bow, pursued by a Thunderhawk displaying the leering daemon face of the Latros Sanctum splashed across its hull, and Baranov hauled on his controls. A bank of lascannons aimed at the interceptor struck the *Rapture* in its port thrusters, sending the shuttle careering off course. Warning lights flashed up, and fire roared through the rear cabins. The air within the shuttle was suddenly sucked from the ship, and only the safety bulkheads slamming closed, sealing the control cabin from the rest of the ship, stopped Marduk and Baranov from being dragged out into space.

'Take it in, fast,' shouted Marduk, and Baranov dragged the damaged shuttle back under his control, aiming it towards the gaping launch bay that was looming up before them, filling their vision.

Assault batteries alongside the launch bay pivoted towards the *Rapture* as she screamed towards the ship, and they began to fire. The shuttle was struck twice, shearing one of her wings off in an explosion of sparks and flame, and then the *Rapture* was inside the Word Bearers' launch bay.

Indentured workers scurried from their path as the *Rapture* slammed down onto the launch bay landing zone, and a shower of sparks rose as the shuttle skidded and spun across the metal flooring. It smashed into a wall and ricocheted off, shearing its left side completely away before coming to a screeching halt.

'Nice landing,' said Marduk.

Two full coteries of Word Bearers Space Marines stood with bolters trained on them as Marduk and Baranov stumbled from the twisted wreckage of the *Rapture*. Marduk grinned and slapped Baranov on the back heavily, knocking the man to his knees.

'It's good to be home,' he said.

The First Acolyte was still naked from the waist up and his flesh was a tattered ruin, hanging from his body in bloody strips. The gathered warrior-brothers stood with bolters levelled at Marduk, for a moment, not recognising him, before they dropped to their knees, bowing their heads to the ground before him.

'THE TRAITOR ASTARTES are attempting to disengage, admiral,' said Gideon Cortez, flag lieutenant of the *Hammer of Retribution*.

'How many have we lost?' asked Admiral Rutger Augustine.

'Two frigates and a destroyer. Another two destroyers have taken severe damage. The captain of the *Implacable* wishes to pursue.'

'Order him to disengage,' said Augustine, somewhat reluctantly. 'We need those ships to protect the line.'

'The mass transports have pulled free of the Perdus moons' atmospheres,' said Gideon, reading the communiqué from a data-wafer that was passed to him from a subordinate.

'Finally,' said Augustine. He looked out towards the moons. A fierce battle was underway, as the bulk of the tyranid fleet converged on the doomed worlds, moving into firing range of the main blockade line.

'Your order, admiral?' asked Gideon.

Augustine sighed.

'Exterminatus,' he said wearily.

SOLON WATCHED THE rays of dawn lift above the horizon for the first time in over five months, relishing the sensation of natural light upon his face. The storms had all but cleared, and from his position he had a clear view across the ice flows. The white glare was almost painful, even through the tinted windows of the spaceport, and he was awed by the sublime view.

For the past hour he had watched the alien chrysalides falling from the sky. The xenos enemy could be seen now, approaching Phorcys like a living tide. People were screaming in panic, but Solon did not bother himself. There was no army here to face the enemy for it had long evacuated the moon, and there was nowhere left to run.

Above the living carpet of the enemy, trails of fire were roaring down from the sky, as if the burning tears of the Emperor were falling from the heavens to smite the never ending xenos horde.

The cyclonic torpedoes, fired by more than a score of battleships in high orbit, slammed into the surface of Perdus Skylla, and the moon was instantly engulfed in flames.

Solon and all those who had not managed to secure passage off-world died instantly, and more than eight million tyranid organisms perished in the hellish conflagration.

'THE EMPEROR'S WILL be done,' said Admiral Rutger Augustine as he watched the moon ignite from the bridge of the *Hammer of Righteousness.*

CHAPTER TWENTY-TWO

BENEATH A SKY of fire and blood, the Basilica of the Word rose impossibly high into the air, hundreds of barbed spires piercing the roiling heavens. Each spire was more than five kilometres high, and studded with jutting, rusted spikes. Ten or more living sacrifices were impaled on each spike, and they moaned in agony and torment as their flesh was torn from their bones by skinless daemons. Thousands more kathartes circled the basilica, filling the air with their screeches and deathly cries.

The sound of the daemons mingled with the morbid chanting of countless millions of proselytes within the basilica, their voices accompanied by braying daemonic choirs and the pounding of industry. Lurid flames burst forth from daemon-headed gargoyles as an endless stream of sacrifices were slain in the blood-chambers deep within, and the deep baritone of Astartes voices lifted in morbid cantillation.

Outside the temple, the lines of sacrifices, ten million strong, shuffled forwards, a never ending stream of humanity that wound its way through the blood-soaked avenues. Deathly cherubs with skeletal wings growing from their bloated, childish bodies swooped low over the masses, and foul-smelling incense billowed from the censors hanging from the chains that pulled at their skin. Ever more penitents were constantly added to the lines, slaves and odalisques taken from a hundred thousand worlds on which the Word Bearers had fought, bringing the holy word of Lorgar to all, willing or not. Most were already utterly corrupted to the worship of dark gods and went to their deaths willingly, eagerly, yet twisted, black-clad minions of the Word Bearers continued to stalk the lines, stabbing their needle-like fingers into any that shuffled forward too slowly, urging them on.

Discords floated along the lines, mechanical tentacles waving gently, and the rapturous blare of Chaos in all its insanity assaulted the eardrums of the condemned from their grilled speakers. Relentless mechanical pounding boomed from the discords, overlaid with daemonic bellows and roars, voices whispering of death and the glory of Chaos, weeping of children and hate-filled screams.

Eight immense gehemahnet towers surrounded the monstrous temple, and the doleful tolling of their bells resounded across the hellish landscape. Hundreds of thousands of rapturous voices rose in glorifying chants as the colossal bells pealed, the sound torn from raw throats.

For as far as the eye could see, from horizon to horizon, towering shrines and temples to the dark gods rose from the blood soaked earth of Sicarus, daemon home world of the XVII Legion and seat of power of the Primarch Lorgar. Kilometre-high obelisks hanging with thousands of lifeless bodies and daubed with infernal runes had been erected in every quarter, and grand mausoleums, cathedrals, and giant statues surrounded by squares teeming with worshippers spread out around the basilica.

Spider-legged cranes picked their way across the horizon, each one accompanied by half a million slave-workers that toiled to raise ever more impressive structures of devotion and worship to the gods of Chaos, constructing new temples, fanes and sacrariums atop older, crumbling edifices and cathedrals. The work was constant, level built upon level, so that the majority of the buildings were subterranean, an impossibly deep, labyrinthine warren of interconnected structures, all devoted to the worship of Chaos in all its guises. Indeed, millions of slaves toiled below ground, never seeing the surface at all, carving out more caverns of worship, crypts and deep, hidden sanctums many kilometres beneath the surface of the daemon world.

The rogue trader, Ikorus Baranov, was down there somewhere, thought Marduk in amusement, if he was not already dead. He had enjoyed the look of horror and betrayal on the weakling mortal's face when he had ordered him to be taken into the slave gangs. The human had served its purpose, and was less than nothing to Marduk.

Two moons hung low in the burning skies, their jet-black surfaces wreathed in hellfire, like the eyes of the gods staring down upon Marduk.

He stood on a high balcony constructed from human bones, staring down upon the glory of the Host, arrayed below him on one of the immense terraces that extended down the sides of the basilica: *his* Host.

It was gathered in all its might, standing in serried ranks, and Marduk felt pride as he looked upon them. Pennants of flayed human flesh fluttered from back-banners, and all within the Host had repainted their left shoulder pads, the ones that had previously been stained black in mourning for Jarulek, Dark Apostle of the Host. They were no longer in mourning, Marduk thought with a smile.

At the front of the power armoured bulk of the warrior brethren stood the Anointed, the warrior elite of the Host, and armoured divisions interspersed the ranks. Rhinos, Land Raiders, Predators, Vindicators, all had had their battle-scarred hulls repainted, and fresh sigils to the ruinous powers and litanies of the true word had been daubed and inscribed upon their ancient, armoured skins. Hundreds of slaves and chirumeks worked upon the hulls of these armoured divisions, patching damage and sanctifying their hulls anew in the blood of unbelievers.

Daemon engines and Dreadnoughts clawed at the flagstones of the terrace to the side of the bulk of the Host, each titanic amalgamation of machine and daemon kept in place by chains held in the hands of hundreds of straining slave-proselytes.

This is my Host, thought Marduk with pride and satisfaction. *Mine.*

MARDUK STOOD WITH his eyes lowered as he awaited the judgement of the Council. None but the Dark Apostles were allowed to look upon the sacred members of the Council when it was in session, and he kept his eyes dutifully cast down as he awaited the outcome that would determine his fate, for now and forever.

The wounds he had suffered under the knives of the eldar haemonculus had long since healed, leaving just faint scars upon his flesh, joining those that he had earned from fighting on a thousand worlds. His body was armoured in archaic plate, a holy relic that had been chosen from the armoury of the *Infidus Diabolus*. Marduk had spent long hours in solitude scrimshawing the litanies of Lorgar upon their surfaces.

He held his skull-faced helmet under one arm, the helm that had been worn by the blessed Warmonger before him, and over his armour he wore an unadorned robe the colour of bone, as the ritual required. His face was sunken and pale, for he had partaken of neither food nor water for a month, just one part of the arduous tests that he had been subjected to in order to prove his suitability.

He had been on Sicarus for almost three months, and since the commencement of the rituals of testing and purification, he had not spoken to a living soul, though his days were filled with acts of penitence, recitation of the Great Works and communion. He had endured all manner of ritual debasement, as his soul was stripped bare and he was reborn into the dark faith.

He was subjected to solitary confinement for weeks on end, sealed within the ossuary sepulchre deep beneath the Basilica of the Word, interred within a crawl-space little larger than his body, walled in with bricks and blood mortar. Hallucinogenic smoke coiled around him in the tomb, and as he breathed the fumes in deeply and his body passed into a catatonic state nearing death, his spirit had soared free. Garbing himself in armour of the soul, he had fought an endless army of daemons that sought to test his resolve, armed with a gleaming sword in one ethereal hand, a shield of darkness strapped across his other. How long the infernal gods had directed their minions against him he knew not, but finally he was brought back to the land of the living, his imprisonment shattered. He awoke a new warrior, weak in the body from his confinement, but strong in faith and spirit.

Endless days of ritual torment and study followed, when every aspect of his mind, faith and body were tested to breaking point, but through it all Marduk remained strong, refusing to succumb to the daemonic whispers that taunted him, telling him that he had already failed, that his soul would be consumed by the ether and his name forgotten by history.

All that was behind him, and he stood before the Council, proud and noble, as he awaited their final word.

'Kneel,' came a growled command, and Marduk fell to the ground, impelled by the sheer dominance of the voice.

A figure moved before him, and a hand was placed upon the crown of his head, pushing it backwards to expose his throat.

I have failed, thought Marduk, though he could not believe it.

A serrated khantanka knife was drawn and its cold blade placed against the carotid artery of his neck, but he did not flinch. He would face death with pride, though still he refused to believe that such was his fate.

The knife slashed the artery, and Marduk gasped as blood fountained from his neck. Bright blood pumped from the wound, spraying out around him. It gushed over his breastplate, running down over his torso and onto the floor, pooling around his knees.

Marduk swayed, still shocked that it had come to this, and all colour drained from his face as the pool around his knees spread outwards.

His pristine skull helmet dropped from numb fingers, splashing into the pool of warm blood, and he fell forwards. He threw a hand out to catch himself, but his strength was fading, and it was all he could do to stop himself from sprawling face-first into the already congealing pool of his lifeblood. Anger swept through him.

Marduk used the anger swelling through him to give him strength, and he pushed himself up off the floor. If he was to die, he would not die scrabbling on the floor like a dog. Even as more blood pumped from his neck, he retrieved his blood-smeared helmet from the floor and shoved it back under his arm.

He blinked, staring at the pool of blood in which he kneeled. There was so much blood that he was amazed that there was any within him at all, and his vision wavered.

This is the end, he thought.

The mark of Lorgar on his forehead began to burn, smoke rising from his skin as the searing rune blistered his flesh.

A hand was placed against his neck, and the wound was closed as warmth suffused him.

'Arise, Marduk,' said the domineering voice, and Marduk felt hands on his shoulders, helping him to his feet. He was weak with loss of blood, and did not realise that he had passed the final test, and had received Lorgar's blessing.

Lifting his gaze, he stared into the impossibly dark eyes of none other than Erebus, he who had been first Chaplain of the Word Bearers when Horus had lived, he who had brought the true faith to so many.

'Welcome, brother,' said Erebus.

Other than Lorgar, and arguably the Keeper of the Faith, Kor Phaeron, Erebus was the most powerful, revered and influential member of the XVII Legion, and at his word countless millions had perished.

Erebus's head was shaved smooth, and covered in intricate script, his flesh a living Book of Lorgar, and Marduk stared at him in confusion and wonder, still not understanding what was taking place.

The other seven Council members stepped forwards, surrounding Marduk, and he gazed around at their hallowed, revered faces in awe. He knew them all by name and reputation: the Dark Apostle Ekodas, the craggy-faced holy leader of the 7th Company Host, who had led a holy crusade of retribution upon the Black Consuls, almost wiping the Cursed Chapter, a successor of the hated Ultramarines, from the galaxy; at his side was the Dark Apostle Paristur, shrewd and savage, who had killed the Blood Angels Chaplain Aristedes in single combat on the walls of the Emperor's palace. Mighty heroes of legend all, the Council members closed ranks around Marduk, touching their fingertips upon the already congealing blood and daubing unholy symbols upon his armoured plates. Erebus dipped his thumb in the blood and marked Marduk's cheek, and he felt his skin blistering beneath the touch.

One of the Dark Apostles, Mothac, encased in ensorcelled daemon armour, a gift from Lorgar, held a thick book in his arms, its weight immense. The book was bound in the skin of Ultramarines, and Marduk gasped as he looked upon it.

'The Dark Creed,' he murmured, overcome with awe. These were the holy writings of the daemon primarch of the Legion.

Finally, realisation dawned on him. He had succeeded!

Mothac's face was solemn, and the Dark Apostles gave him some room as he hefted it before him.

'Swear your undying allegiance upon the Dark Creed and you will be one with us, Brother Marduk,' said Erebus.

Marduk placed a bloody hand upon the hallowed book, his eyes blazing with faith.

'I swear it,' he intoned.

* * *

'DARK APOSTLE,' SAID Burias, and Marduk, standing on the balcony over-looking his Host, turned towards his icon bearer with a smile.

The newly appointed Dark Apostle wore a cloak of flayed flesh, and his right hand leant upon the butt of the mighty crozius arcanum that had been wielded by Jarulek before him. It felt good to wear the deadly weapon, the icon that represented his new-found position.

'That will take some getting used to,' he said.

Burias smiled savagely at Marduk, and inclined his head towards the archway leading from the bone balcony.

'The sorcerer comes,' said Burias, a note of distaste in his voice.

The archway led into his private shrine within the immensity of the Bastion of the Word. All Dark Apostles had their own quarters within the immense structure. This one had belonged to Jarulek, and it now belonged to him.

With a glare of warning to Burias, Marduk turned to receive the Black Legion sorcerer.

Kol Badar stood by Marduk's side, immense and strong, his face unreadable. Only the clenching and unclenching of his mighty power talons gave away a hint of the Coryphaus's thoughts, and Marduk smiled. Kol Badar had not taken Marduk's ascension well, but he had knelt before Marduk, as had all of the Host, and sworn his life and soul to him.

Darioq-Grendh'al stood at his other side, garbed in robes of black, his face hidden beneath a deep cowl. The fallen magos was still changing, though his corruption was all but complete, and Marduk marvelled at how far he had fallen. He was truly a creature of Chaos, both in body and in spirit, and his mighty servo-limbs quivered as if beneath a mirage, their form subtly changing from one second to the next.

Burias stood alongside the champions Sabtec and Khalaxis. Burias was tense and eager to be away, and Marduk sensed too that Khalaxis was yearning to battle once more. Soon, he thought. Sabtec's face was set in his usual stoic expression. Marduk had been impressed by his skill, and knew that he would achieve great victories in his name.

To the side, dwarfing them all, was the immense bulk of the Warmon-ger, standing immobile, his heavy weaponry held at the ready.

These are my warrior faithful, thought Marduk, my officers and advi-sors. He knew they would serve him well, and if they didn't, he would sacrifice them, and none would be able to question his actions, for he was their Dark Apostle and he held their lives in the palm of his hand.

Marduk turned his attention to the new arrival, Inshabael Kharesh, sorcerer of the Black Legion. His gaze met piercing blue eyes that glinted with hidden secrets and knowledge, and Marduk affected a feigned smile of welcome. The Dark Apostle did not like the man, for he saw sorcery as a weakness – the only true power lay in faith, not conjurer's tricks and magic – but he was not one to argue with the will of the Council.

'You will extend him all the courtesies that such an esteemed envoy demands in the coming crusade,' Lord Erebus had said. 'He is the emissary of the Warmaster, and though Abaddon is but a pale shadow of Horus, we must show the requisite respect. This sorcerer could be a great ally for the XVII Legion. See that he is treated with courtesy.'

'It will be as the Council demands, my lord,' Marduk had replied, bowing.

'The... artefact is ready to be tested upon the warriors of the false Emperor?'

'It is, my lord.'

'Do not fail me, Marduk. Should this crusade falter I will be *most* displeased,' said Erebus, his voice soft, yet carrying a potent weight of menace.

The sorcerer nodded his head in respect to Marduk, dipping his staff, which bore the unblinking eye of Horus, low to the ground.

'Welcome, Inshabael,' said Marduk smoothly. 'I am honoured that you will be joining us for this crusade. It is always good to fight alongside our brothers of the Black Legion, and I am sure that your wise council will be invaluable in the coming days of blood.'

'I extend my gratitude to you for your kind words, Dark Apostle Marduk,' replied the sorcerer, his Cthonian accent harsh. 'The Warmaster is keenly interested in your... xenos curio.'

Marduk bowed his head, a pale smile on his lips. Abaddon had clearly sent the sorcerer to watch over the Word Bearers, but Marduk did not allow his anger to be reflected on his face.

The sorcerer's eyes drifted skywards, towards where the *Infidus Diabolus* hung in low orbit, and Marduk followed his gaze. The battleship was but one of many there, hovering motionless in the burning skies of the daemon world. There were thirteen battleships in all, and again Marduk felt his breath stolen by their awesome sight.

Thirteen battleships of the Word Bearers; five full Hosts, each led by a Dark Apostle.

The Thunderhawks and Stormbirds of the other Hosts were already flocking skywards, each one filled with bloodthirsty, zealous warriors. Heavier shuttles rose ponderously towards the waiting battleships, battle tanks and screaming daemon engines looked within their holds or hanging beneath them from metre-thick cables and locking clamps.

Immense transports lifted from the surface of Sicarus, emerging from beneath the parade grounds around the basilica, which slid aside to reveal gaping, subterranean crypt-holds below. The giant tubular vessels were powered by roaring engines that scorched the buildings below them as they rose into the air, defying the powers of gravity that strained to pull them back to earth. Kathartes swirled around the behemoths, filling the air with their piercing screams, for the daemons knew what was held within, and were hungry for them to be awoken. God-machines worshipped as physical representations of the powers that be, the titans of the dark Mechanicus rose towards the battleships, and Marduk relished the time that would soon come when the demi-legion of immeasurably destructive war machines would be unleashed. Long had it been since he had marched to war with the immense forms of titans striding behind him, each step covering fifty metres of ground, and their weapons laying waste to entire Imperial cities.

'An impressive sight,' said the sorcerer.

'Indeed,' agreed Marduk, a satisfied smile on his face. 'Once more the Imperium will tremble.'

The Dark Apostle lifted his skull-faced helmet from under his arm and pulled it over his head. It connected with a hiss, and he breathed deeply of the acrid, recycled air.

'The Black Legion are keeping their eye on us?' growled Kol Badar in a low voice across a closed circuit vox that none bar Marduk could hear.

'Something like that,' said Marduk, replying across the closed circuit. He glanced towards the hulking Coryphaus.

'Don't think for a moment that I don't know what you tried to do, Kol Badar; your little attempt to usurp me,' said Marduk mildly, his voice oozing menace.

The Coryphaus stiffened, but made no response.

'I am your Dark Apostle, with the full backing and confidence of the Council,' continued Marduk calmly. 'I will no longer tolerate or indulge *any* insubordination. I will warn you only once.'

Then he turned to his comrades and broke off the closed communications.

'Come, my brothers,' he said, his voice booming. 'It is time.'

'We go to war?' inquired the Warmonger, its voice booming, sepulchral and eager.

'To war,' confirmed Marduk.

EPILOGUE

Marduk stood with his arms folded across his chest as he watched Darioq-Grendh'al at work.

A series of dark metal rings, each as tall as a man and inscribed with Chaotic runes of power, were aligned above a pentangle of blood, held in mid-air by the servo-arms of the magos. There were three rings in total, each fractionally smaller than the last, and they were aligned to form a single, large circle. Mechadendrite tentacles steadied the rings, holding them motionless with snapping, barbed claws and daemonic mouths. Another tentacle, black and smooth, emerged from within the ex-priest of the Machine-God's body, squirming from a bloody rent that opened up on his metal chest, reaching towards a control column that rose beside the magos.

A blinking eye appeared at the tip of the tentacle, and it peered down at the controls. Then the eye melted back into the fleshy tip of the tentacle, and it keyed in a sequence of buttons on the console.

A red light rose from the centre of the pentangle, and a similar light stabbed down from the ceiling above, where a similar daemonic symbol had been daubed. The two beams of light met, passing through angular holes within the sides of the dark metal rings, and Darioq-Grendh'al released his grip on them.

Marduk half-expected the metal rings to fall to the ground, but they hung in place, perfectly motionless as the magos stepped away. A pair of black-robed chirumeks, their wasted flesh augmented with mechanics, stepped forwards and presented the magos with a featureless stasis box.

Mechadendrites stabbed a series of buttons, and the lid of the stasis box slid aside, smoke rising from within.

Then, with delicate care, the magos brought forth a perfect, silver sphere from within the box. The chirumeks scurried back into the darkness, and Darioq-Grendh'al moved back towards the rings hanging suspended in mid-air.

The magos extended his mechadendrites, reaching towards the joined beams of red light, and placed the silver sphere in their centre, where they had joined. It hung there, caught between the two beams, and Darioq-Grendh'al retreated once more.

The dark metal rings began to rotate, three rings moving in separate arcs that rolled around one another, moving smoothly and with increasing speed. The sound of air being displaced by the spinning rings got louder as they rotated faster, and soon the sound became a solid hum. The red light of the twin beams became diffused, filling the sphere created by the rotating rings as they spun ever faster.

Marduk's eyes were locked on the silver sphere, the Nexus Arrangement that hung motionless in the centre of the rapidly spinning rings. At first nothing happened, but then glowing green, xenos hieroglyphs appeared across the perfect silver sphere. They glowed with intense light, and the sphere appeared to melt, its faultless, seamless exterior becoming seven rings that began to rotate around a centre of glowing green light.

The rings began to turn, mirroring the movements of the larger rings constructed by Darioq-Grendh'al, though their movements were slower.

Turning a dial, the red beams of light began to intensify and thicken, turning the green light at the centre of the xenos sphere a daemonic, bruised purple colour.

'It works,' said Marduk, with a grin. It was his to command.

GREEN LIGHTNING FLICKERED across the tip of the black pyramid as the prison of the ancient being known as the Undying One was shattered. A billowing cloud of dust rose from the ground as the immense pyramid began to rise, green hieroglyphs glowing into life upon its sides. Larger than any battleship, it lifted towards the dark sky, powered by engines far beyond human comprehension, for it was created by beings that had been in existence before the stars had been formed.

The majority of its bulk had been hidden beneath the rock, and it shattered the earth as it rose to the heavens, casting a shadow over the continent below. It rose higher into the air, green lightning still crackling across its sheer sides.

Directed by the Undying One's immortal will, it turned towards the angry red blemish that scarred the night sky, towards the Eye of Terror, towards the one that had released it from its imprisonment.

DARK CREED

PROLOGUE

THE ANIMAL STINK of humanity rose up the bladed sides of the Basilica of the Word, borne on hot updrafts, mingling with the heavy scent of incense and the metallic bite of freshly spilt blood. Behind it, the electric tang of Chaos hung in the air.

A balcony jutted from one of the basilica's great spires, five kilometres above the heaving masses below. The surface of the daemon world Sicarus was a honeycomb of mausoleums and temples, though from this height, it was partially obscured by blood-red clouds that whipped around the spires. Two holy warriors stood side by side upon the balcony, gazing across the skyline of their adopted home world.

Immense towers and shrines strained towards the burning heavens as far as the eye could see, and ten thousand mournful corpse-bells tolled. Moans of pain and rapture rose from the millions of proselytes in the streets, the morbid sound carried on rising thermals exhaled from the subterranean blood-furnaces and daemonic forges.

Skinless daemons circled overhead. Others stripped the flesh from the tens of thousands of living sacrifices impaled on the flanks of the basilica's spires.

The flayed skin curtain behind the pair of holy warriors rippled.

'Let them expose themselves,' said Erebus, First Chaplain of the Word Bearers. His voice was low and dangerous. 'Find out how deep the river of their corruption runs.'

The holy demagogue's head was shaved and oiled. The skin across his scalp was inscribed with intricate cuneiform, his flesh forming a living *Book of Lorgar*. Erebus's eyes were cold and dead, giving away nothing. In their reflective darkness Marduk saw himself, the lurid flames of the æther burning behind him.

'As you wish, my lord,' said Marduk.

'They will seek to deceive and to confuse. They will undermine you, and try to sway your loyalty and the loyalty of your captains. Trust only your own council and judgement.'

'I understand, my lord,' said Marduk. 'I shall not fail you.'

'See that you do not.'

Erebus's gaze remained fixed on a point beyond the horizon, and Marduk followed it.

Though there was nothing to be seen bar the endless landscape of spires, domed cathedrals and gehemehnet towers, Marduk knew where Erebus's thoughts lay.

It seemed an eternity had passed since blessed Lorgar had removed himself from his adoring Legion. It had been thousands of years since the golden-skinned daemon-primarch had isolated himself within the Templum Inficio, forbidding any to disturb his meditations. Great had been the lamentation within the Hosts when the holy daemon-primarch had made his will known, for never had they been without the glorified one, the *Urizen* as he was known amongst the warrior brethren. Surrounded by a desert of bones, the Templum Inficio had been constructed by eight million slave-adepts, all of whom had given their lives upon its completion, staining the temple stones with their blood. As the voices of the Legion rose as one in mourning, the great doors of the templum were sealed, never to be opened until Lorgar's vigil was over.

Centuries rolled into millennia, yet every day hundreds of thousands of blood-candles were still lit in Lorgar's name. His name was whispered on the tortured lips of ten million penitents praying for his return.

In his absence, the Council of Sicarus continued to guide the flock, ensuring that the Legion maintained its adherence to Lorgar's teachings.

'He will return to us, my lord?' asked Marduk.

'In his own time,' assured Erebus. 'Have faith, Apostle.'

Marduk touched the glyph of Lorgar branded on his forehead, murmuring a prayer. He lifted his gaze, squinting into the burning atmosphere and the glory of the raw immaterium.

Thirteen immense battleships hung in low orbit overhead, motionless and menacing; five complete Hosts, ready to embark upon a dark crusade against the hated Imperium. His ship, the *Infidus Diabolus*, was amongst the deadly shoal, her flanks bristling with cannons and launch bays, steeples and shrine towers rising above her armoured hull.

'The crusade awaits you, Marduk,' said Erebus. 'May the blessing of Lorgar be upon you.'

'And you, my master,' said Marduk, bowing low. He turned and strode from the balcony, sweeping the flayed skin curtain aside.

Erebus watched him go then turned to face the distant horizon.

'Come then, my brothers,' he said. 'Make your play against me.'

BOOK ONE: THE BOROS GATE

'Five there shall be, by blood, sin and oath, five cardinals Col-chis born, united in bonds of Brotherhood. Hearken! Rejoice! Harbingers of darkness they, augurs of the fall. And lo! With fury of hellfire, truth, and orb of ancient death, the gate shall be claimed. And so it shall come to pass; the beginning of the End. Glory be!'

– Translation from the Rubric Apocalyptica

CHAPTER ONE

Fanged mouths of a dozen grotesque misericords exhaled incense, filling the dimly lit shuttle interior. Seated shoulder to shoulder, their genetically enhanced bodies encased in thick plate the colour of congealed blood, the warriors of the Host sat in meditative silence, breathing the heavy smoke.

Hunched figures shuffled up the aisles, daubing the warriors' armour with sacred unguents. Their features were hidden beneath deep cowls. They hissed devotional prayers and blessings as they went about their work.

Kol Badar waved them away with a snarl, sending them scurrying.

Heavily scarred from thousands of years of bitter warfare, his face was lit from below by the ruby-red internal glow of his ancient Terminator armour. His head was dwarfed by the immensity of the armoured suit within which he was permanently sealed. Segmented cabling pierced the necrotised flesh at the base of his neck and at his temples.

'Initialising docking sequence,' croaked a mechanised voice. Kol Badar was jolted as the shuttle's retro-thrusters kicked in.

Uncoupling himself from the bracing restraints, Kol Badar rose and stalked down the darkened aisles of the Stormbird. Each heavy metallic step was accompanied by the whir of servo-motors and the hiss of venting steam. Seven holy warriors of the cult of the Anointed, the warrior elite of the Host, had been chosen to accompany the Dark Apostle and his entourage, and they bowed their heads low in respect as Kol Badar passed them.

The Anointed were the blood-soaked veterans of a thousand wars. Proud and zealous, each was a holy champion of Lorgar in his own right. They wore ancient suits of Terminator armour, their heavy gauge ceramite plates inscribed with scripture and hung with fetishes and icons. This armour had been in the service of the Legion since before the fall of Horus, lovingly maintained and repaired over the long millennia by the Legion's chirumeks.

Stabilising jets roared, and the Stormbird shuddered as docking maglocks clamped into place. Burning red blister lights flashed, and the scream of the engines began to subside. Reams of data scrolled before Kol Badar's eyes. He reviewed the information feed swiftly before blinking it away.

'Honour guard, at the ready.'

As one the Anointed brethren released their restraints and stood to attention as the shuttle lowered to the deck of the immense battleship. Mechanical clicks and whines accompanied final diagnostic tests. Weapons were checked and loaded.

The pneumatic stabilisers of the shuttle settled. With a hiss of equalising pressure and a burst of super-heated steam, the assault ramp of the shuttle unfolded and slammed down on the deck. Kol Badar led the Anointed down the ramp. Tracking for targets, they stepped aboard the *Crucius Maledictus*.

An Infernus-class battleship, one of the largest vessels to have fought in the Great Crusade, the *Crucius Maledictus* was the flagship of the Dark Apostle Ekodas. The battleship had suffered calamitous damage fighting against the fleets of the Khan in the last days before Horus's fall, but had managed to limp to the safety of the Maelstrom. Extensively repaired, modified and re-armed upon the daemonic forge-world of Ghalmek, it now ranked amongst the most heavily armed and armoured battleships in the Word Bearers arsenal, rivalling even Kor Phaeron's *Infidus Imperator*.

The docking bay of the *Crucius Maledictus* was immense, with curved arches rising a hundred metres overhead. Ancient banners and kill-pennants hung down the length of giant pillars, recounting the victories of the 7th Company Host. Two other assault shuttles had already docked. They seemed small and insignificant within the vastness of the docking bay, which was far bigger than any aboard the *Infidus Diabolus*. Kol Badar merely scowled, unimpressed, and glared at the serried ranks of Astartes waiting for them.

There were more than two thousand Word Bearers, standing motionless, bolters clasped across deep red chest plates. The 7th was one of the largest and most decorated Hosts in the Word Bearers Legion, and their Dark Apostle Ekodas was counted as close confidant of the Keeper of the Faith, Kor Phaeron. Ten ranks deep on either side, the warrior-brothers of the 7th formed a grand corridor leading towards the titanic blast-doors at the far end of the docking bay, four hundred metres away. A blood-red carpet had been rolled out between them along its length.

There was no welcoming party, no fanfare to honour them as they came aboard the *Crucius Maledictus*. Annoyed, Kol Badar barked an order to his brethren. The Anointed fell into line at the foot of the Stormbird's assault ramp, four warriors to a side. The sound of them slamming their fists against their chests echoed sharply. Kol Badar turned his back on the warriors of the 7th to wait for Marduk, his Dark Apostle and master, to emerge from the Stormbird.

His expression darkened. Master, he thought hatefully. The whelp should never have risen so far. He would have killed the whoreson that day on the moon of Calite long ago had Jarulek not restrained him.

Marduk appeared at the top of the ramp. Kol Badar's power talons twitched involuntarily.

Dark Apostle of the 34th Grand Host, the third leader to have borne such a title, Marduk wore a cold, disdainful expression as he gazed upon the might of the 7th. His deathly pale features were aristocratic and noble, the gene-lineage of blessed Lorgar blatantly apparent. His left eye was red and lidless, bisected by a narrow pupil. His jet-black hair was oiled, and he wore it long, hanging in an intricate braid down his back.

A thick fur cloak was draped over his shoulders and he wore a cream-coloured tabard secured around his waist with a heavy chain.

His red power armour was ornate and heavily artificed, a bastard-ised blend of plate from various eras, ranging from his segmented MkII Crusade-pattern greaves, to his reinforce-studded MkV-era left shoulder plate. Every centimetre of it had been painstakingly etched with ornate script. Hundreds of thousands of words were carved around his vam-braces and upon his kneepads – litanies, scripture and extracts from the *Book of Lorgar*. His left vambrace was engraved with the third book of the Tenets of Hate in its entirety, and dozens of sacred passages and psalms encircled his pauldrons. Strips of cured skin bearing further epistles and glyphs were affixed to his plate by rune-stamped blood-wax.

In his hands, Marduk bore his sacred crozius arcanum. A hallowed artefact consecrated in the blood of Guilliman's lapdogs, the dark cro-zius was a master-crafted weapon and holy symbol of awesome power.

Flicking his cloak imperiously over one shoulder, Marduk began to descend the Stormbird's assault ramp towards the floor of the docking bay. Following a step behind him came two other power-armoured fig-ures.

The one on the left, Burias, moved with a swordsman's grace. Gene-born in the last days of the Great War, Burias was a flamboyant, vicious warrior. His black hair was combed straight and hung to his waist, and he bore the sacred three-metre-tall icon of the 34th in both hands. There was not a scar or blemish upon the Icon Bearer's cruelly handsome face; Burias was one of the possessed, and his powers of regeneration were impressive.

The other was more of an unknown to Kol Badar, and was a stark contrast to the Icon Bearer. Shorter and with a heavier build than most warriors of the Legion, his broad face was a mess of scar tissue. His downcast eyes were set beneath a protruding brow, giving him a brutish appearance at odds with his genetic heritage. His almost translucent skull was shaved smooth and covered in jagged scars and pierced with cables. A black beard bound into a single, tight braid hung half way down his barrel chest. His armour was without ornamentation and he wore an unadorned black robe. His hands were hidden within heavy sleeves. A double-handed power maul hung over his shoulders, and a chained and padlocked book dangled at his waist.

While Kol Badar had fought alongside Marduk, Burias and every other member of the Host during the Great War, First Acolyte Ashkanez had only joined the 34th recently. His combat record was impressive but Kol Badar had yet to fight alongside him in battle, and it was only in battle that true brotherhood was forged.

Ashkanez had only been with the Host since they had left the daemon world of Sicarus, seven standard weeks earlier. Deeming that the 34th lacked a suitable candidate from amongst its own ranks, the Council of Sicarus had appointed Ashkanez to the position of First Acolyte to serve under Marduk.

'What a fine spectacle Ekodas has arranged for us,' said Marduk, looking towards the silent ranks of Word Bearers. 'Such an unsubtle reminder of his strength.'

'Hardly necessary,' said Kol Badar. 'He is of the Council, after all.'

Only eight individuals sat upon the Council of Sicarus, the holy ruling body that guided the Word Bearers in Lorgar's absence, and each was a dark cardinal of great authority and power.

'Intimidation is in his nature,' said Marduk.

With a roar of engines, another shuttle breached the shimmering integrity field of the docking bay. Banks of cannons bulged from beneath the snub nose of the heavily modified craft, and flickering remnants of warp presence – semi-transparent, semi-sentient globs of immaterium that pulsed with inner light – clung to its hull.

'Cadaver-class,' said Kol Badar, assessing the arrival with a glance. '18th Host.'

'Sarabdal,' said Burias.

'*Dark Apostle* Sarabdal, Icon Bearer,' corrected Ashkanez.

Burias snarled and moved towards the newly appointed First Acolyte but Ashkanez remained motionless, offering no confrontation.

The debarkation ramp of the old Cadaver-class shuttle extended in four clunking sections and slammed onto the deck. A trio of corpselike cherubs bearing smoking censers flew from the red-lit shadows of its interior, their pudgy childlike faces twisted into grotesque leers. Their eyes were sutured shut with criss-crossing stitches. Snarling, they exposed tiny barbed teeth. The cherubs began a circuit of looping dives and swoops, heralding the arrival of their master.

Dark Apostle Sarabdal stepped from his shuttle and took in the cavernous docking bay at a glance. He wore a heavy cloak of chainmail and his armour had been painstakingly sculptured to resembled flayed musculature. Every vein, tendon and sinew of it bulged in stark relief.

Sarabdal strode towards Marduk and his retinue fell in behind him. Marduk met him halfway, his own entourage moving with him.

The two Dark Apostles slowed as they approached, sizing each other up before stepping in close and embracing as equals and brothers. Sarabdal, the taller of the two, leant in to kiss Marduk on both cheeks. His skin tingled as the Dark Apostle's burning lips touched his flesh.

'Brother Erebus speaks highly of you, Marduk,' said Sarabdal, in a hoarse whisper.

Marduk inclined his head to accept the compliment.

'My lord,' murmured Ashkanez, and Marduk turned to see a skeletal figure making its way towards them.

Marduk's lip curled at the cyber-organic creature. Four mechanical, insectoid legs protruded from its bloated abdomen and propelled it forwards in a stop-start motion. Bone-thin arms were spread wide in an overly sincere gesture of welcome. The creature's lips had been hacked off, leaving its mouth set in a permanent rictus of teeth. Spine-like sensor arrays protruded from the back of its head, and the buzz of data-flow erupted from the emitters in its modified larynx.

Twitching, the vile creature came to a halt before the pair of Dark Apostles and performed an awkward bow, head flopping forwards. It righted itself and began to speak, though the words bubbling from its lipless mouth had no relation to the crazed articulation of its jaws.

'Welcome, brothers of the 34th and the 18th, to the *Crucius Maledictus*,' it slurred. 'Grand Apostle Ekodas, blessed be his name, regrets he could not welcome you himself, but he humbly requests that you follow this lowly mech-flesh unit to his audience chambers.'

'*Grand* Apostle Ekodas?' said Marduk.

'The arrogance!' fumed Sarabdal. He spat onto the deck floor in disgust. The thick wad of black phlegm began to eat through the metal, hissing and steaming.

The cyber-organic beckoned and twitched impatiently.

'Let me be the one to tear its head off,' said Kol Badar under his breath, and Marduk smiled.

'Depending on how this conclave goes, gladly,' said Marduk.

'Can't we do it now?' said Burias, as the insectoid-legged creature grinned inanely.

'Come,' said Sarabdal. 'Let us get this over with.'

CHAPTER TWO

GARBED IN FULL parade regalia, Praefectus Verenus stood in the centre of Victory Square beneath the baking sun and awaited the arrival of the White Consul.

At his back, four thousand soldiers of the Boros 232nd stood to attention. Proud, royal blue banners hung limp in the still air. Alongside the Guardsmen were the ancillary support vehicles of the regiment: Chimera APCs, reconnaissance Sentinels, Trojan workhorses.

Rearing up behind the regiment, at the top of almost four thousand stairs, was the immense, white marble edifice that was the Temple of the Gloriatus. A golden statue of the Emperor looked resplendent at its soaring peak.

Verenus stood alongside his commanding officer and support staff in total silence.

With his mighty physique, Verenus was the epitome of Boros gene-stock, an imposing officer and soldier. His eyes were ice-blue and hard. His skin was deeply tanned. His nose had been broken a dozen times and poorly set, and his sandy blond hair was clipped short in a regulation cut.

Verenus swallowed heavily as the heat of the twin suns beat down upon him. He had forgotten how unforgiving Boros Prime's summers could be. It had been ten long years since he had been home. He indulged himself and let his eye wander over the majesty of the city before him.

Sirenus Principal was a gleaming bastion-city of white marble and manicured arboretums, and it stretched beyond the horizon in every direction. Home to more than eighty million citizens, all of whom willingly served at least a single five-year term in the Guard or PDF, it was one of the great cities of Boros Prime, and indeed of the entire Boros Gate subsector.

Perfectly symmetrical boulevards, a hundred metres wide and lined with towering statues of Imperial heroes and revered saints, ran past colossal architectural wonders, replete with columns, arches and gleaming alabaster sculptures. Tree-lined flyovers curled between soaring schola progenium collegiums and ecclesiastic shrine-wards, and tens of thousands of dutiful citizens could be seen coming and going, as they hurried to lectures and work. Mass-transits snaked soundlessly along curving aqueduct bridges, whizzing past mighty cathedrals that reached towards the heavens in praise of the God-Emperor. Each day millions of wreaths and aquila tokens were laid before hundreds of grand monuments scattered around the city that celebrated Imperial victories and honoured the valiant fallen.

Gleaming white fortress walls bisected the city. Far from being oppressive and domineering, they were sculptured masterpieces of classical design, with gently sweeping buttresses climbing their flanks.

Lush gardens fed by subterranean hydroponics butted up against the city walls, colonised with exotic flowering plants and broad-leafed shrubs. Fountains surrounded by grassy arboretums were located in each district, water spurting from the lips of cherubs.

Thousands of ordered PDF units marched across the tops of the walls, sunlight glinting off helmets and lascarbines. Their blue cloaks, the same as those worn by all members of the Boros PDF and Guard, were bright upon the pristine white stone. In all, Sirenus Principal boasted nearly fifteen million active soldiers; one in six inhabitants was a Guardsman, and it was the same all across Boros Prime. Few Imperial systems had such numbers.

The entire city was a blend of simple beauty and practicality, of form and function; an elegant and wondrously designed metropolis that was essentially a mighty and brilliantly conceived fortress, yet one that was aesthetic and pleasant for its populace to live within.

The city summed up all that it meant to be a citizen of Boros Prime: strong, determined, ordered, refined, noble.

Verenus's gaze was drawn heavenwards, towards the distant shadow of Kronos. As potent as all the ground defences of Boros Prime were, its true strength lay in the immense star fort orbiting overhead.

Bristling with weaponry and the size of a small moon, Kronos was the largest space station in Segmentum Obscurus. It was an ever-present sentinel that was both a comfort to the people of Boros Prime and a constant reminder of Imperial authority, for it was the seat of the system's governorship: the Consuls.

The White Consuls ruled with a benevolent hand, and the citizens of the Boros system – all eighteen inhabited planets and two-dozen colonised moons and asteroids – were afforded liberties and a quality of life undreamed of in many regions of the Imperium. Civil unrest was all but unheard of.

Two Consuls ruled Boros – the Proconsul Ostorius, and his Coadjutor, Aquilius. The highest authority in all matters military and political, they were regarded with awe bordering on worship by the bulk of the Boros citizenry. Such devotion was not officially encouraged, but neither was it discouraged – was it not true that the Consuls were formed in the image of the God-Emperor himself?

The Proconsul and his Coadjutor were responsible for somewhere in the realm of four hundred billion Imperial citizens, as well as the security of the vital Boros Gate subsector itself.

Verenus spied several shapes approaching from the star fort, gleaming like falling stars, and snapped to attention. He could hear them now, jet engines screaming as they penetrated the atmosphere, the sound rising from a distant drone to an ear-splitting roar.

Three strike aircraft streaked out from the glare of the suns, flying in tight formation, wingtip to wingtip. Verenus recognised them as agile Lightning fighters by their forward sweeping aerofoils and distinctive wail. Slicing effortlessly through the air, they dived low and screamed over the heads of the Boros 232nd. Contrails of white vapour chased their progress like ribbons. Having shot overhead, the fighters peeled off sharply, turning in a wide sweeping motion. A blast of hot, displaced air struck the gathered soldiers of the 232nd a second later, sending their capes and banners fluttering.

As the scream of the Lightnings subsided, it was replaced with the resonant drone of bigger engines. A minute passed and a pair of Vulture gunships hove into view, their wings heavy with tubular rocket-pods and autocannons. They were escorting a smaller Aquila lander. The Lightning strike fighters made another pass before pulling up and disappearing from sight.

The Aquila was resplendent gold, and Verenus was forced to squint against the glare reflected upon its gleaming metal skin. With vectored engines swivelled downwards, the lander and its gunship escort descended upon the gleaming white parade ground twenty metres in front of the Legatus and his officer cadre, landing gear unfolding beneath them.

They touched down smoothly, and even before their engines died, the golden-hulled Aquila was lowering its passenger compartment to the ground.

'*And behold, an Angel of Death walks among us,*' quoted the Legatus in a quiet voice. Verenus recognised the line from his years in the schola progenium, though he could not recall which scrivener had penned it.

All thoughts of ancient poets and their epics were forgotten as the blast door of the Aquila's passenger compartment slid open with a hiss of equalising air pressure.

A huge figure appeared in the doorway, so big that it was forced to duck to exit the landing craft. Only as it stepped onto the parade ground did it rise to its full height, and Verenus's eyes widened.

The praefectus knew that the Consuls were big – he had seen countless holo-vids of their public appearances, and he had seen them commemorated in frescoes and sculptures his whole life – but nothing had prepared him for just *how* big. The warrior was a giant.

The Space Marine was encased in heavy plate armour as white and flawless as the marble of Sirenus Principal. He stood easily two heads taller than Verenus. His shoulders were immense, protected by huge pauldrons and the twin-headed eagle shone on his breastplate. He wore a royal blue tabard over his power armour, emblazoned with the eagle-head heraldry of the White Consuls Chapter. Its hems were stitched with delicate silver thread. Verenus recognised the Space Marine as Coadjutor Aquilius.

The Coadjutor's head was bare. He had a broad face that was solid and youthful. Carrying his helmet under one arm, he strode towards the Legatus of the 232nd. Verenus fought the urge to step back.

'*And fear incarnate is his name,*' Verenus heard his Legatus murmur.

The Coadjutor halted a few steps before the regimental commander and his entourage. He stared at the Legatus, his expression inscrutable and his colourless eyes hard.

'A quote from Sueton,' said the Space Marine. His voice, Verenus noted, was deeper than a man's. It seemed apt given his immensity. '*In Nominae Glorifidae*. Seventh act?'

'Ninth,' said the Legatus.

'Of course,' said the Coadjutor, bowing his head slightly in respect. A discussion on classical literature was the last thing that Verenus had expected.

At a barked order, the soldiers of the Boros 232nd saluted the Coadjutor with perfect synchronicity. The Space Marine returned the salute. Upon a second order the regiment snapped back to attention.

A robed adept of the Ministorum, the left half of his face hidden beneath a mass of augmetics, stepped to the White Consul's side. A servo-skull hovering at his shoulder beeped indecipherable date-code.

'Legatus Cato Merula, 232nd Regiment, Boros Prime Imperial Guard, rotated from battlefront Ixxus IX of the Thraxian campaign, under Lord Commander Tibult Horacio,' intoned the adept from a half-bow, gesturing towards the regimental commander with one outstretched arm. His fingers were needle-like mechanical digits, and they buzzed with exloading data. 'One month resupply, re-indoctrination and recruitment before return to frontline duties. Execution status XX.V.II.P.C.IX.'

The adept swung around to face the Coadjutor and abased himself, dropping to one knee and lowering his head towards the ground.

'Lord Gaius Aquilius, 5th Company White Consuls of the Adeptus Praeses, Dux Militari, Coadjutor of Boros Prime,' intoned the adept in his monotonous voice. 'Praise be to the God-Emperor.'

'Praise be,' murmured the Legatus.

'Praise be,' said Coadjutor Aquilius.

'It is an honour to address you, sons and daughters of Boros,' said the Coadjutor, his resounding voice easily reaching the ears of every soldier of the 232nd without the need of vox enhancement.

'The Proconsul was due to address you himself, but duties of state precluded him from being here,' said Coadjutor Aquilius. 'I pray my presence instead does not disappoint.'

Verenus knew that not one of the soldiers of the 232nd would have been even slightly disappointed. Only a few amongst them had ever laid eyes upon a Space Marine, and then only from afar.

'I am humbled to be in the presence of such noble soldiers as yourselves,' said the Coadjutor. 'You have given all that I could have asked of you, and more, and I have faith that you shall continue to do so. I salute you, men and women of the illustrious 232nd.'

An adjutant of the Coadjutor stepped forward bearing an exquisite, ornate regimental standard. A golden aquila gleamed atop the standard pole above the ornate crosspiece of carved bone. The banner itself was tightly furled and affixed with studs. The adjutant dropped to one knee and offered the standard to the commander of the 232nd, who gestured for one of his younger officers, the regiment's overawed aquilifer, to step forward and take the standard.

'It was with great sadness and regret that I learnt of the loss of the 232nd's standard during the Daxus Offensive on Thraxian Minor,' said the Coadjutor. 'I had my own personal artificers construct this replacement. May it serve your regiment faithfully.'

With a nod of encouragement from his Legatus, the regiment's young aquilifer began to release the studs of the standard with shaking hands. With a flourish, he lifted it high in the air, allowing the banner to unfurl. A tapestry of such beauty was unveiled that it brought a gasp from the regiment. The glorious image of a winged saint, the martyred Ameliana – the regiment's official patron – was emblazoned in gold and silver thread upon a field of blue. In the upper left corner was the unit's regimental insignia, along with the four-dozen campaign badges of the regiment's long history. The names of every Legatus that had led the regiment into battle since its founding – all three hundred and seventy-four of them – were picked out in silver thread on the back of the banner.

Verenus had not known exactly what to expect when meeting one of the revered Consuls face to face, but seeing such humility in one so far above the humble ranks of Guardsmen such as he was certainly not it.

The next few minutes passed in a blur as the Coadjutor was introduced by name to each of the 232nd's officers. Suddenly the White Consul was standing before Verenus. Few men were the equal of Verenus's height, but he felt like a child as he looked up into the broad face of the Space Marine.

The Coadjutor offered his hand, and Verenus clasped forearms with him. It was like gripping the arm of a statue. He could feel the terrifying strength in the Space Marine's grip.

Finally, the Space Marine saluted the 232nd, and made his way back to his shuttle. Awestruck, Verenus watched the golden Aquila lander ascend towards the Kronos star fort, like an angel returning to the heavens.

ABOARD THE AQUILA, Brother Aquilius drummed his fingers on his armrest.

'Where was the Proconsul?' he said.

'Regretfully, I am unable to say, Coadjutor,' said Aquilius's heavily augmented aide.

Aquilius took a deep breath.

'The banner was a nice touch,' he said a moment later.

'I thought that it would be appropriate, Coadjutor. It seemed to be appreciated.'

'It was. Thank you.'

The White Consul peered out through the narrow portal beside his seat. Kronos star fort filled his view.

Even several hundred kilometres out, the space station was immense. It rendered the tiny gold lander utterly insignificant. Aquilius could see a dozen Imperial Navy vessels of Destroyer-class and higher docked there. Even the two battlecruisers of Battlegroup Hexus, *Via Lucis* and *Via Crucis*, each more than three kilometres in length, were dwarfed by Kronos.

'Would you like me to run through the day's remaining commitments, Coadjutor?' said his aide.

Aquilius's gaze lingered on the massive launch bays and banks of gun-batteries lining the space station's heavily shielded flanks.

'Coadjutor?' said his aide, offering the Space Marine a data-slate.

Aquilius turn away and nodded.

TWO HOURS LATER, his mind numb from meetings with bureaucrats and Ministorum adepts, Brother Aquilius walked the length of a brightly lit corridor, deep within the heart of the Kronos star fort. He came to a halt and pressed his palm against a matt-black sensorii tablet. Blast-doors opened with a hiss in response, and he went into the training chambers.

The stink of perspiration and ozone was heavy in the air.

Moving to the third and only occupied training cage, Aquilius stopped. He glanced down at the data-slate readout on the control pulpit, and pursed his lips.

From the cage came a high-pitched squeal of discharging energy as a training servitor was dispatched.

The warrior within moved with a subtle blend of power and grace. Every strike flowed into a parry or another blow, his every thrust precise and deadly. He displayed an astounding economy of movement, with no unnecessary flourish or extravagance. He fought with combat shield and sword, and his head was lathered in sweat. Four training servitors circled him, their blank-helmed heads and swift-moving bodies blurred by their humming shield-units. Bladed arms cut through the air as they sought to land a blow against the sublime swordsman. Programmed to complement each other, the training servitors attacked as one.

Far from being dim-witted protocol mech-organics, these training servitors were vicious combat models, their aggression heightened with stimms and Rage injectors.

Aquilius knew the damage they could inflict with those slashing blade-arms – he carried more than a few scars from their touch – and he watched the Proconsul with a mixture of respect, awe and frustration.

Until twenty-one months ago, Veteran Brother Cassius Ostorius had been Company Champion of 5th Company. He had held the post for forty-seven years, having been inducted into the White Consuls three hundred and thirty-four years earlier.

When Aquilius had first learned that he would be serving as Coadjutor to Veteran Brother Ostorius, he was overjoyed. Ultramar-born, and one of the White Consuls' most respected warriors – arguably its finest swordsman – Ostorius had been Aquilius's idol as he rose from the neophyte Scout to fully fledged battle-brother.

That enthusiasm had waned significantly in the subsequent months.

With enviable skill, Ostorius turned aside a slashing blade with his combat shield. Spinning, he deflected a second and a third blow coming in at him from different angles and cut his sword across the face of one of the training servitors. Its shield registered the hit in a blaze of electricity and the servitor stepped backwards stiffly, powering down.

Ostorius kept moving, closing on another servitor. He executed a perfect kill with a thrust to its chest, before turning and dropping to one knee to perform a disembowelling thrust on another, a blade whipping just centimetres above his head. The last of the active servitors came at him and he rose to his feet. Sidestepping a vicious slash, he swung for its neck. His blow was turned aside and the servitor lunged, its reflexes and strength augmented with clusters of servo-muscles.

With a deft circular motion of his sword Ostorius turned aside both blades as they jabbed at his chest and braced himself, lowering his centre of gravity. Rising, he lifted his shoulder into the servitor's midsection. The weighty mech-organic lifted off the ground and was sent staggering backwards. Ostorius dispatched the machine with a brutal blow to the head.

'Pause combat,' said Ostorius before the combat servitors could come back online. He went to the side of the training cage and replaced his sword and combat shield on a weapons rack. Wiping a hand across his sweat-slick head, he glanced across the array of weapons before choosing a heavy double-ended polearm. It had an axe-blade at one end and a curving crescent-moon blade at the other. Ostorius swung it around him with deft flicks, gauging its weight and balance.

'You come to train, brother?' he said, though he paid Aquilius little attention, continuing to take practice swings with the polearm.

'No, Proconsul.'

'You come to watch *me* train?' Ostorius looked through the cage at Aquilius for the first time. His left eye was augmetic and he bore several long scars that distorted his lips into an ugly sneer. His left ear was missing, replaced with an internal augmetic. He was a brutal-looking warrior, intimidating in appearance and manner.

'No, Proconsul.' Aquilius always felt so young and inexperienced next to his senior Proconsul and fought against the heat rising in his cheeks. 'I came to check that all is well,' he said, diplomatically. 'You didn't make inspection this morning. I was concerned that something was the matter.'

'Recommence combat, threat level eight,' commanded Ostorius. The four training servitors jerked back into motion, circling him again. 'I had other matters to attend to,' he replied, raising his voice above the mechanical din of the servitors. Aquilius glanced down at the date-slate readout upon the command pulpit.

'You have been training for seven hours and twenty minutes.'

'A battle-brother can never train too much, Coadjutor,' growled Ostorius. The younger White Consul bristled at the implication.

'I train as many hours per day as the Codex stipulates,' he said. 'I would train more but for the duties and demands of my office.'

Ostorius spun, sweeping the legs from under one servitor before smashing another to the ground with an emphatic blow to the head.

'I judged that you were capable of conducting this morning's inspection without me,' said Ostorius, parrying a swift blow before kicking the servitor away from him with a heavy boot. 'Or was my belief in you misplaced?'

Aquilius bit his tongue, accepting the rebuke without complaint.

'Proconsul, there are matters that demand your attention,' he said, humbly, looking down at the data-slate in his hands. He was forced to raise his voice above the escalating clamour inside the training cage. 'Nine more regiments returning from the Thaxian Cluster are due in over the next two hours – six infantry, two armoured, one artillery. There are also military dispatches from the Assembly that require your attention, and depositions to be viewed from the Daxus moon conglomerate. Mechanicus emissaries from Gryphonhold that await…'

'Aquilius,' barked Ostorius, knocking the last of his opponents down with a series of stabbing thrusts.

'Yes, Proconsul?' said Aquilius, looking up from his slate.

'Not now.'

OSTORIUS EXHALED WHEN Aquilius had left. He knew his dark mood had nothing to do with his Coadjutor. Aquilius was merely doing his duty – he had no right to belittle him. Indeed, he had less than no right; as Proconsul, it was his place to mentor Aquilius.

Not for the first time, Ostorius questioned why he had been removed from his beloved 5th Company and dispatched to the Boros system. Every battle-brother served as a Coadjutor in the years after rising from the rank of neophyte, but only a selection of veterans were chosen to act as Proconsuls. To be chosen was a great honour, and a requirement of those harbouring ambitions to become a sergeant or captain within the Chapter. Nevertheless, it was not something that Ostorius had ever desired.

He had no wish to be a sergeant, let alone a captain. He was a warrior, and desired to be nothing more than that. He was Company Champion of the 5th, and that was all that he ever wanted to be. Protecting his captain in the midst of battle, that was his duty. That was what he had trained for and that was what he was good at, not governing some wealthy bastion system or trying to be a suitable role model for a young White Consuls Coadjutor.

Ostorius lifted a heavy, double-headed hammer from the weapons rack.

'Recommence combat, threat level nine.'

The training servitors powered up once more.

Thirty years, Ostorius thought. In the life of a Space Marine, thirty years was nothing.

To Ostorius, it felt like an eternity.

CHAPTER THREE

Soaring almost fifty metres high, the observation portal of the Sanctum Corpus offered an unobstructed view up the length of the *Crucius Maledictus*. The castellated superstructure of the hulking battleship looked like a city, as if an entire quadrant of Sicarus had uprooted and taken flight. Scores of buttressed cathedrals rose above its hull, replete with spires, glittering domes and grotesque statuary. Multi-tiered banks of defence cannons and gun turrets, half-hidden within ten-storey alcoves, protruded like bristling spines along its flanks.

The battleship was forging through the roiling madness of the warp, parting the pure stuff of Chaos before its sweeping, skulled prow. A handful of the other ships of the redemptive crusade could be seen off to the port and starboard, though the immaterial realm through which they sailed blurred their ancient hulls. Daemons of all size and shape swam along in their slipstream, an ever-changing escort of the infernal.

Talons scraped against the outside of the observation portal, and sticky tongue-like protuberances slobbered against its surface. A flock of kathartes flew past on feathered white wings, angelic and glowing from within. Only in the aether did they appear in their true form. When they crossed into realspace, they appeared as skinless harpies, not these beautified creatures of elegance and deadly allure.

Even the majestic view of the warp in all its infernal glory could not appease Marduk's frustration and growing anger.

'This is an insult,' snapped Dark Apostle Belagosa from across the gaping Sanctum Corpus chamber, putting voice to Marduk's thoughts. 'He goes too far.'

Belagosa was a tall, gaunt figure. In an act of devout faith the Apostle of the 11th Host had clawed out his own eyes centuries ago. Nevertheless, he turned in Marduk's direction. Those empty eye sockets were still far from blind and bled red tears down his cheeks.

'Patience, brother,' said Dark Apostle Ankh-Heloth of the 11th Host. He spoke from behind the barbed lectern of his own pulpit, his voice a hoarse whisper. 'I'm sure that Grand Apostle Ekodas will not–'

'*Grand* Apostle,' spat Sarabdal. The holy leader of the 18th Host stood with his arms folded. 'Such hubris. It is a slight on our order that he affects such airs.'

'It was the Keeper of the Faith himself, revered Kor Phaeron, that bestowed the title, honoured brother,' said Ankh-Heloth.

A severe-looking warrior with a cruelly barbed, black metal star of Chaos Glorified hammered into his forehead, Dark Apostle Ankh-Heloth's flesh was a living canvas upon which he had performed his grisly, sacred arts. He bore numerous cuts and welts, the angry disfigurements evidence of ritual flagellation. Older scars lay beneath the fresher wounds. Marduk guessed that the Dark Apostle rubbed poisonous balms and linaments into his self-inflicted cuts in order to hamper the regenerative qualities of his physiology, for many of his wounds were open and raw. Such practices were not uncommon within the Legion.

'He can call himself what he likes,' said Belagosa. He gestured to Ekodas's empty pulpit. 'But when will the most honoured and revered Grand Apostle decide to grace us with his presence?'

Ekodas's rostrum was ringed with balustrades and spiked railings. It was far larger than those of the other Apostles, and occupied the central position of dominance in the Sanctum Corpus. Held aloft on skeletal arches, it extended thirty metres from the wall opposite the towering viewing portal, giving it an unobstructed view over and beyond the lesser rostrums. Clouds of incense billowed from the maws of hideous gargoyles carved into its underside.

The octagonal Sanctum Corpus chamber was a vertical shaft that dropped away into darkness. Over a kilometre from top to bottom, it bored right through the centre of the mighty battleship. The Apostle pulpits were at its very top, just fifty metres beneath the glittering red-glass dome at its peak. They protruded over the seemingly bottomless chasm from vertebrae-like pillars set at the corners of the chamber.

Though the chamber was around eighty metres in diameter, the sheer height and depth of the Sanctum Corpus made it feel oppressive, even with the gaping viewing portal in its front wall. The walls were lined with books, codices and leather-bound holy writs.

Tens of millions of sacred works were crammed into alcoves and stacked upon shelves, with no apparent semblance of order or cohesion.

Ancient, dusty tomes filled with Lorgar's teachings and scripture were piled in perilous heaps, and tens of thousands of annals and holy texts were stuffed into every crevice. They were all bound in human or xenos skin of various hue and texture. Many of these priceless books had been penned by the proselyte scribe-slaves of Colchis long before the launch of the Great Crusade, in time immemorial; before the blessed Primarch Lorgar had come to Colchis, before even the rise of the hypocritical and fraudulent False Emperor.

Fresh volumes were constantly added to this staggering conglomeration of the Legion's knowledge and wisdom, new tomes bearing more recent teachings and devotional scripture. Outside Sicarus, the scriptorium of the *Crucius Maledictus* was the greatest repository of the Word Bearers' holy teachings in the universe.

Loathsome archivist-servitors, wasted cadavers held aloft by humming suspensor impellers, floated up and down the endless rows of holy tomes, lovingly tending their allotted sections.

Huge, spider-web-like arches stretched up between the bookcases towards the domed ceiling above the conclave of Apostles. Ten thousand skeletons were fused into those arches, their contorted spines calcified with the marble structures. Their skulls were thrown back in voiceless agony, and they held their skeletal arms up in silent appeal to the gods. In their open palms was a thick candle of blood-wax. Twenty thousand glittering flames cast their light down upon the gathered Apostles.

'I'm sure Grand Apostle Ekodas has no wish to keep us waiting long,' said Ankh-Heloth.

'Just long enough to impress upon us that it is in his power to *make* us wait,' said Marduk.

'Barely elevated past First Acolyte and already he passes judgment on an honoured member of the Council,' hissed Ankh-Heloth, glaring at Marduk across the open space of the Sanctum Corpus.

'Better to see things as they are than to accept them blindly,' said Sarabdal.

'Speak your meaning,' said Ankh-Heloth.

'I mean,' said Sarabdal, 'that our newest brother Apostle speaks what we were all thinking. I grow tired of Ekodas's games.'

'I am sure that the honoured Grand Apostle has no intention of angering his devoted brother Apostles,' said Ankh-Heloth.

'Ever the sycophant,' said Belagosa. 'Your grovelling at Ekodas's feet is quite pathetic.'

'You cannot goad me into breaking the truce of Sanctus Corpus,' said Ankh-Heloth. 'You speak nothing but poison and bile.'

'Brother Belagosa has a point,' said Sarabdal, mildly.

'Oh? Please enlighten me,' said Ankh-Heloth.

'You are a puppet,' said Sarabdal. 'Nothing more than Ekodas's pet, and the 11th Host is nothing but an extension of his own. Like a dog, you grovel whenever your master deigns to throw you his scraps.'

The dull humming of the archivist-servitors' impellor motors reigned over the chamber. Belagosa was grinning broadly now, and Marduk too found it hard to hide his amusement as the blood drained from Ankh-Heloth's face. His entourage had gone very still.

'These are not *my* words, of course,' said Sarabdal mildly, pretending not to have noticed the effect on the incensed Dark Apostle of the 11th Host. 'Just… what I have heard said.'

'Who says such things?' hissed Ankh-Heloth.

'Everyone knows you are Ekodas's whipping boy,' said Belagosa, relishing Ankh-Heloth's incandescent rage.

Marduk had heard through Jarulek, his one-time master and the previous holy leader of the 34th Host, of the dubious manner in which Ankh-Heloth had come to power. Jarulek had told Marduk that while it was the Council of Sicarus that had instated Ankh-Heloth as the First Acolyte of the 11th Host, this was only at Ekodas's insistence. Less than a decade later Ankh-Heloth ascended to the position of Dark Apostle after his predecessor was killed under circumstances engineered, many believed, by Ekodas.

Marduk smirked, thinking of how he himself had come to power.

'Something amuses you, Apostle?' said Ankh-Heloth, staring venomously. His body was quivering with rage.

'Of course not, honoured brother,' said Marduk, his tone mocking. 'Such *obviously* slanderous rumours against one weaken us all.'

'We all know that the only reason we suffer your presence on this crusade,' spat Ankh-Heloth, 'is because you have in your possession the device that Jarulek unearthed. Let's hope it was worth the trouble.'

'That is the only thing that you've said here that has made any sense,' said Belagosa.

'Agreed,' said Sarabdal.

Marduk swallowed back his fury.

'I have fought and bled to attain and unlock the secrets of the Nexus Arrangement, dear brothers,' said Marduk, glaring at the other three Apostles. He clenched the barbed railing of his pulpit with such force that he threatened to tear it loose. 'Tens of millions have died in order that it came to me. Worlds have perished. It will win us this war, and when it does, it will be I who shall reap the rewards. In time, you will all bow your heads in deference to me, hearken to my words.'

Belagosa laughed, deep and rumbling. Sarabdal looked amused at the outburst.

'Tread warily, Marduk,' warned Ankh-Heloth. 'An Apostle can fall from grace very quickly if he does not learn to respect his betters.'

'His betters?' snarled Belagosa, quickly turning back on his favoured target. 'And you include yourself in that mix? Marduk may well be nothing more than a whelp, but remember it was not so long ago that you yourself were a lowly First Apostle, Ankh-Heloth. I can still remember when you were first inducted into the Legion. Even then you were a self-aggrandising worm.'

Ankh-Heloth turned his cold eyes on Belagosa. His entourage, standing in the shadowed alcove behind his pulpit, was tense. Ankh-Heloth's hulking Coryphaus clenched his hands into fists, the ex-loaders of his gauntlet-mounted bolters *chunking* as they came online. The warrior resembled a hulking primate, his back hunched and his augmented arms grossly oversized.

Belagosa's honour guard responded in kind, the daemons within their bodies straining to break from their bonds, just waiting for the trigger word from their master that would release them.

'You go too far, Belagosa,' hissed Ankh-Heloth. 'But I shall not be the one to break conclave peace, as much as you might wish it.'

'Still the coward,' said Belagosa.

'Enough!' snapped Sarabdal, forestalling Ankh-Heloth's reply. 'This bickering demeans us all.'

Of the four Apostles present, it was Sarabdal who had led his Host the longest, Sarabdal who had been groomed to become Dark Apostle of the 18th by none other than blessed Lorgar himself. Raised in the scriptorums of Colchis, Sarabdal had been little more than a child when he had taken part in the brutal Schism Wars that fractured the Covenant, the dominant religious order of the feudal planet. Impressed with the youngster's fanaticism and fiery demeanour, Lorgar had taken the boy under his wing and once reunited with his Legion, had personally chosen Sarabdal for indoctrination into the Word Bearers. Few Dark Apostles garnered more respect than Sarabdal, and Belagosa and Ankh-Heloth fell into sullen silence at his rebuke.

It was a formidable gathering of might here in this chamber, Marduk thought, and a slight smile touched his lips.

Between them, the four Dark Apostles commanded the loyalty of over five and a half thousand Astartes warriors. Together with the might of Ekodas's Grand Host, that number swelled to over nine thousand. Add onto that the battle tanks, Dreadnoughts, daemon-engines and assault craft of the five Hosts and the number was swollen further.

Over a million fanatical cultists of the Word accompanied the Hosts, brainwashed men and women crammed together like cattle in hulking slave vessels. These pitiful wretches were subjected to an endless torrent of maddening warp noise by floating Discords. After months and years of such unceasing abuse, their free will and resistance had long been broken, and they were now true devotees of Chaos. Of little tactical worth, they would be herded into the guns of the enemy, across minefields and sacrificed by their Astartes masters, and they would do it willingly.

Last of all, the fleet was accompanied by a single bulk-transporter of

Legio Vulturus, a grim vessel twice the size of the *Crucius Maledictus*. Within its cavernous stasis hold resided a full demi-Legion of god-machines: twelve of the most potent war engines ever constructed on the forge-worlds of the Mechanicum. As part of the Ordo Militaris wing of the Collegia Titanica, they had fought in nigh on constant battle since the start of the Great Crusade. The Legio Vulturus had declared their allegiance with the Warmaster Horus, turning their guns against their brethren mid-battle, wreaking terrible havoc among the Legios Gryphonicus and Legio Victorum, destroying nigh on forty battle engines in that one unexpected engagement. This particular demi-Legion of Vulturus had fought alongside the Word Bearers since the start of the Crusade, and many within the XVII Legion credited Erebus himself with turning them to the cause of the Warmaster.

'This is outrageous,' snarled Belagosa. 'If I have to wait one more minute for Ekodas to grace us with his presence, I'll–'

His words were cut off as the blast-doors behind the domineering rostrum above them slammed open, venting steam and oily, incense-laden smoke. A procession of Terminator-armoured veterans stamped through the open portal. They stepped deferentially aside, and Ekodas walked forwards to take his place at his podium.

Ancient and heavily augmented, Ekodas's face bore the ravages of thousands of years of war; his features were cratered and cracked. There was nothing flamboyant or extravagant about his appearance. A simple black robe hung over the plain, austere plates of his armour. His only adornment was a handful of charms looped around his neck. These fetishes of bone and blood-matted hair were strung upon lengths of sinew, and Marduk recognised the characteristic style of the shamanistic priests of Davin. He carried no weapon or staff of office. It was said he preferred not to dirty his hands, preferring to let his underlings fight his battles.

'Don't let me interrupt,' said Ekodas. 'I am most interested to hear what you have to say.'

Ekodas looked down at Belagosa, his black eyes burning with contained fury. His sizeable entourage, vastly outnumbering those of the other Apostles, continued to file in behind him. It was an unsubtle display of military strength.

Belagosa's jaw twitched.

Ekodas's attention shifted and, as the full force of the Grand Apostle's gaze struck him, Marduk fought the urge to kneel. He was a Dark Apostle of Lorgar, he reminded himself angrily; he need bow to no one but the Urizen himself. He saw amusement written in Ekodas's burning orbs and his anger flared, hot and potent.

There is great strength to be found in anger, said Ekodas, jolting Marduk as the words stabbed painfully into his mind. Ekodas's lips didn't move, but Marduk heard the words as if they had been spoken directly, and he knew instinctively that no one else had heard them.

An Apostle's mind was like a fortress. It had to be so that he would not be overwhelmed by the crushing power of the warp, nor his sanity ripped apart by any of the billions of deadly entities that dwelt beyond reality. With walls erected by centuries of mental training and conditioning, with ramparts constructed of unshakeable faith and utter belief, an Apostle's mind was virtually unassailable, yet Ekodas had torn straight through those defences as if they were nothing.

Yet always be certain that your anger is directed at the real enemy, young Apostle, continued Ekodas, his voice pounding. He continued to hold Marduk's gaze, his eyes burning with the fires of fanaticism, even as Marduk struggled to look away and reassert control.

Ekodas broke contact suddenly and painfully. Marduk clenched the pulpit railing as a wave of vertigo crashed over him. He felt physically drained, and a dull headache throbbed behind his eyes.

'Is everything well, my lord Apostle?' said Ashkanez, leaning forwards to whisper in Marduk's ear. Ignoring the First Acolyte, Marduk glared up at Ekodas. He was angry at being taken by surprise, that Ekodas had so easily breached his mental defences.

Had Ekodas gleaned anything of import? Had he learnt of Marduk's promise to Erebus, of the shocking suspicion that the First Chaplain had?

It was doubtful, for even the most talented psykers were generally only able to read those thoughts uppermost in an individual's mind with any consistency. Even then it was difficult to gain any coherency amidst the bewildering array of random images and emotions. Still, there was no way of truly knowing what Ekodas might have gleaned.

He realised then that he had misjudged the Apostle. He had always seen Ekodas as an unsubtle priest, a sledgehammer that overcame his opponents, both in war and in politics, through confrontation. Now, Marduk was forced to readdress his preconceptions.

'You have nothing to say then, Belagosa?' said Ekodas, his attention returned to the other Dark Apostle. Who knew what silent communication was being conducted between them. 'There is nothing that you wish to say to my face, *brother*?'

'No, my lord,' said Belagosa finally, lowering his gaze.

Ekodas flashed a glance at Marduk full of staggering, domineering force.

I am not your enemy, his voice boomed. A trickle of blood ran from Marduk's nostrils.

THE CONCLAVE WAS short and to the point. Ekodas's Coryphaus, Kol Harekh, ran through the final assault plans, his words spoken with the calm authority of one used to being obeyed.

In the open space between the Apostles' pulpits hung a three-dimensional hololithic projection of a binary solar system; the target of the crusade's wrath. The image flickered with intermittent static, and flashes of warp interference occasionally overlapped the visual feed, showing screaming daemons and other horrific images.

Ignoring these anomalies, Marduk stared intently at the hololithic projection. As the details of the attack were laid out, he watched the tiny planets and moons of the binary system slowly orbiting each other, revolving lazily around the two suns at its heart. One was a massive red giant in its last few billion years of life and the other, its killer, a small parasite that burned with white-hot intensity.

Twenty-nine planets circled the two suns, as well as a handful of large moons. Streams of data scrolled down the screen of Marduk's lectern, relaying geography, population, defences and industry for each of the planets as he tapped its surface. Eighteen of the planets were inhabited. Three of those were naturally conducive to carbon-based life forms, while others had been terraformed to create atmospheres suitable for human habitation. The populations of the other inhabited moons and planets existed within domes large enough to have their own weather systems, within hermetically sealed stations pumped with recycled air or labyrinthine subterranean complexes.

An asteroid belt a thousand kilometres thick formed a ring within the solar system, dividing it into the inner core worlds and those beyond. The inner core worlds constituted the bulk of the inhabited planets, with only a few isolated mining and industrial facilities located on those celestial bodies in the cold outer reaches.

'The Boros Gate,' said Ekodas, 'staging ground of the End Times, according to the *Rubric Apocalyptica*. For ten thousand years Chaos has tried to take this system. For ten thousand years we have been denied. Until now.'

Throbbing red icons overlaid the hololithic system map, marking warp routes to and from the system.

Streams of information bled across the data-slate of Marduk's lectern, and across the lesser terminals accessed by Kol Badar behind him. Desiccated servitors hardwired into the control feeds coralled this constant flood of data with serpentine tentacle fingers.

The information regarding the system and its defences was as accurate as could be obtained by the small, shielded drones that had been dropped out of warp orbit into the outer reaches of the enemy system. Almost invisible to conventional scans and relay sweeps, they were currently hugging the system's thick asteroid belt and sending back steady streams of valuable information. It was a delicate process: too much data-flow and the enemy would register the feed and be ready for them; too little and they would be blindly entering one of the Imperium's best defended regions of space – only the Cadian Gate was more fiercely guarded.

The system was not particularly rich in mining deposits, nor was it an agri-hub that fed other systems. No sacred shrineworlds existed within it that needed defending, nor did it house any forges vital to the Imperium's ongoing existence. It was heavily populated and very rich, certainly, but that in itself was not enough to warrant such protection, nor the ferocity with which the XVII Legion desired it.

The key to the importance of the system was its wormholes. They were the sole reason it was so hotly defended and so jealously regarded by the Legions that had been loyal to the Warmaster.

Even for the Legions dedicated to Chaos, the warp routes through the immaterium were often convoluted and difficult to navigate. Thousands of overlapping routes existed through the warp, twisting and turning in constant flux. There were fast moving streams that wound their way through the immaterium, allowing remarkably swift passage from one area of realspace to another, but also stagnant areas of null-time where a fleet could become becalmed for years or decades at a time. Skilful Navigators were able to predict and read the warp like a living map. The best of them were able to remain fluid, adapting to the changeable flow of the immaterium and making the most of its fluctuating ways. Often, a fleet would be forced to slip sidewards across several streams, being buffeted to and fro, pulled months off-course by the malign forces that dwelt there before slipping into the warp route that would take them to their destination.

However, there were some rare warp routes that remained stable and unchanging through all the passing centuries and millennia. Highly prized, and violently defended at their egress points, the most favoured of these stable wormholes allowed entire fleets to be shifted from warzone to warzone almost instantaneously, utilising the routes like mass transit highways that bridged the gaps between distant subsectors. The Imperial system that the crusade was soon to descend upon was the hub of one such cluster of wormholes.

In essence, the system was a transportation hub, a waypoint that allowed impossibly swift transference between almost two-dozen other, vastly distant locations. Anyone who controlled it would be capable of practically instantaneous travel to positions millions of light years away.

One such location was only a relatively short jump from Terra, the birthplace of mankind and the centre of the Imperium itself. The very thought of what it meant should they take the system made Marduk salivate.

Several Word Bearers crusades had tried to gain control of the region, but none had ever returned. In all, seventeen Hosts of the XVII Legion had been thrown against this system over the past centuries, and all had been wiped out. The Black Legion had lost double that number trying to find a way around the heavily guarded Cadian Gate. Other Legions too had suffered when attempting to strike at the region, most notably the Death Guard of Mortarion and the Iron Warriors of Perturabo.

A substantial fleet was docked at a devastatingly powerful space bastion orbiting the system's capital planet. That bastion alone had enough firepower to destroy half the Word Bearers crusade, but it was neither the fleet nor the bastion that was the system's most formidable defence. Nor were the standing armies that protected each of the inner core worlds, nor their fortress-like cities, warded by potent defence lasers, cannons and orbital battery arrays. Nor even were its Astartes protectors and stewards, the genetic descendants of those that Marduk and his kin had once called brother.

The true strength of its nigh-on impenetrable defences lay in the wormholes themselves.

Allowing practically instant transportation between a score of other systems, they also allowed the full might of the Imperium to marshal at a moment's notice. As soon as the system registered that an enemy fleet was attempting to breach from the warp, an alarm call would be sent out. Hours after an enemy fleet made realisation into the binary system's outer reaches, an Imperial armada of truly titanic size would emerge from the wormholes to combat the threat.

To go against this region was not merely to go against one system's defences and its Astartes guardians, but rather to go against the fleet of an entire subsector. It was to go against the entire force of the Astartes Praeses – an order of Space Marine Chapters that permanently patrolled the flanks of the Eye of Terror, ever vigilant for incursions from within. Utilising the wormholes of this region, the Adeptus Praeses were a thorn in the side of the Chaos Legions, able to quickly manoeuvre their companies to wherever they were needed.

However, with the Nexus Arrangement, the xenos device that Marduk had secured in his possession, that greatest strength would be completely undone.

'The Boros Gate is a staging ground,' Ekodas confirmed. 'As the gods will it, it will be *the* staging ground; the site where the fall of the Imperium begins.'

Marduk felt a shiver of anticipation.

'We, my brothers are the vanguard of the End Times, its heralds and harbingers. In consultation with the Warmaster Abaddon, the Council of Sicarus has appointed *us* to take the Boros Gate. Five cardinals of Colchis born, united in Brotherhood – such is the prophecy.'

None of the Dark Apostles spoke. All attention was locked onto Ekodas, all petty grievances and feuding temporarily forgotten.

'Others have believed that they were the chosen ones, that it was their destiny to fulfil the prophecy, blinded by greed and ambition. But where they failed, we shall succeed. For we have with us what the *Apocalyptica* foretold: the "*wondrys orb of ancynt death*".'

'The Nexus,' breathed Marduk.

With a gesture, Ekodas turned the revolving hololith of the Boros Gate system into images of war. Word Bearers marched through crumbling shells of bombed buildings, bolters barking soundlessly in their hands. 'And we know that the device works. The lifeless husk of Palantyr V is testament to that.'

'Palantyr V was a poorly defended backwater, my lord,' said Belagosa, his tone noticeably more deferential. 'The scale of what we attempt at the Boros Gate bears no comparison.'

'It doesn't matter,' said Ekodas. 'Once the device was activated, Palantyr V was doomed. The device shut the region down completely. The effect will be the same at Boros.'

Marduk nodded.

'And if it fails?' asked Belagosa.

'We'll be dead,' answered Sarabdal.

'It will work,' said Marduk. 'It is prophesied.'

'"With fury of hellfire, truth, and orb of ancient death, the gate shall be claimed",' quoted Ekodas.

'We are committed to this now,' he continued. 'The Warmaster Abaddon watches our progress closely. Already his envoys are gathering support, scouring the Eye and the Maelstrom for all who will fight under his banner. Rivalries and blood feuds are being put aside, for all can feel that the End Times draw near. Our triumph at the Boros Gate will herald the last Black Crusade. Because of us, the heavens shall burn and the Imperium of man will be dust.'

A heavy silence descended. Ekodas glared, as if daring any of his Dark Apostles to oppose him. After a moment, he nodded to his Coryphaus, Kol Harekh.

'We take these planets in turn,' Kol Harekh said, indicating the outlying planets of the system. 'Once they have fallen – it should not take longer than a month – then we converge here.'

He stabbed a finger towards one planet, five from the centre of the system.

'Boros Prime,' he said, 'is the lynchpin. It is the heart of the system. Take that, and we take the Boros Gate.'

Marduk peered at the sandy-coloured planet, rotating on its endless loop around the system's two suns. It appeared such a little thing. He need only reach out to grasp it. What looked like a silver moon orbited around the planet.

'The Kronos star fort?' he asked.

'A relic of the Dark Age of Technology,' said Kol Harekh with a nod. 'Its size and firepower is prodigious. It serves as the docking station for the system's battleships. It must be neutralised before planetfall can be achieved. We'll use Kol Badar's strategem for tackling it.'

'Prepare the way for Abaddon's Black Crusade,' said Ekodas, resuming his authority. 'Glorify the Legion and bring about the end of mankind. Warp transference commences within the hour. Ready your Hosts. That is all.'

* * *

DARK APOSTLE SARABDAL strode alongside Marduk as they marched back towards their shuttles. He spoke in a low voice so that only Marduk could hear.

'We must talk, but not here,' he said. 'Ekodas's influence even spreads into my Host. Doubtless it also grows within your own.'

'Impossible.'

'It is not,' said Sarabdal. 'Be wary. Things are moving beneath the surface.'

'Ekodas–' began Marduk.

'Ekodas is carving out an empire within the Legion,' said Sarabdal, interrupting him. 'He seeks to bend us to his cause.'

'"His cause?" I don't see–' said Marduk.

'Not here,' hissed Sarabdal. 'I fear this is bigger than any of us could have imagined, perhaps bigger than Ekodas himself. I am close to uncovering its secret, but–' said Sarabdal. He fell silent as Ekodas's veterans, providing an escort for the Apostles, closed in around them.

'Be wary. Be vigilant,' he said after a minute, before boarding his shuttle. 'We cannot act until we know. As soon as we make transference, we shall talk. Then you too shall understand what is at stake.'

'Lorgar's blessing upon you, brother,' said Marduk.

'And upon you, my friend,' said Sarabdal. 'We must speak, soon, you and I.'

'It shall be so.'

Turning away, Marduk strode up the embarkation ramp of his Stormbird.

BACK ABOARD HIS own battleship, the *Anarchus*, Ankh-Heloth knelt within his prayer cell. The doors were shut and sealed, and he had activated the null-sphere that would ensure that nothing that was spoken within could be heard from outside. He was alone in the room, and his eyes were tightly closed. A droplet of blood dripped from his nose onto the floor. His voice echoed off the bare cell walls.

'I believe that Belagosa will turn, given the right leverage, my lord,' said Ankh-Heloth.

I agree, pulsed Ekodas, his voice spearing through Ankh-Heloth's mind, making the Apostle wince.

'Marduk I am unsure of. Nevertheless, once the captains of the 34th are turned, the Host will belong to us.'

How far along are we?

'Our order grows steadily within his Host, my lord. Several officers within the 34th were most eager to turn. It seems that some of them harbour personal grudges against their Dark Apostle.'

Good. That is something that can be exploited.

'Which leaves us with Sarabdal,' said Ankh-Heloth. 'I fear that he will not be swayed. Already he has exposed several members of our cult within his ranks. Its growth stifles.'

He knows, pulsed Ekodas. *He is a danger to us.*

'What would you have me do, my lord?'

I believe that we can solve the problem of Belagosa and Sarabdal in one. Be ready.

'And Marduk?'

Let the Brotherhood do its work.

THE ASTROPATH SCREAMED and went into wild convulsions.

Hands held him down and the hilt of a knife was jammed between his teeth to stop him biting his own tongue. He registered them only dimly; his mind was filled with the horrific after-images of the searing vision that had brought on his fit.

It was more than an hour before his convulsions ceased, leaving him shivering and aching all over. He lay immobile on a pallet, his arms and legs strapped down.

A shape loomed over him and a voice intruded on his nightmare. It was insistent, and would not leave him in peace. He cried out for death, cried out for the Emperor to take him. He had seen too much, much too much, and he begged for release.

'You shall be granted the Emperor's mercy,' said a deep voice. 'Just tell me what you saw.'

The words tumbled from him in a torrent, and while only perhaps every tenth word was decipherable, they painted a clear picture; death was coming to Boros Prime. He spoke of eyes of fire, of a burning flame upon an open book, of living flesh inscribed with symbols that made his stomach clench painfully even to think of it. He babbled insanely, speaking of souls devoured by ravenous gods that dwelt in the dark beyond. He spoke of spinning silver rings that rotated within themselves, conjuring darkness, and how hell was coming to claim them all. Finally, sobbing, he begged for release.

The tortured astropath smiled in relief as the barrel of a bolt pistol was pressed to his temple. The shot was deafening in the holding cell. Blood splattered the walls.

'What is it, Coadjutor?' came the voice of Proconsul Ostorius over the grainy vox-unit. 'What did the astropath foresee?'

'Chaos,' was all that Aquilius said as he holstered his bolt pistol.

CHAPTER FOUR

BURIAS HURRIED TO catch up with Marduk as he stormed through the corridors of the *Infidus Diabolus*.

He glanced at Marduk's face, which was a furious mask.

'Will it work?' he asked.

'It has to,' said Marduk, 'else we are all dead.'

Sirens blared, and Stormbirds and Thunderhawks were prepped for launch. The Host's Dreadclaws had been roused, their daemon essences stirred for the coming engagement in case of potential boarding actions. The Host's warrior-brothers were undergoing final preparations, mournfully intoning catechisms of defilement and retribution.

'I don't trust Ashkanez,' said Burias.

Marduk's silence invited more.

'I do not understand why you allowed him into the Host. He is not one of us. It is bad enough that Kol Badar still lives, but Ashkanez?'

'I don't need to explain myself to you, Burias.'

The Icon Bearer scowled. 'They will betray you. Mark my words. The First Acolyte covets power, and Kol Badar hates you enough to help him take it. Then, the 34th will become just another subservient Host under Ekodas. Let me deal with them.'

'I will deal with Kol Badar myself. For now, he serves a purpose. As for Ashkanez, he is First Acolyte. Of course he seeks to replace me, just as I sought to replace Jarulek, and he the Warmonger before him. It is our way.'

'Let them do it? You need warriors around you that you can trust! You need a Coryphaus–'

'I trust no one!'

'You trust me,' said Burias.

'You I trust less than most, Burias,' Marduk replied.

The possessed warrior looked affronted. 'I am your loyal comrade and friend. I always have been.'

'A Dark Apostle has no need of friends,' said Marduk.

'My loyalty has and ever will be to you,' said Burias, 'and as long–'

'Don't think me a fool, Burias,' snapped Marduk. 'You are loyal to me only as long as it benefits you. I know this. *You* know this. Let us not pretend.'

They glared at each other for a long moment before the Icon Bearer lowered his eyes.

'You are a warrior, Burias, a fantastically gifted one, and you serve me well in that regard. The same can be said of Kol Badar. Ashkanez has yet to prove himself. If he does not, then I will dispose of him. Be my champion, Burias. Forget the rest. Now get out of my sight,' said Marduk. 'Go do something useful.'

'Whatever you wish, *blood-brother*,' said Burias, before stalking away.

THE CHAMBERS SET aside for Magos Darioq-Grendh'al's workshop were located deep within the stern of the *Infidus Diabolus*. They were crowded and claustrophobic, packed with salvaged mechanics, tech-implements, crippled servitors, discarded weaponry and engines of all kinds. Cylinders filled with bloody amniotic fluid stood in rows against the walls. The magos's experiments bobbed inside, vile blends of living flesh, metal and daemon. Further products of his enthusiastic tinkering crawled amongst the heaps of machinery, repulsive by-blows that moaned and twitched.

Once, Darioq had been a devotee of the Cult Mechanicus of Mars, a tech-magos worshipping the so-called Omnissiah, the God in the Machine. Now he was much more than that. Now he was Darioq-Grendh'al.

His body was concealed within a black robe, its edges hemmed with bronze wire. A single gleaming red eyepiece shone from within his deep cowl. As bulky as one of the Terminator-armoured Anointed, Darioq-Grendh'al moved with stilted, mechanised movements. Four immense, articulated arms extended from the servo-harness affixed to his frame, one pair curving over his shoulders like the stabbing tails of a desert arachnoid, the other extending around his sides like pincers. A pulsing cluster of umbilical cords and semi-organic cables trailed behind the tainted magos, hard-plugged into his spine.

Spread-eagled upon a table before the magos was a slave, arms and legs restrained. The magos was working on the figure, clinically cutting and dissecting flesh and organs. The tortured slave's skin had mostly been ripped from its body, exposing musculature, and it moaned in torment beneath the magos's ministrations.

Banks of brain-units sat in bell jars within refrigeration tanks, thin needles puncturing their lobes. The magos had up to five brains plugged into his mechanised body at any one time, picking and choosing which of the hemispheres would best suit his current pursuit. Many of them bore evidence of corruption.

Unfettered by petty moral constraints, the corrupted magos revelled in a universe of studies that had formerly been disallowed, and he now worked at a feverish, obsessive pace.

Thinking machines, xenos tech, mech/daemonic blends, experimental warp-based weaponry, engines utilising the immaterium itself as their power source; all these things had been deemed heretical and blasphemous, outlawed as deviant and fundamentally incompatible with the reverence of the Omnissiah. None of the strict and uncompromising edicts of Mars mattered to him any more.

Servo-arms, fleshy protuberances and mechadendrite tentacles worked independently of each other as the corrupted magos busied himself at his work. He needed no rest and gained what sustenance he required from the bodies of the slaves. Day and night the magos toiled. The Mechanicus code inhibitors implanted in his brain-stems had long been removed, and he found himself with a whole wealth of new areas of study now open to him – enough work for a thousand lifetimes.

None of this mattered to Inshabael Kharesh, sorcerer of the Black Legion. He was Warmaster Abaddon's personally appointed envoy, and all that interested him was the device.

The sorcerer's face was devoid of colour. Black tendrils pulsed within his flesh, runes of Chaos that were in constant flux. His hair was straight and long, as pale as spiders' silk. The colourless hue of the sorcerer's skin and hair made the glittering brilliance of his sapphire eyes all the more startling.

The sorcerer was staring at the device.

It hung motionless in mid-air, caught in a beam of red light. It was a perfect silver sphere roughly the size of an unaugmented human heart.

The Nexus Arrangement.

Three immense hoops of black metal surrounded the sphere. Each was carved with Chaos icons and runes of power. It was this construct that bound that device to the will of the Word Bearers. Those rings were currently motionless. Only when the device was activated would they begin to turn.

'It is remarkable,' said Inshabael Kharesh.

'The power the device harbours is like nothing recalled in any Mechanicus data-record,' said Darioq-Grendh'al. 'Nothing stored in any of Darioq-Grendh'al's brain-units compares to this sublime construction. Darioq-Grendh'al is only able to tap into the smallest fraction of its power – no more than 8.304452349 per cent of its attainable output – and yet even so it can achieve much.'

'The Warmaster is very interested in the device,' said the Black Legion sorcerer. He had to raise his voice to be heard over the cries of the slave the magos was torturing.

'My lord will be interested in you as well, Darioq-Grendh'al,' Kharesh added.

'Lord Abaddon, Warmaster of the Black Legion and genetic descendant of Horus Lupercal, will be interested in the mech/flesh unit daemon symbiote Darioq-Grendh'al, formerly Tech Magos Darioq of the Adeptus Mechanicus?' said Darioq-Grendh'al, his emotionless voice overlaid with the growls and snarls of the daemon infused into every muscle, fibre and cell.

'Of course,' said Kharesh, smiling. 'You are a singular creature, a true blend of human, machine and daemon.'

The magos did not answer, intent on his plaything. The slave's cries had been stifled now, which pleased Kharesh. One of Darioq-Grendh'al's tentacles had pushed down its throat, and it pulsed with peristalsis as it bored through the slave's stomach lining, feasting upon organs.

'You have no ties to Marduk or his 34th Host,' said Kharesh, picking his words carefully.

'It was Marduk, Dark Apostle of the 34th Host of the Word Bearers Astartes Legion, genetic descendant of the glorified Primarch Lorgar, who brought Grendh'al forth from the empyrean,' said the corrupted magos. 'It was Marduk, Dark Apostle of the 34th Host of the Word Bearers Astartes Legion, genetic descendant of the glorified Primarch Lorgar, who released Darioq from the shackles imposed upon him by the Adeptus Mechanicus of Mars,' he added.

'True,' said Kharesh, smiling. 'But it is also true that the Warmaster Abaddon has a far greater access to archeotech caches and Dark Age technology than the XVII Legion.'

The magos paused. Only for a second, but it was enough to show the Black Legion sorcerer that he'd been heard.

'The Warmaster is benefactor to many Dark Mechanicus adepts,' he added, 'and many Obliterator cults. I think you would find much to your appreciation were the Warmaster to become your benefactor, Darioq-Grendh'al.'

'That is a most interesting notion, Inshabael Kharesh, sorcerer lord of the Black Legion, formerly of the Sons of Horus, formerly of the Lunar Wolves, genetic descendant of Warmaster Horus Lupercal.'

'Something to think about,' said the sorcerer, hearing the mag-locked doors hiss as they opened.

Marduk strode in, closely followed by his First Acolyte and Coryphaus.

'And how is Darioq-Grenhd'al today?' said Marduk.

'Darioq-Grenhd'al,' said Darioq-Grenhd'al, 'has been having an interesting conversation with Inshabael Kharesh, sorcerer lord of the Black Legion, formerly of the Sons of Horus, formerly of the Luna Wolves, genetic descendant of Warmaster Horus Lupercal.'

'Oh?' said Marduk. 'And what pray has the sorcerer got to say for himself?'

'The fallen magos was telling me how he has yet to access even ten per cent of the potential power of the Nexus Arrangement,' interposed Kharesh. 'Its potential is quite… staggering.'

'I see,' said Marduk.

'Inshabael Kharesh, sorcerer lord of the Black–' began the magos.

'I know who you mean,' interrupted Marduk.

'–has informed Darioq-Grendh'al that the Warmaster Abaddon is benefactor to many Dark Mechanicus adepts and many Obliterator cults,' said Darioq-Grendh'al. 'He thinks that Darioq-Grendh'al would find much to his appreciation were the Warmaster to become his benefactor.'

'Really,' said Marduk.

Inshabael Kharesh merely shrugged his shoulders, refusing to be cowed by the Dark Apostle.

'Would you deny the truth of the statement, Apostle?' he said.

'The device is *mine*, sorcerer,' said Marduk, 'Just as Darioq-Grendh'al is mine. I will not let either of them leave the 34th Host.'

'We shall see,' said the sorcerer, smiling.

'Yes, we shall,' said Marduk. Idly, he picked up something from one of the magos's workbenches. His eyes widened as he recognised the spherical device.

'A vortex grenade?' he said in wonder. The most powerful man-portable weapon ever conceived by the Imperium of Man, a vortex grenade was a priceless artefact capable of destroying anything – *anything* – that it touched.

'A gift,' said Inshabael Kharesh, reaching out to take it from Marduk's hands. 'For the magos.'

Marduk refused to relinquish his hold on the deadly artefact, and for a moment the Dark Apostle and the sorcerer were locked together, unwilling to back down. Finally, Inshabael shrugged and let go.

'A bribe,' growled Ashkanez.

'You would dare bring such an item aboard my ship without my knowledge?' said Marduk, holding the vortex grenade under the sorcerer's nose.

'It is a bauble, nothing more,' said the sorcerer. 'I thought the magos might like to study it.'

'Secure this,' said Marduk, handing the vortex grenade to Kol Badar. The Coryphaus took it gingerly.

'One cannot help but wonder why the creators of the Nexus Arrangement – the *necron* – had not used the device themselves,' said the sorcerer, changing the subject.

'It hardly matters,' said Marduk.

'Perhaps not,' said Inshabael Kharesh with an enigmatic half-smile.

Marduk suppressed the urge to strike him.

For the millionth time in the last few months, Marduk cursed the day that the Council of Sicarus had agreed to allow the sorcerer to accompany Marduk's 34th Host.

While it was true that the Word Bearers and Black Legion had once been close, much of that good will and brotherly respect had evaporated upon the death of the Warmaster Horus. While Abaddon might have claimed the title of Warmaster for himself, it afforded him none of the respect that Horus had garnered from the XVII Legion. Of course, the Black Legion's strength was unparalleled – their ranks outnumbered those of the Word Bearers almost ten to one – yet many within the Word Bearers regarded it as but a pale shadow of its former glory, its self-proclaimed Warmaster worthy of contempt. Nevertheless, it was all but certain that it would be the Black Legion who would form the mainstay of the final crusade against the hated Imperium, and because of that, the Word Bearers held their peace.

Marduk begrudged Kharesh's presence upon his ship. He hated the self-satisfied, mocking gleam in the whoreson's crystalline eyes as he observed the daily rituals of the 34th Host and studied Darioq-Grendh'al's work on the xenos Nexus Arrangement device.

Perhaps more than anything else, he hated the fact that there was someone aboard the *Infidus Diabolus* whose life was not his to take.

He shifted his attention towards the twisted magos.

Darioq-Grendh'al's head was turned to the side, staring down in morbid curiosity as he prodded the now lifeless slave laid out before him. His tentacles continued to burrow through the corpse's innards, chewing and slurping. Part metal, part living tissue, part daemon, the mechadendrites were sinuous and writhing things, moving with a life of their own.

The stink of Chaos was strong on the corrupted magos, and though his heavily augmented body was fully swathed in heavy black cloth, Marduk could see it bulge and swell, writhing from within as Darioq-Grendh'al's body altered its form, in constant flux.

Marduk smiled to see the magos so changed, to see such a being of order, uniformity and structure released to become a true creature of Chaos.

'We make transference within the hour, Darioq-Grendh'al,' said Marduk. 'The device will be ready?'

'Yes, Marduk, Dark Apostle of the 34th Host of the Word Bearers Astartes Legion, genetic descendant of the glorified Primarch Lorgar,' said Darioq-Grendh'al. 'It will be ready.'

THE ROOM WAS dim and circular, with tiered steps around the edge. A two-headed eagle, the symbol of the Imperium marked the marble floor, but otherwise the room was bare of ornamentation. Marble columns supported the high domed ceiling. The walls of the room had been raised, hiding the view beyond from sight, and their photo-chromatic panels had been dimmed; in direct sunlight, the hololithic figures arranged around the room were difficult to see.

There were over forty figures standing on the circular steps, the higher-ranked individuals positioned on the lowest tiers. Only ten of those figures were physically in the room, including Aquilius himself and his Proconsul Ostorius, both fully garbed for war. The other six were officers of the Boros Imperial Guard and the Fleet Commanders of the Imperial Navy stationed at the Kronos star fort.

Aquilius recognised the Legatus and Praefectus of the Boros 232nd from his inspection of their ranks. Though neither was of the highest rank, and they stood on the upper tiers, the 232nd's combat record was faultless and the high legate of the Boros Guard had requested their presence personally. Ostorius had acquiesced to the appeal, and Aquilius had been pleased to see that Praefectus Verenus had accompanied his Legatus. He had seen something in the man, something akin to the pride of a White Consul. A shame that he was too old for indoctrination into the Chapter, for he believed he would have made a fine Space Marine.

The other thirty figures standing on various tiers around the room were all hololiths, the monochromatic projections of those that could not be present because of their distance. There were many gaps upon the tiers; those gathered were only the ones that were available at such short notice, and all were high-ranking individuals. There were admirals and lord high commanders, all positioned only a step or two from the floor, and high-grade officers of the Commissariat and Ecclesiarchy positioned higher up.

Some of the images were clearer than others. At a glance, some appeared completely solid, excepting their monochrome colouring. Others were like ghosts, transparent and incorporeal, while others were thick with static and jerky with time-lapse, their mouths out of synch with their speech.

Upon the lowest tier were Adeptus Astartes, the Emperor's angels of death. All belonged to the Adeptus Praeses, the fraternity of Chapters that had been created for the sole purpose of guarding against incursions from within the Eye of Terror. They formed the first line of defence against the inhabitants of that hellish realm, responding to any threat with bolter, chainsword, unshakeable faith and the fury of the righteous.

Once there had been twenty Chapters of the Adeptus Praeses; now there were eighteen. The Archenemy had annihilated one Chapter and, more shocking still, another had been branded Excommunicatus Traitorus.

Aquilius's gaze strayed around the circle of these august Space Marines. Chapter Masters, senior captains, Librarians, Chaplains; all were present here, members and representatives of the Adeptus Praeses. Never had he been in the presence of such prestigious individuals.

The Chapter Master of the Marines Exemplar, twin scars ritually carved down his cheeks, stood alongside captains of the Iron Talons, barbarous-looking in their skin-draped power armour, yet utterly devoted to the Imperium. The Chief Librarian of the insular Brothers Penitent stood alongside the captain of the First Company of the Knights Unyielding, his ornamental armour plastered with purity seals and oath papers. A hooded member of the Crimson Scythes stood apart from the others, as was the way of his Chapter. Aquilius could not discern his rank.

Finally, Aquilius's gaze came to rest upon the last two Astartes warriors, the revered Chapter Masters of the White Consuls, Cymar Xydias and Titus Valens.

Unusually amongst the Adeptus Astartes, the White Consuls had not one but two Chapter Masters. While one patrolled the fringes of the Eye of Terror or partook in holy warfare, the other was located back at the Chapter's home world, Sabatine, governing the Chapter from its fortress-monastery high in the mountains. The Consuls were spread far and wide, battle-brothers and companies located across more than fifty systems at any one time, and it had served the Chapter well to have its pair of co-rulers, for the Chapter Master engaged in the theatre of war was able to concentrate his attentions fully upon the task at hand, confident that the Chapter was being run efficiently.

The Chapter Masters were a dramatic contrast in both appearance and demeanour.

Cymar Xydias, who had reigned as Chapter Master for almost twelve hundred years, and currently oversaw the Chapter's movements from Sabatine, was a severe warrior with an angular face. With a piercing gaze and cutting insight, Xydias was a strategic genius; his understanding of both the flow of battle and the politics of the systems the White Consuls oversaw was masterful and inspiring. He wore a long cloak and a metal wreath of ivy upon his balding head.

Xydias had won countless wars for the White Consuls over the centuries, glorious victories that had been forever documented in the annals of the Chapter. His perfectly executed stratagems were studied by White Consul neophytes and initiates, and he was renowned for his ability to outthink the enemy, always a dozen moves ahead. Weaving an intricate and often bewildering web of attack and counter-attack, of feint and rapid redeployment, his strategic ploys had achieved unlikely victory time and again. His strategic acumen was far beyond the ken of any regular battle-brother, and Aquilius had studied every battle that Xydias had overseen.

Where Cymar Xydias was lean and hawk-like, Chapter Master Titus Valens was a thick-necked warrior, his massive frame encased in an exoskeleton of Terminator armour that made his bulk even greater.

His face was broad and blunt, his short-cropped hair sandy blond and speckled with grey where Xydias's was white and sharply receding. His left shoulder plate bore the Crux Terminatus, the holy icon that every suit of revered Terminator armour bore, each containing a tiny fragment of the golden armour worn by the God-Emperor himself ten thousand years earlier. The Chapter symbol, a resplendent blue eagle's head, was emblazoned upon his right, and a gleaming double-headed eagle was sculpted into his chest plate, every feather carved in immaculate detail.

Xydias's strategic brilliance came from a combination of natural talent, intense tutorage under the finest minds of the White Consuls and the Ultramarines in his youth, and a lifetime of study and experience. Valens's strength lay in his instinctive comprehension of the ebb and flow of battle.

While Chapter Master Titus Valens was as highly educated and classically trained as the most learned of the White Consuls, his true talents, as Aquilius understood it, lay in his innate understanding of warfare and its psychology. Valens always seemed to know the exact moment to press the assault in order to demoralise the enemy, the exact moment when a line was close to breaking and needed bolstering. He led the Chapter from the fore, an inspiring and prominent figure capable of turning defeat into a resounding victory with one well-timed charge.

Aquilius idolised Xydias, emulating his logical, strategic mind. Proconsul Ostorius was a fervent supporter of Titus Valens.

Aquilius had listened intently on the odd occasion that Ostorius spoke of the battles he had fought alongside the Chapter Master. Ostorius's eyes would shine with passion then, and Aquilius could picture the battle in his mind's eye as if he had been there himself. He felt the thrill that Ostorius had experienced as Valens had hurled himself into the breach at Delanok Pass time and again, heroically rallying the thirty White Consuls battle-brothers as they held for sixty-two days against a force of over ten thousand, desperately holding the line until reinforcements from the 6th and 9th Companies arrived and flanked the enemy, cutting them down mercilessly between their controlled lines of fire.

'Give your report, Proconsul Ostorius,' said Chapter Master Titus Valens.

The room descended into silence, every present member of the caucus listening to the Proconsul intently.

'Honoured brethren,' said Ostorius in a loud clear voice, addressing the gathered personages. 'Twenty-three minutes ago a considerable Chaos fleet was detected transferring from the warp. It is predicted that it will realise in thirty-five minutes time, emerging on the dark side of the Trajan Belt. I request the aid of the Adeptus Praeses to defeat this threat.'

'From the incoming information, I see that this fleet consists of between eleven and fifteen warships of cruiser size or larger,' said Chapter Master Absalon of the Marines Exemplar. 'Do we have any ship recognition yet?'

'We do,' said Ostorius. 'Archive scouts have found two matches, with more pending. The first, the battlecruiser *Righteous Might*, which disappeared from Imperial records in M32.473. Its last transmission announced an attack from an unidentified raider-fleet, attacking from the Maelstrom.'

'And the second?' said one of the captains of the Iron Talons, in a thick, guttural accent.

Ostorius nodded to the commodore of the Boros Naval Fleet, who cleared his throat before speaking.

'A positive match on an Infernus-class battleship,' said the commodore, which caused an outbreak of muttering and consternation. 'One of only seven ever launched from the forge docks of Balthasar XIX. An inefficient design. Monstrously powerful, though.'

'We have matched the call-signature of this Infernus to that of the *Flame of Purity*. According to our records, the *Flame of Purity* turned traitor during the Heresy and suffered grievous structural damage during its aftermath care of the White Scars – your father Legion, noble captains,' said Ostorius, nodding towards the two Space Marines of the Iron Talons.

'We know this ship,' snarled the First Captain of the Iron Talons. 'We pledge our oath to support Boros Prime. We send six companies.'

Ostorius bowed to the Iron Talons before continuing.

'Since M33.089 the *Flame of Purity* has had confirmed sightings in eighty-four documented confrontations,' said Ostorius. 'It has since been redubbed the *Crucius Maledictus.*'

'The Word Bearers,' spat the warrior-brother of the Crimson Scythes.

'So it would appear,' said Ostorius.

'Between eleven and fifteen battleships,' said the Chapter Master of the Knight Unyielding. 'A sizeable force.'

'The *Crucius Maledictus* was present during the destruction of the Black Consuls,' said Chapter Master Xydias. 'Undoubtedly, the Word Bearers know that Boros is under the control of the White Consuls.'

'The bastards have a taste for your bloodline,' growled one of the Iron Talons captains.

'It would seem so,' said Chapter Master Xydias.

'From the number of ships we are reading, I would hazard that there are around five or six Word Bearers Hosts bearing down on Boros,' said Ostorius.

'If that is true, we may be facing anywhere between five and fifteen thousand Word Brother zealots,' said Chapter Master Valens. 'Plus whatever foul allies they have brought with them.'

'Engines?' said a senior Imperial Guard warmaster.

'Highly likely,' said Chapter Master Xydias. 'The traitorous Legio

Vulturus has been codified as fighting alongside the Word Bearers on dozens of occasions, often in the same systems in which the *Crucius Maledictus* has been sighted. It would be wise to expect to face Titans if the enemy was to make planetfall.'

'Pray it does not come to that, brother,' said Absalon of the Marines Exemplar.

'With the Emperor's grace, it will not,' said Chapter Master Valens. 'But we must be prepared for the eventuality.'

'I will notify Lord Commander Horacio and the Princeps Senioris engaged in the Thraxian campaign,' said the Chapter Master Absalon. 'I shall request that they spare some of the Princeps' Legios, upon the off-chance that the Archenemy makes planetfall. I am certain that the Legio Gryphonicus would relish the opportunity to exact their revenge upon the engines of their dark kin.'

'My thanks,' said Chapter Master Xydias, graciously. 'I need not remind you all of the importance of the Boros Gate. If the enemy were to claim it, then they would have an open path into Segmentum Solar and the heart of the Imperium. All available White Consuls battle-brothers will be marshalled to meet this threat head on. The only warriors of our Chapter who shall not answer this call are those officiating as Proconsuls and Coadjutors of our protectorate systems, and the Praetorian squads of Sabatine itself. The 8th and 9th reserve Companies are already mobilising here, for immediate transference. Brother Valens?'

'The war here in Bellasus VII is almost done,' said Co-Chapter Master Valens. 'Astartes presence is no longer required to complete the pacification. I shall disengage and lead the four battle companies with me to the Boros Gate immediately. The *Divine Splendour* shall lead my armada.'

Aquilius was impressed. The White Consuls were a fleet-heavy Chapter with three immense battle-barges and more than a dozen strike cruisers at their disposal. Fully two-thirds of the fleet was always scouring the fringes of the Eye of Terror, ever vigilant for incursion. That two of the Chapter's three hallowed battle-barges, the *Divine Splendour* and the *Righteous Fury*, were being rerouted to the Boros system, together with virtually the entirety of the White Consuls Chapter, spoke of the level of threat that the enemy posed.

'When can Boros expect the first of these reinforcements, noble lords?' said Ostorius. 'I have already mobilised the defence fleet, and it is closing on the expected warp translation location of the enemy fleet even now. If the enemy attempts to push through towards the core worlds, my fleet could engage as it emerges from the Trajan Belt, but it will not last long in a full engagement without support.'

'We are relatively close, Proconsul. With time adjustment, we will be there in approximately...' the co-Chapter Master's voice trailed off as he received information off-screen. He snorted and shook his head in wonderment. 'Truly the Boros Gate wormholes are a marvel. We will be there within the hour, Boros real-time. It will take us seven weeks of warp travel once we have mobilised, yet it will take less than an hour in realspace until seven full White Consuls companies make transference.'

'My thanks for the swift mobilisation, my lord,' said Ostorius with a bow of his head. 'And it pleases me that my brothers of 5th Company, aboard the *Implacable*, will be joining the armada.'

He wishes he were onboard the *Implacable*, realised Aquilius, hearing a note of bitterness in the Proconsul's voice. He would rather be out there with their brothers of 5th Company, taking the fight to the enemy, than standing here, impotent, watching the battle on the holo-deck of the Kronos Star fort.

'Why are they attacking here?' said Proconsul Ostorius. 'We know they covet the Boros Gate, and yet while the Word Bearers are many things, they are not stupid. They know of its defences. They know that even now we will be moving against them. They will be obliterated before they get within hours of the core planet, and yet still they come.'

'You overestimate them, White Consul,' snarled the Iron Talons 7th Company captain. 'The Word Bearers are fanatics. Perhaps their daemon-gods tell them to die. Who can predict them?'

Aquilius was not certain that he agreed, but he did not voice his concerns. The Word Bearers were known zealots, but they were not fools.

'You do not give them enough credit, captain,' said Chapter Master Harkonus of the Knights Unyielding. 'Don't let your hatred blind you. The Word Bearers would not sacrifice themselves needlessly. If they are attacking here, it is because they believe they can win.'

'I agree,' said Cymar Xydias. 'We must assume that they have a plan to bypass our defences. We must proceed with caution.'

A handful more hololiths had appeared during the conference, including more Astartes upon the lowest tier. Two of those were White Consuls, the captains of 5th and 2nd Companies. Aquilius stood straighter beneath the gaze of his direct superior, Captain Marcus Decimus of 5th Company.

The flickering holo-image of the Subjagators Chapter Master had materialised alongside the other brothers of the Adeptus Praeses. Blood was splattered across his face, and his armour bore evidence of recent battle.

Nevertheless, it was the last arrival that made Aquilius's breath catch in his throat.

'Throne,' he muttered, eyes widening.

The newcomer was bedecked in ornate Terminator armour of a style unique to his order, and this Grand Master of the daemon-hunting Grey Knights bore an immense force halberd and appeared truly ancient. A devotional tattoo was plastered across his forehead and he introduced himself as Grand Master Havashen. He spoke only briefly, informing the caucus that a full company of his brethren would rendezvous with the others in the Boros system forthwith to combat the Word Bearers threat. With that, his hololith promptly disappeared.

The Adeptus Praeses Chapters swore their oaths of support, pledging what companies they could. Battlefleet Gorgon was to be redirected to bolster their strength, and the details of the defence were finalised.

The Boros Defence Fleet, bolstered now by the strike cruisers of the White Consuls 2nd and 5th Companies, was already ploughing at full speed towards the thick band of asteroids, the Trajan Belt, which divided the Boros Gate system. The enemy were expected to make translocation through a warp exit beyond the belt. If the enemy did not attempt to breach the Trajan Belt, then the Boros fleet would wait for the bulk of the Astartes Praeses fleets, and the devastating power of the Darkstar fortress that accompanied Battlefleet Gorgon, before pushing through to engage. If the Word Bearers attempted to breach the Trajan Belt, which was riddled with mines and defence installations, then the Boros Defence Fleet would engage, punishing them as they emerged piecemeal through the notoriously hazardous asteroid band.

With the stable wormholes, the exact moment of the supporting Fleet's arrival had been calculated, and so the Boros Defence Fleet could engage the enemy with confidence, knowing the precise moment when help would arrive. If all went to the meticulously detailed and coordinated plan that had been agreed upon by the caucus, then the enemy would engage the heavily outnumbered Boros Defence Fleet, confident of victory.

The full force of the Imperial reinforcements would hang back, massing just beyond the gate until the enemy was fully engaged. Then they would emerge from the warp and fall upon the flanks of the enemy.

It required perfect timing and was a dangerous ploy, placing the defence fleet of Boros Prime, and the accompanying White Consuls strike cruisers of the 2nd and 5th, in a precarious position.

It was deemed a worthy risk, however. By showing its full strength too early, they risked scaring the enemy fleet off, losing the chance to destroy a sizeable force of the hated Word Bearers.

'Good hunting, brothers,' said Chapter Master Titus Valens at the conclusion of the caucus, and Aquilius felt a thrill of excitement run through him at the prospect of the forthcoming battle, even though he would only be able to view it from afar.

It would be glorious.

CHAPTER FIVE

LIKE A MONSTER rising from the depths, the *Infidus Diabolus* broke from the warp, its hull creaking and groaning as reality crashed in upon it. Phosphorescent waves of warp energy cascaded along its bow. Shimmering void shields blurred the edges of its outline as fragments of debris and wreckage battered against them.

'What in the name of the Urizen?' snarled Marduk from his command pulpit on the bridge as a chunk of twisted metal the size of a hab-block glanced off the prow of the ship with an unnerving squeal of the forward shields. 'Report.'

'Systems coming online,' drawled a servitor hardwired into the control hub of the ship. It was little more than the armless torso of a skeleton, with a thick bundle of pulsating tubes, wires and cables protruding from its ruptured skull, connecting its exposed brain to the cogitation units in front of it. It drooled yellow syrup as its blackened lips moved. 'Scanning in progress… scan complete at 10.34… 13.94…. 18.23…'

'Plasma core at 85% and rising,' barked another servitor unit, a thrashing creature that jerked back and forth, pulling at the leaking plugs that connected its limbless torso to the humming banks of sensor arrays to either side of it.

'Internal comms established, external pulse ignition in five,' intoned another in a mechanised voice.

'Port battery cognition online.'

'Establishing fleet contact.'

Screens of data-flow filled with scrolling diagnostic reports and internal mechadialogue as the systems of the *Infidus Diabolus* slowly came online. A ship was always at its most vulnerable before its navigational and comms arrays were up and running.

Scanning the bewildering array of codeform and binaric data inloading across dozens of screens, Kol Badar frowned.

'Well?' said Marduk.

'I'm reading heat signatures and plasma bleed. Something is wrong,' growled Kol Badar.

'Is it us?' said Burias.

'No,' said Kol Badar. 'Our readings are fine.'

'Where did all this come from?' said Marduk in rising concern as the grating squeal of the shields continued. 'We were meant to realise two hundred thousand kilometres from the asteroid belt.'

'We did,' said Kol Badar, scanning the inloading data being transferred onto the console in front of him. 'This is something else.'

'Where is the *Mortisis Majesticatus*?' said First Acolyte Ashkanez, accessing the in-flood of data via a nerve-spike inserted into a plug in his left vambrace.

Marduk looked out through the viewing portal that dominated the bridge. The *Infidus Diabolus* was positioned towards the rear of the fleet, and he could see the shapes of the other Word Bearers ships beyond, flickering immaterium residue still clutching at their hulls. They had come through in battle formation, wary of potential attack, with the crude proselyte slave-ships on the outside, and the hulking monstrosity that held the Legio Vulturus protectively in the centre.

Ekodas's immense Infernus-class battleship, the *Crucius Maledictus*, was located to the fore, but of the Dark Apostle Sarabdal's strike cruiser, the *Mortisis Majesticatus*, he could see nothing.

Kol Badar's brow furrowed, and he studied the data-floods, eyes scanning quickly.

'Well?' snapped Marduk. 'Where is it?'

'It's not here,' said Kol Badar.

'It didn't make realisation?'

Kol Badar shook his head.

'It came through before us. It should be here.'

'Could it have veered off course?' said Burias. 'Made realisation elsewhere?'

'Not possible,' said Marduk. 'Well, my Coryphaus? Where in the name of the nine hells of Sicarus is Sarabdal and the 18th Host?'

'The *Moribundus Fatalis* is here,' said Kol Badar, stabbing a finger against a data-slate showing the positioning of the fleet. 'So half of Sarabdal's Host is with us. Wait…'

Kol Badar traced the flow of information with one ceramite-encased finger, before turning to face Marduk. His face was grim.

'Spit it out,' snapped Marduk.

'The *Mortisis Majesticatus* is all around us,' said Kol Badar finally.

'What?' said Burias.

Marduk leant backwards and licked his lips as more wreckage was repelled by the shields of the *Infidus Diabolus*.

His mind reeled. He had not thought that even Ekodas would go that far, at least not so blatantly. He realised how much he was relying on his alliance with Sarabdal. Without him, he felt exposed and vulnerable. Worse, whatever secret that Sarabdal had uncovered regarding Ekodas's plot had died with him.

'The murderous bastard,' he hissed.

'Surely you do not suspect one of our own being responsible, my Apostle?' said Ashkanez.

Marduk glanced over at his First Acolyte, but did not say anything.

'I'm reading heat discharge from the cannons and torpedo tubes of the *Crucius Maledictus* and the *Anarchus,*' said Kol Badar.

'Ekodas and his wretched toad, Ankh-Heloth,' murmured Marduk.

'No, First Acolyte,' he said, his voice thick with derision. 'I would never dream of suspecting one of my brothers.'

'The *Mortisis Majesticatus* had been destroyed?' said Burias.

'Very good, my Icon Bearer,' said Marduk. 'As you can see, Ashkanez, I keep Burias around for his cutting, fierce intellect. Nothing gets by him.'

Burias scowled, and Marduk felt the daemon within the Icon Bearer straining to be released.

'Is there such disunity within the XVII Legion that brother fires upon brother?' said a deeply resonant voice, and all hostility within the room was suddenly directed towards this newcomer. First Acolyte Ashkanez flexed his fingers, and Marduk knew that he longed to reach for his weapon; he felt much the same way.

Kol Badar, ignoring the sorcerer, continued to survey the incoming data.

'There is an Imperial fleet moving towards our position from co-ordinates X3.75 by 9 from inside the asteroid belt. Advancing at engagement speed.'

'Warmaster Abaddon would be disturbed to learn that his favoured brother Legion was fractured,' continued the new arrival, the Black Legion Sorceror Inshabael Kharesh.

'If there was any disunity within the XVII Legion,' said Marduk coldly, 'then it would be the business of the XVII Legion, and no one else, sorcerer.'

Kharesh merely smiled in reply, a thin-lipped grimace exposing his bloodstained teeth.

'Incoming transmission,' said Kol Badar. 'From the *Crucius Maledictus.*'

'Bring it up,' said Marduk.

The crackling image of Ekodas filled the viewscreen. The comm-link was dropping in and out, perhaps as a result of the shrapnel interference surrounding the *Infidus Diabolus*.

'...brothers... regret to inform you of the tragic loss... *Mortisis Majesticatus*... suffered catastrophic... destruction at the hands... enemy... minefield... tricks, dishonourable and ignoble. Sarabdal and all hands... joined with Chaos almighty.'

'A minefield, of course,' said Marduk mockingly. He saw Ashkanez's frown deepen.

'...advocate that the remainder of...' continued Ekodas's broken transmission. '...Host be transferred under... Belagosa's wing, becoming... brothers of the 18th.'

'He's disbanded the 18th,' said Kol Badar. 'He's amalgamating them into Belagosa's Host.'

'A bribe?' said Burias.

Marduk did not answer. His mind was whirling. Ekodas must have learnt that Sarabdal was close to uncovering his plotting, and taken measures to silence him. The Brotherhood, Sarabdal had said. Marduk had believed that the Dark Apostle had been misled somehow, for the Brotherhood had not been in existence since the cleansing of the Word Bearers ranks, before Horus had turned. Why would it have been reformed? He realised now that Sarabdal knew something. Marduk had lost the support of that powerful Dark Apostle. He was alone.

'...arduk, the Nexus Arrangement... ready to be activated on my command?'

'Yes, Grand Apostle,' said Marduk, sending the vox to all receiving channels. His words would be broadcast to the bridge of each Dark Apostle within the fleet. Each *remaining* Dark Apostle.

'Good... Continue as planned...' came the crackling order from the *Maledictus Confutatis*. '...in attack formation, penetrating the... belt at co-ordinates FZ3.503.M... combat speed...'

'No turning back now,' murmured Burias.

The ships of the Word Bearers fleet began to advance, engines burning with the white-hot intensity as they moved towards the asteroid belt in the distance. The outer region of the binary solar system was in perpetual shadow, for such was the density of the asteroid belt that it virtually blocked out all light from the two suns at the system's epicentre.

'What is your order?' said Kol Badar, belligerently.

'You will refer to the Dark Apostle by his Council-ordained title at all times, Coryphaus,' rumbled Ashkanez.

'Or what, First Acolyte?' snapped Kol Badar, glaring down at Ashkanez.

'Or you will be duly chastened,' said Ashkanez, his gaze unwavering.

'By who?' snorted Kol Badar. 'You?'

'If such is the Dark Apostle's will,' said Ashkanez. Marduk could smell the adrenaline coming off the First Acolyte's skin as his body readied itself for combat.

'Enough,' snapped Marduk, conscious of the cynical smile that had appeared on the pale face of the Black Legion sorcerer as his underlings bickered. 'This is not the time. The *Infidus Diabolus* shall continue on course. Maintain formation. But reroute additional power to the shields. A precaution against... further *enemy* attack.'

'The disposition of the enemy defence fleet has been confirmed,' said Kol Badar, consulting his information feed. 'They have been bolstered by two Astartes strike cruisers. White Consuls.'

'Good,' said Marduk. 'It has been too long since I have killed any sons of Guilliman.'

'Those two cruisers will be just the start,' said Kol Badar. 'The defence fleet is heavily outnumbered – they will be hoping that we plough head-long through the asteroid belt like blood-crazed savages to engage them. As soon as we do, their reinforcements will drop in via the wormholes, coming through en masse. That is what I would do. There will be no chance of retreat. We will be annihilated.'

'Except it will not be us who are annihilated when their reinforce-ments fail to appear,' said Marduk.

'I shall believe that when I see it,' said Kol Badar.

'Have faith, my Coryphaus,' said Marduk.

'My faith in the gods is not in question,' said Kol Badar. 'It is my faith in the magos and that xenos device that is weak.'

'The engagement is beginning,' said the Black Legion sorcerer. He was staring through the viewing portal. Marduk followed his gaze.

A thousand kilometres in front, the lead elements of the Word Bearers fleet had reached the immense wall of asteroids. The hulking slave ships were expelling vast clouds of smaller craft, poorly armed shuttles and transports for the most part. Like a swarm of insects they entered the asteroid belt, urged on by the whim of their Word Bearers masters. The first explosions lit up the darkness.

From within the asteroid belt, scores of self-powered mines acceler-ated towards the intruders, drawn to their heat-signatures like flies to a corpse. Each was half the size of a Thunderhawk gunship and easily capable of inflicting catastrophic damage to even a well-armoured ship. They attached themselves to the hulls of the cult ships before detonating with catastrophic effect, coronas of red fire flaring across the battlefront. The larger slave hulks were ripped apart as dozens of mines clamped onto them.

Cannon batteries erupted, targeting incoming mines as the slave ships continued to plough ever deeper into the asteroid belt. Scores of mines detonated prematurely, their explosions prickling the darkness, but oth-ers weathered the storm of incoming fire, zoning in on the invading ships and blasting them into oblivion.

Lance batteries hidden within the hollowed out centre of the larg-est asteroids began to fire, concentrated beams searing through shields and cutting slave hulks in two. Asteroids exploded into dust and scores of ships were ripped apart as more white-hot beams of light speared through the mayhem, and more explosions deeper into the asteroid belt erupted as the ships pushing ahead drew more mines to them.

Thousands died in the first moments of the fusillade. Tens of thousands died in the next.

None of the ships of the Hosts had yet entered the asteroid belt – only the sacrificial slave vessels of the cultists had advanced into that deadly arena. Now, as they drew nearer, the Word Bearers unleashed the power of their battleships. An indiscriminate blanket of fire was directed into the asteroid belt. The weight of ordnance was staggering, destroying everything in its path: mines, asteroids, concealed lance batteries and slave ships alike were ripped apart.

The wretched slave-ships had done their duty. Singing praises to their XVII Legion benefactors and with prayers of thanks upon their tortured lips, their crews had gone to their deaths willingly, desperate to serve their infernal masters. Their deaths had cleared a path for their masters and revealed the hidden guns of the Imperials.

'We are being hailed,' said Kol Badar.

'Bring it up,' ordered Marduk.

The image of Ekodas reappeared, the five-metre-high vid-screen free of interference and filled with his glowering face. His jet-black eyes were filled with reflected hellfire.

Marduk began running through conditioning exercises and mantras, trying to seal his mind against intrusion. He didn't know if Ekodas were capable of penetrating his thoughts from afar, but he wanted to be prepared.

'Activate the device on my command,' ordered Ekodas.

'I know the plan, Apostle,' snapped Marduk. 'What happened to the *Mortisis Majesticatus*?'

'Transferral error,' said Ekodas. 'The *Mortisis Majesticatus* made realisation into a minefield. Sarabdal's death has not unnerved you, has it, Marduk?'

Ekodas's eyes were mocking, and Marduk seethed inside. Ekodas was barely making an effort to conceal the fact that he had been responsible for the death of Sarabdal.

'Not at all, Grand Apostle,' said Marduk. 'One must always be vigilant for attack. From any quarter.'

'Indeed,' said Ekodas. 'Sarabdal was a fool. He did not even realise the danger he found himself in until too late. I would hope that one such as yourself would not make such a mistake.'

'As would I,' said Marduk. He could feel the leech-like tendrils of Ekodas's mind worming their way into his thoughts, probing his defences.

'The enemy fleet advances, confident of their reinforcements,' said Ekodas. 'I want the device activated the moment we engage. Be ready for my word. I do not want any of them escaping.'

Marduk could feel the defences of his mind slowly crumbling. In seconds, they would be bypassed. Marduk was certain that Sarabdal had been killed to silence him. Doubtless Ekodas was seeking to learn what, if anything, Marduk already knew.

'I will await your order, my lord,' he said and slammed his fist down upon a glowing blister upon his console. The transmission feed was instantly severed, and Ekodas's glowering visage faded to black. The invasive tendrils of Ekodas's mind instantly receded, and Marduk clutched at his console in order not to stagger as they scraped at the inside of his skull, clawing to maintain their hold.

'My lord Apostle?' said Ashkanez, stepping forward to aid him.

Marduk shrugged off his First Acolyte's attentions. His mind was whirling. What was it that Sarabdal had stumbled across?

He snarled in frustration, knowing that whatever it was, it was now lost to him.

THE CHAOS FLEET contracted its width as it entered the asteroid belt, moving into the breach it had created with the force of its bombardment. Rock dust, spinning chunks of shattered asteroids and twisted metal hung in that gap, repelled by flickering void shields as the battleships of the dark crusade passed through the breach without slowing.

The flanks of the twelve remaining Word Bearers battleships were guarded by a second wave of smaller cult ships that had been ushered forward as sacrificial lambs into the mine-riddled field. They were poorly maintained, and their overcharged and unshielded reactor cores burnt fiercely, slowly irradiating their crew in order to maintain the speed of the battleships they guarded. These ships were mostly ex-transports, mining ships or rogue trader vessels that had been claimed by the Legion over centuries of raids, their crews slaughtered. Now they served the crusade as its ablative armour.

Occasionally, one of the sacrificial vessels that guarded the crusade's flanks was destroyed in a blazing corona of light and fire as isolated mines that had yet to be detonated latched on to their hulls. Sporadic fire stabbed from deeper in the asteroid belt, off to either side of the gateway the Word Bearers had created. Blazing white lance strikes took their toll on the cult vessels, but in doing so exposed their own position and were dutifully targeted by the Word Bearers battleships, immense cannon arrays blasting them apart.

The light of the system's twin suns could be seen now that the way before the fleet was all but clear of obstruction, making the dust of the destroyed asteroids glow a rich orange. Shafts of light speared through gaps in the asteroid belt, the light glinting off the spires and castellated fortifications of the Word Bearers battleships as they ploughed through the thick dust clouds. The sight was breathtaking in its beauty. It looked as if the light of the gods was shining upon the crusade fleet. A good omen, thought Marduk.

'The enemy is advancing at combat speed to engage,' said Kol Badar. 'Main cannons are running at full power, and boarding parties are ready.'

'Transfer power to the forward shields,' said Marduk.

'Clear of the belt in ninety seconds,' said Kol Badar. 'We'll have a better idea of the enemy positioning then.'

'No indication of Imperial warp transfer as yet?' said Inshabael Kharesh.

Kol Badar glared at the sorcerer, then glanced at Marduk who nodded.

'Nothing yet,' said Kol Badar. 'We're advancing right into the mouth of one of the wormhole exit points though. If and when they do appear, they will have us completely surrounded.'

'Encoded transmission inbound,' croaked a servitor.

Marduk tapped his console. A message appeared on screen.

<Be ready. Activate device on my mark.>

Marduk prayed that the magos would be ready.

THE ENEMY WAS emerging from the Trajan Belt and expanding its frontage to face the incoming Boros Defence Fleet, which looked pitifully small in comparison, despite the addition of the two White Consuls strike cruisers.

Proconsul Ostorius felt frustrated as he watched the three-dimensional hololith that showed the two fleets closing with each other. His brother Space Marines were out there preparing to face the brunt of the enemy's attack. Even now the company Chaplains would be conducting their blessings, readying the minds and spirits of the Chapter's warriors for battle.

Ostorius missed the rituals of pre-battle. He missed the surge of adrenaline as the moment of combat drew near. He should be standing with them.

Focussing on the flashing icon that represented the cruiser that held 5th Company in its entirety, Ostorius clenched his fist. He was Company Champion of the 5th – his place was by his captain's side. No, he corrected. He was Company Champion no longer; that duty was now that of another. He was Proconsul of Boros Prime. This was his place now.

Still, he felt a sense of guilt that he was not standing alongside his brothers, regardless of the fact that he had never enjoyed fleet engagements. He disliked them for the same reason that he always felt a vague unease being carried into the thick of battle within the Rhinos, Land Raiders, Thunderhawks and drop-pods of the Chapter. He understood this unease. In the mayhem of the battlefield, amidst the roar of chainswords, the screams of the dying and the rumble of weapon fire he was master of his survival, but in a fleet engagement, or while being ferried into battle, he was at the mercy of dangers beyond his control.

He could sense Aquilius's excitement as the fleets closed with each other. He could understand his Coadjutor's emotions, for the enemy should be annihilated in the forthcoming battle. The trap was set. As soon as the enemy were engaged, the full force of the Adeptus Praeses would descend on them like a hammer.

'How long, do you think?' said Aquilius.

All contact with the incoming ships of the Adeptus Praeses, Battlefleet Gorgon and the battle-barge of the Grey Knights had been cut, so as to give the enemy as little forewarning as possible. Most of the reinforcements were ready for transference, anchored just beyond the veil of reality. They merely waited the order to come through, and fall upon the enemy.

Yet Ostorius could not help but feel a sliver of apprehension, as if there was something at play here that he, that all the members of the caucus, had missed. He prayed to the Emperor that he was wrong, but he could not shake the pervading sense of doom that was descending upon him.

'Not long,' said Ostorius.

ALONE, THE HULKING monstrosity that held the Titans of Legio Vulturus hung back within the protection of the asteroid field, guarded by a flotilla of smaller vessels as the bulk of the Word Bearers fleet advanced to meet the incoming Imperial fleet head on.

The *Maledictus Confutatis* was at the centre of the formation, with the other eleven battleships of the XVII Legion forming an arc to either side of it, reaching out to envelop the smaller defence fleet.

Hurtling towards the foe out in front were the last remnants of the cult ships, their reactors reaching dangerously critical levels as they expended the last of their energy reserves to close the distance. Not much was expected of them, but the enemy could not ignore them. Even unarmed they posed a threat; a ship could suffer serious damage if it were rammed by one of the slave vessels.

The Imperial fleet swung towards one of the advancing wings of the XVII Legion battleships so as not to advance into the centre of their formation, and the first shots of the engagement were fired. Massive torpedoes were launched from cavernous tubes sunk into the armoured prow of the Imperial vessels, the missiles speeding through the emptiness of space towards the *Crucius Maledictus*. The Chaos battleships responded in kind, launching torpedoes of their own as the right arm of its force swung around in a wide arc to engulf the enemy.

Hundreds of thousands of kilometres separated the fleets, yet prow-mounted laser batteries opened up, stabbing lances that shredded dozens of cult vessels. Several more exploded in blinding detonations as they advanced into the paths of incoming torpedoes.

The barrage of fire intensified as the Imperial fleet split into two and unleashed the power of its broadsides upon the slave vessels caught stranded between them. Within minutes of ferocious firing, immense cannon batteries laying down an impenetrable blanket of fire, the cult ships were gone.

Swivelling defence cannons mounted upon the battleships of both fleets swung around and began to rain fire upon incoming torpedoes. Fleets of fighters were exhaled from gaping launch bays like angry insects rising to protect their hive.

The fleets banked and turned, altering their trajectory as they reacted to the torpedoes and the movement of the enemy. Within minutes the symmetrical lines of the fleets were disrupted as the battleship commanders manoeuvred their ships into the best attack position.

Dozens of torpedoes were scythed down by the weight of fire from the *Crucius Maledictus* and the other Word Bearers ships. Others flew wide, exploding upon the walls of the Trajan Belt behind the Chaos fleet. A handful found their mark, exploding upon the monstrous battleship's forward shields.

The Imperial fleet came back together and swung around to form two fronts, turning their flanks into the face of the advancing Chaos fleet. The ships of XVII Legion ploughed on into the broadsides of their foes, and the battle began in earnest.

The Imperial fleet consisted of a single Retribution-class battleship, the *Dawn Eternal*, four Lunar-class cruisers and a host of escorts, and was bolstered by the two strike cruisers of the White Consuls. The enemy still heavily outgunned them. Regardless, it unleashed its fury into the face of the Chaos fleet, stripping void shields and crippling one battleship, the *Dominus Violatus* of Ekodas's Host.

Flights of Starhawk bombers hurtled from the yawning launch bays of the Imperial fleet, accompanied by Fury interceptors. The boxy shapes of Thunderhawks and larger, heavier armed Stormbirds spat forth from the Chaos ships to meet them.

A furious exchange erupted as the fighters and interceptors engaged. Thousands of las-beams stabbed through the mayhem of battle like needles of light, and bank upon bank of cannon unleashed their salvos, their firepower growing ever more destructive as the fleets closed.

The two strike cruisers of the White Consuls veered off from the Imperial line to target the *Dies Mortis*, Dark Apostle Belagosa's ship. They started stripping its void shields with concentrated bombardments. The powerful Chaos vessel began turning on its axis, attempting to bring them under its broadsides.

The nova cannon of the *Crucius Maledictus* roared like an angry god, and a massive blaze of light comparable to the output of a small sur-rounded its barrel as it fired. The beam of blinding light tore through the Imperial line, engulfing two cruisers and an escort, ripping them apart with seeming disdain.

* * *

'CONFIRMED KILL ON the starboard wing,' droned a servitor.

'Shields holding at eighty per cent stability,' said another.

A horrific wailing sounded within the bridge of the *Infidus Diabolus*.

'The enemy fleet is making transference,' growled Kol Badar.

'Lorgar's blood,' said Burias, looking over Kol Badar's shoulder. 'There are thirty-two vessels zoning in!'

An evil grin split Marduk's face. They had the Imperials by the throat. By the time they realised their reinforcements were not going to make the jump from warp space, they would have no chance of extracting themselves from the engagement. The slaughter would be glorious.

'Patch me a link through to the magos,' said Marduk.

'Link established,' gargled a servitor.

'Be ready, magos,' said Marduk.

'Darioq-Grendh'al is unable to comply,' came the reply.

'What!'

'Regretfully that action cannot currently be performed,' returned the corrupted magos's voice.

'Enemy fleet realisation in progress,' drawled a servitor on the bridge of the *Infidus Diabolus*.

Marduk swung around and slammed his fist into the servitor's face. Its skull collapsed like a moist shell, the Dark Apostle's fist pulping the rotting brain within.

'That was helpful,' commented Kharesh. Marduk glared at him.

'Darioq-Grendh'al,' said Marduk. 'Activate the device, now!'

'Re-calibration is required of the support brace X5.dfg4.234g enshrining the device designated "Nexus Arrangement" – recovered from xenos pyramidal structure classified c6.7.32.N98.t3, upon planet c6.7.32 "Tanakreg", suspect of mech-organism species NCT.p023423.2234.x, "Necron-tyr", origin incomplete – due to binary system atmospheric inload frequency disparity–'

Now! came Ekodas's order.

Marduk took a deep breath

'*Darioq-Grendh'al,*' he snarled, exerting his power over the possessed magos. 'Activate the device now, or we are all dead.'

'Summary: Darioq-Grendh'al regrets to inform Marduk, Dark Apostle of the 34th Host of the Word Bearers Astartes Legion, genetic descendant of the glorified Primarch Lorgar that the xenos artifice device designated "Nexus Arrangement" will take longer to activate than previous estimation.'

'We do not have time to fire up the warp engines for transference,' hissed Kol Badar. 'We are committed to this engagement.'

'How long, Darioq-Grendh'al?' growled Marduk.

'Re-calculated estimate: the device will be active in 1.234937276091780 minutes. Clarification: this is an estimated supposition only, and has a variance of 0.00000234 seconds.'

'Too long,' said Kol Badar, shaking his head. 'The Imperial fleet could be ten times its size by then. We should never have put our trust in the cursed magos or that damned xenos device. This crusade is going to end in disaster.'

'No,' said Marduk forcefully. 'I have come too far.'

The Word Bearers within the bridge of the *Infidus Diabolus* waited in tense silence.

'Incoming transmission,' warned Kol Badar. 'It's Ekodas.'

'Block it,' said Marduk, foetid ichor dripping from his knuckles. 'Darioq-Grendh'al – get that damned thing operational, now!'

'Regretfully that action cannot currently be performed, Marduk, Dark Apostle of the 34th Host of the Word Bearers Astartes Legion, genetic descendant of the glorified Primarch Lorgar,' returned the corrupted magos's voice. 'There is a type XP3.251.te5 code error that requires calibration adjustment of the–'

'It will not end like this!' said Marduk. 'Magos, I am sending Burias down to you. If the device is not active by the time he gets there, he will tear you limb from limb. Get it working. *Now!*'

He swung towards Burias.

'Go,' he said.

The change came over the Icon Bearer in an instant, his features blurring with those of the daemon Drak'shal.

'Launching attack craft,' said Kol Badar as a wave of enemy Starhawks rose to greet to *Infidus Diabolus*. 'Defensive turrets engaging.'

Another incoming transmission from the *Crucius Maledictus* was rebuffed.

'How close are the enemy from making realisation?' said Marduk.

'Close,' replied Kol Badar, his eyes filled with accusation. *You have brought us to this precipice*, they said.

'The gods of Chaos shall deliver us,' said Ashkanez. Alone on the bridge, he seemed unaffected by the tension, as if resigned to whatever fate the gods decreed.

A pair of Imperial Cobra frigates were torn apart by concentrated broadsides, and the *Infidus Diabolus* shook as impacts from incoming Starhawks struck home.

'It shall not end like this,' snarled Marduk. 'This is not my fate.'

'Enemy fleet realisation commencing,' said Kol Badar.

Five new enemy blips appeared on the holo-screens. 'First realisation complete. Astartes vessels. Two battle-barges, three cruisers. More inbound.'

The Chaos fleet began to splinter, reacting to the sudden appearance of these new threats.

Marduk swore then dropped to his knees as pain blossomed in his mind.

Activate the device now, roared Ekodas.

'We have been target-acquired by the *Crucius Maledictus*,' said Kol Badar, his voice a warning growl. 'Its nova cannon is re-energising.'

You dare defy me? roared Ekodas, making blood ooze from Marduk's nose, ears and eye sockets.

'This... is... not... my... time,' gasped Marduk through clenched teeth.

BURIAS-DRAK'SHAL BOUNDED DOWN the corridor, skidding as he rounded a tight corner, his talons gouging deep wounds in the latticed floor. He burst through the doors of the workshop, shattering plate glass.

Magos Darioq-Grendh'al was standing before the spinning hoops rotating with increasing speed around the Nexus Arrangement, his four articulated servo-arms spread wide. His mechadendrites waved languidly around him as the Nexus, hanging motionless in the air, began to vibrate and spin. Burias-Drak'shal hurled himself at the corrupted magos.

The red beams of light transfixing the Nexus in place expanded, filling the sphere formed by the spinning hoops of ensorcelled metal so that it looked like a globe of hellish light, a sun with a gleaming metallic centre.

The perfect silver orb of the xenos device shimmered, and glowing green hieroglyphs of alien design appeared upon its spinning surface. The speed of its rotation increased exponentially, so that the hieroglyphs were soon nothing more than a gleaming green blur, and then it seemed to melt and come apart, forming seven rapidly spinning rings.

Green light spilled from the device. As the Nexus spun faster and faster, it let off a keening wail that was at the upper echelon of augmented hearing. The noise was painful, and Burias-Drak'shal roared as it cut through him, Still, he came on. He leapt, bony talons extended to impale the corrupted magos.

In mid-leap, Burias-Drak'shal heard the corrupted magos say, 'Completion.'

Then everything changed.

Burias-Drak'shal was hurled against the far wall by the force of the blast from the Nexus Arrangement, blinding white light spilling from it in a sudden, devastating burst. Burias felt the daemon within him scream in agony as it retreated deep within him and his hyper-evolved and augmented physiology struggled to maintain consciousness.

Amid the blinding inferno of light and sound stood Darioq-Grendh'al, arms and tentacles spread wide, and he began to laugh, a horrible clucking sound akin to the grind of rusted pistons.

A ripple in realspace burst from the Nexus Arrangement and expanded outwards, gathering speed exponentially as it grew. It exploded outwards from the *Infidus Diabolus* and engulfed both warring fleets, knocking out communications and scanning relays aboard every vessel in an explosion of sparks and fire. All those with even a modicum of psychic ability fell to their knees, lesser minds bursting with aneurisms and clots, those of stronger stuff suffering intense pain and temporary blindness. Those who had been peering into the warp, notably the astropaths of the Imperial fleet, fell into sub-catatonic states, their minds wiped of all notable activity, collapsing at their posts.

The ripple continued to expand, engulfing nearby planets and moons. Within seconds it had spread across the entire solar system. Only when it reached neighbouring solar systems, over four light years away, did its strength waver.

'ENEMY REALISATION HAS failed,' said Kol Badar, blinking at the sensor array in front of him as it flickered and came back online.

A feral grin spread across Marduk's face, despite the lingering pain and emptiness that the ripple had caused him.

'It worked,' he said.

Kol Badar shook his head in wonder. 'The wormhole has been shut down. The whole of the Boros Gate has been shut down.'

'Open up a link with the *Crucius Maledictus*,' said Marduk.

'Warp-link down. Switching to conventional hail.'

'Ekodas,' said Marduk as the hail was received. 'I'd ask you remove that target lock on my ship now.'

'Marduk,' said Ekodas. 'A second later and–'

'You're most welcome, Grand Apostle,' said Marduk, cutting Ekodas off and severing the link.

The Imperials had no hope of further reinforcement now, and were committed to a battle in which the XVII Legion held the advantage, despite the additional White Consuls ships that had arrived before the Nexus had been activated.

Yet a lingering doubt hung over him like a cloud. In the moment of activation, something had happened. He'd felt a stabbing pain in the core of his being. It felt as if his link to the warp had diminished. But then, that was a minor thing when set alongside what the Nexus had achieved. He pushed his concerns aside.

Marduk smiled broadly. 'Let's get to killing, my brothers.'

'IN THE NAME of the Throne,' said Proconsul Ostorius as the hololith display and all the data-slates bearing incoming fleet transmissions went dead. With a strangled cry the astropath maintaining the link collapsed to the ground.

Coadjutor Aquilius went to his aid. As he rolled the astropath onto his side he saw that blood was leaking from the man's nose and ears. He felt for a pulse – it was weak. The astropath began to twitch and convulse.

'Repair the links now!' barked Ostorius.

'We're trying, my lord,' replied a robed tech-adept as he and a dozen others worked frantically over the dozens of consoles and cogitation units.

'Try harder! I need an astropath!'

'None are responding, my lord,' said an exasperated comms technician.

Ostorius looked down at the twitching astropath on the floor of the chamber. 'Communications?'

'Sir, it… it is as if the entire system has been cut off.'

'What?'

'There are no transmission links into or out of the Boros Gate, Proconsul,' said the man, paling. 'We are alone.'

Alone.

What had happened to the incoming Adeptus Praeses reinforcements? Battlefleet Gorgon? Had they made realisation?

With the astropaths down, communications were limited to standard transmissions – at a sluggish light speed. He cursed. Transmitting at that speed, he would not hear word from the fleet regarding the outcome of the battle out on the Trajan Belt for over three hours. The enemy may have annihilated the defence fleet and be ploughing towards Boros Prime by then.

'Alone,' he breathed grimly.

HALF A GALAXY away, an immense black ship suddenly altered its trajectory. It began to accelerate at an exponential rate, swiftly reaching, then surpassing, the speed of light. Impossibly, its momentum continued to increase.

It streaked through the cold darkness of the universe, guided by inhuman will. It passed through dazzling solar systems in the blink of an eye and crossed vast empty tracts of space in seconds. On and on it hurtled, moving faster than any Imperial tracking station could follow.

As if responding to some distant siren's call, inexorably, it closed on the Boros Gate.

BOOK TWO: THE BROTHERHOOD

'Our fraternity represents divine change. On ancient Colchis, a billion souls were released from earthly flesh in the Brotherhood's purge of the Covenant, and great was the rejoicing; and stronger did Colchis become. The second cleansing saw the Legion's ranks purified of Terran taint; and stronger did the Legion become, its chaff cast aside. Change is inevitable; the Brotherhood's return is inevitable. So shall the Legion be strengthened once more.'

– *The Arch-Prophet Baz-Ezael, recorded during his torture/death-vigil after being condemned by the Council of Sicarus for heresy and blasphemy*

CHAPTER SIX

THE BATTLE OF the Trajan Belt was short and brutal, the furious exchange seeing a dozen cruisers and battleships crippled within the space of ten minutes, yet to those involved it seemed to last an age.

The Boros Defence Fleet realised too late that reinforcements were not coming, yet by then it was already fully committed. As they tried desperately to extricate themselves from the engagement, the Chaos battleships exacted a terrible toll.

Of the expected relief force, only the White Consuls battle-barges *Sword of Deliverance* and *Sword of the Truth* made realisation, four full companies of White Consuls borne within them, plus an attendant flotilla of Gladius- and Nova-class frigates. The Imperial allied fleet that had been ready to make the transition from the warp would have obliterated this Chaos fleet in the space of minutes, such was its size, but no other vessels had made it through before the entire region had been shrouded by the Nexus Arrangement, ensuring that no further warp traffic was able to enter or exit the Boros Gate binary system. Within the bridge of the *Sword of Deliverance*, Chapter Master Valens, 5th Captain Marcus Decimus, and the captain of the 7th reserve company, Cato Paulinus, viewed the enemy fleet with dawning horror.

Outnumbered and outgunned, the reeling Imperial fleet sought to pull back. The White Consuls ships hurled themselves into the maelstrom of battle with guns blazing, attempting to buy the beleaguered defence fleet some relief. Powering into the middle of the Chaos battlefleet, the White Consuls ships brought their full battery arrays to bear, blasting away at close range.

The battleship *Sanctus Diabolica* was ripped apart between the concentrated fire of the two Space Marine battle-barges, and another Chaos ship, the *Dominus Violatus*, was rendered defenceless by the combined weight of fire of the Chapter's strike cruisers and frigates.

The monstrously powerful *Crucius Maledictus* annihilated the light cruiser *Scythe of Faith*, and a further four Boros Defence Fleet cruisers and frigates were destroyed as they tried to disengage. A desperate swathe of torpedoes, fired at extreme close range, critically damaged Dark Apostle Belagosa's *Dies Mortis*. Squadrons of Starhawk bombers riddled her hull with plasma detonations before themselves being obliterated by the battleship's cloud of daemon-infused fighters.

More manoeuvrable than the larger Chaos battleships, the White Consuls strike cruisers cut through the field of destruction like knives. They focussed their weapon batteries on the isolated and defenceless *Dominus Violatus*, pummelling it with bombardment cannons and las-batteries until it was a shattered wreck. The strike cruisers retreated as the heavier Chaos ships lurched around to bring their broadsides to bear, though the *Eternal Faith*, holding the entirety of the Chapter's 2nd Company, suffered grievous damage as she was caught at the edge of a nova cannon blast from the hulking *Crucius Maledictus*.

The *Pride of Redolus*, a truly ancient Avenger-class grand cruiser, was surrounded by three Chaos ships that circled it like sharks. They pounded it into submission as it attempted to disengage. Under the calm direction of its captain, it inflicted major structural damage upon Ankh-Heloth's flagship, the *Corruptus Maligniatus*, and stripped the shields of the *Infidus Diabolus* before it died, exploding in a series of catastrophic plasma-core detonations.

One of the White Consuls battle-barges, the *Sword of Deliverance*, caught a glancing blow from the *Crucius Maledictus*, knocking out almost half of its starboard cannon arrays and sending it keening off course as it came to a new heading. It collided with the *Dies Mortis*, and the powerful ships were locked together for some minutes before the *Sword* blasted its way free.

Now isolated from the Boros battlefleet, the *Sword of Deliverance* was rounded upon by the Chaos fleet, which battered it with ordnance and waves of heavy cannon fire. As powerfully armoured and shielded as the mighty battle-barge was, even it could not stand against such overwhelming hatred, and it reeled as its shields were torn apart and its hull hammered by the heavy incoming fire. Gleaming towers and castellated sensor arrays were ripped from its body, and its port-mounted lance batteries were shorn off, spinning into space.

Formations of Thunderhawks erupted from the launch bays of the *Sword of Deliverance*, but they were not enough to hold off the plague of fighters and Stormbirds that descended over her like a vicious swarm of predatory insects, tearing at the battle-barge's hide with plasma charges and cluster bombs. The proud vessel's core was approaching critical, and fuel and air bled from the gashes in its side. Still it continued to fight on, its active turrets and gun batteries blasting away at the enemy swarming around it.

The *Sword of Truth* and the surviving frigates of the White Consuls Chapter turned back into the face of the Chaos fleet. Desperate to save Chapter Master Valens and the mighty battle-barge, they launched a swift strike back into the fray. The desperate manoeuvre cut through the Chaos line, and while the White Consuls ships took heavy damage, the *Sword of Deliverance* managed to limp out of the danger zone under the protective fire of the Chapter's gunships.

As the survivors of the Boros Defence Fleet pulled away, finally extricating themselves from the slower vessels of the XVII Legion, the Chaos fleet vented its fury upon the White Consuls, enveloping them and pounding them with thousands of tonnes of ordnance. Having bought enough time for the *Sword of Deliverance* to extricate itself from the heaviest fighting, the heavily outnumbered Consuls vessels veered away sharply, attempting to pull back. The strike cruiser *Sacred Blade* was severely damaged in the firefight, and almost half the Chapter's frigates were destroyed in that one engagement as they attempted to fight their way free of the Chaos fleet surrounding them.

Slowest to turn and pull away was the retreating battle-barge *Sword of Truth*. Thanks to her guns, her sister-ship, the *Sword of Deliverance*, had managed to get away, bearing Chapter Master Valens to safety, but now the ship was suffering for its heroics.

A hugely powerful yet heavy vessel, the *Sword of Truth* did not have the speed or manoeuvrability of the smaller Astartes vessels. Pounded from all sides, its shields and armoured hull taking a hammering, the *Sword of Truth* nevertheless exacted a heavy toll on the Chaos ships, rotating turrets drilling its attackers with relentless fire. Diverting huge amounts of energy to its overloading shield arrays, it could not pull away fast enough, and like circling predators, the Chaos ships moved to cut it off from its brethren.

Chapter Master Valens wanted to turn the *Sword of Deliverance* back around to aid its sister-ship, but the battle-barge was in no fit state, and he knew in his heart that if he did so both battle-barges would be lost.

Realising that he was cut off, Captain Augustus of 2nd Company, the most senior officer aboard the battle-barge, signalled his intentions to his Chapter Master and ordered the *Sword of Truth* to come about to a new heading, turning and ploughing straight towards the Trajan asteroid belt. The sudden move threw off most of its attackers, and Imperial battle platforms within the asteroid belt began to fire past the approaching battle-barge, zeroing in on its pursuers.

Alone amongst the Chaos fleet, Kol Badar had predicted the move, and the *Infidus Diabolus* had already been turning as the *Sword of Truth* swung for the safety of the asteroid belt.

Marduk's ship did not have the firepower to cripple the vessel before it was in amongst the asteroids, but the Dark Apostle had no intention of destroying it.

'Remember, Apostles, we need one of their ships left intact,' Ekodas had said in the conclave aboard the *Crucius Maledictus*. Marduk intended to be the one to claim the glory of achieving that goal.

The *Infidus Diabolus* turned on her side as she came astern of the mighty White Consuls battle-barge, raking her flanks with cannon fire. Then, as the roaring of the cannons died down, waves of Dreadclaws were launched from assault tubes, spat towards the battle-barge which could do little but brace for the inevitable impact, the vast majority of her Thunderhawks having already fallen and her defensive turrets now offline.

With pinpoint accuracy the Dreadclaws hurtled towards the battle-barge, their target locations designated by Kol Badar. The Coryphaus of the 34th knew the layout of the enemy battle-barge well, for he had orchestrated the destruction of its like in battle before, and the XVII Legion had several similar vessels in its flotillas. He knew precisely where to hit to inflict the most damage, precisely where to aim in order that the boarding parties secreted within the Dreadclaws would cause the most havoc. He knew where to strike to take control of the ship's engines, and the precise deck locales he needed to secure in order to bring the vessel to a halt.

A score of boarding pods screamed towards the neck of the battle-barge, while others dipped beneath its looming hull to strike in deep towards its belly. These would assault the shield generators and the engine-core respectively, while other waves hurtled towards other locations as identified and marked by Kol Badar – boarding parties designated to take control of gun decks, to cut off expected counter-attack routes, to knock out communications, and others to isolate the warp drives.

A last burst of Dreadclaws powered towards the towers atop the hulking stern. Rising over a kilometre above the rear of the battle-barge's superstructure, this tiered, crenulated location was not unlike a fortress-monastery in its own right. The warrior-brothers packed into those assault pods readied themselves for combat, preparing to fight their way onto the bridge.

Leading the assault, Marduk roared the Catechisms of Defilement and Hate as his Dreadclaw screamed towards its target. Projected across all channels, his impassioned recitation drove his warriors into a fanatical blood-rage. Spouting psalms of debasement and vitriol, Marduk whipped them into a frenzied state of hyper-aggression, further heightened by the combat drugs pumping through their systems and the blaring roar of Chaos that thundered from the grilled vox-amplifiers of the Dreadclaws.

With colossal force the Dreadclaws struck the outer hull of the battle-barge, talon-like claws latching on tightly, gouging great rents in its metal skin. Phase-cutters hissed like monstrous serpents as they carved through the *Sword of Truth's* thick armour, metres of dense plating turning molten beneath the blinding arcs of energy. Blobs of liquid metal drifted off into space around the ships as the Dreadclaws burrowed through the outer shell, and unleashed their deadly cargo within.

In a tide of screaming hatred, the 34th Host boarded the *Sword of Truth*.

EXALTED CHAMPION KHALAXIS of the 17th Coterie was the first of the Word Bearers to step foot aboard the *Sword of Truth*. His cheeks were carved with fresh cuts inflicted by his own ritual *khantanka* blade, and his mane of thick dreadlocks swung wildly as he hurled himself into the enemy, roaring in hatred.

Always the first into any engagement, and invariably the last to be extracted, the 17th Coterie were brutal warriors all, savage berserkers who wore the grisly trophies of those they had defeated around their waists. Their shoulder pads were draped with skins ripped from the corpses of powerful enemies overcome in personal combat; it was an old Colchis belief that by donning the flesh of powerful defeated enemies, you were able to harness a portion of their strength.

While the Word Bearers as a Legion worshipped Chaos in all its glory, Khalaxis and his brood had a tendency to gravitate towards the sole worship of great Khorne, the Bloodied One, the Skull Taker, the brazen god of destruction and brutality. For the most part Marduk overlooked this failing, as had his predecessor Jarulek, merely for the fact that Khalaxis and his squad were such devastating shock troops, and that their pre-battle blood-rituals honouring Khorne lent them unmatched fury and savagery.

With an animalistic roar of pure rage, Khalaxis hacked his chainaxe into the chest of a White Consuls Chapter serf, the screaming teeth of the weapon ripping apart carapace armour and hungrily shearing through his rib cage in a glorious explosion of viscera and bone. Hot blood splattered across Khalaxis's face, which was twisted into that of a monster by battle-lust, the heady, metallic scent of the man's lifeblood merely fuelling his frenzy further. He fired his bolt pistol at close range and another two serfs were slain, exploding from within as bolt rounds penetrated their bodies and detonated.

The Chapter serfs that served aboard the *Sword of Truth* were bigger, stronger and more disciplined than regular men, and had arms and armour equivalent to Imperial Guard stormtroopers. Even so, they were like children next to the fury of the power armoured juggernauts of muscle and rage that were the members of Khalaxis's 17th Coterie, who smashed into them with the force of a sledgehammer. Limbs were hacked from bodies and warrior-serfs were tossed aside like rag-dolls, arms and spines shattering as the force of the 17th's charge hit home.

Automated defence turrets emerged from the battle-barge's decks and autocannons began to scream, shredding the armour of several Word Bearers, misting the air with blood. More Dreadclaws struck home, filling the air with acrid black smoke as they cut through the hull plating of the battle-barge to disgorge their Coteries upon the enemy.

Within moments, the silence of the lower deck corridors had erupted into roars and screams of pain, the deafening whine of autocannons and the deeper thump of bolters, as well as the painful grind of chainaxe and sword carving bone and armour. Word Bearers bellowed prayers and passages from their holy scripture. Khalaxis snarled as his enhanced hearing picked up the shouts of White Consuls sergeants as they barked their orders.

From the deck floor rose thick armoured barriers, angled shields of dense ceramite, adamantium and rockcrete designed to aid in repelling boarding actions. Through the smoke, Kalaxis saw armoured figures in white power armour taking up positions behind these barricades, dropping down behind them and hefting bolters up, bringing them to bear on the invaders. In a microsecond he had noted their number and position, and as he hacked the head from the shoulders of another hapless Chapter-serf, he registered an enemy Devastator squad moving up to join the defence, hauling their servo-balanced heavy weapons. Their sergeant ducked down behind a barricade and pointed in Khalaxis's direction as the last of the Chapter serfs were cut down, and the four heavy bolter-toting Space Marines accompanying him set their feet wide, bringing their immense weapons to bear.

With a snarl of hatred, Khalaxis threw himself into a roll as heavy bolter fire began to rake across the battle line, the deep percussive roar of the weapons deafening. Great chunks were gouged out of the walls and deck floor beneath the explosive barrage of heavy fire. Three of Khalaxis's Coterie were ripped apart, torn limb from limb by the annihilating rate of fire unleashed upon them.

Khalaxis slammed down behind a steel-plated storage crate, spitting in fury as bolter rounds screamed through the air around him. He thumbed a pair of grenades into his hand and rose from his position, hurling them towards the Devastator squad before ducking back behind cover. As quick as he was, a bolt round struck him in the neck, a glancing hit that passed through his flesh and out the other side. It penetrated one of the exhaust arms of his power-plant backpack, which exploded in a shower of superheated shrapnel, peppering the back of his skull with razor shards.

The grenades detonated, and while none of the White Consuls dropped, they were forced to hunker down behind cover. It would be a second or two before they had set themselves again, and Khalaxis launched himself towards them, bellowing in blood-frenzy as he closed the distance, the last of his Coterie a step behind.

A bolt round whizzed past his ear, scant centimetres away, and one of his brethren was felled as a burst of plasma caught him in the head, turning his horned helmet molten. Khalaxis leapt a barricade, planting his foot upon its top and leaping towards the Devastators that were even now swinging their heavy weapons in his direction.

They began to fire a moment before he got there, taking down two more of his brethren before they were overrun.

Their sergeant, whose helmet was royal blue with a white laurel painted around its crown, rose to meet the charging Word Bearers, and Khalaxis threw himself forwards to meet the challenge.

Chainaxe met chainsword in a clatter of rapidly spinning ceramite teeth. The White Consul was Khalaxis's equal in height and strength, and he turned his blade expertly to the side, using the exalted champion's momentum to sidestep him. The White Consul fired a plasma pistol blast square into the chest of another of Khalaxis's Coterie as the blood-crazed champion staggered, sending the warrior-brother flying backwards, his armour a molten ruin.

Snarling in anger, Khalaxis recovered quickly and slammed a kick into the sergeant's midsection, knocking him back into the barricade. His brethren were amongst the Devastators now, hacking them down without mercy, hot blood splattering across the White Consul's alabaster armour plates. The sergeant lifted his chainsword defensively, but the arm holding it was hacked off as Khalaxis struck downwards with his chainaxe, the biting teeth of the weapon grinding through power armour, flesh and bone.

Blood pumped from the wound and Khalaxis brought his knee up hard into the sergeant's groin, cracking ceramite. With a backhand slap he knocked the plasma pistol from the sergeant's hand, sending it spinning across the deck floor and planted the barrel of his bolt pistol against the White Consul's chest plate, right over his primary heart.

'See you in hell,' said Khalaxis, and he squeezed the trigger.

It took three shots to penetrate the thick power armour and the bonded ribcage of the White Consul, but the fourth detonated within the warrior's chest cavity, pulping the organs within. Still, the Consul was Astartes, and did not die. He continued to grapple with Khalaxis, who pounded his fist repeatedly into the White Consul's helmet, shattering one lens and caving in his rebreather.

With a wrench, Khalaxis tore the Space Marine's ruptured helmet from his head, so that he could see the face of the one he was about to kill.

The Consul's face was noble and proud, and three metal service studs protruded from his brow. His genetic lineage was readily apparent, for he had the same arrogant cast to his features as had the despised Primarch Roboute Guilliman, making Khalaxis's hatred surge all the more hotly.

'For Calth,' hissed Khalaxis, drawing his fist back.

'You did not win then, and you shall not win here, infidel,' said the White Consul, his voice defiant and haughty.

With a snarl of rage, Khalaxis drove his fist into the Astartes's face, killing him instantly.

Breathing hard, Khalaxis rose above the now unrecognisable White Consul. He spat upon the corpse and gave it one last kick.

There was a series of concentrated explosions as krak grenades were used to neutralise the automated turrets still peppering the warriors of the XVII Legion with heavy calibre fire, until the last of the guns were silenced.

'Deck secured,' growled one his warriors.

'We move,' said Khalaxis. 'We have our orders.'

With that, the warrior-brothers of the XVII Legion advanced deeper into the hulking battle-barge, moving inexorably towards the main engine-core, their mission briefing explicit – bring the *Sword of Truth* to a halt.

IN THE UPPER collegia decks, the push towards the plasma core was faltering. The Word Bearers Coteries were pinned down between carefully staggered lines of White Consuls defence, their lines of fire overlapping.

Another Dreadclaw penetrated the hull, its talons piercing the inner skin of the ship and spitting the thick circular drilled core of the battle-barge's armour. The bladed arcs of the assault pod slid aside, belching smoke, but before the Coterie cloistered within could launch itself into the fray a missile was fired into its interior. It exploded inside, fire billowing forth in a rapidly expanding cloud, and the survivors staggered out, their armour blackened and peeling.

Concentrated bursts of bolter fire tore through the Word Bearers, cutting them down mercilessly as they fought to gain some cover. The last of them crawled across the deck, trailing blood in their wake, before carefully aimed shots took them in their heads.

'Assault group X5.3, requiring assistance,' said Sabtec, champion of the exalted 13th Coterie. His voice was calm and measured. 'We are at location P3954.23, facing heavy resistance. We are pinned down. Request heavy support.'

'Acknowledged, Sabtec,' came Kol Badar's voice, crackling through the vox-comms integrated into Sabtec's helmet. The sound of bolter fire could be heard accompanying Kol Badar's voice; the Coryphaus was currently marching his way towards the bridge of the *Sword of Truth*, accompanying the Dark Apostle himself with his Anointed brethren. 'Secondary Dreadclaw launch initiated. Heavy support inbound.'

'Received, my Corpyhaus,' said Sabtec.

With a quick glance around the barricade, he saw that the enemy were flanking them, moving into position that would catch the pinned-down warrior-brothers in a brutal enfilade. Assessing the situation instantly, he passed his orders with short, concise commands relayed through his vox-comms, shifting the position of three of the pinned Coteries under his command to counter the threat.

'Brother Sabtec,' came the warning from one of his sub-champions.

'I see them,' he replied.

Moving up in support of the White Consuls were more Space Marines, several of whom had heavy plasma cannons.

'Brother Sabtec,' hissed another champion, his voice tense as the destructive cannons were brought to bear.

Sabtec checked the flood of data being projected down the head-up display array of his helmet with a glance.

'Twelve seconds,' he said.

The plasma cannons hummed, powering up, but didn't fire.

They are waiting for more support, Sabtec assessed. Good. They were not the only ones.

The seconds passed with painful slowness, then the battle-barge shuddered as more Dreadclaws struck home.

As before, a missile speared into the yawning aperture of the first Dreadclaw that penetrated, but this time there were no warrior-brothers stumbling from the flames to be cut down by bolter fire. No, this time there was a deep roar of outrage that reverberated deafeningly from the confines of the assault pod. As other Dreadclaws burrowed through the thick outer plating of the *Sword of Truth* to disgorge their lethal cargoes, Sabtec smiled in anticipation.

The deck shook as the immense armoured form of the Warmonger advanced out of the Dreadclaw, emerging unharmed through the inferno unleashed by the missile fired into the assault pod's interior, which had been modified to accommodate the hulking Dreadnought.

'For the Warmaster Horus!' blared the Warmonger, the booming, sepulchral sound projected from grilled vox-amplifiers to either side of the sarcophagus that forever held his shattered body. Bolts ricocheted off the Warmonger's armoured shell and the Dreadnought advanced through the weight of fire, seemingly oblivious.

With an ungodly wail, a plasma cannon fired. Sabtec's monochromatic auto-compensators reacted instantly to the painfully bright white/blue expulsion, dimming his vision momentarily so as not to blind him. The blast glanced off the Warmonger's armoured left shoulder, melting the outer casing of his thick plates but doing little substantial damage.

The blow rocked the Dreadnought back a step. With a bellow of fury, the Warmonger set its clawed feet wide and began firing. Heavy-calibre cannon slugs tore across the deck, shredding barricades and several White Consuls. The White Consuls' plasma cannon exploded with a sucking roar, spraying super-heated plasma as its core was breached.

With a bellow the Warmonger broke into a loping charge, smashing barricades aside. A missile glanced off its angled armour plates and veered up into the ceiling before exploding harmlessly. The heavy flamer slung beneath the Warmonger's crackling power talons roared, pouring burning promethium. Pristine white plate blackened and peeled beneath the inferno.

Sabtec rose from his cover and charged forward, his bolter bucking in his hands as he fired it from the hip. His 13th Coterie were with him, moving swiftly from cover to cover while laying down a blanket of suppressing fire, and other squads moved up in support.

Several Word Bearers were cut down by bolter fire. One warrior-brother screamed in anger when his left arm disappeared from the searing blast of a meltagun. Sabtec slid his serrated power sabre from its scabbard and thumbed its activation rune, firing his bolter one-handed. Hot energy vibrated up the length of the blade, and the champion of the 13th Coterie closed the distance with the nearest White Consuls swiftly.

The potent weapon had been gifted to him personally by Erebus after the 13th's heroics upon the stinking death-world of Jagata VII, when the Coterie had brought down the defences of a war shrine of the Adeptus Sororitas, ensuring a crushing victory against the hated sisters holed up there. Every last sister had been stripped of their armour and their flesh ritually debased before being staked out around the outskirts of the defiled shrine, their bloodied forms affixed to crosses hammered into the earth. There they were left to perish, vast swarms of blood-sucking insects rising from the surrounding death-marshes and descending upon them. Their screams had been sweet music to Sabtec that night.

The humming blade passed effortlessly through the power armour of a White Consuls warrior as Sabtec brought it slicing down into his neck. The sabre cut down through the gorget and deep into the tactical squad member's flesh. Arterial blood pumped from the wound, an injury that would have been fatal to any but a Space Marine. Sabtec planted a bolt in the White Consul's brainpan to finish the job, and turned smoothly to deflect a stabbing combat knife aimed at his sternum. With a deft twist of the wrist Sabtec disarmed his attacker before running him through, sliding the blade of his power sabre through the Space Marine's body all the way to the hilt.

Whipping the blade from the body of the White Consul, Sabtec turned and dropped to one knee. A pistol raised to blow his head apart fired over the top of his helmet harmlessly, and Sabtec swept his blade around in a low arc that sliced the legs of the warrior from under him.

The Warmonger was in the middle of the enemy now, and the mighty Dreadnought backhanded one Astartes warrior into a wall with a sweep of its crackling talons. The sheet plating of the wall buckled inwards and the White Consul was crushed to pulp, his armour wrenched out of shape by the force of the blow. Another warrior was snatched up in the Warmonger's grasp, lifted clear off his feet. His bolter barked as the warrior fired frantically, but it dropped from lifeless fingers a moment later as the Dreadnought clenched its bladed talons, the Space Marine falling to the deck in half a dozen separate pieces.

The Dreadnought fired into the other members of the tactical squad as they pulled back in the face of the rampaging behemoth, knocking several of them off their feet and bathing the others in flame.

More Coteries of Word Bearers emerged from Dreadclaws, heavy weapon toting Havoc squads bearing missile launchers and autocannons. Faced with the sudden reinforcements and seemingly unable to halt the enraged Warmonger, the White Consuls began to pull back, under the covering fire of Scout snipers located further back. It was no rout; the Consuls fell back in good order, moving from cover to cover and laying down fields of fire to allow their brethren to extricate themselves. Sabtec had to admire their coordination and discipline, even as he hated them with every fibre of his being.

A final Dreadclaw gnawed its way onto the deck before disgorging its sole occupant. Immense and shrouded in black robes, the corrupted Magos Darioq-Grendh'al stepped heavily aboard the White Consuls battle-barge, mechadendrites waving excitedly and four heavy servo-limbs curving around from his servo-harness as if ready to stab anything that came near him.

'Escort the magos to the central cogitation chamber, Sabtec,' said the Dark Apostle Marduk in his ear. 'Let no harm befall him.'

'Your will be done, Dark Apostle,' said Sabtec, motioning for a pair of Coteries to form an honour guard around the corrupted magos.

He needn't have bothered.

Darioq-Grendh'al strode straight towards the retreating enemy, eschewing any form of cover. Each step was heavy and mechanical, accompanied by the grind of motors and the whine of servo-bundles.

'My lord Sabtec?' questioned the champion of one of the Coteries he had designated to guard the magos.

'Leave him,' said Sabtec, shrugging.

A cough of a sniper rifle firing echoed through the deck, and a bubble of coruscating energy appeared around Darioq-Grendh'al, absorbing the force of the incoming shot and stopping it short of hitting home.

In response, the corrupted magos's four servo arms began to reform, the metal/flesh of his articulated limbs running like molten wax as they remoulded themselves. Oily, black blood dripped from the servo-arms as their skin split, but the magos seemed unaffected, continuing to stride with slow determination towards the enemy. The protective bubble of his refractor field flashed again as more fire was directed towards him.

Mechadendrites attached themselves to the gun-forms manifesting on the magos's four servo-arms, bulging and changing shape to become energy cables and power conduits. Gone were the grasping power clamps and las-cutters as four deadly weapons replaced them, their power drawn from the warp and the magos's own potent internal powerplant.

Darioq-Grendh'al began to fire, his servo-arms blasting in diagonal pairs, first one pair then the other. They fired blinding gouts of hellish energy drawn directly from the warp, and spitting red ichor dripped from the infernal barrels of his newly formed weapons, hissing and smoking as they struck the deck.

'Somehow I think it might be the magos that will be protecting us,' said Sabtec.

'Come, little brother,' growled the immense form of the Warmonger as he stalked by Sabtec, having slaughtered all the enemy within his grasp. 'We must gain the palace walls. The cursed betrayer of the Crusade, the self proclaimed Emperor of Mankind, will fall this day.'

Sabtec shook his head. With every passing century it seemed that the Warmonger's grip on reality slipped further. Often in the midst of battle the ancient warrior believed he was refighting the battle for the False Emperor's palace, ten thousand years ago. The Warmonger had been amongst those within the palace when the battle had commenced in earnest, the fools unaware that there was an enemy within.

Sometimes Sabtec wished that he too could lose himself in the dreams and delusion of battles long past. Perhaps in them the outcome would be different, and the False Emperor thrown down. It would be the Legions loyal to the Emperor that were hunted to the galaxy's fringes, and the Great Crusade would be re-launched, deviants and xenos exterminated in glorious warfare that would set the universe ablaze. All of humanity would be united behind the teachings of his master Lorgar, and a new era of unity and rapturous praise of the Gods of Chaos would emerge. All who spurned the teaching of the primarch of the XVII Legion would be sacrificed. There would be war, of course, but without war humanity would become weak.

Sabtec bitterly dispelled such thoughts, and ordered his Coteries on, plunging deeper into the belly of the *Sword of Truth*.

HATE-FUELLED BATTLE ERUPTED all across the *Sword of Truth*. Resistance was heavy, and equal numbers of XVII Legion warrior-brothers and White Consuls fell in the brutal, close-quarter fighting. Nowhere was the fighting more fierce than upon the corridors leading to the bridge. Here, the loyalist Astartes were dug in, determined to defend the bridge until the last. Through them marched Kol Badar's Anointed, carving a bloody path for their Dark Apostle.

Wrenching his unholy crozius arcanum from the shattered skull of a White Consuls Scout, Marduk urged his brethren on with roared quotations from the *Book of Lorgar*.

'We have reports that the *Corruptus Maligniatus* is advancing into close range,' said Kol Badar, speaking of the Dark Apostle Ankh-Heloth's personal warship. Marduk alone heard his voice across the closed channel.

The Dark Apostle activated his holy weapon, and the blood and brain matter that had gathered upon its spikes was burned off by the surge of power.

Was this how it was to end then? Had Ekodas chosen to dispose of him and his Host while they were aboard the enemy battle-barge, ensuring that the Nexus Arrangement remained unharmed, safely ensconced aboard the *Infidus Diabolus*?

'Does she target the *Sword of Truth*?' he said in reply, also using the closed channel.

'Negative,' reported Kol Badar. 'The *Corruptus Maligniatus* is opening her Dreadclaw tubes. Assault pods are being launched.'

'Where?' snarled Marduk.

'They are targeting the corridors higher up the command spire,' said Kol Badar.

'The bastard is seeking to take the bridge from under our nose,' said Marduk. 'We draw the ship's defenders, and he takes the glory of claiming the ship.'

'Your orders?' asked Kol Badar.

'We advance on the bridge, double speed.'

You will not steal my glory, Ankh-Heloth, he thought.

'It shall be so,' intoned the Coryphaus.

'Come, sorcerer,' said Marduk.

The Black Legion sorcerer, Inshabael Kharesh, looked up from where he was kneeling over a fallen enemy. He had his hands clasped around the Space Marine's head. The sorcerer released the warrior, his hands still smoking with infernal power, and the Space Marine fell face first to the floor, dead, his liquefied brain oozing from his nose and ears.

Marduk had wanted the sorcerer to stay aboard the *Infidus Diabolus*, yet he had little real power over him, and when he had expressed his desire to accompany the strike force he had agreed, albeit somewhat reluctantly.

The sorcerer rose with a cynical smile on his lips.

'Your wish, Dark Apostle,' said the Black Legion sorcerer, his tone mocking.

Remembering Erebus's words to ensure no harm befell the sorcerer, Marduk swung away, his First Acolyte at his side.

He would take his anger out on the Space Marine captain.

CHAPTER SEVEN

KOL BADAR SNARLED as the blast of a combat shotgun fired at close range struck him, peppering his armour. The powerful kick of the weapon was unable to knock him back even a step, and he continued on through the hail of fire, combi-bolter roaring.

Another White Consuls Scout moved up from behind the barricade, combat shotgun booming. They were lightly armoured, their bodies not yet fully ready to bond completely with power armour. Doubtless most had only begun their indoctrination a decade or so past. To Kol Badar they were children, inexperienced and worthy only of contempt. His combi-bolter barked, taking the Scout's head off.

From further up the heavily defended corridor – one of three that the Word Bearers were advancing up towards the bridge – a blinding lascannon beam struck, punching a cauterised hole straight through one of his Anointed brethren. Even mighty Terminator armour afforded little protection against such a weapon.

Waves of bolter fire struck the advancing Terminators, and though few of his warriors fell to the unrelenting swathe of fire, it was slowing their progress. The enemy fell back before them, taking cover behind barricades that rose from the corridor floor. As the Word Bearers advanced, the barriers retracted, denying the XVII Legion their cover. Kol Badar cared not. The thick ceramite and adamantium plating of the Anointed's Terminator armour could withstand easily as much incoming fire as the barricades themselves.

Behind the enemy squads up ahead, towards the four-way junction

578

roughly forty metres in front of the advancing Terminators, Kol Badar could see a White Consuls Techmarine at work, setting up a series of Tarantula sentry guns.

A stabbing lascannon beam struck down one of his warriors, and another lost an arm to a plasma gun. Kol Badar snarled in frustration. A dozen target markers were blinking red before his eyes as the head-up targeting display of his quad-tusked helmet identified threats, and he selected the lascannon-wielding enemy Space Marine with a blink.

'Suppressing fire,' ordered the Coryphaus, allocating the target to one of his Anointed squads.

'Target confirmed,' came the growled reply from the squad's champion.

A second later a Reaper autocannon began to scream, the heavy underslung cannon swinging towards the allocated target. The twin barrels of the devastating weapon spat a torrent of high-calibre fire towards the enemy squad, and the deck floor around the Terminator was showered with countless hundreds of spent shell casings in seconds.

A grenade rolled to Kol Badar's feet but he ignored it and continued his advance. It detonated in a blinding fireball, spraying the area with super-heated shrapnel. He marched on through the fiery conflagration without concern, ignoring the fact that his armour was now alight and riddled with debris. He didn't even feel the heat of the blaze through the thick insulated layers of his exo-armour.

Emerging from the flames, he gunned down two Scouts as they ducked back to the next barricade before switching his attention as his auto-senses flashed him a warning. He turned to see a combat squad of power-armoured Astartes advancing up to flank him, using a dimly-lit side-passage filled with cables and pipes. The two enemies in the lead both carried meltaguns, potent weapons easily capable of liquefying even Terminator armour. Kol Badar activated the flame unit of his combi-bolter, sending burning promethium down the corridor to meet them. The rolling fire filled the narrow service tunnel, engulfing the enemy Space Marines. The Coryphaus pumped bolts through the inferno. His targeting array revealed that the flamer had only incapacitated two of his enemies.

With a clipped order to his Anointed to advance, Kol Badar stomped into the service tunnel and unleashed another burst from his flamer. He came upon the first White Consul within the blaze. The Space Marine's armour was blackened and smoking. Kol Badar's crackling power talons clenched into a fist and he smashed the warrior backwards, crumpling his thick power-armoured chestplate like foil.

A meltagun seared a glancing blow across his shoulder, making Kol Badar hiss in sudden pain, and he launched himself forward as the enemy squad frantically back-pedalled. His combi-bolter created gaping craters in the armour of two of the White Consuls, not penetrating but knocking them off-balance, and he grabbed the arm of one of them as the meltagun was turned again in his direction.

With a sharp twist, Kol Badar ripped the White Consul's arm off at the shoulder. He kicked the warrior square in the face, shattering the front of his helmet before planting a fatal bolt through the ruptured rebreather grille.

A chainsword hit him on the arm, its teeth screaming as they sought to shear through his thick armour amid a spray of ceramite chips. Kol Badar backhanded the warrior into the wall and gunned down the last White Consul in the corridor.

Angry at having been slowed, Kol Badar turned around awkwardly, snarling in frustration as his massive shoulder plates ground against the service tunnel walls. He stormed back out into the main thoroughfare, crushing the corpses of his bested enemies beneath his tread.

The Tarantula sentry guns had been deployed and were now online, and the White Consuls were falling back towards the bridge under the cover of the automated turrets. They fired at an incredible rate before falling silent momentarily, turning with mechanised precision to pick a new target as one fell and they unleashed their fury once more. Huge drums of ammunition spooled, and smoke rose from the spinning barrels of the guns as they raked the Terminators of the Anointed with heavy weapon fire.

One of the turrets was destroyed as Reaper autocannon fire shredded its armour and ignited its ammunition store, sending it catapulting backwards as it exploded. The Anointed's advance ground to a halt as the White Consuls, having taken up new positions further up the corridor, just outside the armoured entrance to the bridge, began to add their weight of fire to those of the remaining sentry guns. The corridor was filled with tracer fire, gouts of plasma and the contrails of missiles that screamed down its length to explode amongst the warrior-brothers of the XVII Legion, and Kol Badar ground his teeth in frustration.

'We are too slow,' came Marduk's unnecessary assessment from further back, conveyed in Kol Badar's earpiece via vox-link. His talons clenched in anger at the implicit rebuke in the Dark Apostle's voice. 'I will not let Ankh-Heloth take the bridge before us.'

'I am well aware of the situation,' snarled Kol Badar as a line of assault cannon fire stitched across his breastplate.

A wealth of information bombarded the Coryphaus, scrolling down his irises as reports from elsewhere within the *Sword of Truth* flooded in. He expertly sent his orders through to all the champions serving under him, coordinating their efforts to achieve the swift control of the enemy vessel, while still advancing and engaging the enemy. His ability to maintain a strategic overview and continue directing the elements of the Host even when engaged in the fiercest conflict was part of what made him such an effective Coryphaus. From the data updates and visual feeds he was receiving from the other members of the Anointed, he could see that the advance up the other corridors too had stalled.

Another Tarantula sentry gun was silenced, and Kol Badar once again began to stride forward, ordering his Anointed on. A missile spiralled past his shoulder, exploding just metres behind him but he ignored it, pumping bolt shells towards the dug-in White Consuls up ahead. The twin-linked assault cannons of a spider-legged turret ripped across the Anointed, felling one of them and forcing another to his knees, but the remainder came on, combi-bolters bucking in their hands.

The turret began to walk backwards, its movements stilted and jerky, and Kol Badar knew that it was being remotely operated by the White Consuls Techmarine, who was undoubtedly back with his brethren at the bridge doors. The Tarantula turned and unleashed its cannons into one Anointed brethren who was within metres of it now, the powerful weapon tearing his armour apart at such close range.

Still, the Terminator-armoured cult-warrior had not died purposelessly, and Kol Badar broke into a heavy run as the turret spun towards another warrior of the Anointed bearing down on it, power axe crackling with energy.

Kol Badar reached the turret as its smoking assault cannons began firing once again, and he smashed it backwards with a sweep of his talons, knocking the field cannon off its mechanised feet. The turret weighed well over a tonne, yet Kol Badar tossed it aside as if it were nothing, his prodigious strength augmented by the thick servo-bundles and hydraulic amplifiers of his Terminator suit.

Thirty metres ahead he saw the heavy blast-doors leading to the bridge, and bellowed his orders as he began striding through the enemy fire towards them. Missiles belched from behind barricades, and the intensity of the incoming bolter fire was considerable, even to his heavily armoured brethren. Taking the bridge was going to be costly.

In addition to the enemy foot troops, there was a pair of vehicles parked in front of the thick blast-doors. He knew that service elevators ran from this wide corridor down through the ship. Clearly, these vehicles had been raised from the ship's armoury depot in the lower decks to guard the wide corridor's approach.

Kol Badar recognised them as Razorbacks, Rhino APC variants that had come into production in the millennia since the end of the Great War. Atop the boxy white Rhino chassis, replete with blue eagle-head Chapter designs and campaign markers, were twin-linked heavy bolter turrets. They began to roar, adding to the heavy weight of fire directed towards the Anointed.

'Burias,' Kol Badar growled into his vox-comm. 'I am target-marking a location. I want you there now.'

No reply was forthcoming, but that did not concern the Coryphaus. He could see from his trackers that Burias and his possessed kindred were responding to his order, and the Icon Bearer clearly did not wish to risk giving away his position by sending a vox response.

Kol Badar fired towards one of the enemy squads, his shots blowing chunks out of the barricades, forcing them to duck. A red target-laser appeared on his chest plate and he saw the White Consuls Techmarine with his ornate bolter a fraction of a second before he fired. Kol Badar snarled as he was knocked back a step, warning signals announcing a breach in his exo-skeleton's integrity. The Techmarine was using non-standard anti-armour shells, their explosive tips replaced with melta-charges.

He fired in return, grimacing in pain, but his shots went wide, missing their target.

'Anytime, Burias…'

IN THE WAKE of the Anointed vanguard, Marduk moved up more cautiously. Ducking behind cover, he slammed a fresh sickle clip into his Mars-pattern bolt pistol. The White Consuls had wrapped around behind the advancing strike force, threatening them from the rear as they plunged deeper into the battle-barge. A sniper round impacted with the wall scant centimetres from his head, gouging a heart-sized crater out of the smooth plascrete surface.

'Get down, you fool,' he snapped at the Black Legion sorcerer accompanying him.

Inshabael Kharesh strolled calmly through the mayhem. Trailing white smoke, a missile screamed towards the sorcerer but he merely flicked a hand dismissively as it neared him and it was deflected into the ceiling.

Marduk scowled and broke cover, snapping off a shot and taking down a White Consul who was dashing towards a better firing position.

The Coteries accompanying Marduk fell in around him, bolters roaring as they kept the White Consuls dogging their progress at bay.

Behind them a combat squad with a pair of heavy bolters hustled into position under the covering fire of their brethren, falling in behind a barricade to bring the heavy weapons to bear up the corridor.

Inshabael Kharesh turned towards them, mouthing his infernal magicks, and Marduk saw his eyes flickering with violet electricity. The Dark Apostle could feel the power growing within the sorcerer, the sensation tingling at the base of his neck. The sorcerer continued mouthing his incantation, flexing the fingers of his hands. Marduk shook his head, but then Kharesh took a step forwards, bracing his legs as the power surging within him was unleashed.

It leapt from his fingertips in a crackling violet arc that struck one of the distant heavy bolter-armed Space Marines as he readied his weapon, cooking his flesh within his power armour. More arcs leapt from the White Consul's convulsing form to strike his companions, and Kharesh sent a further purple lightning bolt slamming into them as he thrust his other hand towards them, lifting one of them off his feet and slamming him back against the wall behind. The sorcerer hurled three more bolts into the enemy, relishing their pain as they collapsed to the ground, twitching and jerking as the last vestiges of warp energy sparked across their bodies. The sorcerer then turned away, flashing Marduk an arrogant glance.

'Cheap tricks,' muttered First Acolyte Ashkanez.

Marduk grunted.

Turning, he saw the Anointed's advance slowed by the weight of fire they were drawing, and he snarled in impatience.

'Kol Badar,' he growled, opening a vox-link to his Coryphaus.

'I know,' came the snarled reply before he could say any more.

BURIAS SLITHERED ALONG the vent, worming his way forward. His arms were by his sides and he squirmed through the tight confines by relaxing and flexing his genetically enhanced muscles. He came to a junction and turned to the right, continuing another hundred metres through the lightless pipe before coming to a halt. He could hear his kindred coming up behind him. The sound seemed deafeningly loud to his ears. Still, the enemy was unlikely to hear a thing over the gunfire.

Burias exhaled a long breath as he released the shackles that bound the ravaging daemon Drak'shal, and the change came over him. His modified power armour expanded as his musculature bulged and swelled, his arms thickening and his fingers fusing into broad talons. The air recycling pipe groaned in protest as his body expanded, the metal wrenching out of shape. Curving horns extended up from his now bestial face, and drool ran from lips that were pulled back to expose a maw heavy with fangs and tusks.

He sniffed, hatred growing, as he tasted the unmistakeable scent of loyalist Astartes on the air. His talons extended and he punched them through the constricting embrace of the pipe. With a wrench, he tore the pipe apart and launched himself down onto the grilled sheeting below. He crashed down through the metal roofing as his brethren emerged behind him, dropping down into the midst of the enemy position.

Burias-Drak'shal landed on all fours atop the armoured hull of a Razorback, and he let out a blood-curdling roar, throwing his head back like an unfettered beast howling at the moon.

The White Consuls spun, turning their bolters towards this new threat without panic or fear, and bolts sliced through the air around Burias-Drak'shal. One took him in the side, gouging a deep wound in his daemonic flesh, but he ignored the injury. Bounding across the top of the armoured vehicle, talons ripping into its hull plating, he tore the twin-linked heavy bolter turret from its housing with a surge of warp-fuelled strength. He hurled the sparking turret aside and leapt from the tank.

He landed amongst the White Consuls, roaring his hatred, and bore one of them to the ground beneath his talons. His jaw distending unnaturally, Burias-Drak'shal clamped his teeth around the warrior's helmet. With a wrench, he tore helmet and head from the warrior's shoulders. Blood spurted like a fountain.

His possessed kindred dropped down among the enemy, their forms altering as they allowed the daemons lurking within them to surge to the fore, inviting them to sate their hatred upon the foe. Astartes were ripped apart, torn limb from limb by the brute force exhibited by these monsters.

One of the possessed was lifted into the air by the clamping jaws of the White Consuls Techmarine's servo-arm, kicking and screaming in rabid fury, before the Techmarine tore it in two with a burst of fire from his master-crafted bolter. Its lower body continued to kick as it dropped to the deck in a shower of blood, while its upper half was hurled away.

Marduk broke into a run as the weight of fire dropped. First Acolyte Ashkanez ran at his side, immense power maul clasped in both hands. The rest of the Coterie members accompanying the Dark Apostle were only a step behind, quickly overtaking the slower Anointed brethren. While Terminator armour turned an Astartes into a living tank, able to shrug off incoming fire and march staunchly on enemy positions, it slowed a warrior down considerably – an acceptable compromise in situations such as boarding actions and close-quarter firefights.

The possessed carved a bloody swathe through the White Consuls, and their roars and bellows echoed sharply up the corridor. Still, there were only a handful of the daemonically infused warriors, and the Consuls were reacting quickly to their presence, squads falling back into disciplined fire channels that hammered them with bolter fire. Another two possessed were torn to shreds by the concentrated weight of fire. Their forms mutated wildly as they perished, the daemons within seeking desperately to maintain control over their dying host-bodies.

Nevertheless, the possessed had done their job and cracked the enemy formation, allowing the Word Bearers to close the distance.

Marduk holstered his pistol and drew his chainsword. Barbed thorns set into the daemon weapon's hilt pushed through the perforations drilled into the palm of his gauntlets, and a tingle ran though him as they pierced his flesh. His blood mingled with the daemon-blade, and he felt a surge of fury and power as he and the daemon Borhg'ash bound within the roaring blade became one. Borhg'ash's anger and desire to feed flooded through him, and he revelled in the sensation, more powerful than any hyper-stimm or combat drug.

'Death to the False Emperor!' Marduk roared, and wielding the daemon weapon in one hand and his humming crozius in the other, he leapt a barricade, hurling himself amongst the White Consuls. His chainsword roared, carving power armour and flesh, and his blessed crozius was wreathed in dark energy as he laid about him with it.

Ashkanez was only a step behind, and a powerful blow of his power maul took a White Consul under the chin, lifting the Space Marine off his feet and sending him flying backwards. The weapon's power source surged on impact with a sharp crack of discharging energy, splitting the warrior's power armour and shattering his jaw.

A White Consul deflected Marduk's next strike with his bolter, the teeth of his daemon-blade ripping chunks out of the gun's casing. The Dark Apostle slammed his crozius into the warrior's side, puncturing power armour and lungs with its spikes and hurling the Consul into the wall. Before he could finish the warrior, a bolt pistol wielded by another Consul boomed, the shot taking Marduk in his shoulder, spinning him half around. His own blood sprayed out around him for a moment before the potent hyper-coagulants in his bloodstream sealed the wound, and he growled in pain and outrage.

The bolt pistol was raised for another shot, but the White Consul's arm was shattered by a heavy double-handed blow of Ashkanez's power maul, splinters of broken bone gleaming brightly within the messy wreckage of power armour and flesh. The First Acolyte's return blow crunched down upon the Consul's white helmet, killing him in a splatter of gore.

'Apostle!' growled Ashkanez in warning, and Marduk turned, hissing at the pain in his shoulder, but managed to lift his crozius up to deflect a buzzing chainsword that was aimed towards his neck. He smashed his own chainblade up into his attacker's groin, and blood sprayed as the hungry teeth of his daemon weapon ripped through power armour.

The White Consul fell to the deck, his plate armour covered in blood, and Marduk spun away from him, deflecting the thrust of a combat knife before stepping in close and ramming his elbow into the Consul's face.

'Guilliman's weakness resides within you, *brother*,' sneered Marduk. Still, the warrior was Astartes, even if he was descended from the False Emperor's bastard lapdog primarch, and he recovered quickly, spitting teeth and blood from his mouth. With a roar he hurled himself at Marduk, lunging for the Dark Apostle's neck with his combat knife.

Marduk battered him aside with his crozius and struck out with his chainblade in a blow intended to rip his enemy's neck apart. The Astartes warrior felt Marduk's intent a fraction of a second before the attack was launched, and lifted an arm into the path of the daemon weapon. The weapon screamed as it tore through ceramite and flesh, biting deep into bone. The White Consul grimaced in pain, but dragged the chainsword away from his neck and lashed out with his knife. Marduk threw his head back, avoiding the worst of the blow, though a deep slash was carved across his face just under his left eye.

'Heathen filth,' snarled Marduk as hot blood ran from the wound, and he brought his crozius crashing down upon the White Consul's shoulder, pummelling him to the ground. Before the warrior could rise, he stepped forwards and brought his weapons together, catching the warrior's head between them.

Behind him, Burias-Drak'shal grabbed hold of the Techmarine's servo-arm and lifted the Space Marine off the ground, smashing him into a wall. The red-armoured adept lost his grip on his weapon and fell to the floor, the sheet plating of the wall behind him a crumpled ruin. He reached for his gun, but before he could lift it Burias-Drak'shal was on him, snarling and spitting. He grabbed the Techmarine's head in one hand and rammed the talons of his other into his face, transfixing him to the wall for a moment before the possessed warrior ripped his talons free with a tortured wrench of metal.

One of the Razorbacks was thrown into reverse, its engines roaring, but Kol Badar held it in place, his power talons digging deeply into its fore armour. Tracks squealed as they spun, and smoke rose from the vehicle's engines, but Kol Badar held it firmly in place, allowing his chainfist-wielding Anointed brethren to close in, carving a gaping hole in its side. Heavy flamers roared, filling the interior and cooking the driver and gunner inside.

Smoke was pouring from the other tank, from grenades that had been hurled into wrenched open hatches.

Anointed brethren with roaring chainfists had moved on to the blast-doors and begun to carve through its thick layers, but their progress was slow, and Marduk snarled in frustration. In the time it would take to breach the doors their position might have been overrun or, perhaps worse, the bridge might have fallen to Ankh-Heloth's boarding party, coming at it from a different angle.

'Quickly now!' snarled Marduk.

He cast another glance down the corridor, seeing the White Consuls inching their way forwards there. The enemy were gathering for a counter-attack from the rear, but they were holding back as they waited for more reinforcements.

'What are you waiting for, you whoresons?' he roared. 'Come to us and die!'

He was answered almost immediately. Red light began to strobe from a pair of warning beacons mounted in sconces thirty metres back down the corridor. Grinding gears announced the arrival of two service elevators, and steam and smoke belched from within them as their doors clattered open. The deck shook beneath heavy, reverberant footsteps, and Marduk swore under his breath.

From out of the steam and smoke, a pair of immense shapes emerged.

'I think they may have heard you,' said the Black Legion sorcerer dryly, and Marduk cast him a dark look.

'Dreadnoughts,' snarled Kol Badar.

These were clearly the reinforcements that the White Consuls had been waiting for, and the battle-brothers of the hated Chapter began to advance behind the two behemoths, bolters roaring.

One of the Dreadnoughts was armed with an assault cannon that whined as it began to spin, muzzle-flare spitting from its barrels. Its exhaust stacks belched fumes as it heaved itself forward with titanic steps, its massive power claw clacking open and shut in eagerness. Its sepulchre was carved in the likeness of a stylised winged Astartes warrior, bolter clasped in its hands.

The other Dreadnought was draped in regal blue banners depicting scenes of victory. It planted its heavy feet and stabilising maglocks slammed down, rooting it in place. A second later it began to lay down a withering barrage, missiles streaming from launchers and superheated blasts screaming from the scorched double barrels of its multi-melta.

Marduk threw himself into a roll as the newcomers' fire tore across the breadth of the corridor.

Bolters roared in response, spraying the enemy Dreadnoughts, and Reaper autocannons tore chunks out of their hull plating, yet they were barely scratched. The floor shook as the advancing Dreadnought's momentum increased, while the screaming of its assault cannon reached a deafening pitch.

Meltaguns integrated into combi-bolters fired, blurring the air with waves of heat, causing blistered welts to appear upon the Dreadnought's ceramite plates. Cables and servos melted, dripping steaming gulps of liquefied metal onto the deck floor, but the Dreadnought did not slow.

Still firing its assault cannon, it grabbed the first Anointed brother it reached, its massive paw closing around his Terminator-armoured body and lifting him into the air. The warrior slammed his power axe into the mechanical beast's armoured forearm, embedding it deep, before he was hurled away.

The Dreadnought smashed another cult warrior aside with a sweep of its massive arm, knocking the Terminator into a pillar. Even such a blow was not enough to finish the heavily armoured Chaos Space Marine, and he rose to one knee and blasted white-hot plasma from his combi-bolter into the Dreadnought's sarcophagus. It was merely a last-ditch act of defiance and the damage it caused was negligible. The Dreadnought's assault cannon roared and the warrior was torn apart. The mechanised behemoth's armoured bulk rotated towards Marduk, and it began to advance upon him, stitching the corridor with lines of fire.

Krak missiles streamed up the corridor, obliterating all they touched in devastating explosions. Ignoring the danger, XVII Legion warriors moved to interpose themselves between the advancing Dreadnought and their hallowed Dark Apostle, but they were swatted aside like children and cut down by the torrent of fire spitting from the whirling barrels of its assault cannon. The torso of one warrior, a battle-scared veteran who had fought as part of the Host since its inception, simply disappeared in a cloud of bloody vapour as a multi-melta blast struck him square on. The super-heated mist of blood splattered across Marduk, who stood snarling up at the Dreadnought as it bore down upon him.

Ashkanez leapt past him with a defiant roar, smashing at the Dreadnought with his power maul. He scarcely dented its armoured plates, and the Dreadnought swept him aside with a heavy blow. He crashed into an exposed girder, which buckled beneath his weight, and fell heavily to the deck floor.

Servos and pneumatics wheezing, the White Consuls Dreadnought drew back its massive power fist. If it struck, it would crush Marduk utterly. The Dreadnought struck with a speed that belied its bulk, and Marduk only barely avoiding the blow, throwing himself into a roll that took him beneath the strike. There was a mighty crash and the sound of wrenching metal, and as Marduk came to his feet, he saw the Dreadnought's fist embedded deep in the buckled metal of the blast-doors.

It struggled to pull itself free, and with one arm still embedded in the metal door, it dragged its assault cannon around, tearing up everything in its path as it sought to bring the heavy weapon to bear on Marduk.

With a curse, Marduk threw himself flat as thousands of rounds ripped across the corridor, leaving a smoking line of impacts where they struck.

Another warrior was melted beneath the intense heat of the other Dreadnought's multi-melta, fusing him to the thick armoured blast-doors. Missiles roared from the launch tubes, engulfing a Coterie in a series of explosions that tore them to pieces.

Marduk heard Kol Badar's coldly detached and calm orders to the Host, the Coryphaus confident of victory even when faced with such odds. He was directing the other assault parties, advising them and passing on fresh orders as enemy dispositions came to light.

Burias-Drak'shal and his possessed kindred were leaping towards the advancing White Consuls, tongues lolling from distended jaws and claws gouging deep furrows in the deck in their eagerness to close with them. Bolters tore great chunks out of their armour and flesh, and more than one was cut in half by concentrated fire, but only killing shots dropped them. They shrugged off lesser injuries and tore into the hated descendants of Guilliman.

The Icon Bearer himself closed the distance with the enemy Dreadnought with bounding leaps. The hulking construct fired a trio of krak missiles at Burias-Drak'shal. With unholy speed, Burias ducked beneath the first two missiles, and swung his horned head to the side to avoid the last, which missed him by less than half a hand's breadth.

Maglocked stabilisers unhooked themselves from the deck and the Dreadnought began to back up, attempting to put more space between it and the possessed warrior bounding towards it. Its multi-melta screamed, but Burias-Drak'shal swayed to the side to avoid the blast and launched himself into the air.

He landed on the Dreadnought's chassis, claws digging in deep. With a bestial roar, he drew back one fist and smashed it into the armoured sarcophagus. The blow did not breach the thick armour, but he clung on as the Dreadnought swung from side to side, trying to shake him loose. Nor did his second or third blow penetrate the Dreadnought's armour, but his fourth produced a crack.

More possessed warriors, their hulking bodies rippling with mutation, closed in around the Dreadnought. Like a rabid pack, they snarled and roared as they leapt upon its massive form, tearing armour plates loose, ripping at cables and wiring.

Marduk grinned as his chainsword carved through the midsection of a charging White Consul, relishing the rich taste of Astartes blood as it sprayed onto his lips. Blood was eagerly sucked up into the innards of his daemon blade, the beast within gorging on this feast and roaring its pleasure in the revving motor of the chainsword. He could feel the daemon pulling at his hand, urging him to kill again.

Burias-Drak'shal punched a talon into the widening crack of the Dreadnought's sarcophagus, still clutching on to the front of the immense war machine like a horrid gargoyle. He hooked the claws of both hands into the crack and heaved at it, his entire body straining. Muscles mutated and swelled to twice their size as Burias-Drak'shal sought to rip open the sarcophagus.

More White Consuls were moving up steadily now, and a flamer was brought to bear on the Icon Bearer, liquid promethium spraying across the front of the Dreadnought. Even as his armour and flesh caught fire, Burias Drak'shal continued straining, using all his warp-enhanced strength to tear the Dreadnought's armoured shell apart.

With a series of violent yanks, the possessed warrior tore off a cracked section of the sarcophagus, sending it clattering to the deck floor. With a roar of victory, he reached inside, grabbing the shattered form of the White Consul within and kicked off backwards, tearing the pitiful semi-living corpse from its protective housing.

He landed five metres away, patches of his skin still on fire, and looked down at the thing clutched in his talons. It was pathetic to think that once it had been an Astartes warrior.

It had no arms or legs, and its head was that of a cadaver, flopping limply over its wasted, skeletal chest. Its troglodytic skin was pulled taut across its bones, pallid and lifeless. Its eyes were sutured closed, though Burias-Drak'shal could see them moving spasmodically behind the eyelids, like a man trapped in a nightmare. A wealth of cables and wires protruded from its body, emerging from plugs inserted along its spinal column and seemingly at random all over its torso and head. Torn from the life-support and internal controls of the Dreadnought, they leaked stinking milky paste and oily fluid.

Burias-Drak'shal snarled in disgust as the thing twitched in his hands.

With a powerful wrench he corkscrewed its head from its shoulders and tossed it aside.

The Dreadnought was lifeless now, as if waiting for the shattered master that made it whole to return. Marduk saw Burias-Drak'shal grin in feral satisfaction.

A bolt took Burias-Drak'shal in the thigh half a second later, and he snarled in anger and pain as he dropped to one knee.

Marduk gunned down a White Consul and ducked back behind a pillar as carefully laid down bolter fire pushed him and the Coterie members around him back.

They were taking heavy casualties now. From the reports flooding in from the other areas of the ship it was the same story: Word Bearers and White Consuls selling their lives dearly, with an XVII Legion warrior falling for each loyalist scum that was killed.

The assault cannon-armed Dreadnought was still struggling to free its fist, allowing a Coterie to approach its exposed rear. Arming melta bombs one-handed, they closed in and affixed the potent grenades to the Dreadnought as it strained to turn to face them, almost tearing its arm off at the shoulder.

Finally it freed itself with a sickening sound of protesting metal, and staggered around, assault cannon screaming as it raked its attackers with fire. Then the melta bombs detonated. The Dreadnought stood for a moment, half its engine and drive mechanics melting down its legs onto the floor, before it tipped forwards and collapsed, belching black smoke.

The deck shuddered as the monster fell, and as if this were a signal, the locking mechanisms of the immense blast-doors were suddenly released, maglocks grinding. Interlocking serrated teeth unclamped, and like the jaws of a yawning beast the doors parted, retracting into the floor and ceiling to reveal the bridge of the *Sword of Truth*.

There in the doorway stood the figure of a White Consul. A tall white crest rose above his gold-edged helmet. His pristine white armour was heavily artificed, and a rich blue cloak with gold thread was thrown back over his shoulders. Gleaming claws slid from the sheaths of his power gauntlets, energy dancing along the elongated, gently curved blades. Behind this defiant warrior stood a semi-circle of veterans, their helmets regal blue and their spotless white armour swathed in blue tabards. One held aloft their company standard, and all were bedecked with purity seals and military decorations.

Marduk licked his lips in relish.

'For Guilliman!' the captain of the White Consuls bellowed, a cry echoed by his bodyguard before he broke into a charge, leading his warriors into the ranks of the Word Bearers. The other Consuls pressed in behind them shouting war cries of their own.

The warrior-brothers of the 34th Host welcomed this test. It had been too long since they had met foes their equal. The prospect of killing the enemy Chapter's captain was intoxicating. With verses of hatred upon their lips, the brethren of the XVII Legion surged forwards to meet their foe head on.

Ashkanez smashed one of the charging veterans from his feet with his double-handed power maul, and Marduk brought his crozius crashing down on a White Consul's arm with a sickening crunch. The warrior's arm flopped uselessly, blood leaking from his ruptured power armour, and Marduk ripped his chainsword across the warrior's throat as he staggered. The eager revving of the chainsword rose to a fever-pitched squeal as adamantium teeth shore first through armour and flesh, then vertebrae.

Marduk was battered sideways as a charging veteran slammed a crackling storm shield into him. Recovering quickly, Marduk parried the warrior's follow-up thrust, batting a power blade away with his crozius, and he swayed aside to avoid a hissing burst from the bulbous barrel of a plasma pistol.

A Word Bearer nearby spat a curse as he was impaled upon a humming falchion blade, and another died as the back of his head exploded, a bolt fired at close range detonating inside his helmet.

Another warrior-brother staggered back, clutching at the thick ropes of innards spilling from his abdomen. The captain of the White Consuls came after him, energy dancing across the tips of his lightning claws. Cradling his intestines in one arm, the Word Bearer lifted his bolter towards the captain. With a blinding slash, the arm was severed, falling to the ground, and in a heartbeat the warrior-brother was dead. The captain's fist smashed up under the Word Bearer's chin in a brutal uppercut; the blades of his lightning claws penetrated his brain and speared out through the top of his helmet.

Marduk blocked another stabbing blow and launched a lightning riposte, which his enemy took on his crackling storm shield. The percussive shock of the impact jolted Marduk's arm, numbing it to his shoulder. At his side, First Acolyte Ashkanez flattened a veteran with a heavy overhead blow of his flanged power maul and turned on Marduk's opponent. A two-handed blow clubbed the storm shield-wielding Consul to his knees, and Marduk dispatched him with a heavy blow to the side of his head that splintered his helm.

The captain of the White Consuls took down two more Word Bearers. The first fell heavily, half his head sliced away. The second died as the Space Marine captain's lightning claws sank deep into his chest. The Word Bearer was lifted off his feet and hurled contemptuously away. Marduk snarled in rage and moved towards the enemy captain.

Kol Badar was bleeding from several wounds, but continued to fight with a cold-burning fury, destroying every White Consul that came within his reach. A humming power sword slashed towards him, but he caught the blade in his talons, halting it mid-strike. With a wrench he ripped the blade from his opponent's hand, and as the White Consul staggered back, raising his pistol, hurled the power sword after him. It spun once, end over end, before embedding deep in the warrior's chest, sinking to the hilt. Bringing his combi-bolter up, Kol Badar finished off the White Consul with a concentrated burst of fire.

Marduk could not close with the enemy captain, whose bodyguard were holding tight rank around him. The Dark Apostle gave vent to his frustration, his fury giving him strength. Swinging up his crozius, he knocked aside a bolter aimed at his head and brought his chainsword around in a bloody arc that struck his enemy in the shoulder. The daemon entity residing within the blade was raging, adamantine teeth whirring madly as they sought to tear through the warrior's power armour.

The White Consuls captain killed another Word Bearer, tearing him to shreds with his slashing claws before kicking him away to find another victim.

'The enemy press in behind us,' said Ashkanez, as bolter fire peppered off one of his shoulder plates. 'We are caught between them. Our position is untenable.'

'Where are our damned reinforcements, Kol Badar?' replied Marduk through gritted teeth, glancing behind him. His First Acolyte was correct – the enemy were moving up solidly, pressuring their position, and it would not be long before they were overrun. 'Shouldn't they be here by now?'

'They are delayed,' replied Kol Badar. 'They have encountered higher enemy concentrations than expected.'

'A flaw in your plan? I'm shocked.'

'They will be here.'

'Not fast enough,' said Marduk, battering a sword aside with his crozius.

The Black Legion sorcerer released the helm of a White Consul, his hands glowing with warp energy. Coiling blue-grey smoke whispered from the Space Marine's ruptured lenses as he fell to the ground, a lifeless, burnt-out husk. The stink of burning flesh rose from the corpse, mingling with the electric tang of Kharesh's warp sorcery.

'If I may?' the sorcerer ventured.

Marduk flicked a glance towards the sorcerer. It was impossible to gauge his facial expression, hidden as it was behind his sickeningly ornate battle-helm, but he was sure it would be mocking.

'I may be able to slow them,' the sorcerer said.

'Do what you will,' said Marduk, his attention diverted as he was forced to sway to the side to avoid a falchion blow.

He heard the sorcerer begin to incant, speaking in the infernal tongue of daemons. It felt as though skeletal fingers were clawing at the back of Marduk's mind, but the sensation was not unpleasant. He struck a heavy overhand blow towards his foe, who blocked the strike with a standard overhead parry, as he knew he would. He slammed a kick into the warrior's chest, knocking him back into one of his comrades, unbalancing them both. Kol Badar, talons balled into a fist, punched the head off the shoulders of one, and the other was downed by a sweep of Ashkanez's power maul. Marduk finished him off, planting a kick into the side of the fallen warrior's head. The sound of his neck cracking was audible even over the battle's din.

Marduk felt the hairs across his flesh stand rigidly to attention as the Black Legion sorcerer completed his spell, and he glanced back to see what the invocation heralded. A rippling wall of black mist was stretching out to block the corridor behind them. It moved like a living entity, tendrils reaching out like wriggling worms to bridge the expanse. Forms could be vaguely discerned amongst the smoke, swirling within it in a seething mass. Marduk saw sinuous bodies writhing around each other before disappearing once more, fanged mouths opening and closing and eyes glinting like stars within the thickening darkness.

He could still see the enemy advancing beyond the veil of warp-spawned mist, but no gunfire seemed able to penetrate it. A feral grin cracked Marduk's face as he realised that the sorcerer had brought forth a minor warp rift into existence, a link to the holy æther itself. Bolts and plasma fire disappeared in small puffs of smoke as they struck the ethereal wall, transported to the gods only knew where.

One of the White Consuls attempted to push through the insubstantial barrier, and his body was instantly the focus of frantic movement within the mist. Smoky claws and tentacles latched onto the warrior's armour, which began to run like melted wax. The warrior's battle-brothers tried to drag him back, but this merely ensnared them as well, and they were all dragged into the hellish warp rift. In the blink of an eye, they were gone.

Marduk nodded appreciatively towards the sorcerer, who inclined his head in acknowledgement. With the threat from the rear at least temporarily held at bay, the Word Bearers spread out, encircling the enemy captain and the last of his veteran battle-brothers.

One by one, the blue-helmeted warriors were cut down, dragged to the ground and butchered. Held aloft by one of the few remaining veterans, their Chapter banner burst into flames at a word from Inshabael Kharesh. In a heartbeat, nothing remained of it but its skeletal standard pole, the ancient design rendered to ash. The banner bearer was dropped a second later, Marduk's crozius buried in his skull.

The captain's champion was next to die, ripped limb from limb by Burias-Drak'shal. The possessed warrior's wounds, deep cuts sustained from the champion's slender power blade, began to heal instantly. His long, forked tongue lapped at the blood on the side of his face and he looked towards the lone figure of the White Consuls captain with undisguised hunger.

The captain stood alone, the bodies of his comrades piled around him. Even facing certain death, he showed no fear. Sparking energy danced across his bared lightning claws.

'Now you die, like the dog you are,' said Marduk, relishing the moment. The enemy captain tensed himself, dropping into a crouch.

'Face me, heretic,' said the captain. 'One on one.'

'No,' Marduk said. The enemy captain seemed momentarily taken aback by the unexpected answer.

'Have you no honour?' said the White Consul. 'Do you fear to face me, to be humbled before your brethren?'

Sheathing his chainsword, Marduk reached up and removed his skull-faced helmet. His face, an ugly mess of scar tissue, regrafts and augmentation, was amused. He cleared his throat and spat a thick wad of black phlegm at the captain's feet. The floor plating began to sizzle and melt beneath the impact.

'Coward,' taunted the White Consuls captain.

'You are the bastard get of the thrice-cursed Guilliman,' said Marduk. 'You do not deserve an honourable death.'

'Let me take him,' growled Burias-Drak'shal.

'No,' said Marduk.

'Let me face your warp-spawned pet,' said the White Consul. 'In the Emperor's holy name, I shall cut it down and spit upon its corpse.'

Burias-Drak'shal snarled and stepped forward. Marduk halted him with a word.

'No,' he said. 'He wishes to die a noble death. Therefore, he shall not have it. Gun him down.'

Marduk smiled as he saw the shock and outrage written in the eyes of the enemy captain. The White Consul made to leap at Marduk, but he was cut down before he could move, struck from all sides by gunfire.

The bridge belonged to Marduk, and he grinned in savage pleasure as a second blast door exploded inward less than a minute later.

'Too slow, Ankh-Heloth,' he said with relish as the rival Dark Apostle and his warriors stormed through the breach, weapons raised. 'I have already informed Ekodas that the 34th has taken control of the vessel.'

ANKH-HELOTH HAD DEPARTED the *Sword of Truth* in a rage, and the last White Consuls still holding out against the Word Bearers were isolated, bulkheads locking down around their positions as the dark magos Darioq-Grendh'al linked with the ship's controls. Marduk had felt the unspoken question from his warriors that these last survivors were not killed, but the Dark Apostle felt no need to explain his actions. The ship's communications had been severed before the bridge had fallen, ensuring that the enemy had not learnt its fate. For all they knew, the battle-barge had made it to the safety of the asteroid belt, escaping the wrath of the Chaos fleet.

The Dark Apostle was standing upon the bridge of a White Consuls battle-barge, gazing upon its cogitator banks and data-screens in distaste. He spied a shrine to the Emperor, a small statue surrounded by candles and papers of devotion, and his lip curled in loathing.

'First Acolyte?' said Marduk, nodding his head in the direction of the shrine.

In response, Ashkanez stepped forwards and smashed the statue to dust with his power maul, intoning the psalms of desecration. A second sweep saw the candles and papers scattered.

'Kol Badar,' said Marduk through his vox. The Coryphaus was located half a kilometre distant, assessing the weapon caches of the White Consuls vessel.

'Yes, Apostle,' came the reply.

'Where is the sorcerer? I wish to speak with him.'

'I believe he has already returned to the *Infidus Diabolus*, Apostle,' said Kol Badar. 'He returned on one of the first shuttles.'

'Find him,' said Marduk.

'It will be done,' said Kol Badar.

Marduk cut the communication, irritated that he had no real authority over the Black Legion sorcerer's movements. He felt a presence behind him and turned to see his Icon Bearer, still in the thrall of his daemonic possession.

'Yes?'

'I am your champion,' snarled Burias-Drak'shal, forming the words with difficulty. He shook his head and his face returned to his own regular, slender, handsome features as he pushed the daemon back within. 'That was my kill.'

'Do not question my decisions, Burias.'

'And as for your precious Coryphaus… His plan to take the bridge almost saw us killed. So much for his being a master strategist.'

Burias once more held the heavy Host icon in his hands, having snatched it from the Anointed brother who had borne it in his absence. The heavy base of the tall, dark metal icon thumped into the floor repeatedly as Burias paced back and forth alongside Marduk, his free hand clenching and unclenching into a fist. His face was flushed and his cruel mouth set in a deep scowl.

'We just took a fully manned Astartes battle-barge in under thirty minutes,' said Marduk. 'That is hardly the result of an incompetent Coryphaus.'

'I don't know why you show the whoreson such favours,' snapped Burias. 'Be rid of him! You know he will betray you.'

With a single word, Marduk dismissed all the warriors of the Host from the bridge.

'You too, First Acolyte,' said Marduk.

With a bow, Ashkanez left the room, leaving Marduk alone with the Host's Icon Bearer.

'I see I am going to have to spell this out to you, Burias,' said Marduk. 'You are my blood-brother, and for this reason I have given you much leniency, but I'm not prepared to take any more.'

'You are making a mistake,' said Burias, his voice tinged with bitterness. 'Be rid of Kol Badar, before he turns on you.'

'You think there is someone more suitable to be Coryphaus within the Host than Kol Badar, Burias?' said Marduk.

The Dark Apostle had considered the option long and hard. Sabtec was the obvious candidate, but Marduk did not believe that even he, the exalted champion of the glorified 13th Coterie, was anywhere approaching Kol Badar's equal, at least not yet. There was no one that came close. The taking of the *Sword of Truth* confirmed Kol Badar's pre-eminence, had Marduk harboured any doubt.

'We are brothers, sworn in blood,' said Burias. 'I am the only one you can trust.'

'You honestly thought that *you* would become Coryphaus upon my ascension? Is that really what all this is about?' said Marduk.

He had always known that Burias was a devious and ambitious warrior who hungered for power and prestige, and that he had always planned to rise up the ranks of the Host, buoyed by his close relationship with Marduk, but... Coryphaus? He turned back towards his Icon Bearer, a look of exasperation on his face.

'You are important to the Host, Burias, and you have a role to play. But Coryphaus? Really?' said Marduk.

Burias's jaw jutted forward stubbornly, and though he did not speak, his silence was confirmation enough to Marduk.

The Dark Apostle shook his head and chuckled. He placed a hand upon Burias's shoulder.

'Ah, my brother, you do so amuse me,' he said.

Burias shrugged off his hand.

'I do not see what is so amusing,' Burias said, his voice heavy with bitterness. 'We are blood brothers. You owe me–'

The Icon Bearer silenced himself, perhaps hearing the words spilling from his own lips, perhaps seeing the murderous light that was flaring in the Dark Apostle's eyes.

'I owe you?' said Marduk in a quiet, deadly voice.

'What I meant–'

Burias didn't see the blow coming. Marduk slammed his fist into Burias's face, snapping the Icon Bearer's head back sharply, breaking his nose. He staggered, and touched his fingers to the blood dripping down his face.

'You dare–' he began, but Marduk struck again, the blow catching him on the temple as he tried to turn away from it.

'*I* dare?' snarled Marduk. '*I* dare? I am your Dark Apostle, you insolent wretch. You dare question *me*? You dare suggest that I *owe you* somehow?'

'I felt that–' began Burias, but Marduk did not let him finish. His face was a mask of fury. He stepped in close to Burias and raised his hand to strike him. The Icon Bearer stepped back instinctively.

'Do not recoil,' snarled Marduk, and Burias froze, waiting for the blow to fall.

Marduk unclenched his fist, and sighed. 'Burias, you are my champion, and the Host's finest warrior. Is that not enough?'

The anger simmering in Burias's eyes said that it was not.

'I had hoped that we would not need to have this conversation, Burias,' said Marduk. 'I had hoped that you would come to accept your place in the Host, but I see now that I will have to speak even more plainly. Accept what you are, Burias, and stop trying to become something you will never be. Let me make this perfectly clear: you will never be Coryphaus, Burias. Kol Badar is Coryphaus, and your superior, and that is not changing.'

Burias stood glowering at him.

'You are my champion, and the Host's Icon Bearer, but you are a warrior, Burias, just a warrior. You will never be more than that. Never.'

Marduk let these words sink in, holding the Icon Bearer's gaze, before he added, 'Now get out of my sight. Six hours on the pain deck. Perhaps that will help you learn to accept your place.'

Without a word, Burias turned and marched from the bridge. Marduk stood there silently for a moment, before slamming his fist down onto a console.

Standing unseen in the shadows outside the bridge, having overheard the entire exchange, First Acolyte Ashkanez smiled.

A BLINKING VOX-BEAD interrupted Marduk's brooding. It was Kol Badar.

'What?' he said.

'I have just received word from Sabtec. The Black Legion sorcerer has been found.'

'Have him wait for me in my quarters. I am returning to the *Infidus Diabolus* now.'

'There is a problem,' said Kol Badar.

ANGER RADIATED OFF Marduk in waves. Together with Sabtec and Kol Badar, he stood inside a little-used, dimly lit storage space located on one of the lower decks of the *Infidus Diabolus*. Humming fan units spun overhead. All three of the Word Bearers were focussed on the body strung up in the centre of the room. It hung there like a martyred saint, arms wide, wrapped in razor wire that cut deep into its armoured wrists and ankles.

It was the body of Inshabael Kharesh, Warmaster Abaddon's personal envoy within the Host. Blood had pooled and congealed upon the deck floor beneath him.

Kol Badar made a warding gesture. The killing of a sorcerer was a blasphemy said to bring down the ire of the gods.

'It is a bad omen,' said Sabtec.

'You think?' said Marduk.

He lifted the sorcerer's head. His neck had been slashed open, a cut so deep that it had reached the spine. The sorcerer's eyes had been put out, and there was a runic icon carved into his alabaster forehead. It was Colchisite cuneiform in origin, he knew that, but the symbol meant nothing to him.

'Abaddon will have our heads for this,' said Kol Badar.

Marduk's mind was reeling – first his only ally, Sarabdal; now the Black Legion sorcerer.

'Why would anyone want him dead?' said Kol Badar.

'To dishonour the 34th? To spread disharmony and doubt?' said Sabtec.

'Or to ignite antagonism between us and the Black Legion,' said Marduk.

'What is this symbol?' said Kol Badar.

'I don't know,' said Marduk.

'There were more than two hundred warrior-brothers onboard the *Infidus Diabolus* at the time when this took place,' said Sabtec. 'I will begin verifying the whereabouts of each of them.'

'We do not have the time,' said Marduk, shaking his head. 'This is what they want – to sow confusion and dissent.'

'Ashkanez,' said Kol Badar. 'He's the only one of us who is not of the 34th.'

'The First Acolyte was aboard the White Consuls ship,' said Marduk.

'If not him, then we must face the fact that there is one – or more than one – working against us from within the Host,' said Kol Badar.

The thought was not a comforting one.

BURIAS WAS LYING upon his spike-rimmed pallet, his flesh awash with agony, when there came a knock on his cell door.

'Wait,' he said, and dragged himself to his feet. His pain receptors were still burning with residual agony from the ministrations of the black-clad wraiths of the pain deck. Serums had been injected into his spinal column that retarded the accelerated healing of his body, ensuring that he felt every nuance of his punishment. It was not the physical pain that bothered him – in truth, its purity was welcome – but rather the fact that his blood-brother had humiliated him so. Anger seethed within him, coiling around his twin hearts like a serpent.

Rising to his feet, nerve endings searing, he pulled a robe around his body.

'Come' he said, his voice raw, as he tied the black rope of his robe around his waist. First Acolyte Ashkanez entered.

He gazed around the cell, taking in its few details. A MkII bolter and twin bolt pistol hung upon one black iron wall, and a heavy chest was at the foot of the Icon Bearer's austere pallet. A small bookshelf holding scripture and texts hung upon one wall, and a myriad of sacred symbols of Chaos and assorted severed body parts dangled from chains overhead. A buzzing red blister shone its dim light down upon the cell. The tanned flesh of a human being was splayed out across another wall, the skin covered in tiny scripture. There was a scent of blood and meat in the air, detectible even above the incense.

'What do you want?' snarled Burias.

'You are the Host's champion. It was a slight on your honour not to face the enemy captain. The Dark Apostle shamed you.'

The First Acolyte kept his eyes upon Burias, studying the reaction to his words.

Burias felt the serpent of hate tighten its grip around his heart.

'And you have come here why? To gloat?'

'Not at all,' said Ashkanez. 'I feel that the Dark Apostle erred in his judgement. You have fought together for a long time, have you not?'

'A long time,' agreed Burias.

'He's holding you back,' said Ashkanez.

Burias said nothing, eyeing the First Acolyte warily.

'We understand each other, you and I, I think,' said Ashkanez.

Burias opened his mouth to rebuke the First Acolyte, but he held his tongue. His eyes narrowed. Was this some trick? Had Marduk sent his First Acolyte down here to test him, to see if he needed more time in the pain deck?

'There is something that I would like to show you, Burias.'

The First Acolyte opened the door to Burias's cell and stepped outside, looking up and down the corridor beyond. He turned back towards Burias, who had remained motionless, eying him suspiciously.

'If you wish your eyes opened, to see the true face of things to come, then come with me. If you wish to remain blind in ignorance, stay here,' said Ashkanez, shrugging his shoulders. 'The choice is yours.'

The First Acolyte turned on his heel and walked out of Burias's cell. He paused outside.

'Well?' he said.

Moving warily, Burias stepped out of his cell. Its gate clattered shut behind him, and the First Acolyte smiled.

He led Burias deep into the bowels of the *Infidus Diabolus*. The Icon Bearer tried to ask Ashkanez several times where he was leading him, but his questions were answered with silence.

Their route was circuitous and indirect, backtracking on itself a dozen times as if the First Acolyte was wary of being followed. Finally, in the lowest of the ship's dimly lit sub-decks, Ashkanez drew them to a halt.

'We are here,' he said.

'Where?' said Burias.

Ashkanez pointed at a small symbol scratched into a rusted wall-panel besides a narrow side-passage. He would never have noticed it had it not been pointed out.

'What does it mean?' said Burias.

'A meeting place,' said Ashkanez. 'For like-minded souls.'

Without further explanation, Ashkanez pulled his hood over his head, hiding his features in the gloom. He gestured for Burias to do the same, and stepped into the dimly lit side-passage.

From the shadows, a voice challenged them. Burias could easily make him out in the darkness, though a deep hood obscured his face too.

'Who goes there?'

'Warriors of Lorgar, seeking the communion of brotherhood,' answered Ashkanez.

'Welcome, brothers,' came the voice. The figure backed away, and Ashkanez swept past.

'What the–' began Burias, but Ashkanez gestured for silence.

Burias was led into a dark cave-like room. Immense pistons rose and fell within the gloom above, filling the air with their hissing and venting steam, and Burias realised that they were located beneath the fore-engine drive shafts. Withered fingers protruded from beneath the grilled decking, desperately seeking the attention of the Word Bearers walking above them, and their pitiful cries ghosted up from below.

As his eyes adjusted to the gloom, Burias came to a halt as he saw that there were other figures located here in the dim confines, hugging the shadows, their faces obscured by hoods. There must have been several hundred gathered, and more were filing in from side-entrances and service tunnels; a sizeable chunk of the Host was arrayed here, warriors that Burias had fought alongside for thousands of years.

'What is this?' he growled.

'This,' said Ashkanez, spreading his arms wide and speaking at last, 'is the Brotherhood.'

BOOK THREE: THE CLEANSING

'Faith, hate, vengeance and truth; these are our tenets. Embrace them.'

– *Keeper of the Faith, Kor Phaeron*

CHAPTER EIGHT

'I PRAY THAT Boros Prime will pose more of a challenge,' said Kol Badar. 'Taking this backwater was beneath us.'

The Coryphaus stood alongside the Dark Apostle Marduk upon the world known locally as Balerius II, the ninth planet of the Boros Gate. A tall, gleaming hab-spire could be seen in the distance, breaching the jungle canopy. Smoke was billowing from its ruptured sides.

'I yearn for the challenge,' said Kol Badar. 'Not one of the White Consuls cowards dared face us here.'

'We will face them again soon enough,' said Marduk.

Having defeated the Imperial armada at the battle of Trajan Belt, the XVII Legion pushed deep into the Boros system, spreading like a malignant cancer, and the process of subjugation and indoctrination was begun in earnest. Each Host struck out for a different quarter of the system, and world after world fell before them. Spouting catechisms of revilement and hate, the Dark Apostles had led their Hosts against the PDF and Imperial Guard regiments, butchering tens of millions – a grand sacrifice to the insatiable gods of the aether.

In less than a month, over half the Boros system's inhabited worlds had fallen to the advancing Word Bearers, as planned. On worlds where the Astartes of the White Consuls stood side by side with the PDF the battles were fierce and bloody, but the loyalist Space Marines were but few and scattered, isolated beacons of hope trying to hold back a ravening tide of destruction. All they had achieved was merely to forestall the inevitable.

One by one the core worlds of the Boros Gate binary system fell. The enemy fell back before them, towards Boros Prime, the core planet in the system. A steady stream of escape pods, mass transits and shuttles ferried Imperial Guard regiments and citizens towards the fortress world. Of those left behind, the millions who died in the fierce bombardments and firestorms were the lucky ones; those that survived to see their planets overwhelmed by the Word Bearers were either sacrificed in mass killings dedicated to the Dark Gods, or were enslaved, chained together in endless lines and subjected to unspeakable horrors.

The XVII Legion had already taken millions and once pristine core worlds were being steadily reduced to hellish realms of madness and despair. Hives, cities and entire continents were levelled, their remains used to construct immense towers and monuments of unholy significance, and the ritual debasement and insidious corruption of Imperial citizens advanced steadily. The minds, bodies and will of the slaves were slowly broken down, all hope and faith ground out of them, their souls as tortured as their flesh by the horrors unleashed upon them.

Discords drifted amongst them, horrific floating constructs trailing tentacle-like limbs blaring a barrage of noise from their speaker-grilles, a maddening cacophony of deafening roars, screams and pounding heartbeats – the sound of Chaos itself. Voices within this insane din whispered into the hearts and minds of the slaves, corrupting their souls even as their bodies were corrupted. In time they would come to understand the truth of the Word that the XVII Legion bore, giving in gladly to Chaos.

A dozen naval engagements had been fought as the ships of the White Consuls launched lightning attacks upon the Chaos fleets, but these were little more than skirmishes. The Imperialist Astartes were unwilling to stand and fight in a full-blown engagement, preferring to strike hard and fast before pulling back when the enemy fleets turned to engage. They were irritating, and the Consuls managed to destroy and cripple a handful of Chaos vessels in their hit-and-run strikes, but these skirmishes had little bearing on the overall outcome of the war.

The Boros Defence Fleet and the ships of the White Consuls had drawn back to the protection of the star fort orbiting Boros Prime. The stage was being set for a grand confrontation.

The time drew close for the Hosts of the Dark Apostles to come back together, to converge on Boros Prime. There, the final battle for the Boros Gate would take place.

From out of the jungle, a Land Raider rolled towards Marduk and Kol Badar. It growled like an angry beast as its massive tracks crushed a path through the thick undergrowth. Its armoured hull bristled with rotating sensor arrays and antennae, and its assault ramp opened like a gaping maw as it came to a halt before them, belching blood-incense.

First Acolyte Ashkanez stepped from the red-lit interior, Icon Bearer

Burias, sullen and brooding, behind him.

'Well?' said Marduk.

Ashkanez held a data-sheaf out to Marduk, the bone-coloured parchment punched with holes. The Dark Apostle gestured to Kol Badar, who stepped forwards and took it. The Coryphaus fed the data-sheaf into the reader unit inbuilt into his left forearm, and the information was relayed across his irises.

'Finally,' said Kol Badar.

Marduk raised an eyebrow.

'We move on Boros Prime,' said Kol Badar. 'The 34th has been chosen to act as vanguard. It is our role to achieve planetfall.'

'Ekodas honours us,' said Ashkanez.

Marduk grunted in response, certain that there was more to it than that.

'What of the other Hosts?' asked Ashkanez. Marduk scrutinised him, certain that his First Acolyte had already read the dispatch. Indeed, it's what *he* would have done in his place, when he were First Acolyte. The heavy-set warrior-priest gave away nothing, his expression a blank.

'Ankh-Heloth and Belagosa will make planetfall once we have established a landing zone. The 11th Host will assault the frozen polar north, the 30th will land on the dark side of the mega-continent and push towards the equator. Ekodas will take the star fort itself.'

'*Grand Apostle* Ekodas,' said Ashkanez in a low voice, making Burias scowl.

'He gets the glory, while we bleed,' observed Kol Badar.

'Fine,' said Marduk. 'The 34th will not shirk from this challenge. Ready the Host.'

ALMOST FOUR HUNDRED warriors were gathered within a long unused underdeck slave pen deep within the bowels of the *Infidus Diabolus*. All were cloaked and hooded. In the time since Burias had been embraced into the Brotherhood, its numbers had swollen, and more brothers of the 34th Host were being sworn into the sacrosanct, secretive ranks of the cult with each passing week. It had become a close-knit community, a brotherhood within a brotherhood.

'We are the legacy of Colchis,' said First Acolyte Ashkanez to the hooded gathering of Astartes brethren. 'The blood of our home world flows in the veins of each and every one of us. We are brothers in faith, and brothers in blood. Twice before has the Brotherhood been needed. Twice has it performed its duty.'

Burias was in the front row, his hood pulled low and his eyes filled with fanaticism as he listened to the First Acolyte's sermon.

'The Great Purge,' growled Ashkanez, 'was a time of blood and faith, a grand cleansing that saw one in three men, women and children of Colchis burn. In their arrogance, there had been those amongst the holy

Covenant that had sought to defame our blessed primarch, blinded by jealousy. They led their devoted, ignorant flock against Lorgar, who wept as he was forced into conflict with those who ought to have been his brothers. With great reluctance he empowered the Brotherhood, warrior-monks handpicked and indoctrinated by our lord himself, to act as his foot soldiers, and thus began the first great cleansing. Over a billion souls perished in that grand conflict, but it only made us stronger. Our faith became as iron.'

Ashkanez stalked back and forth as he addressed the gathered suppliants, his hands balled into fists at his sides.

'The Second Purge came a century later, after our blessed lord, the Urizen, had been reunited with his Legion; after our glorified primarch's eyes were opened to the lies of the golden-tongued so-called Emperor of Mankind,' said Ashkanez. He spat in loathing, as if expelling a foul taste from his mouth, before continuing.

'With realisation came the understanding that the old beliefs of Colchis were the only truth in the universe; that the old gods were the only powers worthy of our faith and worship. There were those amongst our blessed Legion that would not have understood these things, brainwashed and conditioned as they had been in their formative years. Our lord Lorgar once more reformed the Brotherhood, again with great mourning and remorse. Thus were the Legion's ranks cleansed and unified. In one week, thus were all warrior-brothers of Terran birth eradicated, leaving only those of Colchis blood behind.'

Ashkanez licked his lips and glared around at his audience, his eyes blazing with passion.

'Great was the Urizen's lamentation, for those warriors slain were his sons, his flesh and blood, children of his own gene-code. And yet, through no fault of their own and as a direct result of being raised in isolation from him, they had to be removed. Their will had been utterly corrupted by the lies of the False Emperor. Their souls had been closed off to the great truth.'

Burias leant forward, absorbing every word. For millennia, such knowledge had been denied him, denied all those who had not themselves taken part in the great cleansing. He himself had been born and raised in the monastery-prisons of Colchis but only indoctrinated into the Legion during the first great influx, once the old beliefs had been re-embraced wholeheartedly. He had only ever known of the Great Purge – of the second, he had only ever heard insinuations. Now that this knowledge was being freely given, he was soaking it all in like a sponge. Truly, he could not understand why the Council had forbidden it.

Even Marduk, his oldest comrade and *faithful* friend – who had, he had learnt, been an active part of the Brotherhood itself during the Second Purge – had kept these secrets from him, holding him back with ignorance.

'Ignorance is control. Ignorance is slavery,' Ashkanez had said to him when he had broached the subject with the First Acolyte, and Burias had long pondered the words.

'We move towards a grim time in our Legion's history, my brethren,' said Ashkanez. 'Once more, the Brotherhood has been reformed, at the will of Lorgar himself. The third purging of our ranks approaches, brothers, and its us, you and I, who have been chosen to enact it.'

FLANKED BY WARRIORS of the Anointed, Marduk stood on one of the cavernous launch decks of the *Infidus Diabolus*, his arms folded across his chest.

An ancient Stormbird was crouched before him like an immense, predatory beast. Its assault ramps were lowered, and a score of warheads were being carefully emptied from its hold on tracked crawlers, under the supervision of Kol Badar. Just one of those warheads would have crippled the *Infidus Diabolus*. Dozens more had already been stowed away within the ship, delivered to them by a score of separate shuttle runs.

However, Marduk's attention was elsewhere; his focus was on the Nexus Arrangement. The xenos device and its weighty housing unit had been loaded onto a similar tracked crawler unit, and it was slowly being led towards the now empty hold of the waiting shuttle. The hulking form of Darioq-Grendh'al moved ponderously alongside it, physically attached to the crawler unit by a swathe of cables and fleshy pipes.

'I am not happy about this,' said Marduk.

'And your opinion has been noted,' replied Kol Harekh, Ekodas's Coryphaus. 'Nevertheless, the Grand Apostle has decreed that the device will be taken aboard the *Crucius Maledictus*, for safekeeping.'

'Safekeeping,' sneered Marduk. 'Ekodas wants the device for himself, so that he can claim its success as his own.'

'Think what you will, Apostle,' said Kol Harekh. 'The device is being requisitioned. He is Grand Apostle, and has a seat on the Council. You have no authority to refuse him.'

'It is *mine*,' said Marduk. 'My Host has bled for it. *I* have bled for it.'

'The Grand Apostle thanks you for your loyal service. You do your Host proud. However, the device belongs to the Legion, not to you. And the Grand Apostle feels that it will be safer aboard the *Crucius Maledictus*. The death of the Black Legion envoy, Inshabael Kharesh, has made the Grand Apostle doubt your ability to keep the device secure.'

'I did not know that Ekodas was already aware of the sorcerer's death,' said Marduk.

Kol Harekh smiled coldly.

'I am merely here to supervise the safe passage of the device,' he said. 'Is there going to be a problem here, Apostle?'

Kol Harekh appeared unconcerned that he was standing upon the deck of Marduk's own ship and heavily outnumbered. On Marduk's word, Kol Harekh and his entourage would be butchered where they stood.

Marduk did not answer Ekodas's Coryphaus. Kol Harekh shrugged his shoulders and broke eye contact, turning and ordering his warriors to ready the Stormbird's engines.

Marduk watched in silence as the Nexus Arrangement was loaded aboard Kol Harekh's Stormbird. Sitting atop the slowly moving crawler unit, the Nexus Arrangement continued to spin smoothly, its silver rings revolving in mesmerising arcs. The air vibrated with each turn, like the huffing of some immense infernal beast. Where they crossed they blurred together like quicksilver, only to reform themselves instantly on the other side. The green light exuded by the alien device was held in thrall by the harsh red light projected into it from the daemon-machine that the fallen magos had constructed, creating a malignant, diffuse glow.

The corrupted magos stepped onto the Stormbird's ramp. It groaned under his weight.

'Darioq-Grendh'al…' said Marduk.

'That is the last of the warheads,' said Kol Harekh. 'You have established the teleportation link?'

'Of course,' said Marduk.

'Kol Badar's plan is a good one. See that it is enacted successfully.'

Marduk glared at Ekodas's Coryphaus.

'You have what you came for,' he said. 'Now get off my ship.'

COADJUTOR GAIUS AQUILIUS of 5th Company looked back and forth between the gathered White Consuls, reading the tension upon their faces. While he knew rationally that, as Coadjutor of Boros Prime, it was only right for him to be involved in the discussions of its defence, he still felt out of his depth amongst the senior battle-brothers and captains, let alone in the presence of one of the Chapter Masters and a high-ranked Librarian.

The discussion was taking place high within a three-kilometre-tall spire that protruded above the Kronos star fort, orbiting Boros Prime. Floor-to-ceiling observation portals granted a panoramic view across the orbital bastion. From here it resembled an immense cathedral city, bristling with defences. More than twenty-five kilometres from side to side and octagonal in shape, it was the largest construction of its kind in the entire sector. Hundreds of shuttles and transports darted over its superstructure like tiny bees around their hive. Docking arms extended outwards around the orbital fortress, coupled to more than a score of battlecruisers and heavily armoured mass transports. For all the majesty of the view, none of the White Consuls paid it any mind, intent as they were upon the holograph. The tension in the room was palpable.

'Relays confirm it,' said Chapter Master Titus Valens. 'It is the *Sword of Truth*. It is approaching at combat speed, bearing directly upon us.'

'The *Sword of Truth* was lost. This is clearly a ploy,' said Ostorius, his arms folded across his chest. 'We should target it and bring it down as soon as it comes into range.'

'It is one of our own,' protested Aquilius, 'One of the three battle-barges of our noble Chapter. We cannot destroy it out of hand.'

Ostorius threw him a glance.

'You have much to learn, Coadjutor,' he said. 'The enemy are cunning. This is a trick.'

Aquilius bristled to be spoken to in such a manner in front of the senior Consuls.

'We must be wary, but I will not authorise its destruction out of hand,' said Chapter Master Titus Valens. 'We have had no confirmation of its loss to the enemy, and it is one of ours. Marcus? Your view?'

'I agree with Ostorius,' said Marcus Decimus, Captain of 5th Company, stroking his grey beard thoughtfully. 'We have to suspect this is a ploy. Our hubris has already lost us too many battle-brothers.'

'Agreed,' said Titus Valens. 'We underestimated the foe. I do not intend to do so again. The Trajan Belt massacre shall forever tarnish my honour. And yet, we feared the *Sword of Truth* lost. Now, it appears before us. If there is a chance that there are battle-brothers aboard, I dare not destroy it out of hand.'

'The last we saw, Brother-Captain Augustus was attempting to disengage by manoeuvring the *Sword of Truth* into the Trajan Belt,' said Sulinus, Captain of 3rd Company. 'As unlikely as it seems, there is a chance that he managed it.'

'And successfully evaded destruction in the last month?' said Captain Decimus. 'Without making any contact with us in the intervening time? I cannot see that happening.'

'Perhaps her communications were knocked out in the engagement,' suggested Sulinus. 'I know it is unlikely, but it is possible. Do we take that risk?'

'It's a fool's hope, Sulinus,' said Captain Decimus.

'For all we know, Captain Augustus is still onboard and alive, along with Throne-knows how many battle-brothers. Can we in all faith destroy the ship if there is even the slimmest chance of that?'

'Epistolary Liventius?' said Chapter Master Valens, turning towards the blue-armoured Librarian stood alongside him. 'Can you confirm that for us?'

Liventius nodded, and closed his eyes, touching the fingertips of one hand to his temple. Aquilius felt a disconcerting prickling sensation at the base of his neck, and he shivered involuntarily.

Aquilius held all Librarians in awe and reverence, for they were masters of powers the like of which he could barely conceive. Liventius's face was heavily lined and drawn, as if all the moisture had been drained from his flesh. He leant upon a tall force-halberd, a weapon charged with a portion of his awesome psychic mastery. His hairless scalp was pierced with diodes and wires connecting him directly to his psychic hood.

Holding the rank of Epistolary, the highest attainable for an Astartes Librarian barring Chief Librarian, Liventius was held in high regard amongst the Chapter, both for his fearlessness and skills in battle and his potent psychic abilities. His wise council was greatly respected by battle-brother and Chapter Master alike.

The Librarian opened his eyes a moment later, and Aquilius felt the prickling sensation dissipate.

'There are battle-brothers alive onboard,' he confirmed.

'Captain Augustus?' said the Chapter Master.

'I am not sure,' said the Librarian. 'Maybe. Something clouds my vision.'

'More proof that this is nothing but a ploy of the enemy, surely,' said Ostorius.

'Perhaps,' said Liventius, 'but there are White Consuls alive onboard the *Sword of Truth*. Of that there can be no doubt.'

'How many?' asked Chapter Master Valens.

'More than thirty,' said Liventius.

'Are they in control of the *Sword of Truth*, or are they imprisoned upon it? Has the enemy kept them alive merely to use them as living shields?'

'I cannot say,' said the Librarian.

Aquilius looked out of the towering observation window, but the *Sword of Truth* and the ships closing in behind her were still well beyond even his enhanced vision. In his mind's eye he imagined the White Consuls battle-barge ploughing towards the Kronos star fort, explosions and coronas of light flashing upon her flank as the enemy targeted her. Even considering firing upon the noble vessel felt like sacrilege, let alone doing so if there were any White Consuls still alive on board.

'*Sword of Truth* closing at eleven hundred kilometres,' blurted a mechanised servitor hardwired into the operational panel of the Kronos deck.

Aquilius's gaze took in the expanse of the Kronos star fort, bristling with laser batteries, cannons and torpedo tubes. Its architecture was studiously practical, yet still pleasing to the eye with its militaristic, classical aesthetic. Protected as it was with immense armour and copious layers of void shields, Kronos was virtually impenetrable, and with such potent defences, nothing short of an entire battlefleet would pose a threat.

The curve of Boros Prime could be seen out of the observation window, and its beauty briefly distracted Aquilius. Blue atmosphere gave way to the sprawling continents below, which the Kronos station watched over like a benign god, ready to unleash its fury upon any who wished the planet harm.

It was unfathomable to Aquilius that the enemy would dare attempt a frontal assault upon the planet or the star fort itself – Kronos would obliterate any such attempt, surely.

Aquilius's gaze moved back towards the holo-screens. They showed the *Sword of Truth* being pursued by one massive battleship – the *Crucius Maledictus* – three strike cruiser-sized vessels and a handful of smaller craft. The enemy were harrying the valiant White Consuls battle-barge, and he saw flashes of colour that indicated the Word Bearers ships firing upon the *Sword of Truth*.

One of the smaller enemy ships disappeared from the screen.

'Look!' said Aquilius. 'The *Sword of Truth* retaliates! One of the enemy ships has been brought down!'

'Sacrificial,' said Ostorius. 'They seek to fool us.'

'Even if that is the case, I do not believe that we can risk it,' said Brother-Captain Sulinus.

'White Consuls battle-barge is in range of orbital cannons,' said one of the grey-uniformed Kronos personnel. 'Do we take it down, sir?'

Chapter Master Titus Valens balled one of his hands into a fist in frustration.

'Damn them,' he said. 'They know that we cannot gun down one of our own, not with battle-brothers still living on board.'

'They know that, and use it to their advantage,' said Ostorius. 'They are banking on us having just this dilemma. If we shoot it down now, then we take back the advantage. It is what the enemy would do were they in our situation,' said Ostorius.

'And that is what sets us apart from them,' said Epistolary Liventius severely.

'I do not believe that Augustus would want us to compromise Kronos for his wellbeing, nor those of any of his brothers,' said Decimus.

The Chapter Master sighed, the weight of responsibility falling to him. While Ostorius was the Proconsul of the Boros Gate system, in the presence of his captain and one of the White Consuls Chapter Masters, his authority naturally deferred to them.

'Let it get closer,' said Chapter Master Valens after a moment, 'Lock gun batteries on the ship. One false move, and we destroy it. But I will not order its destruction until we know, not with battle-brothers on board.'

'The closer the *Sword of Truth* gets, the more damage it could potentially achieve,' said Ostorius.

'Our shields can absorb anything that she could unleash,' said Sulinus.

'What damage could the *Sword of Truth* do to this installation if it rammed it?' said Decimus. 'That would bypass our shields, wouldn't it?'

'The damage would be negligible,' said one of the Kronos officers.

'Scan the *Sword of Truth* for evidence of atomic warheads,' said Chapter Master Valens.

'The scan reads negative,' said the officer a moment later.

'Are you sure?' said Ostorius.

'One hundred per cent accuracy, sir,' said the officer.

'Thank you,' said Ostorius. 'At least that is something.'

'Send a flight wing out to meet the *Sword of Truth*,' said Titus Valens. 'Order them to cripple her engines if she does not slow her advance.'

'Incoming transmission,' announced another of the Kronos personnel.

'Bring it up,' said Ostorius.

The screen crackled with static before the bloody face of Captain Augustus of 2nd Company flashed up. The linkup was rough with interference, but it was irrefutably the captain.

'...under heavy fire... immediate assistance...' came the accompanying vox-stream, as patchy and unclear as the visual feed. '...immediate assistance, repeat... half company still live... transmissions failure...'

'Well, that settles it, then,' said Sulinus as the link dropped.

'With respect, brother-captain, I think you are mistaken,' said Ostorius.

Aquilius could scarce believe that Ostorius was so bold as to speak in such a way to a captain. Ostorius was an honoured veteran, true, but he was far down the line of command from a company captain.

'That was Captain Augustus, Proconsul,' said Sulinus hotly. 'We were inducted into the Chapter from the same sub-hive. I've known him since childhood. I'd recognise him anywhere.'

'The *Sword of Truth* is within firing range,' came a warning report.

'Continue to hold, but keep scanning her for any evidence of weapons powering up,' said Chapter Master Titus Valens. 'I will not fire upon our own until it is beyond doubt that this is an enemy trick.'

'The Word Bearers continue to fire upon the *Sword of Truth*, but their ships are holding back,' Sulinus noted, nodding at the vid-screens. 'They are wary of our weapon systems, as they should be.'

'Nor are they attempting to descend towards Boros Prime,' said Decimus.

'They are not stupid,' said Ostorius. 'As soon as they attempted that, we would obliterate them. Nothing can descend on Boros Prime without coming into range of Kronos.'

The *Sword of Truth* was looming ever larger, ploughing towards the star fort at speed. Explosions detonated upon her bow as the Word Bearers continued to direct their fire towards the ship.

'Distance five hundred kilometres,' came a servitor's voice.

'Get that link with the *Sword of Truth* back up,' said Valens. 'I want contact with 2nd Company.'

'Trying, sir,' came the reply. 'We are having trouble establishing a link. There might be a communications malfunction at their end.'

'Keep trying,' said Valens.

'She is not slowing down,' warned Ostorius.

'Order the flight wing to target her engines on my mark,' ordered Titus Valens.

'In doing so, my lord, we leave her at the mercy of the enemy,' said Sulinus. 'It's as good as a death sentence.'

'Two hundred kilometres.'

'What is Augustus doing?' said Chapter Master Valens. 'Control malfunction?'

'The *Sword of Truth's* shields are still up.'

'She is too close,' said Valens. 'Take out her engines.'

'Sir! The enemy ships are accelerating en masse! They are within range and coming fast!'

'Fire upon them,' said Chapter Masters Titus Valens. 'Bring them down. All guns.'

'Torpedoes have been launched towards Kronos.'

'They'll not get anywhere near us,' said Sulinus dismissively.

'Sir, the flight wing is taking casualties. Do we continue to cripple the *Sword of Truth*?'

'Keep at it,' said Valens.

'One hundred kilometres.'

'Any readings of heat build-up in her weapons?'

'No, sir,' came the reply from an officer sat before one of the scanner arrays.

'Another of our escorts is down! The *Sword of Truth's* engines are at fifty per cent, but it will not be enough! Fifty kilometres, and closing! She is going to hit us!'

Warning klaxons blared through the star fort, warning of immanent impact.

'We have to take it down,' said Ostorius, urgently. 'It poses too much of a risk!'

'No!' shouted Captain Sulinus. 'We cannot! Our brothers are aboard that ship!'

'We cannot risk Kronos!' said Captain Decimus.

'Twenty seconds to impact!'

'May the Emperor forgive us if we are wrong,' said Chapter Master Valens. 'Take it down.'

Hundreds of cannon turrets, each the size of a Titan, rotated towards the incoming battle-barge, but the Chapter Master held off from giving the order. The utter wrongness of killing a brother Astartes was ingrained in them all.

'Transmission! It's the *Sword of Truth*!'

'Hold your fire!' shouted Valens as the blurred image of Captain Augustus of 2nd Company again flashed up.

'...lacking reverse thrusters... malfunction... not fire, attempting emergency...' the captain was saying.

'Torpedoes closing. Commencing defensive barrage.'

'Lance batteries locked and ready to fire upon encroaching enemy fleet, sir!'

The dark void of space lit up as the first incandescent beams of energy stabbed towards the incoming Word Bearers ships.

'Ten kilometres! Five!'

Aquilius's eyes widened as he stared out of the deck window, watching the rapidly approaching battle-barge.

'Sir?' called one of the deck officers suddenly.

'What is it?' said Ostorius.

'Teleport signature!'

'What? Where? Onto Kronos? Our jammers are operational, aren't they?'

'Not onto Kronos, sir! The signature is locking onto the *Sword of Truth*!'

'What are they doing?' asked Decimus, his eyes narrowing.

'I don't know,' said Ostorius. 'Scan the *Sword of Truth* again, officer.'

'In progress, sir!'

'One kilometre!'

'Sir! We are reading... Throne! Sir! Massive readings of atomic warheads aboard the *Sword of Truth*!'

'Guilliman's blood, they've teleported them across,' said Ostorius, the colour draining from his face.

'Is such a thing even possible?'

'Apparently so.'

'Five hundred metres and closing!'

'Bring it down!' shouted the Chapter Master.

Aquilius looked out of the observation window towards the battle-barge, looming large and coming in fast. Turrets began to fire upon it, but it was already too close...

'Throne above,' he breathed.

Half torn apart from close-range cannon fire, but still coming, the *Sword of Truth* ploughed into the side of the Kronos star fort. The timed warheads that had been teleported across into her holds detonated and the battle-barge's plasma core exploded in a blinding corona.

MARDUK SMILED FROM within the dead flesh of the White Consuls captain. As the *Sword of Truth* ploughed into the side of the immense orbital bastion, mere seconds before the atomic warheads that had been teleported across were detonated, Marduk retreated from the corpse. Without his spirit animating it, the dead body collapsed to the floor moments before being consumed in the immense explosion.

The Dark Apostle slammed back into his body aboard the *Infidus Diabolus*, and he felt a moment of dislocation before full control and feeling returned. He stood, and moved forward to observe the destruction.

Through the forward bridge observation portal he witnessed the massive explosion upon the enemy star fort, engulfing several enemy battleships that had been sluggish in disengaging from their docked positions. Secondary detonations rippled outwards from the point of impact, rolling flames bursting into space briefly as oxygen vented before being sucked inwards, hungering for more air to feed upon. Bulkheads would be crashing down within that massive orbital fortress, isolating shattered decks.

The weight of incoming fire directed towards the Word Bearers ships dropped markedly, the overwhelming destructive barrage reduced to a trickle of sporadic fire as explosions continued to ripple along cannon arrays and laser batteries.

Marduk narrowed his eyes against the brightness as another detonation exploded in the heart of the star fort, larger than any other so far.

'Plasma reactor,' said Kol Badar.

When the flame cleared, Marduk could see a massive gaping wound in the flank of the mighty star fort, exposing a mess of twisted metal and exposed sub-decks. A thick cloud of debris and wreckage spiralled outwards from the blast, and Marduk saw with amusement the tiny figures of people blasting out into the emptiness of space alongside twisted metal scrap and ruptured gun turrets. The orbital bastion was still operational, but it had been dealt a terrible, near fatal blow, and it would be long minutes before it would be able to rotate to bring its undamaged weapons to bear on the advancing Chaos fleet.

'Commence planetfall,' said Marduk, savouring the words.

CHAPTER NINE

Aquilius picked himself up from the deck floor, using the command podium to haul himself back to his feet. The air was thick with smoke, and flames were all around. His white armour was scorched and peppered with shards of scrap metal. He was bleeding from the temple, but the blood flow halted within seconds thanks to the hyper-coagulants in his bloodstream.

The Coadjutor's eyes were watering from the smoke, but he could see the carnage around him well enough. White Consuls were picking themselves up from the floor, surrounded by flames and twisted girders. He saw Chapter Master Valens still standing, scowling darkly as he hauled Captain Decimus to his feet.

Aquilius's augmented senses picked up the unmistakeable odours of blood and burnt flesh before he saw the bodies or registered the agonised screams. The officers of the Kronos star fort who had been within the room were scattered across the deck floor, their flesh torn to bloody ribbons. Protected by their battle plate, the White Consuls had merely suffered scratches and abrasions, but these men and women had no such aegis. The Coadjutor began moving around the room, checking for life-signs. Three of the seven officers were still alive, at least for now, and he echoed Ostorius's cry. One of them had, miraculously, escaped all but unscathed. Dutiful even in the face of such destruction, the man climbed unsteadily to his feet and moved back to the consoles, checking to see if any of them were still operational.

'Apothecary!' Aquilius shouted, doing what he could to staunch the bleeding of one officer, a woman in her middling years.

A still form, garbed in white power armour caught his attention, and Aquilius rose to his feet, moving swiftly towards the sprawled figure and dropping to his knees beside him.

A heavy girder had fallen atop the figure, pinning the warrior-brother to the ground. He saw it was the captain of 3rd Company.

'Help me,' Aquilius shouted as he strained fruitlessly to budge the heavy weight.

Chapter Master Valens was at his side a moment later. The Chapter Master grasped the girder one-handed and heaved it aside as if it were made of balsa.

'God-Emperor, no,' said Aquilius as he rolled the motionless figure of Captain Sulinus onto his back and looked into staring, dead eyes. A shard of metal thirty centimetres long was embedded deep in his left eye.

'Damn,' said Chapter Master Valens.

Tracked servitors trundled into the room, bathing the flames with foam.

'Status update!' shouted Ostorius.

'Aft shields at twenty-five per cent!' shouted the sole standing officer on deck, having found a working cogitator unit. 'Re-routing power from the subsidiary banks!'

'Torpedoes incoming, contact in thirty seconds!' called the captain of 5th Company, Decimus, having taken the place of one of the fallen officers.

'Emperor damn them!' said Chapter Master Titus Valens.

'Kronos rotation underway. Sixteen per cent completion.'

'Too slow!' said Ostorius, standing and looking out through the cracked observation portal. 'The traitors are already descending towards the surface.'

Aquilius glanced out into space, and saw that several of the Word Bearers vessels had taken the opportunity in the sudden cessation of fire to cut away from the other incoming traitor vessels and drop towards Boros Prime.

The coadjutor knew as well as any White Consul the procedure for an Astartes strike force launching an attack upon a hostile planet, and though the enemy were vile and corrupted, an abasement of the Adeptus Astartes, he suspected that their modus operandi would be sickeningly close to how such an engagement was dictated in the *Codex Astartes*.

Within minutes, streaming fire would be launched from bombardment cannons, targeted at key lance batteries upon the planet's surface, softening the way for the drop. On the back of this bombardment, the first wave of drop-pods would be launched, striking hard and fast, their mission to gain a foothold upon the surface and take out anti-air and flak emplacements. Further drop-pod waves would help establish this goal and eliminate prime enemy targets, before Thunderhawks descended towards designated landing zones, deploying more troops, support and armour in preparation for a counterattack.

In all, a well-coordinated attack could be launched in minutes, giving the beleaguered ground forces little time to react. It was part of the reason why the Astartes were so devastating – they might be outnumbered a million to one, but the sheer force that could be brought to bear on one location, and the speed of its deployment, was almost impossible to counter. There was little in the universe that could resist against a determined Astartes spearhead. Still, if any world could hold, it was Boros Prime.

Alarms sounded, preceding the stream of incoming enemy torpedoes. Unable to do anything, the White Consuls looked out over the star fort from their spire in horror as they struck home. Less than a third of the torpedoes were taken down by the severely depleted defensive fire, the rest slamming into already straining void shields, overwhelming and tearing rents through them. A score passed through and impacted upon the tiered, castellated sides of the Kronos star fort already ripped asunder by the explosion of the *Sword of Truth*.

'Ground fire will not be enough to stop the Word Bearers drop,' said Captain Decimus. 'Not without the firepower of this installation.'

'I want 5th Company down there on the ground, captain,' said the Chapter Master. Decimus slammed his fist against his chest in salute.

'I believe Pollo Dardanius is the most senior of 3rd Company's sergeants?' said the Chapter Master.

'Yes, my lord,' replied Captain Decimus.

'Inform him that he is now acting captain of 3rd Company. Get him here, now, for briefing.'

'It will be done,' said Decimus.

'I want 3rd Company stationed here. The enemy will attempt to take Kronos. It is 3rd Company's duty to ensure that does not happen. I will accompany 5th Company planetward.'

'You will stay here as well,' said Proconsul Ostorius, addressing his Coadjutor. Aquilius nodded his head solemnly. 'You will be in charge of coordinating the station's defence, deferring to brother Captain Sulinus's original tactics.'

'No,' said the Chapter Master. 'Aquilius will accompany us down onto the planet's surface. You will remain here to oversee the Kronos's defence, Proconsul.'

'My lord?' said Ostorius. His face remained stoic, but Aquilius could see the tension around his eyes.

'You will remain here, Proconsul.'

'My lord, I must protest,' said Ostorius. Aquilius could see that he was struggling to maintain his composure. 'I am the Proconsul of Boros Prime. It is my place to fight on the front line, and to be seen doing so.'

'How many soldiers of your world do you know by name, Proconsul?' said the Chapter Master.

'What?' said Ostorius. 'I do not see–'

'How many?'

Ostorius fell silent.

'I have read the reports,' said the Chapter Master, his voice softening. 'The men of Boros know Aquilius. They will follow him. I am not saying that they would not follow you, but he knows them better. It will do the defenders of this world good to know that the star fort is being held by their Proconsul. As long as Kronos holds, so too will their morale. Your Coadjutor will descend to the surface, and will marshal the Imperial Guard and PDF regiments there. He will do you proud.'

Ostorius was silent for a moment, glaring at the Chapter Master. Then, as if remembering himself, his lowered his gaze.

'I am a soldier, not an administrator,' he said at last. 'I have never had any desire to be more than that. I understand Astartes, but of these unaugmented men of Boros, its Guardsmen, its officials, I know little. I cannot relate to their short lives, nor their fears and mundane concerns. I know that once I was the same as them, but I can remember little of that time. It is as if they are a breed apart.' He snorted. 'Whereas in truth it is we who are the breed apart, are we not?'

'Did you never think that perhaps it was to learn empathy for these people that I posted you here? They share our blood,' said the Chapter Master. 'They are as important, nay, more important than we. We exist merely to protect them. *They* are our reason for being. We are warriors, yes, but we must be more than that, Ostorius.'

The Proconsul hung his head.

'Aquilius understands them better than I,' he said, finally. 'It is right for him to lead them upon Boros Prime. Forgive me, Chapter Master, I realise that I have performed my duties here poorly.'

Aquilius stared at Ostorius in surprise. Never would he have expected the taciturn veteran to speak so openly of his own shortcomings, and despite himself he felt a sudden devotion to him.

'There is nothing to forgive, Proconsul,' said the Chapter Master. 'Hold Kronos. Make the enemy bleed as they try to take it.'

'On my honour, my lord,' said Ostorius, dropping to one knee before his Chapter Master.

'They've bypassed Kronos, and will be hitting the planet in minutes,' said Chapter Master Valens. 'Once they are established on the ground, we will not beat them. All we will be able to do is stall them.'

'There are close to five billion trained Guardsmen on Boros Prime, my lord,' said Aquilius. 'We will grind them into the dust.'

'They are Chaos Space Marines, Aquilius,' said the Chapter Master. 'And there might be as many as fifteen thousand of them. Even by conservative estimates, there will be at least five, six thousand. Imagine it.

That is the same as five or six loyal Chapters descending in their entirety upon one world. Nothing could stand against that – not five billion Guardsmen, not even ten. We need Astartes to fight them, and we ourselves number less than three hundred.'

Aquilius dropped his gaze, accepting the truth in the Chapter Master's words.

'Our only hope is in identifying and nullifying whatever it is that has shut down the Boros Gate,' said the Chapter Master. 'With that veil removed, the Adeptus Praeses could make transference instantly, and we would crush these traitors. Ensuring that comes to pass is our only hope here now. We hold until such a time as that goal is achieved.'

'Are you any closer to identifying the source that shrouds the Boros Gate, Epistolary Liventius?' said Ostorius.

'My attempts are being thwarted, Proconsul,' said Liventius, shaking his head. 'There is a powerful warp presence working actively against me. One of the traitorous Apostates, I would presume. His psychic defences are staggeringly powerful.'

'What help do you need?' said Chapter Master Valens.

'Were I to have a circle of psykers at my disposal, working together, it might help me breach the Apostate's defences.'

'Do it,' said the Chapter Master. 'Gather whoever you need – Navigators, astropaths, sanctioned psykers. Find the source, Liventius. The future of the Boros Gate depends upon it. Now come, my brothers. Let us take the fight to the enemy.'

MARDUK RECITED PASSAGES from the *Canticles of Mortification* as the Dreadclaw reached terminal velocity, his voice barking out over the deafening roar of turbine engines and the groaning of its super-heated, armoured sides. The assault pod screamed down through the upper atmosphere, hurtling towards the planet's surface, bringing death to Boros Prime. G-forces pulled at the ten warriors ensconced within the armoured shell; any unaugmented human would have long succumbed to them and blacked out. Opposite Marduk, Burias grinned with savage pleasure and howled like a beast, his face hellishly lit by the red light emitted by the pulsing blisters above.

'Impact thirty seconds,' croaked the infernal, mechanised voice of the Dreadclaw through vox-grilles.

Marduk roared his hate-filled sermon at the top of his lungs, his voice further enhanced by the vox-amps within the grille of his gleaming skull helmet. Down through the intensifying barrage being directed up at them from the ground the Dreadclaw screamed, shuddering and shaking violently, yet Marduk's sermon never once missed a beat. He spat out his words with passion, hatred and vitriol, fuelling the fury of his warriors. Combat stimms and adrenal glands sent their serums surging through the augmented warriors' systems, further preparing them for the glorious worship of battle.

The Dreadclaw was struck a glancing blow from below, sending it careening off course for a moment, before righting itself and accelerating downwards once more. A further impact ripped one of the side-panels completely off the assault pod, filling the interior with glaring sunlight and roaring wind. One of the warrior-brothers within was ripped away with the panel, the scream of shearing metal sounding for a moment before both disappeared.

Scores of other Dreadclaws hurtled planetwards like meteors, their undersides glowing with heat and burning contrails streaking behind them. Tracer fire stitched across the skies, strafing up from below, thousands of kilotonnes of ammunition being fired indiscriminately heavenwards in a desperate attempt to destroy the Dreadclaws before they struck home. Retina-searing defence laser beams stabbed upwards, and a Dreadclaw no more than ten metres away simply evaporated as it was engulfed in one of these beams, every devoted warrior-brother within perishing instantly.

Still Marduk continued his fiery exhortation, the death of his brothers merely adding fuel to his sermon, his voice heard over the roar of engines and the deafening wind.

The Dreadclaw tilted its trajectory slightly, its guidance controls struggling to keep it on target, and as it rotated its occupants were afforded a view across the sprawling city below them.

Bathed in sunlight, the city below was a gleaming expanse of white marble and parapets, and streaming defensive fire scythed up at them from hundreds of castellated towers, fortified bastions and rotating turrets set atop domed cathedrals and spires. Like industrious ants, people could be seen moving purposefully through tree-lined streets and along colonnaded boulevards and arched bridgeways, though whether they were soldiers or mere civilians, Marduk neither knew nor cared – they would all die.

The ground was approaching with alarming swiftness as the Dreadclaw screamed downwards, and even as he bellowed his hateful catechisms and psalms of defilement, Marduk prepared himself for disembarkation. With a glance he assessed the combat readiness of his comrades, and ran a swift diagnostic check of his weapons and armour, information feeds scrolling across his irises.

His heart was pounding with anticipation, and he could detect the scent of eagerness being exuded by his gene-brothers. Cannon fire screamed by them, missing the Dreadclaw by scant metres, and then the view outside was obscured by marble and sculpture. Retro burners kicked in, filling the air with flame and screaming engines, and their rapid acceleration was reduced, slowing the descent just before the moment of impact.

A fraction of a second later the Dreadclaw hit the ground with spine-compacting force, its talons embedding deep into marble.

Restraint harnesses were retracted instantly and the Word Bearers piled out of the assault pod behind Marduk, roaring with fury and hatred.

Enemy soldiers were falling back away from them, and Marduk's pupils contracted as he focused on this prey.

'Come, my brethren!' he bellowed. 'Let us murder them!'

The Dark Apostle hurled himself into the fray, hacking and cutting like a berserker. Bolters bucked like angry beasts in the hands of the Word Bearers, and chainswords revved furiously as their hunger was sated on the blood of these pathetic specimens of humanity. Only after these first soldiers were slaughtered did Marduk take in his location.

They had landed in the middle of a large column-edged square, overlooked by towering arched bastions and profane temples. Soaring arched bridges and flyways crossed far overhead, and huge weighted royal blue banners stitched with Imperialist propaganda and symbols were draped down their sides. Statues stood atop the massive columns, and Marduk snarled in hatred as he saw that they were depictions of White Consuls and Ultramarines, standing sentinel in heroic poses, bolters clasped in hands and heads wreathed in ivy.

Other Dreadclaws were streaming down from the heavens. Several crashed nearby, causing the ground to crack beneath them. One of them brought a towering statue of a Space Marine captain plummeting to the ground as it hit it with the force of a falling meteor, smashing it to splinters. Another struck one of the high arched bridges and broke straight through, leaving a gaping hole before slamming down into the middle of an ostentatious fountain. A great spume of water and steam was sent up as the glowing red assault pod hit home.

One drop-pod was shredded by flak as it descended, and came apart in mid-air, trailing black smoke, flames and debris. Astartes figures could be seen silhouetted against the fire as they tumbled from the shattered Dreadclaw.

It took Marduk a moment to assess his location, estimating that they had been driven several hundred metres off course. He saw their target up ahead and with a roar led his warriors in its direction, sprinting across the square as the sky overhead was torn apart by gunfire, streaming missiles and rapidly descending drop-pods.

Their objective loomed up ahead of them, and Marduk stared up at it hatefully. The gigantic, broad-based tower squatted at the north end of the square, replete with statuary and bas-relief of famous White Consuls battles. Fifty-metre-high lance battery barrels protruded from its gleaming, golden dome, and dozens of flak cannon turrets and missile racks bristled down its sides. The weight of fire from this tower was immense, and Marduk saw several Dreadclaws ripped apart. There were a dozen such towers within the landing zone, and each of them was marked as priority targets for the assaulting Chaos Legion.

The air tingled with electricity and there was a sudden influx of air before the lance battery fired. Were it not for the auto-sensors of his helmet dimming his vision at the sudden burst of light, Marduk would have been blinded temporarily as it fired. A beam of pure light stabbed upwards towards the distant Word Bearers fleet in high orbit. Concentrated fire from lance batteries could cripple even the largest battleships; neutralising them was of paramount importance.

Even without the immense firepower of the enemy star fort, Boros Prime's ground defences were more than enough to see off the most determined orbital assault. As such, merely bombarding the world into submission was not an option. The *Infidus Diabolus* would unleash its payload and launch the warriors of the 34th Host from its hangar bays and Dreadclaw tubes, but once done, it would pull away and join Ekodas's attack upon the star fort.

Lasfire stabbed from the buildings overlooking the square, fired from behind crenulations and through vision slits. Marduk hissed in anger as one of the shots struck him, scorching his shoulder plate black and causing several of the devotional oath papers nailed there to burst into flame, the scripture reduced to ash.

He could see figures running to take up position above them, lining up along the fortified rooftops overlooking the square, but Marduk ignored them, focussing on his target. One of his brethren stumbled and fell as he was struck by a dozen white-hot las-beams, penetrating and igniting the external cabling and tubing of his power armour. None of the Word Bearers deigned to stop to help their fallen brother; the Gods of Chaos had clearly seen weakness in his soul, and had thus failed to protect him. Further beams struck Marduk on his shoulders and back, making him grit his teeth in fury. Burias was struck a glancing blow across the side of his skull, taking off his left ear and leaving a cauterised burn down the side of his head. He snarled in anger and the change came over him in an instant as the daemon Drak'shal surged to the surface.

Autocannon fire from armoured turrets upon the immense defence tower began to rip across the square, tearing up chunks of marble and smashing XVII Legion warriors from their feet. The sacred power armour of the Word Bearers caught in the enfilades was torn to shreds and their flesh riddled with bullets, but most battled on, the pain merely adding to their hate. A spray of autocannon fire struck Burias-Drak'shal in the shoulder and side, and he roared in defiance, lifting the 34th's holy icon high over his head as his daemon-infused bellow echoed out across the square.

'Incoming!' came the shout from one of Marduk's warriors.

A moment later, a modified Dreadclaw smashed down in front of Marduk and his Coterie, striking with colossal force, cracking the marble slabs beneath it. Its sides, blistered and charred from atmospheric entry, exploded outwards, slamming heavily down onto the ground. Marduk dropped down to one knee behind it, taking cover from the intensifying fire.

'Greetings, young one,' boomed the Warmonger, stepping heavily from the modified drop-pod. 'The Emperor's Palace will fall this day. I feel it in my bones.'

The holy Dreadnought had been rearmed for this mission, heavy bolters replaced with an immense breaching drill, studded with adamantine teeth capable of tearing through even the most heavily fortified bastion. The apex of the fearsome weapon was formed of a dozen separate, rotating adamantine cones, studded with coral-like teeth. Designed by the warsmiths of the Iron Warriors to crack the defences of the Emperor's Palace long ago, Marduk was not surprised to discover that armed in such a manner, the Warmonger was again locked in one of his delusions of times past.

Anything struck by the breaching drill, be it a reinforced rockcrete bunker, a front-line battle tank or the leg of a Titan, would be torn apart. Underslung beneath the potent weapon, a twin-linked meltagun protruded.

'The gateway, revered one!' shouted Marduk, pointing towards the golden doorway leading into the defence tower. 'It must be opened!'

'If such is Lorgar's will,' boomed the Dreadnought, turning towards the gateway. Lurching into motion, the war machine began to walk steadily forwards, cracking paving stones underfoot with every step, ignoring the autocannon rounds and stabbing las-rounds that stung its immense armoured form. Marduk and his warriors broke into a loping run, using the Dreadnought as mobile cover.

The golden doors were wide enough for a super-heavy tank, and over thirty metres in height. A twin-headed eagle had been sculptured in bas-relief upon its surface, and Marduk felt the rage build within him as he stared at the hateful icon, the symbol of the Imperium and the cursed False Emperor, the Great Betrayer.

The Warmonger struck the doors like a battering ram, lowering one shoulder and driving its full weight into the golden surface, which buckled – but held – under the impact. With a mechanical roar, the Dreadnought slammed its madly whirring breaching drill into the slim fissure where the two doors came together. There was a hideous sound of screeching metal, and sparks and glowing splinters of gold plating and the underlying bonded ceramite and adamantium spat out around the Dreadnought. Lascutters and melta shears built into the drill carved through the door. Lasbeams stabbed ineffectually at the Warmonger from narrow slits either side of the gateway's alcove. Marduk hurled a grenade through one of those slits high overhead and grinned in satisfaction as he heard the panicked shouts within, followed by the muffled explosion.

Then a breach the size of the Warmonger was carved in the gateway, and Marduk and his brethren followed the Dreadnought through, roaring their fury.

Soldiers wearing blue tabards over grey carapace armour were waiting for them, arrayed in overlapping serried ranks, lasguns lowered, and they unleashed a barrage that saw several Word Bearers fall. Another one dropped, his chest plate melted beneath a searing plasma blast.

'For Lorgar!' bellowed Marduk, and led the charge.

The enemy began to fall back. They maintained good discipline but were unprepared for the sheer ferocity of the Word Bearers, who raced headlong into their fire, bolters and flamers roaring.

Marduk snapped off a trio of bolts, each a killing shot, before he reached the enemy lines and the blood began to flow in earnest. None of the soldiers stood even to his shoulder, and he smashed two of them aside with one sweep of his crozius, bones turned to powder beneath the force of his first blow. He smashed his bolt pistol into the face of another, the man's features disintegrating as his bone structure crumpled inwards, before knocking aside a lasgun pointed at his head and planting a foot squarely into the chest of another, shattering the soldier's ribs and pulping the organs within.

It was amazing that they had ever achieved anything at all, Marduk thought as he slaughtered the hapless soldiers. He and his brethren were so far beyond these wretched, redundant, pathetic creatures. The only possible purpose of their meaningless lives was as slaves and sacrifices.

The Word Bearers tore through the tower guards without mercy. With curt orders, Marduk sent them spreading throughout the enemy structure. The entire tower was constructed around the immense defence laser protruding up through its middle, and the air was electric as the mass energy capacitors buried beneath the structure powered up to fire once more.

'I want this place silenced and secured!' he roared, stamping towards a spiralling stairwell. 'Every moment it remains operational more noble sons of Lorgar perish!'

FIVE KILOMETRES TO the north-east, Kol Badar broke the spine of a Guardsman with a twist of his power talons before tossing the broken body aside as if it weighed nothing at all. He stalked forwards, glass crunching beneath his footfalls. He ignored the butchered enemy soldiers and adepts strewn across the floor and slumped at their machinery, and looked out of the control room window.

The control room was positioned atop another of the defence laser towers, and he stared out across the war-torn city. In the space of ten minutes it had been turned into hell, but Kol Badar felt no particular satisfaction. After millennia of constant warfare, after organising the deaths of a thousand worlds, he felt nothing. The sky was still being torn apart by missiles and tracer fire and he grimaced as defence lasers continued to send their searing blasts heavenward.

'Target secured and silenced,' he growled. 'Strike groups, report.'

One by one, the reports came filtering in. The attack was going well. Each of the defence lasers designated as the prime targets should fall silent within the next five minutes, creating a safe corridor for the heavier mass transports to descend. Still, they should have been silenced already.

A report from high orbit was relayed to him, the information scrolling before his eyes, and he swore.

'Objective update,' Kol Badar growled, re-opening the vox-channel to all the champions leading the various strike forces. 'The enemy star fort has almost completed its rotation, faster than predicted. Our ships in high orbit will be coming under heavy fire within five minutes, and must pull back. Mass transporters en route. The window for their safe deployment has been reduced dramatically. Silence those damn guns! Silence them now!'

MARDUK SWORE AS he received Kol Badar's update, and he grunted with effort as he slammed his foot into the heavy-gauge door, half tearing it off its hinges. Sparks spurted from damaged cabling, and the door crashed inwards as Marduk kicked it again.

A pair of robed acolytes, their shaven heads tattooed with binary code, rose in alarm, and Marduk gunned them both down, his bolt pistol kicking in his hand. Their chests exploded, blood and bone spraying across the walls as the mass-reactive tips of the bolts detonated.

The interior was dark and filled with the mechanical whine of gyro-stabilisers and grind of ammunition feeds. This was one of the dozens of flak turrets on the exterior of the defence tower, and as the powerful weapon began firing again the room was lit up harshly. The sound was deafening. Two gunners were strapped into the rotating turret. Their control harness was a framework capable of swivelling up and down and through one hundred and eighty degrees, powered by wheezing servos. Flickering green screens hung before them, showing targeting matrices and data-streams, and they gripped the pistol-grip controls of the flak-turret tightly, thumbs depressed upon triggers.

Intent upon their targeting monitors and with their ears muffled from the roar of their guns, the gunners had no clue that their pitiful lives were about to end.

One of the men gave a whoop as he brought down a target, and Marduk growled. Stepping forward onto the turret, he grabbed one of the gunners by the front of his flak-vest and ripped him from his seat, snapping his restraint buckles. He pounded the man headfirst into the turret's framework, and tossed the lifeless corpse aside. The other gunner, seeing the fate of his comrade, struggled to release himself from his restraint. Marduk punched his hand through the soldier's chest, fingers straight as a blade. Closing his hand around the man's heart, he ripped it free with a yank. The man stared incomprehendingly at his own beating heart in his moments before death.

Marduk dropped off the turret, which fell silent as its one remaining, lifeless gunner slumped backwards in his seat.

Marduk strode back into the corridor. Adepts were being dragged from side rooms and butchered. Conserving ammunition, warrior-brothers broke necks and shattered skulls with clubbing blows from bolters and fists. Others had their throats torn out or were cut from groin to neck with knives the length of a human's thigh. Others were merely slung into walls, their skulls caving in from the force, or tossed over the gantry banisters, falling to the distant floor below.

More doors were kicked in as one by one the turrets of the tower were silenced and the occupants butchered or beaten to death.

The entire structure shuddered as the defence laser fired, and Marduk swore once more.

'Khalaxis,' he growled. 'Why is the defence laser still active?'

KHALAXIS STOOD AMID a scene of absolute destruction, blood covering every surface of the room deep below the defence tower. The bodies and limbs of over a dozen adepts and soldiers were strewn around him. His chest was rising and falling heavily, and he was crouched over one of the bodies, his hands and forearms glistening with gore. His lower face was caked in blood.

Licking the blood coating his lips, the towering champion moved towards the humming power array.

He looked it up and down for a moment then swung his chainaxe around in an arc, smashing it into the controls with a satisfying crunch. He pounded his madly whirring axe into the panels again and again, smashing and ripping them apart amid a burst of sparks and electrical smoke, and the strip lighting overhead flickered and died.

Even in darkness, Khalaxis could see quite comfortably.

'Better?' said Khalaxis, establishing a link with his Dark Apostle.

'Better,' agreed Marduk. 'Now get yourself topside. The enemy gather for a counterattack.'

Khalaxis slammed his chainaxe into the control panel one more time for good measure. With a nod to his Coterie, he led them loping out of the room, on the search for fresh prey.

KOL BADAR WATCHED as the Hosts' assault screamed towards the surface of the planet, coordinating their deployment from his position atop the defence tower he had just conquered. Cannons fired as they descended, targeting the gathering enemy ground forces, and hunter-killer missiles were launched from beneath wings, along with hellfire bombs and streams of missiles.

Armoured columns of enemy Guard were moving swiftly through the city towards them, but Kol Badar was unconcerned. With all of the defence towers silenced within the fifty-kilometre radius he had designated as the landing zone, few of the Host's shuttles were shot down on the descent. Those that had made the drop unscathed were barely touching down upon the boulevards, flyovers and colonnaded squares of the enemy city before releasing their deadly cargo.

Hundreds of the Legion's warrior-brothers streamed from embarkation ramps, taking up defensive positions in the face of incoming enemy ground forces. Rhinos and Land Raiders were dropped in, tracks skidding on marble when they ripped free of their couplings. Daemon-engines and Dreadnoughts stalked from transports as their binding chains and wards were loosened, roaring in fury and hatred.

High above them, just visible in the upper atmosphere, were the immense mass transports housing the potent engines of Legio Vulturus.

Movement out of the corner of his eye attracted his attention, and he glimpsed boxy white shapes moving at high speed through the city streets towards the Word Bearers position.

'Enemy contact,' he warned. 'Moving at speed towards the north-western cordon.'

'Acknowledged,' came the reply from Sabtec, the battle-brother in command of the strike teams controlling the location.

'Coryphaus, we have additional inbound contacts sighted, approaching from the west,' said a warrior-brother nearby, an auspex held in his left hand. He was splattered with blood, and one of the horns had been shorn from his helmet in the recent gun battle. 'They are coming down from the orbital bastion in force.'

'Show me,' said Kol Badar, and the Word Bearer passed the auspex to the hulking warlord.

'It is hard to lock onto them,' said the warrior. 'They are coming in fast, below our scans, and they are actively jamming our signal, but you can see their ghost presence sporadically... there.'

'I see them,' said Kol Badar. 'Look at the heat distortion. Thunderhawks.'

Kol Badar glanced up at the immense mass transporters slowly making planetfall. He gauged that it would be at least another twenty minutes before they were down safely. The Host's warriors had to hold the towers until then.

'White Consuls counter-attack inbound,' said Kol Badar, patching through to all the Host's champions and commanders. 'Prepare yourselves. Dark Apostle, Sabtec, Ashkanez; they are converging on your locations. Rerouting reinforcements in your direction.'

'Let them come,' replied Marduk, his voice tinny over the vox-channel.

'This location is our foothold in taking this cursed planet,' said Kol Badar. 'It is our beachhead. If we fail to hold it, then our entire attack will stall. We will not get another chance.'

'Then we had better hold,' replied Marduk.

Kol Badar grunted. Leaving a skeleton defence to guard the defence laser he had claimed, he descended the wide stairs onto the square below, barking orders as he went and coordinating the deployment of the Host's warriors. His personal Land Raider rumbled forwards to meet him. It was adorned with spikes, chains and crucified Imperial citizens. Some of the poor wretches were still alive. The huge machine rolled to a stop, its red headlights burning with fury before they dimmed in bestial servitude, the way a beaten dog would cower before its master. Kol Badar had no doubt that the daemon inhabiting the mighty war engine – it had had no need for a driver or gunner for over four thousand years – would turn on him the moment he let his guard down, but that day had not yet come.

With a submissive growl, the Land Raider lowered its assault ramp. Accompanied by his Anointed brethren, Kol Badar ducked as he embarked. The assault ramp slammed shut, cutting off the painfully bright light outside, and the immense war machine began advancing towards the location of the enemy attack.

In the red-tinged darkness within, Kol Badar smiled. The taking of the *Sword of Truth* had merely whetted his appetite. Killing pathetic mortals did little to raise his interest. Astartes, on the other hand, now *there* was a foe worthy of his attention.

CHAPTER TEN

THE AIR WAS filled with the whine of incoming artillery, followed by the reverberating thump of explosions as they tore their way across squares and boulevards, demolishing statues, turning arboretums to muddy ruin and toppling gold-veined pillars. From his position on the crenulated battlements of the captured defence tower, Marduk could see the warriors of the XVII Legion in the streets below taking cover behind their Rhinos and in the lee of buildings as the Imperial artillery barrage began. He knew it would be a constant presence in the war from here on in.

Few of his brothers would fall in these attacks, but that was not the point; the barrage was chiefly designed to ensure the Word Bearers were pinned down, taking cover rather than concentrating on targeting the incoming enemy forces.

Marduk was unconcerned, confident that whatever the White Consuls could throw at his Host, they would emerge victorious.

'There,' said Burias, pointing.

The Icon Bearer had joined Marduk a moment before, his face and arms caked in drying blood, and he stood alongside his Dark Apostle, staring westward across the gleaming marble city. Marduk looked where Burias indicated, and the targeting matrices built into his helmet flashed momentarily as they locked onto fast-moving shapes, flying low and jinking around columns and statues, before he lost them again within the maze of streets.

'Land Speeders sighted,' relayed Marduk.

The anti-grav vehicles were moving at great speed as they roared through the city, closing the distance swiftly. They had split into two groups, one gunning their engines towards Sabtec's position and the other moving towards Marduk's.

Through the thick artillery smoke, larger shapes could be seen flying low over the rooftops, approaching fast – Thunderhawks, gleaming white and adorned with the blue eagle head motif of the White Consuls. Missiles streaked from beneath their stubby wings, and heavy battle cannons roared.

Marduk glanced up at the mass transports and heavy shuttles descending through the upper atmosphere. They were coming down painfully slowly, retros burning fiercely to control their momentum, and he knew that they were at their most vulnerable now. The contents of those transports were incalculably valuable; ensuring their unmolested arrival was of paramount importance for the success of this war.

The enemy's intention was obvious – take these towers back and blast those mass transports to pieces before they landed. They were not fools, clearly; they understood how much of an impact the precious engines held within those transports would have in the forthcoming ground war.

The Land Speeders appeared again suddenly, only a few hundred metres away, banking sharply around the corner of a domed cathedral and roaring towards the defence tower, heavy bolters barking. They were about twenty metres off the ground, and as soon as they appeared, dozens of bolters and heavier weapons began to target them. They jinked from side to side, avoiding the worst of the incoming fire, and Marduk was forced to duck as heavy bolter rounds stitched across the battlements of the tower, ripping out chunks of marble.

One of the enemy vehicles was struck by a lascannon, taking the driver's head off and ripping a hole through its engines. The Land Speeder veered sharply and spun out of control, trailing black smoke, before smashing into a towering Space Marine statue atop a pillar, shattering like glass as it struck the stone figure at full speed.

The remainder kept coming, and split smoothly into three distinct groups.

One group, using the buildings opposite the defence tower to protect them from ground fire, rose to be level with Marduk's position and hovered in place, raking the walls with assault cannons and heavy bolters. Under this cover, a handful of speeders – their chassis longer than the others – rose and banked sharply, heading westward over the rooftops before lingering over a heavily defensible building nearby. As the sights in his helmet zoomed in, Marduk saw lightly armoured Scouts rappelling from them onto the building's roof, sniper rifles slung across their backs.

The third group dipped low, and disappeared from sight.

'Enemy snipers moving into position,' Marduk said. 'I have target-marked their last sighted location.'

'Acknowledged,' came Kol Badar's reply. 'Sabtec, be wary; that is near your position.'

'Understood,' said the exalted champion of the decorated 13th Coterie.

Marduk rose and snapped off a shot with his bolt pistol, which glanced off the armoured screen in front of an enemy gunner. One of his brethren nearby rose and fired a missile from his launcher that ripped apart a Land Speeder in a blinding explosion.

As if that had been a signal, the others dropped sharply, engines roaring and they disappeared from sight.

Marduk glanced over the parapet and saw White Consuls vehicles moving swiftly up the streets, having been dropped in by Thunderhawks. He also saw Rhino APCs, Predators and other vehicles that he had no name for, variations of the Rhino pattern that he had not encountered before.

'Enemy armour, moving on my position,' said Marduk.

'Received and moving to intercept,' replied Kol Badar.

Further communication was forestalled as hissing static interference suddenly washed the comms-network across all channels.

'Curse them,' snarled Marduk. 'We are being jammed.'

There was a roar of engines close by, and a strong downdraft struck Marduk. He looked up to see a Land Speeder hovering directly overhead. White Consuls Scouts were rappelling from it onto the roof of the tower.

"Ware the sky!' roared Marduk, as he began to fire. He caught one of the Scouts in the back of the head, killing him instantly, before the remainder ducked out of sight. He saw four Land Speeders veering away, just a fraction of a second before a hail of small projectiles were lobbed towards his position.

'Grenades!' roared Marduk, throwing himself back inside the tower. The concussive explosions of the frag grenades picked him up and hurled him inside, razor-tipped shards of shrapnel embedding in his power armour.

He crashed down, red warning lights flashing before his eyes. One of his brothers was nearby, armour blackened and filled with fragmentation shards. Marduk barked a warning as the warrior rose to his feet. Before the warrior could respond, his head was pulped by a shotgun blast fired at close range.

Burias was picking himself up off the floor nearby, snarling. The left side of his face was a blackened ruin of charred flesh, and he was about to hurl himself back out onto the battlements when there was a crash behind them, and a shower of plasglass.

Marduk spun to see a white-armoured Astartes figure on one knee behind him, smoke billowing from its bulky jump pack, plasglass surrounding it. Before he could fire, Marduk saw looming shadows appear outside, and more Space Marines suddenly crashed through the plasglass, jump packs and chainswords roaring.

Acrid exhaust fumes filled the interior of the control room, and

Marduk rose to his feet, firing. He hit one of the Assault Marines in the chest, but the bolt was unable to penetrate the thick ceramite armour, merely knocking the warrior back half a step.

Marduk felt a surge of warp energy as Drak'shal rose to power within Burias's flesh. Roaring in infernal fury, the possessed warrior leapt past him, bowling one of the Assault Marines to the ground, talons digging through power armour. A bolt hit Marduk in the shoulder, half spinning him, and he snarled, firing a pair of shots in retaliation.

Holstering the sidearm, Marduk took hold of his crozius in two hands and leapt forwards to meet the advancing Assault Marines head-on, bellowing his hatred. He ducked beneath a buzzing chainsword and slammed his crozius into the side of his attacker, the spiked head of the holy weapon penetrating ceramite and crackling with energy as it knocked the White Consul aside.

Marduk swayed backwards and a chainsword, roaring furiously, tore through the air where his head had been a fraction of a second earlier. He only just managed to get his weapon into the path of the return blow, his muscles straining against the strength of his opponent. The teeth of the madly whirring chainsword ripped at his crozius, threatening to tear it from his grip. Marduk kicked the White Consuls Assault Marine away from him, straight into the path of Burias-Drak'shal, who impaled the warrior upon the Host's icon, lifting the spitted enemy warrior off his feet before hurling him aside.

A chainsword tore into Burias-Drak'shal's neck, ripping at power armour and flesh, and blood sprayed out. He roared in fury and pain and spun, dropping to one knee and smashing the legs from under his attacker with a sweep of his bladed icon. Before he could leap upon the downed warrior and finish him, a bolt hit him in the back, making him stumble forwards, and he lost his grip on the icon.

A bolt pistol was levelled at the possessed Icon Bearer's head, but with preternatural speed he swayed to the side, avoiding the shot, and as another chainsword roared in at him, Burias-Drak'shal merely grabbed the whirring blade in one hand, blood splattering as he pulled the wielder towards him. With the palm of his other hand he struck the White Consul under the chin, snapping his head back sharply and exposing his neck. Still holding the chainsword tightly in one hand, blood continuing to splatter out as its mechanisms strained to rip the flesh from his bones, Burias-Drak'shal lunged forwards and tore the White Consul's throat.

A shotgun blast took one of Marduk's companions in the back, knocking him forwards and into the path of the blue helmeted veteran sergeant of the Assault Marines, who used his full body weight to deliver a powerful punch with a massive power gauntlet. The blow sundered the Word Bearer's chest plate and the fused ribcage within, pulping his twin hearts and sending him crashing to his back, flickers of electrical energy dancing across his exposed chest cavity.

Marduk deflected a swinging blow aimed at his head and risked a glance onto the battlements, seeing several squads of Scouts dropping down onto the area he had recently vacated, combat shotguns held in their hands. More Assault Marines crashed through the tinted plasglass, and another of his brethren went down, impaled on a chainsword that ripped and tore at his flesh, splattering hot blood across the room.

'Back!' shouted Marduk, swallowing down his bitterness. 'Pull back!'

WITH SMOKE SPEWING from its daemon-headed exhausts, the Land Raider smashed through the wall, rockcrete and marble crumbling around it. It came down hard, powering onto a quad-laned road, and with a sickening crunch ploughed straight into the side of a White Consuls Rhino. The smaller APC was slammed sidewards, tracks skidding on the rockcrete roadway before it was rammed at speed into the corner of a building and came to shocking halt.

Dust and rock crumbled from the building, crashing down upon the vehicle's armoured roof. The Rhino's engines spluttered and died, and smoke rose from its buckled chassis. The Land Raider roared, tracks spinning into reverse, kicking up rocks and dust as it spun around to face the other enemy vehicles in the convoy.

Two Rhinos had slewed to the side and ground to a halt, their occupants spilling from within. The White Consuls dropped into cover on either side of the road, bolters bucking in their hands. The Word Bearers Land Raider fired and its twin-linked lascannon struck one of the Rhinos as it started to reverse, punching a pair of gaping holes through its armour and engine block. Its heavy bolters chased the White Consuls as they ducked into cover.

The Land Raider's assault hatch slammed down on the rubble strewn across the road. Kol Badar was first out, his combi-bolter blazing. He ordered his Anointed forward, while he strode towards the Rhino that his Land Raider had just rammed.

Smoke was rising from the wreck, and as Kol Badar reached the vehicle its side hatch slammed open. He grabbed the first White Consul to emerge by the head, his power talons closing around the Astartes's helmet. With a wrench, Kol Badar dragged the warrior out and lifted his combi-bolter, spraying bolts into the crowded interior. Kol Badar twisted his power talons, ripping the head off the White Consul held in his clutches, and continued firing. When he had exhausted a full clip he switched to the flamer affixed to his combi-bolter and filled the inside of the APC with burning promethium.

Satisfied, Kol Badar turned away, and began stalking towards the other enemy warriors, who were engaged in a brutal, close range firefight with his advancing Anointed brethren. Four lascannon beams hit the second Rhino, and it exploded in a blinding fireball, flipping end over end ten metres into the air before smashing back to the ground as a blackened, twisted heap of metal.

Targeting icons flashed as they identified heavily armoured tanks further up the roadway, turning southward.

'Tanks moving on your position, Sabtec,' he said, reloading.

'UNDERSTOOD,' SAID SABTEC, his hand held to his ear. He had formed a perimeter around the outside of the silenced defence laser turret that he had been assigned to secure, his warriors hunkered down behind makeshift barricades.

'13th!' he shouted. 'Incoming armour!'

'The attack on my position was a feint,' came the crackling voice of First Acolyte Ashkanez across the vox. 'Moving to support you.'

Seeing the enemy tanks hove into view, Sabtec gritted his teeth.

'You had better hurry, First Acolyte,' he replied. 'The 13th will hold as long as able.'

Half a dozen enemy vehicles had rounded a bend three hundred metres from his position, and were rumbling towards his cordon. At the forefront was a pair of Predators, Destructor-pattern: heavily armoured front-line battle tanks with rotating autocannon turrets and heavy bolter side sponsons. The autocannon turrets began to fire towards his position, tearing huge chunks out of the tower behind him, and Sabtec grimaced.

With clipped orders he organised his defence, redeploying the two Havoc squads accompanying him into enfilading fire positions and picking out the prime targets. With a nod, he ordered the lascannon-wielding heavy weapon specialist within his own 13th Coterie to fire, but just as the warrior's finger squeezed the trigger he jerked backwards, the back of his head blown out.

'Sniper!' roared Sabtec, throwing himself towards his fallen brother to commandeer the heavy weapon. '27th Coterie, do you see them?'

A burst of heavy bolter fire from atop the defence tower roared in answer.

'Three confirmed kills, Exalted Champion Sabtec,' replied the squad champion of 27th.

'Be vigilant,' said Sabtec. 'There will be more of them up there.'

He hefted the lascannon onto his shoulder and flicked out its optical sight. He did not unhook the heavy power generator from his fallen brother's back – he did not have time – and the insulated cables connecting the bulky weapon hummed as he linked to its targeting systems.

The enemy tanks had fired smoke and blind grenades; broad-spectrum electro-magnetic radiation blinding both sensors and scans as well as blocking conventional sight. Sabtec swore.

He aimed the lascannon into the thick smoke that confused his auto-sensors. The edge of the smoke was no more than a hundred metres off, and he panned left and right as he sought a target.

Abruptly, he saw headlights appear through the smoke and his target icons flashed red. He swung the lascannon around towards them and fired

The shot glanced off the Predator's angled fore-armour. Sabtec gritted his teeth in frustration as the weapon began to power up again, venting steam.

'Come on,' he said as more enemy vehicles materialised out of the blinding fog, moving at speed towards him.

Missiles streamed from the Havoc team on his left, and an enemy Rhino ground to a halt as its tracks were torn clear. Autocannons ripped across armoured plates and tore a barking heavy bolter sponson loose from a Predator. The turret of the battle tank turned molten, dripping down over its hull like wax as a plasma cannon found its mark.

The heavy vehicles gunned their engines and accelerated.

The Predator unleashed a torrent from its weapon systems, raking fire across the Word Bearers line, and bolters began to roar as White Consuls disembarked from their Rhinos. A melta blast seared a burning hole through the marble balustrade that Sabtec knelt behind, but he remained unfazed as he calmly waited for his weapon to reach full power.

Bolts ricocheted off the marble around him, and as a blinking red icon turned green, he took careful aim and squeezed the lascannon's trigger.

The shot hit a Predator in its armoured vision slit, burning straight through the high-compound reinforced plasglass and killing the tank's driver instantly. The Predator slewed to the side and struck a Rhino, half spinning it, before ploughing up a bank of marble stairs and ramming into a wall. The tank's turret started to turn, but a well-aimed missile hit the Predator's exposed rear. There was a muted explosion and smoke and flames began pouring from inside, and the turret froze.

No more than two metres from Sabtec, a warrior dropped without a sound as a result of sniper fire, half his helmet blowing out in a blossoming cloud of blood. Sabtec ditched the lascannon and threw himself to the side as a Rhino, an immense dozer blade painted in yellow and black chevrons affixed to its front, ploughed towards him. Bolts and autocannon rounds pinged off the thick protective dozer blade, and the APC drove straight through the balustrade, debris, chunks of masonry and fallen statues smashed out of its path.

Side hatches slammed open and enemy Astartes leapt out, bolters barking. A shot took Sabtec in the side of the head, obscuring his vision as sparks and smoke filled his helmet. Firing his bolter one-handed, he ripped his helmet off, and the full sound and scent of battle crashed in on him.

Blood was dripping down his face as Sabtec ordered the 13th to reform and fall back now that their defensive position had been compromised.

He saw two of his brothers torn to shreds by concentrated bursts of close-range fire, but continued to issue his orders with cool detachment.

'I could really do with that support, First Acolyte,' said Sabtec, calmly.

'Hold on, brother,' came Ashkanez's voice across the vox. 'Closing on your position. One minute.'

Sabtec drew his power sword. Its hilt resembled bones blackened in fire. It hummed into life as he thumbed its activation rune. He dropped to one knee as a burst of bolter fire tore through the air above him, and fired his bolter one-handed, the shot taking a White Consul in the head, then rose to his feet again, slashing upwards with his power sword.

The humming blade caught another White Consul under the chin, slicing up through his power armour like a lascutter and carving his jaw in two.

Flamers roared, bathing the assaulting White Consuls in burning pro-methium, scorching battle plate black. A roaring chainaxe hacked the head from a loyalist, but the victorious Word Bearer was then himself slain, a plasma pistol fired up close slamming him backwards.

Another enemy vehicle was halted, a missile impacting into its side and slewing it sidewards. The enemy attack was faltering, Sabtec real-ised, and he ordered his warriors to converge. He emerged from cover and began to advance upon the enemy, who had taken up position behind the same cover that the 13th had been using moments before.

The concealing smoke fired by the enemy vehicles was drifting down the avenue, becoming patchy, but it suddenly cleared as the huge shape of a White Consuls Thunderhawk came screaming low over the rooftops and descended sharply. The downdraft of its powerful engines sent eddies of dust and smoke fleeing before it, and multiple heavy bolters opened up, their heavy thuds barely heard over the deafening Thunder-hawk's engines.

Before the Thunderhawk's landing gear touched the ground, the Land Raider held tight to the gunship's belly was released, couplings unlocked, and it dropped the last few metres to the ground, where it bounced once before settling.

More heavy weapon fire stabbed into the Thunderhawk's hull, shattering one of the windows of its cockpit and damaging one of its engine turbines, and it lifted off again, engines roaring. It banked vio-lently as it rose, and was gone.

The massive Land Raider's flanks were gleaming white and adorned with gold, and royal blue banners hung from its side. It was rumbling forwards, and unleashed a heavy fusillade that ripped one of his Havoc squads to pieces.

'Enemy Land Raider has dropped in at my position,' said Sabtec coolly, raising his voice to be heard over the roaring gun battle.

Backing away towards cover, snapping off shots with his ornate bolter one-handed, Sabtec gave clipped orders to target the heavy battle tank.

A squad of Word Bearers was almost completely annihilated as the Land Raider unleashed its fury. It had a weapon outfit that Sabtec was not familiar with. Ranks of bolters had replaced the standard lascannon side-sponsons – six bolters per side – and twin-linked assault cannons were built into its front turret. Clearly, it was a pattern designed for frontal assault, and it performed that role admirably.

Missiles and lascannons struck the Land Raider as it powered forwards, but they had little effect. It came through the heavy barrage like an enraged beast, shaking off everything that the Word Bearers threw at it. It smashed the smoking chassis of an immobilised Rhino out of its path. Sabtec gunned down another White Consul, then grunted in pain as a bolt hit him in the wrist. The explosive round took his hand clear off. It landed some metres away, still clutching his ornate bolter, and he frowned in irritation at having been disarmed.

The hulking behemoth smashed a path towards the 13th Coterie, crushing a low wall beneath its tread. Sabtec registered that there were explosive charges set to either side of the Land Raider's assault ramp a fraction of a second before they were fired, and he threw himself down behind a fallen statue. Above him, the air was suddenly filled with shrapnel as the assault launchers detonated, unleashing a swathe of destruction that tore one of his 13th brothers to shreds.

Then the assault ramp of the Land Raider slammed down, and Sabtec glimpsed a massive warrior striding from within, bedecked in gleaming Terminator armour, a billowing blue tabard across his body. A golden metal halo framed his head. In his right hand he held a thunder hammer. Across his left arm was strapped a crackling storm shield shaped like an oversized crux terminatus. A Chapter Master, Sabtec realised.

A Librarian emerged alongside the heavily armoured commander, a nimbus of shimmering light emitting from his psychic hood. A command squad followed them. Caught between these newcomers and the other White Consuls closing in to either side, there was nowhere for Sabtec to fall back to, no room for manoeuvre. For all his tactical savvy and strategic brilliance, all the experience garnered from thousands of years of constant warfare, he had few options.

Nevertheless, death held no fear for him.

'Thirteen!' he roared, rising from his cover, one side of which was pockmarked with shrapnel. 'With me!'

His surviving Coterie brothers rose from cover and charged after him. Bolters pumped shots towards the Chapter Master and his entourage, then Sabtec broke into a run, brandishing his humming power sword.

He saw one of the enemy, an Apothecary, lose an arm, and a dozen holes were shot through the banner that was unfurled as its bearer stepped from within the Land Raider. The banner bearer was felled a moment later, his faceplate shattered by a concentrated burst of fire. The standard of the Chapter teetered and started to fall.

Everything seemed to be happening in slow motion.

Bolts screamed past Sabtec's head, missing him by centimetres, and he registered one of his 13th brothers' dying roar as he fell beneath a meltagun blast. Another brother fell as the twin-linked assault cannons of the Land Raider tore him in half at the waist. Sabtec heard the warrior still shouting litanies of Lorgar as he crawled towards the enemy before a bolt silenced him.

A warrior armed with power sword and buckler, his blue crusade-era helmet adorned with a red crest of stiffened hair, stepped in front of the Chapter Master, his voice ringing with challenge.

Sabtec rolled beneath the enemy's attack and smashed his power sword into the enemy champion's head as he came to his feet. The warrior fell silently, leaving the path to the White Consuls Chapter Master clear.

With a snarl, Sabtec leapt forwards. His first blow was smashed aside by his enemy's heavy storm shield. His second was cut short as the White Consul's immense thunder hammer smashed down on his forearm, shattering his bones. His power sword, that revered weapon that had been gifted him by Erebus himself, dropped from fingers that no longer worked, and Sabtec stared up into the face of the White Consuls Chapter Master.

'Emperor damn you, heretic,' said the White Consul.

'We're all damned,' Sabtec breathed, 'You, me, all of us. This whole galaxy will burn.'

'That time is not yet upon us,' growled the White Consuls Chapter Master, and hefted his thunder hammer to deliver the killing blow.

A plasma blast struck the Chapter Master's hammer-arm, distracting him just long enough for Sabtec to roll away. He rose to see the arrival of First Acolyte Ashkanez, firing a plasma pistol. Two-score warriors charged behind him, and now outnumbered, the enemy began to fall back.

'Your timing is impeccable, First Acolyte,' said Sabtec.

MARDUK CURSED AS he slammed his last sickle clip into his MkII bolt pistol.

Almost half the warrior-brothers that had accompanied him in taking the enemy defence tower had fallen. He and the last survivors were holed up in the lower levels, guarding the way down to the defence laser's controls, ensuring that the potent weapon did not come back online.

Another of his brothers fell, a crater in his chest, splattering Marduk with blood.

'Kol Badar,' snarled Marduk as he leant around a corner and fired. He ducked back as White Consuls returned fire. 'How long until those damned transports are down?'

'Five minutes more,' came the reply.

'Five minutes,' said Marduk. 'And how long until I get some support?'

'Entering the compound now,' said Kol Badar. 'Two other towers have fallen. It's just minutes before their defence lasers are back online.'

'Perfect,' said Marduk.

The sound of distant gunfire and shouting came to Marduk's ears.

'You are in?' said Marduk.

'Affirmative. Perimeter breached,' said Kol Badar.

'Come brothers,' snarled Marduk. 'Let us drive these loyalist filth before us like dogs.'

'We go to kill the Emperor?' said the hulking Warmonger, standing before the defence laser's control panels, clenching his power talons in eagerness.

'His minions,' said Marduk. He motioned towards the corner. 'After you, revered one.'

The Dreadnought growled and broke into a run that made the ground shake. He rounded the corner, smashing loose marble slabs from the walls, and hundreds of bolt rounds pinged off his armour.

'Kill them all!' roared Marduk, right behind the Warmonger.

A HUNDRED SOLDIERS of the Boros Imperial Guard surrounded Coadjutor Aquilius as he pushed on the enemy position. He could feel the pride of the soldiers to be fighting alongside Astartes, and he smiled grimly. He towered over them, like an adult amongst a sea of children. One of the defence lasers that the Guardsmen, *his* Guardsmen, had retaken fired suddenly with a crackling boom that made his ears ache.

One of the huge, cylindrical mass transports descending planetward was struck, shearing a devastating wound up its side and destroying one of its mass stabilisers in an explosion of fire and sparks. They were the largest drop-ships he had ever seen, and he felt some consternation as he looked upon them, knowing the terrible machines they contained. Consternation was about as close to fear as he had ever come since his indoctrination into the Chapter. He vaguely remembered the emotion from childhood, but it meant nothing to him now.

With some satisfaction, he saw the mass transport begin to accelerate towards the ground, tipping to one side as it came down, its stabilisers unbalanced. It accelerated past the other transports, its velocity increasing rapidly. In satisfaction, he saw another defence laser strike a second of the descending transport cylinders.

'Brace yourselves,' said Aquilius.

The container struck the surface of Boros Prime fifteen kilometres away. A section of the city five hundred metres in diameter was crushed beneath its weight. An obscuring cloud of dust and smoke spread in all directions like a widening ripple in a pond, shaking the city to its foundations. The ground shuddered and a rising mushroom cloud of dust erupted hundreds of metres into the air. The deafening boom of the impact reached them a moment later, so loud it was as if the planet were splitting in two.

As the sound of the collapsing city section subsided, there came the horrible death cry of something unnameable. Images of the warp, of tentacles flailing from the void, filled Aquilius's mind.

'What do they contain, sir?' said the recently promoted trooper, Verenus. The soldier's superior, the regiment's ageing Legatus, had died just minutes earlier, his torso torn apart in a bloody explosion as a bolt detonated within his chest. Aquilius had promoted Verenus to the position as acting regimental commander of the Boros 232nd.

'Corrupted engines of the Adeptus Mechanicus,' said Aquilius.

He regarded the trooper. Verenus was still in shock at his sudden rise to power, but was handling it well. The poster child for the ideal Boros Prime Guardsman, Verenus was strong and self-assured, his eyes an icy blue and his hair bleached pale from sun and radiation. Aquilius had been impressed by the 3rd Prime Cohort's combat record, but it had been because of Verenus that Aquilius had chosen them to accompany him on this mission. The man had impressed him on the parade grounds of Boros Prime months earlier.

Throne, he thought. Had it been only months? It seemed like a lifetime. There were few regiments on Boros Prime that had as much combat experience as these men, and they had not disappointed. Aquilius could see the effect that fighting alongside Astartes was having on them – the Guardsmen stood taller, their chests puffed out proudly, despite having recently lost their commanding officer.

A great cheer went up from the Guardsmen as the mass transport crashed to earth, but Aquilius's mood was still grim. One had been destroyed and another was plummeting to the ground, but that still left three untouched.

They descended to the ground seemingly in violation of the laws of gravity, coming down slowly and steadily, grav-motors, stabilisers and thrusters bearing them sedately towards the surface of Boros Prime. They were hateful, vile things, with giant, mechanical tentacles beneath them that waved lazily in the air like sea-fronds in a current.

The first of the massive transports touched down in the middle of a distant square, causing another violent earth tremor. Instantly, giant tentacles flailed, ripping at the armoured sides of the cylinder, tearing the armoured sheath away like it was sloughed off skin.

Until now, the reality of the situation had not been fully driven home to Aquilius. The enemy had a foothold on his beloved home world. Worse, they had unleashed terrors of such power entire cities would be razed to the ground.

A ululating roar echoed across the city, followed by another. Aquilius glimpsed two of the terrible engines as they loped from their cylindrical cages. They stood as tall as a five-storey building, and though he knew these were but the smallest of the enemy Titans – corrupted Warhounds – he felt again a stab of consternation.

'Titans,' hissed Verenus, his eyes widening.

'They are the remnants of one of the cursed Legios that sided against the Emperor in ages past,' Aquilius told him.

The White Consul felt the resolve of the soldiers around him waver in the face of the daemonic Titans.

'By the grace of the Emperor,' breathed one soldier.

'Titans?' muttered another. 'What hope have–'

'There is always hope,' Aquilius said forcefully, cutting the soldier off. '*Always*. I am a son of Boros, as are you. As are we all. Our bloodline is a bloodline of heroes, and this is our world. The enemy thinks they can take it from us, but we will show them their error. We will punish them for every metre of ground they take, striking hard and without fear, for we are sons of Boros, and we shall not falter. The Emperor is with us, my brothers, and mark my words: Boros Prime *will not fall*.'

MARDUK'S EYES BURNED with zealous fury as he picked his way through the sea of bodies left in the wake of the Warmonger. Belagosa and Ankh-Heloth were inbound, leading their warriors against the other prime targets. He smiled grimly, exposing serrated, shark-like teeth. It had been costly, but Marduk had gained their foothold on the planet.

Now its corruption would begin.

BOOK FOUR: THE TAINT

'A man can be convinced to do anything, no matter how abhorrent, with the right motivation.'

– First Chaplain Erebus

CHAPTER ELEVEN

THE CLEAR BLUE skies of Boros Prime were long gone. In their place, the atmosphere was thick with rust-coloured haze, choking pollutants and vile toxins. The twin suns, bright and clear before the arrival of the Word Bearers, were now barely discernible, hidden behind the festering cloud. The temperature and humidity of Boros soared. An ever-thickening pall of smoke hung low over the war-torn cities of the Imperial world, heavy with cinders and ash that caught in the throat and made breathing for the unaugmented difficult and painful.

Tens of millions had already perished, and the corruption of the planet and its occupants was well underway.

Legatus Verenus, acting regimental commander of the Boros 232nd, slammed the butt of his lasgun into the face of the cultist, splintering the traitor's nose across his face. The man refused to go down, growling and hissing like an animal, hands like claws scrabbling for Verenus's eyes.

The traitor's face was so twisted with hatred that it was barely human at all. Fire-blackened hooks pinned the man's eyelids open, and an eight-pointed star had been cut into his forehead, leaking blood. He was a vision of depravity, but what sickened Verenus most of all was that the man wore a breastplate of the Boros Guard; once, mere weeks or days past perhaps, this man had given praise to the Emperor of Mankind and fought alongside him. What had the enemy done to him to make him fall so low?

Verenus smashed away the man's clutching hands and again slammed the butt of his lasgun into the man's face. The savage cultist staggered back a step, giving Verenus the space he needed. He reversed his grip on his weapon and shot the man in the chest. The traitor collapsed with a gargled sigh, a searing black hole burnt through his chest. The stink of melting plastek and charred flesh stung Verenus's nostrils.

More cultists were rushing his position, a veritable flood of heretics that bayed for blood like wild dogs.

'Back!' roared Verenus, snapping off shots into the mob as he walked steadily backwards. 'Move to the fallback position!'

The Guardsmen of the 2nd Cohort fell back along the war-torn street, gunning down scores of screaming heretics as they moved. Explosions from grenades and rockets rocked the ground beneath Verenus's feet, and aircraft screamed overhead through the smoke and fire. Heavy stubbers positioned behind shuttered windows above opened up, providing covering fire for the retreating soldiers. Muzzle flare spat from barrels of the clattering weapons, and empty shells fell down to the street below in a deluge, the sound of them hitting the ground like the jingling of wind chimes. In the distance, the heavy thump of siege mortars and Whirlwinds could be heard, followed a few seconds later by the shriek of incoming artillery.

The street was a shattered ruin, lined by the skeletal shells of buildings. Rubble was piled high, and the dead littered the ground, piled in gutters and at the base of crumbling walls. An all-pervading stink hung in the humid air, rancid and foul, like rotting meat. Verenus blinked soot and sweat out of his eyes as he backed away, snapping off shots with his lasgun, too busy just trying to keep his soldiers alive another day, another hour to allow the direness of his situation to press upon him.

It had been two months since the enemy had first descended upon Boros Prime, and the beautiful cities of Verenus's home world were almost unrecognisable. They had been turned into a living hell, once majestic tree-lined boulevards reduced to scorched rubble, the clear blue skies thick with black smoke and wheeling creatures that defied description.

The once proud citizens of Boros Prime – or at least those that had not yet been slaughtered or taken – now bore haunted, hunted expressions. Every citizen of Boros Prime of eligible age, no matter his or her standing or profession, underwent years of military training. Every able man, woman and child had been issued with a lasgun and formed into auxiliary units to support the PDF and Guard units.

Nevertheless, it was one thing to know how to arm and fire a lasgun, another to face an enemy such as they faced, day in day out, and to see one's home world torn apart by warfare. The enemy's corrupt presence could be felt everywhere, a vile, malignant touch that plagued the minds of every one of the Imperial world's defenders.

Verenus had not had a decent nights sleep since the enemy's arrival, plagued with violent nightmares filled with blood and malevolent, skin-less daemons that had him awake and screaming minutes after closing his eyes. It was the same with everyone and Verenus knew that these were no normal dreams – they were an insidious weapon of the enemy, designed to sow terror and despair amongst the regiments. Damn them, but it was working, Verenus thought.

It had become so bad that Verenus was starting to see those skinless daemons while he was awake. He saw them leering at him from the cor-ner of his eye, but whenever he turned towards them there was nothing there. Sleep deprivation, he told himself. You are imagining things. If he, a veteran with decades of fighting against the minions of the Ruin-ous Powers under his belt, was becoming unnerved by the dreams, then he could only imagine what it would be doing to the minds of those not trained for war. Indeed, suicides had already accounted for one man in twenty within the Guard units, a staggering total when one considered how many soldiers were fighting here on Boros.

Tens of millions had been killed in battle. Millions more, the unlucky ones, had been taken by the enemy. Verenus grimaced to think of their fate. He'd put a las-round in his head before he allowed such a fate to claim him.

He could hear the enemy chanting as they approached. It was a deep, mournful sound, filled with hatred. An even worse sound accompanied them – a hellish blare of insanity that made Verenus's flesh crawl. It felt as though something was scratching painfully behind his eardrums, penetrating his head and reverberating within his mind. It made him feel sick, and his gorge rose.

The infernal chanting was deeply unnerving, and he had already seen more than a dozen soldiers succumb to its madness, men that the com-missars were forced to put down as insanity claimed them.

It sounded like a faulty vox-unit, amplified a hundred times louder, deafening static overlaid with screams, whispers, roars, the sound of children crying. The pounding industrial clamour was overlaid with the sound of women screaming in unwholesome pleasure, of bones break-ing, of animals howling in pain and terror.

Verenus had come to associate it with Chaos itself, the sound of bed-lam and despair. He heard it when he slept, insinuating itself into his dreams, and it was always there in the back of his head, even when the hideous floating machines that projected the discordant sound were nowhere nearby.

Verenus ducked around the corner of a building and pressed himself back against the wall. Weapon lifted to his shoulder, he glanced around the corner. Most of the cultists his cohort had ambushed were dead, but it was not them that drew his attention. Through the fire and smoke he saw first one, then more of the hellish, red-armoured enemy, their faces obscured behind horned helmets fashioned into the horrific visage of beasts and daemons. The huge figures moved forward steadily, bellowing their hateful catechisms as they came.

'Move it, soldiers! Move,' Verenus bellowed. Then the enemy Astartes began to fire, and his words were drowned out by the noise.

A dozen soldiers of the 232nd were gunned down before Verenus's eyes as they raced for cover, their bodies ripped apart as bolter fire raked across their backs. One of his men stumbled only metres from the corner as a ricochet clipped the back of his knee; the soldier fell with a cry.

Verenus swore and ducked back around the corner, snapping off a pair of shots as he moved to the soldier's aid. He saw one of his shots strike an enemy square in the forehead, but it did not even slow the warrior. The wall behind Verenus collapsed as a bolt struck it, showering him with dust and rock. Verenus kept moving, and dropped to one knee before the fallen soldier. He fired off another hastily aimed shot, and gripped the soldier by the scruff of his uniform, hauling him back into cover.

Heavy stubbers ripped across the advancing enemy, buying the retreating soldiers precious moments, but the traitors kept advancing steadily, gunning down more Boros Guardsmen with every burst of fire. One of the Word Bearers fired up at a window, almost casually taking out one of the heavy weapon operators. His head exploded, spraying blood and brain matter across the face of his shocked comrade, reams of ammunition still held in his hands.

There was only a handful of the traitor Space Marines, Verenus saw. Even so, it was enough. He had learnt the hard way that each of those cursed giants was easily the equivalent of thirty or forty of his own battle-hardened veteran Guardsmen, or more than a hundred auxiliary draftees. More, perhaps. Each one of the bastards that his regiment took down was cause for celebration.

He had been engaged with the enemy in constant battle for the past two months, and though the war had devolved into a horrid, bloody grind, he knew that they were winning.

Tank companies and hundreds of millions of soldiers fought the enemy toe-to-toe, day in day out, and it had become an exercise of military logistics, a constant rotation of regiments to and from the front in order to maintain pressure. The Word Bearers could not keep up this pace forever, and would eventually be ground down, or at least Verenus prayed that this would be so, but how many Imperial citizens would be lost in the meanwhile? What would be left of Boros Prime once the dust settled? Nothing worth salvaging, he thought darkly.

'Thank you, sir,' said the soldier that he had just hauled to safety, and he nodded to him. A pair of Guardsmen lifted the man from the ground, and hurried him away from danger.

Verenus signalled, and broke into a run, his soldiers scattering into the ruins at his order. He threw himself over a smashed low wall into what had once been a beautiful garden, and propped himself behind it, keeping his head down. Blackened skeletons of trees stood sentinel above him. With curt hand signals, he moved his troops into position. Soldiers hefted heavy tripod-mounted autocannons into cover, slamming them down behind low walls and piles of rubble and hurriedly loading them with fresh spools of ammunition.

'Come on, you bastards,' said Verenus.

He was lathered in sweat and grime, the unbearable Boros Prime heat only emphasised by the oppressive black smoke filling the sky. There was a horrible stink in the air, something akin to burnt flesh and bones. Verenus thought again of the men and women that the enemy had forced into servitude, slaving away upon the horrific construction works that were sprouting up all across the continent, corrupting them into base creatures that spurned the light of the Emperor.

There seemed to be some form of pattern to the location of the enemy's construction, but Verenus was damned if he knew what it was. He snorted without humour as he realised he probably *would* be damned if he understood.

A corrupted Guardsman was the first around the corner, diabolical symbols of the Ruinous Powers smeared in blood and faeces across his helmet and breastplate. He held a standard-issue lasgun in his hands, but was gunned down before he could raise it. Another heretic appeared, his face contorted with hatred and loathing, his blackened cheeks streaked with tears. He too was shot down, smoking burns riddling his chest and face.

The first of the Word Bearers rounded the corner, a hulking traitor encased in gore-splattered plate. Curving horns of obsidian rose from his helmet, which had been fashioned to resemble a snarling beast. Verenus fired. His lasgun beam struck the immense warrior in the chest, to little effect. From all around, dozens of blue lasbeams were fired as more of the hated traitors appeared. The heavy thump of autocannons joined the fusillade, spraying bullets across power-armoured foes.

One of the enemy went down, peppered with bullet craters and covered in lasburns. Verenus grinned savagely. That grin turned into a grimace as he saw the enemy warrior push himself back to his feet, blood and oil leaking from his wounds.

A handful of the Boros infantrymen were cut down with short bursts of enemy fire. The man next to Verenus was struck as he raised his lasgun to fire, the shot tearing his arm off and creating a gaping hole in his chest. He gaped up at Verenus in the second before he died, a look of shock on his blood-drenched face.

The enemy were moving steadily forwards, conserving ammunition as they took their shots with robotic precision. Few of their bolts did not find their mark, and any of his warriors that were hit suffered horrendous injuries. He fired another shot then ducked into cover as one of the enemy swung a bolter in his direction. Verenus dropped flat and began to crawl arm over arm to a new position as bolter fire smashed into his cover, blowing it away in explosive detonations.

'Armour in position, sir!' shouted one of his sergeants, a heavy vox-caster unit strapped to his back.

'Finally,' said Verenus. He turned and shouted, 'Back! Fall back!'

His soldiers responded instantly, slipping back into the rubble of the shattered buildings, snapping off occasional shots as they scrambled into heavier cover. Verenus pushed himself to his feet, and began running, keeping his profile low. A man further along the street turned and shouted something, but Verenus couldn't make it out. Then the man was killed, his torso becoming one huge, bloodied crater, and he fell without a sound. Glancing back, he saw the enemy perhaps halfway along the street. Verenus hurled himself over a fallen statue and dropped in behind it, his heart pounding, and gunfire zipped past him.

He heard the grind of engines nearby, followed closely by a crash that shook the ground. There was a whoop of joy from one of his soldiers, and he peered over the top of the fallen statue. His fire-blackened face broke into a smile as he saw a wall collapse, brought down by the dozer blades of three tracked armoured vehicles.

The tanks, a support division of the 53rd armoured company, were Hellhounds, close support vehicles based on the Chimera STC chassis. Armed with their flame-throwing Inferno cannons, they had proven themselves invaluable in the brutal, close quarter fighting on Boros Prime in the last months. While some battle tanks had proved unwieldy within the tight confines of the cityfight, the Hellhounds had excelled.

They rumbled through the dust and smoke, crunching over the rubble of the fallen wall. A half-cohort of the 232nd swarmed in their wake, scrambling to take position amongst the debris. Inferno cannons spewed liquid fire across the Word Bearers, who stoically refused to back away, bolters roaring even as they were consumed in flame.

Their armour cracked and blistered, but still they gunned down almost a score of Guardsmen before they fell. Their resilience and their absolute refusal to back down even in the face of certain death never ceased to stagger Verenus. One of the Hellhounds exploded in an incandescent plume of fire as krak grenades ignited its fuel reserve.

Only two of the enemy Astartes were still standing, bolters blazing in their hands when there came a hideous screeching sound from overhead.

'The sky!' shouted one of his men.

Verenus panned his weapon across the smoke-filled heavens. For a moment he saw nothing, then a blood-red flock of skinless, winged horrors swept over the rooftops, screaming towards the Boros soldiers.

'In the name of the Throne,' breathed Verenus, seeing his nightmares come to life.

The daemons, for they could have been nothing else, descended in a screeching rush, leathery wings tightly furled as they dropped towards the ground. They were horrific creatures, their glistening exposed musculature a perverted mockery of humanity. Lipless mouths were twisted into feral grins, exposing needle-like fangs, and barbed, serpentine tails of wet muscle trailed behind them as they hurtled towards the horrified soldiers below. Their forms shimmered like a mirage, as if they were at once there but not there, or perhaps existed simultaneously in more than one realm.

Cold fear gripping him, Verenus began to fire wildly up at the incoming daemons. His soldiers began to run.

The monsters swooped down low over the Boros 232nd, unfurling blade-like talons to slash at their prey. The face of one soldier was ripped off as claws hooked into his flesh. Several soldiers were lifted off their feet, talons locking around their necks and shoulders, and others fell screaming as daemons dropped upon them, bearing them to the ground under their weight, biting and ripping.

A wild shot from Verenus hit one of the creatures in its skinless head. Its flesh, the colour of raw liver, turned grey and black as it cooked, and it crashed to the ground, the bones of its wings snapping as it impacted and rolled, bowling one of his soldiers over in the process. The man screamed horribly as the creature tore at him, slashing with its talons and biting with its needle-fangs.

All semblance of order was lost. The Guardsmen of the Boros 232nd scattered blindly, and the daemons continued to sow their terror, ripping the soldiers apart in a gory frenzy.

Verenus was shouting orders, but no one heard him. Hot blood splashed across his face as the man at his side was slain, his throat torn out. Talons raked his shoulder, and Verenus screamed in pain, dropping his weapon. Wild with panic, one of his own soldiers ran into him blindly, desperate to escape, and Verenus was knocked to the ground. All hope was lost. Death had finally come for him.

A shadow descended on Verenus and he dropped to one knee, raising an arm protectively as a hideous, screeching fury hurtled overhead, talons slashing. He gasped as the daemon's claws locked shut around his forearm, digging deep into his flesh. His shoulder was almost torn from its socket as he was dragged to his feet. Leathery wings covered in a spider web of red and blue veins flapped heavily, and Verenus felt a sudden panic as his feet lost contact with the ground.

The fury looked down at him, snarling. Its eyes were yellow and catlike and oozed steaming, milky tears. It opened its mouth wide – too wide – and strings of saliva dripped from its needle-teeth. A dozen worm-like tongues squirmed in its throat, and Verenus felt its hot breath upon his face. It smelt like sulphur, rotting meat and electricity.

A heavy weight suddenly pulled the fury back down towards the earth, and it screeched in anger. It released Verenus, who fell to the ground heavily, and coiled around to slash at the figure that had a solid grip upon its tail.

From the ground, Verenus looked up to see an imposing figure surrounded in a halo of light, a holy aura that made his breath catch in his throat. For a moment it was as if time stood still. Verenus was not alone in witnessing this divine vision; all the soldiers of Boros Prime nearby saw it, this holy figure bathed in seraphic light.

The glowing nimbus lasted just a fraction of a second, and while the rational part of Verenus's mind insisted it was nothing but a momentary trick of the light reflecting off alabaster armour plates, the impression was indelible.

The halo bathing the figure dissipated, and the immense figure of a White Consul stood there, defiant and unwavering. Brother Aquilius, Coadjutor of Boros Prime, held the daemon by one of its hind legs. As it turned to swipe at him, spitting in hatred, he slammed his bolter into the side of its head. The force of the blow smashed it to the ground, crushing its skull.

Still alive, it landed heavily upon its back, and in one swift, violent movement it flipped itself over, snarling, crouched on all fours. Its tail cracked like a whip as it readied to spring, but before it could, Aquilius planted his foot upon its back and pinned it to the ground.

The White Consul pressed the barrel of his bolter against the back of its skinless head. It thrashed wildly but could not escape the crushing weight of the Space Marine.

'Begone daemon-spawn!' said Aquilius. The infernal beast's movements ceased as he planted a bolt in its head. Within seconds, the creature had rotted away, its flesh ridden with maggots and worms before liquefying, leaving just a foetid pool of foulness upon the ground.

'Be strong, men of Boros!' shouted the White Consul. 'The Emperor is with us!'

Verenus snatched up a lasgun from a fallen Guardsman and began firing on full auto, all fear evaporated. Other soldiers of the Boros 232nd fell in around Aquilius and Verenus, forming a tight knot of defiance anchored around the holy Astartes warrior.

One by one the screaming daemons were cut down, hissing ichor bursting from their Chaotic bodies, and Verenus felt savage joy to see the deviant, unholy beasts banished back to the warp.

In the aftermath of battle he felt exultant, invigorated and inspired. He had felt the presence of the Emperor in that battle, and he saw the same glow of belief reflected in the eyes of his soldiers.

'We are going to win this war, aren't we?' said one of his men.

'We are,' said Verenus, for the first time actually believing it. He turned his gaze towards Aquilius, talking softly with some of his soldiers. 'The White Angel is with us.'

* * *

To the Word Bearers, the battlefield was their most sacred church, and Boros Prime had become one immense battlefield. The full Hosts of three Dark Apostles had descended upon it, hatred in their hearts. Every death was a sacrifice, and Marduk could feel the gluttonous pleasure of his infernal deities. Yet he could also sense their impatience, mirroring his own, and those of his captains.

Marduk's chainsword was glutted with blood, but it still hungered for more. He was crouched low, moving towards the enemy position. He saw the enemy gathering for another assault, he knew that the daemon within his weapon, Borgh'ash, would not have long to wait.

'It offends me that we have not yet won this war,' came Kol Badar's voice in Marduk's ear. 'This wretched planet resists us with every step!'

Marduk and Kol Badar were communing over a closed vox-channel, their words heard by none but each other. The Coryphaus was located over a hundred kilometres away, in the north-east of the sprawling city known as Sirenus Principal, fighting to hold a key landing-zone from Imperial counterattack. The Imperial Guard, bolstered by White Consuls, had been battling for six solid days to retake the location.

'Their resistance is frustrating,' said Marduk. 'But it cannot last.'

He rose to his full height and dropped two Guardsmen with carefully aimed shots from his bolt pistol. Shouts and gunfire erupted all around him, and Marduk broke cover, closing the distance with the enemy swiftly.

'They threaten to overrun us at a score of key locations, through sheer numbers,' continued Kol Badar. 'The other Hosts too are struggling to maintain their footholds.'

'Our faith is our armour,' growled Marduk as he killed, tearing apart the chest of a Guardsman with his chainsword. He stepped forward and gunned down two more Guardsmen who were backing away from him, horror written across their faces. 'With true faith, nothing can harm us.'

'Empty rhetoric,' came Kol Badar's crackling reply. 'It means nothing.'

'Speak not such heresy, Kol Badar,' said Marduk, breaking the arm of a Guardsman with a backhand swipe, before clubbing him to the ground with his bolt pistol. He slammed his boot down upon the warrior's neck, breaking it with an audible crack. 'Armoured with true faith, nothing can defeat us.'

'All your praying will not stop their Bombards and Basilisks from ripping the Host to pieces, little by little.'

'We will break them,' said Marduk. 'Their world is falling around them. It will be only a matter of time before their will is broken.'

The Dark Apostle lowered his smoking bolt pistol as the enemy routed before him.

'Casualties?' he said over his shoulder.

'Two,' replied Sabtec, champion of the exalted 13th. 'Shulgar of 19th Coterie, and Erish-Bhor of the 52nd.'

'The enemy?' said Marduk, surveying the carnage before him. Bodies were strewn across the open square that the Imperials had been trying to retake.

Sabtec shrugged, the servo-motors of his power armour whining as they tried to replicate the movement.

'Two hundred, give or take.'

'A goodly sacrifice,' said Marduk.

Sabtec grunted in response, and the Dark Apostle could feel what his champion was thinking.

'Every one of their deaths brings us closer to victory,' he said. His words sounded hollow, even to his own ears.

Sabtec saluted and spun away, barking orders.

A hot wind clawed at Marduk's blood-matted cloak, bringing with it the redolence of butchery and oil, industry and suffering, and the insidious electric tang of Chaos itself.

The world was changing, and it would never again be the same. Like a worm wriggling its way through the core of an apple, the taint of Chaos was now rooted in the very substance of Boros Prime. Even if the Word Bearers were to leave, the Imperium would be forced to abandon it.

Even so, Marduk's face was grim. Victory was a certainty, he was sure of this, and yet with every passing day it seemed further from their grasp. The acidic taste of defeat was in his mouth, no matter how he tried to deny it.

His warriors were genetically enhanced killers armoured in the finest power armour. Each was more than a match for fifty or a hundred lesser mortals. Their weapons slew tens of thousands with every passing day, and their war engines sowed terror and destruction across the length and breadth of the world. A demi-Legion of Titans marched behind them, laying waste to entire cities.

Nevertheless, the number of XVII Legion warrior-brothers fighting upon the surface of Boros Prime numbered less than seven thousand all told, whereas Imperial vermin infested this world.

Boros Prime was home to more than twelve billion, and almost another two billion had been evacuated to the relative safety of the planet from its surrounding moons. More than half of that number served in its armed forces, or had been drafted into service. Every citizen of eligible age served a tenure in the Guard – even the bureaucrats and public servants knew their way around a lasgun and basic small-unit tactics. By Marduk's reckoning, the five thousand warriors of Lorgar faced off against nigh on ten billion soldiers. Added to the mix were the White Consuls, and while there were no more than three companies engaged here on Boros – three hundred loyalist Astartes – their mere presence bolstered the resolve of the Guardsmen, and they were always to be found in the thickest fighting. In these battles, neither side gave any quarter, their fury and hatred fuelled by ten thousand years of mutual loathing and bitterness. It was glorious.

Industrious forge-hives located towards the poles spewed out a constant stream of weapons and armour, and the smoking plains outside the world's sprawling cities were dominated by massive tank formations. The Titans of Legio Vulturus had stalked out to meet one of these grand tank companies, and had notched up a kill-tally numbering in the thousands. Nevertheless, these confirmed kills were rendered insignificant against the sheer number of tanks taking the field. Four Titans, ancient war engines that had stalked across battlefields for ten thousand years, were brought down and three others suffered crippling damage as their void shields and armoured carapaces were hammered by ordnance and focused battle cannon fire. One of the Titans, one hulking Warlord-class engine, now a daemonically infested monster, was laid low by a devastating barrage from super-heavy Shadowswords. Suffering these losses, the Legio had been forced from the plains back into the relative safety of Boros's cities.

Far to the north, in the frozen wastes, the Dark Apostle Belagosa, the ranks of his host swollen with the warriors of Sarabdal's Host, fought a bloody siege against the largest of the world's industrial forge-hives. Five thousand kilometres southward, Ankh-Heloth's 11th Host ranged eastward, occupying and destroying the equatorial city-bastions in turn.

Every day tens of thousands of enemy soldiers perished, but every day scores of Word Bearers fell, and their loss was felt keenly. On all three fronts, the Word Bearers suffered.

Marduk's gaze lifted. Though he could see past the choking fumes engulfing the lower atmosphere, he knew that beyond, hanging in orbit like a malevolent sentinel, was the Kronos star fort. It too still held out, fighting Ekodas and his Host to a standstill. Like clockwork, every hour the star fort would unleash its barrage upon the world below, decimating everything within a three-kilometre radius of its target. The constant need for Marduk's Host to shift its battlefront to avoid annihilation was growing tiresome, and while on one hand he wished that Ekodas would hurry up and take the orbital bastion, there was a part of him that relished the Apostle's failure.

Nevertheless, Marduk felt his anger rise as he gazed heavenward. If the star fort had fallen, then the Chaos fleet would have been able to move into high orbit and commence a devastating bombardment upon the planet below that would have quickly changed the tide of the war. As it was, no Chaos warship was able to move into position without coming under fire from the Imperial star fort. For the thousandth time, Marduk cursed Ekodas's name for his weakness.

Like rolling thunder, artillery batteries in the distance began to roar.

'They attack again, Dark Apostle,' called Sabtec.

'Let them come,' said Marduk.

* * *

Ashkanez stalked back and forth within the centre of the gathering of hooded Astartes of the 34th Host, the strength of his faith and conviction obvious in every inflection, in every movement.

The clandestine meeting was taking place in the dead of night within the burnt-out shell of a bunker complex. The ground shook with intermittent artillery shelling in the distance, and flashes lit the night sky. Aircraft could be heard roaring overhead. It was a small group, numbering less than twenty of the cult members. With the war raging, it was difficult for Coterie members to slip away from their warrior-brothers unobserved, yet even so, the Brotherhood met in dozens of small congregations like this whenever it could.

Burias draw his hood up over his face as he ghosted in to join the gathering.

'In the aftermath of the cleansing, the Legion shall be stronger,' Ashkanez was saying. 'The Legion shall be unified once more.'

Ashkanez stopped stalking back and forth and lowered his voice.

'But more than this,' he said, 'it is prophesied that the Urizen shall once more walk among us.'

Burias's eyes widened, and there were gasps and muttering from amongst the gather warrior-brothers.

'Yes, my brothers,' said Ashkanez after a moment. 'Once the cleansing has been achieved, our lord and Primarch Lorgar shall rejoin the Legion. Once more he shall lead us in glorified battle, striding at our forefront and setting the universe aflame with faith and death.'

'Then let us begin!' growled a voice in the crowd, which was greeted with murmurs and foot-stamping in agreement. Burias found himself nodding and lending his own voice to the proclamation. Ashkanez lifted a hand for silence.

'I understand your eagerness, my brothers, for I feel it too. But no, we must not act yet. We must gather our strength, for the reach and cunning of our enemy is great.'

'Who *is* the enemy of the Brotherhood, lord?' said a voice from nearby.

Burias smiled, for he recognized that voice – it belonged to the brutal champion Khalaxis, a mighty warrior. He was pleased that Khalaxis too had been embraced into this noble fraternity.

'I cannot say,' said Ashkanez. 'Not yet, at least. The enemy has ears everywhere. Perhaps even amongst us here.'

A heavy silence descended on the gathering. Ashkanez's gaze fell upon Burias, noticing him for the first time. Even hooded as he was, Burias felt the First Acolyte's eyes burrowing into his own.

'But know that the day draws near, my brothers. And when it comes, we will all have our part to play.'

Ashkanez's eyes lingered on Burias as he spoke these last words, and the Icon Bearer knew that they were spoken for him in particular. He would be ready, he swore to himself.

'Return to your Coteries, my brothers,' said Ashkanez. 'All will be revealed soon.'

As the hooded warriors began to filter out of the shattered bunker-complex, Burias almost bumped into a towering warrior. Burias had noted his presence at several other Brotherhood conclaves, and though the warrior had always been careful to keep his identity concealed, as did all the brethren, from his size he was clearly garbed in Terminator armour – one of the Anointed.

'My pardon, brother,' said Burias.

The warrior did not respond, but as he looked up into the dark shadow of the warrior's hood his eyes widened. The hulking warrior turned away, pulling his cowl down lower, and moved off.

'It surprised me as well,' said Ashkanez in a low voice, suddenly at the Icon Bearer's side. Burias had not heard the First Acolyte's approach. 'But he has been with us since the beginning.'

'But…' said Burias. 'You promised me–'

'This changes nothing,' said Ashkanez.

Burias's face split in a daemonic grin, though hidden within the darkness of his cowl, it was all but invisible.

CHAPTER TWELVE

PROCONSUL OSTORIUS'S HUMMING power blade was a blur as he cut through the melee. Wave after wave of boarding parties were assaulting the Kronos star fort in this, the latest attack by the Word Bearers, and as ever Ostorius was in the thick of it.

Ostorius fought with astonishing economy of movement, expending no more energy than was required. For all his skill, there was no flourish or showmanship in his combat style; he merely killed, effectively and efficiently, again and again.

He slashed his sword across the faceplate of a Word Bearer, cutting deep into flesh and bone, before spinning and driving his blade into the throat of another enemy. Blood bubbled up from the wound, spitting off the super-heated power sword's blade.

Ostorius whipped his sword free, and before the Word Bearer had even hit the ground he was already away and moving, engaging a new foe. With his combat shield he turned aside a blade stabbing for him and cut down the Word Bearer with a stroke that sliced the enemy open from right shoulder blade to left hip.

Another Word Bearer leapt at Ostorius, animalistic growls emitting from the vox-amps set into his helmet. He hefted a massive chainaxe in both hands, and brought the screaming weapon down towards Ostorius's head.

The Proconsul of Boros Prime swayed aside at the last moment, the roaring teeth of the chainaxe missing him by centimetres. He ducked beneath a second blow and severed one of the traitor's legs above the

658

knee, his power sword shearing through armour, flesh and bone. The Word Bearer fell with a snarl, blood pumping from the terrible wound, and Ostorius moved on.

The next minute passed in a blur of motion and blood, until Ostorius came to a halt. Blood splattered his armour, and he was breathing heavily, his heart beating fast. Dimly he felt pain receptors flaring, and glanced down to see the rerebrace protecting his left upper arm shorn completely through, the flesh beneath a bloody ruin. He could see the white of bone, but could not even remember being struck.

He glanced around the deck as pain nullifiers flooded his system. A dozen White Consuls, all splattered with blood and carrying injuries, moved amongst the fallen, dispatching those Word Bearers that still lived without mercy.

Twenty-five Word Bearers lay strewn across the deck floor, all dead. Eighteen White Consuls had fallen. Nine of those would recover, given time – Astartes did not die easily. Nevertheless, only one, perhaps two, of the fallen White Consuls would be able to fight again within the next few days or weeks, and time was not a luxury that Ostorius could afford.

Kronos had held out for two months now – an astonishing feat given the force besieging it – yet the Proconsul knew that it would be but days now before it was overrun. He prayed that Librarian Epistolary Liventius would uncover the source that shrouded the Boros Gate soon. If he did not, then Boros would fall, it was as simple as that.

His gaze was drawn to the enemy Thunderhawk, sitting idle on the deck. A carefully aimed shot had taken out its pilot as it had attempted to pull away. A foul reek emerged from within its gaping assault ramp pods, along with a growling sound of static that made Ostorius feel faintly sick.

The enemy was growing bolder. Previously, all attacks had been launched via Deathclaw, corrupted drop-pods that burrowed through the thick armour plating of Kronos like flesh-eating maggots. However, with Kronos's shields failing, they were now able to launch attacks directly into its launch bays, with Word Bearers delivered right into the heart of the star fort via Thunderhawk and Stormbird.

'Shall we set explosives to destroy it, Proconsul?' said a battle-brother.

'Not just yet,' said Ostorius, eyeing the Thunderhawk thoughtfully. Apart from some exterior damage it had sustained in the assault, it was mostly intact. With minor repairs, it would again be spaceworthy.

An Apothecary was kneeling beside the bodies of dead White Consuls, extracting their precious gene-seed, the lifeblood of the Chapter. His narthecium whirred and crunched as he cut through plate and flesh.

Vox-chatter from elsewhere upon the star fort crackled in his ear; the latest assault had been underway for perhaps fifteen minutes, and already the enemy had breached the star fort's defences in more than a dozen places.

'Not today,' said Ostorius under his breath.

Never in his life had Ostorius felt this weary, and his mind was hazy with exhaustion. He had not slept – not truly slept – since the start of the siege. He had snatched moments of rest here and there, in between attacks, and during those lapses in battle he allowed isolated sections of his brain to shut down, but it was not real, healing rest. Plenty of time to rest when he was dead, though, he thought, morbidly. He was sure that time would come soon enough.

Frantic calls for reinforcements were broadcast suddenly from a deck location eighty floors below his current position, and Ostorius snapped back to full alertness. He responded curtly, and was moving purposefully a moment later.

'Come brothers,' he called. 'We are needed. Deck 53b-E91.'

MARDUK'S SPIRIT RIPPED away from the prison of his flesh, soaring free.

The release had been more difficult than usual to attain, and this caused him a moment of disquiet. It was forgotten when he was overwhelmed with stimuli.

The material world around him was now nothing more than a shadowy presence rendered in shades of grey, yet his witch-sight afforded him a vision richer and more alive with colour and movement than mortal eyes could ever realise.

His aural senses too were overwhelmed. Billions of voices screamed out in terror and fear, joining the sublime cacophony of the Discords, which could be heard in both this plane and the real. Theirs was an unholy, rapturous din.

He could hear the leathery flap of wings as kathartes circled around him, brushing his soaring soul affectionately. A hundred kilometres away, a corrupted Titan of the Legio Vulturus let out a cry, the reverberant bass note shaking the doomed planet to its core.

Invisible to mortal sight, daemons in their tens of millions had descended upon Boros Prime, and Marduk saw them now in their full glory, a dizzying panoply of radiance and majesty, of horror and despair. Like a swarming tide they had come here, attracted by the sheer scale of the savagery being enacted in the name of the gods of Chaos, summoned by the powerful emotions being unleashed across its continents.

Invisible to all but those with the witch-sight and will to see them, these daemon spirits swarmed across the skies like a hellish, ethereal living soup, and waited in great, menacing groups around the living. Even those pathetic mortals unable to perceive them felt their presence, perhaps as nothing more than a shiver or a breath of ice across the back of their necks. They suffered the nightmares that the daemons brought with them, their minds giving voice to their doubts and their fears.

The scale of fear, revulsion, hatred, terror and panic of the system's inhabitants had drawn the daemons to this world, like flies to a corpse.

They fed off these raw emotions, gluttonously supping at them, but more delectable still were the souls of those dying in torment and fear.

The daemons licked their ethereal lips in hunger, clustered in eager packs around the glowing soul-flames of those about to die. As the mortal soldiers of Boros Prime perished, the hellspawn descended upon them in a whirlwind of hunger and savagery, rending, tearing and feeding. Whether they fell on the field of battle, killed beneath the blades of the faithful or merely took their own lives, all were consumed to feed the insatiable hunger of the true gods, for these lesser daemons were but aspects of the greater powers. In the depths of the warp, the gods rumbled their pleasure.

But Marduk was not spirit-journeying merely to witness the majesty of Chaos, as glorious and inspirational as it was.

Turning his attention away from the beauteous carnage, he streaked across the heavens, the monochromatic war-torn planet blurring beneath him. He hurtled invisibly across the ravaged planet's continents, rising up higher and higher into the airless upper atmosphere, drawn towards a dark nimbus of power that called to him like a siren. He could see it from afar, a malignant blot upon reality, oozing potency.

At last, he slowed his ascent, and hovered in the air before this powerful warp presence.

Greetings, Apostle of the 34th Host, boomed the shadow-soul, making Marduk's spirit waver.

My lord Ekodas, answered Marduk.

The amorphous, insubstantial shape of Ekodas's soaring shadow-soul coalesced into a shape more recognisable, an anthropomorphised form projected from his mind. He appeared before Marduk in the guise of a giant, robed figure hanging effortlessly in the sky, his head that of a snarling beast. Flames surrounded him, and the sheer brutality and force of the power Ekodas radiated buffeted Marduk's spirit like a gale.

Two other soul-spirits coalesced in view alongside Marduk.

Belagosa's presence was hazy and flickering. He took the form of an archaic warrior-knight, his body encased in ancient plate armour. Ankh-Heloth's presence revealed itself as a coiled serpent, eyes glinting with malign light.

This war threatens to slip from our grasp, boomed Ekodas into the minds of the gathered Apostles.

If there is any failure it is yours alone, shot back Marduk.

Ankh-Heloth's avatar bared its fangs, hissing and spitting, but Marduk ignored him.

We are making progress, said Belagosa. *So long as the Nexus holds and the warp gate is kept shut, there is no hope of salvation for the followers of the Corpse-God. This world's corruption is assured.*

I want this world to burn, roared Ekodas. *Its continued defiance offends me. The spirit of the Imperials is not yet broken. There is one amongst them who is their talisman; their so-called White Angel. Find him, my Apostles. Find him, and bring him to me.*

We are not alone, said Belagosa suddenly.

Marduk looked around him, probing with his mind's eye. An insubstantial flicker played at the edge of his vision.

There, he said.

Ekodas spun, ghostly arms extended and flames of the spirit roared. Amidst the inferno, a glowing figure armoured in silver plate appeared. A shining tabard of white was worn over his armour. The flames licked at this newly revealed presence, but they could not touch him, for a glowing bubble of light surrounded him.

Spying on us, Librarian? said Ekodas. *It will avail you little.*

This world shall never belong to you, traitors, pulsed the White Consul.

It already does, boomed Ekodas. *And now, you die.*

I think not, heretic, replied the Librarian.

Ekodas grew in stature, his bestial face twisted in hatred. His arms sprouted insubstantial claws and he flew at the Librarian's soul-presence, flames flaring all around him.

There was an explosion of blinding light that made Marduk and the other Apostles shrink back. When it cleared, the Librarian's presence had disappeared.

He is gone, said Belagosa.

How much did he hear? pulsed Ankh-Heloth.

It matters not, boomed Ekodas.

Go now, my Apostles. Find their White Angel. We destroy him, and we destroy their hope.

With his dictate conveyed, the blaze surrounding Ekodas burst outwards, slamming into Marduk and the other two Apostles with the force of a psychic hurricane. Marduk fell, spinning out of control, and slammed involuntarily back into the cage of his earthly flesh.

He collapsed to his knees, blood dripping from his nostrils.

'My lord?' said Ashkanez, kneeling beside him. Marduk waved him back.

'Get Burias,' he said hoarsely. 'I have a job for him.'

THE SOUND OF the battle was loud even kilometres from the nearest of the ever-shifting front lines, dull explosions that shook the planet to its core. Thunderbolts and Marauders roared overhead, heading towards the warzones with full payloads, while others chugged back towards the scattered airbases, trailing smoke, their ammunition spent. The screams of the wounded and dying echoed from makeshift medicae facilities, and corpses were strewn throughout the streets.

Aquilius gazed around him as he marched. The sky was filled with smoke and cinders. The once pristine, gleaming white marble of Sirenus Principal, his birth-city, was now pocked and chipped from small-arms fire, scarred by ordnance and covered in soot and blood. The beautiful gardens and arboretums were now little more than charred wastelands of scorched earth. The blackened skeletons of trees protruded mournfully from the ash, like headstones, and lakes and fountains were now cesspools of foulness, choked with scum and unnatural algae blooms. Corpses floated face down in the waters.

Boros Prime was changing. Aquilius could feel the change in the air itself, and it had nothing to do with anything as mundane as pollutants, ash and death. The taint of Chaos had taken hold of Boros Prime, and he despaired as to what would be left here, even if they were victorious. A week ago, one in ten thousand had been identified as exhibiting some unnatural taint, planet-wide – tens of millions of citizens and soldiers. All had been removed from their units and habs and transported under guard to the quarantine sanitation camps – death camps by any other name.

The number of the afflicted had risen sharply in the last days, and it was judged that the taint was now affecting one in five thousand, and rising daily. Paranoia was rife within the ranks of the Imperial Guard and the citizenry, for no detectable pattern to determine who would be affected was apparent. Where would it end? *Would* it end?

So far no warrior-brother of the White Consuls had suffered any visible or detectible taint, but not even Astartes were immune to the perverting effects of Chaos if exposed to it for long enough.

It was like a plague that the invaders brought with them, an insidious creeping sickness that had infiltrated Boros Prime. It was worse than the Word Bearers themselves, perhaps, for it was an enemy that could not be fought with bolter or chainsword.

Rebreathers had been issued, but already the supply of filter plugs was running short. In truth, the insidious, corrupting effect of Chaos was not transferred through the air – it was far more insidious than that – but it had been deemed an appropriate calming measure.

In consultation with the Chapter's Apothecaries and the Guard's senior medicae officers, Aquilius had rolled out daily screening and purity testing for all soldiers, to be conducted in the presence of a superior officer. Any individual exhibiting any taint was removed from their unit. Commissars prowled the ranks, and each day Aquilius read depressing communiqués tallying the numbers of soldiers executed for exhibiting hostile effects of taint, or for concealing and avoiding screens.

Coadjutor Aquilius moved through the press of soldiers. He towered head and shoulders above them, and conversations died as he passed.

His armour was battle worn, his cloak was tattered and burnt, yet he walked with his head held high, his blue-crested helmet tucked under one arm. A melta burn scarred the left side of his face, and his short-cropped blond hair was blackened from fire.

Aquilius saw the soldiers' expressions lifting as they moved reverently from his path. He nodded to them. Hands blackened with grime and ash touched his armour plates. Murmurs spread like ripples on a lake as he made his way through the press of stinking, battle-weary soldiers. They spoke in hushed tones, but Aquilius could hear them all. The White Angel, they whispered. That was what the men were calling him now. He had tried to stop them, but it had done no good.

He did not feel worthy of their adoration, but it didn't matter. It was Chapter Master Valens who had made him realise that, and his respect for the warrior had grown immeasurably.

'This is not about you,' Chapter Master Valens had said. 'This is not about what you need, or what you deserve. This is about what those soldiers need. They need hope, Aquilius. The *White Angel* is that hope. The men must hold until the veil over the Boros Gate is lifted.'

He had not understood the Chapter Master's words at first but as weeks passed he slowly came to.

Amidst the horror and darkness of this escalating, planet-wide war, the White Angel had become a beacon of hope.

In the months since the enemy had attacked, Aquilius had fought fearlessly alongside the regiments of the Boros Imperial Guard, fighting as one of them. He faced the dangers they faced, and was ever at the forefront of the most intense battles, and he – or rather the fiction that was the White Angel – had become a legend.

The Imperial propaganda machine was in full swing. Printed leaflets were distributed amongst the ranks speaking of the White Angel's exploits, all highly exaggerated, and how the enemy was being slowly repelled. It made him intensely uncomfortable, but he could see the positive effect it was having on the men. Spirits lifted wherever he went, and soldiers that had been about to break redoubled their resolve in his presence.

He understood his role here now, and had come to accept its burden. It was his job to ensure that the Guard and the PDF, the tank companies and the auxiliary regiments were operating at their peak, that their morale held, and that their will to fight was not eroded by the insidious tools of the enemy. If that meant that he must become their talisman, their *White Angel*, then so be it.

The soldiers and citizenry of Boros Prime saw the White Angel as their saviour, their divine protector. While Aquilius stood, there was hope. Despite everything, that ray of hope was burning brighter with every day that passed, with every day that victory was denied the enemy.

As he moved through the regiments, making himself seen, he could not shake the feeling that hostile eyes were watching him. He stopped and scanned the rooftops and damaged battlements. He told himself he was being foolish, but the nagging impression would not budge.

The vox-bead in his ear clicked.

'Coadjutor Aquilius,' came a voice as he accepted the incoming communication. It was Chapter Master Titus Valens, located halfway around the world, engaged in the frozen north.

'Yes, my lord?'

'We are close to unearthing the secret that locks down the Boros Gate. Librarian Epistolary Liventius believes it is a device, something called the Nexus. Our brother Librarian is launching an attack upon it as we speak.'

'This is auspicious news, my lord!'

'Hope is at hand, Coadjutor. Pray that the Librarian is successful. But there is more.'

'Yes, my lord?'

'The enemy have learnt of the White Angel. The enemy is coming for you, Aquilius. Be vigilant.'

The Coadjutor's gaze never left the rooftops. Something *was* watching then.

'Let them come,' he said.

'I myself am returning to Sirenus Principal,' said Chapter Master Valens. 'My Thunderhawk should reach you in six hours. You will rendezvous with me, Aquilius. I cannot allow you to fall. You are too important.'

'I am a Space Marine, my lord,' said Aquilius. 'I need no protection.'

Hidden in the shadows of a high alcove, Burias-Drak'shal crouched like a malignant gargoyle. A bestial snarl issued from his lips and his daemonic eyes narrowed as he focussed on his prey.

THE CLOISTERED ANTECHAMBER of the Temple of the Gloriatus had been sealed with psychic wards, and incense billowed from censers. The only light came from hundreds of brightly burning candles. Wax pooled beneath them.

Thirteen psykers of various abilities and specialities knelt in a circle, as if in prayer, their minds linked. They had been gathered from all across Boros Prime as the embattled fleet still fought to protect the Kronos star fort. Their number was made up of four blind astropaths, three haughty navigators from the Imperial Navy, three sanctioned psykers of the Boros Guard command, and three young inductees of the schola progenium who showed marked psychic abilities. All of them had been vetted by Librarian Epistolary Liventius, and judged worthy. The White Consul himself sat crosslegged in the centre of the circle, like a shaman of the old times.

It is time, said Liventius.

Those arrayed around him readied themselves, conducting their own rituals in preparation of the coming conflict, lending Liventius their strength. Each of them knew that the chances of them surviving this encounter were slim. Maddening glimpses of their thoughts and fears flashed through the Librarian's mind.

Focus, he said, gently nudging the psykers' minds with his own.

As their united trance deepened, the temperature in the room dropped markedly. Hoarfrost began to crystallise upon the blue plates of Liventius's armour. Deeper he drew the psykers into him, focussing their power and uniting them, until he was no longer a single entity, but rather all of them bound together as one.

For two hours, the trance continued before Liventius judged them ready to proceed. He surged from his body and passed on up through the ceiling, striking heavenward.

Up and up and up he soared, cutting through the atmosphere of the tortured planet, passing effortlessly through its gravity and out into the airless vacuum beyond.

He saw the beleaguered Kronos star fort, and could see the glowing souls of every individual on board. Even as he watched, he saw scores of the glowing soul-flames snuffed out, blinking out of existence as they perished.

Liventius turned his attention towards the Chaos fleet. For weeks and months he had been probing their defences, attempting to locate the origin of whatever it was locking down the Boros Gate's wormholes. At last, he had narrowed his focus down onto one ship, the hulking Infernus-class battleship, the *Crucius Maledictus*. From what he had garnered from overhearing the gathering of the enemy Apostles, he now had a name for whatever it was – the Nexus.

With a thought, Liventius closed the distance to the immense warship. Immediately he came up against a wall of psychic force, an almost impenetrable barrier that actively resisted his presence. However, bolstered with the strength of the thirteen minds linked to his own, he began pushing through the defences, focusing all his will on worming his way through its intricate layers of protection.

Stabbing pain erupted in his mind, and he heard the psychic scream of one of the astropaths linked to him as he perished. Shielding himself and the other minds linked to his own from the trauma of the dying man, Liventius pushed on. It was like swimming though a viscous pool of acid, and agony rippled across his spirit-form.

He was less than halfway through the potent wall of psychic force when he felt a malignant presence swell into being around him. This was the psyker who had erected the barrier, and Liventius siphoned off a portion of his prodigious power to hide himself from its soul-eyes; for all his strength, he was as a child next to this being.

You cannot hide forever, boomed the presence. *I will find you.*

Liventius continued burrowing through the force wall, but even as he did, he felt the resistance against him redouble. He began losing ground, the wall repelling him, and he screamed out soundlessly as psychic shockwaves of pain flowed through him.

Another of the astropaths perished under the strain, further weakening

Liventius. Knowing that he would never penetrate the ever-strengthening barrier while still trying to conceal his presence, he dropped his shielding completely, focussing all his will into cutting through the barrier before him.

There you are, little man, boomed the voice, and Liventius screamed in torment as his spirit was bathed in incandescent flames. Two of the minds linked with his own were instantly fried, blood exploding from their eyeballs.

Nevertheless, with all his strength now focused, Liventius was making headway once more, and with a final surge, he penetrated the psychic barrier surrounding the *Crucius Maledictus*.

Suddenly free, he surged through the corridors of the battleship, touching every mind that he passed, seeking answers. Roaring in fury, the spirit of the apostate dogged him, surging behind him like a tidal wave, threatening to drown him.

From what Liventius gleaned from the repulsive minds that he touched, there was something unnatural aboard the vessel. As he got closer to its source, he felt its touch, and he was at once repelled and attracted to it. It was anathema to a psychic's mind, and yet he was drawn towards it, like flotsam pulled inexorably into a whirlpool. Rather than resisting its pull, Liventius went along with it, hurtling towards the source at a speed far beyond anything capable of physical matter. He burst into a high-ceilinged room located centrally within the *Crucius Maledictus's* bloated belly, and came to an abrupt halt, desperately pulling up short before he was consumed.

Here was the source that had locked down the Boros Gate, he knew that instantly. It appeared to him as a pulsing sphere of utter darkness, drawing all psychic energy into itself. It was all Liventius could do to hold himself back from being sucked into that emptiness. Two of the minds linked with his own were not so strong. Their souls were dragged into the darkness screaming and snuffed out, as though they had never been. The blackness shuddered, growing stronger.

A number of souls burned fiercely in the room, one so bright it caused him pain just to look upon it. Word Bearers.

With a thought, Liventius slammed into the mind of one of the traitors. It was vile and repellent, and the Word Bearer struggled against him, but he drove into him with all the focus of an assassin's knife, overcoming his will completely.

He blinked and turned his meat-puppet towards the psychic black hole, so as to see it with physical eyes.

It appeared before him: a spinning orb of silver held captive within a series of rotating arcs.

Seven other Word Bearers stood in a circle around the device, but if they realised an impostor was within their midst, they did not show it. There was another being within the room, reclined as if in a trance upon a high-backed throne, and Liventius knew instantly that this was the psyker who had erected the defences around the Word Bearers fleet, the one who was hunting him now. He dared not let his gaze linger, lest the monstrously powerful psyker feel his touch.

Not yet fully in command of this borrowed flesh, Liventius's movements were sluggish and awkward. He took one ponderous step forwards, breaking the circle of Word Bearers. He felt the attention of the others turn towards him. In his hands he held a corrupted bolter, and this he lifted towards the spinning silver device, the source that held the Boros Gate in its thrall. His finger tightened upon the trigger of the borrowed weapon.

The awesomely powerful mind of the Word Bearers apostate caught up with him, slamming into him with staggering force. He was almost dislodged from the flesh of the Word Bearer, but he clung on, ignoring the searing pain. He was desperate to finish his task, knowing the fate of the Boros Gate rested with the destruction of this infernal device.

The Word Bearers puppet was fighting him once more, attempting to regain control of his own movements, and he began to lower his weapon. Redoubling his efforts, Liventius dragged the bolter back up towards the spinning device.

Bolt rounds struck him as the other Word Bearers turned their guns on their brother, and he staggered. Again, the Apostle struck him psychically, this time with even more force, and he was knocked out of the borrowed flesh.

Now you are mine, thundered the voice of the Apostle.

Liventius roared in agony as his spirit was wracked with soul-fire. Agonising psychic shackles closed around him, but he thrashed and struggled against them, until with a final surge he tore himself free.

WITH A GASP, Librarian Epistolary Liventius opened his eyes. Agony crashed in upon him, and his vision wavered. Steadying himself, wiping blood from his nose, he looked around him. All the candles in the antechamber were out, but even in the near pitch darkness, Liventius could see the thirteen psykers that had aided him were dead.

He had failed.

CHAPTER THIRTEEN

OSTORIUS KNELT BEFORE the holo-images of Chapter Master Titus Valens and his Captain, Marcus Decimus of 5th Company. His head was bowed, and he held his power sword flat in his hands as he waited for an answer.

'If I allow this,' said the ghostly image of the White Consuls Chapter Master, 'it will leave Kronos critically undermanned.'

'If you do not allow it, we stand no chance of ending this war,' said Captain Decimus. 'Liventius failed in his attempt. A direct assault upon the device is the logical next step.'

'If it fails, Kronos will belong to the Word Bearers.'

'If it fails, then none of this matters anyway,' said Decimus.

'Were it practical, I'd lead the attack myself,' said Valens. Ostorius could hear frustration in the Chapter Master's voice. 'But I believe you two are right. This is our best chance to end this war. Do it.'

'Assemble your kill-team, Ostorius,' said Captain Decimus.

'Thank you, my lords,' said Ostorius.

'May the Emperor guide your sword, Proconsul.'

BURIAS-DRAK'SHAL RACED ACROSS the battlements in bounding leaps, his claws gouging deep rents in the marble. Like a shadow chased by the sun, he moved across the rooftops in a blur.

Bunching his powerful leg muscles, he exploded off the top of a bastion, his leap carrying him clear over the wide-laned street far below. Chimeras and front-line Leman Russ battle tanks were advancing along that boulevard, completely unaware that their movement was being shadowed by the possessed warrior high overhead.

Arms bulging with daemonic muscle, Burias-Drak'shal came down hard, clearing the thirty-metre expanse with ease. He turned in the air, landing on the rooftop of the lower bastion. He rolled and came to his feet smoothly, and again was off, bounding and leaping on all fours.

He launched himself off another vertigo-inducing drop-off and landed halfway up the side of a vertical antennae-pylon, clinging to the sheer surface like a spider. With swift movements, barely pausing to find handholds, he scurried up the vertical incline, pulling himself hand over hand to its peak. There he paused, tasting the air and cocking his head to one side, listening. All his daemon-enhanced senses were utterly focussed on the hunt.

The sound of battle was loud; a major confrontation was playing out less than ten kilometres away. It was a battle that the Chimeras were angling towards.

He was ahead of the armoured column now, and as it rounded a corner, it was forced into single file to navigate past a fallen building.

Burias-Drak'shal's eyes focussed on the third Chimera in the line. The APC had a cluster of communication arrays rising from its hull, like the spines of an insect, differentiating it from the others. This was the one that Burias-Drak'shal had seen the White Consul enter, several hours earlier.

The possessed Icon Bearer dropped off the pylon, falling like a stone. He landed thirty metres below, crouched on all fours. His bestial head turned from side to side, sniffing. Then he set off once more, closing inexorably with his prey.

THE FULL EXTENT of the 34th Host had come together, and the warrior-brothers of the Host fought shoulder-to-shoulder, laying waste to all that dared oppose them.

The turrets of corrupted Predator battle tanks rotated, spewing torrents of high-calibre shells down boulevards and byways, killing hundreds. The air crackled as Land Raiders unleashed the power of their lascannons, targeting armoured columns and tank formations.

The heavy, bipedal forms of Dreadnoughts ranged out in front, roaring with mechanised insanity as they killed, gunning down scores of Guardsmen with heavy gauge weapon systems and ripping them apart with power talons and electro-flails. The Warmonger stalked amongst them, bellowing catechisms and holy scripture, reliving the days when he was a warrior of flesh and blood, fighting upon the walls of the Emperor's Palace and exhorting his Host to kill and kill again in the name of Lorgar and the Warmaster Horus, ten millennia earlier.

Daemons numbering in their thousands had been summoned forth from bleeding rents ripped in the fabric of reality, and they brayed in fury and bloodlust as they charged into the densely packed ranks of Guardsmen. Kathartes descended upon the Imperial soldiers in flocks a hundred-strong, dragging their victims high into the air before ripping them limb from limb and dropping them into the streets below.

Titans as tall as buildings stalked in the distance, their bestial howls reverberating across the city. Their princeps and moderati had long been subsumed into the substance of the Titans, and powerful daemonic entities bound and infused with them, making the mighty engines more living, breathing beasts than mechanised constructs.

Heavily armed Warlord- and Reaver-class engines laid waste to entire city blocks with the power of their ordnance. Their armoured hulls were pitted from ten thousand years of warfare, and kill-pennants hung from their weapons.

Comparatively smaller Warhound-class Titans loped through the streets, hunting. Unnervingly stealthy for engines four storeys high, they stalked through the mayhem of battle, annihilating colonnades of battle tanks, and butchering entire brigades of Guardsmen with salvoes of their Inferno cannons. Their bestial howls ululated across the city as they claimed another kill.

Somewhere out there was the enemy that had come to be known as the White Angel. That individual was the lynchpin of the enemy's resolve. Kill him, and the world would soon falter.

'Come on, Burias,' Marduk hissed.

THE TAINTED STENCH within the Word Bearers Thunderhawk was vile, yet Ostorius repressed his revulsion. He had claimed the assault shuttle a week earlier, and although he could not have said why at the time, he had not ordered its immediate destruction.

Now, as it carried him and his carefully chosen kill-team of White Consuls across the gulf of space between Kronos and the largest of the enemy battleships, he hoped that his decision had proved a wise one.

Priests of the Ecclesiarchy had cleansed the shuttle of the worst of its taint, yet Ostorius could still feel its corrupting touch all around him. It made his skin crawl, and he repressed a shudder of disgust. He wore his helmet so as not to breathe the foetid air within the Thunderhawk, yet even so he could taste the poison of Chaos in his throat. He was not alone in his discomfort. The White Consuls of his kill-team murmured prayers of purification, and several of them held holy icons tightly in their hands.

At any moment Ostorius expected the Thunderhawk to be gunned down. Even as the shuttle entered the shadow of the monstrous enemy flagship, the *Crucius Maledictus*, and began to angle down towards one of its gaping launch bays, he still expected the enemy to see through the ruse and obliterate them.

His fears proved to be unfounded, and after what seemed like an eternity, the Thunderhawk's landing gear touched down. They were onboard the enemy vessel.

'Move out,' he said grimly.

THERE WAS AN almighty crash that shook the occupants of the Chimera, and it ground to a halt. Voices were raised.

'What was that?' said Aquilius. It had not sounded like ordnance.

Gears ground together, and the Chimera began slowly backing up.

'Apologies, my lord,' said one of the other occupants, Versus of the Boros 232nd. 'There is a blockage ahead. This area has suffered heavy shelling, and is structurally unsound. We are being forced to reroute in order to rejoin the column.'

'Casualties?'

'None, my lord.'

Aquilius shifted his weight in discomfort, and cursed as his head hit the roof with a dull thud. The APC had not been designed to hold the bulk of a Space Marine.

'I'm going up,' he said, and began clambering awkwardly across the tight enclosed space within the Chimera towards its cupola.

Climbing the slender ladder, his shoulders only barely fitting through its aperture, Aquilius popped the cupola hatch and pulled himself up. He breathed in deeply, pleased to be out of the enclosed space. A pintle-mounted heavy stubber lay at rest within arm's reach.

A massive statue lay smashed across the boulevard twenty metres in front of the Chimera. Dust filled the air. Shielding his eyes, Aquilius looked up to see from where it had fallen.

There was a heavy thump behind him, and the Chimera rocked. Aquilius's first thought was that more falling masonry had struck the APC, but then the tainted smell of Chaos reached his nostrils.

'Enemy!' he shouted, reaching for his bolt pistol.

There was a blur of movement behind him and he caught a glimpse of a horrific, daemonic creature crouched upon the back of the Chimera's hull. He lifted his bolt pistol as the thing snarled and leapt towards him, but the weapon was smashed out of his hand. A taloned claw grabbed him around the neck and he was hauled out of the Chimera and hurled aside.

Aquilius hit the ground hard, crashing down onto a pile of rubble that had been pushed up against a shattered building wall. He heard frantic shouting above the growl of the Chimera's engines.

He came to his feet quickly, reaching for his blade, but his daemonic foe was faster. It leapt from on top of the Chimera and tackled him to the ground again, snarling and spitting. The Astartes was hauled back to his feet and slammed face-first into the side of his turning Chimera, denting its armoured plates and shattering Aquilius's nose.

The Chimera's rear hatch was thrown open, and he heard boots hitting the ground as the APC's occupants leapt out to aid their Coadjutor.

A lasgun burn seared across the back of the possessed warrior's head, and he snarled in anger. It drove Aquilius's head into the Chimera once more before releasing him and leaping towards these new enemies, its jaw opening wider than should have been possible.

Screams and the sickly sound of meat being hacked apart reached Aquilius's ears as he steadied himself. He drew his thick-bladed combat knife and rounded on his foe.

Four men were down, screaming as blood poured from their horrific wounds. One was missing his left arm, the limb having been ripped from its socket, while another was clutching vainly at his savaged throat. The daemon's maw closed around the head of another, helmet and all. It popped like an overripe fruit, and blood splattered across the beast's face and chest.

Aquilius bellowed a challenge and leapt towards the unholy creature that was butchering his men. It turned towards him as it heard his cry, eyes narrowed to blood-red slits.

The butt of a lasgun slammed into the side of the monster's head. It was a powerful blow, delivered with all of Verenus's strength, but for all his size and strength, he was but a man. The daemon grabbed him around the neck and hurled him away, throwing him deep into the ruins. Still, Verenus had distracted the creature long enough for Aquilius to close the distance.

He lowered his shoulder and slammed into the possessed Word Bearer, throwing him back into the Chimera. He knew that his combat knife would have no chance of penetrating his enemy's power armour, so he wielded it like a dagger, driving it down towards his foe's exposed neck.

The blade bit deep, sinking to the hilt, and hot blood spilt over Aquilius's gauntlet. The beast roared in pain and fury, and one of its curving horns slashed across Aquilius's face as it bucked and struggled in his grasp. He ignored the pain and stabbed again but the daemon spun him around, slamming him up against the Chimera, and the knife missed its target, glancing off the Word Bearer's shoulder plate.

Using all of its infernal strength, the Word Bearer slammed its knee up into Aquilius's mid-section, cracking ceramite. The White Consul gasped as the wind was driven from him, and sank to his knees. The possessed warrior dropped his elbow into the back of his neck as he went down, slamming him to the ground.

The beast bent over him, and Aquilius felt a warm rivulet of drool upon his cheek. He strained to fight on, but he was helpless. The beast drew back one of its hands, thick talons poised to kill.

'Their hope will die with you,' snarled the beast, in a guttural voice.

'Hope never dies,' managed Aquilius.

The beast's lips curled in a sneer. Then a blue-hot lasgun burst took the beast in the side of the head, and it was thrown off Aquilius.

He struggled to his feet to see Verenus advancing, lasgun raised to his shoulder. The beast was crouched low, snarling.

Dust rose as a deafening gale roared around them, and Aquilius glanced up, shielding his eyes, to see a Thunderhawk dropping in on his position. It came down, its pilot carefully navigating its way between the steep sides of the ruins.

When he looked back, the possessed Word Bearer had gone.

His vox-bead clicked in his ear.

'Go ahead,' he said, shouting to be heard over the roar of the Thunderhawk's engines as it touched down.

'The enemy have your position surrounded,' came the voice of Chapter Master Titus Valens as the assault shuttle's main ramp slammed open. 'Get your men inside.'

THE BLASTDOOR EXPLODED inwards as melta charges detonated, and Ostorius was through them in a heartbeat, humming power sword in hand.

The directions that Liventius had given him were perfect, and he and his kill-team had made steady progress through the repulsive hallways of the *Crucius Maledictus*. They had encountered less opposition than the Proconsul had envisaged, for which he was thankful. The vast majority of the Word Bearers were evidentally fighting on the planet below, or intent on taking Kronos. It seemed that the last thing the Word Bearers were expecting was a direct attack upon their flagship.

Even so, only five of Ostorius's kill-team still lived. Moving warily, the Proconsul led them into a wide, circular room, taking in its details in a quick glance.

The roof was high and domed, and it was ringed with huge stone pillars. One wall was dominated by an immense view portal that looked out across the exterior of the ship. Beyond its armoured prow lay Boros Prime.

A tracked crawler unit was positioned centrally within the room, at the bottom of a stepped dais, and it was to this that Ostorius's gaze was drawn. Humming arcs of black metal revolved around each other with the hum of displaced air. Within these spinning rings was the device that he had been tasked with disabling, even though Liventius wasn't certain that nullifying the Nexus would reopen the Boros Gate. To not make an attempt to destroy the device, no matter how futile, would have been akin to conceding defeat. For a moment he was lost in its form, mesmerised by its rotating silver rings, but he dragged his attention away as he registered that there were other beings in the room.

A massive robed figure plugged into the crawler unit turned towards the intruders, tentacled mechadendrites rising threateningly. He was a corrupted mirror image of the tech-adepts that served on Kronos. Ostorius's gaze flicked towards a circle of Word Bearers standing sentinel around the device, bolters held across their chest.

Finally, Ostorius's eyes darted up the steps of the dais, and he looked upon what must have been the corrupted Chaplain leading the Word Bearers fleet.

The Apostle sat upon a high-backed throne crafted from the bones of some immense, draconic beast. His eyes were closed, as if he were in some form of trance.

Ostorius took in all this information in the space of single heartbeat, and before any of the Word Bearers could lift their bolters, he was sprinting forwards, power sword singing in his hands.

BURIAS-DRAK'SHAL ROARED HIS frustration as the Thunderhawk lifted off. His scowl turned to a vicious grin as he saw the immense shape of a Reaver Titan rear up from within the shell of a ruined building one street down.

The monstrous war-engine's weapons fired, glancing the Thunderhawk and shearing off one of its stabiliser wings. The shuttle began veering sharply in an uncontrolled nose-dive.

Burias-Drak'shal roared again, this time in triumph, and set off once more through the ruins.

'MASTER,' SAID ASHKANEZ, pointing.

Marduk followed his First Acolyte's gaze, and saw a White Consuls Thunderhawk in the distance. It was spewing smoke and going down fast.

'Let's go,' said the Dark Apostle.

OSTORIUS WAS BLEEDING from a dozen wounds, but he felt no pain. He knew he was not going to live beyond this fight, but it didn't matter. All he cared about was that he completed his mission.

The bodies of three Word Bearers lay upon the floor behind the Proconsul. He spun gracefully, and killed another of the enemy warriors, impaling his head on the blade of his humming power sword. The sword penetrated the Word Bearer's skull and burst through the back of his helmet. Ostorius slid the blade clear and the warrior crashed to the deck floor.

Two more of the White Consuls battle-brothers that made up his kill-team were down, but there was only a handful of Word Bearers now standing between Ostorius and his goal. The Apostle was still seated motionless in his high-backed throne atop the dais, apparently lost in a trance.

A bolter came up and Ostorius threw himself into a roll, the bolt pistol clasped behind his combat shield booming. His shot hit the Word Bearer in the arm, throwing his aim off, and Ostorius felt the passage of displaced air as a bolt round accelerated past his ear. He came up to his feet in front of the Word Bearer, spinning his power sword up as he came, hacking into the Traitor's groin. The blade cleaved through power armour and flesh, lodging itself halfway up the Word Bearer's abdomen. Kicking the body away with the flat of his boot, Ostorius freed his weapon and spun ever closer towards the device.

A power axe sliced in for his neck, but he turned it aside with his combat shield and beheaded his opponent with a powerful sweeping blow.

'Cover my back!' he roared, seeing a gap appear through the melee. His battle-brothers closed in behind him as he darted towards the spinning device atop the tracked crawler unit.

The corrupted tech-magos heaved itself between Ostorius and his goal. As wary as he was of this one now, having seen it tear one of his battle-brothers apart, he needed to end this fight quickly.

Servo-arms snapped towards him, but Ostorius was already moving at speed. He ducked the first of them and leapt over the second, his sword carving an arc through the air.

He took the tech-magos in the throat, his power blade shearing through altered flesh and arterial cabling. Milky blood and oil spurted, and Ostorius swept past the hulking robed adept as he reeled.

The Proconsul hauled himself onto the back of the crawler. He could feel the rush of displaced air over him, and he drew back his sword, preparing to thrust it between the spinning arcs and impale the silver device at its centre.

'For Boros,' he said.

At that moment, the Apostle seated upon the skeletal throne atop the dais rose to his feet.

'Enough!'

An invisible force struck Ostorius, lifting him off the crawler unit and slamming him to the deck floor.

The Apostle was descending the steps of the dais now, throwing off his robe.

Ostorius struggled to rise, but there was a numbing pain in the back of his mind and his vision was wavering.

The other White Consuls were down, their precious lifeblood leaking out across the deck.

The Apostle descended to the floor of his inner sanctum. He approached Ostorius as he struggled to his knees.

'Lower your weapon, Kol Harekh,' the Apostle said to a Word Bearer aiming a bolter at the White Consul.

Ostorius understood his words, though the Traitor's guttural accent was thick and archaic.

Like a blade of fire, a piercing pain jabbed into his mind and he clutched at his temples in agony.

'I could kill you with a thought,' said the Dark Apostle, twisting the invisible psychic needle inside the Proconsul's head, 'but that would not placate my rage. Get up.'

The pain suddenly left Ostorius, and he rose to his feet, holding out his power sword. The unarmed Apostle marched on him. With a gesture, the Word Bearer ordered his minions back. A space developed between him and the White Consul.

Without ceremony, Ostorius leapt forwards to cut down the apostate.

The Word Bearer caught the humming power sword between the flat of his hands, halting its descent centimetres from his face. Ostorius had not even seen him move.

The blade was pushed to the side and released, and the Word Bearer slammed the palm of a hand into the grille of Ostorius's helmet, which cracked and crumpled inwards.

The White Consul tore his helmet free and tossed it aside, eyeing his foe with newfound respect.

'I'm going to enjoy this,' said the Word Bearer, closing in on Ostorius.

CHAPTER FOURTEEN

Upon the steps of the Temple of the Gloriatus, Titus Valens made his final stand.

The temple-fortress was one of the largest and most impressive structures in the south-eastern quadrant of Sirenus Principal, and it dominated the landscape. The expansive victory square before it was almost five kilometres across, and titanic columns lined its approach. Not a single one of the mighty marble pillars still stood intact, however, and the defiant statues of Astartes heroes that had stood atop them were in ruin.

It seemed like a lifetime ago that Aquilius had stood on this square inspecting the ranks of the Boros 232nd.

The smoking carcass of the Thunderhawk lay in the middle of the square behind them. It had been brought down by a glancing blow from a gatling blaster, fired from a feral Reaver-class Titan lurking in the streets. Nine battle-brothers, including its pilot, had perished as the devastating fire ripped through the assault shuttle as if it were made of tinfoil. More had died as it had fallen from the sky like a bird with its wings clipped and ploughed into the square, smashing through colonnades in its spiralling descent.

Nevertheless, there had been only a handful of survivors. Chapter Master Titus Valens, Librarian Epistolary Liventius and six Sternguard veterans had crawled from the wreckage, along with Coadjutor Aquilius. Against all odds, Verenus of the Boros 232nd had also survived along with three of his soldiers. 'Status report,' growled the Chapter Master as he stomped up the steps of the temple.

'We are cut off and completely surrounded,' said one of the Sternguard veterans, accessing an auspex built into his bionic left arm. 'Captain Decimus of 5th Company is moving on our position, coordinating Guard platoons and armoured companies. A Thunderhawk is inbound to pick us up.'

'We move into the temple and hold out for reinforcements,' said the Chapter Master. 'Now.'

Supporting their injured, the cluster of Space Marines and Guardsmen began hurrying across the open square towards the steps leading up to the Temple of the Gloriatus.

'Any word of Proconsul Ostorius yet?' said Titus Valens.

'Not yet,' came the reply.

'The enemy,' warned Librarian Epistolary Liventius.

Aquilius lifted his gaze towards the top of the stairs to see Word Bearers marching into view, blocking their access to the Temple of the Gloriatus.

Chapter Master Titus Valens called a halt, and the cluster of Space Marines readied themselves, slamming fresh clips into bolters and unsheathing chainblades. The Chapter Master activated his thunder hammer, and the sharp odour of ozone reached Aquilius's nostrils.

'Aquilius, you must not fall,' said Chapter Master Valens. 'The White Angel is all that is holding Boros together. We have to buy Ostorius the time to finish his mission. All else is of secondary concern.'

'My lord,' said Aquilius. 'What are you saying?'

'Liventius, get him to safety,' said the Chapter Master.

At the top of the stairs, the Word Bearers gave way deferentially, bowing their heads and stepping aside. A savage-looking warrior-priest appeared atop the stairs. The Word Bearer wore a skull-faced helmet and bore a profane mockery of a Chaplain's crozius arcanum in one of his armoured fists. The Traitor's plate was bedecked in unholy oath papers and insane scratchings. Aquilius felt a surge of hatred and revulsion. This foul warrior must have been who they were waiting for.

'A Dark Apostle,' Aquilius spat.

'Listen to me,' said Chapter Master Valens. 'There is a fortified landing pad within the golden dome of the Temple of the Gloriatus. It is accessible via subterranean tunnels. There are service elevators less than two kilometres south-south-east of here.'

Librarian Epistolary Liventius raised an eyebrow.

'I trained here as a novitiate,' the Chapter Master said in answer to the unspoken question. 'I am target-marking the location for you now.'

'My lord, you are coming with us?' said Liventius, frowning.

'It has been an honour to lead you, my brothers,' said the Chapter Master.

'My lord,' said Liventius. 'Titus! You cannot be considering this!'

'I am giving you an order, Epistolary,' growled the Chapter Master. 'All of you. I will hold them here. Keep Aquilius alive.'

Aquilius's eyes were wide. He looked between the Chapter Master and Librarian Epistolary Liventius.

'I cannot–' said Liventius.

'I am giving you an order!' barked the Chapter Master, beginning to climb the stairs towards the waiting Dark Apostle. 'Go!'

Aquilius and the other battle-brothers stood in silence, indecision clawing at them.

'Go!' boomed their Chapter Master. 'Liventius! I am ordering you to lead these men to safety.'

MARDUK SMILED BEHIND his skull helm as he watched the Chapter Master of the White Consuls climbing the stairs to meet him. The Space Marine was garbed in gold-edged Terminator armour and rivalled Kol Badar in size.

He wore no helmet, and his face was broad. As he drew closer, Marduk could see the shadow of the primarch Guilliman within the Chapter Master's features, and hatred swelled within him.

The Chapter Master carried a thunder hammer and storm shield, and his ornate armour was hung with a blue, battle-scorched tabard. Several of his pathetically small retinue of veterans moved to interpose themselves between their lord and Marduk, but they were ordered curtly back by their Terminator-armoured commander.

'Do we shoot him?' asked Kol Badar, at Marduk's shoulder.

'No,' the Dark Apostle said. 'Let him approach.'

At Marduk's urging, the Word Bearers backed away, forming a wide semi-circle at the top of the stairs. Warily, the White Consuls stepped into the circle, gaze locked on Marduk's.

'Burias!' barked Marduk, not taking his eyes off the White Consuls. The slender Icon Bearer, having recently regrouped with the Host, stepped forward instantly. 'You want him?'

Burias smiled broadly in response, and handed the Host's icon to Khalaxis. He allowed the change to come upon him and became one with the daemon within.

THE CIRCLE OF Word Bearers stood in silence as Burias-Drak'shal and the White Consul circled each other. Daemons looped overhead.

The White Consul was easily three times the Icon Bearer's weight, and he stomped around heavily, keeping his storm shield between them. Burias-Drak'shal stalked around him, moving in a low crouch. He bore no weapon. He needed none. His fingers had fused into elongated talons easily capable of punching through ceramite, and his distended jaw erupted in a savage display of tusks.

He loped left and right, bestial head low, seeking a weakness in his enemy's defence. The White Consul kept his storm shield up, his thunder hammer held at the ready.

When the possessed warrior struck, it was with all his preternatural speed and strength. With a roar, he flew at the White Consul, little more than a blur. The storm shield sparked, and the Icon Bearer was thrown backwards, landing heavily. He was on his feet again in an instant, leaping at the Chapter Master with talons extended.

He landed on the White Consul Terminator's storm shield clawed feet first, and clutched at the top of it with the talons of his left hand. Barbed claws hooked around the edge of the storm shield, dragging it low even as the stink of scorched flesh filled the air. With his free hand, the Icon Bearer slashed at the Chapter Master, thirty-centimetre talons raking across his gorget.

The White Consul slammed the haft of his thunder hammer into Burias-Drak'shal's face with staggering force, dislodging him from his shield. The Icon Bearer dropped to the ground, landing on all fours. The Chapter Master moved after him, hammer crackling with arcs of electricity.

Burias-Drak'shal leapt backwards, talons scratching deeply into the marble slabs beneath him as he scrambled to avoid the hammer blow. The head of the White Consul's weapon slammed into the marble slab with a sharp crack of discharging power. Stone splintered beneath the strike.

Burias-Drak'shal caught the next blow with a taloned hand, halting it mid-swing, his warp-spawned musculature straining to keep the weapon at bay. The Chapter Master smashed his storm shield into him, knocking him backwards.

Moving with surprising swiftness, the White Consul followed up on the momentarily stunned possessed warrior and struck a brutal blow towards his chest. Burias-Drak'shal tried to sway aside, but the hammer caught him on the shoulder. There was an explosive, percussive shock, and he was thrown to the ground. When he came back to his feet, his left arm was hanging uselessly at his side. His shoulder pad had been torn loose, and his plate armour underneath was sundered and leaking red-black ichor that hissed as it dripped onto the marble underfoot.

Within seconds the possessed warrior's arm was healing, but he was in considerable pain.

When it came, the end of the fight was brutal and abrupt. A hammer blow ripped one of Burias-Drak'shal curving horns from his head, and hot daemon blood sprayed from the wound. A droplet struck the Chapter Master in his left eye, burning into the retina, and for a fraction of a second the White Consul turned his head away, eyes closing reflexively. That was all the opening that Burias-Drak'shal needed.

Ducking beneath the Chapter Master's backhand swipe he leapt in close, talons ramming into the warrior's side. He could not penetrate the thick armour, but using the momentum of the blows, he swung his mutated body up around the heavier Marine's back like an ape, coming to rest in a crouch atop the White Consul's broad shoulders, the claws of his feet digging deep.

Stabbing downwards with all his might, he punched the talons of his left hand through the top of the Chapter Master's skull, killing him instantly. With a tremendous crash, the warrior fell.

Burias-Drak'shal mounted the Chapter Master's chest in an instant, pounding at the already dead warrior's face over and over. The White Consul's skull collapsed beneath his blows, even super-hardened Astartes bone unable to withstand the sheer brutality Burias-Drak'shal unleashed upon it.

'Enough,' said Marduk, finally.

Breathing heavily, the Icon Bearer rose to his full height. The blood liberally coating his face matched the colour of his armour. He lifted both arms high into the air and threw his head back, howling his victory to the heavens, that the gods might witness his triumph.

AQUILIUS AND THE other White Consuls heard that cry as they reached the bottom of the temple stairs. The young Coadjutor made the sign of the aquila. Atop the stairs, the hateful silhouette of the Dark Apostle could be seen. More than one of the veterans seemed ready to run back, but Librarian Epistolary Liventius forestalled any such rash move.

'More Traitors moving in,' warned one of the veterans. Rhinos and Predators were rolling up the boulevards and causeways leading into the square, threatening to box the White Consuls in.

The Librarian held for a moment and put his hand to his face. He pulled it away to find splashes of crimson coating the fingertips of his gauntlets. Trickles of blood flowed from his nostrils.

'Liventius…?' said Aquilius.

'I sense something.'

'More of the enemy?'

'No. This is something… new. I've never felt a presence like this before. Let's move. Now, brothers,' said Liventius.

Aquilius cast one last glance up towards the top of the stairs.

'Let him not have died in vain,' he said. 'Everything rests with Proconsul Ostorius now.'

ANY LESSER MAN would already have been dead.

Ostorius was a bloody ruin, his body broken and his face unrecognisable. One eye was swollen shut, and his nose had been broken in three places. His left cheekbone was fractured and splinters of bone pressed through his flesh. His skull was cracked and leaking. Blood and spit dribbled from his mouth, and he spat a handful of teeth out onto the deck floor as he pushed himself unsteadily back to his feet once more.

His left arm was broken and hanging useless at his side. Nevertheless, he still clasped his power sword in his right hand. He lunged at his foe, the tip of his sword stabbing for the Word Bearer's heart.

With a dismissive backhand slap, his attack was knocked aside. A thunderous open hand strike hit Ostorius square in the face. A chopping blow to the side of the White Consul's neck sent him crashing back to the floor.

Grand Apostle Ekodas was completely unscathed, though his hands were covered in blood. He stalked back and forth as he waited for Ostorius to pick himself up.

Again and again, Ostorius got up, attacked and was knocked down. The circle of Word Bearers watched impassively as their lord dismantled the White Consul piece by piece, breaking bones and rupturing organs at will.

At last, Ekodas tired of his sport. He caught Ostorius's arm as he launched a weak overhead strike. Spinning in behind his opponent, Ekodas wrapped an arm around his neck.

'All over now,' said Ekodas in Ostorius's ear. The brutalised White Consul's unfocussed gaze lingered on the Nexus Arrangement.

With a violent twist, Ekodas broke the Proconsul's neck.

MARDUK'S EYES WERE narrowed as he watched the pitiful cluster of White Consuls and Guardsmen scurrying across the square below.

'Take them,' he said, and the warriors of the 34th Host broke into a charge, leaping down the steps in pursuit.

They were halfway down when the heavens exploded.

Like a star going supernova, the Kronos star fort detonated in an almighty explosion that lit up the planet below in blinding, harsh white light.

'What in the name of the gods?' breathed Ashkanez.

Something changed in the quality of the air. Marduk could feel it even within his hermetically sealed armour. It was as if the air were suddenly charged with electricity, making the thick, matted hairs of his cloak stand on end.

A hot wind blew down from above, sending eddies of dust and ash spinning across the square. The heavens had began to roil like an angry whirlpool, clouds of ash, smoke and toxic pollutants swirling madly. Directly overhead, they began to spiral in an anti-clockwise direction, as if a cyclone of tremendous proportions were brewing. It looked like a giant maelstrom, a vortex that began to rotate with increasing volatility. Marduk felt unease begin to form within his gut. His natural response to such an unfamiliar emotion was aggression and violence, and fresh combat drugs were pumped through his veins, flooding his system.

'Are *we* doing that?' growled Burias, once again holding his revered icon in his hands, the daemon pushed back below the surface.

'No,' said Marduk. 'I feel no touch of the warp here. None at all. It is... something else.'

Anthony Reynolds

Whatever it was, it began descending into the atmosphere. And it was *huge*.

BOOK FIVE: RETRIBUTION

'We are all eternal, my brothers. All this pain is but an illusion.'

*– Dark Apostle Mah'keenen, scrawled
in blood on the eve of his sacrifice*

CHAPTER FIFTEEN

At first it was nothing more than a shadow in the heavens, obscured by the crimson miasma hanging in the atmosphere of Boros Prime. It blotted out the twin suns, casting darkness as deep as night across the city below. It loomed large, seeming to spread from horizon to horizon, and it got nearer.

At first, Marduk thought perhaps it was a battlecruiser crashing down to earth, a casualty of the ongoing war in orbit above Boros, but he saw that this shape was bigger than that, larger even than Ekodas's flagship, the immense *Crucius Maledictus*. The star fort itself?

The spiralling downwind intensified and a gap in the centre of the maelstrom appeared. This break in the cloud cover should have afforded those upon the surface of Boros Prime their first unobscured glimpse of the sky since the arrival of the Word Bearers. The angry welt of the Eye of Terror should have been visible across the heavens, but something blotted out the view. Blue skies should have been visible within that growing gap, but all that could be seen through it was darkness, an enveloping emptiness that seemed to swallow all light.

It was the underside of a vessel so vast as to put the largest battlecruiser to shame, yet Marduk knew instantly that this was not the falling Kronos star fort. Whatever this vessel was, it had destroyed the orbital bastion, utterly and completely. The rotating clouds continued to part before it. As it descended ever closer, eerie glowing green lights lit up along its black underside. Marduk felt a spike of trepidation.

The last of the clouds were sent fleeing over the horizon, and the xenos vessel was finally fully revealed. It must have been easily fifteen kilometres across, and it cast its shadow over the entire city. The dull glow of the obscured suns framed it like an eclipse, giving all those below a sense of the vessel's shape.

It was an immense, perfectly geometric crescent, curving like a sickleblade, and it hung in low atmosphere, an executioner's axe ready to fall. Something so large should not have been able to descend so close to the planet's surface without being dragged down by the planet's gravity, no matter how powerful its engines were. Yet still it descended.

The energy it must have been exerting to resist the pull of gravity and keep its immense bulk from crashing to earth was beyond imagining, far in excess of anything that could be fathomed by a human mind. Nevertheless, while the fierce downwind continued to buffet the city below, they were hardly of the scale that Marduk would have imagined necessary to keep such a structure aloft. Indeed, there appeared to be no blazing engines burning with the heat of a thousand suns upon the vessel's underside at all.

How it was controlling its descent was beyond his understanding, and yet in defiance of all natural law and rational thought it continued to penetrate the low atmosphere, drawing steadily nearer the surface of Boros Prime.

The immense xenos vessel was so utterly black that it seemed to absorb the light, and this darkness made the glowing green lines that spread across its underside in alien, geometric patterns all the brighter. Tens of thousands of glowing hieroglyphs could be discerned upon its sheer underside, symbols that might have been some form of inhuman picture writing consisting of lines, circles and crescents. One symbol was larger than the others – a circle with lines of differing lengths projecting from it, like the stylised beams of a sun.

Marduk had seen this symbol before on an Imperial backwater planet called Tanakreg. There, it had appeared upon the sheer obsidian flanks of an alien structure deeply embedded in the rock of an evaporated ocean floor. He knew what manner of beings resided within: undying constructs of living metal, devoid of fear, compassion or mercy, unfettered by mortal concerns. They were a deadly foe, nigh unstoppable, and his blood ran cold as he realised for what purpose they had surely come here.

'Call in our Stormbirds,' ordered Marduk as he reached the bottom of the Imperial temple's stairs. His voice was tense. 'Have the *Infidus Diabolus* readied. I want full and immediate extraction. *Now.*'

'WHAT NEW HORROR is this?' breathed Coadjutor Aquilius, eyes wide, pausing just before he dropped down into the sub-tunnels that would lead into the lower levels of the Temple of the Gloriatus.

Librarian Epistolary Liventius too was looking up. His face was grave.

'Come, brothers,' said the Librarian at last.

Moving warily, weapons at the ready, the cluster of wounded White Consuls and Guardsmen ducked their heads and moved into the tunnels. The heavy blast-doors slammed behind them with grim finality.

KOL BADAR'S EYES were locked on the immense shape hovering low in the atmosphere overhead. He had offered no argument to the Dark Apostle's order to abandon this world. Marduk knew that he too recognised the nature of this vessel hovering oppressively over the city. Marduk heard the crackle of vox-traffic as the Coryphaus began ordering the evacuation.

'Master?' said Ashkanez, scowling darkly. 'What is this? We are going to abandon all we have fought for?'

Ignoring his First Acolyte, the only member of the 34th Host who had not fought on Tanakreg, Marduk began barking orders, commanding his forces to pull back and regroup, ready for extraction.

'Master!' said Ashkanez more forcefully. 'We must finish what we started! The sons of Guilliman cannot be allowed to live!'

Marduk continued to ignore him.

'This world is not yet ours,' growled Ashkanez. 'We cannot make extraction before Grand Apostle Ekodas gives us leave to commence the–'

The First Acolyte was silenced as Marduk spun around suddenly and clamped a hand around his throat, snarling. The broad features of Ashkanez flared with anger and for a moment Marduk thought – even hoped – that his First Apostle would strike out at him, but the stony mask of composure fell across Ashkanez's features once more, and the First Acolyte lowered his gaze.

'No, this world is not yet ours, and nor will it be, not now. You have no comprehension of what that is,' said Marduk, gesturing up at the immense shape looming ever larger in the heavens, 'nor of what its appearance portends. We leave *now*. Ekodas be damned.'

'So the Imperials have unexpected reinforcements,' said Ashkanez. 'What does it matter? We must finish the Consuls while they are weak and vulnerable.'

'Ignorant fool,' said Marduk. 'These are no Imperial allies.'

He released his First Acolyte with a shove, sneering.

He saw Ashkanez glance over Marduk's shoulder, and only then did he register the hulking presence of someone standing threateningly close behind him. With a glance he saw it was the berserker Khalaxis, exalted champion of 17th Coterie. The big warrior's chest was rising and falling heavily, and his ritualistically scarred face, framed by matted dreadlocks, was contorted in a bestial snarl.

'Is there a problem, Khalaxis?' growled Marduk, glaring up into the champion's red-tinged, frenzied eyes. He was amongst the tallest warriors of the Host, and Marduk came barely to his chin.

Out of corner of his eye, Marduk saw Ashkanez glance skyward, then back at Khalaxis. The First Acolyte seemed indecisive for a moment, then gave a brief shake of his head – reluctantly, it seemed to Marduk.

'Move away now, brother,' said Sabtec, stepping protectively in front of Marduk. The champion of the hallowed 13th had his hand on the hilt of his sword.

The massive exalted champion refused to back down, still glaring over Sabtec's head at Marduk, violence written in his gaze. Marduk was very aware of the immense chainaxe clasped in the towering warrior's hands and blood-rage that Khalaxis clearly held only barely in check.

'Khalaxis,' snapped Ashkanez.

With a last threatening glare, the berserker swung away, stamping off to rejoin his Coterie.

'Do not be too hard on Khalaxis, my lord,' said Ashkanez. 'His choler was in the ascendant. He meant no disrespect.'

'When we get out of this, you and I are going to have... words, First Acolyte,' said Marduk.

Ashkanez bowed his head in supplication.

'As it pleases you, my master,' he said, his tone neutral.

Marduk saw Burias smirk.

'Assault shuttles inbound,' confirmed Kol Badar.

Marduk glanced across the expanse of the square. The White Consuls were long gone now. Ever since Calth, the desire to kill and maim the sons of Guilliman, to destroy all that they stood for, had consumed him. Now he was allowing these gene-descendants of the Ultramarines to escape him, but he swallowed back his hatred, for there were issues of more pressing importance that demanded his attention. Namely, keeping himself alive. His gaze ventured skywards once more.

On Tanakreg, a xenos pyramid of ancient, inhuman design had sat deep within an abyssal trench located far beneath the acidic oceans of that backwater planet. There it had resided for countless millennia, dormant and lifeless. Its location had been revealed after the oceans had been boiled away by the actions of the 34th Host, under the leadership of Marduk's predecessor, the Dark Apostle Jarulek. Marduk, Jarulek's First Acolyte, had been amongst those that had penetrated the alien pyramid, descending into its claustrophobic interior. It was a tomb, Marduk had realised, and by penetrating into its dark heart, the Word Bearers had awakened its guardians from their eternal slumber.

It had been there, deep within the alien crypts of the xenos pyramid, that he had entered the inner sanctum of a being the ancient apocrypha of the Word Bearers named the Undying One. This being was unimaginably ancient, a thing that Marduk suspected was as old as the heavens themselves. There in the Undying One's insane realm, a place far beyond his understanding where distance and time seemed as malleable as living flesh, Marduk had discovered the Nexus Arrangement, the potent piece of alien technology that had made this attack on the Boros Gate sector possible. There too, Marduk had left his master, Jarulek. The Dark Apostle had turned on him once his usefulness had passed, but it had been Marduk that had emerged triumphant.

Marduk had long plotted Jarulek's downfall. It might not have happened the way he had planned, but it mattered little. Jarulek had perished, and Marduk had escaped from the Undying One's maddening realm, taking with him his prize, the Nexus.

A niggling doubt remained, buried deep within his consciousness, that the malevolent sentient being had *allowed* him to leave its realm. Always, Marduk had refused to entertain the errant thought, but now, seeing this immense vessel descending down towards the city, the whisper of doubt returned. Instinctively, he knew the malign intelligence that commanded this vessel was the same as that he had encountered beneath the alien pyramid. Doubtless it came to reclaim what had been stolen from it.

The immense xenos vessel was now so close that Marduk imagined he could almost touch its obsidian underside, yet it was still at least a kilometre above the city.

It is not my fate to die here, Marduk thought, defiantly. Nothing in the portents had spoken of his death.

The immense alien vessel had come to rest some two hundred metres above the city, looming claustrophobically low overhead. No hint of the sky beyond it could be glimpsed now. It felt as if the planet had an unsupported low roof that might drop to crush those beneath it at any moment.

Green-tinged lightning arced across its underside, dancing across its obsidian surfaces. Geometric designs throbbed, growing brighter and then dimming, like a heartbeat, and thousands of alien hieroglyphs flared into glowing, green life.

'Where are the Stormbirds?' hissed Marduk.

'Incoming, one minute,' said Kol Badar. He pointed into the distance. A flock of dark craft could be seen hurtling in their direction, flying low over the city. 'There.'

A high frequency electronic whine that made Marduk's skin crawl sounded in the distance. Its pitch ascended sharply, and as it moved beyond the range of Astartes hearing, a column of ghostly light as wide as a city block stabbed downwards from the alien vessel, perhaps two kilometres away to the north. Arcs of electricity danced along the shaft's ethereal edges. The light of the column did not dissipate, but stayed firmly targeted on the city, like some immense, motionless spotlight.

'What in the hells of Sicarus is that?' said Ashkanez.

A second whine sounded and another spotlight stabbed downwards, this time appearing perhaps five kilometres south of their position.

Further whines heralded more columns of ghostly light, until there were a dozen of them projected blindingly downwards, linking the alien craft to the city below. They shone like divine pillars in the darkness, as if holding the xenos vessel aloft.

A further electronic whine began to sound, piercing in its intensity, louder than any other so far. Gazing upwards Marduk saw a ring of light burning brightly on the underside of the xenos vessel, directly overhead. It grew steadily more intense, and while the auto-reactive lenses of his helmet compensated for the sudden, white-hot light, dulling it back to a manageable level, he nevertheless raised an arm to shield his eyes. If it were some form of weapon, a lance-beam of monstrous scale, Marduk realised that he and his brothers would be directly beneath the blast.

Setting his feet firmly, Marduk roared his fury at the heavens. If he were to die, then he would do so defiant and unrepentant to the last.

Blinding, diffused light surrounded Marduk and his brethren, and the air crackled with a powerful electrical charge. It took Marduk half a second to realise that he lived still, that the column of light was not destructive in nature, and he gave a short prayer of thanks to the gods of the æther.

The moment's respite did not last.

The air around him shimmered and crackled with intensity, as if the particles of the air were vibrating violently, and sparks of bright light danced across the armour plates of the uneasy Word Bearers.

'Energy readings are off the scale,' said Sabtec, his brows furrowed, looking at the daemonically-infused auspex in his hands.

'Something is making transference,' hissed Kol Badar, the bladed lengths of his power talons clenching and unclenching reflexively. 'I can feel it in my bones.'

'Stand ready!' said Marduk, hefting his crozius.

'Something is coming through,' shouted Sabtec, turning around on the spot, eyes locked on the throbbing red blister-display of his auspex. He stopped abruptly, and his eyes lifted. 'There! Three hundred and twenty metres! Elevation 3.46!'

Marduk looked where his champion pointed. At first he saw nothing. Then a ball of crackling energy blinked into existence, hanging perhaps twenty metres above the city. It was positioned in the centre of a wide boulevard that led up towards the square. The Word Bearers began to back away, weapons raised. The air around the sphere of flickering energy wavered, and sparking electricity stabbed outwards from its centre.

'What–' began Ashkanez, but he never finished.

With a deep whoosh, the crackling ball of light expanded suddenly to a hundred times its former size. Coronas of lightning sparked madly within it, and the Word Bearers fell back a step defensively as the blast overtook them. It lasted only a fraction of a second before it contracted sharply once more, accompanied by a deep sucking sound like air being vented into a vacuum. It shrank in upon itself, collapsing to something the size of a pea before exploding.

With a deafening crack, blinding white light burst out in all directions, and the sphere of energy was gone. In its place was a slowly spinning flat-topped pyramid roughly the size of a super-heavy tank, hovering ten metres above the ground. It was formed of light-absorbing black stone, and green electricity played along its blank, sheer surfaces.

It hung there in the air, turning lazily, and then its form began to alter. Glowing green lines appeared upon its smooth surfaces, and four oblong pillars of black stone rose from the corners of its top, rising like battlements atop a fortress. Rib-like sections of the prism's sides slid upwards, forming a hollow cage atop it. A single wider arc, like an architectural buttress of unearthly design, glided smoothly upwards to position itself over the hollow cage.

A massive dark green crystal, easily three metres in height, rose up from within the prism until it was hanging unsupported within this hollow cage-like formation. This crystal was perfect in its angular symmetry, and flickered with inner light. Sparking green electrical impulses darted between it and the rib-like buttresses enclosing it, tentatively at first, then building in frequency and power. The light within the crystal intensified, until it was glowing brightly, and the shower of sparks coalescing around it crackled like sheet lightning.

Hieroglyphs and pictograms pulsed into life upon the sheer sides of the prism, and weapon-turrets emerged from crenellations that appeared upon the four corners of the pyramid. They began to rotate mechanically, and green lightning flickered along the length of their barrels. Targeting reticules within Marduk's helmet flashed, locking onto these weapons.

'Take it down!' he roared.

COADJUTOR AQUILIUS EMERGED with his brethren from the service elevator. They stood upon the high crenulated battlements of the designated landing pad the incoming Thunderhawk was aiming for, high atop the Temple of the Gloriatus. A golden dome rose behind them, topped with a gleaming statue of the Emperor. How it still remained intact among the destruction was a minor miracle in itself, Aquilius thought.

Standing nearly thirty metres tall, it was to view this that so many of the devout made the pilgrimage to Boros Prime. It was said that to look upon the statue was to look upon the divine. So skilled had its artisans been that the sublime expression upon the statue's face brought tears to the eyes of all who looked upon it. Aquilius felt some comfort to be standing beneath its gaze.

One of the injured Sternguard veterans was lowered to the ground. The battle-brother propped himself up with his back to the crenulations and Aquilius stood, looking out over the battlements across the square below. What he saw made his breath catch in his throat.

The Word Bearers below firing upon a slowly revolving black pyramid hovering above the ground. Where the xenos thing had come from, Aquilius knew not.

Missiles detonated ineffectively upon the structure's sheer, black surfaces, and he watched as autocannon rounds stitched across its sides. The heavy-calibre shells ricocheted harmlessly off the dark stone, causing not so much as a crack in its surface. Lascannon beams struck its angled sides, yet the energy was merely absorbed into the alien structure, making its hieroglyphs momentarily glow brighter.

A widening circle was cleared before the alien prism as the Word Bearers spread out into cover as it descended towards the ground. It came to rest a metre above the marble square, and began to return fire.

An arc of lightning erupted from one of its rotating armatures, striking a cluster of Word Bearers who had taken cover behind a low balustrade. There was a blinding explosion of light and half a dozen of the traitor Space Marines were sent flying, their bodies blackened and smoking. They hit the ground hard, their bodies twitching as remnants of green electricity flickered across their armour. The marble balustrade was completely obliterated, and a circle of smoking ash marked where the potent arc had hit.

The other rotating armatures fired, causing destruction to all and sundry, striking anything within a thirty metres radius. A Predator battle tank, a crucified White Consul nailed to the front of its armoured chassis, was reversing away from the deadly xenos prism, its turret-mounted twin lascannons firing desperately and ineffectually. A lightning arc whipped out and struck the Predator, sending it flipping backwards, end over end, a blackened shell flickering with sparks.

A doorway of shimmering light appeared within one side of the black prism, and Aquilius watched in horrified fascination as a pair of deathly, robotic skeletons marched from within, stepping down onto the marble surface of Victory Square, their movements in perfect synchronicity.

Their gaunt, skeletal bodies appeared to be formed of dark metal, and glowing green light oozed from their empty eye sockets. They held long-barrelled weapons across their hollow chests, and the light of gunfire and electricity reflected sharply off their silver craniums and bones.

In pairs, skeletal soldiers marched from within the prism in a steady stream, and they began to form a phalanx. Several of them were felled by concentrated Word Bearers fire, but many of the undead warriors simply rose back to their feet seconds later, the damage they had sustained repairing itself seamlessly. Severed limbs reattached themselves and craters caused by detonating bolt rounds in heads and chests disappeared as if they had never been.

Still more skeletal warriors stepped through the doorway of flickering light, far more than could have possibly fitted within the prism, moving steadily, their pace unhurried and relentless. Aquilius realised the prism must be acting as a form of gateway, linking to the immense ship hanging in low orbit overhead. His mind boggled as he imagined the number of humanoid sentinels that a vessel of such size might contain.

More of the black-sided prisms blinked into existence above Victory Square, spinning lazily as they descended slowly towards the ground. Each began undergoing the same transformation that the first had, glowing crystals rising from their centres and rib-like buttresses sliding up their sheer sides as they powered up.

A krak missile struck the crystal emerging from the inside of one of the xenos prisms before it had come fully to life, and it exploded into a million shards. Like a marionette with its strings cut, the prism dropped like a stone, its glowing hieroglyphs fading to darkness. By the time it hit the square below, it was nothing more than an inert, lifeless hunk of stone.

Smaller spheres of light glimmered in the air, like a host of sparking fireflies, before contracting sharply, and other shapes blinked into reality.

Spider-like robotic constructs the size of Dreadnoughts appeared, looming above the Word Bearers, their arachnid, metal legs clicking beneath them. Clusters of glowing green eyes blinked and locked onto the milling traitors below. Binaric clicks issued from their silver mandibles, and they descended upon the enemy's ranks, huge metal pincers snapping Traitor Astartes in two.

Other xenos beings materialised, resembling some kind of bizarre, mechanised centaur. From the waist up they were the manifestation of horrific skeletal humanoids, while their lower bodies were some form of anti-grav skiff. Their right arms had been replaced with multi-barrelled cannons, pulsing with intense, green electrical currents. Moving with unhurried grace, their movements conducted in perfect unison, these new arrivals hovered several metres above the heads of the Word Bearers. They began to unleash the power of their alien weaponry, and Aquilius felt a mixture of horror and awe as he witnessed the beams of light passing right through the bodies of the Traitors, leaving gaping holes in ceramite armour and flesh alike.

Victory Square was now a chaotic warzone, with traitors battling furiously with the xenos constructs.

A flight of traitor Stormbirds and Thunderhawks, their gore-splashed hulls hung with chains and daemonic symbology, came screaming in low over the rooftops, engines spewing orange flame. One of them was instantly struck by a whiplash of discharging electricity, sending it into a spiralling death spin. It came down hard, one wing ripping off as it struck a soaring buttress of the Temple of the Gloriatus. The fifty-tonne piece of masonry came crashing down in a shower of marble, and the Stormbird ploughed into the square, killing dozens of traitors and skeletal xenos warriors as it exploded into a towering fireball.

The other shuttles dropped down through the mayhem, weapon systems firing, and the Word Bearers began streaming towards them as their assault ramps slammed down onto the square.

'Thunderhawk inbound,' said one of the blue-helmed Sternguard veterans, his white crest shivering from the amount of electricity pulsing through the air. 'Three minutes.'

Aquilius wondered briefly what the point was anymore. Ostorius had failed. There was no hope of salvation.

He felt a hand on his arm, and looked down into the strong face of the Imperial officer, Verenus of the Boros 232nd.

'As long as the White Angel is with us, there is always hope,' said the solder, with a smile.

Aquilius shook his head, smiling despite himself.

Then Verenus's head disintegrated, ripped apart molecule by molecule as an arc of green energy struck it.

Aquilius swore and fell back, scrabbling for his bolter.

A TRIO OF skeletal constructs hove into view, flying along at the same level as the temple's battlements. Aquilius was dragged backwards as the xenos constructs fired again, and a head-sized chunk of the battlements disintegrated, right where he had been standing a fraction of a second earlier. One of the Sternguard veterans fell, a gaping hole torn through his body.

The veteran that had pulled Aquilius back fired his plasma pistol, taking one of the mechanoids in the head. Its leering skull face was replaced with a molten crater as the white hot burst of plasma struck it, and it dropped out of sight, falling to the ground thirty metres below the wall.

Bolts pattered off the chests of the other two, and the Imperials fled before them, retreating inside the temple precinct. Aquilius glanced back over his shoulder to see the fallen construct rising from the ground, its skull reforming before his eyes.

'Emperor above,' breathed Aquilius.

'How long till that Thunderhawk arrives?' barked Liventius.

'One minute, Epistolary!' came the reply.

It seemed like a lifetime.

'HURRY, REVERED ONE!' bellowed Marduk, urging the Warmonger up the ramp of the Stormbird. The Dreadnought clomped its way into the shuttle's assault bay, even as more warrior-brothers bolted up the ramp to take their seats.

'Full!' shouted Sabtec, and Marduk nodded.

'Go!' roared Marduk.

He was standing in the doorway of the Stormbird, firing his bolt pistol. He slammed his fist onto a panel on inner wall, and the embarkation ramp began to close. Retro thrusters roared, and the heavy assault craft lifted off.

He could see First Acolyte Ashkanez and his Icon Bearer, Burias, some distance away, boarding another Stormbird. He raised his hand as Burias looked in his direction, but the Icon Bearer turned away.

All the Word Bearers within the square were streaming towards the assault shuttles that were touching down. Rhinos accelerated up embarkation ramps, tracks skidding, and Land Raiders and Predators were grasped by coupling claws beneath Thunderhawks, ready for transportation

Before Marduk's Stormbird could pull away, a giant mechanical pincer tore into the closing assault ramp, punching through the reinforced plasteel. In one violent motion the entire hatch was ripped off its pneumatic hinges, and Marduk came face to face with one of the immense, robotic spider-constructs, hovering outside. Its cluster of green eyes glimmered with malign intelligence. Its mandibles quivered and it emitted an indecipherable torrent of electronic clicks and whistles. It lifted its other slender fore-claw, which ended in a long barrel flickering with energy.

Marduk swore and threw himself sidewards as the mechanised construct fired into the cramped interior of the Stormbird. Three Word Bearers were consumed in the blast, and they roared in pain. The searing beam took apart their power armour molecule by molecule, before setting to work on the flesh, flaying skin and muscle exposing the skeleton beneath. In turn, even the warrior-brothers' bones were atomised. It was a deeply unsettling sight, even to one such as Marduk.

Kol Badar planted his feet wide and unleashed a burst of fire into the spider's head, and a dozen of its glowing eyes darkened. It twitched, gliding backwards in the face of the fusillade, and then the Stormbird's engines fired at full power, lifting the assault craft away from the corpse-strewn square, which was still bathed in cold diffused light projected from above.

As the Stormbird rose, it passed through a thick cloud of dust that manifested out of nowhere amid a million tiny flashes of light.

No, not dust, Marduk realised. The particles were too large, and shone with reflective light. It was a cloud of tiny metallic insects, he realised, a million buzzing, robotic scarabs.

They swarmed in a tight-knit cloud that obscured his vision as the Stormbird rose through it. Hundreds of them swarmed through the gaping rent left in the side of the Stormbird where the assault ramp had been torn loose, tiny metal wings buzzing and thoraxes vibrating. Marduk staggered back away from the opening, keeping his centre of gravity low and swatting at the massed insects.

The scarabs, most no larger than the palm of a hand, some so small as to be almost invisible, skittered across every surface of the Stormbird's interior, their tiny silver legs and mandibles clicking. They flowed like a tide up the legs of the Word Bearers locked into the harnesses nearest the doorway and burrowed into their thick ceramite plates. One warrior screamed as he was covered from head to toe, the mechanical insects crawling up over the lip of his breastplate and down the inside of his armour, tunnelling into his flesh. The Word Bearer threw his restraint harness clear and rose to his feet, slapping and scratching at his armour. Marduk saw a bulge of scarabs beneath the skin of the warrior's face. He saw one of the tiny creatures emerge, its silver carapace slick with blood, burrowing out through his left eye socket.

The warrior turned around on the spot, grimacing, slapping and tearing at his own skin. As the Stormbird's angle of ascent steepened, he lost his footing and was sucked out of the gaping hole in the shuttle's hull.

'Flamers!' roared Kol Badar, and controlled bursts of promethium bathed the interior of the Stormbird. Scarabs squealed as they were consumed, and within a minute, the majority of the tiny constructs were gone.

The Stormbird continued to rise, leaving the chittering cloud behind.

Gripping onto guide rails tightly, Marduk moved to the gaping hole where the assault ramp had been torn away and leant out into the deafening wind, studying the lay of the land below. The full spectacle of the xenos' arrival could be seen as the Stormbird rose above the city.

Thousands of skeletal warriors were marching through the streets below, moving in perfect phalanxes. Tens of thousands of Guardsmen flooded the streets, fleeing before them. As the Stormbird pulled higher, Marduk could see hundreds of the black-sided prisms dotted all over the city, and even more xenos constructs were marching from them onto the streets with every passing minute.

As the Stormbird gained altitude, he saw a Reaver Titan of Legio Vulturus surrounded by six of the monoliths. The fire-blackened forms of two Warhounds lay twitching in smoking heaps nearby, buildings crushed beneath their carcasses. Arcs of energy struck the Reaver repeatedly. It brought one of the pyramids down with a concentrated burst of missiles launched from the pod upon its shoulders. Another was swatted aside by the Reaver's immense chainfist, the blow tearing the alien prism in half and sending it smashing into a fortified tower, bringing it crashing down. But even the mighty Reaver could not last against the monoliths, and one by one its flickering void shields were brought down by the relentless barrage it was sustaining from all sides. Like a cornered beast, it turned one way and another, seeking escape. It howled its fury as it came under direct assault again, arcs of green electricity ripping one arm away and tearing into its black carapace. It was finally brought down, and its ululating death cry rang out across the city.

Marduk whistled through his teeth as he witnessed the death of the ancient engine.

Reports flooded in. All across Boros Prime, the xenos were making their presence known. Ekodas's order came through, ordering all Hosts to evacuate immediately.

The planet belonged to the xenos.

IN THE CENTRE of the square below, unseen by mortal eyes, the thick cloud of metal scarabs was swarming into an ever denser, impenetrable cloud, hovering just metres above the scorched stonework. Robotic warriors formed up in precise ranks around this violently writhing shoal of mechanised insects. These warriors were larger and more heavily armoured than the other deathly automatons, and they clutched glaive-like weapons in their skeletal hands, their blades formed of flickering green light

The scarabs started to latch onto each other, barbed legs and mandibles locking together, and a vaguely humanoid shape began to take form. Insectoid bodies seemed to melt as if under an intense heat, their bodies turning to molten metal as they blurred together, sacrificing their individual forms to create something altogether more terrible.

Ghostly green light began to burn within hollow eye sockets. Coldly, the ancient being known as the Undying One turned to watch the Word Bearers retreat before it.

CHAPTER SIXTEEN

'Look at the size of it,' exclaimed Sabtec. The champion of the exalted 13th Coterie stood next to Marduk, peering out of the port side window of the Stormbird's cockpit.

The surface of Boros Prime was receding away below them as the heavy assault shuttle hurtled up through the tortured planet's atmosphere, angling towards the *Infidus Diabolus*, which was on an intercept path with them in orbit above. They were three thousand kilometres from the ground and rising steadily, and from their vantage point they were afforded a view across the immense, crescent-shaped vessel of the enemy xenos-constructs.

It was truly massive, larger than any ship that Marduk had ever laid eyes on. It rivalled the bulk of a Darkstar fortress. Having witnessed the effectiveness of the enemy's weapons upon the ground, the thought of what this titanic vessel might be capable of was horrifying. Marduk prayed to the Weaver of the Fates that they were out of range of whatever weapons system it might have at its disposal.

Blinding pillars of light beamed from the ship's underside down onto the city below, deploying its inhuman armies across the city in a spread of more than fifteen kilometres. Marduk shook his head in wonder. Less than ten minutes after first appearing in the upper atmosphere, the enemy had deployed tens of thousands of its troops and established complete dominion within the city below. Not even Astartes were able to deploy in such force at a speed to match that feat.

'How did they make translocation?' growled Kol Badar, removing his heavy, quad-tusked helmet. 'Has your precious Nexus Arrangement failed? Are the gates to the warp open?'

Marduk's eyelids flickered as he reached out with his soul-spirit. His entire body jolted a moment later as he slammed back into his body.

'No,' he said. 'The device remains effective. Nothing could have entered the system through the aether.'

'Well, it came from *somewhere*,' said Kol Badar.

'Perhaps it does not need the warp at all,' commented Sabtec.

Marduk shrugged.

The Word Bearers continued to study the enemy ship, their silence broken only by the crackling hiss of scanners, and the guttural growls and mechanical wheezing of the piloting servitors hardwired into the controls of the shuttle.

They were almost on a level with the xenos vessel, separated now by the three hundred kilometres of curved space. From this angle they could see three black-sided pyramids rising from the rear of the ship's crescent shape. Marduk judged them to be its command decks, and it was the largest of these that attracted his interest. He narrowed his eyes, and nodded his head slowly.

'I have seen this ship before,' said Marduk.

'What? Where?' said Kol Badar.

'On Tanakreg,' said Marduk.

'I do not recall seeing any such thing,' said the Coryphaus.

'That pyramid,' said Marduk, stabbing a finger onto the transparent, ice-cold surface of the port window. 'We have been inside it, Kol Badar.'

The Coryphaus nodded slowly, realisation dawning.

'Only its tip was exposed,' said Kol Badar. 'The rest of the ship was hidden beneath the ocean floor.'

'The gods alone know how long it was buried there,' said Marduk. The roar of the main drive engines subsided marginally, and stabilising jets kicked in, adjusting the Stormbird's angle of ascent.

'We've broken atmosphere,' confirmed Sabtec with a glance at the hissing display screens. As the shuttle came to a new heading, and the crescent shape of the xenos ship disappeared from view behind them. Ahead of them, just appearing over the red-tinged curvature of the world, they could make out the dark shape of the *Infidus Diabolus*, ploughing to meet them.

A veined blister in the ceiling began to blink.

'Transmission,' said Kol Badar, keying a sequence of buttons with the bladed tips of his power talons, his touch surprisingly delicate. 'It is from the *Crucius Maledictus*.'

'Ekodas,' said Marduk. 'Ignore it.'

'How many of our brothers made it off the ground?' asked Sabtec.

'Not enough,' said Marduk.

* * *

HALF A DOZEN assault shuttles had already docked as Marduk's Stormbird passed through the shimmering integrity field and entered one of the lower launch bays of the *Infidus Diabolus*. The deck was a hive of activity, with black-clad overseers and slave-gangs hurrying to attend to the newly arrived craft. Tracked crawlers ground across the floor, loaded high with fresh ammunition and fuel cells. Limping mecha-organics shrouded in black robes wafted incense, and hunched chirumeks attended to the wounded.

As the landing gear of the Stormbird touched down, Marduk marched from the shuttle, attended by his Coryphaus and a bodyguard of Anointed. He saw the burly figure of First Acolyte Ashkanez emerging from a nearby smoking Thunderhawk, Burias and Khalaxis flanking him. Marduk sneered, shaking his head.

Seeing him, the First Acolyte angled his march to meet him.

'I have had contact from Grand Apostle Ekodas,' said the First Acolyte by way of greeting. Marduk did not slow his pace, forcing Ashkanez to fall into step beside him. 'Fresh orders. We are to form up with the rest of the fleet and fall back out of range of the xenos ship. If it is Boros Prime that they want, then let them have it.'

'It is not the planet they want,' said Marduk. 'It is the Nexus.'

SIX SLAB-SIDED NECRON monoliths had formed a perfectly equidistant perimeter around Victory Square. Thousands of gleaming, skeletal warriors stood in serried, outward-facing ranks between these structures, silent sentinels that guarded all routes leading to the square. They stood in perfect, deathly stillness. If it was their master's wish, they would stand there for all eternity. They existed solely to serve, any semblance of will long having eroded to nothingness within the cold, lifeless shell of their bodies. Formations of destroyers patrolled the area, gliding soundlessly in perfectly coordinated patterns over the heads of the phalanxes below.

The being referred to in the ancient texts of the Word Bearers as the Undying One was positioned centrally within the square, the beaming light from its tomb ship overhead reflecting sharply off its gleaming, silver skeleton. Alone amongst its undying legions, it moved with grace and suppleness as it stretched its long, slender limbs. Alone amongst its kind, it retained some semblance of its former self, from a time long past, before the rise of man or eldar, when it had been a creature of flesh and blood.

From the waist up the ancient, hate-filled being was humanoid, a deathly parody of what it had resembled in life. From the waist down, however, its body was akin to one of the great tomb spyders that tended the undying legion across the emptiness of passing millennia. The Undying One's curving spine ran along the top of its insectoid lower body, which was covered in a series of protective armour plates of gleaming black, their smooth surfaces inscribed with intricate geometry. A dozen slender, arachnoid legs hung beneath its bulky dark silver abdomen, the long, multi-jointed limbs narrowing to slender blade-points.

A reflective obsidian breastplate had formed across the Undying One's thin, cadaverous chest. Upon this lustrous plate were fine, golden lines representing a sun and its life-giving rays. It wore a circlet of gold upon its silver skull, a regal crown of rulership that seemed to burn with the contained power of an enslaved sun. A death shroud billowed lazily around it, as if waving gently in an undersea current, the sheer material glistening with iridescence.

The ancient being's limbs were inscribed with arcane geometry and hieroglyphs, and it stretched its arms upwards, long, skeletal fingers unfurling. In response, the Undying One's immortal guardians began to emit a deep, reverberant note, a sound at once mournful and hollow.

A swirling wind picked up, and dust and ash eddied around the Undying One. Its death shroud was unaffected, wafting languidly in the air around it.

As the low bass note continued unabated, darkness descended over the square. The glowing eyes of the Undying One and its minions burned more fiercely in the deepening shadow. Green light spilled from the Undying One's underbelly, throwing the ancient being's body into silhouette.

Rolling its deathly head back, the terrifying being began to emit an unnatural shriek, making the air visibly vibrate. A shiver seemed to ripple out across the shadowed square, and filled with diabolic impulse, the wailing cry lifted up into the heavens, reaching out in all directions. Subtle vibrations were sent out like a fine mesh, and deep within the bowels of the *Crucius Maledictus*, the Nexus Arrangement responded to its master's summons.

GRAND APOSTLE EKODAS stood at the view portal, his expression unreadable.

'Grand Apostle,' said Kol Harekh, his Coryphaus.

'What is it?' Ekodas said over his shoulder, not taking his eyes off the xenos ship in the distance. Despite the distance, it still loomed impossibly large.

'I think we may have a further problem.'

Ekodas turned towards his Coryphaus, who gestured at the Nexus Arrangement, positioned centrally within his circular throne room. The corrupted magos worked feverishly, babbling nonsensically in his monotone drone.

The Grand Apostle stepped over the brutalised body of the White Consuls fool that had somehow managed to penetrate his inner sanctum and moved towards the magos, frowning. There was something happening, but he was not immediately sure what it was.

'The device, it looks unstable,' said Kol Harekh.

It was barely perceptible at first, but as he narrowed his eyes, Ekodas could see what his Coryphaus meant. The Nexus Arrangement was vibrating, and that movement was becoming more violent with every passing second, as if it were fighting to free itself from the contraption the magos had used to ensnare and control it.

Ekodas felt an uncomfortable pressure tugging at his soul, and he redoubled his potent psychic defences.

The kathartes daemons crouching in the alcoves high overhead clearly felt something too, and they began screeching.

'Are you doing this, magos?' said Ekodas.

Darioq-Grendh'al was hissing in agitation, his mechanised limbs shuddering and his mechadendrites a blur of motion as they danced across keypads and control dials. Bloody organic data-spikes were thrust into the cognifiers. A torrent of data, both spoken and clicking binaric cant, spilled from the corrupted magos's dead lips, a ceaseless flow of noise that Ekodas found for the most part indecipherable.

'Previously inert beta power levels surging beyond charted magnifiers, peaking at 99.224952 gamma-parsecs, expanding exponentially, outside source unknown, controlling mechanisms failing to compensate, capacitors levelling out, gone, failure, dead,' blurted the magos, his agitated voice interspersed with frantic clicks and beeps.

'Do something!' Ekodas said. 'You are losing it!'

Abruptly, one of the spinning rings that surrounded the Nexus seemed to wilt, the integrity of its shape compromised. Its rotation was thrown out as the ring became ovular in shape, and it began to list around unevenly. The light spilling from the Nexus Arrangement surged, becoming painfully bright, forcing Ekodas to turn away.

A keening wail echoed through the room, making the walls and workbenches shudder and vibrate.

'What in the gods?' said Kol Harekh, backing away.

The rings spinning around the Nexus exploded, riven into a thousand shards that burst outwards, embedding themselves deep into the room's walls, and into ceramite armour plates. Darioq-Grendh'al was thrown backwards, mechadendrites flailing. Two of his tentacles, still attached to control panels with umbilical data-spikes, were ripped from his spine as he was knocked backwards.

Ekodas hissed in pain as one of the shards impaled his thigh, the sliver of metal passing clean through his armour and flesh to protrude out the other side.

The housing that had been constructed to control and temper the alien device was a shattered ruin, electrical sparks leaping across its broken rings.

The Nexus Arrangement hung in mid-air. It was still for a moment. It had reverted back to its seamless orb form, and its violent vibrations had died down, leaving it utterly motionless.

Then, moving at a speed that not even an Astartes could follow, it began to accelerate.

THE SILVER ORB punched its way clear of the *Crucius Maledictus*, moving at tremendous speed, tearing clean through metre-thick bulkheads and countless levels of decking. It ripped straight through everything in its path, causing untold damage. It rent a gaping hole through the engine decks, coming within scant centimetres of penetrating the plasma core. It cut straight through the cavernous expanse of the ship's cavaedium, instantly killing a warrior-brother of the 64th Coterie as he knelt in prayer. It ripped through the lower slave pens, killing dozens, before passing on through the sepulchres, filled with the raging screams of shackled daemon-engines. Down it plunged, until finally it tore out through the thick armour plates of the immense ship's underhull. Over a hundred slave-proselytes were slain as they were sucked out the fist-sized hole before bulkheads slammed shut, isolating the integrity breach.

With a streaking tail of fire arcing out behind it, the silver sphere hurtled down through the atmosphere of Boros Prime like a shooting star.

Moving at such velocity, were it to strike the surface of Boros Prime it would cause a crater tens of kilometres wide, but before it struck it came to a sudden halt, its velocity arrested instantly.

Glowing with pale light, it hovered between the Undying One's outstretched hands.

DARIOQ-GRENDH'AL WENT BERSERK, his body mutating wildly as his stress-levels increased exponentially.

'It is mine!' he bellowed. 'Mine! Bring it back to me!'

New tentacles burst from his flesh, barbed and fleshy and dripping with blood. They flailed around him wildly as the corrupted magos railed against the loss of the Nexus Arrangement. Effortlessly, he flipped one of the workbenches bolted to the ground, tearing up sheets of the metal flooring in the process. He hurled it into a far wall, which collapsed beneath the sheer force.

Snarling in anger Ekodas ducked beneath a scything, toothed tentacle that would have taken his head off had it connected.

'Restrain him,' Ekodas barked.

Kol Harekh stepped in close and backhanded the magos across the head, using all of his strength. There was a heavy metallic clunk, but Darioq-Grendh'al was not felled. With surprising swiftness, the two servo-arms that extended over the magos's shoulders darted down and forwards, taking hold of the Coryphaus by the shoulders. Ceramite armour groaned beneath the pressure, and Kol Harekh was lifted off of his feet.

Kol Harekh's bolt pistol came up, levelling at the corrupted magos's head, even as a dozen tentacles altered their form, their tips becoming elongated, barbed prongs, poised to impale.

'*Enough!*' barked Ekodas, his intonation carefully weighted to convey a portion of his gods-given power.

The magos froze, though he strained to finish his the killing blow.

'*Put him down*,' he ordered, and the magos gently lowered Kol Harekh to the ground. The Coryphaus lashed out, fingers encircling the magos's scrawny neck. Ekodas knew that it would take little effort for Kol Harekh to tear the magos's head loose.

'Don't do it,' he growled. 'We may need him yet.'

The Coryphaus released Darioq-Grendh'al with a snarl.

Ekodas gritted his teeth as he used his psychic powers to drag the length of metal impaling his leg clear of his flesh. His armour squealed in protest. Telekinetically, he lifted the razor-sharp spike up before him. It was slick with blood. Carefully, he ran his tongue along its length before he hurled it aside with a flick of his mind, sending it clattering to the deck.

'My, my,' said Ekodas. 'That *was* quite a tantrum, wasn't it?'

He walked slowly around the now motionless figure of Darioq-Grendh'al. The magos's mechadendrites quivered with suppressed rage as he struggled against Ekodas's will, straining to break loose and unleash their fury.

'Locate the device,' said Ekodas. His Coryphaus nodded and opened a vox-channel to the bridge, barking orders.

Still maintaining his hold over the magos, Ekodas walked to the view portal staring out into the void of space.

'I have a lock on it,' said Kol Harekh, finally.

'Well?' said Ekodas.

'The device is on the planet's surface.'

'Without the device, we are not going anywhere,' said Ekodas. 'Get a hold of Marduk. Perhaps it is time for him to prove himself useful.'

THE BRILLIANT LIGHT of the Nexus Arrangement reflected sharply off the metallic body-shell of the Undying One. The silver sphere spun impossibly fast, hovering steadily between the ancient being's elongated fingertips, which tapered to curving needle-like nails. It caressed the air around the device, fingers moving like the legs of some metallic arachnid, and it tilted its head to one side, as if captivated by the device.

For untold millennia, the Undying One had been trapped within the prison of its crypt. So long had it been confined that the heavens it now looked upon were strange and unfamiliar. A billion new suns had been born since the time of its imprisonment, and tens of thousands had burnt out, becoming lifeless, wasted husks or light-sucking black holes. Everywhere, it saw the taint of the Old Ones. Their engineered Young Races were spread across the universe in a verminous tide. Hatred, cold and ancient, burnt within its cavernous heart.

Now released, it would take up the old fight, and finish what had been started millions of years earlier.

With a slow, deliberate movement, the Undying One drew the Nexus Arrangement in towards its chest. The centre of the sun-disc emblazoned upon its breastplate sunk inwards, forming a half-moon depression, and the spinning device slotted neatly into place.

The Undying One's body was jolted with the force of the connection, its metal spine curving backwards violently, and its head thrown back. A patina of shimmering iridescence rippled across its metallic limbs, and a web of intricate, golden lines burning with hot light crept across its every surface, delicate labyrinthine veins forming shifting, geometric patterns across its living-metal skin.

The solid, silver orb embedded within its chest seemed to blur, its seamless surface melting and reforming to become a series of delicate rings arrayed around a miniature, green-hued sun. Those rings began to spin around each other, liquid metal rotating faster and faster.

The glowing sun at its centre seemed to swell, spilling light outwards in a blinding wave, and as the Undying One threw out its hands, the Nexus Arrangement began to operate as its creator had intended... and a psychic black hole was torn open.

ACROSS THE CONTINENTS of Boros Prime, unaugmented men and Astartes reeled as the effects of the Nexus Arrangement washed over them. Many of them fell to their knees, gasping, as a terrible, aching pain clutched at the very fibres of their being. It felt as though their souls were being wrenched from their bodies and cast into the abyss, leaving them empty and hollow, mere shells.

A terrible, all-pervading pall of utter futility descended upon Boros Prime, affecting even the most fervent and strong-willed individuals. Millions of soldiers and civilians simply gave up, their will to fight fading, their will to even *live* deserting them. Some, men who moments before had been fighting for their lives, dropped their weapons and sank to the ground, a fugue of hopelessness overcoming them. With haunted, unfocussed eyes they stared into the distance, oblivious or simply not caring about what was occurring around them. Others turned their weapons on themselves, unable to live with this gut-wrenching emptiness in their souls.

Tens of thousands were slaughtered by the merciless necron warriors marching steadily through the streets, gunning down every living creature that they encountered, whether they resisted or not. It was a harvest of sickening proportions. The streets were awash with blood, and mutilated corpses and severed limbs were scattered about like discarded toys.

Those with the strongest warp presence suffered the worst. Blood clots blossomed within the minds of Imperial astropaths and the sanctioned psykers attached to the command sections of the Boros Guard, and they collapsed to the ground, their bodies wracked with violent convulsions, screaming incoherently as their souls were torn from their fragile bodies.

'What in the Emperor's name has happened?' breathed Aquilius, clutching at a marble railing for balance.

Librarian Epistolary Liventius's eyes were clenched tightly shut, and his teeth were bared in a grimace of pain. A droplet of blood ran from his left nostril.

'My lord?' said Aquilius in concern. The Librarian was leaning heavily upon his force staff, and after a moment he opened his eyes. They were bloodshot and sunken. He placed a hand to his temple, a shadow passing across his face.

'My powers,' breathed the Librarian. 'They are gone.'

IN ORBIT ABOVE Boros Prime, the *Infidus Diabolus* shuddered as if it had been struck with cyclonic torpedoes. It listed heavily to one side, its hull groaning in protest as the daemons that had infused its essence since before the outbreak of the Horus Heresy were banished. The strike cruiser's central processing cogitator units sputtered and died. Reliant on the daemon essences bound into its mainframe, the ship's thinking computers and hard-wired servitors were unable to function as the malicious spirits were driven out. The ship threatened to come apart at the seams, so intrinsic was the warp to its very existence.

Marduk dropped to his knees, a terrible empty pain clutching at his hearts as he felt his connection to the warp stripped away.

Aboard the *Crucius Maledictus*, the corrupted magos, Darioq-Grendh'al, seemed to shrink, his fleshy, daemonic appendages withering and beginning to rot at an accelerated rate as the daemon within him was sent screaming back to its plane of origin. Cancers and tumours long kept at bay by the infernal spirit that had become a part of the tech-magos began to bloom, and his life-support system began to bleat plaintively.

Skinless kathartes daemons took flight, but they had barely stretched out their flayed-flesh wings before they blinked out of existence, dragged back to their own turbulent realm of Chaos.

Arachnid-legged daemon-engines fell lifelessly to the floor, rendered utterly inert, their hulls nothing more than empty shells, the daemons bound into their iron skins dragged into darkness by the power of the Nexus Arrangement.

There was not a warrior-brother within any of the Word Bearers ships that did not suffer as the link between the material universe and the empyrean was severed. Isolated from their gods, they were utterly and terribly alone.

Marduk regained his balance, steadying himself. Pain throbbed through his mind, but he forcibly pushed it away. Twice before he had experienced this emptiness, this complete isolation from the blessed warp.

'The æther is being blocked,' growled First Acolyte Ashkanez, massaging his temples. 'We are cut off, adrift. It is... It is an abomination! Such a thing should not be.'

Burias was pale and drawn, and he stared at his shaking hands, the expression upon his face one of rising panic. Marduk could only imagine the horror of separation that the possessed warrior was experiencing.

Kol Badar was down on one knee, steadying himself with a hand to the floor. Never one to have been strongly attuned to the warp at the best of times, the Coryphaus was nonetheless shaken, his face waxy and an even more deathly shade than usual.

Marduk unsheathed his chainsword and studied it closely, turning it over in his hands. There was no familiar daemonic presence within the weapon; the daemon Borhg'ash was gone.

A blister light throbbed weakly on one of the few still functioning command consoles of the bridge. Kol Badar pushed himself to his feet and moved to it.

'A message from the *Crucius Maledictus*,' he said.

'And what does the Grand Apostle have to say?'

'Gods,' swore the Coryphaus. 'He has lost the device.'

'What?' said Marduk. 'How?'

'It does not say. He has identified its location, however. He is ordering us to retrieve it.'

'Of course,' he said. 'Where is it?'

'On the surface.'

Marduk scoffed, shaking his head.

'He wants us to go back and get it, cut off from the warp completely, as we are? It would be suicide.'

'It is suicide if we do not,' said Kol Badar.

'Explain yourself.'

'The *Crucius Maledictus* has us in her sight. The message says that it will fire unless an attempt is made within the next fifteen minutes.'

'He's bluffing. His systems will be offline, just as ours are.'

'Perhaps,' said Kol Badar.

'Gods!' swore Marduk. 'Fine. How do we do this?'

'The daemon-infused guidance systems of the Dreadclaws will be non-operational,' said Kol Badar, shaking his head. 'We cannot use them.'

'Damnation!' growled Marduk, seething. 'Assault shuttles, then.'

'Five Thunderhawks and three Stormbirds were destroyed attempting to get us *off*-world,' said Kol Badar. 'None of those that made it out are undamaged. It will be weeks before they are ready to be redeployed. It would be futile to launch an assault using them. We will be annihilated.'

'Then what do you propose, Coryphaus? Tell me! We must reclaim the device! Failure is not an option!'

The deck shook as the towering shape of the Warmonger stepped forwards from the shadows.

'There is another way...' the ancient Dreadnought boomed.

WITHIN THE DARKENED expanse of the Temple of the Gloriatus, Aquilius and the handful of Sternguard veterans of 1st Company were fighting back to back, desperately seeking to keep the necrons at bay. They had abandoned their location atop the temple half an hour earlier, when they had seen the Thunderhawk that had been closing on their position blasted out of the sky. It had crashed into the city below in a blossoming explosion of fire, killing all the battle-brothers on board.

They fired their bolters in short, concentrated bursts to conserve ammunition, but all were running perilously low. The inhuman automatons came on relentlessly, their movements unhurried and in perfect unison. In the darkness of the temple, their soulless eyes glowed brightly, and the flickering energy of their infernal weapons was reflected upon their silver skeletons.

Aquilius held the scrimshawed pole of the unfurled Chapter banner tightly in his left hand. Only in death would he relinquish his hold on it, and even then, the enemy would be forced to pry his fingers open before he dropped the holy standard. The young Coadjutor felt both fierce pride and an awed humility even to be in the presence of the holy relic, let alone to be holding it aloft in battle.

Were the situation not so dire, he would have been overawed to be surrounded by such vaunted heroes as now fought at his side. He could not imagine a better death than to fall fighting alongside these 1st Company Veterans, and death seemed a certainty.

The huge, gold-plated doors of the Temple of the Gloriatus had been obliterated, exploding inwards as arcs of green energy struck them, and the ranks of the deathly xenos had marched inside. Their mere presence was an affront, and the White Consuls had met them with bolter and chainsword, yet they were but a handful, and arrayed against them was a numberless tide of evil.

The White Consuls had been pushed further and further back. They had chosen to make their stand upon the stairs of the central dais, and it was here that Aquilius had planted the Chapter banner, swearing that while he drew breath, it would not fall.

The temple was immense, the largest cathedral in the Boros system, and tens of thousands of men and women made the pilgrimage to its hallowed halls every month, many using their entire life savings to make the passage. The arched ceilings soared impossibly high overhead, before disappearing into darkness. Each of the four expansive wings of the cathedral had their own pulpits, chapels and choirs, but it was within the central nave that Aquilius and the battle-brothers of 1st Company now stood. The sound of the enemy's metal-boned feet upon the marble flooring echoed loudly through the cavernous temple.

Seven levels of tiered seating looked down upon them, and hundreds of low benches were arrayed upon the floor of the temple below the steps. All told, more than two hundred thousand worshippers could be accommodated comfortably within the temple walls. On holy days, a hundred times that number packed into Victory Square to hear the choirs of the Gloriatus and witness the sermons on flickering holo-screens. Now the floor was seething with deathly abominations, marching resolutely upon the White Consuls, death spitting from their ancient weapons.

'Out!' shouted one of the White Consuls as the chambers of his weapon emptied. The veteran battle-brother swung his ornate bolter over his shoulder and drew his power sword, itself a holy relic of the Chapter. Coruscating arcs of green energy took down two of the blue-helmeted veterans, stripping them to the bone.

Scores of the skeletal automatons were felled by the disciplined fire of the Sternguard, but more were advancing into the cathedral, their numbers beyond counting. The twisted wreckage of destroyed necrons was piled at the base of the broad stairs, which soon resembled an island amidst a sea of skeletal, metallic corpses.

The necrons were incredibly difficult to put down, each one soaking up enough fire to drop an Astartes before their implacable advance was halted. Even then, many simply rose back to their feet moments later, all evidence of the damage they had sustained gone.

Aquilius saw one of the necron warriors stoop and pick up its own arm, which had been blown off with a meltagun blast. Sparks spat from the robotic xenos's shattered shoulder, but as the severed limb was placed back against the joint the sparks stopped. Metal ran like quicksilver as the joint reformed. Within the space of a heartbeat the limb was reattached, and the necron continued its relentless advance, climbing the stairs towards them.

The front ranks of the enemy were only metres away now, each heavy step bringing them ever closer.

Apart from the echoing stamp of their metal feet striking the marble in perfect unison and the crackling discharge of their weapons, the necrons made no other sound as they advanced. The lack of battle cries, the absence of screams of pain and cries of victory was, to Aquilius's way of thinking, more ominous and unnerving even than the frenzied ranting of the traitor Word Bearers.

Step by step, the necrons closed the distance, until they reached the cluster of White Consuls at the feet of the golden statue of the God-Emperor. They hefted their weapons over their heads, intent on bringing them crashing down upon the blue helms of the Astartes. Aquilius saw that curving axe-blades of alien design jutted from beneath their deadly guns, and while the xenos were neither particularly swift nor skilled, they wielded them with deadly intent, their blows heavy and powerful.

Power swords hummed as they carved through skulls and alien rib-cages, melting easily through living metal. Chainswords tore chunks out of skeletal limbs, and bolters fired at point-blank range sent obliterated necrons tumbling back down the stairs into their comrades.

Aquilius fired his bolt pistol, blowing out the back of the skull of one enemy before switching targets and gunning down another necron with a burst of fire. The mass reactive explosive rounds detonated within the xenos's skeletal chest, ripping it apart. It fell without a sound but was replaced by another, stepping mechanically forward to take its place.

The ammunition counter on the back of his pistol was counting down steadily, and he was on his last sickle clip. His last few shots were measured and deliberate, careful to ensure that every last bolt took down an enemy. With his final bolt, he gunned down a necron as it hefted its heavy weapon back over its head to strike him down. The shot struck it in one of its baleful, glowing eyes, and its head was split in two as it exploded, the ruin of its skull hanging from its spinal column. Still, it did not fall.

Aquilius gave a grunt of frustration as the two halves of the necron's skull came back together, the damage self-repairing seamlessly. Tossing aside his bolt pistol, the Coadjutor grasped the pole of the Chapter banner in both hands, wielding it like a spear. The base of the pole was spiked, and with a grunt of effort, he drove it into the necron's chest, smashing it backwards.

Something clutched at Aquilius's leg, and he looked down into the inhuman, emotionless face of a necron. Its slender, skeletal hands scrabbled at his armour, seeking purchase. The wretched thing was missing its entire lower body and had only one arm, but its eyes still burnt with cold, alien fury. Even rent limb from limb, the inhuman imperative to kill drove the creature on. The Coadjutor kicked it away from him in disgust, and drew his chainsword.

Looking out across the nave, Aquilius saw a sea of glowing witchfire eyes in the gloom, closing in around them inexorably. There seemed to be thousands of the alien warrior-constructs closing in around them, far too many for them to have any hope of survival.

It would only be minutes at best before it was over, Aquilius realised.

As if to emphasise the hopelessness of the situation, the Coadjutor heard a gasp of pain and, as he kicked the body of a necron off the wildly revving blade of his chainsword, he glanced over his shoulder to see Librarian Epistolary Liventius fall to his knees, blood pumping from his chest. A gaping hole ran completely through the aged Librarian, and a necron warrior stood over him, its weapon raised. Aquilius cried out and tried to turn, to interpose himself between them, but he was too slow.

With a devastating force, the necron warrior brought the heavy axe-blade of its weapon down upon the Librarian's skull with a sickening, wet crack. The dark blade was embedded down to the teeth, and while the automaton struggled to pull it free, Aquilius stepped forward and smashed his chainsword across its face. It reeled backwards, but the damage had been done, and Liventius fell face forwards to the ground, the weapon that had slain him still embedded in his head.

There were only four White Consuls left alive now. So many of his brothers had died, so many warriors that were far more important than he – Chapter Master Valens, Librarian Epistolary Liventius, Captain Decimus, Proconsul Ostorius. It seemed perverse that such mighty warriors had been slain while he yet lived.

Aquilius gritted his teeth. If he were to die this day, and it seemed a certainty that such would be his fate, he swore that he would take as many of the enemy down with him as he could. He swore that he would make his ancestors proud.

'For the Emperor!' he roared, before hurling himself into the fray.

THE UNDYING ONE's head snapped around sharply. The baleful pinpricks of its soulless eyes glowed brightly, and they roamed across the square, searching. Hovering a metre above the ground, the ancient being rotated smoothly on the spot, head turning to and fro as it sought the origin of the energy build-up that it detected nearby.

With an elegant movement it extended one of its slender limbs, and a cloud of tiny scarabs burst from the darkness beneath its shroud. The tiny, robotic insects flew up to the Undying One's hand as its long, needle-like fingers unfurled. They began to latch onto each other, each scarab grasping its neighbour with barbed leg and mandible. The tiny creatures locked into place and became motionless, forming a two-metre-long staff. Its shape completed, the scarabs melted together to create a smooth, seamless implement. At either end of the weapon, green light flared, creating a pair of energy blades that crackled with barely contained potency.

With a grace far beyond that of its servants, the Undying One swung the twin-bladed staff around it in a glittering arc and waited for its enemy to appear.

Responding to the unspoken orders of their master, the Undying One's bodyguard stood to attention, energy surging through their long-bladed warscythes.

SURROUNDED ON ALL sides by endless phalanxes of motionless necron warriors, a shimmering light began to materialise within the centre of the square, swiftly followed by a hundred others. They gleamed and flickered, like dense clusters of fireflies, and within a fraction of a second they began to solidify into ghostly figures. With a sharp crack of displacing air, a hundred Terminator-armoured warriors of the cult Anointed teleported in from the *Infidus Diabolus*.

The immense shape of the Warmonger appeared amongst them, the immense killing machine one of the few remaining Dreadnoughts capable of such deployment. At the Word Bearer's fore materialised the Host's war leader and Coryphaus, Kol Badar, Dark Apostle Marduk at his side.

The Dark Apostle was encased within an ancient suit of Terminator armour, its deep red plates lustrous and gleaming. The armour was edged with barbed dark metal, and thousands of holy passages from the *Book of Lorgar* had been painstakingly engraved across its plates in tiny Colchisite cuneiform script. His own matted fur cloak was thrown over the immense shoulders of his new armour, and in his right hand he held his staff of office, his deadly crozius arcanum, its bladed tip crackling with energy. In his left he held an archaic, daemon-mawed combi-bolter, a weapon last wielded by the Warmonger himself during the battle for the Emperor's Palace on Terra.

The Terminator armour had not been worn for over nine thousand years, not since the Warmonger – then the 34th Host's Dark Apostle – was fatally wounded and had been peeled from it before being interred within his eternal sarcophagus prison. The revered suit of armour had been dutifully repaired, yet no one had ever been bold enough to have donned it since. For millennia it had remained dormant, empty and unused, locked away in the sepulchre of the great hero. Now, at the urging of the Warmonger, it tasted battle once more. Within his skull-faced helm, Marduk grinned savagely, rejoicing in the feeling of power that the suit conveyed. He felt like a god.

His eyes fell upon the Undying One, less than one hundred metres distant. He had faced the creature once before, and recognised it instantly. Even from this distance, he could make out the spinning orb of the Nexus Arrangement set into its chest plate.

'There!' roared Marduk, levelling his crozius in the direction of the enemy xenos lord.

'Target acquired,' confirmed Kol Badar, his combi-bolter roaring in his hand. 'Come, my Anointed brothers! Kill for the living, kill for the dead!'

More than three hundred necron warriors separated the Terminators and the Dreadnought from their target. Thousands more surrounded them. As if being suddenly awoken from their slumber, the necrons turned as one to face the Anointed, and in an instant, battle was joined.

'Death to the betrayer of the crusade!' boomed the Warmonger, reliving once more battle of days past.

KOL BADAR SNARLED as he gunned down necrons, ripping dozens of them to pieces with each concentrated burst of fire.

'Close formation! Keep moving!' he bellowed. Deeper into the enemy formation the Anointed strode, destroying dozens of the xenos machines for each step of ground they gained.

Hot blood pumped through Kol Badar's veins, his twin hearts hammering in his chest. He closed his power talons around one of the necron's heads, and with a savage twisting motion ripped it clear. He backhanded another of the xenos automatons, smashing it heavily to the ground. As it struggled to rise, he placed the twin barrels of his combi-bolter against its head and squeezed the trigger.

One of the necrons was lifted off its feet as an Anointed warrior rammed his chainfist into the hapless robotic being's chest, sending shards of metal spitting out in all directions before it was torn in two. Another was liquefied as combi-melta fire turned its body molten.

Half a dozen of the Anointed were down, felled by the brutally effective gauss weapon fire of the necrons. None of their brethren made any move to aid them. Kol Badar saw more of his battle-brothers, warriors he had fought alongside through countless campaigns spanning the galaxy, fall under the devastating weapons of the necrons. It was horrifyingly effective, even Terminator armour proving to be little protection against their touch. Under each searing volley of crackling energy, armour was stripped away layer by layer, until pallid flesh was exposed and stripped to the bone; a fraction of a second later, and bone too was torn apart at a sub-atomic level.

A beam of energy sliced across his shoulder, cleaving through his armour plating. Kol Badar turned and gunned down his attacker, driving it backwards, only for it to be finished by one of his brethren, who smashed its head from its shoulders with a blow of a power maul.

The Warmonger barrelled through the orderly ranks of the enemy, smashing dozens of the skeletal warriors aside with each sweep of its massive talons. Dozens more were ripped apart as the Warmonger's heavy bolters tore a swathe through their ranks. Emotionless and seemingly oblivious to the danger they faced, more necrons moved forward to fill the gaps left by their fallen comrades, stepping into the path of the rampaging Dreadnought. Arcing green beams stabbed at the Warmonger's armoured hull, ripping gaping holes in his carapace that exposed the Dreadnought's inner workings, but it was not slowed.

A necron warrior before Kol Badar raised its weapon over its head, bringing the axe-head underslung beneath its barrel down towards his shoulder. The Coryphaus caught the blow in his power talons. He clenched his hand into a fist and the weapon crumpled, ghostly green energy leaping in all direction. He smashed the necron across the side of the head with the barrel of his combi-bolter with a sharp, metallic clang, and then stabbed his bladed talons into its chest.

Crackling with energy, his fingertips passed through the gaps of the necron's ribcage, and with a flick of his hand he sent the corpse-machine flying.

Death was assured. There was virtually no chance that any of them would make it out alive.

Kol Badar began to laugh. He had not felt this alive in centuries.

MARDUK SMASHED HIS crozius into the head of a necron, exposing sparking wiring and circuitry as it was sundered by the force of the blow. As the robotic corpse collapsed to the ground, a space was momentarily cleared before him, affording him a glimpse towards his target.

The ancient being of living metal was gliding smoothly towards him and the Anointed and Marduk saw that there was only a thin line of enemy constructs that separated him from his immortal foe.

The warriors that marched before the Undying One were unlike any that he had faced thus far. Their bodies seemed to be an armoured mockery of the living, rather than reflections of death as were the other necrons. They moved differently as well, their movements smooth and natural, more like those a living foe, rather than the stilted movements of the lesser warriors. They were tall and slender, easily matching the height of the Terminator-armoured Anointed, though they were a fraction of their bulk, and in their hands they wielded halberd-like warscythes, their blades flickering with green energy.

The Anointed and the elite bodyguard of the Undying One came together with a crash, energised warscythes meeting power mauls and chainfists. The enemy moved with supple grace, their weapons leaving gleaming contrails in their wake as they were whipped around in blinding arcs.

Those weapons proved utterly deadly, shearing through Terminator armour with ease. Marduk glimpsed one of the Anointed raising a barbed power sword to parry a blow scything in towards its neck, only to see the blade of the power sword neatly sheared away. The energised necron weapon continued on into the body of the veteran Word Bearer, slicing him open from neck to sternum.

Having witnessed the shocking power of the warscythes, Marduk swayed backwards out of the way of a hissing blade rather than attempt to block it. His movement was slowed by the sheer bulk of his newly donned Terminator armour, though not as much as he had initially expected.

Marduk turned aside the next blow aimed at him, careful only to allow his crozius to touch the metal haft of the warscythe rather than its energised blade. His return blow all but tore the necron's head from its shoulders, and the Dark Apostle grinned savagely. What he had lost in speed was more than made up for by the boost in sheer brute strength that the tightly bound servo-muscles of his Terminator armour gifted him.

Battering another enemy aside, his combi-bolter scoring deep wounds across its armoured chest, Marduk surged forward, desperate to close the distance with the Undying One.

The dull ache in his chest, the pain of separation from the warp, seemed all the worse in close proximity to these deadly warriors. He wanted to end this battle swiftly. He did not know how long he could endure the gaping void that seemed to fill him.

The Undying One glided smoothly into the brutal melee, double-bladed staff spinning in its hands. With consummate ease, two of the Anointed were instantly cut down. Both of the warriors were sliced neatly in two with a contemptuous lack of effort. The spinning Nexus Arrangement embedded in the ancient being's chest spilt its ethereal light before it, taunting Marduk.

Another Anointed warrior was slain, the Undying One's bladed staff slicing neatly from shoulder to hip, and the two parts of the warrior slid to the ground. The necron lord spun the staff around in a blinding arc, levelling one of its tips at another Chaos Terminator, and a searing blast of energy slammed into the unfortunate warrior. The Anointed warrior reeled backwards, a head-sized hole punched clear through his chest.

Marduk snarled and launched himself forward, coming at the Undying One from the side. He saw the hulking form of Kol Badar moving to attack the ancient being from its other flank, combi-bolter roaring in his hand, and he felt a surge of rage at the thought of his Coryphaus stealing his kill.

The Undying One's head was turned away from him, focussed on Kol Badar. He stepped in close, lifting his crozius arcanum with all his might, aiming his strike at the fell being's delicate-looking, slender skull. The blow never landed, for without so much as turning its head, the necron lord parried the blow with one of the energy-bladed tips of its staff, even as the other blade sliced across Kol Badar's torso, almost eviscerating him.

Turning with a deceptively languid, smooth movement, still hovering a metre above the ground, the Undying One fended off the attacks of both Marduk and Kol Badar with ease. A third warrior entered the fray, power maul striking out. The Anointed brother was instantly slain, an energy blade plunged through his head.

Blood welling from the deep wound slashed across his torso, Kol Badar lifted his combi-bolter, spraying bolts from its twin-barrels. The Undying One's shroud billowed out around it as it turned, and a dense cloud of scarabs was unleashed upon the Coryphaus, biting and clawing at him. Though the miniscule, robotic insects could do little real damage to him, encased as he was within his Terminator armour, they soaked up the fury of his weapon fire, the bolts detonating well before striking their intended target.

Marduk aimed another strike at his enemy. But again the double-bladed staff came around in a blinding arc, turning his weapon aside. Marduk had prepared for this reaction, and swiftly altered his angle of attack, but this too was blocked, a deft circular parry disarming him neatly, sending his crozius arcanum spinning away, landing several metres away.

Still turning, the Undying One cut another Anointed brother in two as he stepped forward to attack the ancient being, before neatly ramming one of the energy-blades straight through Kol Badar, impaling him on its length.

Marduk lifted his combi-bolter towards his enemy, squeezing the trigger. Before the first bolt was launched from the chamber, the Undying One slid its blade clear of Kol Badar and swung it around. Marduk was knocked back a step, and it was only when he saw blood spraying out in a geyser that he realised something was wrong.

The pain kicked in a heartbeat later, and the Dark Apostle gazed down in disbelief at his severed arm lying on the ground. His combi-bolter was still clutched in his hand.

On the other side of the Undying One, Kol Badar dropped to one knee, blood pumping from his chest wound. The ancient being twirled its staff around in a deft display of skill. A ring of bodies surrounded it.

Necrons closed in on all sides, gauss flayers spitting death, and Marduk, refusing to accept defeat, felt his anger build.

'Face me, betrayer!' came a booming cry and the immense figure of the Warmonger burst through a cluster of necrons, smashing them out of its path with a sweep of one massive, mechanised arm. Heavy bolters spewed a torrent of fire before it as it charged.

THE WARMONGER'S VOICE was hoarse from leading the Host in their battle psalms, yet it still carried great power and authority. His eyes were locked on the hated figure of his foe, bedecked in fluted, golden armour.

His crozius dripped blood from its barbed tips, and his armour was pitted with battle damage. He was exhausted, for this battle had been raging for weeks. He could not recall when he had last rested. But none of that mattered, not now that the being that was the focus of all his hatred and bitterness was within his reach.

The bodies of his defeated foes lay strewn about him, their yellow armour splattered with blood. None of them stood in his way now.

As far as the eye could see, the battle raged on, brother fighting brother. It was glorious, and yet it filled him with a deep burning hatred for the one who had, in his arrogance, been the cause of it all.

He licked his blood-flecked lips and clenched his hand tightly around the haft of his crozius as he looked upon the one whose hands were stained with the blood of every noble brother Astartes that had fallen.

Once he had called this man Emperor. Once he had even worshipped him. He spat, as if his mouth were suddenly filled with a vile poison.

Liar. Betrayer of the Crusade. Betrayer of the Warmaster.

He had deceived them all.

'Now, it is over,' he said. 'Your lies shall lead no more brother Astartes to their deaths, false one.'

On the walls of the largest palace ever constructed, he hurled himself at his mortal enemy, determined to be the one that killed the False Emperor.

'Now, IT IS over,' the Warmonger boomed. 'Your lies shall lead no more brother Astartes to their deaths, false one.'

The Undying One turned smoothly to face the Dreadnought rampaging towards it, and with inhuman speed and suppleness, it contorted its body like a dancer's. Bolts sprayed around it, tearing holes through its billowing shroud, but failing to strike its body.

On the Warmonger came, roaring incoherently as it pounded forward, a ten-tonne behemoth of metal and brutality.

The Undying One ducked neatly beneath the Dreadnought's swinging talons, its double-bladed staff slicing out, striking across the Warmonger's armoured chassis amid an explosion of sparks and the agonising scream of rending metal.

The Warmonger struggled to arrest its forward momentum, which took it past the Undying One. The Dreadnought's damaged chassis was rotating before it had yet ground to a halt, dragging its heavy bolters around. The heavy weapons roared, belching an impenetrable curtain of high-calibre shells around in a wide arc, chasing its elusive foe. The Undying One was too swift, always a fraction of a second in front of the devastating salvo.

Hefting its double-bladed staff like a spear, the Undying One glided forward, heavy bolter rounds ripping at its shadow-cloak. With inhuman strength and speed, the Undying One rammed its weapon into the heart of the Dreadnought's chassis. The glowing energy blade slid effortlessly through the Warmonger's thick armour plates, impaling it.

Marduk roared in outrage and denial but was helpless as the Undying One ripped the glowing energy blade free, tearing it out sideways in a disembowelling stroke that ripped open the Dreadnought's sarcophagus. Stinking amniotic fluids gushed from this fatal wound, and Marduk caught a glimpse of the Warmonger's corpse within, shrunken, pallid and foetal.

It was hard to believe that once this had been one of the Legion's proudest warriors, a Dark Apostle no less. It now looked like an exhumed cadaver, a half-rotten corpse cruelly kept lingering in some horrific unlife. Wires, cables and tubes connected this lifeless, drowned thing to the Dreadnought's nervous system. It was only this spider web tangle that kept it from flopping out onto the ground. It was little more than a wasted torso, upon which a skeletal head hung loosely.

Most of its skull was gone, either from the extent of the injuries that had seen it interred or surgically removed, and the exposed brain matter

– a horrible colour, like rotten fruit – was pierced with dozens of needle-tipped wires. It was missing its lower jaw. Only its visible fused ribcage and the gigantism of its skeleton revealed that this had once been a proud Astartes warrior.

The Warmonger's mechanised Dreadnought body shuddered and twitched, sparks bursting from damaged wiring and cabling.

Marduk hooked his sacred crozius at his waist and dropped to one knee, prying the archaic combi-bolter from his own dead hand. He fired at the back of the Undying One's head as he rose, snarling in hatred.

Displaying unnatural prescience, the Undying One swayed aside from the burst of bolter fire, twirling its energy scythe around its hands as it turned.

It was unable to avoid the Warmonger, however.

The Dreadnought was not yet finished and as the Undying One turned away, the Warmonger lashed out, clamping its immense power talons around the body of its adversary. The necron lord struggled, its double-bladed staff flailing, but it could not escape. It was completely enclosed within the Warmonger's grasp.

'Death to the False Emperor!' the Dreadnought roared, clenching its fist.

The Undying One's humanoid form splintered, exploding into a million scarabs. In the centre of the buzzing cloud of metallic insects hovered the Nexus Arrangement.

Sparks and sickly black smoke rose from the Warmonger as the Dreadnought twitched spasmodically. The Undying One's bodyguard stepped forward, warscythes flashing as they tore into the Warmonger's armoured flanks.

Marduk roared in anger, stamping forwards, combi-bolter roaring in his hand. Kol Badar smashed a pair of Immortals and stepped into the midst of the scarab swarm, swatting at the robotic insects.

He only registered the Coryphaus when his power talons closed around the Nexus Arrangement, plucking it out of the air. As the hulking warlord's bladed fingers closed around the spinning orb; the device once more took on its prior form, that of an inert, solid sphere.

Reality shuddered, and Marduk gasped as he felt the blessed touch of the æther crash in upon him once more. The Dark Apostle whispered a prayer of thanks to the gods that he sensed around him.

Kol Badar held the Nexus Arrangement within his power talons, gunning down a pair of necrons with his combi-bolter. The blood around the hole in his chest was already scabbed and dry, the Larraman cells in his bloodstream having sealed the wound.

The angry buzzing of the scarab cloud became more insistent, and Marduk saw it begin to coalesce into a tight, dense swarm once more, forming the unmistakeable outline of the Undying One.

'We need to leave. Now,' said Marduk, firing his combi-bolter on full auto, blasting holes in the reforming necron lord. Even as he did so, he knew it was futile – the Undying One was reforming, and no matter what he did, nothing would halt its progress.

'Ashkanez,' said Kol Badar. 'Initiate teleport return. Now!'

'Do it,' said First Acolyte Ashkanez, nodding his head towards Burias. All around them, the ship was repowering, coming back to unholy life as the daemons that had for so long been infused with it returned.

'Why not just leave them?' growled the hulking figure of the champion Khalaxis. 'Let the xenos finish this for us?'

Burias's hand hovered over the activation rune upon the teleporter's control panel, waiting for the First Acolyte's response.

'Don't be a fool,' snapped Ashkanez. 'They have the device. And besides, the Anointed are ours. Do it.'

Burias slammed his fist down onto the glowing rune.

Like droplets of molten metal coming together, a million tiny scarabs gave up their individual form as they combined, until once more the Undying One hovered in the air before Marduk, gleaming, untarnished, perfect. Pinpricks of light began to glow malevolently within darkened eye sockets. The necron lord turned its head from side to side, as if stretching its neck, before its inscrutable gaze locked onto Marduk. The air shimmered as the immortal being spun its deadly, twin-bladed staff, and it began to glide towards the Dark Apostle.

'Any time now, Ashkanez,' hissed Marduk, backing away, still firing with his archaic combi-bolter. His twin-sickle clip ran dry and he holstered the revered old weapon, drawing his crozius once more.

Then there was a sudden feeling of vertigo, and a bright light obscured his vision.

When it cleared, Marduk was standing upon a dimly lit sub deck of the *Infidus Diabolus*, staring down the barrel of a meltagun.

'Welcome back, Apostle,' growled First Acolyte Ashkanez.

CHAPTER SEVENTEEN

First Acolyte Ashkanez stood five metres away, the meltagun in his hands levelled squarely at Marduk. The weapon was designed as an anti-tank weapon. At such range, even Terminator armour would offer little protection.

Without making any threatening or sudden move, Marduk turned his head to glance around him, careful to keep the First Acolyte within his frame of vision. Kol Badar stood at his shoulder, but of the other brethren of the Anointed there was no sign. The five of them were alone.

'You *dare* draw a weapon against your Dark Apostle?' snarled Marduk, his voice quivering with barely contained fury. 'What is this?'

'This is your hour of judgement, Apostle,' replied Ashkanez.

The First Acolyte's face was hidden in the shadow of his hood. In the gloom behind Ashkanez stood Burias and Khalaxis. Both were hooded, but easily recognisable.

'*You* seek to pass judgement upon *me*? You arrogant whoreson. Look at you,' said Marduk, his voice thick with scorn, 'unwilling even to show your faces. You are cowards, worthless cowards who bring nothing but shame upon XVII Legion.'

The towering form of Khalaxis stiffened, his hands clenching tightly around the haft of his huge chainaxe. Burias pulled away his hood angrily.

'You brought this upon yourself, *master*,' the Icon Bearer snarled.

'You have always been a treacherous dog, Burias,' retorted Marduk. 'I should have put you down long ago.'

'Enough,' growled Ashkanez. 'Where is the device?

'I have it,' said Kol Badar.

'Good,' said Ashkanez. 'Remove your helmet, Apostle. I want to see your eyes as you die.'

Marduk glanced down at the stump of his left arm, then at his sacred crozius still clasped in his right hand, then back up at Ashkanez.

'I might need a little help. Would you care to step closer and take my crozius from me, Acolyte?' he said. 'It is clear that you intend to claim it anyway, why not now?'

'I think not,' said Ashkanez, clearly having no intention on closing the distance between himself and the huge figure of the Dark Apostle, ensconced in the Warmonger's ancient Terminator armour.

'Coward,' mocked Marduk.

'Prudent,' corrected Ashkanez. 'Your helmet, Apostle.'

Marduk hooked his crozius onto his barbed chain belt and reached up to remove his skull-faced helmet. It came loose with a hiss of pressurised air. The malignant red glow of his helmet's lenses faded as he hooked his helm at his waist. The Dark Apostle's eyes simmered with hatred.

'Happy?' he snarled.

The First Acolyte nodded.

'Where are my Anointed brothers?' growled Kol Badar.

'Does their blood stain your hands as well, Acolyte?' said Marduk.

'Their deaths would serve no purpose. They have been teleported back safely,' said Ashkanez. 'I did not feel it necessary for them to witness any of this.'

Marduk licked his lips, and glanced between the three warriors ranged against him.

Ashkanez still had the meltagun levelled squarely at Marduk.

'You rate yourself rather highly, First Acolyte,' he said. 'Do you really think that the three of you can take us both?'

'No,' said Ashkanez. 'I do not.'

Marduk opened his mouth to speak, then shut it as Kol Badar stepped away from him.

'You bastard,' he snarled as the Coryphaus bowed his head in deference to the First Acolyte. His eyes were murderous as he watched Kol Badar take a position alongside the others, a step behind the treacherous First Acolyte.

'This day has been a long time coming, Marduk,' said Kol Badar.

'They have all turned against you, Apostle,' said Ashkanez, unable to keep the smirk from his voice. 'All your most trusted captains.'

'Not all. Sabtec would never turn,' said Marduk.

'True,' said Ashkanez. 'I believe the fool would maintain his deluded loyalty to you to the end. A shame. He is a fine warrior. But in this war, sacrifices must be made. He will die soon enough. You are all alone, Apostle.'

'No,' said Marduk. 'The gods of Chaos are with me. And hell's torments shall be as paradise to the pains that I shall unleash upon you. I'll see you all burn for this outrage.'

'No,' said Ashkanez, 'you won't.'

'You are a traitor and a whoreson, Ashkanez. How long will it be before he turns on you, Burias? Or you, Khalaxis?' said Marduk. 'Once he has control over the Host, your usefulness will be over.'

'I've heard enough,' growled Khalaxis. 'Let's kill him now and finish this.'

'The Council will see through this petty mutiny,' said Marduk. 'They will never endorse you as Dark Apostle of the Host, Ashkanez.'

'Traitors?' said Ashkanez. 'No, you are mistaken, Apostle. We are not traitors; we represent the future. The Legion has stagnated under the Council's rulership, its ideals have corrupted. Only a fool could fail to see how Erebus has twisted the Legion's ideals to his own end, corrupting the Council to his will. We represent a new order, one that will cast down Erebus's grip upon the Council.'

'Ekodas has been filling your head with lies,' said Marduk. 'His little uprising will go nowhere. You will be hunted down like the traitorous dogs you are.'

'You are wrong, Marduk. This is no petty uprising. We are the Brotherhood. The time of the Third Cleansing draws in.'

'The Brotherhood?' said Marduk, in surprise. 'The Brotherhood is a relic of the past. It died out ten millennia ago.'

'And now it is reborn, under a new High Priest.'

Marduk laughed.

'You are more deluded that I had thought,' he said. 'Ekodas thinks he can rebuild the Brotherhood in some petty grab for power? Does he truly think he could ever pose any sort of risk to the Council? That he could ever be a threat to Erebus and Kor Phaeron?'

'It is you who is deluded,' said Ashkanez, grinning. 'This goes far beyond Ekodas.'

'I find that hard to believe.'

'That is of no consequence to me. But before you die, know that the Keeper of the Faith, Kor Phaeron himself, is the one that has raised the Brotherhood once more.'

'Impossible,' hissed Marduk, though his blood ran cold at his First Acolyte's words.

'More than twenty Hosts have sworn their allegiance to the Brotherhood,' said Ashkanez. 'Dozens more will join before Erebus has any idea of the danger he is in.'

'It will never work,' said Marduk.

'Erebus's perversion of the Council draws to an end. Under Kor Phaeron's leadership, the Legion shall be guided back to Lorgar's true teachings.'

'The Keeper of the Faith would drag the Legion into civil war?' said Marduk. 'He would cause a schism within our ranks merely to overthrow his brother? Such a path is madness!'

Ashkanez smiled.

'Too long has Erebus manipulated our Legion from the shadows. His time has come to an end.'

'Enough of your poison, traitor,' snapped Marduk, lifting his head high. Without fear, he stared into Ashkanez's eyes. 'It is as Khalaxis says: it is time to finish this. Would you not agree, Kol Badar?'

'Yes,' said the hulking warlord, standing at Ashkanez's back. 'I would.'

Before anyone could react, the Coryphaus stepped forward and rammed the electrified lengths of his power talons into Ashkanez's back.

Ashkanez was lifted up into the air. The tips of Kol Badar's power talons burst from his chest, hot blood dancing off the blades. The meltagun in Ashkanez's hand fired, and Marduk hurled himself to the side to avoid its searing blast. Curse papers affixed to his shoulder plate burst into flame as the shot glanced him, melting a furrow across his armour as if it were butter.

Dark energy flickered across the barbed spikes at the head of Marduk's holy crozius as his hand closed around its hilt, thumbing its activation rune.

Burias was the first of Ashkanez's conspirators to react. The change came over him instantly, his features blurring with those of the daemon within. With a dismissive flick, Kol Badar sent Ashkanez crashing into the Icon Bearer, momentarily taking him out of the fight. The meltagun in the First Acolyte's hand went flying.

The dimly lit chamber suddenly resounded with the deafening roar of Khalaxis's chainaxe. The towering champion launched himself at Marduk, his face twisted in berserk fury.

Marduk met the murderous, double-handed blow with one of his own, dark crozius and chainaxe coming together with awesome force. Marduk's strength was augmented by the tightly knit servo-bundles of his newly donned Terminator armour, yet even so his arm was forced back as Khalaxis exerted his strength. The teeth of the chainaxe tore at the crozius, and sparks flew.

Khalaxis's face was close to Marduk's, flushed with hatred and battle fury. His teeth were bared.

'I'm going to rip you apart, *master*,' growled the towering, dreadlocked aspiring champion, spittle and foam glistening at the edges of his mouth.

'In your dreams,' spat Marduk, stepping forward and slamming his forehead into Khalaxis's face, breaking his nose with a sharp crack and splatter of blood.

The berserker snarled in fury and reeled backwards, letting go of the haft of his axe with one hand. Marduk stepped forward to crush his skull, but walked straight into a thundering backhand. Khalaxis's spiked gauntlet hammered into the side of his face, snapping his head around, and he tasted blood in his mouth.

Stepping backwards, Marduk brought his crozius up instinctively, blocking the madly whirring chainaxe slashing towards his neck. With impressive speed, Khalaxis turned, spinning on his heel and bringing the axe cutting around to strike from a different angle. Still recovering from the previous blow, Marduk had no hope of getting his weapon in the path of the new attack, and so turned his shoulder into the chainaxe. It hacked deep into his armour plating, ripping and tearing furiously, but did not penetrate to the skin.

Marduk slammed his crozius into Khalaxis's side, the bladed points punching through his armour with a sharp discharge of energy that hurled him backwards. The stink of burnt flesh rose from the wound, but the champion leapt forwards once more, pain merely adding fuel to his rage.

As the chainaxe roared, scything through the air towards Marduk, the Dark Apostle brought his crozius down hard, smashing it down onto one of Khalaxis's arms. Bone and armour were splintered, knocking his strike aside, and stepping back to give himself more space, Marduk swung his weapon around in a brutal arc that connected solidly with the side of Khalaxis's head.

The bladed spikes penetrated the champion's skull, which crumpled inwards as the heavy head of the mace slammed home. Blood splattered across Marduk's face and Khalaxis staggered drunkenly. He looked strange, his features caved inwards, like wax melting under a hot sun. The dreadlocked champion swayed on his feet for a second, then fell in a crumpled heap at Marduk's feet, dead.

Ashkanez's power maul smashed into Marduk from behind, battering him to his knees. A second blow, delivered with malice, crashed down onto his arm and he lost his grip on his sacred crozius. Moving faster than Marduk, bedecked as he was in hulking Terminator armour, the First Acolyte stepped swiftly forward and kicked the holy weapon across the floor.

Marduk regained his feet and rounded on Ashkanez, his expression furious.

'You don't know when to stay down, do you?' he hissed.

The First Acolyte's face was pale from blood loss, and red foam bubbled at the corners of his mouth. The four terrible bloody wounds in his chest were leaking his lifeblood, but they would close soon enough. Still, Marduk was surprised that the Icon Bearer was still alive, let alone fighting on.

With a roar, bloody spittle spraying from his mouth, the First Acolyte stepped forward and brought his power maul crashing down towards Marduk's crown.

The Dark Apostle caught the blow in his gauntleted hand, holding the crackling weapon at bay. Electricity ran up and down the length of his arm, but still he held on. The veins in the First Acolyte's neck bulged as he exerted all his considerable force to bring the maul down upon Marduk's, but his strength was fading, and they both knew it.

Marduk slammed a heavy kick into the side of one of Ashkanez's knees, snapping tendons and ligaments, and the First Acolyte fell to the ground, snarling in agony. The Dark Apostle stepped forward and kicked him hard in the side, lifting him off the floor. The First Acolyte crashed into a nearby control panel, which crumpled beneath his weight.

The meltagun that Ashkanez had been holding was lying on the ground nearby, and Marduk stooped to retrieve the deadly anti-tank weapon. Ashkanez pulled himself from the crumpled wreckage of the control panel, struggling to rise. His shattered knee would not support his weight, however, and he was forced to cling to the control panel merely to keep upright. Marduk grinned evilly as he hefted the meltagun in his hand and stalked towards him. He came to a halt within a few steps of the First Acolyte.

'Whether I live or die, it won't affect the days to come,' Ashkanez snarled up at him, blood foaming from his lips. 'The Brotherhood is already moving. You cannot do anything to stop it.'

Marduk levelled the meltagun at Ashkanez's intact knee and squeezed the trigger. The heat from the weapon was staggering, making the air shimmer with haze. Marduk kept his finger depressed on the trigger for a good two seconds, cutting his First Acolyte's leg off neatly above the joint and searing the wound shut. Marduk chuckled in good humour.

Ashkanez refused to scream out, even as the searing blast turned his armour and flesh molten, his bones to ash. He collapsed, gritting his teeth in pain.

'With or without the 34th Host, the Brotherhood will cleanse the ranks of our Legion,' hissed Ashkanez from the deck floor. The stink of burnt flesh was heavy in the air. 'This changes nothing.'

Marduk snorted, and turned away to witness the outcome of the conflict between Burias and Kol Badar. Ever since Burias's rise to the station of Icon Bearer, so long ago, the pair had been needling each other. Now they let a millennia of hatred spill out.

Burias-Drak'shal was crouched on all fours, his shoulders and arms swollen out of proportion with his body. Ridged horns curved backwards from his forehead, and his needle-like teeth were bared in an animalistic snarl. His armour was hanging off him in bloody tatters. Deep gouges were carved across his chest, but even as Marduk watched, they began to heal, his flesh closing up as his warp-spawned flesh regenerated itself.

With a snarl, the Icon Bearer leapt sidewards as Kol Badar brought his combi-bolter up, twin barrels roaring. Burias-Drak'shal leapt onto the nearby wall, his neck bent at an unnatural angle to keep his hellish, altered eyes locked on the Coryphaus. His claws had hardly touched the wall before he had sprung off again, leaping directly at the Coryphaus. Kol Badar tried to follow the possessed warrior's movement with his combi-bolter, tearing chunks out of the metal walls and smashing delicate display screens, but he was too slow.

The three middle fingers of each of Burias-Drak'shal's hands had fused into thick talons, and with his arms at full extension he struck the Coryphaus in his wounded chest, punching the daemonic claws deep. The force of his attack knocked Kol Badar back a step, but the Terminator-armoured warlord did not fall. Burias's clawed feet sank into Kol Badar's chest, and he squatted there like a hellish primate. With one clawed hand holding him in place, he punched several holes in the Coryphaus's chest with his free hand before Kol Badar sent him flying, swatting him off with a backhand blow of his power talons.

Burias-Drak'shal spun in the air then landed hard, snarling, his powerful leg muscles bunched beneath him. With an explosive movement, he sprang back at the Coryphaus, but Kol Badar's combi-bolter was raised, and he was slammed back down into the floor as a heavy burst of fire impacted with his chest.

Bloody craters were blown in his armour and flesh, exposing muscle and bone, and Burias-Drak'shal shook his head in anger and pain. Part of his jaw was ripped away, exposing shark-like teeth and glistening flesh. As he tried to rise to his feet, another burst of fire sent him reeling back again, mass reactive-tipped bolts ripping into him. The Coryphaus's weapon jammed suddenly, falling silent in his hands, smoke seeping from its twin barrels.

A vicious grin split Burias-Drak'shal's brutally damaged face, and his flesh began to reform. He spat a gobbet of flesh and blood to the ground as Kol Badar hurled aside his daemon-mawed combi-bolter in disgust.

'Now you're in some trouble,' said Burias-Drak'shal, forming the words with difficulty as thick tusks began to emerge from his lower jaw.

Kol Badar scoffed derisively. 'I've waited a long time for this,' he said, flexing his power talons.

Both warriors were bloody, their armour compromised in a dozen places, yet while Burias's wounds continued to heal even as he sustained them, the Coryphaus was starting to slow.

With a sigh, Marduk turned the meltagun in his hand on Burias-Drak'shal. Without ceremony, he fired a searing blast that hit the Icon Bearer in the lower back.

The shot melted through his plate armour and deep into his flesh. It knocked the Icon Bearer forwards a step, and off-balance, he stumbled straight into Kol Badar's power talons. The half-metre blades impaled Burias-Drak'shal through the throat. They sank in deep, almost to Kol Badar's fist, and their tips emerged from the back of his neck.

'Who's in trouble now?' snarled Kol Badar.

Blood bubbled up around the energised lengths of his talon, and Burias-Drak'shal stood there transfixed upon them. Kol Badar's combi-bolter barked deafeningly, and Burias-Drak'shal was hurled backwards, his chest cavity exploding from within.

'The Council *will* be overthrown,' gasped Ashkanez through clenched teeth, and Marduk turned to regard the pitiful creature once more. 'It is just a matter of time. Erebus will be brought to justice.'

'You fool,' said Marduk. 'Do you really think that Erebus could be so duped? He knows all about this pathetic uprising within our Legion's ranks. All he needed was for it to expose itself, and learn how deep it ran. All the Hosts will unite against the Keeper of the Faith once the full extent of his treachery is known.'

Ashkanez's eyes narrowed, and Marduk laughed.

'Did you never question why the Council appointed me to accompany this crusade? It was to draw out the serpents within the Legion, to bring their treachery to light. I knew what you were doing from the start.'

'You'll never get word back to Sicarus,' he said.

'Enough talk. I grow weary of your presence. Goodbye, First Acolyte.'

Marduk fired the meltagun, killing Ashkanez instantly. The stink of burnt flesh rose from his corpse.

KOL BADAR HAD Burias-Drak'shal pinned to the ground beneath one knee, and had encircled the Icon Bearer's skull with his power talons. With one squeeze, Burias would be no more – not even his prodigious regenerative qualities could save him from such an injury. As if knowing that its host body was about to perish, the daemon Drak'shal abandoned the Icon Bearer, and his flesh seemed to shrink as he took on his natural form. His injuries were many, and blood pooled beneath him. His chest was splayed open, and while his primary heart was nothing but a pulp, his secondary heart still beat weakly.

'You… you used me,' snarled Burias, looking up at Marduk. Blood was leaking from his swollen lips, and one of his eyes was filled with blood and rolling blindly in its socket. 'You knew about the Brotherhood all along.'

'I knew about the Brotherhood, yes,' said Marduk, kneeling down besides the broken Icon Bearer. 'But I did not drive you into its arms. You made your decision. Nevertheless, you have done me a great service, brother. For that, I thank you. You played your role to perfection.'

'I was your… blood-brother,' spat Burias. 'I would have followed you… anywhere.'

'But instead you chose to stand against me, all because you could not stand to accept your limitations,' said Marduk.

'Kill me then,' snarled Burias. 'Finish it.'

'Oh no, my dear Icon Bearer,' said Marduk, grinning evilly. 'Your pain is only just beginning. An eternity of suffering awaits you for this treachery, have no fear of that.'

Burias spat into Marduk's face, his eyes blazing.

Marduk smiled, wiping the bloody, stinging sputum from his cheek, and rose to his feet.

'You know, for a moment there,' he said to Kol Badar, 'I thought you were going to forget our little pact.'

'For a moment there, I almost did,' said Kol Badar, heaving himself to his full height with a groan.

For the first time, Marduk thought the warlord looked old. He kept Burias pinned to the ground beneath one heavy foot, but he needn't have bothered. The Icon Bearer was a broken figure, exposed and ruptured organs pulsing within his blasted chest cavity.

'What stopped you?' said Marduk.

'You are a devious whoreson, Dark Apostle,' said Kol Badar. 'And one day I *will* kill you.'

Marduk snorted.

'That does not answer my question.'

'Let me just say that I'd rather follow a devious bastard than a dog like *that*,' he said, gesturing towards the body of Ashkanez, sprawled upon the floor. 'At least *you* are of the 34th.'

'We must get word to Erebus of Kor Phaeron's place in this rebellion,' said Marduk. 'This runs deeper than even the First Chaplain could have expected. Contact the bridge. Ekodas will soon know that Ashkanez is dead. I want to put as much distance between us and the *Crucius Maledictus* as possible.'

'We will have a reckoning one day, you and I,' growled Kol Badar as he rose to his feet, dragging the broken body of Burias up with him. Hatred simmered in his eyes as he stared down at Marduk.

'We will,' said Marduk. 'And that will be an interesting day indeed.'

CHAPTER EIGHTEEN

THE INFIDUS DIABOLUS ploughed through the vastness of space away from Boros Prime, plasma engines burning with hellish white-hot ferocity as every iota of power was eked out of them.

'We are being hailed,' said Sabtec. The champion was standing to the fore of the Chaos strike cruiser's darkly shadowed bridge. 'It is the *Crucius Maledictus*.'

'Bring it up on screen,' growled Marduk.

The glowering visage of Dark Apostle Ekodas appeared, filling the curved vid-screen. Intermittent static and blaring white noise interrupted the visual feed before it came into full focus.

'Apostle Marduk,' said Ekodas. He covered it well, but Marduk could tell that Ekodas was surprised to see him.

'You expected someone else, Apostle?' said Marduk, mildly.

'The retribution is not yet complete,' snarled the broad-faced Grand Apostle, ignoring Marduk's question. 'Our job is not yet done. Once we bring the xenos down, the pacification of the Boros Gate shall be recommenced. Move the *Infidus Diabolus* back into formation, now, or I will not hesitate to target you.'

'It cannot be destroyed,' said Marduk. 'Stay and fight if you will. It will be the death of you all.'

'Coward!' hissed Ekodas. 'You would flee before foul xenos?'

Marduk cast his gaze towards the slowly spinning three-dimensional display showing the relative positions of the Chaos battlefleet. He paid particular attention to the blinking icon that represented the massive xenos vessel. For now, at least, it remained stationary. Already, the Chaos battleships had begun pummelling its flanks with torpedoes and ordnance, but they had thus far elicited no response; nor had they caused any noticeable effect.

Marduk returned his focus back onto the glowering face filling the vid-screen before him.

'It's over, Ekodas,' he snarled. 'The attack on Boros has failed. You have failed. And your worm, Ashkanez, has failed.'

Marduk lifted his First Acolyte's head aloft for Ekodas to see.

'Where do you think you can run, Marduk?' said Ekodas, his face looming threateningly upon the vid-screen. 'The wormholes remain inactive. This system is still cut-off. You cannot escape.'

'You and all of your conspirators will burn,' hissed Marduk. The Dark Apostle of the 34th could already feel Ekodas worming his way into his mind, breaking down his defences. 'Once the Council learns of your treachery, the Brotherhood will burn.'

'And how, may I ask, will the Council learn of its existence? From you? I think not.'

The psychic pressure that Ekodas exerted was building, and Marduk could feel dark tendrils plundering the depths of his mind, writhing like razor-worms.

'Enough,' said Marduk, struggling to maintain his control. 'Good-bye, Ekodas. See you in hell.'

Marduk cut visual feed and stood clutching at his command podium as the barbed claws of Ekodas's mind were forced to retract. He breathed deeply as he recovered his composure, wiping a bead of blood from his nostrils.

'The *Crucius Maledictus* is coming around,' warned Sabtec. 'Correction; the entire fleet is redeploying to take up the pursuit. I think you might have displeased him, my lord.'

'Good,' said Marduk. 'We continue as planned. All power to the rearward thrusters. I don't want them overtaking us before I am ready.'

Kol Badar stood stock-still, his eyes clouded.

'What?' snapped Marduk.

'If this does not work, then you have damned us all,' said the Coryphaus.

'Wondering if you made the right decision after all?' said Marduk.

'Too late now,' said Kol Badar.

'Keep a watch on the xenos vessel,' said Marduk as he swung away. 'Inform me the moment it moves.'

'What now?' said Kol Badar.

'I want the names of every damned warrior-brother that is part of the Brotherhood. Now is the time of their reckoning.'

* * *

'Out,' said Coadjutor Aquilius, hurling his spent bolt pistol aside and drawing his broad-bladed combat knife, determined to fight to the very end.

The young White Consul was bleeding from a score of wounds that even the blessed Larraman cells within his bloodstream could not seal. He knew that death was coming for him, yet still he held the Chapter banner tightly in his grasp.

Only two other battle-brothers remained alive at his side, Brother Severus Naevius and Brother Lucius Castus. Both were Sternguard veterans of 1st Company, and figures that Aquilius held in awe. Together, the trio fought back to back, facing out in all directions. The number of necrons assailing them was beyond counting, and it was only a matter of seconds before they were overwhelmed.

The darkness within the Temple of the Gloriatus was alleviated in sudden flashes as weapons discharged, sending shadows fleeing to the hidden corners of the temple. Brother Castus blasted a necron warrior to liquid with his plasma gun, before hurling the weapon aside, its core emptied.

The 1st Company veteran unsheathed a humming power sword smoothly from its scabbard at his waist.

'Ammunition one per cent,' said Naevius. His ornate bolter kicked in his hands, and after two final short bursts of fire, he too discarded the sacred weapon in favour of a revving chainsword that he clasped in both hands.

The three White Consuls stood together facing outwards as the circle of deathless robotic constructs closed in around them.

The necrons closest to the trio lowered the barrels of their weapons as they stepped forward. Green lightning flickered along their lengths, reflected across the xenos's gleaming skeletons.

'It has been an honour, brothers,' said Aquilius, lifting his head high. A dry wind rasped through the open doorway of the temple, ruffling the banner clasped tightly in his left hand.

'The honour has been ours, Coadjutor,' replied Brother Severus Naevius. 'You have done the Chapter proud.'

Aquilius stood a little taller for the praise.

Abruptly, every necron warrior halted mid-step. Aquilius tensed, eyes darting between the array of enemies before him, and his fingers flexed on the hilt of his knife, waiting for the necrons to unleash the barrage of destruction that would flay the White Consuls apart molecule by molecule.

It never came.

As one, the necrons lifted the barrels of their weapons skyward, the movement performed by every one of them simultaneously.

They turned in an abrupt about face, and commenced marching uniformly from the temple, filing out in ordered ranks.

'What is this?' said Brother Castus.

Veteran Brother Naevius shook his head in wonder. 'The Emperor protects,' he breathed.

Moving warily, unwilling yet to allow hope to lodge itself within them, the three White Consuls followed the departing necron warriors out of the grand golden doors of the temple, keeping their distance.

As they ventured out onto the mighty stairs leading to the temple's face, they could see the ordered echelons of necron warriors in the square below filing back into the black-slabbed monoliths, marching in unhurried, ordered lines. One by one, the monoliths began to fade, and Aquilius had to blink his eyes several times to make sure that he was not imagining it. But no, the monoliths *were* fading out, each in turn, until they had all disappeared, like mirages fading into nothingness. Nothing but corpses remained on the square. Even the skeletal warriors that had fallen had now faded, disappearing without a trace.

Silence descended over the city like a shroud.

Unmoving and exhausted, the trio of White Consuls stood and watched the xenos depart Sirenus Principal. Only when the immense crescent-shaped vessel hanging threateningly overhead began to lift away did it sink in to Aquilius that he had survived. His sudden euphoria was short lived as he reflected on the full horror of the war; almost five full companies of the Chapter had fallen, along with one of its hallowed Chapter Masters. It would be centuries before the Chapter recovered.

'By the blood of Guilliman,' breathed Aquilius. 'Is it over?'

'It will never be over,' said Veteran Brother Severus Naevius.

'THE XENOS VESSEL is moving,' came Sabtec's voice from the bridge. 'Accelerating fast. It will be upon us within minutes.'

'Understood,' said Marduk.

The Dark Apostle was caked in blood, and his chest was rising and falling heavily, his breath ragged. Accompanied by Kol Badar and twenty of the Anointed, he had spent the last two hours isolating each warrior that had been identified as Brotherhood. Already, he had killed over a hundred and eighty of his own brothers, and his *khantanka* blade was not yet done.

'I hope this plan of yours works,' said Kol Badar.

It had been a close-run thing, and at full burn the *Infidus Diabolus* had only barely managed to keep out of range of the Chaos fleet's weapons.

'Have faith, my Coryphaus,' said Marduk.

THE INFIDUS DIABOLUS speared inexorably towards the Trajan Belt, the thick ring of asteroids that divided the Boros Gate system into inner and outer worlds. Only as the mighty Chaos ship approached the detritus of the previous battle with the Imperials did it slow its progress. The carcasses of dozens of ships hung here, a veritable graveyard of devastated vessels. Slowing, the *Infidus Diabolus* slipped amongst the wreckage like a grave robber, an unwelcome intruder into the silent realm.

Immense sections of destroyed battleships and twisted hunks of scrap spun lazily in the vacuum, and as the *Infidus Diabolus* glided into the midst of the flotsam, Marduk ordered all systems, primary and second-ary, to be shut down. Shimmering void shields flickered and dissolved one after another, and all internal lights, air-recycling units and weapon systems went offline. Deep within the slave pens, thousands gasped as they rose from the floor as the ship's inertial anti-gravity inhibiters pow-ered down and their oxygen supply was cut.

Within minutes, the ever-present hum of the engines subsided into silence as the beating warp drive at the heart of the vessel was silenced. All that was left behind was the sound of the ship's hull contracting and expanding alarmingly. Dull echoes boomed through the silent hallways of the ship as debris stuck the *Infidus Diabolus*.

'Unshielded, we'll be crushed if we are hit by anything of considerable size,' growled Kol Badar. Marduk could see the shape of the Coryphaus clearly, despite the darkness.

'Silence,' said Marduk.

In the darkness, they waited.

'THEY SEEK TO hide from our scans,' said Dark Apostle Ankh-Heloth from the bridge of the *Anarchus*.

'It buys them a few minutes, nothing more,' replied Belagosa, from his own flagship, the *Dies Mortis*.

'Commence the bombardment,' transmitted Ekodas.

EXPLOSIONS DETONATED WITHIN the field of space wreckage as the Chaos fleet's weaponry was brought to bear, firing indiscriminately into its midst.

The *Infidus Diabolus* was jolted as a detonation nearby peppered its hull with debris.

Marduk and his captains stood upon one of the ship's assault decks, a dozen Deathclaw drop-pods waiting patiently for the order to launch.

'We won't last long in this barrage,' said Kol Badar.

'They are in position, my lord,' said Sabtec.

'Give me the device,' said Marduk.

Kol Badar produced the Nexus Arrangement and Marduk took it from him. It looked so insignificant now, just a simple silver orb. He had been through so much to attain the device and unlock its secrets...

It had surprised him that, even still, the device was holding back the warp, disallowing transference. He prayed fervently that what he had planned would work, though in truth he had no idea whether it would or not. Still, in a few minutes it would not matter either way.

'Are you sure about this?' said Kol Badar.

'It is the only way,' said Marduk, his voice tinged with bitterness. 'We must get word to Erebus about Kor Phaeron's treachery. He must learn how deep the Brotherhood runs. Nothing else matters. Not even this,' he said, holding aloft the Nexus Arrangement.

'How many brothers have we lost because of that device?' said Kol Badar. He snorted, shaking his head. 'And it comes to this?'

'There is no other way,' said Marduk. 'Gods damn it!'

Marduk looked down at the violently shaking device in his hand. His search for the Nexus and unlocking its secrets had seen him battle all manner of foe, entire worlds burn, and thousands of loyal warrior-brothers perish. He had been through so much to claim the device. So much had been prophesised of the power it contained within its inscrutable form. For what?

What was he thinking? How could he even contemplate going through with this?

The device began to vibrate in his hand, almost imperceptiibly at first, but it was getting stronger.

'The xenos approach,' hissed Marduk. 'They are calling it to them.'

'If we are going to do this, we need to do it now,' said Kol Badar.

Another explosion shook the *Infidus Diabolus*.

'We cannot take much more of this,' said Kol Badar.

Marduk came to a decision.

'Do it,' he said.

Sabtec held the vortex grenade that Marduk had claimed from magos Darioq-Grendh'al, the most potent man-portable weapon that the Imperium had ever produced. He prayed that this was going to work. Sabtec readied the device, thumbing its activation code and timer, his movements precise and careful. It began to blink with a repetitive red beacon.

'Armed!' said Sabtec.

Marduk muttered a prayer to the gods and tossed the Nexus Arrangement through the gaping, spherical aperture of one of the Deathclaw assault pods.

Sabtec lobbed the vortex grenade in behind it, and Kol Badar slammed his fist onto the launch press-switch.

The Deathclaw's hatch slid closed with a metallic screech.

'Now, we pray,' breathed Marduk.

Half a second later, the assault pod fired, shooting down the launch tube at high speed. Spiralling like a bullet, the drop-pod screamed down the fifty metres of tube before launching out into space, engines roaring.

Marduk held his breath as he watched the Deathclaw blasting out away from the *Infidus Diabolus*.

Three seconds later, the vortex grenade detonated.

A sphere of absolute darkness appeared, swallowing all light as the vortex grenade created a miniature black hole three hundred metres off the starboard bow. Its hemisphere touched a twisted mess of space debris half the length of the *Infidus Diabolus*, and it was instantly consumed. Marduk shuddered to think what would have happened had the device detonated prematurely.

The Deathclaw was swallowed instantly, crumpling to the size of an atom and blinking out of existence.

The Nexus Arrangement was destroyed along with it, and with it gone, its hold over the Boros Gate was lifted.

'WE HAVE MULTIPLE contacts!' bellowed Ankh-Heloth. 'Mass transference is underway!'

'Gods above!' swore Belagosa. 'The gateways are open!'

'No!' roared Ekodas as his scanners lit up with dozens of flashing icons. Gazing out of the curved portal before him, he saw the first of the Imperial ships materialise on his starboard bow, the Astartes battle-barge emerging from the rent that had been ripped in realspace, its hull blackened and the iconography of a bared sword plastered across its prow. Its hull was bathed in warp light and it lurched towards the *Crucius Maledictus* as its weapons powered up.

'We must fight clear! We cannot win here!' yelled Ankh-Heloth.

'No!' spat Ekodas. 'I will not flee the enemy like a coward! Target them! Take them down!'

Ignoring his order, Ekodas saw the flickering icon of the *Anarchus* begin to turn away, desperately attempting to extricate itself from the soon to erupt firestorm. Ekodas knew that it would be too slow. They were all dead.

'Nova-cannon ready to fire,' drawled a servitor hardwired into the battle control systems of the bridge.

'Target the battle-barge,' Ekodas bellowed, gesturing frantically. With painful reluctance, the *Crucius Maledictus* began to swing around, even as the first shots began to pound at her shields.

Dozens of enemy ships were making transference now, materialising all around the *Crucius Maledictus* and its beleaguered fleet. He saw a massive starship, a Darkstar fortress, emerge directly in front of his own hulking flagship.

'New target!' roared Ekodas.

Cross-hair reticules upon vid-screens blinked as they locked onto the massive battle station.

'Fire!' ordered Ekodas.

The *Crucius Maledictus* shook as her mighty nova cannon was unleashed, and the Darkstar was momentarily hidden within its blast. Then it emerged, unscathed, though more than half its shields had been stripped. He saw the *Anarchus* explode in a billowing corona, targeted by the combined fire of two newly arrived Astartes battle-barges and four

Imperial battle cruisers. The battle would be over in seconds.

'Ready the cannon for another shot!' bellowed Ekodas. He did not see the silver strike cruiser blink into existence on his flank, nor see it turn and begin angling towards his vessel.

The first he knew of the Grey Knights' attack was when twenty Terminator-armoured battle-brothers of the Chamber Militant appeared on his bridge, teleporting across the empty gulf between their own vessel and the hulking Chaos flagship in the blink of an eye.

Garbed in their archaic armour and with Nemesis force weapons clutched in their gauntleted hands, the Terminators of the Ordo Malleus obliterated everyone on the command deck in a devastating salvo.

Alone, Ekodas rose from the hail of fire.

'A curse upon your name, Marduk,' snarled Ekodas. He stepped forward to meet the Grey Knights. He did not even make it two metres before he was cut down.

MARDUK LAUGHED OUT loud as he witnessed the destruction of his brethren. The spectacle was awe-inspiring.

'The xenos?' said Kol Badar as the lights began blinking back into life upon the bridge's control dais.

'Gone,' said Sabtec, studying the vid-screens. 'They disappeared as soon as the Nexus was destroyed.'

'Power up the warp drive,' Marduk ordered, not taking his eyes off the scene of glorious destruction occurring beyond the curving view-deck. 'Set coordinates for Sicarus. We are going home.'

EPILOGUE

MARDUK MARCHED BESIDE First Chaplain Erebus through the high vaulted halls of the Basilica of Torment. The sound of their footsteps echoed hollowly in the high vaulted space. Immense vertebrae-like pillars towered above them. Robed adepts skulked in the shadows, prostrating themselves as the holy duo passed them by.

'The loss of the device is disappointing,' Erebus was saying. 'But it served its purpose. The enemies of the XVII Legion have been exposed.'

'Will the Council declare war upon Kor Phaeron?' said Marduk in a low voice. Bedecked in his ancient suit of Terminator armour, he loomed over the compact figure of Erebus.

The First Chaplain's head was shaven smooth and oiled. Every inch of exposed skin was covered in intricate cuneiform.

'The Brotherhood and all who gave them succour shall burn, have no doubt of that,' said Erebus. 'But my brother shall not be touched. He has already distanced himself from the Brotherhood, severing all links that tied it back to him. He has left them to the wolves, and there shall be no reparations against him. And if I ever hear you refer to the Keeper of the Faith by name again, Marduk, I will see you flayed alive.'

The First Chaplain had not raised his voice, and spoke in a calm, matter-of-fact voice, yet Marduk paled.

'I do not understand, master,' said Marduk.

Erebus smiled.

'The Keeper of the Faith and I have known each other for a very long time,' he said. Every Word Bearer knew that Erebus and Kor Phaeron were the first and closest comrades of their lord primarch, Lorgar. 'It has always been like this between us. Our little struggles against each other mean nothing.'

Marduk walked in silence, baffled. For long minutes the pair marched through the basilica. The immense, carved bone doors of the Council chambers loomed up ahead of them.

'The death of the Black Legion sorcerer displeases me, however,' said Erebus finally, and Marduk's blood ran cold. 'It will have consequences. But no matter. What's done is done.'

'Will the Black Legion seek amends?'

Glancing sideways, he saw that Erebus was smiling. It was a mocking and sinister sight, and Marduk's unease redoubled.

'Abaddon seek amends against us? No,' said Erebus. 'But he will not be pleased. It will raise his suspicion. We will have to be more… circumspect in the coming days.'

Marduk felt like a child, not understanding a half of what Erebus implied.

'There are some who feel that Abaddon is not worthy of bearing the title Warmaster any longer,' said Erebus. 'Some feel the time approaches for him to be… relieved of the position.'

Marduk's eyes widened in shock.

'Ekodas's death leaves a gap on the Council,' said Erebus, and Marduk looked at him in surprise. Erebus's face gave away nothing. His eyes were as cold and dead as those of a corpse. 'I want someone that I know I can trust to take his place.'

Marduk's heart was beating hard in his chest.

'I can trust you, can't I, Marduk?' said Erebus, coming to an abrupt halt and turning towards the Dark Apostle. His voice was silken with threat and promise.

'Implicitly, my lord,' said Marduk, dropping to one knee. 'My life is yours.'

'Good,' said Erebus, laying his hand upon Marduk's crown in a casual benediction. 'There is much work to be done.'

TORMENT

DEATH WAS NOTHING to be feared. Death he would have welcomed. It was the in-between place that that filled him with dread.

To some it was the Undercroft, Tartarus, or Limbo; to others it was Sheyole, the Shadowlands, or Despair. On old Colchis it was known as *Bharzek*. Translated literally, its meaning was simple and direct – Torment.

Those condemned to wander its ashen fields were said to be cursed above all others. They lingered there, haunted, confused and lost, suffused with impotent rage, longing and regret. Unable to move on, yet equally unable to move back to the lives they had left behind, they were trapped in that empty, grey wasteland, doomed to an eternity of emptiness.

He knew now that the old stories were wrong, however.

It *was* possible to come back...

'Burias.' That voice was not welcome here. It was an intrusion. He tried to ignore it, but it was insistent.

'Burias-Drak'shal.'

HE AWOKE TO pain. It blossomed within him, building, compounding, multiplying, until every inch of his body was awash with fire. He was blinded by agony, yet he grinned, bloodied lips drawn back in a leering grimace.

Pain was good. Pain he could endure. He was alive, and not yet confined to the hell that the Dark Apostle had promised him. Burias embraced his pain, letting it draw him back from the brink of oblivion.

743

He knew where he was – deep within the Basilica of Torment, on Sicarus, adopted homeworld of the XVII Legion. He'd been dragged here in chains by his former brothers, but he had no concept of how long ago that had been. It felt like an eternity.

Gradually his senses returned.

The smell hit him first. Hot, cloying and repellent, it was the stink of a dying animal. It hung in the unbearably humid air like a fog, something that could be felt on the skin, oily, clinging and foul. He could taste it. Sickly stale sweat, charred meat and burnt hair; none of it could quite mask the stench of bile and necrotising flesh.

But more than anything else, he could smell blood. The room reeked of it.

He discerned low whispers and chanting, and the hushed shuffle of feet on a hard stone floor as his hearing returned. He heard the clank of chains, the hiss of venting steam, and the mechanical grind of gears and pistons.

This is not your fate.

The words were spoken with the confidence of one who does not need to raise its voice in order to make itself heard. It was familiar, but he could not place it. He tried to answer, but his lips were dry, cracked and bleeding, his throat raw and painful. He swallowed, tasting blood, and tried again.

'Who are you?' he managed.

I am the Word and the Truth.

'Your voice... is inside my head,' said Burias, wondering if his torture had driven him to insanity. 'Are you real? Are you a spirit? A daemon?'

I am your saviour, Burias.

The haze of his surroundings was slowly coming into focus. He was staring straight up at an octagonal, vaulted ceiling. It was shrouded in darkness, lit only by a handful of low-burning sconces mounted upon the eight pillars surrounding him. Oily smoke coiled from these fittings, rising languorously.

He lay spread-eagled upon a low stone slab, bound in heavy chains bolted to the floor. The links that bound him were each the size of a Space Marine's fist and heavy manacles were clamped around his ankles, wrists, and neck. The flesh around these bindings was blackened, raw and weeping, burnt almost to the bone.

The manacles were inscribed with ancient Colchisian cuneiform. Painstakingly replicated from the Book of Lorgar, the potent runic script glowed like molten rock, and the infernal heat radiating from them made the air shimmer. Yet more of the angular ideograms were carved directly into Burias's tortured flesh, and these too smouldered with burning heat.

His body was a ruin of raw scar tissue, burns, cuts, abrasions and welts. His sacred warplate had been torn away piece by piece, with all the eagerness and hunger of feeding vultures. Where over the years it had become fused to his superhuman frame, it had been crudely hacked off with cleavers and blades that he suspected had been purposefully dulled to make the work longer and bloodier.

Every conceivable torture had been inflicted on him. But he had not been broken.

You are already broken, yet your mind refuses to accept it.

'You lie,' Burias gasped.

I do not. I am here to help you.

'Then help me!'

Look to your left. That is your way out.

With some difficulty, his movement painfully restricted, Burias turned his head. Before him was the reinforced door of his cell. It was closed and bolted, and rust and corrosion was sloughing off its surface like dead skin. The door was massive, thick and solid, and the stonework around the lintel was carved with runic wards.

A pair of hulking executors were slumped in shadowed niches to either side of the door. Huge even compared to a Space Marine and vaguely simian in appearance, these mecha-daemon sentinels appeared completely lifeless except for their eye-sensors which blinked unceasingly in the darkness. They were behemoths of armour and barely-checked fury, mechanical constructs built around a brain and nervous system that had once been human, though daemonic entities had long since been bound within their steel bodies.

When roused, they were easily capable of ripping him in half with their immense powered mitts. Even in his weakened state, chained, tortured and stripped of his armour, Burias stared at them with eyes narrowed; an apex predator sizing up its rivals.

His muscles tensed as his body responded to his desire to fight, yet he was bound securely and he knew that any attempt to break his bonds was futile. There was no hope of escape.

All that imprisons you is your own perception, Burias, and nothing more. You believe that there is no escape, and so there is none.

'You can hear my thoughts,' said Burias.

Yes. You are not speaking aloud now, you realise?

'Who are you?'

Burias's question was met with silence.

'Are you Drak'shal?'

Again, silence.

His view of the dormant executors was abruptly blocked as a dark figure shuffled in front of him, chattering incoherently. More of these robed figures moved around him, attentive and whispering, their faces hidden in the shadow of deep cowls. They were loathsome creatures, emaciated and hunched, the definition of their ribs and vertebrae clearly visible through their black robes. Their arms were corpse-thin and grey. Rusting cables and tubes that leaked milky fluids protruded from their flesh, and their bony fingers were tipped with a plethora of needles, hooks, blades and callipers. All were stained with blood. *His* blood.

Lobotomised cantors were hard-wired into hooded alcoves positioned half way up the chamber's eight pillars. They chanted litanies of binding and containment in long, monotonous streams, their entire existence focused solely on this duty. Their eyes were wired open, and their grossly obese bodies were the pallid shade of a creature that had never seen daylight. Reams of parchment unfolded endlessly before them, and their mouths bled from the potency of the words they read aloud.

Everything about the cell, from the runic chains to the inscriptions upon the cell door and the drone of the cantors, had been designed with a singular purpose – to ensure that the daemon Drak'shal remained tightly bound, suppressed and quiescent.

With the daemon dormant within him, Burias was as any other warrior-brother within the Host; a demi-god of war in comparison to lesser, unaugmented beings, yes, but nothing more than a shadow of his former self. He could hardly feel the daemon's presence at all, and this cut him more deeply than any physical torture. It felt like he was missing a part of himself, something so integral to his being that he felt like he had been hacked in two.

The daemon had been bound to his flesh in the early days of his induction into the Legion. He had been one of the special few, chosen for this path with great ceremony and care. Few warrior-brothers were able to survive the rituals of possession. Fewer still were able to master the daemon once joined.

There had been a period of struggle when Drak'shal had fought to gain ascendency, of course, but Burias had won out, asserting his dominance. He had been reborn. Everything of his former life was forgotten.

Drak'shal had given him strength – great strength – as well as speed, cunning, and rapidly accelerated healing that had seem him walk away from injuries that would have killed any other Space Marine. He'd fought in wars across a thousand battlefronts, and yet he bore not a single scar to show for all the countless wounds he had sustained – until now.

Fused with the daemon, his every sense had been heightened beyond anything he could ever have imagined. He could see in total darkness without the aid of his helmet's optic augmentations. He could taste a drop of blood in the air at a hundred metres. He could run as fast as a Rhino APC and maintain his pace for days on end. His strength was easily that of five of his Word Bearer brothers.

'You are nothing without Drak'shal,' Marduk had said, standing over

him as the manacles that now held him had been welded shut. Burias and Drak'shal had roared as one, knowing what was to come, but powerless to prevent it. The Dark Apostle had smiled as the runes had burst into flame, pushing the daemon back into enforced dormancy. *'This is the punishment for your treachery, Burias.'*

His muscles tensed at the memory, his lips curling back in a snarl.

It is your choice what path you take, Burias. To your left lies freedom; to your right, slavery.

Somehow Burias knew what he would see to his right, but he was still compelled to look.

For a moment the horror of the sight carried him somewhere else entirely; drowning, blinded, screaming.

The moment passed as quickly as it had come, and he was staring into a cavernous alcove, like the lair of some great beast. Slumped motionless in the shadow was the mechanical prison that would be Burias's tomb for all eternity.

A Dreadnought.

War machines of colossal power, with a chassis of heavy ablative armour and toting weaponry comparable to that of a front line battle tank, the Dreadnoughts had been conceived early in the Great Crusade. Every time a Legion lost a battle-brother, particularly a captain or veteran, a wealth of hard-won knowledge and wisdom was lost along with them. The Dreadnought was designed to ensure that the greatest warriors and heroes of a Legion might live on even after suffering fatal wounds.

It had been a noble aim, one that seemed to hold great merit, but the machine's creators on Mars had not foreseen the terrible, tortured existence that those interred within were forced to endure. Denied physical sensation, their existence was hollow, empty, and without end. They were cursed never again to experience physical sensation, and were cut off from everything and everyone.

To these poor unfortunates, the one thing that they had been gene-bred and trained for – war – was now a soulless and dissatisfying experience. They had become living war machines capable of laying waste to entire battlefields, and yet cruelly they were not able to elicit any satisfaction from doing so. Never again would they experience the rush of adrenaline that came from combat, nor feel the kick of a bolter in their hands, or watch the life leave a worthy enemy's eyes as the shuddering kill thrust was administered.

As years turned to decades, decades rolled into centuries, and centuries became millennia, those pitiful souls condemned to that horrid half-life were driven slowly and inexorably to madness, filled with longing for all that they had lost, and bitterness towards those who had imprisoned them.

It was therefore in an act of pure malice and barbarity that Marduk intended to take Burias, a healthy, living warrior of the Host, and forcibly inter him. It spoke of the Dark Apostle's vindictiveness that he would rather see Burias suffer for all eternity than have a fatally wounded warrior-brother saved from death's grasp.

Burias stared at the immense, motionless machine with rising terror.

It stood upon squat, armoured legs, and its massive torso was almost as wide as the machine was tall. Both of its arms ended in immense power talons that hung dormant at its sides. A helmet – one of the early Mark II helms, brutal and archaic – was half-hidden behind a gorget of reinforced adamantium. The lenses of the Dreadnought were dark.

The machine was an ancient relic, a shrine to the dark gods, and its armour plating was a work of peerless artifice. Every centimetre of its deep crimson hide was covered in intricately carved scripture, and barbed metal bands edged each individual plate. Strips of vellum hung from wax seals, each covered in long tracts of illuminated text.

The chest of the Dreadnought was a gaping cavity. That was where the sarcophagus would be secured. That was where Burias would be entombed, and not as a glorious martyr of the Legion – the only injuries he bore were the result of his torture at the hands of the Host's chirumeks. No, he was being interred within the Dreadnought as punishment for having dared turn against his sworn master Marduk.

Located behind his own was a second altar, mirroring the slab to which he was chained. Upon it rested a sarcophagus. *His* sarcophagus.

It was filled to the brim with liquid and ribbed pipes, cables and tubes spilled over its edges. Some of them connected into tall glass cylinders filled with murky amniotic fluid; others hung limp and lifeless, like parasites waiting to be affixed to a host.

The casket was not large – his arms and legs would be amputated in order for him to fit within. Cables and wires would be rammed into his nervous system, impulse-needles pushed into his cortex. Feed-tubes, ribbed-pipes and cables would be inserted into him, and oxygen-rich liquid would fill his lungs. Once sealed, his tomb could never be re-opened.

In times of war he would be interred within the Dreadnought and unleashed upon the foe, but at all other times his sarcophagus would lie dormant, collecting dust in the undercroft of the *Infidus Diabolus*. Denied outside stimuli, he would yet remain conscious, trapped in Torment...

Nothing is real but what you've chosen to accept.

'You speak nothing but riddles!' Burias snapped. 'You said you were here to help me.'

I am.

'Then tell me how to be free of his prison.'
Break your bonds.
Burias paused. 'What?'
Break your bonds, and you will be free.
As simple as that, thought Burias, mockingly.
As simple as that.
Burias smirked, and shook his head slightly. Humouring the disembodied voice, he pulled against the chains binding him. He gritted his teeth and groaned with the effort, but there was no give in the metal links at all. He gave up. They were too strong.

They are not too strong, Burias. Belief is the path to freedom. Believe that you can break them, and you will.

Burias breathed in deeply, gathering himself. *'Break, you bastards,'* he whispered, then hauled on the chains with all his prodigious, gene-enhanced strength. His abused, flayed musculature strained, veins protruding monstrously, like bloodworm parasites burrowing beneath the skin. He roared, pulling against his chains with reserves of strength that he did not know he had left.

He felt something stir within him.

The cuneiform runes carved upon his manacles burst into flame, their smouldering power surging. The droning intonation of the cantors lifted a pitch, becoming more strained, and the pair of slumbering mecha-daemon executors set to guard over him were roused, leaning forward on immense metal knuckles, emitting snuffling clicks from their vox-registers.

Burias's vision was red, and the sound of his blood pumping in his ears drowned out all else. He could not hear himself roaring, though he knew that he still was. The runic wards turned white hot, and Burias dimly registered the smell of burning flesh – his skin around the manacles being seared anew by the heat of the metal. He barely felt it.

The executors were advancing, the rotary-barrelled autocannons mounted in their forearms clicking and ratcheting as they moved towards him. He lifted himself up off the slab, his back arching with the strain.

The first weakening in the wards came when one of the cantors began to spasm, its words faltering as it began to convulse. Blood burst from its nostrils and ears.

Whatever affliction had struck the cantor down was evidently contagious, as those adjacent to it began to shake and stammer. The chant lost all coherence and was suddenly a confused mess of conflicting, stuttering voices. The burning runes that bound Burias flared erratically, and the executor's rotator cannons began to whine and spin.

With a scream that made reality shimmer, the daemon within Burias surged to the surface, rising like a monster from the deep. The warding runes exploded into blinding, glittering shards, and the chanting cantors' brains burst in one mass collective haemorrhage.

Drak'shal was unleashed.

The change came over him quickly. Burias's form shimmered and distorted like the display of a faulty pict-viewer, flicking back and forth between two incompatible images. It was as if two beings of vastly differing physiology were fighting to share the same location and the laws of reality did not know which to give precedence. Instead of a decision being made, the two images blurred together to become one.

Curving horns rose from Burias-Drak'shal's brow, and his shoulders were suddenly bulging with additional musculature, flesh remoulding like wax. Barbed spines pushed from his elbows and down his spine, and ridges of bone sprouted down the blade of his forearms. His fingers fused to form thick talons, each as long as a mortal man's thigh. Crimson hellfire burnt in eyes which were suddenly elongated slashes carved into a bestial visage, and thin lips drew back to expose the serrated teeth of a predator.

The whole change occurred within the space of a millisecond, faster than the time it took the guardian mecha-daemons to register the danger and open fire.

With a brutal surge of warp-spawned power, Burias-Drak'shal hauled himself upright. His arms and neck ripped free of the chains binding him, tearing the thick links effortlessly. One of the chain lengths held, and the heavy bracket securing it was instead ripped from the floor, bringing with it a torso-sized chunk of rockcrete.

With his legs still shackled, Burias-Drak'shal swung the chain around like a flail as the executors fired. The swinging rockcrete lump took the first in the side of the head, splattering blood and cancer-ridden brain matter as its armoured cranium crumpled.

The sheer brutal force of the blow almost tore the construct's head from its servo-thick neck. Knocked off balance, its autocannon sprayed a burst of heavy-bore shells across the room, ripping through the bodies of black-robed attendants and tearing gouges along the far wall. A rain of expelled shell cartridges fell to the floor.

The second executor was spraying wild gunfire at Burias-Drak'shal, but the possessed Word Bearer was already moving, too fast for mortal eyes to follow. He used his momentum to wheel himself off the blood-stained stone slab, ripping the chains that bound his legs free. Detonations chased him as he spun away from the shots.

With a casual shove Burias-Drak'shal sent one of his craven, black-cowled tormentors flying backwards, hurling it ten metres through the air to strike one of the pillars with a sickening wet crack. With the same movement, he brought the weighted chain swinging around towards the executor that still stood.

The mecha-daemon ceased firing and reached up to grab the chain early in its swing. The heavy links encircled the armoured gauntlet of its fist three times, and the rockcrete lump crashed against its armoured forearm and shattered. With a savage yank, the executor snapped the chain, and Burias-Drak'shal stumbled to his knees.

The bestial construct bellowed in triumph and surged forward on all fours, moving with surprising swiftness. It lifted one immense fist high and brought it down hard, intending to pound Burias-Drak'shal into the floor.

The possessed warrior rolled, and the executor's blow struck the flagstones, sending cracks rippling out from the impact and making the whole room shudder. Burias-Drak'shal scrambled to get away, but the executor managed to grab the short length of chain still attached to his left leg. With a triumphant roar that reverberated deafeningly in the confined space of the chamber, it hoisted him off the ground and swung him first into one of the stone pillars, then into the opposite wall.

Rock crumbled and dust fell as Burias-Drak'shal was pounded from side to side. One of the black-robed attendants cowering in a corner was crushed, brittle bones pulverised under the possessed warrior's weight as it was caught up in the executor's wild fury.

Then the Word Bearer was hurled violently across the chamber. He slammed against the far wall, which cracked under the impact, and fell to the floor. He spat blood as he pushed himself to one knee, momentarily blinded by pain.

The executor bellowed and came at him again.

Move. Leap to the right.

Burias-Drak'shal hurled himself aside as the voice commanded, and the executor thundered into the wall with tremendous force. Masonry dust fell from the ceiling, and cracks spread across the wall like veins. The monstrous executor's shoulder was embedded half a metre into the stonework, and it appeared momentarily stunned by the colossal force of impact.

Kill it.

With a snarl, Burias-Drak'shal scrambled up the executor's armoured body, climbing onto its hunched shoulders as it struggled to pull itself free of the crumbling wall. An outraged growl of scrap-code burst from its vox-grille and it whirled around, seeking to dislodge him, but Burias-Drak'shal clung on, holding tight to the edge of its armoured shell with one hand, claws digging deep into ceramite.

The executor's armoured hide was as thick as the frontal glacis of a predator battle tank, but its joints were comparatively vulnerable. Its design compensated for this deficiency with overlapping, sheathed plating and a high gorget to shield its neck, but while this was powerful defence against an enemy facing it, there was little to protect against an enemy standing upon its shoulders.

With his free hand, Burias-Drak'shal began punching his talons into the executor's exposed neck, hacking into the thickly bunched mass of fibre-bundles, servos and ribbed cables. Oil, milky fluid and stinking synth-blood sprayed outwards, splattering across Burias-Drak'shal's face. Sparking electrical discharge arced from the wounds, and the executor went wild.

Spinning dementedly, roaring and bellowing, it sought desperately to throw off its smaller foe. It tried to slam him into one of the pillars, driving itself backwards at full force, but he clung on, hacking into its neck, ripping away cables and synthetic muscle-fibres, digging towards the vulnerable neural wiring deeper within.

The mecha-daemon's data-roars become a pitiful, crackling whine, and it stumbled as its nervous system began to fail. It collapsed to the floor, twitching as its life-fluid pooled beneath it, running freely from its savaged neck. It clung to life, trying vainly to push itself upright, but it had lost all coordination and was unable to rise.

Burias-Drak'shal finished it off by driving one of his talons through the back of its armoured cranium, then turned his feral gaze towards the cluster of lesser creatures cowering in the corners of the chamber, determined to vent his fury on their flesh.

Go now. The others are coming for you.

Snarling, he advanced towards the terrified acolytes.

THE IMMENSE CELL door exploded outwards, wrenched out of shape and torn from its hinges. It slammed against the opposite wall, and Burias-Drak'shal sprang through the gaping doorway into a wide shadowed corridor. Gore caked his arms from talon to elbow, and bright blood was splashed across his chin.

There were four sentinels on guard outside his cell. Burias-Drak'shal did not stop to think why they had not entered his cell at the cacophony of mayhem that had been unleashed within, though if he had he might have guessed that in this place such sounds were not unusual. They came at him with falchion blades that hummed with power, and they died with those weapons still in their hands.

When his flesh was his own, Burias was a consummate and graceful warrior, elegant and poised. When he was one with the daemon, he was pure bestial rage.

He tore the head from one of the sentinels and ripped the throat out of the next with his teeth. The third died with the daemon-talons of his fist through its armoured chest, and the last was hurled away with a backhand blow, its spine shattered by the force of it.

Without pausing, Burias-Drak'shal swung his heavy head from side to side, tasting the air.

The ceiling was high and arched. Katharte daemons crouched high up along spiked buttresses like gargoyles, watching over him indifferently. The darkness hid their skinless forms from mortal eyes, though

Burias-Drak'shal saw them clearly, and acknowledged them with a snarl.

Clusters of robed curators and indentured servants fled before him, wailing and falling over themselves in their haste. Penitents, their flesh criss-crossed with self-inflicted wounds, dropped to their knees in worship, crying out to him, skeletally thin arms raised in supplication. He ignored them, cocking his head to one side and listening intently.

Mournful bells of alarm were echoing up through the halls. He could hear raised voices barking orders in the war-cant of Colchis, and the stamp of heavy nailed boots on stone, coming in his direction. The sound reached him of weapons powering up – he discerned the unmistakeable hum of plasma weaponry; the electric crackle of submission whips.

With a snarl Burias-Drak'shal launched into motion, bounding down the hall towards the sounds. Each leap tore up the stonework as his talons dug deep, propelling him onwards, urgency and rage lending him speed. He rounded a corridor at full tilt, his momentum forcing him up onto the wall. Rather than slowing, his pace increased.

He hit the approaching warriors with all the elemental force of a thunder strike, leaping in amongst them and starting to kill before they had even registered his presence or thought to raise a weapon.

They were indentured Sicarus warrior-clan, enhanced post-humans bred by the XVII Legion for devotional combat. Their faces were obscured by clockwork rebreather masks and external optical targeting arrays, and hyper-stimms flooded their nervous systems. Though they could never have matched one of the Legion, they were a highly trained, elite force that was worthy of respect.

Nevertheless, there were children next to the fury of Burias-Drak'shal. Three of them were dead without even raising a hand in defence.

Burias-Drak'shal towered head and shoulders over them and ploughed through their ranks, ripping and killing. He smashed gun barrels aside as they were swung up towards him, and warrior-clansmen inadvertently slew their own brethren with high-powered hellguns and plasma blasts in the frenzied mayhem. He punched heads from shoulders, and ripped arms from sockets. He crushed skulls against the passage walls, and slashed throats with his blood-slick talons.

Writhing submission whips sought to ensnare him, but he was too fast for their touch, and those wielding them died, their hot blood splattering up the walls.

All the while, Burias-Drak'shal kept focussed on one figure at the back of the regiment, the hulking warrior whom he had heard barking orders in the language of dead Colchis. He was one of the Host, a brother Word Bearer that Burias had fought alongside for countless years. His name was Eshmun, and he was of the 16th Cohort.

A respected veteran, Eshmun was a stoic and capable warrior who, Burias-Drak'shal recalled, had been marked out for greater things after butchering three White Consuls, bastard gene-descendants of the Ultramarines primarch Guilliman, in close combat on the Imperial world of Boros Prime. In a hundred wars they had been comrades, fighting across innumerable worlds against all manner of foes. But here in these dark, sweltering corridors those bonds of brotherhood were forgotten.

Eshmun unslung his chainsword as Burias-Drak'shal leapt through the crush towards him, holding the weapon in a two-handed grasp. The blade's engines roared, adamantium teeth a blur of motion as they spun in combat readiness. 'Time to die, whoreson,' growled Eshmun, his voice wet and throaty.

Eshmun was fully armoured in battle plate, yet even it proved unable to withstand Buras-Drak'shal's fury. The possessed warrior took the swing of Eshmun's chainsword in his forearm, allowing the whirring blades to rip into his flesh. It bit deep, screaming and spraying gobbets of blood and shards of bone, and then stuck fast.

With his weapon effectively disabled, the warrior was unable to deflect Burias-Drak'shal's return strike, which punched straight through the front of his horned helmet and drove a half-metre long talon through his skull.

Eshmun died instantly but remained standing until Burias-Drak'shal withdrew, at which point the Word Bearer collapsed to the floor like a puppet with its strings cut.

Burias thought that killing one of his own Legion would have resonated powerfully within him... but it did not. It was merely another kill.

More of his kinsmen were closing in. He could taste their scent on the air.

It is the Anointed.

A part of him wanted to fight, but it was not a battle that he could win, and he knew that oblivion would not be granted to him; the Dark Apostle was too spiteful for that. He would fight, and a good number of them would die at his hands – Kol Badar included, if the Coryphaus dared face him – but Burias-Drak'shal would eventually fall.

Bloodied and broken, he would be dragged back to the cell, and once again he would be bound and shackled with wards and runes. The cantors would be replaced, their droning intonation would begin anew. Once Marduk grew bored, he would be torn limb from limb and sealed within the armoured sarcophagus that had been chosen for him.

Eternity in a box, going slowly and inexorably mad, was not a fate that he would welcome.

You must move quickly.

He stepped over the corpse of Eshmun and slaughtered a path free of the remaining clan warriors without a second thought.

Then he ran, the voice in his head guiding his every step.

COUNTLESS SIDE CORRIDORS, hallways and tunnels branched off the main thoroughfares, like so many capillaries, veins and arteries. Each turn revealed ever more; thousands of passages spreading out in a bewildering, interconnected maze like an intricate spider-web.

Always, the voice guided him on.

It was impossible to fathom how many individuals were locked away down here, suffering, tortured and brutalised for all eternity. Still, he gave the matter just the barest moment of thought. What did he care? He was free – everything else was an irrelevance.

He passed by hundreds of heavy doors and cells, most of which were locked and barred. Agonised screams, wails and cries echoed from many. The curators of this hellish place knew their art well.

The corridors seemed to stretch out forever. It would have been possible to wander lost for a dozen lifetimes on any one level and never see the same corridor twice, and there were many hundreds of levels below ground, dug deep into the stifling, burning core of the daemon planet, and yet more were being excavated all the time.

Chained bondsmen, their eyes and mouths sutured shut, paused and raised their pallid heads blindly as he surged past them. Black-clad cenobites whipped them back into subservience, their faces obscured by masks of dead flesh.

Malforms with braziers surgically sculpted into their fleshy backs wandered the darkest corridors, existing merely to bring light where shadow lingered. In hidden alcoves, grinning chasteners scourged the bodies of proselytes, lashing them with barbed whips that grew from their wrist-stumps.

Tens of thousands of penitents shuffled along in endless lines, patiently and willingly awaiting ritual sacrifice, their minds turned to palsied mush by the blaring incoherence of floating Discords. Many of them had been standing in line for weeks on end. Flesh-eating cherubs circled around the weak and the sick, waiting for them to fall.

Burias-Drak'shal met his captors in battle once again at the foot of a majestic, sweeping staircase that spiralled up into pure darkness. Strobing lasfire puckered the air, and autocannons wielded by mono-tasked guardian-slaves tore apart the ornate, frescoed walls as they tried to lock onto his rapidly moving shadow.

He slaughtered everything that stood in his path, and bounded up the great stairs, taking them eight at a time. Up into the higher levels of the

Basilica of Torment, Burias-Drak'shal climbed.

The scent-traces of the Anointed pursued him always.

HE DIDN'T KNOW how long he'd been running. Drak'shal had departed for now, receding back within, leaving him drained and aching.

Time was always difficult to judge on Sicarus. It was not a reliable measure here, its flow dictated by the tidal flow of the ether. It ran slower within the basilica than elsewhere on the daemon-world, the winds eddying around its buttressed flanks becoming torpid and slothful. This was no accident – the edifice's location had been carefully chosen so as to maximise and extend the torment of those within.

Nevertheless, Burias had never been as disoriented as he was now. He might have been running for minutes, or it may have been weeks. Everything that had occurred since his escape from his cell had melded together into one confusing blur.

He vaguely recalled a restless urgency that had driven him up through the basilica. Sometimes he had ascended narrow, spiralling staircases echoing with ethereal wails and screams. At other times he hauled himself up yawning elevator shafts, climbing hand over hand up chains slick with grease and oily grime; he crawled through pipes gushing with liquid foulness, and shimmied up vertical chimneys where corpses were routinely dumped, broken bodies tumbling down into the bowels of the planet. He had fought and killed everything that sought to halt his progress.

Was any of that real? It seemed like a dream.

He tried to focus on his elusive, deceptive memories, but they were as insubstantial as smoke, dissipating like ghosts as he sought to grasp them. It felt like knives were twisting in his mind as he struggled to comprehend what was going on.

He rubbed his shoulders, feeling a ghost-ache there – residual pain from his torture, he guessed – along with a disconcerting recurring numbness in his arms and legs.

There was a heavy, wet feeling in his lungs, making his breathing painful and laboured. He could hear a dull repetitive thumping sound from somewhere nearby, as of metal striking stone. He dropped to his knees, an intense nausea threatening to overwhelm him.

Shaking his head, he struggled to focus on what was real – what he could see, hear, touch and feel. He could not allow himself to slip. Not now.

'Are you still there, spirit?' he growled.

I am no spirit. But I am here.

'What is going on?' he breathed. 'What is happening to me?'

You teeter on the edge of Torment. You must keep moving, lest you succumb.

'I cannot bear this,' Burias said. 'How can I know-'

Focus on what you feel. The stone beneath your hands, the ache of your muscles. The blood in your mouth.

Burias did as the voice bade him, and the nausea and throbbing pain in his head receded, along with the metallic pounding.

His strength slowly returning, he rose back to his feet.

Your pursuers are closing in on you once more.

'Then guide me away from here,' Burias replied.

AFTER WHAT SEEMED a lifetime he emerged, blinking, from the darkness.

He found himself upon a section of spiked battlement, high up on the basilica. Immense spires, turrets, towers, and domes soared above him, kilometres high, reaching up into the burning sky. Twin obsidian moons wreathed in hellfire stared down like the unblinking eyes of gods. Kathartes rode the heat-currents and swirling updrafts, circling lazily, descending occasionally to feast upon the twitching bodies of sacrifices.

He'd been guided up into the giant cathedral, driven ever higher by his relentless pursuers. The exits on the lower levels had been heavily guarded by warrior clans, sentry guns, and battle-brothers of the 34th Host. There had been no chance of escape there.

He allowed himself a moment, gazing across the surface of Sicarus, the adopted homewold of the Word Bearers. Vast cathedrals, temples, fanes, and gehemahnet towers stretched out across the scorched world, tightly clustered as far as the eye could see. Many of these grand structures were a dozen kilometres or more in height, yet the Basilica of Torment reared up over them all.

The surface of Sicarus was always changing, climbing ever higher into the heavens and the realms of the gods. Larger and more extravagant temples of worship were constantly being raised, constructed on top of the older, crumbling structures like the trees of a forest straining up to the sun and strangling out their rivals.

Ancient battleships, many of which had served the Legion since the Great Crusade, hung in low orbit like circling void sharks. Beyond them, the maddening heavens whirled.

The warp was alive with burning incandescence and surging, ethereal power. Semi-divine entities that defied description could be half-seen in the roiling fire out there, immense forms coiling and writhing, dwarfing the battleships below them. Their grasping tentacles reached down low in places, stretching toward the rising structures of Sicarus.

Burias leaned out over the battlements, gazing down. Cloying yellow cloud hugged the towers and flying buttresses below, obscuring the firmament and lower structures completely. Immense daemonic faces materialised within the fog, snarling and roaring in soundless fury. They seemed to be straining to rise and devour him, but they could not break free of the cloud bank. He found himself mesmerised by their languid, malevolent shapes.

The Anointed are upon you.

A whickering bolter shot whipped past Burias's head, and he hurled himself to one side, ducking for cover. The concussive thump of impact reached him a fraction of a second after the self-propelled shell had passed him by.

He cursed himself for not having sensed how close his pursuers had come.

Stealing a glance around the edge of the archway, he saw the Anointed – hulking Terminator armoured Word Bearers looming out of the gloom, striding belligerently toward his position with weapons raised. The lenses of their helms shone red as their auto-targeters locked onto him.

He ducked back behind the corner of the balcony, cursing. A crackling melta blast struck, liquefying the rockcrete and making it drip like syrup.

'You've led me to a dead end, spirit,' he snapped.

Death is no end for us, Burias.

More gunfire struck the corner at his back, ripping at the stonework.

'Where now, then?'

Up.

Drak'shal returned in an instant and Burias sprang vertically, talons latching onto a jutting ledge six metres above the balcony. The ledge began to crumble beneath his talons, and he scrabbled for purchase, feeling the dizzying pull of the void below...

Finding a foothold, he leapt powerfully upwards again, and latched onto the underside of a horned statue with one hand. As he hung there, he glimpsed the Anointed emerging onto the balcony below. He hauled himself up the daemonic stone figure as they raised their weapons and unleashed a torrent of fire towards him.

The statue fractured beneath the withering fusillade. Bolter rounds and splinters of rock sliced the thin air around him. He snarled as his blood was drawn.

Burias-Drak'shal pushed off from the head of the statue as it shattered, grabbing onto a jutting plinth and continuing his rapid ascent, bounding up the exterior of the basilica, leaping from handhold to handhold.

He swung out over a deep overhang, climbing hand over hand along stone ribs that formed arches supporting the underside of a protruding wing of the basilica. He could no longer see the Anointed or the balcony he had left below – both had been inexplicably swallowed up by the thick cloudbank that hung beneath him.

With a grunt of effort, he hauled himself up onto a ledge, disturbing a roosting Katharte. The daemon beared its teeth at him and dived off the ledge, drawing its skinless wings tightly in to its body.

Moving swiftly and silently, Burias-Drak'shal slid in through an arched window and found himself in a long shadowed corridor. There was no living soul to be seen, though flayed human flesh was pinned to the walls, hair and fingernails still attached.

As he drew near, fresh ruinous symbols carved by unseen hands were cut into these skins. Blood ran from the wounds, dripping down the walls. The flesh began to ripple and twitch, and a large milky eye slid open to regard him impassively. Mouths tore open, and the dead flesh began to wail and gibber, flapping and twitching spasmodically.

Burias-Drak'shal picked up his pace, loping quickly along the corridor as more mouths opened, adding to the toneless wail.

Outside, a floating Discord descended, drawn to the sound, and hovered several metres beyond the portico's windows. It turned its brazen vox-grille toward him, a tangle of mechanised tendrils trailing behind it. A deafening blare of sound burst from the thing, a cacophonous wall of sound that made his eardrums vibrate painfully. It was the sound of Chaos itself, filled with ungodly screams, wailing children, pounding industry, and the beating of the dark gods' hearts.

Amongst the din, a familiar voice spoke his name. *'Burias.'*

In confusion, Burias-Drak'shal stared at the hovering Discord.

'Marduk?' he said.

Do not listen. It will speak only lies and falsehoods. The deceiver seeks to draw you back to Torment.

A second blast of noise rolled over him, and he reeled as if struck a physical blow. Blood dripped from his ears. Again he heard the voice of his former lord and master, coaxing him back to… where…?

The choking, drowning sensation rose within his throat once more, threatening to engulf him.

Focus, Burias. All that is real is here.

Stumbling blindly away from the aural assault, Burias staggered through an archway into shadow. It was cooler here in the cloistered darkness, and a rasping wind seemed to pull him eagerly along. Within moments, the blare of the Discord faded away.

He paused in his flight, breathing heavily, until he was back in control of his senses. His ears were ringing from the din.

A familiar scent reached his nostrils, and his lips pulled back in a snarl, exposing his serrated teeth. He spun, lashing out… but too late.

His strike was knocked aside contemptuously, and powered talons clamped around his neck.

'Hello, Burias,' snarled Kol Badar.

Burias-Drak'shal was hoisted half a metre off the ground to match Kol Badar's height, and his feet kicked futilely beneath him. The Coryphaus was wearing his quad-tusked Terminator helm, and his voice was a low, mechanised growl.

'It is time to go back, Burias,' said Kol Badar. 'You cannot keep running forever.'

Burias's windpipe was being crushed and his arteries compressed, stemming the flow of blood to his brain. Dimly he saw a distorted reflection in the elliptical lenses of Kol Badar's helmet, but it was not his own face that stared back at him – what he saw was a wasted, grimacing cadaver. Tubes and ribbed pipes emerged from its nostrils and mouth, and its hairless scalp was pitted with plugs, cables and wires. Blood, oil and dark mucus leaked from the crudely drilled holes in its skull.

Burias-Drak'shal cried out, thrashing and striking out wildly, but he could not break the Coryphaus's crushing grip. Kol Badar laughed at his frantic struggle.

His vision grew hazy and indistinct, his brain starved of blood and oxygen. Whispering shadows danced around the periphery of his vision, like grim spectres awaiting his death. His surroundings faded, the walls melting away, and flames erupted all around him. He gripped the Coryphaus's talons, straining to loosen them, but his strength was fading, along with his consciousness.

With a sickly crack, a vertical slit opened Kol Badar's helmet from chin to crown, yawning into a gaping, daemonic maw filled with rows of ceramite teeth. The jaws of this mouth distended impossibly, and Burias was dragged in towards it. Wriggling black worms emerged from deep in the monster's throat, straining toward his face.

If you surrender now, you will be lost to Torment forever.

'No!' roared Burias, straining to turn away. Surging with a last burst of desperate strength, he managed to wrench apart the daemon's talons, and he fell to the ground at its feet.

He rose fast, lashing out, but he hit nothing. He was alone.

The corridor was empty.

STILL GASPING FOR breath, Burias staggered down a narrow side tunnel and into an antechamber crowded with robed proselytes. Their heads were bowed as they hurried on their way, paying him no attention at all. The air was thick and cloying with smoke and incense, and the walls seemed to be closing in on him.

At the far end of the chamber, he could see the hellfire glow of the open sky, and he pushed his way towards it. He was battling against the flow of proselytes, and he roughly barged his way through the stinking press of bodies. Still they paid him no mind, not even complaining as he shoved them out of his path. Several fell to the ground and were instantly lost beneath the living tide.

Burias realised he was getting no closer to his goal, and he began to lay around him more forcefully, battering aside those in his path, breaking bones and limbs with sickening cracks. He trampled over those that fell and crushed them with his heavy steps.

At last he emerged into the light to find himself upon a wide bridge spanning the gap between two cathedral spires of the basilica. Statues of Word Bearers, each more than five metres tall, lined the bridge, each with hundreds of prayer papers fixed to their armour. Doleful bells sounded, reverberating across the maddening cityscape of Sicarus.

The flow of the faithful broke upon him, streaming around him like liquid. He was an island, a lone motionless figure in the midst of a migration as the bells called the faithful to worship.

'*Burias.*'

Again he heard someone speaking his name and he turned, scanning the sea of downcast faces for its source.

His legs gave way beneath him. They were completely numb, and the same loss of sensation was tingling up his arms. He felt suddenly confined, claustrophobic and trapped in the midst of the crowd. '*Burias-Drak'shal.*'

Shut it out.

Burias clutched his head, confused and disoriented. 'What is happening to me?' Bodies pressed in around him, bustling past.

You are being called back.

'Back to where?'

Torment.

The immense Word Bearer statues began to move, stepping off their plinths with stonework crumbling away from their forms to reveal blood-red armour beneath. They strode through the crowd, moving toward Burias in step with the pealing of the distant bells, giant bolters clasped across their chests.

'This cannot be real,' he whispered, dragging himself to his feet.

The crowd turned, as if seeing him for the first time. In a rush they surged forwards, babbling and speaking in tongues. They crowded around him, their eyes burning hot with faith and fever, reaching out to touch him.

'Bless us, great one,' a scrawny proselyte begged, clutching at his leg. Burias kicked the wretch away, snapping the man's bones.

'This cannot be real!' he said again, pushing away from the crowd, making his way to the edge of the bridge.

This is all that is real, Burias. Everything else is Torment.

The giant Word Bearers were closing, making the bridge shudder with every footfall, crushing any who did not get out of their way quick enough.

Run. Fight. Kill. Do this, and you can live on here, forever.

Burias laughed at the absurdity of it all, and climbed up onto the edge of the soaring bridge's low wall and glanced down. The sickly cloud bank below was impenetrable even to his daemon-sight.

'To hell with this,' snarled Burias.

'*Burias-Drak'shal,*' said every proselyte in unison, speaking with the Dark Apostle Marduk's voice. '*Come to me.*'

The immense statues hefted their bolters, closing in all around him.

The voice cut through Burias's mind, tinged with desperation.

Do not do this!

'And to hell with both of you,' said Burias, speaking to both the spirit-voice and the voice of his master. He turned away from the crowd of believers.

With his head held high, he extended his arms out to either side. He closed his eyes, and breathed in deeply.

The thunderous fire of gigantic bolters echoed all around, but Burias had already let himself topple forwards.

The proselytes screamed as one. *'No!'*

No!

Burias pushed off hard, and holding his cruciform pose, he plummeted down into the fog. The air rushed past him, yet he kept his eyes shut, giving himself over to the Ruinous Powers.

It felt as though he were flying, soaring the ether with the kathartes. Not the foul, skinless harpies that filled the skies of Sicarus and frequented the *Infidus Diabolus*, but the beauteous angelic beings of pure light that those daemons became in the deep flow of the warp.

He was drowning.

Thick, viscous fluid filled his lungs, lukewarm and repulsive. He coughed and spluttered, crying out in shock and anger. The sound was muffled by the thick bundles of tubes and pipes that filled his throat and nostrils. All he achieved was to expel what little air he-

'No!' ROARED BURIAS, kicking and thrashing against his confinement, and then he was falling through the void once more.

Abruptly, the cloud bank parted and he smashed through a great dome of coloured glass. Coming down fast, he rolled and skidded along the length of a flying buttress to rob the fall of its impact, tumbling to the floor and ending the movement on one knee. Shards of coloured glass studded his flesh, and more showered down around him, filling the air with its tinkling music.

He found himself in a tiny chapel. It was a humble, ascetic space, a simple shrine to the dark gods that lacked the grandeur and ceremony that infested the rest of Sicarus. A plain altar was carved into one wall, atop which sat a skull with a simple eight-pointed star of Chaos burnt into its forehead.

Beneath a shadowed arch stood the lifeless, immense form of the Warmonger. Burias's skin began to itch as he looked upon the Dreadnought, his arms and legs tingling.

'You should not be here,' said a woman's voice, and Burias-Drak'shal snarled, turning sharply. He had not sensed a presence in the room.

He could tell by her manner of garb and bearing that she was a seer. She stood in the shadows, bedecked in robes the colour of congealed blood. Her hood was down, revealing an angular, pale face. Gaping, empty hollows were located where her eyes should have been, yet she seemed to stare at him unerringly. 'You have gone too deep.'

Drak'shal was raging within him, urging him to attack, to brutalise this witch and be away, but he resisted. He forced the daemon back. It struggled, attempting to gain ascendancy, but it was an old battle, and one that Burias had won long ago. Resentfully, Drak'shal receded, sinking within.

The daemon's presence had ensured that the wounds of his torture had now healed. All that remained was his dried blood upon his skin. No scars marred his flesh.

For a moment he thought he heard a distant voice speaking his name. He shook his head, clearing it of these errant distractions.

'There is someone waiting here for me,' he said. 'Who is it?'

'You do not need me to answer that question,' said the seer. 'You already know the answer.'

'I do not have time for riddles,' muttered Burias, turning to leave.

'Time is meaningless here,' she replied. 'You know this.'

'Speak plainly, witch, or do not speak at all.'

'It was he who released you from your bondage,' she said, her words giving him pause. 'It was he who brought you here.'

'Released me?' Burias snarled over his shoulder. 'I released myself!'

'No,' said the seer, shaking her head. 'He burnt away the wards holding you, opening the door for you to come here, to come to him. But I see that your mind refuses to accept what your heart already knows is true. You need to *see* in order to believe.'

The seer stepped away from a simple wooden door, and gestured towards it.

Burias frowned, his anger piquing, but he stepped past her and placed a hand upon the door's rough hewn panels. It swung inwards easily, revealing a narrow passage. Lowering his head, he stepped within.

He moved up the narrow passage until he came to a circular, windowless prayer-room lit by a single candle in an arched alcove. It was small, the kind of room used by fasting penitents or hermetic recluses. The walls were covered in tiny neat script-work. He recognised the hand-writing. He had seen its like before.

'*Burias. Burias-Drak'shal.*' That voice again...

Burias's twin hearts began to pound. He could not breathe. He heard metallic pounding in the distance, beating in time to his hearts.

His gaze fell upon a figure kneeling in the centre of the room. Its back was turned to him, and it wore a plain robe of undyed, coarse fabric. Its head was smooth and hairless, the bare scalp glinting like gold in the candlelight.

The figure rose to its feet. It seemed to expand to fill the circular room, as if it were magnifying in volume to gigantic proportions. Then the illusion passed, and Burias realised that the figure stood no taller than he.

As the figure turned, Burias looked upon the golden face of a demi-god.

His eyes began to bleed and his mind rebelled. His soul lurched, and he was driven to his knees, breathless and suffocating.

A veil seemed to be ripped aside, and the walls of the shrine disappeared, replaced with roaring flames and darkness. A maddening cacophony of screams and roars assaulted him from all sides.

'Urizen? Lord?' he breathed.

The flames seared his lungs, but he did not care. His mind was reeling. He did not understand. The primarch of the XVIIth had been locked in self-imposed isolation within the *Templum Inficio* since long before Burias's creation. How could he be here? Where, in fact, were they?

Burias's hearts were thundering, beating erratically and dangerously fast. He couldn't breathe. He was drowning. He was blind.

Look.

The voice was velveteen and smooth, once again calm and measured. It was the same voice that had guided him to freedom, yet it seemed more potent, more vital. There was a controlled intensity to it that was almost painful.

LOOK.

He opened his eyes. The figure that stood before him was not the holy primarch of the XVII Legion. He was staring at himself.

He jolted, and the vision was gone. He was alone in the cold darkness.

'Burias.'

That voice was not welcome here. It was an intrusion. He tried to ignore it, but its power was impossible to resist. He rebelled against it, but it dragged him back towards consciousness.

'Burias-Drak'shal.'

He was drowning.

Thick, viscous fluid filled his lungs, lukewarm and repulsive. He coughed and spluttered, crying out in shock and anger. The sound was muffled by the thick bundles of tubes and pipes that filled his throat and nostrils. All he achieved was to expel what little air he had left.

In panic, he registered that he was completely submerged, and as he struggled to rise he struck a hard, unyielding metal surface. He thrashed wildly, smashing against the sides of his containment, desperately seeking escape. There was none to be had. He was sealed in and drowning.

His hands refused to respond to his commands, and he could not move his arms. He could see nothing but darkness. He tasted oil and blood, battery acid and bile. He vomited violently, but the acidic foulness had nowhere to go.

His strength was fading, along with his consciousness. Metallic clangs, hammering and the whine of engines echoed loudly around him. Behind it, he heard the muffled murmur of voices, but could make no sense of the words.

The end was close now, and his struggles weakened. His lungs rebelled against him, causing him to reflexively suck in a deep breath of liquid and his own vomit. He began to convulse, shuddering and jerking violently.

Oblivion came for him then. But it was not to last.

HE AWOKE TO darkness. There was no pain. There was nothing at all, and he knew then that he was in hell.

He roared in a voice that was not his voice. He heard that mechanical, grinding, anguished bellow with ears that were not his ears; external sensors translated what they heard into electrical impulses and were transmitted directly into his cortex.

He clenched a hand that was not his hand into a fist, and an immense, blade-fingered power talon clenched. He pounded this great fist into the stone walls of his prison once again. It made a dull sound, metal on stone. *That sound...*

'Burias,' said a voice. 'Burias-Drak'shal.'

It was the voice that had called him back. It was the voice that had brought him into this hell. He swung towards it, servos whining.

'Back in the land of the living, finally. In a manner of speaking, at least.'

Optic sensors interpreted what they saw. A figure stood nearby, one that he recognised.

'You were in deep this time,' said the figure. 'I was not sure you were coming out. You resisted my call for the longest time yet. I am impressed.'

Burias lunged at the figure, pneumatic piston-driven legs driving him forward and giant claws reaching out to crush it, but immense chains bound with burning runes held him fast, restraining his mechanical strength.

Dark Apostle Marduk laughed. 'Now, now, Burias. Mind that temper.'

Hatred surged through what was left of Burias's body – amputated, rotten and curled foetus-like in the amniotic fluid sloshing within the sarcophagus implanted at the heart of the machine.

Hatred. *That* was something he was still capable of feeling. His mighty fists were clenching and unclenching unconsciously. With every last remaining fibre of his being he wanted to smash the author of his torment to paste.

'How long this time?' Burias managed, his voice deep and sepulchral, the sound of immense rocks grinding together.

'Not long. Ninety-seven years, unadjusted.'

To Burias it had felt like an eternity. He wondered how he could possibly endure.

'Why do you rouse me now?' he growled. 'There is no torment that you can unleash upon me that would make my suffering any more complete.'

'Torment, old friend? No, you mistake my purpose,' said Marduk. 'I come to you because the Host marshals for war. I am, for now, *releasing* you from torment. It is time you killed again for the Legion.'

Death was nothing to be feared. Death he would have welcomed. But denied that, the next best thing was the chance to kill once more. Burias ceased his struggles.

'War?' he boomed, unable to keep the eagerness from his grating, mechanical voice.

'War,' agreed the Dark Apostle.

A silken voice spoke in Burias's mind.

None of this is real.

ABOUT THE AUTHOR

After finishing university **Anthony Reynolds** set sail from his homeland Australia and ventured forth to foreign climes. He ended up settling in the UK, and managed to blag his way into Games Workshop's hallowed design studio. There he worked for four years as a games developer and two years as part of the management team. He now resides back in his hometown of Sydney, overlooking the beach and enjoying the sun and the surf, though he finds that to capture the true darkness and horror of Warhammer and Warhammer 40,000 he has taken to writing in what could be described as a darkened cave.

His online blog can be found at
http://anthonyreynolds.wordpress.com/
or you can follow him on Twitter *@_AntReynolds_*

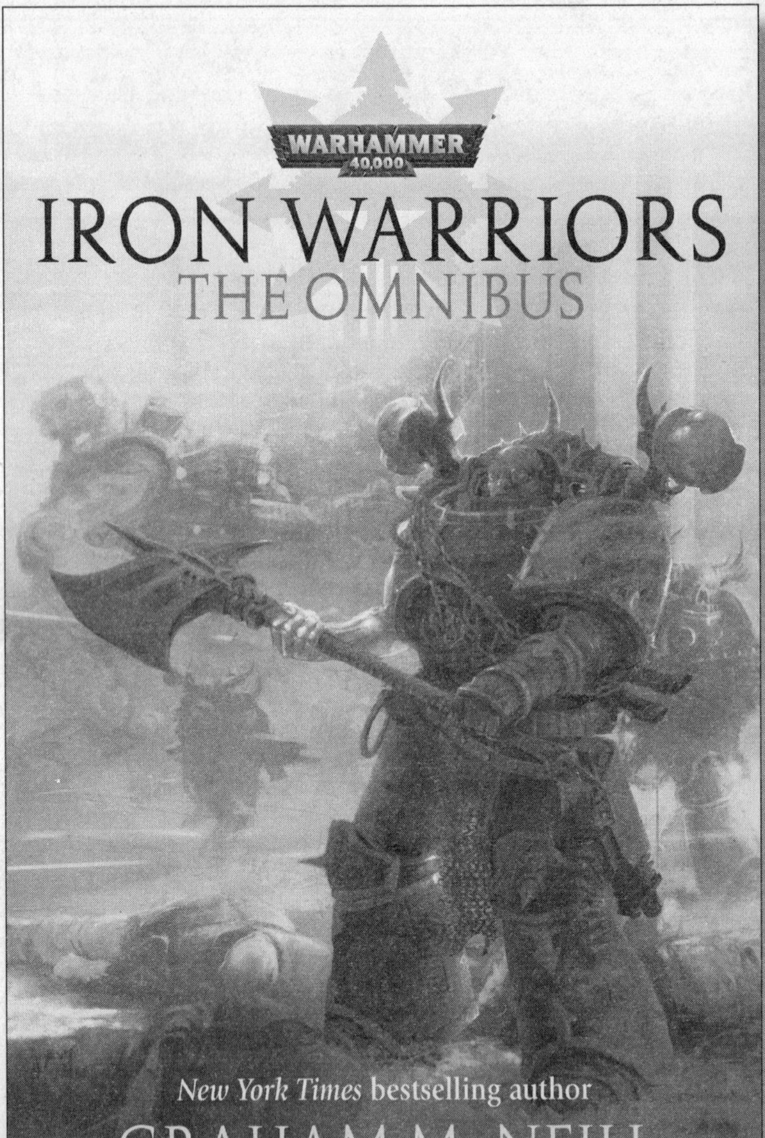

UK ISBN: 978-1-84970-138-9 US ISBN: 978-1-84970-139-6